"[An] excellent debut novel . . . This is historical fiction at its most convincing."

—Regina Marler, *The New York Observer*

"Grandly old-fashioned . . . Bernstein maintains firm control of his plot and painstakingly re-creates the historical landscape."

—*The New Yorker*

"[A] spellbinding first novel . . . Bernstein [is] a novelist with a penchant for ideas. The complex challenges he sets himself in this book, and the flair with which he meets them, make this first novel a compelling, enjoyable read, and create high expectations for his next effort."

—Harvey Blume, *The Jerusalem Report*

"Compelling . . . exquisitely detailed . . . the lost province of Galicia comes vividly clear."

—Dan Glover, *The Toronto Globe and Mail*

"*Conspirators* is a deeply original novel, grand and far-seeing in its conception, comprehensive in its close examination of life in a Jewish community in eastern Austria. The blind ardor of the conspirators is matched by the blindness of fate, and the intensifying fever of their plots is linked to the onset of the First World War. The qualities of the writing suggested to this reader the work of Musil and Mann and, in the closeness of its observation, Proust."

—Paula Fox, author of *Desperate Characters* and *Borrowed Finery*

"Those who delight in leisurely, literary reads will welcome this book."

—*The Reporter*

"Clever analogies and juxtaposition are drawn in mesmerizing prose."

—Susan Farrington, *The Sanford Herald*

CONSPIRATORS

CONSPIRATORS

Michael André Bernstein

PICADOR

FARRAR, STRAUS AND GIROUX

NEW YORK

www.picadorusa.com

Picador® is a U.S. registered trademark and is used by Farrar, Straus and Giroux under license from Pan Books Limited.

For information on Picador Reading Group Guides, as well as ordering, please contact the Trade Marketing department at St. Martin's Press.
Phone: 1-800-221-7945 extension 763
Fax: 212-677-7456
E-mail: trademarketing@stmartins.com

Designed by Jonathan D. Lippincott

Library of Congress Cataloging-in-Publication Data

Bernstein, Michael André, 1947–
        Conspirators / Michael André Bernstein.
            p. cm.
        ISBN 0-312-42437-X
        EAN 978-0312-42437-4
        1. Europe—History—1871–1918—Fiction. 2. Galicia (Poland and Ukraine)—
Fiction. 3. Aristocracy (Social class)—Fiction. 4. Intelligence officers—Fiction.
5. Jewish preaching—Fiction. 6. Revolutionaries—Fiction. 7. Conspiracies—
Fiction. 8. Rabbis—Fiction. I. Title.

PS3552.E737C66 2004
813'.54—dc21   2003012713

First published in the United States by Farrar, Straus and Giroux

First Picador Edition: April 2004

10 9 8 7 6 5 4 3 2 1

OVERTURE

1925

C rossing into middle age, a successful writer is expected to enter his custodial phase, in which he services and maintains his prior accomplishments. Is that really what he was agreeing to now? The thought vexed Alexander too much for him to continue answering either of the letters lying open on his desk, so he got up from his chair by the window to stretch his legs, certain that at this hour he could walk down to the lake without meeting anyone.

Initially, Alexander had been flattered by his publisher's suggestion that this might be a good time to reissue all of his early works. He could easily visualize them displayed in a bookstore window, boxed together in one of those solemn-looking, uniform editions that middle-class Viennese households always seemed ready to buy, even when money was scarce. It was the closest such families could come to the rows of sumptuous, privately bound leather volumes, decorated with the family crest, that they were able to admire in the libraries of the nobility, now that former Imperial palaces like Schönbrunn had been opened to the public. Clearly, almost a decade as a republic had done nothing to diminish people's fascination with the Habsburgs. Quite the contrary: Images of the Emperor Franz Josef and his bride were even more prevalent than during their lifetimes, used to peddle everything from boxes of chocolate to tickets for an outdoor concert. A citizen could be excused for believing that nothing of interest had occurred since the end of their reign. The traffic in imperial nostalgia was one of the country's few stable industries, surviving every economic crisis, and for the better-off purchasers with aspirations to advanced taste, one of Klimt's erotic sketches, a Josef Hoffmann rocking chair, or a piece of Wiener Werkstätte jewelry fed the same nostalgia for lost glamour as the formulaic picture postcards of the Imperial family did in poorer homes. But so too, Alexander admitted ruefully to himself, did his own plays and stories.

In the first, hard days after the war, he had been terrified that no one would care for his writing anymore. The fear of being dismissed as obsolete had made him send out discreet feelers to the most important socialist journals, assuring them of his support and reminding the editors that he had always used his pen to satirize the absurdities of the old regime. All completely unnecessary, as it turned out. His work had never sold so well or received such glowing reviews, not even fourteen years ago, when the whole weight of the Interior Ministry was behind him and the newspapers secretly controlled by the government were crowning him one of the country's most promising young writers. If Baron von Kirchmayr, Franz Josef's last Chief of Police, were still alive, he would be astonished, and probably unpleasantly so, to see just how well his former protégé was doing without his backing. Lately at least one of Alexander's plays was always in repertoire somewhere in the country, and a few months ago a clumsy stage farce like *The Jew's Misfortune*, cobbled together from old notebooks at breakneck speed during his first penniless months in the capital, had been successfully revived for extended runs in both Salzburg and Vienna. Now, if a suitable English translation could be commissioned, there was even talk of a London production.

By the standards of a Thurn und Taxis or a Rotenburg, Alexander could hardly consider himself rich, but he had done well enough so that very little remained of the anxious young provincial who had arrived in Vienna from Galicia, dreaming only of finding a publisher for his short sketches and being allowed to sit in the same room with the famous writers who frequented the Café Central. But within less than a year—as though his career were itself an episode from one of his own half-melancholy, half-cynical fables, in which, for reasons Alexander himself could never fathom, Viennese of all classes seemed to rediscover some forgotten part of their dream lives—he found himself almost as well known as any of the authors he used to admire from a distance. Soon the knowledge that his royalties were beginning to exceed theirs by a sizable margin created just as wide a gulf between Alexander and the writers who congregated in the literary coffeehouses as his lack of reputation and money had done when he first walked through the heavy wood and glass doors of the Café Central and found himself instantly relegated to the worst table in the room. As his means increased, Alexander became a kind of restless urban Gypsy, the Wandering Jew of a single city, as he described himself in one of his letters home to Asher Blumenthal, the only friend from his adolescence with whom he continued to keep in close touch. He moved from district to district, always insisting on a short-term lease, although the rent was inevitably higher that way, until more out of weariness than anything else, he settled on the second floor of an elegant house on the Bäckerstrasse, one of the cloistered Viennese neighborhoods famous for having housed some of the greatest composers of the nineteenth century, and ever since, notoriously unwelcoming to living artists of any sort. When the earnings from his second successful opera libretto, *Flowers for the Hanged Men*, finally let him buy the vacation home that he had long coveted, situated on the most beautiful lake in the whole Salzkammergut, he intended to follow the same rhythm as all the other prosperous seasonal visitors and use it only during the summer months. But every autumn, when it came time to board up the house until next Easter, he found himself increasingly reluctant to return to the capital. Eventually Alexander simply decided to give in to his longing for solitude, and he now lived year round in the countryside outside Salzburg. The only time he returned to Vienna these days was when a new piece was in rehearsal at the Burgtheater, and he had to be on hand to supervise the production and be agreeable to all the important reviewers. Toadying to the rich, ruthless, and wellborn who controlled a writer's career under the Habsburgs had been replaced by toadying to the poor, ruthless, and ill-bred who controlled an author's career in the new parliamentary republic. With only the slightest adjustment of vocabulary and tone, Alexander found that the same phrases he had used successfully with aristocrats like Director von Bruck and Baron von Kirchmayr, now worked just as well with Herr Nebehaye from the liberal paper the *New Free Press* and even with the formidable Fräulein Ruth Zuckerman, the principal literary critic for the Austro-Marxist *The Voice of the Worker*. The chief difference, as far as Alexander could tell, was in the quality of the coffee and pastries that were served at their meetings and in the bluntness with which the required quid pro quos were outlined to him.

Except for the faint glow of his own stubby cigar and the slightly hazy light from his study window overhead, everything on this side of the lake looked as though it had vanished into the waves of blue-black darkness that seemed to flow down at dusk from the circle of the surrounding mountains to the waterline. There were still a few lights visible on the other side, in Sankt Wolfgang, where the hotels and summer boarding-houses were located, but seen at such a distance, they only intensified the stillness through which Alexander was glad to walk undisturbed until he had regained his composure. The offer to put out an interim *Collected Works* made him feel as if he were being asked to help design his own cenotaph, all the more so since his publisher wanted him to compose a se-ries of prefaces to his texts specially for this edition. The idea of such a retrospective self-appraisal appalled Alexander. Unlike most of the writers he knew, he had very little interest in talking about himself and still less about what the journalists called his sources of inspiration. No doubt that was why, though he was never entirely able to shake a certain discomfort dealing with actors and directors, he had ended up writing so much for the theater, where he could represent his characters' words and passions without the need for any intrusive meddling in his own voice.

But the prospective tedium of composing a handful of new forewords to his prewar works was not really the source of Alexander's agitation. If that were all, refusing the suggestion would be simple enough. He was making too much money for the Europa Publishing House for them to press him too hard, and besides, they could always hire some academic from the university, who would be glad of a few extra schillings to write the critical introductions in Alexander's place. A preface by some distin-guished Herr Professor X or other might actually be preferable as a stimu-lus to sales, giving the edition the ponderous armature of an authentic classic. No, what had driven him out of his warm study into the chilliness of the August night, where he was already smoking more than his doctor allowed him, was an obscure sense that Broderson's proposition was somehow linked to the small newspaper picture that had been haunting him ever since his visit to Berlin six months ago. He had spent an inordi-nate amount of time since then trying alternately to verify the identity of the man in the photo and to put the whole question out of his mind, with-out succeeding in either.

He had traveled to Germany at the invitation of the *Berliner Funkstunde*, a radio program paying well-known authors princely sums to read from their works. He could never hope to earn as much in Austria for a few sessions in front of a microphone, and the opportunity of intimacy without actual personal contact offered by the new medium was irre-sistible. The broadcasts had gone even better than he and his employers at the station had hoped. Somewhat to Alexander's astonishment, the vogue for his urbanely risqué vignettes about life in the old Habsburg Empire had spread to Germany as well, perhaps because people there found little to look back on with affectionate nostalgia in their own deposed dynasty. Clearly some lost causes were more marketable than others. For whatever reason, the audience had been so enthusiastic that Alexander received an open invitation to return for more readings.

The next morning, feeling thoroughly pleased with the trip and only a little piqued that none of the other passengers seemed to recognize him as the famous foreign author whose books were on sale everywhere in the city, Alexander stood at a kiosk in the train station, buying half a dozen newspapers to browse through on the ride back to Salzburg. The managing director of the radio station had boasted that there were now over two thousand different periodicals available, and it seemed that at least a third of them were folded up in large bundles near the ticket counter to tempt travelers of every taste. He had planned to buy mainly literary journals and some of the specialized radio reviews to see if any of them might be a suitable outlet for his new work. But just as he was getting ready to pay, he caught sight of a thin, cheaply printed tabloid titled *Exiled Voices* and on an impulse added it to his pile. He did so mostly because it contained a new article by Alicia Chudo, a White Russian émigrée, whose accounts of her experiences in the months between the fall of the Czar and the Bolshevik seizure of power he had enjoyed reading a while ago. Instead of the gloomy self-pity that seemed to characterize so many of these reminiscences, Chudo had impressed him with her wit and a wickedly disabused lucidity that saw the absurdity in her own camp as much as the evil in her enemies. That probably explained why she had been banished from the more prestigious White newspapers and forced to place her pieces in obscure journals like this unattractive quarterly of which Alexander had never heard.

He didn't turn to her piece until well into the late afternoon, when something about the delicate curvature of the timbered farmhouses, the small balconies decorated with tulips in full spring bloom, and the familiar pale yellow walls of the local stations past which their express train rushed without stopping made him realize that they were approaching the Austrian border. The new article was quite different in tone from Chudo's earlier work and dealt entirely with a dreadful episode from just before her permanent expulsion from Russia, when she had been arrested and questioned by the Cheka as a suspected counterrevolutionary agent. Unlike some of her friends, she hadn't been physically tortured, but for days on end she had been interrogated by changing teams of inquisitors without ever being permitted to sleep more than an hour or two at a time, until the exhaustion, together with anxiety over the fate of her husband and teenage daughter, made her try to kill herself in her cell. As a piece of writing, Alexander found Chudo's description powerful enough, but there were so many similar stories coming out these days that halfway through, he found himself beginning to skim the rest of the piece. So he nearly missed the small, out-of-focus photograph in the lower-right-hand corner with the startling caption "Group photo including the writer's principal interrogator." Unaccountably, as soon as his eyes fell on the picture, Alexander felt himself start to sweat with nervousness. He almost tore the flimsy paper in half trying to find where she switched from chronicling her prison experience to identifying the man in the image. After he had calmed down enough to look more systematically, he saw the text right away, set off by a thin black border and given a column of its own on the same page as the three-line biographies that served as the journal's "Notes on This Issue's Contributors": "This photo of the Soviet trade delegation visiting here last month was obtained by our own photographer, whose camera was nearly smashed out of his hands by local KPD thugs when they saw what he was doing. The man standing with his head partly turned away, directly behind the chief commercial representative, Georg Sklarz, is listed in the official protocol as Avrakham Shubin and described only as a specialist in foreign trade. But several trustworthy people in the émigré community have come forward in support of Alicia Chudo's accusation, and we now believe that he is one of the most ruthless leaders of the Soviet OGPU, possibly even Felix Dzerzhinsky's right-hand man."

The picture was far too blurry for Alexander to be confident, especially after so many years, but the longer he stared at the photo, the more he found himself unable to shake the thought that however the man was identified now—whether it was as Trade Delegate Shubin or as Alicia Chudo's unnamed tormentor of the Lubyianka Prison—he had once been Jakob Tausk, the brilliant former rabbinical student whom Alexander had gotten to know shortly before his own departure for Vienna.

They had been inseparable for only a few months, but those days were charged with the peculiar intimacy, half mutual admiration, half thinly concealed rivalry, of two desperately poor, ambitious young Jews in a town that had no use for their talents. At least Alexander had always known he

8

wanted to be a writer, a profession for which Tausk never bothered to disguise his contempt. Remembering the Tausk of those days, what lingered most in Alexander's mind was how little value he had placed on worldly success of any kind, especially the sort of acclaim for which Alexander hungered. But when Alexander challenged him to come up with a worthier ambition, Tausk refused to answer, shrugging off the question as though it were too frivolous to take seriously. To Alexander, it was clear Tausk had no idea of what he intended to do except lie in bed most of the day, smoke his endless succession of foul-smelling cigarettes, and brood over his expulsion from Rabbi Pelz's seminary. He never explained why he had been driven out, or rather, he came up with a dozen different versions, depending on his mood. But the one time Alexander had made a crude joke at the rabbi's expense, echoing, or so he thought, Tausk's own tone, Tausk simply stared back at him in disgust as though he were looking at some diseased animal and said quietly that if Alexander ever spoke like that about his teacher again, it would be the last time he would have a tongue to use. Then, just as abruptly, as though nothing unusual had occurred, Tausk began to speculate about where they could borrow enough money to go have dinner at Meir's restaurant, at one of whose greasy communal tables they had originally met.

Alexander no longer remembered whether they were successful in their quest or not, but soon after that evening he stopped visiting Tausk. He made no effort to write to Tausk from Vienna and was shocked when he first heard a rumor that the province's Count-Governor had hired Tausk to help protect him from assassination. Poor Asher Blumenthal eventually confirmed the rumor and admitted that Tausk had terrorized him for a whole year, forcing the reluctant accountant to act as a police informer, just as, to be perfectly honest, von Kirchmayr had done with Alexander himself. By the time of the notorious Cathedral Square murders in April 1914, Tausk had risen to the rank of chief spy for Count Wiladowski, and oblique references to him surfaced occasionally in the newspapers. At first these murders, committed on the very steps of the church, attracted the curiosity of the entire Empire, but their fame was almost immediately eclipsed by the much greater madness that soon engulfed the whole continent. Since the killings took place on Tausk's watch, so to speak, Alexander had always assumed that the spymaster must have been discreetly cashiered for incompetence and sent to the same jail with which he had threatened so many townsmen during his brief time in office. To Alexander, there was something offensive in the possibility that such a person, a figure belonging to the realm of Habsburg fables that Alexander had made his own literary property, should simply have changed uniform and script and reemerged on a much larger stage with the power to terrorize a whole country.

As soon as he got home, Alexander set about trying to discover what really had become of Jakob Tausk. His former patrons had taught Alexander the trick of being on good terms with men in power, and he was not one to let a useful lesson fall into abeyance merely because of a change in regimes. His relationship with Michael Skubl, the new Viennese Chief of Police, was particularly close, and Alexander promptly wrote to him, requesting assistance in solving the mystery. When Alexander invented the excuse that he needed the information for a new play on which he was currently working, Skubl, as ardent a theatergoer as any of his aristocratic predecessors, put the full resources of his department to work on the question. But to judge by the results, the gathering of intelligence had declined lamentably since von Kirchmayr's day. Instead of the massive dossier on which Alexander had counted, all that Skubl's private messenger was able to deliver to Alexander's lakeside house was a thin sheaf of papers and an apologetic letter, both of which were now lying on his desk beside the contract from the publisher.

Skubl explained that since the province where the crime had taken place was no longer part of Austria, the local archives were unavailable for direct inspection. As a matter of professional courtesy, though, one of his foreign colleagues had obligingly looked into the question but had found no record of legal proceedings involving a Jakob Tausk. Nor were the public record offices in Vienna much more helpful. Documentation finally turned up from a secondary register, confirming that Tausk had indeed been employed by the Interior Ministry from 1912 until sometime in 1914, but the paperwork was surprisingly incomplete, and even before the outbreak of hostilities in August 1914, Tausk's name had vanished entirely from the files. Of course many government papers, especially documents concerning the old government's far-flung network of spies, had been lost or misfiled in the months before the republic was declared, and it would be imprudent to draw any conclusions from one more instance of so widespread a phenomenon.

Alexander stopped reading for a moment to marvel at how thoroughly Skubl had absorbed the rhetoric of his job. "It would be imprudent to draw any conclusions" was a perfect Austrian bureaucrat's phrase, employed by generations of Imperial officials and now just as useful in the mouths of their republican successors. When he came home at night and took off his uniform did Skubl congratulate himself on how well he had played his part that day, or would such a thought interfere with his ability to repeat the role without a slip for the rest of his run? In the little notebook that he kept in his breast pocket for such occasions, Alexander quickly wrote down the formulation, intending to use it, along with some of Skubl's other characteristic sayings, in a small comic sketch set during Maria Theresa's reign, a century and a half ago.

It was, admittedly, an ungenerous way to repay a man who had gone to considerable trouble to help him, but by the time he read that far, Alexander was feeling anything but generous-minded. Nor was his sour mood improved by the last paragraph of Skubl's letter, which was what finally drove him out of the house altogether. As far as the recent, putative sighting in Berlin was concerned, Skubl merely said that given the current political climate in Russia, it was impossible to put much credence in accusations published in a paper like *Exiled Voices*. There was no telling who worked for the OGPU and who didn't, but speaking as a professional, he proceeded on the assumption that everyone coming from Russia was connected to the Soviet secret police in one form or another. Since his colleagues in Germany felt the same way, they kept close watch on all such visitors and had established that although an Avrakham Shubin had entered the country as an accredited member of a trade delegation, he returned home a whole week before anyone else from his group, the very evening, in fact, that his picture had been taken by Chudo's friends. But—and by now Alexander was so sure of what Skubl would write next that he permitted himself a stagey, exaggerated groan even before seeing the actual phrase—"one really mustn't leap to any conclusions from such circumstantial details." An understandable reluctance to encourage unproved rumors made Skubl hesitate to include the final item forwarded from Germany, but since Alexander was interested only in getting background information for his dramatic work, not in making trouble through tendentious political journalism, there was no harm in letting him see how overwrought the émigré community's fantasies were and what kinds of lurid hearsay the police had to look into these days. According to a certain Ekaterina Galitzina, widow of a recent fugitive from Russia who had been killed in an automobile accident shortly after settling in Berlin, her husband had been in possession of indisputable proof that several important Bolshevik leaders, including some now involved in the fight for control of the party, had been double agents for the Czar. He had been on his way to deliver this proof to the newspapers when he was struck by a speeding car and died instantly. Of course, when the ambulance came, no inflammatory documents of any kind were found on him, and a thorough police investigation turned up no sign of anything beyond an unfortunate hit-and-run incident of the kind that was increasingly common, especially in an unsavory district like the Scheunenviertel. But to the crowd at the editorial office of *Exiled Voices*, the explanation was obvious: Galitzine's evidence was so damning that Dzerzhinsky had to send in the one person he could trust to make sure it would never be made public, even if that meant risking his most valuable agent. The man using the name Shubin crossed the border just once to do a single job; as soon as it was done, he disappeared from sight, and it was a foregone conclusion that he would never be heard from again.

Alexander watched the last of his thin cigars arc elegantly into the water and vanish. He had deliberately left the rest back inside, knowing that otherwise he'd go through them all before his walk was over. Nothing in Skubl's letter should have disturbed him this much, but repeating that to himself was not helping matters. Instead of calming down, he became more agitated than ever, mostly at finding himself so shaken by a story that, true or not, really didn't involve him at all. By the time Tausk was fully installed in his position as the Count-Governor's spymaster, Alexander had been in Vienna and out of reach of his machinations. But perhaps not entirely. Alexander had put the whole affair out of his mind years ago, but in those first days, when he used to puzzle about it ceaselessly, he had concluded that the suggestion to entrap him must originally have come from Tausk. An unpublished Jewish scribbler from Galicia, with no political interests or contacts, who shared a sordid little room on the Kleine Schiffgasse, was hardly someone to attract the attention of a man like Baron von Kirchmayr, unless the Police Chief's interest had been steered in his direction by a persuasive voice from Alexander's hometown. And since Tausk had brought in Asher for formal questioning even before Alexander's own "interview" with von Kirchmayr, it was hard not to see the whole affair as a two-pronged campaign, intended to ensnare both of them together. At first Asher was probably the more important catch of the two. Through the Mendelssohn Club, he had a chance to associate with the most prominent Jews in the province, including even the Rotenburgs, and could report on their activities without arousing suspicion. No one, however, could have predicted the extent of Alexander's success, not even if one had taken into account how much help he had been given secretly by the government. Watching Alexander become a celebrated figure in the Viennese literary world was merely an unexpected bonus for all concerned. Tausk, in particular, would have enjoyed following it from a distance, knowing all the while he had the power to ruin Alexander merely by revealing the services to the state that he himself had been instrumental in forcing the writer to perform.

But these were all just insubstantial speculations from long ago, probably quite unrelated to anything in Chudo's story. The tantalizing photograph was just that: an image so indistinct it could plausibly portray half the Jews Alexander knew. In her article Chudo herself admitted that she had never once heard her interrogator's name. None of the other jailors ever mentioned it either or called him anything but Comrade, as though it were dangerous simply to speak his name. He was usually accompanied by a disheveled familiar who seemed to serve him as both personal guard and intermediary to the rest of the prison staff and who appeared, as far as Chudo could judge such things, less terrified of him than the other Chekists. But since the man had not accompanied his master to Berlin, there was no picture of him available to compare with any of Tausk's former acquaintances. The whole time Alexander was going over these facts, trying to understand what, if anything, they really signified, he had the unpleasant feeling that he was revising one of his own intricate plots and turning it into a satire against himself. In the world of his plays and stories, as in the fairy tales and legends on which he deliberately patterned even his most ironic works, everything was deeply connected, and when a particular adventure ended unhappily, readers were nonetheless comforted to find the characters' lives so cunningly intertwined. For Alexander, sophistication was strictly a surface virtue, a tone at which he excelled, but which he used only as a foil to the deliberately simple rhythm of a fable on which his intricacies rested. However, ever since he had left Berlin, that simplifying urge was transforming everything into a macabre parody. What was someone like Jakob Tausk doing killing people for the OGPU anyway? It was as absurd as if figures from his favorite paintings at the Kunsthistorisches Museum decided to wander off into different canvases altogether. He suddenly imagined a group of Bosch's malshapen demons stumbling into one of Vermeer's tranquil kitchens, where they continued to carouse raucously while the morning light flowed gently downward from a high lead-paned window and a single, pensive woman stood pouring milk from an earthenware pitcher into a deep blue and white breakfast jug. That was just how Alexander felt about Tausk's reappearing. He belonged exactly where Alexander had depicted him in dozens of sketches, beside Asher, the Rotenburgs, Count-Governor Wiladowski, and the rest of them, and it was sheer malice on Tausk's part—almost a personal violation—to rewrite himself, as though the whole world Alexander had painstakingly built up in the successive volumes Broderson was so eager to reedit didn't merit so much as a backward glance.

Maybe the tedious hacks at *The Voice of the Worker* were right after all and he really didn't understand anything about people. But they were hardly in a position to give advice, though that seemed to be their house specialty these days. Like that impossible Zuckerman woman, who bullied everyone she knew but was so devoted to her wonder rebbe Marx that she would die rather than utter a single phrase that couldn't be supported by a quotation from one of his sacred texts. Alexander had been forced to listen to enough of her sermonizing over the past two or three years that by dint of repetition he himself had acquired a stock of the master's phrases. If he did end up agreeing to a *Collected Works* and wanted a glowing review from her, maybe he should write to Moscow and see if Comrade Shubin, c/o the Lubyianka Prison, would care to provide an introduction to one of the volumes. What was it she loved to quote from Marx about everything important in history's occurring twice: the first time as tragedy, the second as farce? What drivel. He knew about both farce and tragedy and would stake his professional reputation that Marx had gotten it exactly backward. Actually, how could *any* Austrian believe such nonsense when history clearly showed that in the Danube countries everything occurred *first* as farce and that only later, after its provincial tryout in the comic mode, was it taken up by the rest of the world and replayed as a tragedy. Alexander seemed to recall that Tausk had despised such glib literary analogies, but if he was really working for the Bolsheviks these days, with their theatrical party congresses and florid propaganda, no doubt he would have learned to disguise his repugnance. In fact it was precisely the deliberate literariness of the clues connecting Dzerzhinsky's fearsome agent, Trade Delegate Shubin, and Jakob Tausk that dismayed Alexander the most. The whole story contained elements of a costume melodrama, unpleasantly reminiscent of some of his own facile successes. One detail, in particular, was so embarrassingly familiar that he avoided mentioning it to Skubl. Ever since the first reviews of *The Jew's Misfortune*, Alexander had amused himself by naming his most dull-witted, fatuous characters after anyone who had thwarted him early in his career. The names were sufficiently disguised for Alexander to be able to plead an astonished innocence if one of his targets ever confronted him, and over the years the game had become more of a private joke than a desire for revenge against his critics, most of whom were long forgotten anyway. Only Asher, and perhaps Tausk, if he was still alive, would know about Alexander's little joke. So it was impossible for Alexander to tell whether or not the name adopted by the OGPU assassin for his trip to Berlin was devised according to a similar principle, but anyone who had grown up on the border between the Czar's Empire and Franz Josef's would have recognized that Avrakham Shubin was the perfect Russian equivalent of Avraham Pelz, the name of the one man in whose presence Tausk had said he felt "unworthy." It was Pelz who had driven Tausk forever into the secular world, sentencing his most gifted student to live out his days in what he had taught him to view as a realm of spiritual darkness, where even the words of the Law came out of men's mouths already bearing bestial traces. To take on the name of his teacher for the filthiest purposes would be an act of vengeance—against Rabbi Pelz, against what he himself had become, or against both at the same time—of which the Tausk Alexander had known might just be capable. Alexander was not vain enough to think Tausk's gesture was directed against him. A trivial writerly amusement he indulged in was being used for far more malicious ends. Whether Alexander would ever hear about it would not have mattered to Tausk. It was the act of defilement itself he cared about; the rest was mere anecdote.

Alexander's suspicion that all these threads were being spun only in his own imagination was hardly reassuring. Even the tranquillity of the deserted path between the dense wood forest and the waterline, which usually restored Alexander's spirits, left him as restless as if he had taken the evening ferry across the lake to the Empress Elisabeth Hotel bar. By now the place would have been closed for several hours anyway, and before too long the morning shift would be arriving to set up for breakfast on the terrace. Although he had been pacing outside in the cool night air for several hours, Alexander wasn't tired or hungry, but his shoes had gotten soaked through from the dew on the ground, and he badly craved one of the cigars he foolishly had left behind on his desk. To judge by the first faint traces of red and gold emerging over the Zwölverhorn Mountain, it would be a glorious morning soon down in Sankt Wolfgang. Right now, though, everything—houses, hills, and water alike—was still wrapped in a softly luminous fog, and the trees looked like mere stains under the wash of mist that was thickening the late-night air. It was time to go home. He would never be able to free himself from wondering about Tausk by turning to a man like Skubl. It was not police work Alexander needed, and he had been deluded ever to think so. The people involved in the town's affairs at the time of the Cathedral Square murders would be more helpful, and he intended to contact as many of them as he could in the weeks ahead. In the end the only defense against letting his own story be imagined for him by others was to accept the task of telling it himself. Climbing the narrow staircase, past the ground-floor kitchen to his study, he decided how he would answer Broderson. It was not just his legacy as a writer that was at stake now. He would agree to put out an interim *Collected Works*, but instead of the usual string of separate prefaces for each volume, the introduction to the entire edition would be itself a brand-new book, specially written for the occasion and dedicated "to the memory of the companions of my youth, Asher Blumenthal in Palestine and Jakob Tausk, wherever he may be living today."

· ◆ ·

With each passing week, darkness began to take root earlier. The harvesters had finished scything the fields at the edge of the wood behind Alexander's house, and the short stubble they left behind seemed to trap each shred of light until nightfall. Alexander was calmer now as he gazed out the window of his study. The irritability he had felt ever since seeing Shubin's photograph was gradually dissipated by the delicate task of initiating a correspondence with people he had never met, including distinguished figures like the Countess Elisabeth von Alpsbach, widow of one of the largest landowners in what had been his home province. According to Skubl, who, in spite of Alexander's earlier doubts, proved himself indispensable by coming up with a list of helpful names and addresses, only the late Count's heroic death in the war had made everyone forget that he had been at least indirectly implicated in the Cathedral Square murders. The archives at Police Headquarters in Vienna revealed that there had been considerable debate about arresting Ernst von Alpsbach as an accessory, but his younger brother's self-sacrifice during the murders and the absence of any definitive proof of Ernst's guilt had spared him the ignominy of a public trial. There was even a story going around that his widow was writing some kind of family memoir herself. Her own background was apparently much less distinguished than the von Alpsbachs had hoped for in the wife of the family heir, and perhaps she had taken to writing to compensate for a sense of social inferiority. Alexander decided to seize on this information to approach her as a fellow author, almost, one might say, as a colleague, to solicit her help in better understanding what had gone on behind the scenes in aristocratic circles during the last year before the war. Considering what Skubl had told him about her husband, Alexander was far too discreet to refer directly to the murders, but he was certain that if it was true that the Countess had literary ambitions, she would be sure to leap at the chance of discussing everything she knew, or just imagined, about so dramatic an episode, with a well-known author like him.

In each of the letters he sent out, Alexander tailored his initial approach to what he imagined was likeliest to elicit a response. But since he often had very little information to go on beyond a name and brief description of the person's rank or profession, composing these letters already required a certain amount of novelizing, and although not everyone bothered to answer him, he heard back from enough people to provide him with a rich storehouse of characteristic incidents and points of view on which he could later draw. It was one of Alexander's habitual analogies, and he meant it in a strictly practical, craftsmanlike way. He planned to use whatever his correspondents wrote him much as a painter might incorporate different elements from his various sketchbooks in a single new composition, freely combining, for example, a quick charcoal drawing of an unknown woman's profile at a market stall made years ago with a more recent pencil and ink study of faces at a crowded political rally. Long experience made Alexander take for granted that his correspondents would agree to help him only if each one was assured that his insights alone were indispensable. Alexander was quite ready to flatter everyone on his list, from great countesses to retired minor civil servants, with a lavishly democratic impartiality, but to his astonishment, there was no need for any of this. On the contrary, almost every reply opened with an admission of how partial and fragmentary the letter writer's own understanding of the events had been. Far from their claiming a reliable overview, it was exactly the sense of something left not so much undone as not understood that made many of the people to whom he wrote reply so promptly and at such length to Alexander's questions. Trying to make sense of those frantic months long ago seemed to draw from everyone who made the attempt a similar declaration of puzzlement, apparently as unavoidable, although hardly as reassuring, as the opening "once upon a time" of fairy tales. But these avowals of uncertainty were regularly accompanied by a marked skepticism, sometimes even an open hostility toward other versions of the story potentially in circulation. The full truth might never be known, but according to the various letter writers, that was no reason for Alexander to trust anyone else's self-interested version. There was not even any agreement about who the most important actors in the drama were, and as the letters began to accumulate, the contradictions and barely disguised rivalry among the various stories became as compelling as any of the actual accounts. Still, the adjustment in perspective Alexander resisted longest was also the only one on which virtually all his correspondents seemed united. For them, Tausk was simply not the principal figure in the drama. At most it was as the skillful tool of a corrupt provincial governor that Tausk was granted a measure of importance. Not even Asher, whom Tausk had bullied so pitilessly, saw him as anything more than that. To Alexander, these unexpected revelations were anything but comforting. It was just about possible for him to project a story line linking the shadowy figure able to inspire fear even in the Lubyianka guards to the Tausk who had successfully imposed his will on a whole Imperial province, but not if it turned out that Tausk had only carried out the ideas of some worn-out Habsburg aristocrat. Such a life seemed profoundly unnarratable, at least within any of the terms Alexander had envisaged.

Up until now, as soon as Alexander reached what felt like a dead end with one of his texts, he had taken it as a signal that he was on the wrong path. This time, though, rather than be tempted to abandon the new work, he felt himself compelled forward by the very obstacles that were slowing his progress. The prospect of deliberately writing something that couldn't be read as another piece of Habsburg nostalgia exerted a more powerful appeal than he had foreseen. Alexander's declarations of sympathy with the socialist editors at the end of the war hadn't been as cynical as he liked to pretend to himself these days; his early writings certainly contained numerous satiric scenes ridiculing the old Empire's inanities, sometimes so sharply that von Kirchmayr would call him in and warn him that it was time to rein in his impudence. The Baron himself found Alexander's sketches quite amusing and thought that a reputation for daring could only help confirm the writer's credibility with the radicals on whose activities he was to report back to the police, but others in the government didn't share von Kirchmayr's tolerance for Jewish wit and regarded it as a mistake to permit any mockery from such tainted sources. More powerfully than any censorship, though, time itself seemed to have taken all the sting out of satires like Alexander's. His most biting scenes were now read as affectionately nostalgic recollections, especially by a newer generation, because the world they found depicted there was gone forever and its staunchest representatives had long since been buried in their family tombs or the anonymous mass graveyards of the war. How could his readers' laughter not be layered with affection when history had already passed a far harsher judgment than any Alexander had ever wished upon his characters? The objects of Alexander's mockery seemingly had lost their power to do any more damage, and with that loss they had been transformed into touching figures from a fable, who evoke the protective solicitude with which the passage of time gradually envelops all of one's childhood legends. But what if the old demons hadn't become so harmless after all and were flourishing as much as ever, only in different uniforms and with other titles? There were some things that even the Viennese might not be able to turn into another piece of marzipan confection, and Alexander was gripped by the idea that if he did come up with a way to add this, the final and strangest of his "Galician Tales," to his *Collected Works*, he would have found such a subject.

For all the delight he took in his success, Alexander had never made the mistake of identifying with his titled admirers. There was little that revolted him more than the way the courtiers of the exiled Habsburg claimant to the throne tried to use work like his to further their fantasy of returning to power. Three years ago, when Alexander's *A Casanova of the Provinces* had its premiere at the Burgtheater, the Imperial aide-de-camp, Count Trautmannsdorff, had sent a congratulatory wreath backstage, wrapped in the black and yellow colors of the Habsburgs and with an effusive card signed simply "Trautmannsdorff." At first Alexander couldn't help feeling flattered. When Franz Josef still ruled the Empire, a Trautmannsdorff would have been appalled at the idea of being expected to acknowledge the existence of someone like Alexander Garber. But when

Alexander read out Trautmannsdorff's note and found himself lauded as "a true fighter for the monarchy," his pleasure turned to disgust. "The enemy of my enemy is my friend" had always struck him as a fatuous maxim, and not even the crude badgering of the Fräulein Zuckermans of the world would make him grateful that a Trautmannsdorff now thought him worth a tin wreath.

One thing, at least, was clear from everything he had been able to piece together so far about the Cathedral Square murders: It was an episode that neither Count Trautmannsdorff nor Fräulein Zuckerman would enjoy reading about, and in his present mood that realization was enough to make Alexander press forward in spite of his doubts about whether he would be able to make a coherent story out of it. To Alexander, the formal shapeliness of his work had always been important and no doubt accounted for the mutual impatience between him and the avant-garde critics. But even in this regard, his preferences were purely instinctive. Abstract arguments about art had always left him indifferent, and although he pored over every discussion of his work, no matter how obscure the journal in which it appeared—all the while of course protesting that he never bothered looking at his reviews—he could never understand why someone capable of writing decent prose would want to waste time on a form as tedious, and as badly paid, as literary polemics. Now, though, he confronted a dilemma designed to baffle him. The story to which he was drawn seemed to call for exactly the kind of fractured, shifting perspectives from which he drew so little pleasure as a reader and for which, in any case, he had never shown any flair as an author. It was useless to talk about his problem with practical men like Broderson and Skubl, and ever since he had stopped having to keep von Kirchmayr informed about the literary world, Alexander had avoided personal contact with other writers as much as possible. So it felt like a totally unexpected gift that just when he most needed an attentive ear, Alexander found a passionate ally in Alicia Chudo. She had been among the first people to whom Alexander had written on his return from Berlin, not just to tell her how powerfully her article had affected him but also to admit that he might have once known, indeed even befriended, the man who had caused her so much anguish. Gradually a kind of reserved intimacy grew up between the two writers, aided, he thought, by the fact that they both were content to confine their relationship entirely to the page and not risk jeopardizing it by a personal encounter. To Alexander, her helpfulness sometimes reminded him of one of the wise old women who were regularly appearing in his Galician tales to teach the hero the virtues of a simple peasant life, except, as she mordantly reminded him, she was not old, had never done any manual labor in her life, and thought that Marx's comment about "the idiocy of rural life" was the only accurate observation in the man's entire pernicious corpus. She wasn't religious either, Chudo briskly cautioned him, and would strongly prefer that he never recast her as the voice of some profound spiritual wisdom that came from nightlong prison vigils with only the Gospels and Tolstoy's late stories as her companions. The cells in the Lubyianka were far too crowded for such conversion scenes, and under Dzerzhinsky, unlike in Czarist times, books were completely forbidden. Besides, she detested accounts of spiritual awakenings and held them almost as responsible for her country's woes as the pamphlets of the Red agitators. Her mock annoyance delighted Alexander. Not only was Chudo formidably intelligent, but more usefully, she appeared to delight in exactly the kinds of questions for which he himself had no patience. She was fascinated by Alexander's attempt to find out what had become of Tausk, and when he complained to her about his failure to make any progress at all with that question, let alone to determine if Tausk and Trade Delegate Shubin were truly the same man, her only reply was to ask for a copy of the various letters Alexander had received on the subject. Three weeks after he had sent her a thick package of everything he had put together so far, Alexander received a telegram from Berlin, saying only: "Arriving Salzburg in three days. Staying with Caroline Potiorek 12 Schrannengasse. Come for coffee 3 P.M. Chudo."

· ◆ ·

An invitation to be the best man at the wedding of Count Trautmannsdorff's eldest son would have surprised Alexander less than this unwelcome intrusion into his solitude by one of the few people he had credited with enough discretion not to make a nuisance of herself. Could it be that he was wrong in his judgment of her and that beneath the clearheaded, subtle writer he had admired was just another hysterical Russian émigrée, eager to embroil everyone in her self-dramatizations? Even if he kept their meeting as brief as politeness allowed, the whole day would almost certainly be wasted. He would probably end up having to take a room for the night in order not to have to travel back to Gschwendt after dark. He spent the next few hours reproaching alternately himself for ever having written her and Chudo for having so disappointed him. Gradually Alexander forced himself to calm down and take seriously the possibility that she really had something important to tell him. No matter how he tried, though, he found himself unable to imagine what that might be, and when it finally came time for him to leave for Salzburg, he was thoroughly enervated by the whole situation.

At least the train ride through the steep mountains, with the lake a brilliant Memling blue in the late-fall sunlight, helped restore some of his good spirits, and by the time the great fortress of Hohensalzburg and the towers of the Prince-Archbishop's palace came into view, Alexander felt able to renew his resolution to make the best of Chudo's bizarre whim. At this time of year the old city wasn't too crowded, but Alexander was still glad that Chudo's friend lived on the right bank of the Salzach River, a few minutes' walk across the bridge from the fashionable town center. He found the building without any difficulty and saw by the nameplates that Potiorek lived on the second floor in what appeared, at least from street level, to be a comfortably spacious apartment. Alexander lingered outside a few moments, trying to settle in advance what tone he would adopt to get through the first, inevitably awkward moments of the encounter awaiting him upstairs.

As it turned out, his hesitation was pointless. Before he reached the front door, it had swung open toward him, and a short dark-haired woman, wrapped in an oversize and far from new fur coat, emerged briskly from the building and stood in the street, staring at him for several seconds. "Well, Herr Garber"—she greeted him in a slightly hoarse, amused voice, with only a faint trace of a Russian accent—"since it is obvious that you are too polite to risk disturbing a pair of old ladies by ringing the doorbell, I thought I should come down and save you the embarrassment of standing out here any longer. Although it might have been more comfortable to make our introductions upstairs, I am delighted to meet you and apologize if you were startled by my telegram. I am Alicia Chudo," she added, quite unnecessarily. Then, in a gesture that Alexander would never have expected from someone seemingly so self-assured and that went a long way toward quieting many of the doubts he felt about being there at all, she stretched out her hand to him, accompanied by a slight, but unmistakable curtsy, like one that a young girl might make at her first dance or when greeting her parents' dinner guests. Alexander knew that she must be well into her forties, and she made no attempt to look younger than her years, but the combination of an almost residual coquettishness with her natural formality was so obviously a spontaneous reenactment of who she had once been in another country and epoch that Alexander felt abashed at not having brought any flowers or chocolates to offer her in turn.

But his lack of foresight also gave Alexander an opportunity which he quickly seized. He immediately took her hand in his and bent his face down over it in the symbolic finger kiss of innumerable Austrian stage plays, including many of his own, all the while smiling at the comic exaggeration of the ritual as though he and Chudo were sharing a joke at such a manifestly absurd convention. "Of course, my dear lady, of course, I completely understand." Alexander went on, "I am absolutely delighted to meet you at last and was simply waiting here until I could make up my mind where to invite you and your friend for coffee and cake. We are very close to the Café Bazar, which has decent pastries and a fine view of the river but is also the favorite spot for Salzburg's literary types. Or there's Tomaselli over on the Alter Markt, where there may be a bit more variety in the choice of sweets. But since I don't know where your friend has already taken you, I was in a real quandary what to suggest."

To Alexander's relief, Chudo smiled in all the right places at the self-mocking formality of his speech. Immediately behind her amused look, though, Chudo's gaze was detached and quizzical, her face marked with fatigue kept at bay only by a strong self-discipline. Unlike well-bred Austrian women, who still thought it bad form to wear eyeglasses in public and consequently had a kind of dreamy inward look that was simply the physiological manifestation of taking in the world through a myopic haze, Chudo had on the same pair of thick tortoiseshell glasses that Alexander remembered finding slightly comical in the photograph on the back of one of her books. "I mentioned two old women just now," she replied, leaning in slightly toward Alexander whenever she spoke, as though to shelter her words from anyone within earshot, "but that was just a figure of speech. Actually, I am staying here entirely on my own. Caroline has gone to Munich for a few days and lent me her flat. Otherwise I probably wouldn't have come at all. Ever since my experience with your old friend back in Russia, I have had a horror of sharing a place with anyone. So you see, there's only me to invite. Tomaselli will be perfect." Although Chudo's German was grammatically perfect and, at moments, even elegant, nothing could be further from the rhythmical, continuous rise and fall of Austrian speech than the staccato bursts, framed by brief silences, with which her sentences were fired off. Nor did she sound like someone from Berlin, although that was where she had spent the most time since being expelled from Russia. Listening to Chudo tell him about her trip as they walked together back along the quay, then across the bridge toward the Alter Markt, Alexander had the impression that she inhabited her new language as an extra-nationalist who had mastered its resources but would never be entirely at home within it.

It was astonishing how much cake someone so slight could consume without feeling in the least ill. Chudo was on her third piece, having decided that rather than choose among several Alexander recommended, it would be more logical to sample them in turn. In between the pastries, each of which she accompanied by a fresh cup of strong black coffee taken, to the evident scandal of their waiter, without whipped cream, Chudo looked around at the elegant winter costumes of the ladies who made Tomaselli their regular afternoon meeting place, and instead of the ironic comment Alexander expected, she clearly approved of the atmosphere of well-fed somnolence that reigned there. She caught his surprised expression and shook her head slightly as though to dispel his own sharper comments before he spoke them aloud. "I have learned not to be so quick to pass judgment on people whose only crime is that they are enjoying themselves, even if their conversation isn't exactly the kind in which I am tempted to take part myself," she told him. "No one here cares about what we have come to talk about, and that only makes our own conversation less constrained. Besides, it's hard for me to get indignant about people whose principal vices are a passion for sweets, a little malice, and a great deal of gossip. Do you know how they define a decent man in my former country? Someone who knows he has to behave like a swine in order to survive but who does so without too much enjoyment. Well, I have seen plenty of swine who enjoy their work more the nastier it gets, so I feel at ease knowing I am in a room with people whose only reaction of disapproval of me is to pretend I don't exist. Did you notice how all the women looked away as soon as we came through the door and they saw me in that ridiculous coat I like so much? Especially the lady with the emerald brooch at the center table. She studied us the whole way over here but without ever looking up from her plate. It's obvious she recognizes you and can't imagine what you are doing here with a woman who is dressed like me and so can't be either your mistress or a wealthy patron."

Alexander glanced in the direction Chudo indicated and recognized Johanna von Welden, a woman whose middle-class husband had made a fortune during the war supplying the Imperial army with munitions whose failure rate was such a disgrace he came close to being arrested as a saboteur. Instead, in a solution typical of the war cabinet during those final chaotic months, it was decided to give Welden a title in the hope that it might encourage him to lower his profit margin and improve the reliability of his products. The newly ennobled manufacturer did nothing of the kind, but ever since the Republic was declared, Johanna had reinvented herself as a fanatic Habsburg loyalist, passionate anti-Semite, and living incarnation of the preindustrial values of old Austria. To her infinite sorrow, she hadn't lost a single relative in the war and so couldn't wear a mourning outfit commensurate with her new rank, but after much strenuous hand wringing, first with her confessor and then with a skillful Jewish seamstress she had found, she settled on a severely elegant black hat with a delicate veil that served to protect her from the dirt of the street and simultaneously to suggest, without openly so claiming, that she too had shared directly in the nation's calamity.

Alexander had met enough women like her to doubt that they were quite as harmless as Chudo assumed. If they were ever put in charge of more than the seating arrangements at a nationalist dinner, he was sure his life would take a distinct turn for the worse. But since there wasn't any chance of that happening, Alexander didn't feel like arguing the point with Chudo, who, he suspected, was unlikely to let herself be persuaded by him anyway, not even about people from his own country. Besides, Alexander was enjoying himself far too much listening to his companion's endless flow of theories about everything that crossed her field of vision to think of challenging her conclusions. She was the most theoretically minded person he had ever met, but the savingly fantastical aspect, from his point of view, was that her principal thesis seemed to be the extreme perniciousness of any tendency to overtheorize. While she made impressive inroads into an elaborately sculptured three-tier hazelnut cream cake, Chudo delivered a full-scale lecture on the topic, during which Alexander was glad to smile and nod his agreement, in the hope that doing so would excuse him from having to demonstrate that he grasped what she was saying. "The great vice of my people"—Chudo's tone alerted him that she was in the process of summing up her thoughts, and so Alexander made sure to pay especially close attention—"a vice we originally picked up largely from the Germans, by the way, is to forget that the only truth that matters is always already there, in front of us, hidden in plain view and unrecognized not because of its complexity but because of its very ordinariness. We spend all our time looking for some mysterious law or pattern underneath human existence and so are blind to the random, haphazard contingencies that end up shaping who we are and what kind of world we are making." With admirable timing, both her speech and the last piece of cake came to an end.

"Now here's someone who could get even Ruth Zuckerman to shut up. Why, she could think, talk, and eat Zuckerman into oblivion." Alexander pictured the scene to himself with gleeful anticipation. When it was clear, though, that in spite of all his diligent head nodding and earnest smiles, Chudo nonetheless expected some kind of reply, Alexander decided his safest bet was to make light of her speech by pointing out that especially in Austria, where abstract ideas had always been regarded as having about them a whiff of the vulgar and the seditious, Chudo's notion would certainly be well received. He added that as a Jew, who, in principle at least, was still waiting for signs of the Messiah's coming, he considered the search for hidden omens and arcane meanings in seemingly random events a quasi-religious obligation. But it was a duty he was prepared to set aside at her urging, just as thoroughly as he had already done with all the other injunctions of his faith.

Instead of smiling at his attempted jest, Chudo sat up quite stiffly in her chair and fixed him with the same searching, curious gaze he had noticed when they first met in front of the house on the Schrannengasse. "You write wonderful comedies, Herr Garber," she finally said in a voice that made no attempt to cloak her fatigue, "but that's no reason to play the fool in a room that already has enough of them to go around." With that she nodded her head amiably in the general direction of the von Welden table, whose occupants all were fussing loudly with their stoles and muffs prior to returning home for dinner. "You are the perfect refutation of all the nonsense Wagner wrote about artistic Jews." Chudo seemed to find renewed energy as she launched herself into what Alexander feared was likely to be a disagreeably forceful itemization of his failings. For a moment he wondered whether a fresh pastry might deflect her attention but gave up that hope when he heard her begin another of her unmistakable speech bursts. "You remember how he claimed Jews could never get beyond the rational element in art and so would always remain critics and analysts of what others created? Well, with you, on the contrary, it's been all instinct, talent, and charm, but without any sign of an analytic intelligence or critical faculty at all. But those are exactly the qualities you need now if you are ever going to finish this work you have undertaken. It's perfectly all right for a writer to use his brain, even if he wants to see his works performed in the Burgtheater, own a house on the Wolfgangsee, and be able to invite an exasperating old Russian refugee to Café Tomaselli."

"Do you know the last person who talked to me in almost the same terms?" Her pleased look showed him that she recognized immediately that he had just taken a significant step toward her. "It was decades ago, back in my hometown before I'd gone to Vienna for the first time. There were only two people to whom I showed the writing I had done over the past three years that I was planning on taking with me to the capital: Asher Blumenthal, who praised everything I ever put into his hands as though it were a lost manuscript by Schiller, and a second friend, who kept my notebooks for over a month before returning them to me and, with the utmost seriousness, urged me to burn all of them until I learned how to think like an adult and had something worth writing about."

"Jakob Tausk?" Alicia wasn't so much asking Alexander as trying to hedge the name with question marks as an act of self-preservation, the way a peasant might hold up his rosary when he sensed the presence of something evil.

"Yes, who else but Tausk? The way he was back when I knew him, more lost in his exile from Rabbi Pelz's seminary than you are from your Russia today. At least you were able to take what you believed in along with you when you crossed the border for the last time. For Tausk it was different: He had to leave behind everything important to him in the only place he ever cared about. He may work for Dzerzhinsky these days, but I can't believe the opinions of his new masters matter to him any more than did those of the Count-Governor whom he served before the war."

For a while neither of them spoke. Alexander hoped that his comparison of her fate and Tausk's hadn't pained Alicia, but when he scanned her face, he noticed that on the contrary, she seemed more at peace than at any time since they'd come into the coffeehouse. They sat across the small marble table from each other with the silent intimacy of people who have no need for words to feel at ease. Outside, it had grown pitch-dark, and except for the streetlamps illuminating the cobblestones with slowly diminishing ripples of light, the whole square in front of Tomaselli was completely deserted. As he had anticipated, it was too late for him to return home, and he asked the headwaiter to telephone over to the Goldener Hirsch to confirm the reservation he had made for a room that night and to let them know that he would be checking in quite late. Whatever was important enough for Alicia to have traveled all the way to Salzburg to tell him was almost palpably audible in the hesitations between her sentences, but Alexander knew any effort to rush her would be pointless, and somewhat to his own surprise, he found that the impatience with which he had come into town that morning had largely dissipated.

They had been sitting in one place for a long time without getting up, and Alexander was starting to feel a need to stretch his legs. It seemed too cold to suggest an evening stroll, and there was really nowhere else to go since all the interesting historical buildings would have closed hours ago. For many of his Viennese acquaintances, there was nothing unusual about leaving one's favorite coffeehouse at this time of day, going home quickly to change, then heading directly out to dinner, and he knew several first-rate restaurants in the neighborhood. But living alone out by the lake for several months of the year, Alexander had fallen out of the habit of eating more than a sandwich in the afternoon. He lit a small cigar to help his digestion and contented himself listening to the subdued hum of the waiters clearing the nearby tables. Chudo too seemed to be resting, deeply absorbed in her own thoughts; her eyes were half closed, and her glasses had been carefully folded and set down beside the empty coffee cup in front of her. But after another quarter of an hour she sensed his growing need for a change of scene almost at the same moment as he became fully aware of it himself. She straightened herself, put on her glasses again, and nodded over at him sympathetically, "Well, this place certainly lived up to its reputation, and I am delighted that we came here. What I propose now, though—only if you have time, of course—is that we go back together to Schrannengasse. The walk will do us both good, and I have got to get back to the apartment anyway, since I left all the lights and the heat on and don't want Caroline to be burdened with my extravagances when she returns from Munich. Besides, after such a rich indulgence here, I think it will be quite a while before either of us is ready for dinner. I happened to visit the market earlier today and would be glad to make us a light supper later on. First, though, I think it's high time we put our heads together seriously about this Galician story of yours. What you have just said about Tausk showed me how right I was to come see you."

• ◆ •

The night had turned much colder than it looked from inside the coffee-house, and by the time they reached Schrannengasse, the pair was grate-ful that she had forgotten to turn down the heat. They had extended their walk for a while to admire the city under a brilliantly clear blue-black sky with just a thin curve of moonlight suspended like a half-formed brush-stroke above the domes. Seen only in shadow, the Archbishop's Cathe-dral and the numerous parish churches lost much of their ponderous triumphalism and became, if not translucent, at least less massive, en-veloped in a darkness that was so much more substantial than mere stone. Alexander, who had felt only indifference when he walked by them during the day, found himself quickening with pleasure as he guided his compan-ion through the narrow lanes that opened onto still another empty square decorated like a stage set with elegant townhouses and churches that were themselves sumptuous baroque palaces. They felt no need to com-ment on the various buildings as they came upon them and simply kept on strolling, continuing their earlier conversation as though they had never got up from their table. And yet, when Alexander later thought back on that evening, he realized how strongly everything they saw wove itself into their words, becoming part of what they talked about the way the weave of a particular canvas and the undercoats of paint applied before the artist has fully decided on a subject become part of the final composition.

It was directly in front of the heavy oak door, bound with iron hoops, that served as the side entrance to the Franciscan Church that Chudo abruptly veered from what they had been talking about a moment earlier and said, "I played the fool in there at the end, my dear Herr Garber, not you, and I apologize for having taken you so lightly. I didn't think I would understand myself better from a comment tossed off in a coffeehouse by someone I'd met only a few hours earlier, but that's exactly what hap-pened, and it would be ignoble of me not to acknowledge it. I suppose that must be what makes your comedies linger in my memory even when I don't have all that much interest in the story or the characters. One of them says something in passing, with no connection to the plot, but it

29

stays with me when I have forgotten most of the serious lines from that season's serious plays. But what we are talking about now *is* difficult, and I don't think you can treat it in an aside, no matter how much you instinctively seem to prefer working like that. What you were saying about exile made me want to tell you that what I have learned from my own life is simply that all love is haunted by the possibility of loss. And the deeper the love, the more unremitting the pain when what was once so treasured seems forever gone. Whether it is a person, a stretch of shoreline, or the sound of a language, when something basic to your identity has been torn away, nothing in the world is ever the same again. Not even geographic distance matters. The lost homeland can be as remote as Palestine is to the Jews in Russia today or as near as the distance between your hometown and the seminary from which Tausk was banished. People are always comparing exile with the death of one's beloved, but that seems fundamentally wrong to me. It's more like a betrayal from which it is impossible ever to become fully healed because the prospect of a pathway home continues to exist. For us exiles, hope is itself part of our torment. Doesn't the helpless waiting for a reconciliation, for a change of heart in one's homeland that would make it possible to return, continually deepen the grief of every exile's consciousness? Especially since these dreams are always dreamed uselessly from abroad."

Alexander took on faith that these words were addressed to him, but he was grateful that the darkness made it impossible for Chudo to see how impassive he must have looked. He could tell by her tone that she was speaking from the core of her being, but there was something in him that stayed unresponsive to even the most strongly felt abstractions, and he could make emotional sense of her description only by translating it into a small, personal memory from his own early months in Vienna. He knew that her gift for empathy would let her understand his private recollections as his truest way of replying to her, and as they slowly walked away from the elegant squares of the inner city toward the bridge joining the two banks of the Salzach, he began to talk to her about his first months in the capital. He described the cloying smell of old kerosene and sweat that permeated the whole neighborhood, the grimy, soot-covered back wall and the rotting, blotched roof of the adjoining house onto which the tiny window in his room looked, the sky continuously hung with smoke, coal dust, and fog, and the hunger that left him exhausted before the day had even begun. Yet amid all this shabbiness what he suffered from most was the recurring dread of having to return home to Galicia as a failure. One summer he had shared a small room with an apprentice from a nearby brewery who was bold enough to smuggle his girlfriend in at night past the sleeping landlady. While the two were in bed together, Alexander had to spend the hours before morning, when the girl would sneak out again, wandering alone through Vienna, hoping to avoid being stopped by the police as a vagrant. But as he told Chudo, instead of resenting the imposition, he discovered that "I never felt more myself than when I paced up and down in the waiting room of the Eastern Railway Station pretending to wait for a train or sat in one of the all-night buffets near the station watching the few street whores and out-of-work porters who had come in seeking shelter from the night fog. Even later, when I could afford a study of my own with a serviceable desk and my manuscripts piled up beside me, I didn't recognize myself in my surroundings as completely as I had back then on those hard wooden benches in the third-class waiting room. Something inside me always felt I belonged back there with the other souls who have been permanently abandoned and are somehow still determined to survive. Not just the poor student, the betrayed lover, or the aging mistress who knows that she is losing the man she adores to a younger rival. It's true that those types have always been staples of my comedies, and maybe I have made things a bit too easy on myself, but lately I have been thinking more about a child who is left in the care of indifferent strangers by the mother he counted on to make sense of the world for him or a shell-shocked soldier from a noble family who comes back from the war to a country he no longer recognizes. For both of them, the only experience that really matters has become completely unutterable, and I wonder if I could write a play in which these two appear onstage and never speak a single word while everyone else scurries around loudly diagnosing their problem."

"And would they be joined by a yeshiva student who has been expelled into a realm peopled by demons and soulless husks, and feels himself becoming one of them?" Alicia speculated. "I wonder how he would fit in to your new troupe? Alexander Garber's updated commedia dell'arte. As far as making a play out of these abandoned ones, the answer is probably not—at least not if you want to keep on being produced at the Burgtheater. But before we leave the riverbank for Schrannengasse, I want to take a quick look back toward the old town. Sometimes in Berlin, you know, I have nights like the ones you described when you used to go watch people at the train station. Only what I do then is walk for hours until it is almost dawn, and I find a high ground in a park above the city to wait for sunrise." They walked the last short blocks quite slowly and saw the stars suspended in lucid order high above the Mönchsberg, clear as sparks of snow on an iron railing.

The first thing Chudo did after they had taken off their coats and rubber galoshes was to prepare tea in an enormous old samovar, a present her parents had made to the Potioreks before the war when the two girls were still exchanging annual summer visits. She drank her tea in the Russian manner, picking up a small lump of sugar and putting it in her mouth, where it gradually dissolved with each sip of the strong, hot liquid. When they had thoroughly warmed themselves, she went into the bedroom and returned with what Alexander recognized as the stack of letters he had sent her. She cleared a space on the low table between them, where she put down the dossier, and Alexander could tell by her manner that she was now all business, a professional writer come to give her advice to a colleague who had run into trouble.

"Did anyone in your town actually like the other people living there?" she began. "To judge by how they still talk about each other in these letters, it certainly doesn't sound that way. I kept thinking to myself what ideal terrain it must have been for a police spy since the people he'd have to keep an eye on can't wait to denounce one another. What really stands out, though—and this was very hard for me to see initially, since by whatever name he goes now, your Jakob Tausk is such a terrifying figure in my life—is how puzzled most of your correspondents are that you are inquiring about him in the first place. But they don't seem at all surprised that a stranger should write to ask about what happened over a decade ago. Not at all. Reading between the lines, I have the sense that a few of them spent years expecting to be contacted and had carefully thought out the answers they were prepared to give. And then your letter arrived. Only it contained totally different questions from the ones they were anticipating, and so there is this odd mixture of relief and puzzlement in their replies. Most of them don't seem to remember much about Tausk except that they all thoroughly detested him. It is clear they have not thought about him for ages and are not especially curious what became of him, but they also have no reluctance to talk about whatever they can still recall about him personally. But then I started wondering: If the people you contacted aren't made nervous by questions about their relationship with Tausk, what is it that worries them so much? Why all this effort to put you on guard against anything one of their former neighbors might tell you? It has to be more than just the residue of old grudges. Something in the whole story makes them extremely uncomfortable. I can't say for certain whether it was fear or embarrassment I sensed, but whatever happened out there in Galicia after you left for Vienna and Tausk went to work for the provincial governor still unsettles almost every one of your correspondents. Anyone going over these letters would come to a similar conclusion, and I am sure that if you asked your policeman friend, he would tell you exactly the same thing. But recognizing all these signs of ill ease didn't bring me any closer to knowing their source. I have to admit that I was becoming extremely frustrated. It was as tantalizing as staring for a long time at one of Velázquez's great portraits of Philip the Fourth and making out the clear shadow of a completely different underpainting just beneath the surface without ever succeeding in working out exactly what had been painted over and replaced by the figure of the King. No doubt that is where things would have stayed, except that one of your correspondents inadvertently helped me see the half-obliterated figure I had nearly missed.

"Since it is really your story we are working on, not mine, I should have guessed that the first clue would come as an aside. It is in one of the letters you didn't bother marking up with marginal comments, and I can certainly understand why. But it is an entertaining document in its own right. The writer signs herself Frau Hofrat Simeon Pichler-Ziolkowski (née Sophie Pichler) and tells us several times that her husband is one of the most successful and important lawyers in Vienna. It sounds as though her father had a similar position in Galicia and at least according to her, was a trusted associate of old Moritz Rotenburg. In her recollection, the major event of that whole season was her near marriage to Hans Rotenburg, the heir to all the Rotenburg millions, who was courting her relentlessly, but whom she finally turned down because of his impossible political ideas. She doesn't remember ever seeing Tausk and wonders why you would write to her about him, since "people in my family's position did not have any dealings with the secret police." She does add, though, that if Tausk had done his job properly—and here I was expecting her to say something about his preventing the Cathedral Square murders—he would have arrested Elisabeth Demetz, who was responsible not just for young Rotenburg's unsavory politics but for the moral corruption of some of the town's most eligible aristocratic bachelors. She goes on in the same vein for several more pages, revealing herself as more appalling with each paragraph and cheerfully innocent of what she sounds like. She had me laughing out loud. But then one of her paragraphs struck me more forcefully than anything else in your whole dossier. Toward the end of her letter, just after she winds up another long complaint against the Demetz girl, the former Fräulein Pichler says, 'And anyway, in addition to everyone's being preoccupied with my imminent betrothal to Hans Rotenburg, there was so much else going on that winter, no one in my circle had any time to be concerned about some spy of the Count-Governor's. You may remember that it was the coldest winter for over a decade and the province was suffering from an economic downturn that touched almost everyone. I think the Rotenburgs were the only ones not affected by all the business failures, and I remember hearing my father and mother whispering that somehow Moritz Rotenburg had to be behind all the bankruptcies since he seemed to be doing so well out of them. Papa kept saying that if only he could anticipate Rotenburg's investment strategy, we all could make a fortune out of the slump too.' "

"To me, it doesn't sound as though her father and Rotenburg were all that intimate if Pichler has no idea what the financier was thinking." Alexander interrupted. "That is just one of the reasons I couldn't take anything in her letter seriously. Also, I have heard her husband's name mentioned a few times in Vienna, but never with much respect. He is a second-rate lawyer, always trying to ingratiate himself by doing errands for influential people. Skubl, who is a bit of a snob in these matters, once described him to me as having the temperament of a waiter who always gives the wrong change in his own favor."

"Well of course she is lying about both her father and her husband. Probably about Hans Rotenburg as well, but that has nothing to do with what makes the letter so important. Look again, and you will see what gripped my attention."

Alicia, who had taken advantage of Alexander's outburst to pour herself a fresh cup of tea, set it down and continued reading aloud. " 'Around our table, at least, Papa was much more worried about the risk of violence from the strikers than about anything the police spies were up to. All the reasonable people in town thought the Count-Governor was much too soft on potential troublemakers and wanted the army brought in to keep order. You see, half the workers were turning into Reds, led by a professional agitator called Nathan Kaplansky, and the other half, or at least all

34

the poor Jews among them, were completely hypnotized by a strange wonder rabbi from Russia—I have forgotten his name, but I am sure there are enough people around who still recall it—who they actually believed was the Messiah. And to be totally fair, it was not just the out-of-work Jews. A lot of people who should have known better came under the man's spell as well. He and Kaplansky were two more failures of this Tausk in whom you are so interested, since he didn't stop either of them in time, just as he didn't prevent Elisabeth from ruining my engagement. Personally, I can't see that an unsuccessful provincial spy would make a very interesting subject for one of your plays, but I am sure you know best, and I am always glad to try to help so distinguished a former townsman as yourself. The next time you have a new piece at the Burgtheater, it would be a great pleasure for my husband and me to come to the opening and meet you again in person. Now that we are in touch with one another, and you have our address, I do hope we can count on being put on the official guest list for your premieres.' "

"When the King of England puts on a yarmulke!" Alexander muttered with a smile. But he quickly broke the light mood by repeating that he was as baffled as ever about what was useful in Sophie's letter.

"Not in her letter, exactly," Alicia answered, "in what it made me piece together. I am afraid we émigrés are as bad as your Sophie Pichler. We seem to spend more time squabbling among ourselves about small doctrinal differences than we do organizing against the Bolsheviks or helping one another. Still, there are a few people in our community I have grown to admire, and one of them, in particular, has become a dear friend, although I don't see nearly enough of her. Her name is Sonia Sonnenschön, and she is a doctor in one of the free clinics for the poor out in the Scheunenviertel neighborhood. In spite of her German last name, she is quite Russian. Her family has lived in Odessa since early in the last century. Sonia is one of the most decent people I have ever met, and the only reason I see so little of her is that she works too hard at her clinic. Sometimes, though, I succeed in persuading her to take a Sunday afternoon off, and then we go and have coffee together and stroll down the boulevards, looking in the chic store windows and chatting away. She is very shy and, unlike most of us émigrés, doesn't like to talk about her past, but over time I have managed to get her to tell me about her childhood. There is one strand in Sonia's story that fits in so closely with what the Pichler-Ziolkowski woman wrote you, that when I got to that part of her letter, I jumped up and shouted out so loudly the landlady began pounding at my door thinking I'd had a stroke. For myself, I am convinced that we have found the missing figure whom everyone is trying so hard to paint out of the canvas entirely. But I am so eager to solve the problem that I don't entirely trust myself to evaluate the information objectively, and if you tell me that I am not making any sense, I won't argue. At least not too much."

Alexander waited a few moments before adjusting his gaze to meet hers and, in a tone somehow both impatient and indulgent, urged her to tell him what she had discovered. "I don't know how much longer I can contain my curiosity," he said to her with a smile.

But it was impossible to rush Alicia. She had arrived in Salzburg with a tale of her own, not a single, revelatory image, and her story would unfold only according to its own inner logic.

"Sonia told me that the whole time she was growing up, she worshiped her older brother, Robert, like a hero"—Alicia began again—"and even today she still carries his photo with her everywhere. It must have been taken around 1910 or '11, and he does look quite handsome in it, although maybe that is just because he was still so terribly young, and everyone who was young and healthy back then looks good to me these days. Lately, you know, I have begun to think that the greatest sin of the young is not to be happier when it is all still so possible. In any case, Robert was trying very hard to put on a fierce expression for the photographer, but there was something not quite convincing about the result. At least that is what he seems like from Sonia's photograph. What is unmistakable is the effort he put into making himself a powerful physical specimen. Sonia told me that like a lot of Odessa Jews of her generation, both she and her brother were determined not to let themselves be intimidated by anyone. In spite of all the legal and social restrictions they were going to do whatever they wanted with their lives, unlike their parents. Apparently, Robert became quite well known in the area as an athlete and won several province-wide competitions in gymnastics and pistol shooting, while Sonia was one of the first women from her school to show real promise as a research scientist. But somewhere between finishing high school and entering university, Robert began to go astray. He moved away from Odessa and drifted around the country, occasionally using forged papers to cross over into the eastern Habsburg territories. Robert supported himself with odd jobs and, she was ashamed to say, probably also with smuggling and petty robberies. Although he knew how much she cared for him, or perhaps especially because he knew it and couldn't stand to disappoint her, he stopped writing regularly, and for months at a time she had no contact with him. Then, one day, he abruptly got back in touch and sounded like the brother she remembered, only, if anything, even more optimistic and full of energy than before. At first Sonia and her parents were delighted, but as the letters kept coming, there was something in his ardor that seemed to her excessive, almost manic. She didn't mention her suspicion to her parents, and in any case, Robert soon began writing her separately from them. He told her about how his life had been transformed by meeting a teacher, Moses Elch Brugger, who had pulled him back from an abyss of self-loathing and hopelessness that he could now see had been leading him toward suicide.

"When you and I began our correspondence"—she went on—"I remembered Sonia's stories about her brother and eventually asked her if I might read the letters she had talked about so often. I never had asked her any favors before, and though she obviously thought it odd and a bit intrusive, she agreed, and the next weekend, when we met again for coffee, she brought along a large folder of Robert's letters. That is what I have had here next to me all this time, and now I just have to find the right excerpts to read to you so you can see what got me so excited in the first place. I think I will start with this one, which was written when Robert had just been released from prison. He had been locked up for beating up a man who insulted him in some drunken tavern brawl. Robert had no idea what he was going to do next and describes his situation like this:

" 'One evening, as I was wandering near the outskirts of town, looking for a place to sleep for the night, I sensed someone tap me on the shoulder from behind, but when I wheeled around to lash out at the person, I felt my fist being held by a young woman who, instead of flinching away, smiled at me and said, "The rebbe tells us one should never try to catch a falling knife, but sometimes it is the only merciful thing to do." I have met enough damaged souls in my wanderings not to be interested in striking up a conversation with another one, even if she was as attractive as this girl. But I was exhausted and hungry, and she looked well fed enough to make me think she might know where to get a warm meal and shelter. It's not that I didn't recognize the type; the roads are full of desperate runaways looking for some cause to give themselves to, and in general, you know how repelled I am by weakness and sentimental piety. In my experience, most of the flophouse preachers are anti-Semites who think the

Jews are responsible for all Russia's evils. That is why the word *rebbe* surprised me more than anything. There is no shortage of holy men looking for new followers, but not ones who talk about knives and have such pretty women carrying their message.

" 'I decided to go with her and, to my surprise, found that instead of the usual seedy prayerhouse, she led me to a run-down but fairly large tenement in a working-class neighborhood close to the river. The house had been turned over to the rebbe by one of his local followers who normally rents it out to laborers employed in one of the Rotenburg factories, and when I first arrived, there were about eight people living in it together, all of them completely devoted to their teacher. I was prepared for a lengthy sermon to pay for my evening meal and shared cot. But the rebbe had sequestered himself with one of his recurring attacks of migraine and never appeared at all during the first few days I was in the house. Throughout that whole time the only one to speak to me at length about the rebbe was Hannah Altschuler, the girl who had brought me here whom everyone calls by her nickname, Linnetchen. Except when she is talking about Brugger, Linnetchen seems quite ordinary, but what she said about her first meeting with the rebbe was enough to make me decide to pack up and leave the moment Brugger recovered sufficiently to emerge from his sickroom. "One day in midsummer," she told me, "I heard an unfamiliar voice speaking to some of my fellow students in the courtyard of the Free Jewish Library, and something in the man's tone made me put down the book I was reading and step outside to see who it was. As soon as I was past the front door, the stranger, who was leaning against the small stone fountain, turned away from the others to whom he had been speaking and looked directly at me as though I were the one he had been waiting for the whole time. His face moved into the light. It was beautiful in a way I never believed was possible. I turned away immediately, knowing that if I looked for too long, even just seconds, I would never be able to look away again and that all else would be ugly and horrible to me from that point on. I am sure you think this is an exaggeration, but you did not see his face!" Well, all I can tell you is that her expression of selfless, unlimited adoration—directed toward a man with whom I instantly sensed I had no chance to compete—was more than I could bear, and so I tried to break her mood in the best way I knew: by shocking her with an obscenity. "Did you go home with him and fuck him right away, or did you wait to see if the rest of him lived up to that face?" I asked. Far from being offended, though, Linnetchen seemed grateful that my question gave her a chance to talk more about the first and so far the only time Brugger has touched her body. No doubt her description of sex with Brugger would have been as rapturous as the rest of her account, but just as she was starting to lose herself in her recollection, the door behind her opened, and a slightly weary voice interrupted her. "Not again, Linnetchen, please, or our new friend here will think we are all as crazy as the Russian women who flog themselves into an orgasm and are convinced Christ is taking possession of their souls." Those are the first words I ever heard Brugger speak! Then, in a meditative tone, he added, "It's true, I have always loved the look on a girl's face and in her eyes when she is being entered. It is almost an innocent, mystified sort of stare that comes from her whole body rather than just her face. Not really seeing, but rather staring within. But we are still Jews, after all, and have more stringent standards of ecstasy."

" 'To my eyes, there was certainly no radiance on the face of the man who stepped into the hallway. On the contrary, he looked pale and drawn with traces of his migraine still lingering behind his eyes. But what most surprised me was that he dressed entirely in European clothes with no hint of Hasidic garb. He even does away with the skullcap and wears his hair in a close crop that emphasizes his forehead. All his suits are beautifully cut in the English style, and he reminds me far more of the wealthy patrons who used to come award the annual prizes at the all-Russian athletic club than of any rabbi I have ever seen before. Since he seems to get headaches often, his large brown eyes almost always look as though he has barely slept for days. He speaks to everyone in the house in a courteous, almost formal tone, but lightly, as if all his words amuse him, no matter what their effect on the listeners. I wonder if Linnetchen had already told Brugger all about me because the rebbe dispensed with conventional introductions entirely. Whatever the reason, he began talking to me as though we had known each other for a long time and were simply continuing a conversation started sometime earlier. Brugger walked me over to the large window on the second floor and, pointing to the green copper roof of the great synagogue, said, "You know, we Jews may die solitary deaths, but we dream communal dreams. That is what makes teaching the injured ones who come to me so fascinating. They arrive riddled with feelings of shame, complicity, and humiliation, and you never know what will emerge when they realize that they have always been strong enough to cast all that off: a butterfly, a hawk, or maybe even a vulture. Each story that I hear is unique, but the questions and my answers are always the same: 'Rebbe, can I ever be free?' 'All your choices have always been your own.' But when I see a town like this, I start to wonder how much fear it would take to save people from themselves. Perhaps that is exactly what you have been sent to help me understand. Come, let's go out for a walk together, so I can clear my head of these pains, and you can show me what I need to accomplish the work." Just imagine: he said this to *me!*' "

At last Chudo lifted her eyes from the pages she had been holding close to her face as she read and interjected, "And that of course is what ensnared him! It wasn't the pretty little Linnetchen, although she and Robert became lovers quickly enough, and it wasn't Brugger's strange intensity. No, it was the fact that this man, who was worshiped by his followers, so clearly needed him, Robert Sonnenschön! Isn't that what always emerges as the irresistible temptation? The revelation that *you* have been chosen by the chosen one, that only this amazing leader has had the insight to recognize your rare gifts, and that only he—whom you will henceforth follow anywhere he commands—values you as you truly deserve!" Alexander nodded in agreement, now as engrossed by Chudo's way of telling her story as by Robert's urgency in his letters.

"Robert goes on . . . and I know you are worried I will never get to the point, but you have to understand how I reached my idea," she told Alexander while riffling through the pages until she found the passage she was seeking. " 'Every shtetl in the Pale boasts its own miracle-working rabbi, and Brugger has nothing but contempt for the whole tribe of grasping faith healers. Prayer is only a kind of intent listening, he tells us, not the prelude to a magic show. Once one of the casual visitors who sometimes attend his Sabbath lessons was clamoring for a miracle like the famous one the Buczacz rabbi performed in healing an epileptic girl. Brugger had the man thrown out bodily from the room and then told everyone: "There are no single miracles anymore. I thought I taught you that much, at least. We will either see the fulfillment of everything promised to us as a people or stay slaves forever. When you learn to believe enough to give yourselves completely without demanding parlor tricks, that will be the first miracle and release all the others to come. I tell you, the soul is not the witness of an external event but the very arena in which the event takes place. It took no miracles or revelations to send me among you, and I do not need men and women to kneel before me. All I want is for them to rise with me ever higher to the completion of what it means to be fully human. I am the maker of my own miracles, and so is each of you and has been since time began."

" 'Sometimes, after an especially passionate sermon, Brugger retreats back into his room exhausted, and then none of us sees him for the next few days. It was during one of these absences, without any explicit decisions ever having been voiced, that Linnetchen and I simply took over the day-to-day management of the disciples. We collect the subsidies promised from his well-off supporters in town, arrange for the purchase of the week's provisions, and assign the daily household tasks that Brugger himself has no interest in supervising even when he is well, but whose neglect would irritate him greatly. He loathes the filth and tumult of a typical Hasidic court, the kind that so many "sophisticated" journalists find captivatingly authentic, especially if they are enlightened Jews with a touch of nostalgia writing for like-minded readers in Berlin and Vienna. Brugger's reputation is spreading fast, and some jealous disciples from other long-established Hasidic dynasties occasionally try to disrupt his teaching, and then it falls to me to defend the rebbe. At last all my years in athletic competition finally do me some good, Sonia! I am starting to train the most loyal followers, teaching them how to protect Brugger, with their fists, if necessary.' "

Alicia was beginning to interrupt her reading more frequently to supplement Robert's account with what she had learned from Sonia and broke off again from the letter to add, "Yes, he started with just fists, but as the gang grew more hardened, he included regular practice with small arms as well. His fondness for pistols ended up coming in just as useful as his years learning gymnastics. He must have molded them into quite a cadre!" She picked up the sheaf of papers again and with a look of distaste continued: " 'Ever since we sent home one or two troublemakers from another town with their faces bloodied, there has been no further provocation from would-be rivals. A few of the wealthy merchants who dominate the local Jewish council here are alarmed by anything that risks attracting the attention of the provincial government, but none of them wants to call in the police; all that would do is expose their growing loss of control over their own community. It seems that they are just as weak here as the town elders back home and spend their whole time cringing to the authorities and slandering one another. But you should know that Brugger himself has never given me any direct orders to train anyone. I am afraid you are thinking I have gone mad and am running around here attacking people to

41

ingratiate myself with some charlatan. But it isn't like that, Sonia. Not at all. I know what I am doing, and why. He is the only person who has ever taught me anything important about myself and the world. It is just hard for others to recognize how much he has to offer them because the way he teaches is so different from anything they have ever experienced. For example, a few days ago, toward the end of one of his sermons, his eyes sought me out in my customary place beside the door, keeping a close watch on everyone who came into the room. Staring directly at me, Brugger began to tell the story of Rabbi Akiva's joyous laughter upon seeing wild foxes emerge from the charred ruins of the Temple in Jerusalem. When all the other rabbis burst into tears of anguish at the terrible sight, Akiva chastised them for their lack of faith. "If the desolation prophesied in Lamentations has been fulfilled down to its smallest detail, how can you doubt that the Redemption promised to us won't come to pass just as surely?" Brugger's voice rose, but he never looked away from me. He said all the sages agree that before we see the Redemption, a time of great tribulation will come upon us. In the generation in which the Son of David is to come, the meeting place of scholars will be turned into a brothel, the young will humiliate the elderly, and the old will tremble in fear before the young. In such a time, Brugger told us, "violence becomes the cleanest mode of contact. It allows the pure to touch the defiled without becoming polluted themselves. That is why so many timorous rabbis cry out, 'Let him come, but let me not witness it.' And who can say whether their wish is not heard in heaven, and the day of deliverance delayed because of their cowardice? But now it is *our* time, and we will not repeat their blasphemy. If violence must come, let us greet it as the soul's joy, and if we must see great tribulation, let us welcome it as the gateway to Redemption."

" 'That night I was the one, not Brugger, who slumped down, burning with fever and without the strength to move my limbs. I had to be helped to bed, where I am told I lay semiconscious for over a week, tended by the whole household until I was fully recovered. Don't worry yourself, Sonia, I was never in any real danger. But I was certain the rebbe's words were meant specifically for me and contained a command that could not be spoken aloud. I finally understand now what is expected of me, and I feel such an enormous surge of gratitude that I, who failed at everything, have been chosen for such a task.' "

Alicia again set down the sheaf to tell Alexander that after this letter

Robert began writing to Sonia almost every day, urgent, pleading messages, almost entirely about his teacher. He started begging her to abandon her medical studies to join him, but his letters so terrified her that after a while she found herself unable any longer to answer him. "Sonia has never forgiven herself for her silence. Robert might have been beyond saving, but the guilt of not having tried continues to haunt her. Saddest of all is that even today Sonia still finds herself thinking about certain of Brugger's sayings that Robert quoted to her in his letters, and she is now convinced that the man who had made her brother confront such questions must have possessed an extraordinary soul, whether for good or evil. Just a few weeks ago, on one of our outings, Sonia took out one of Robert's letters from the frayed leather briefcase she carries everywhere and quickly found a passage that she had underlined in pencil years ago when she first read it and to which she has obviously turned many times since. In it, Robert says that Brugger had devoted an entire Sabbath day to a sermon on the concept of a soul and concluded by saying that the only image that had ever helped him to understand the word was as 'the part of the man that sees the dream. What truly matters is to live in such a way that one's whole being, the part that is the dreamer and the part that is the witness to the dream, is equally at stake in whatever one does.'

"When Sonia read me those lines, I couldn't shake the thought that Brugger's way of talking about the soul was close to what I have heard Sonia sometimes says herself! I suggested as much to her, and she admitted that she was not at all certain she would have been able to resist the rebbe's spell any more than her brother had. Perhaps she suspected so even back then, and that was why she convinced herself it was futile to travel to Austria to try to save Robert. If so, it was herself she was rescuing by staying at the university. Robert, who had made ruthless demands on her loyalty the whole time they lived together at home, never reproached her for not answering him—a change she couldn't help attributing to Brugger's influence—but his sorrow at her absence was audible in every letter. He described himself walking over to the train station on the one day each week the express from St. Petersburg stopped there on its way to Vienna, to watch the passengers disembark in the hope that one of them might be his Sonia. Only when every person had left, and the platform was completely empty, did he finally give up and return back to the house. He was haunted by the idea that the time to choose sides was running out and that when the hour came, she would be alone, cut off from her people and her portion in their heritage. Just before Passover she received a last flurry of letters, which he must have dashed off, one after the other, in the space of a few days. There was a subtle but unmistakable change in Robert's tone in those letters; since Sonia has given me permission to let you make a copy of anything you need for your book, you'll see what I mean right away. There comes a point where Robert seems to have given up trying to persuade her, and for the first time in months he actually asks about her studies and wishes her well with them. Although the letters were obviously written in great haste, he sounds less frantic in them than during the preceding months, but also more distant, as though his calmness were that of a traveler already under way on a journey that no longer included her. And then there was complete silence. At first Sonia felt something like relief at not finding another thick envelope awaiting her in the porter's lodge almost every evening. But soon enough her relief gave way, first to worry and then to a sense of dread that was close to panic. There was no one she could turn to for information. The Russian government was not going to help a Jewess locate a missing relative who had gone abroad illegally, and since Robert had entered Galicia without a passport, it would be dangerous to alert anyone on the Austrian side of the border about him. All Sonia had to go on was the name of a town she had barely ever heard of and a general delivery address from which Robert had written her and where he would go to collect his mail. She sent several letters and two telegrams there herself but heard nothing back. Sonia had nearly secured proper travel documents and arranged for a leave from school in order to go bring Robert home with her when she received a polite one-page inquiry on magnificent ivory-colored paper decorated with the Habsburg double eagle, asking if as his only known relative she intended to collect the remains of the deceased prisoner Robert Sonnenschön, convicted of murder and arson and executed in accordance with the prescribed articles of the penal code. If she wished to avail herself of the opportunity, would she kindly inform the prison officials when they could expect her arrival? If she was unable to advise them in writing of her plans within six days, the prisoner would be buried at His Imperial Majesty's expense in the public graveyard in a section reserved for members of the Mosaic faith. I brought that letter too, but just see how it is signed: 'Yours respectfully, Dr. Karl Fernkorn, First Medical Secretary of the State Security Office.' And look"—Chudo's small thumb gestured toward the bottom of the page she held out for Alexander—"immediately below the official seal of the Provincial Governor, Count Otto Wiladowski, you can clearly make out a handwritten countersignature, 'approved as safe for public communication: Jakob Tausk.' "

· ◆ ·

Only now, when Chudo herself put down the mass of papers in her hand, did Alexander take his eyes off her face to stare at length out the window. He was baffled that it could still be completely dark outside. He had no idea how long he had been listening, but to judge by his exhaustion, he assumed it must be almost morning. Yet the sky was not much lighter than when they had come in after their walk through the old town. It was not until a few days later, when he was back at his desk in Gschwendt, writing up his impressions of the evening, that he realized how thoroughly he had started to overlay her story with his own imagined scenes, improvising even while she was still talking. To Alexander, such elaborations were a story's way of reproducing itself, as inevitable and compelling as sexual desire. That evening in Schrannengasse, although Alexander had the clear impression he and Chudo had sat motionless across from each other while she spoke, this too must have been a mistake since the fire was going at full strength and the tea in the large samovar had been renewed. Someone must have gotten up to take care of both those domestic duties while they talked, just as someone—he supposed it could only have been he—must have smoked the cigars whose residue was clearly visible in the ashtray between the two half-filled teacups and the silver sugar bowl. No doubt Dr. Stechel would be disappointed in him for breaking his regimen several days in a row. He had felt almost as if he were being dragged reluctantly out of an overpowering dream when Chudo appeared, looking down at him in his chair and reminding him that the dinner she had promised earlier had been ready for some time now.

A smallish oval table had been set next to the modern-looking stove that took up most of the kitchen. "I hope you don't mind eating here," Chudo said. "Just now I prefer not to deal with the waiters and other patrons. I don't think Caroline cooks at home very often—or if so, she doesn't keep much in the way of spices on hand—but this way we can continue our conversation without having to worry about being overheard." For all her demurrals, she had prepared a meal that, although much simpler than anything they would deign to attempt, could have shamed the haughtiest chefs in Salzburg. Alexander was amused to find that at least in this area she was capable of the most transparently false modesty. Throughout the long years of their subsequent friendship, her cooking remained the single talent in which a justifiable pride in her accomplishments revealed itself through repeated affirmations of uncertainty. Usually Alexander found singing someone else's praises as gratifying an activity as going to the dentist, but he was delighted to tell Alicia how superb he found her cooking, in part, perhaps, because she never failed to blush with pleasure at the compliment. That evening she had made chicken breasts stuffed with cabbage and apples, baked with an aromatic blend of sweet paprika and a touch of cinnamon, accompanied by a perfect sauté of wild mushrooms simmered in white wine. Dessert was an improvisation, imaginatively concocted of that morning's breakfast rolls transformed into a bread pudding dotted with cranberries and glazed with plum jam and sugar.

The whole time they were eating, Alexander scrutinized Alicia as closely as if he were watching a celebrated actress at the Burgtheater triumph in a role as demanding of its audience as it was of the performer. Even now, although her story, or rather, her uncanny ventriloquization of Sonia Sonnenschön's story, had moved him in spite of his instinctive distaste for all that shtetl hysteria, Alexander was not entirely certain what Alicia intended in offering it up to him. He had willed himself not to draw any conclusions, preferring to let her account unfold as though it had no more direct connection with him than any other vignette about the last days of Galician Jewry before the breakup of the Empire. He knew that he risked appearing obtuse, but her impatience to have Alexander not just as her audience but as an equal partner in her excitement was at least as urgent as his own to understand what her story signified. Brusquely Alicia pushed the dessert plates out of the way, leaned in toward Alexander, and with a look that was almost gleeful, said, "Don't you see? Wiladowski's seal and Tausk's note clinch it. Sonia's story must have taken place in your hometown, and that is what they all have been too ashamed to talk about. Not any political conspiracy, but this corrupt preacher who seems to have terrorized half the town into treating him as if he were the Messiah. It is poor, crazy Robert Sonnenschön's rebbe whom they have been busy painting over in their recollections, so that not a trace of him is still visible. Only that is never something one can do with complete success. You don't have to believe in your famous Viennese mind doctor to know that much about human beings! It is not like being a Communist for a few years in one's youth and then settling down to take over the family business. I can't tell you how many respectable old men are enchanted with the legend of their own daring adolescence. No matter how much they resemble their fathers today, they like to think that a youthful fling with radical politics guarantees their status as 'advanced' thinkers for the rest of their lives. To have been on a police list as a 'suspicious character,' even if only for a few months, can be held up as proof of an enviably independent mind, but there is nothing in the least heroic about having been taken in by a street corner redeemer."

By now Alexander's initial skepticism had been swept aside in the headlong rush of Alicia's excitement. What she told him about the rebbe was part of what he had been looking for ever since Broderson approached him with the idea of a *Collected Works*. But it was not really a matter of seeing the story through her eyes. In just the way that there are realizations we do not know we already know until we first hear them from someone else, Alexander found himself entirely at home in the story whose premises Alicia had provided. This legend of hers permitted Alexander to return to his own hometown as if it were a made-up scene, a place of charged possibilities, his own yet entirely invented. And so it was completely natural for him to interrupt her and gloss what she herself was in the midst of explaining.

"No, there is certainly very little heroism in having been duped by someone like Brugger. It is all terribly humiliating, and I can't think of a more powerful motive for silence than that. It is also easy to understand why someone as self-satisfied and soulless as Sophie Pichler-Ziolkowski would have been immune to Brugger's appeal. That is no doubt why she has no trouble mentioning him in her letter when the rest of them need to act as though he had never existed. In any case, she is right. If Tausk served as the Provincial Governor's chief spy and approved Robert's death notice, it is safe to assume he would have had Brugger under surveillance, and his failure to arrest the preacher or to stop the Cathedral Square murders doesn't say much for his efficiency. But that kind of incompetence certainly doesn't sound like the man you met in the Lubyianka, so we must still not be seeing the threads connecting the stories. What you said earlier about the underpainting behind Velázquez's portraits of Philip the Fourth made me think of a different kind of artwork altogether. Whenever I am back in Vienna, even if it is only for a few days, I always set aside enough time to go look at the illuminated manuscripts in the Albertina Museum. I like to think that there is something about the depiction of daily life in a Book of Hours that is not so different from my Galicia—I mean the Galicia of my plays and stories—only without the Jews."

"I don't understand what you mean by that at all," Alicia said, more sharply than she intended, puzzled by the seeming inconsequence of his remark.

"Well, what I am thinking of"—Alexander eagerly explained—"is the way the figures in the different scenes are always completely absorbed in their own activities, oblivious of what their neighbors are doing, even if they are standing only a few feet away, caught up in the most desperate situations. A band of brigands might be waylaying some travelers in the left foreground, while on the right, people are happily skating on a frozen pond or playing beside a small fire, while far in the background, a servant girl blows on her frostbitten hands as she passes a group of hunters returning home with a stag they've managed to bring down. That's how it is in my town too, at least the way I see it. Everyone so entirely caught up in what he is doing, it is no wonder none of them takes in the whole picture. But the anonymous artists who painted those scenes knew it was necessary to include everything, no matter how ridiculous, because that is the only way to represent what is essential and still stay human."

Alicia had regained her earlier equanimity and nodded in agreement. "Yes, I do understand now. Back in Moscow, I had any number of such moments, watching the concentration with which women tried to pick out the unspoiled potatoes from the meager supplies available in the stores. They were doing their best to prepare a cheerful evening meal for their families, all the while wondering on whose door Dzerzhinsky's men would be knocking that night. But one thought still troubles me, Alexander, and I don't see your Book of Hours helping me here: What about someone who wants to experience only what is essential and doesn't care anymore about staying human? How would he fit into your town?"

"Just don't write my novel before I do, Alicia. That wouldn't be fair."

PART ONE

December 1912

1

That year the snow seemed to have begun much earlier than usual. By December, at any rate, normal life in the town was grinding to a complete halt. Fuel was running low, and wood and coal were becoming impossibly expensive, especially for the poorer workers, whose ranks had kept increasing during the past five years until it looked as though soon no one would be left to tend the surrounding farms. Even when the factories stopped taking on new laborers and began to let go those they had recently hired, it was as though all these new arrivals were too stunned by their misery to remember the way back to their villages. One often came across whole families huddling for shelter by the walls of the quays alongside the river, and every day the papers reported another body found dead there of exposure. Throughout the town the water pipes were repeatedly frozen solid, and even among the more prosperous, elaborate schemes were worked out in case it became impossible to take a hot bath or do the household washing. Almost everyone who worked in one of the offices in the business district ate in the nearby restaurants as often as possible. Although they were expensive compared with cooking at home, there was usually a well-stoked fire in one corner, and the crowded tables encouraged a constantly reanimated sociability, no matter how isolating the weather outside. But everyone's nerves were growing frayed, and several long-standing friendships and love affairs revealed themselves as dangerously ragged and at risk of collapsing from the weight of the winter.

It must have been two weeks or so before the Christmas holidays, when Asher Blumenthal, twenty-eight years old and still only a junior accountant at the Sobieski Import-Export Company, left his office early one afternoon, hoping to be able to catch a tram and avoid the long walk home. But once again most of the wagons were frozen on the tracks, and the idea of trudging on foot all the way across the Nepomuk Bridge to his somber flat in the Josef Quarter was too demoralizing. He had wanted to avoid going to the Mendelssohn Club for a few days, but the chance to warm himself free of charge beside the massive old tile oven in the center of the reading room, of seeing the familiar green lamp shades running the length of the rear walls behind the comfortably worn leather chairs, and the certainty of hearing at least a few familiar voices proved irresistible. Asher usually left the club overstimulated, drained and excited at the same time, angry at the fluency of the talkers and even more annoyed at himself for not having the will to interrupt them and show everybody how ridiculous he thought their pronouncements were. The richer their families, the more passionately the club's younger members made a point of insisting on their readiness to leap at any change that would bring about a completely new kind of existence. At one time or another nearly every one of them stood up at the after-dinner meetings and testified to longing for some great, all-transforming crisis, a moment of truth, whether for good or evil, that would smash through the suffocating trivia of their daily routines like a whirlwind. The phrasing would change from time to time, but it always resonated with some equally sonorous and thoroughly conventional flourish.

Asher himself was skeptical about the innumerable programs drawn up for the common betterment. Pretending to know what would help others when his own life felt so thwarted struck him as absurd. But occasionally being present for those exhausting all-night sessions, with their furious exchange of pamphlets with similar clubs in Odessa and Warsaw and their increasingly grandiose plans for redeeming the Jewish people, made even Asher feel somehow significant. For a few hours he tried to make himself ignore the obvious fact that he was listening to a dozen contradictory hopes, all incoherently jumbled together and all of them, really, no more than confused versions of a single complaint: "None of us has ever felt fully alive in our homes or our country. What are we really risking by walking away from something as desolate as the lives our parents and teachers have already planned out for us? We all know how spiritually deadening their values are and how far their expectations are from touching our core. If we first have the courage to change ourselves, we will see how quickly the world will be changed along with us!" Then the cigarettes and pipes would be lit up again, another furious round of debates would start, someone would call out for drinks or for a vote on the latest motion, and before everyone went home for the night, a collection would be taken up to subscribe to another new journal or help send a delegation to a similar meeting in some other town. While people were finishing their last cigarettes, there was the inevitable, protracted struggle over who would have the final word, until the whole affair dissipated, without a clear victor, into a series of irritable farewells. But just underneath all that excitement and breathlessness there was really a calming stupor, as though one had learned to doze quite pleasantly inside while shouting out objections at everyone else. In spite of the deafening volume at which most conversation was conducted, such evenings somehow also felt reassuringly tranquil.

"Argumentative Jews! I am sick of their interminable discussions" is what Asher usually muttered to himself on his way home, much too late and with nothing to show for the hours spent in such company. "Well," he concluded as he set out down the Mariahilferstrasse toward the Mendelssohn Club, "tonight it's better to be an argumentative Jew than a frozen one." In this part of the town all the streetlamps were still functioning, and although there was too much snow for the work crews sent from the prison to keep the sidewalks clear, at least the government made sure the convicts salted the pavement here several times a day. Even though he feared it made him look like a peasant, Asher now always wore an enormous, old-fashioned winter cloak of heavy boiled wool with horn buttons that he had found in a pawnshop in the Josef Quarter. It was much warmer than anything else he could afford, and as he trudged along, his whole body bent forward against the evening wind, he enjoyed the taste of the slightly damp wool collar that he would catch himself reaching down to suck into his mouth. Asher detested the name of the club, chosen by the founding committee about twenty-five years ago in honor of the no doubt eminent but to him completely unendurable Moses Mendelssohn. Asher's father, the community's well-known autodidact, freethinker, and bankrupt Eliezer Blumenthal, had admired Mendelssohn tremendously and used to read out to his children, as his version of an enlightened Sabbath text, page after page of Mendelssohn's boring platitudes about fundamental human goodness and the universal ethical significance of Judaism. "As if any of us children cared about such big words when all we wanted was to be allowed to go outside and play with the other kids," Asher used to complain to his school friend Alexander Garber a few years later, when they were teenagers and walked home together after classes. What Asher found especially amusing is that to almost everyone in town, including probably a large percentage of its Jews, the name Mendelssohn evoked only the philosopher's grandson, the celebrated composer and conductor and, most delicious of all, notorious apostate to Christianity. Whenever he said he was going to the club after dinner, Asher's colleagues from work assumed there was a rehearsal in progress and asked him when he would be putting on a public concert. "Actually," Asher used to tell his prying landlady, "I wish someone would try to organize a musical evening using the club membership. What a splendidly horrific racket that would create."

But both Blumenthals, Eliezer and Asher, found it impossible not to admire the elegance of the club's high-columned entrance, and when Asher was still a boy, they would take a walk together across town just for the joy of standing in front of it, filled with wonder that so fine a place was at the disposal of Jews like them. At such moments Eliezer would sigh contentedly and tell his son how fortunate they were to be subjects of an Emperor like Franz Josef. The whole building was expressly designed to look impressive, erected near the town center by the Allianz Insurance Company before the mania for making everything resemble a reform school or military barracks had become a sign of advanced taste. When the insurance company needed to expand to a still-larger building during one of the intense, but usually short-lived, bursts of optimistic energy to which all of the Empire's different strata seemed subject in an irregular cycle of alternating enthusiasm and apathy, the original headquarters was taken over on a long-term lease, guaranteed by some of the wealthier Jews, and converted to a private club. Since none of the other social clubs admitted Jews, the lack of a fitting place of their own had long been a source of vexation among the community leaders, and the unexpected availability of one of the most attractive edifices in the whole province was interpreted as further proof of the special favor with which their existence was being watched over by the highest powers. In the last few years, though, what had once been fairly predictable cycles of expansiveness and contraction had become increasingly erratic, and everyone had lost track of when another good phase was due. That winter moods previously existing in strict alternation seemed to converge: Total, bone-aching weariness merged into the certainty that something wonderful would break through the exhaustion if only one didn't give in to despair. The most contradictory emotions coexisted and expressed themselves in a jittery, nervous hum, audible like a second, subterranean motif beneath otherwise monotone, predictable conversations.

Since the streets were almost empty, and the falling snowflakes made it impossible to see more than a few footsteps ahead, there was nothing to distract Asher on his walk, and he found himself unable to stop his mind trotting like a well-trained Lipizzaner horse through the familiar routine of its obsessions. Mostly, when he didn't worry about his duties at the office, especially the interminable paperwork involved in importing bars of cheap soap through Trieste from Cosini and Sons, he thought how he was unlikely ever to find a regular mistress, let alone a wife, or to learn Hebrew, or even to get his landlady to starch his shirts properly so that he needn't fret about showing up at work in the morning looking unkempt and slovenly. Although he occasionally succeeded in going out with one of the women from the club for an afternoon coffee, the few whom he had dared approach didn't encourage him to keep after them, and he linked their rebuff to the state of his collar and his ignorance of Hebrew. He was sure that if only he could dress properly, he could make an impression with his elegance; conversely, if he knew Hebrew, he could show his scorn of trivialities like fashionable clothes and turn the conversation to stirring issues like the cultivation of wine in the Galilee and the possibility of obtaining a charter from the Turkish authorities for more Jewish settlements. Lacking both, he tended to linger around the edges of discussions, hoping that someone would notice what he took to be an ironic gaze and the suggestion of a superior smile. If neither of these approaches seemed to be working, he found himself switching to the wish that maybe one of the more sensible women would decide that his mediocre but steady salary and guaranteed pension were, in the long run, more attractive than the wild dreams and empty wallets of the club's big talkers.

In fact Asher had worked at learning Hebrew off and on for several years without much success. Years later, when Alexander asked him to look back on that period, he tried to explain how frustrating the whole experience had been. "I could put up with the bizarre idea of reading and writing from right to left," he wrote, "and even with the strangely shaped letters, but a language that was printed without vowels so that until you already knew a word you couldn't possibly decipher it on the page, or even look it up in a dictionary, just seemed perverse to me. Even today, here in Haifa, it still does. But back then the very unfamiliarity of the language attracted me as much as it stopped me from making much progress. It's not

that I thought of it as a Holy Tongue or the language of Creation or anything remotely similar. I have always had a healthy contempt for mystical
claptrap of any kind—ours as much as the goyim's. That's probably the
one useful legacy my father passed on to his children. But maybe for no
better reason than because they were so obviously archaic, the individual
letters seemed charged with mystery. More than anything else, I think it
was the abstract idea of Hebrew, not the actual language, that intrigued
me. After the club arranged for classes to be offered three nights a week, I
would find myself occasionally enrolling for a while, then losing interest,
and so always having to begin again several months later not much further
advanced than where I had begun the very first time. When I wanted to
ask for a cup of coffee with sugar, I realized I no longer knew, or perhaps
had never learned, the word for 'cup,' 'saucer,' 'pour,' and 'spoon' and so
was left saying something like 'Take that and do that and bring me that
and I'll drink it.' In any case, that was also a time when some loudmouth
could be heard on every street corner of the Empire screaming out the
merits of his particular racial dialect. I often thought my interest in Hebrew was only contributing to an already unhealthy tribalism and was
ready to forgive my laziness accordingly. The newspapers reported that agitators had begun stirring up people to refuse to speak German altogether.
Everyone was now supposed to communicate only in whatever outlandish
tongue he imagined his ancestors had babbled before they'd started enjoying the privileges of Austrian civilization. How would they ever conceive of
something as indispensable as life insurance and pensions, or the plot of a
sophisticated comedy like yours, in dialects that never needed to express
ideas more complicated than sheep farming or distilling grain alcohol?
Listening to some of these polemics, I couldn't help contrasting the neat
and regular German that we all had learned since birth, so useful for
everything from business letters and engineering patents to Schiller's poems and debates in Parliament, with the impossible combination of con-
sonants in the various Slavic languages one was forced to put up with
more and more, not only on the streets but even in respectable business
concerns like Sobieski's. I wasn't convinced that one should make an exception for Hebrew, which I'd scarcely ever heard spoken. The only real
instances were a few half-understood phrases mumbled during prayers on
the infrequent occasions, usually High Holidays, when my father decided
to supplement our dosage of Mendelssohn's ethical writings with a visit to
the synagogue. To these, I could now add the experience of a half dozen

slogans, pronounced with what I thought was annoyingly excessive self-congratulation, by some Zionist speakers who had come to address the club about the moral virtues of swamp drainage and orange farming in Eretz Yisrael. Neither kind of encounter did much to further my zeal as a Hebraist. I do remember that for a while I debated if it might not be strategically advantageous to become an impassioned advocate of Jewish self-determination. Women seemed to find that sort of man very attractive, and I thought that if I could sound sufficiently fiery about an ideal, maybe some of that enthusiasm would transfer directly to me. After all, the arid wasteland of my sex life could have done with reclaiming just as much as the deserts of Palestine, and indisputably, it was a lot closer at hand. Besides, a reputation as a man of deep principles who also happened to have mastered the most advanced accounting techniques might have encouraged one of the businessmen in the club to offer me a better job than the wretched position I had with Sobieski, where I worked for insultingly low wages and with no chance for a meaningful promotion."

The daydreams of success that tormented Asher and prompted him to put in appearances at the Mendelssohn Club more regularly than he wanted to remember were starting to seem even more implausible than usual that winter evening. By the time he passed through the club's imposing front doors, there was already a long row of coats and galoshes in the hallway closet. Asher saw right away that he would have trouble finding a free hook and was anxious that some oaf would walk out with his galoshes and leave his own behind instead. Which of course were bound to be too small. But he also realized that his exasperation had little to do with these petty annoyances and was so vexed at himself for being vexed that he nearly gathered his things together and left again. But after standing for several minutes in the vestibule, blankly staring at the puddles forming on the tiles at his feet, wrapping and unwrapping his scarf from his throat a half dozen times, he decided that an hour or two of company might help dissipate his sour mood. So, trying to clear his expression of its look of irritation, he went ahead into the main salon.

Once inside, he was surprised by how remarkably little was needed to raise his spirits and stop fretting about the galoshes. Nothing more than an unlimited quantity of free tea and a table piled high with sandwiches and damson plum tarts. Wonderfully hot black tea poured into tall glasses with lemon and three cubes of sugar, and delicious plum jam stuffed inside a little swollen bosom of pastry, all laid out in large quantities for anybody who happened to wander into the paneled dining room, although as far as Asher remembered, it was neither anyone's birthday nor an official state occasion. Asher planted himself as close as possible to the tile stove and felt its heat penetrate his frozen clothes, very slowly at first, then, with increasing intensity, until wearing the double-knit sweater he had put on before leaving the office became uncomfortable. Only after his third cup of tea, when he felt so appeased that the only thing missing to complete his sense of physical well-being was a glass or two of plum brandy, did he think of asking a casual acquaintance standing nearby, who, he was relieved to observe, seemed to be eating and drinking everything within reach even more greedily than he was doing, "To whose generosity do we owe this Nebuchadnezzarine treat?"

"Don't you remember?" Fischbein answered him with his mouth still stuffed with pastry, "Moritz Rotenburg's son returned from his studies in Switzerland and London a few weeks ago, and his father is so happy at having him home again that he wants to celebrate the occasion as publicly as possible."

"Well, I suppose that means he finally has found something for Hans to do. If he goes to work for his father, there'll be no more days spent loitering in the elegant stores on the great boulevards of Europe ordering the salesgirls around" was Asher's dismissive reply. Privately he couldn't stop himself from imagining a whole sequence of thrilling pictures of what young Rotenburg did with those fawning salesgirls after the store closed for the night. Yet even to himself his attempt at sarcasm sounded forced. To be jealous of a family as wealthy as the Rotenburgs struck Asher as perfectly normal, part of what everyone there surely felt. His own presence in the club, like Fischbein's, was an act of Rotenburg charity, since Moritz paid the membership dues for some of the poorer Jews from respectable families—two categories that certainly fitted the Blumenthals—and Asher felt the natural resentment of any debtor who knows not only that he will never be able to repay his obligation but that to his creditor the sum involved is too trivial to notice. But along with envy, he sensed in himself a sudden, embarrassing rush of excitement, strong enough to leave him short of breath, at the prospect of actually meeting, and on such intimate terms, the sole heir to one of the largest fortunes in the Empire. Asher couldn't help being mesmerized by the thought of Rotenburg's money and felt sufficiently humiliated by his own awe to suppress any trace of it in his banter with Fischbein. He suddenly recalled one of his father's annoying old proverbs, "The only thing a man gets from rubbing shoulders with the rich is holes in his jacket," and as a kind of homage to a man whose advice he normally thought not even worth mocking, Asher swore that if Hans ever invited him over to the famous Rotenburg townhouse, he would put on the most worn jacket he owned, the one in which he had taken his accounting exam and which was too ragged to wear to work. With so many patches all over it, even Rotenburg's gold was unlikely to add another hole to this garment, no matter how much Asher might rub up against the Jewish stock market princeling.

But if such an invitation were ever going to be extended, it would have to come on a different evening. Although one Rotenburg had provided the means, and the other the reason, for the fête, neither bothered to show up in person. Asher was not the only member to take their absence as a personal insult, and he wandered up and down the stairs exchanging malicious stories about the financier's excessive attachment to his son. He glanced into the different rooms in case someone he knew might be heading home in the same direction and felt like stopping in at one of the many taverns along the way. Downstairs in the dining room, when it became clear that no one wanted any more refreshments, the table was cleared by the fat Slovene maid, whose large bosom and waist promised a hearty cheerfulness that clashed disconcertingly with her calculating, unpersuaded eyes. Gradually the white Meissen stove, its beehive-shaped tiles still radiating heat outward, the lateness of the hour, and the continuous, thickly falling snow outside spread a pleasant torpor through everyone who hadn't already left. Even Asher, who'd been unsuccessful in his search for a late-night drinking companion and had temporarily settled down in the reading room, grew less committed to brooding about Hans Rotenburg's snub and became engrossed in the latest number of *The New Order*, a Viennese journal to which he had persuaded the club librarian to subscribe.

The mood toward Hans was considerably less forgiving in the ornate private suite, looking directly on to the Radetzkyplatz, that had originally served the president of the insurance company as his personal office and now was used by the Mendelssohn Club's Governing Board as its meeting room. Many of the senior members had given up waiting for Hans even before Nicholas, the English butler Moritz Rotenburg had brought back from a business trip a decade ago, arrived with a note conveying Rotenburg's perfunctory apologies for himself and his son. Those who still remained, though, were furious, not simply at having been stood up by a mere boy of twenty-three but still more at the knowledge that they were helpless to do anything about it. To men like Rudi Pichler and Gerhard Himmelfarb, who depended on Rotenburg for their livelihood, Hans's rudeness amounted to a calculated provocation, intended to show everyone his indifference to their opinions. Although it was nearly impossible to see anything out the window except the dimly flickering lights of the Metropole Restaurant across the square, Pichler continued to stand with his face against the glass pane, idly watching the snow shroud the large equestrian statue of Prince Frederick von Schwarzenberg that had been erected half a century earlier. Even Pichler's daughter had become infatuated with Hans, and Rudi feared that this latest bit of insolence was only going to add to his prestige in her eyes. It seemed that the less Hans let himself be seen, the more everyone talked about him. During his fifteen months abroad Hans had become one of those legendary figures without an actual legend. Already before his return contradictory rumors about him were circulating through the town, extending, it was said, from the leaders of the Jewish community to the Count-Governor's own desk. It was taken for granted that Hans, as the future possessor of one of the country's largest private fortunes, would be watched closely by the authorities, and since an important career in the government or the military was closed to him as a Jew, the Political Section of the Foreign Ministry kept him under regular, if delicate, surveillance wherever he traveled. Very little that he said or did was not recorded somewhere in a secret police dossier. His presence at gatherings of political exiles in Zurich and London was carefully noted, and there was talk of summoning him to the consulate and threatening to take away his passport. But since he barely said anything at these rallies, where, in any case, at least half the participants were paid agents of the Russian, German, and Austrian governments, it was decided there was no immediate need for official action. In any case, Hans spent considerably more time accumulating a string of expensive mistresses and apprenticing himself to the heads of some of the large foreign concerns with whom the Rotenburgs did business than he did associating with known revolutionaries. The experts in Vienna were baffled by what to make of him. Opinion was divided as to whether Hans was a spoiled womanizer, posing as a revolutionary to add a different sort of glamour to the already potent appeal of his wealth and good looks, or a cunning political conspirator hiding behind the mask of a carefree seducer. There was of course the further possibility that he was simply acting as his father's emissary, accumulating useful information for the old man's increasingly far-flung business dealings. Since Hans had been known as a passionate Zionist back in his high school days, when several of his teachers secretly reported him to the government for exhibiting "the divided loyalties typical of his race," some elements in the Ministry continued to regard him as a potentially important figure in the outlandish Jewish fantasy of leading the Hebrew people back to their Promised Land. That entire project alternately baffled and annoyed specialists at the Foreign Ministry who never knew how seriously to take it, but since it was not practical to quash the movement out of hand, a way had to be found to make these daydreams serve the Empire's interests. Given the natural rivalry among the army, the Interior Ministry, and the Foreign Ministry, each suspected Hans might end up in the secret employ of the other. The immediate result of all this high-level speculation was a joint decision by the various departments not to interfere, at least for the moment, with Hans's activities, no matter how provocative they might appear. In jail Hans would be of no further use to anyone, but if he believed himself unobserved, he would undoubtedly end up giving away whose interests he was really serving. So perhaps the rumor that Hans had been approached by someone important in connection with the question of a Jewish homeland, or possibly with the promise of a small diplomatic posting in a setting where his race and undistinguished lineage would not constitute an insuperable barrier, had been started by the government itself to discredit him in advance should he later prove more troublesome than anyone had foreseen. More likely, though, no such approach had ever taken place, but once it had entered the eddies of the town's gossip, it became part of Hans's legend, the very multiplicity of stories in which he figured giving him an importance in the minds of his fellow townspeople that went far beyond anything he had actually done.

Hans had heard a few of these contradictory accounts about himself and found them all equally irritating. Unlike his father, he didn't yet realize the usefulness of having mutually exclusive versions of oneself widely disseminated. To secure greater flexibility for his own actions by manipulating discrepancies in the ways others saw him struck Hans as a needless acknowledgment of weakness. He was certain that success came only from the greatest possible audacity. Months before he left on his travels, he had grown disgusted by the passivity of the Mendelssohn Club's talkers—"samovar Zionists" is what he called them—and stopped attending their interminable debates, even when Elisabeth Demetz urged him to continue accompanying her. More speeches, he told her, no longer interested him, unless he could be convinced they would lead to direct action. The argument between them erupted with still more sharpness than usual on a muggy July night a few weeks after she had decided to adopt the name Batya as a pledge of her intention to emigrate to Palestine. She had gone directly from her Hebrew class at the club to visit Hans in the upstairs suite of rooms at the Rotenburg villa that he had converted into a self-contained apartment, separated from the rest of the house. Even as they quickly fell into their by now unhappily familiar litany of reproaches, Batya couldn't help thinking how bitter it was to be quarreling in a room that she herself had been responsible for furnishing. She remembered ordering the dark blue couch with the pattern of soft gold stars on which they were now sitting, as well as her delight when it finally arrived from Prague. In spite of his widespread reputation as a seducer of salesgirls, Hans scarcely ever shopped for himself, and he was glad to entrust all the decisions about his apartment to Batya. A bowl of fruit and a crystal pitcher full of cold water, sparkling with condensation, lay on a gilded tray next to the sofa. Behind them a bottle of white wine stood upright in a graceful terra-cotta holder. The wine holder had been her birthday present to Hans last year, and Batya wasn't sure if his placing it there was a subtle peace offering or if he had simply forgotten she had given it to him. The temperature had barely dropped since midday, and Batya was glad to sit quietly for a few minutes, pressing her glass of wine against her forehead, but Hans had obviously been waiting for her arrival all evening and was eager to plunge directly into his stored-up grievances. At such moments the contrast between the aggressive harshness of his tone and the natural delicacy of his features made his anger all the more disconcerting. Hans strongly resembled his dead mother, although in him Dina's features seemed more angular and assertive, perhaps as a function of his temperament tensing the lines and curves that otherwise would betray more softness than he could permit anyone to glimpse. The two or three times that Moritz had seen Hans asleep as an adult—once when he went into Hans's rooms late one afternoon only to find him napping on top of his bed, completely clothed, including his shoes, and a few times by the fire, in winter, with his arms folded over a stack of papers that were slowly slipping down from his chest—this most self-contained of men felt his heart ache with grief at how fully Hans's resemblance to his mother had surfaced. To

Moritz it seemed that Dina's delicate shyness had been momentarily released in a youthful male face, freed of waking consciousness. Hans's pale brown eyes were framed by wide, softly arcing brows, and Batya often thought that if he had been governed by a different, more inward temperament, Hans could easily have cultivated the look of one of the famous portraits of a musician or writer from the beginning of the last century. She must once have been foolish enough to tell him so, since he now went out of his way to show his indifference to anything connected to the arts. He seemed to enjoy framing his arguments in the crassest, most vulgar terms imaginable, and that night he had found a particularly galling comparison to punish her for having made him wait for so long while she stayed talking to her friends at the club.

"Our politics"—he started in even before Batya put down her wine—"ought to be no more tolerant of failure than my father's businesses. There's nothing noble or romantic about incompetence, and I don't see why I should sit patiently and listen to people's political fantasies when I wouldn't trust any of them to manage a corner tobacco store. But even if that crowd of daydreamers at the club manages to get a few people into Palestine, the idea of remaking the place into a second Galicia, with its own little Mendelssohn Club in every town, is pretty unappealing. Not when there is so much that needs doing right here. Besides, think about whom you'd be emigrating with. A half dozen of those sad-looking clerks my father subsidizes, who walk around the club staring at the women with their wet, pleading eyes and those ridiculously affected smirks? They've all got the kind of defeated look you can't stand, and I don't believe a few months dressed up as Arabs will change that. Don't you remember what you said to me after the Succoth dance two years ago? I haven't forgotten a word of it at any rate. You came over to where I was standing alone in the garden, and you put your arms around my neck, half laughing and half furious, and began talking so loudly people couldn't help staring at us, although we both pretended not to notice. 'Tell me, Hans,' you said in your best mock-quizzical tone, 'why do so many of the young men in this town wear glasses and dress so badly? At least you can see straight without spectacles on your nose, so maybe I will go home with you later on after all. How many centuries of servility do you think it took to produce a face like that fellow's over there? Just imagine what a picture he would make naked, with those long, hairy arms and his cock all droopy and awkward! I am so tired of all that melancholy and introspection. Oversensitive coffeehouse souls ready to run home in terror the moment someone on the street raises his voice to them.' But just a month later, Batya, you suddenly wanted me to start combing my hair to look more like some delicate Romantic poet myself. To me, all these commitments of yours seem like so much playacting. It's as though you are trying on one costume after another to see which one you look best in, and I just can't take it all as seriously as you'd like me to."

At the beginning Batya listened carefully while Hans was berating her, but as he went on, she felt her attention start to drift, and she began looking around the room, prompted by both her fatigue and the sense that it would be the last time she would be there as his girlfriend. Although the room was full of rare curios, gathered from other parts of the house, her eyes lingered on the trinkets she had most enjoyed giving him, especially the small tiger's-eye cigarette holder on his desk and the dark bentwood music stand that he never used, and she suddenly felt immensely tired and eager to get back to her own home and bed. Behind the meanspiritedness of his words, Batya heard how strongly Hans felt he needed to distance himself from her, and she was convinced of the futility of trying to argue him out of his decision. There was a great deal she could answer, much of which ran through her mind as he was talking, but the impulse to prolong their quarrel and prove herself in the right dissipated as the uselessness of the effort became clear to her. Yes, of course, she had said a lot of foolish things the night of the dance, and whether or not anyone really had overheard her—something she was much less certain of than Hans now claimed—she felt ashamed at her cruelty. It was the first time she had ever drunk that much champagne, and the excitement of the evening, the hours spent dancing to a Gypsy orchestra that had been specially hired over the objections of the more conservative club members, and the knowledge that Hans Rotenburg, whom every girl in town wanted, was in love with her had made her as giddy as a fourteen-year-old. When she rushed out to him in the garden, she was really only trying to let him feel some of her own exhilaration while still sounding like one of the brazen, experienced women she loved to read about. None of that excused what she had said, but it was unjust of Hans to use it to brush aside everything she believed in. It was also dishonest. What about everything else she told him in the garden? With his wonderful memory, leaving the rest out could only be deliberate. She might have been tipsy that night, but not so much that she could forget his strange look when she blurted out that all those

64

dejected faces inside only strengthened her conviction that "what we need now are Jewish farmers and laborers, not more lawyers, rabbis, and clerks! I know the next generation is going to look and act completely different, and I want to be a part of that transformation, not just stay here and make a suitable marriage!"

Hans had finally stopped his accusations, and his face was set in an expression she recognized but never expected to encounter when they were alone together: It was stubborn and hard and looked out at whoever had displeased him as though the person were being dismissed from his mind like an unsatisfactory subordinate whose presence had become tedious. But then, as she was gathering her things together, angry and humiliated, Batya suddenly remembered Hans's fury years ago, when he defended poor little Sandor the time the other schoolboys attacked him after class and threw his homework into the snow. And how everyone in the school had gasped at the insolence with which Hans had answered back when that pompous fool of a history teacher made his joke about Jewish war profiteers selling defective rifles to the army. No matter what he now seemed to believe, it was those moments, not the Rotenburg name, that had made her fall in love with him and dream about the two of them going together as delegates to a Zionist convention, helping each other with their speeches, openly sharing a room, both on fire with the excitement of being together as partners in a cause that was entirely their own. She had just enough self-restraint not to remind Hans of those images. Whatever they might have meant to her, to Hans, anything she said about them now would seem only like further playacting. She even agreed with him in part and knew better than he how much she enjoyed her own changeable enthusiasms because of the optimism and energy they brought her. But unlike Hans, for whom passing judgment seemed to have become a pleasure in itself, Batya was naturally ready to be forgiving of whatever made one feel life more joyously. She understood, as well, that none of this had made Hans stop caring for her. He no longer found it pleasurable to be with her, and all the rest was merely an elaboration of that fundamental change in his own feeling. One can defend oneself against almost any charge, but not against having ceased to be desirable. Hans might scorn her theatricality, but nothing that whole dismal evening was more transparently staged than the way she let him help her on with her coat, accompany her down the wide, curving staircase to the front door, and exchange farewells in as nearly normal a tone as possible. It was all polite and ghastly like a scene in some mediocre play, and only when Batya was by herself again, with the door to her room locked and her clothes carefully hung up in the wardrobe, did she throw herself down in the chair by her bed and sob uncontrollably until she fell asleep.

When Hans was back upstairs and realized that Batya was actually gone without the last-minute restatements and reconciliations that had marked all their earlier quarrels, he felt momentarily startled, then relieved, as though surprised at having attained a goal of which he was only obliquely aware when Batya had come over that evening. Until that moment he hadn't made up his mind whether or not to take his father's suggestion and go study abroad, but he was certain now that he needed to get away from this house and town if he was ever going to be more than simply Moritz Rotenburg's son. Breaking with Batya was just as necessary, although he knew that she didn't perceive him the way the others did. But her need to see both of them as part of a story in which he no longer believed felt impossibly constraining. Unlike the heroes of Dostoevsky's novels, which she had raced through in sleepless nights of wonder and admiration, and in which she kept finding what seemed to Hans wildly implausible parallels to their own love affair, he never thought of himself as an anguished seeker after some higher spiritual truth. On the contrary, he was drawn to the kind of aloof sangfroid he conceived of as the antithesis to her Romantic hysteria, which he despised but to which he imagined himself overly susceptible. Like many instinctively calculating people, Hans needed to see himself as so easily overwrought that he had to exercise the strictest control over his own emotions.

It was to protect himself from his own supposedly excessive sensibility that he avoided being alone with Batya in the months before he left for England. In addition to the preparations required for so long a journey and the distraction of a brief, lifeless affair with Sophie Pichler, Hans spent part of each week with various senior assistants in his father's office, learning some of the fundamentals involved in managing the Rotenburg enterprises. When two of his best friends, Ernst von Alpsbach and Christoph von Hradl, with whom Hans had formed a reading group that had progressed from studying older Marxist texts to acquiring an extensive collection of underground revolutionary pamphlets, tried to tease Hans about dividing his time between observing enormous sums of money being made and reading about ways to abolish private property altogether, Hans bristled with annoyance. He insisted that if they bothered to learn anything about the modern world, they would soon realize there was nothing in the least contradictory between his two activities: "I am sure that for aristocrats like you two, whose family money comes from your estates, the principles of modern, rational social organization are deeply alien. That's where being a Rotenburg gives me such an advantage. It has nothing to do with the fact that my father may be richer than yours; it's just that his success depends on being in tune with constantly mutating, implacable economic forces. There is simply no room for sentiment or nostalgia either on the bourse or in a political movement that is serious about seizing power. Everything connected with the work has to be ruthlessly logical and efficient, no matter what gets sacrificed in the process. Marx and my father would probably understand each other pretty well, at least as far as agreeing where real power comes from these days. I have certainly learned more about what it takes to run an organization from working in his offices these past months than I did from any of our debates."

They went on arguing like this the rest of a glorious autumn afternoon, walking together under the double column of ancient walnut trees for which Weidenau, the von Hradl country estate, was famous. From far away the voices of the harvesters reached their ears, and the glass panes of the summerhouse, where Christoph's mother was busy tending her exotic flowers, glowed red and gold in the late sun, as though the light itself had transformed them into the beveled windows of an old village church. If it occurred to either Ernst or Christoph that Hans's presence there as their friend, not to mention their patience letting him lecture them in his sardonic, insistent way, was proof that the Empire's old families weren't all as sclerotic as he claimed, they gave no hint. No Jew would have dared talk to one of their grandparents in such a tone, and Philip von Hradl, Christoph's father, whose debts gave him ample grounds for wanting to stay on good terms with the Rotenburgs, was clearly uncomfortable at the intimacy between his boy and Moritz's. But even the Emperor himself was starting to make such adjustments, and with more humor than one usually attributed to him. According to Count-Governor Wiladowski, who was in Vienna at the time, Franz Josef had been asked to approve the appointment to an important church post of a new bishop named Cohn, and when he saw the name, he merely turned to his aide-de-camp, Count Trautmannsdorff, and in no particular tone inquired, "Is he at least baptized?" Though they would never put it this way, Christoph and Ernst admired Hans for many of the same reasons Batya did, and they were willing

67

to tolerate his not always agreeable sharp irony unleavened by any sense of humor because they thought that he was more serious than they were, and they all were still young enough to regard that as a quality above almost any other.

Hans took it as an auspicious sign that the cities to which his father wanted to send him were also centers of subversive political activity, from which the pamphlets he and his friends read were smuggled into Austria. His natural urge to dominate any group was tempered, though none of the other members realized it, by an acute awareness of how fragile a basis in experience underlay his claims, and he thought that by going to different radical gatherings in England and Switzerland, he could acquire the final polish on his political education. When he at last left, he warned his friends not to expect his letters to include any mention of the various underground contacts he would make abroad, ostensibly out of a fear of being detected by the government's mail censors, but in reality, because he wanted to preserve his independence from any outside constraints, especially the opinions of other members of his group. Hans was not much more inclined to let his friends know exactly what he was doing than his father would have been to let his partners in a business venture know the details of all the other negotiations he was involved in at the same time. Although he listened to the different radical leaders with the curiosity of a bright student eager both to learn from and to test himself against the most renowned teachers of the day, Hans never formally joined any one party, preferring to keep open the possibility of working with a number of them, even though they often regarded one another as bitter rivals. The possible addition to their ranks of Hans's name and funds was enough to persuade otherwise rigidly sectarian party organizers to allow him a leeway they would never have extended toward a less attractive recruit, and Hans took full advantage of his freedom to pick and choose among the various factions. His instinctive preference was always for the most intractable theories. When he finally committed himself to returning home to organize a revolutionary cell entirely on his own, it was the scientific, purely logical authority of the revolutionaries' historical analyses that convinced him, and he trusted in them with the same certainty that he felt watching his father speculate on the movement of iron and steel prices. What thrilled him more than anything he had known before was the confirmation of his belief in a rigorous science of revolution, as irrefutable as the proofs of a mathematical formula.

On his way back from Switzerland, Hans stopped off in Vienna for a few weeks, and then, having first asked his father not to tell anyone the exact date of his arrival, he returned home from the capital on the evening express train, where he was met at the station only by Nicholas, who took him directly to the Rotenburg villa. Over the next few days, and without any of the resistance Moritz had expected, Hans agreed to resume working alongside his father's senior aides in order to prepare himself for the day he would inherit the company. Yet Moritz noticed that his son avoided any intimate conversation that did not touch on business and seemed even more distant and withdrawn than before his departure. Although news of his return spread quickly through the town, as far as Moritz could tell from asking the servants, only four or five of Hans's large circle of acquaintances ever seemed to be invited to the house. According to Dr. Demetz, Hans never bothered getting in touch with Batya at all. Moritz wondered whether perhaps Hans had been more injured than he had let on at the news that Batya and the von Alpsbach boy were known to be seeing each other—a liaison that greatly distressed both sets of parents as well—but if Hans was troubled, he never mentioned it to anyone. If anything, during his time away his sexual tastes seemed to have gravitated from girls like Batya Demetz and Sophie Pichler toward working-class women. He had recently come up with the eccentric notion of renting an apartment in the run-down Josef Quarter, motivated, no doubt, by the need for a place to entertain certain kinds of women whom it was impossible to bring to his father's home. Although Moritz wasn't in the least alarmed by such whims, viewing them as expressions of a harmless frivolity on the part of someone who, for his age, was otherwise altogether too serious and self-contained, he saw no reason for Hans to sever his ties to his old circle either. It was precisely to help reintegrate Hans into the local community that Moritz had arranged for the reception at the Mendelssohn Club, but when his son sent him a two-line note from his new flat, half an hour before they were due to leave together for the party, saying only that he was not feeling well enough to attend, Moritz was too discouraged to go over to the club alone. He sent Nicholas in his place to make the necessary apologies, knowing that since everyone would be furious with him and attribute both his and Hans's absence to arrogance, it was pointless to exert himself to frame an acceptable explanation in person. Moritz had no wish to be morose in the company of people like Gerhard Himmelfarb, who resented him for his money, and Rudi Pichler, who may have been no fonder of him than Gerhard, but who had a daughter to marry off and still futilely dreamed of pairing her with Hans. Moritz found no pleasure in hurting people's feelings. But what anyone at the club thought of him ultimately made no difference to the financier, and in that judgment, at least, although the whole snowed-in town lay between them, father and son were more united that evening than either of them realized.

· ◆ ·

While everyone at the Mendelssohn Club was muttering about Hans's absence, he himself was trying unsuccessfully to get a proper fire going in the apartment he had just rented. Outside his door, in the narrow stairway of the three-story building, everything was saturated with the smell of cheap cooking lard and kerosene, and thick layers of soot clung permanently to the walls like an imitation of the black drapery found in middle-class homes when an important family member has died. Inside, it was nearly as gloomy. The grimy windows hadn't been washed in years, and the room itself was almost completely bare. The only visible objects were two rickety wooden chairs, an old stove, a desk that had been nailed to the floor, and an iron bed frame without a mattress; everything else had been hastily removed by the previous tenants, who had left without paying the rent and taken with them whatever was easily transportable. As he scrambled around, looking for a place to set down the armful of books he had brought with him, Hans found himself regretting his impracticality for the hundredth time since he had come back. It took several tries before he finally managed to get the heap of cheap coal and shreds of old newspaper to catch fire, and he was forced to admit to himself that if he was going to make the place habitable, he would have to hire someone reliable to begin looking after it right away. The landlord would be able to arrange for a cleaning woman to come regularly, but since he could hardly ask Batya Demetz to take care of buying the necessary furniture, he would need to engage Herr Lászny, the manager of Koppensteiner's Department Store, to come and look over the rooms. It would almost certainly be the first time Lászny had ever been inside an apartment in this district, but the Rotenburgs were too important for him to hesitate to offer his services.

By now, though, dusk was falling, and Hans reluctantly concluded that it would be some time before the apartment could be used for anything more than a few hurried, preliminary meetings. Tonight he was expecting only four visitors, Christoph von Hradl, Joachim Gerling, Leo von Arnstein, and Manfred Langer. They were the most loyal members of his old reading group and would have to form the nucleus of the revolutionary cell. They all had wondered if Hans would invite Ernst von Alpsbach, whom everyone, except, perhaps, Ernst and Hans themselves, used to regard as Hans's closest friend. It was true that Ernst was the only one whose intelligence Hans fully respected, but their friendship had been marked from early on by a certain mutual wariness that was more than just the natural rivalry of two extraordinarily privileged and strong-willed young men. Hans had almost completed his internship in London and was making arrangements to go on to Zurich when Sophie Pichler wrote to tell him that Ernst and Batya had become romantically linked. Sophie's malice toward Batya was so transparent it made it easier for Hans to treat her news as something that no longer concerned him directly. He told himself that Ernst and Batya belonged to an earlier phase of his own development. There was even something flattering in the thought that these two figures from his past should have become lovers once he was no longer around. To his surprise, though, now that he was back in town, he sometimes woke up in the middle of the night wondering whether they had been together that day, and before he could go back to sleep, he had to force himself to dispel a series of dismayingly vivid images of them lying naked together in Ernst's room, laughing at some remembered absurdity of his. Christoph and the others all looked up to Ernst as well, and there was no doubt that he had sufficient personal authority to set himself up as a rival in the cell. Nonetheless, Hans had concluded that he had no choice but to invite Ernst; to do otherwise would be an admission of self-doubt, so he made a point of showing all the others the note in which he emphasized how much they were looking forward to Ernst's participation. He was secretly pleased, though, when Ernst had politely excused himself from joining them that evening.

Yet in part Hans genuinely regretted Ernst's absence. Although Hans had decided at the outset to assume sole leadership of their small cell, he was uncomfortably aware of the strain between his scientific confidence in the coming triumph of the movement and his longing to commit an act of "revolutionary justice." Such a gesture would be the best way to legitimize his role in the group. He was hardly the equal of the professional revolutionaries he had observed abroad, and he sensed that his companions were distinguished mostly by an uninspiring mental and emotional slackness. "They are, all of them, mere dilettantes" was how he phrased it to himself while he was waiting for them to find the house. Their very incompetence compelled him to think of ways to harden the group's collective resolve. History, Hans believed, had given him a unique opportunity since at this very moment the country's need and that of his own cell were in perfect harmony: He and his comrades needed to have their resolve forged in some great undertaking, and the Empire required a direct act of revolutionary warfare in order for any meaningful change to occur. It was because he felt ready to provide the first spark for such a war that Hans had bothered to return home at all and work with whatever human material he could recruit.

As if to confirm all of Hans's doubts about them, Christoph and the others had scarcely come though the door when they began to complain about the difficulty of finding the apartment. Not one of them bothered to take off his coat. Instead they all just stood there in an awkward semicircle, pressing themselves up against the stove, visibly baffled at Hans's whim to meet here rather than at home. Even Gerling and Langer, the two middle-class members of the group who were always so respectfully silent in front of their more distinguished comrades that everyone had taken to calling them "our revolutionary Benedictines," made no effort to disguise their discomfort. As he watched them impassively from his position by the window, Hans felt more and more pleased at his decision. Making everyone meet here would end up strengthening his domination over the group. The more they were thrust out of their familiar routines, the more they would turn to him to give them a purpose. Besides, everyone could come and go here much more freely than in his own neighborhood. There were already too many dangerous agitators trying to stir up the unemployed in the Josef Quarter for the police to pay much attention to a group of rich boys from the other side of town. It was an honored national tradition for young men of their background to find working-class mistresses, and Hans was confident he would have no trouble making it look as though that were his own aim in setting himself up in this part of town. Policemen, Hans thought, uncovered only what they were already looking for, so all that was necessary to reassure the government spies was for him to come in drunk some evening, accompanied by his friends and a few girls from a nearby bar. They would make enough noise that one of the families in the neighborhood was sure to lodge a complaint. Then Hans would pay the prescribed fine, everyone's expectations would be satisfied, and no one would take any further notice of his activities.

As Hans watched his comrades look around despondently for something to drink and a place to sit down, it occurred to him that for tonight, at least, there was an additional, if unanticipated, advantage to the flat's condition. Long discussions were impossible under such circumstances. People with chattering teeth and empty stomachs wouldn't feel like engaging him in a debate about revolutionary theory—at least not when they all had comfortable places to go to as soon as they'd heard him out and felt at liberty to leave. After his visitors had been standing together awkwardly for a few moments, waiting for Hans to start matters, he abruptly straightened himself from his semislouch against the window ledge, walked over to the center of the room, and shook everyone's hand with an air of hurried but friendly pleasure. He apologized for the unfinished condition of the apartment, but his tone made it clear that he regarded physical comfort as a matter of no great concern and was certain that they all felt the same way. The crucial thing, he told them, was to have a place to meet regularly away from any supervision by either the police or their families' servants. But when Christoph asked him if it wouldn't make more sense for at least one or two of them to go to Vienna and establish contacts with some of the radical groups there, Hans quickly cut him off and said that if he had learned one thing abroad, it was the necessity for the separate underground cells to work independently of one another so that if one was ever compromised, it couldn't take down any of the others in its wake. "Besides"—he went on—"just think how much time it would take to get established in the capital, make the right contacts, and find something useful to do for the cause. We would obviously be much more productive staying right here, where we already know the situation and can organize for some kind of action without needing to bring in unknown and potentially risky outsiders. With this place in the Josef Quarter to throw the police off guard, we could start getting hold of some weapons to store in the basement, and if any of us could manage to infiltrate the lumberyard and cloth factory and make contact with the comrades who are already agitating there in secret, we'd be able to combine an exemplary act of political terror with a mass strike. But don't make any mistake about it, the strike is a secondary issue for us. Our job—the one I have promised the leadership in Zurich we have both the willpower and the determination to carry out—is the terror itself. Even if the workers themselves aren't fully aware of it yet, you can be certain that they will rise up to emulate whoever sets the boldest example. Mass action always develops after a deed of individual sacrifice, never the other way around."

Though Hans tried to keep his voice level and businesslike, there was no doubting the excitement he felt as soon as he began to talk about terror as a political instrument. The other men all registered it at nearly the same moment and were faintly embarrassed at witnessing so intimate an emotion seize a friend whose self-control they'd often admired. For Christoph, it was unnervingly similar to how he imagined he himself sounded when he was instructing one of the women in a brothel exactly what to do to augment his pleasure. Leo and Christoph exchanged a quick glance, and then immediately looked away, abashed at the similarity in their response. Both were amazed that for Hans, simply the idea of political terror could arouse intensities that they had known only in shameful erotic encounters, and they wondered what it would feel like to have such a powerful depth of commitment to a cause beyond their own momentary pleasures. Hans caught their look, but the decisive point had already been gained. No one had raised any objection to his call for violence, and whatever strategy might emerge, he intended to treat that initial consent by silence as a pledge no less binding than a legal contract. To give the impression of an open meeting, he would have to keep them all busy talking for a while longer, but as far as he was concerned, everything else said that evening would be just so much chatter.

As though he were still a schoolboy, Joachim Gerling instinctively began raising his index finger to indicate a desire to speak, only to blush furiously when he became aware of what he was doing. He pulled his hand partway back down and started tugging at his oversize earlobes as though that had always been his intention. Without Ernst's presence to fortify him, Gerling would always try to attach himself as closely as possible to the strongest man in a group. Hans knew that, but even he was unprepared for the ineptitude with which Gerling set about ingratiating himself. With a look of utmost seriousness, he asked whether, in light of the growing tensions between the organized Jewish workers and the Catholic socialists, the group couldn't use some of Hans's old contacts in the Zionist movement to help build a bridge between the two movements. For an instant Hans was tempted simply to laugh out loud at such nonsense. Instead he decided that pretending to take Gerling's ideas seriously enough to argue with them was the best way to reward a natural follower for his future loyalty and, more important, to impress on everyone there that what made an idea worthy of being discussed was not its intrinsic merit but only how closely it might echo something Hans himself had once said. So he made a special point of nodding thoughtfully at Gerling's words and appeared to reflect before answering.

"Well, at the moment, Joachim, I am far from convinced these divisions are as deep as certain people would like us all to believe." Hans kept his eyes firmly fixed on Gerling and addressed him with the same respectful intimacy he used to reserve exclusively for Ernst. "There's no point jumping to pessimistic conclusions. I don't believe that the so-called race question carries much weight with the working class. We're not talking about peasants after all, but about an industrial proletariat with the most developed class consciousness of anyone in the country. We all have got to learn to analyze a situation more dialectically, not condescend to the workers by imagining them sunk in medieval superstition. It's obvious that all this bigotry is just fomented by the government to set different groups against one another. After the revolution you'll see that all the nationality questions in the Empire will be resolved without any problem on the basis of class solidarity. To take these things seriously now, under our circumstances, is just counterrevolutionary. Why do you think the authorities encourage windbags like the Zionist recruiters? Just think about it, they all have perfectly legal travel documents giving them permission to hop from town to town to hold their meetings. I have never heard of a banned Zionist paper or exiled leader. Why do you suppose that is the case? Because, to speak objectively, their fantasies are completely reactionary; all they'll ever do is draw energy away from genuine revolutionary work. I realize none of you here knows much about it, but I wasted a lot of hours investigating them, and believe me, in the crowd that people like that move— and I am afraid that probably now includes our former comrade von Alpsbach and his new girlfriend—these currents are not without a certain appeal. That's exactly why what we have agreed to tonight is so important. Unlike any of those coffeehouse reformers, what we're doing is planning something immediate and impossible to overlook. Not another scheme for some distant future, but for right away, something we can do by ourselves, a single pure and ruthless action to show that we already have the power to strike at the government whenever we wish. Think of how many workers would rise up spontaneously to join us if they had a sign that Count Wiladowski himself was afraid of us. What counts now is to demonstrate the will to act. A deed that is absolute, above fear, calculation, or self-interest. Remember everything Vera Zasulich accomplished in Russia by shooting just one reactionary swine? When the jury acquitted her, they say, even some of the high army officers were so impressed by her courage that they couldn't help applauding. Who's got the nerve to tell us we can't be just as steely-minded as our Russian comrades?"

Hans abruptly turned away from Gerling and addressed the last question to everyone. It was important to bring them back into the conversation. None of them cared about the Zionists one way or another, and Hans didn't want them thinking the topic was of more than peripheral importance to him either. Christoph, who had inherited the unhappy tendency of the von Hradl males to a prematurely thinning hairline over a small, nearly dome-shaped head, stared out at the others with the puzzled, abstracted focus of someone looking through the wrong end of a telescope at an unfamiliar and not altogether appealing new species. With his habitual half-bored, half-irritated tone, he pointed out that even in Russia, if their own pamphlets were to be believed, most of the revolutionary parties had renounced assassination as a political instrument.

Christoph's skepticism was exactly what Hans had hoped for. From his father Hans had learned that to dominate a meeting without leaving any doubt about one's control always required finding at least one influential adversary around the table to overcome. Several times, before important negotiations, Hans had seen Moritz arrange for one of his own secret partners to play the role of opposition leader and let himself be vanquished so that having witnessed his defeat, no one else would dare challenge Moritz's plans further. Now Hans leaped at the chance and cut von Hradl off before he could make the crucial move from disagreeing with what Hans had proposed to developing a counterposition of his own.

"Listen, Christoph, of course I know as well as you that they've changed their tactics over there. I was at the meeting in Switzerland when the Russian leadership explained the reasons for their decision, and they all emphasized that it was only a temporary measure. But even if that weren't the case, I don't see why we need to feel ourselves bound to follow someone else's example. Obviously the situation in Russia is different from ours. With the percentage of industrial workers in our country increasing every month we are much closer to a real prerevolutionary situation here than they could ever dream about in Moscow or St. Petersburg. They'll still be cowering from the Czar's police long after we have abolished titles and class distinctions. I am thinking of writing a pamphlet about that very question, and when it's ready, I'll circulate it to everyone for comments and then send it abroad to be printed as a collective document from our cell. Soon the whole world will see that our backward little province can produce just as dedicated revolutionaries as any of the famous cities in Europe. And why not? When Saint-Just called for Louis the Sixteenth's head, he wasn't any older than we are. A revolution can't be squeamish about employing terror, and anyone who is afraid of shedding blood belongs with the enemies of human progress. If I have learned anything from all those nights listening to debates in underground meeting rooms that were much colder than this flat—I give you my word for that!—it is that it takes an unwavering clarity of mind to demand real sacrifice of oneself and others. I intend to earn the right to make those demands by my own actions, and I expect the same of each of you. For our next meeting I suggest that everyone come up with a proposal for who should be our first target. By then I'll have had a chance to make this place comfortable enough for a longer discussion, so we can begin to decide on a specific plan of action. It's clear, though, that we need to start learning more about explosives. If we had reliable instructions, we could use the basement here for manufacturing bombs. I will find out everything I can on that score. In the meantime, Leo and Christoph, you ought to go out hunting more with your relatives and old friends from the cadet regiments. That way you will stay in practice with firearms and might also pick up some useful gossip about important visitors to the Castle, extra security details—anything that can help us stay ahead of the secret police. It's really too bad that Ernst is not with us anymore since his family connections would be useful in letting us know what Count Wiladowski was up to. I can see that you all are eager to go somewhere warm, so I won't keep you longer. This has been a productive meeting. Just be careful when you are going down the stairs, and if you make any noise on the way out, be sure it sounds like someone who's had too much to drink. I'll lock up after you have gone and see you back in town tomorrow."

· ◆ ·

Half an hour later, when Hans emerged from the tenement, the snowfall had let up somewhat, but it had been a struggle to open the massive front door against the pressure of the high bank of snow blown up against it by the night wind. Most of the Josef Quarter was still unpaved, and any difference between street and sidewalk had been obliterated weeks ago. Apart from the fresh footprints of his friends, there were no signs of activity anywhere near the house. Even the police spies must have given up and gone inside to write their reports. Glancing down the long, curved street at the row of somber houses, ungainly in the pale clarity of the reflected starlight, Hans couldn't make out a single strand of smoke rising from any of the chimneys in the neighborhood. Placed at what he guessed must be the street intersections, the few gaslights that were still functioning gave off a flickering, anemic glow that only emphasized the cold.

He was glad that it was far too late to stop by and explain to his father why he had been unable to come to the party. Although Hans had never hidden his indifference to social obligations, Moritz's distress at his son's unwillingness to accompany him to any of the Mendelssohn Club's activities left Hans with the feeling of having been somehow in the wrong. Like many people who are compelled by the obvious pain they are causing to recognize that they have acted unjustly, Hans, after an initial surge of compassion, quickly began to think of his father with more annoyance than guilt, and lately he found any contact with him, except on matters of family business, exasperating. "Unless I am incredibly unlucky," Hans reflected as he started walking toward the town center, "he'll be fast asleep by the time I get home, and I won't have to talk to him at all until tomorrow."

Hans hadn't given any thought to how he would get back to his own part of town, and after only a few blocks he began, mostly out of habit, to look out for a carriage that he could hire to take him home. But at that hour there were no vehicles for hire in the Josef Quarter. He continued briskly toward the town center, his naturally long strides leaving a lengthy trail of fresh prints in the snow. In spite of the chill, Hans found that he didn't mind the walk. The near-frozen air served to clear his mind from the strain of the meeting and cut through the accumulated tobacco smoke that he could still taste in his mouth and lungs. A hot tea with brandy, followed by a long bath, would be enough to restore him. Stopping for a moment underneath the arc of one of the rare working streetlamps, Hans turned his fur collar up against the wind, quickly checked his pocket watch, and calculated that he could be home within three-quarters of an hour. But just when he had reconciled himself to not finding a carriage and settled into the rhythm of his rapid walk, enjoying the softness of the fresh powder snow underneath his boots, he was startled by a fiacre pulling up a few yards ahead of him, obviously waiting until he came within hailing range. By the time Hans came closer, though, he saw that there was very little about the shivering coachman or his scrawny horse to suggest much in the way of comfort, and he quickly determined to walk on. But as he passed the carriage without having slowed down, its door flew open, and a man called out his name, obviously expecting to be recognized in turn. Although Hans had no idea who the passenger might be, something in his tone suggested both an aggrieved querulousness should Hans's recognition be in any way tardy and a discouraging certainty that just such an offense was bound to occur. When Hans still made no move to get in, the bundled-up figure inside suddenly reached out an arm and, in his eagerness to help Hans negotiate the icy half step up into the carriage, grabbed him by the shoulders at such an awkward angle that Hans momentarily lost his balance and nearly toppled both of them face forward into the street. He barely managed to stay on his feet and, more baffled than annoyed, allowed himself to be pulled inside to a seat on the wooden bank across from the stranger.

It was too dark in the carriage to see much except for a thin face, completely dominated by a pair of dull brown, aqueous eyes, set below hypermobile eyebrows that seemed to rise and fall in some complex accord with their possessor's emotional state. In spite of the cold, he was hatless but, perhaps in compensation, had wrapped himself up in an immense wool coat that looked large enough to contain someone twice his size. While Hans was still settling himself into his seat and trying to make out whatever he could about his new travel companion, the man leaned over toward him until their faces were almost touching and began speaking at such a breathless pace it was as though he were determined to fasten Hans to his place by the sheer torrent of words.

"Well, are you going to shut the door and warm yourself or not? There's a wool blanket here that doesn't look too mangy, and even a rickety coach like this helps keep the wind out a little bit. It's lucky for you I came along just now. There won't be any other carriages at this time of night around here, especially not in such horrible weather. You probably couldn't recognize me from out there, blinded by all that snow, but I have just been at the club celebrating your return. Yes, yes, it was a great success, though I must say you were much missed tonight, especially by our common friends from the Zionist study groups. But I am glad to be able to give you a lift anyway. Surely you remember when we were introduced at . . . oh, wherever it was, some time ago? In any case, I am Asher Blumenthal. Of course, when I saw you standing there by the lamppost, I knew right away who you were. Is there anyone in town, even among the goyim, who wouldn't recognize Hans Rotenburg? Well, it's a real pleasure to run into you again and be of some small service. I just wish everyone back at the club could see how *my* evening turned out! It seems I am the only one who got to meet you after all! Are you quite comfortable now? Where can I drop you? I live only a few minutes away from here and would be glad to invite you to my flat for a drink, but my landlady, who's a real terror, absolutely will not tolerate visitors after nine. If you are in a desperate hurry to get home yourself, I could just get out when we pass my house and let you continue on, but now that we have met again for the first time in ages, wouldn't it be nice to chat for a while?"

On any other evening Hans would probably have gotten away from a person like Asher Blumenthal as quickly as possible. But something in the man's desperate eagerness made Hans hesitate. Well before he had gone abroad, Hans had begun to train himself to look for qualities in others that might prove useful to him someday, even if he couldn't always be certain how, and with the same rapid calculation that governed most of his choices, Hans decided to let this strange encounter continue for a while longer. If he could listen to Gerling's inanities, why not hear this Blumenthal out? Of course bringing him back to the Rotenburg villa was out of the question, and the only place Hans knew where they could sit and talk in comfort at this hour was the Metropole. He politely asked Asher if he felt like joining him there for drinks, confident that in spite of the lateness of the hour, the fellow would leap at the invitation. Indeed Blumenthal instantly accepted without even pretending to weigh the matter. He shouted out their change of destination to the cabbie up above, his delight in naming the town's most elegant restaurant evident in his voice, and then, as though his energy had already been recharged simply by the idea of what lay ahead, and anxious lest the promised treat be withdrawn at the last moment, he began speaking even more quickly than before.

"Well, I must say that's very generous of you to offer. I didn't know the Metropole served guests as late as this. But you are quite sure there'll be a carriage out front to take me home afterward? Otherwise I'd feel pretty silly to have ridden all the way here only to turn around again and go back on foot more or less to where I started from, don't you agree? It's all settled then. How perfect. Only a little while ago, back at the club, I thought to myself that a nice plum brandy would be just the thing to end the evening on the right note. To tell you the truth, I have never been inside the Metropole at all, though I have often walked by it and debated having a drink there. You are probably wondering what I am doing hiring a carriage in the first place, but you see, I saved so much money by skipping dinner tonight because of the sandwiches and cakes your father bought for the party that I decided to treat myself to a ride home. And now, by being able so unexpectedly to save you from possibly freezing to death out here, I feel as though I have even had the chance to repay Herr Rotenburg, for his generosity."

Although Asher left no time for any actual reply to his outpourings, he clearly expected some acknowledgment from his listener. With Asher, interruption was physically impossible, and silence regarded as offensive, so even someone much more concerned to indulge him than Hans would have found it a challenging task. Hans, who had no interest in humoring Asher, just stared at him silently with the vague smile that he always put on when trying to make up his mind about a person without committing himself in any way. After a few more sentences Asher began to grow increasingly uneasy at not getting back whatever signs of encouragement he was waiting for, and almost in mid-sentence, with only the slightest pause to draw fresh breath, his tone abruptly veered from excited anticipation to injured complaint.

"Well, I can certainly see that none of this interests you, but there's no need to make it so obvious. You probably think it's true what they say, that we talk too much about money. It's like my sister's old joke that whenever a Jew is complimented on a new suit or watch, he immediately feels the need to declare that he actually bought it on sale and paid only half the asking price. But she said it with affection, from inside, as it were, with a warm heart, and that's quite different from the way you are sitting there judging me. I am sure it's easy to sneer at such topics when one is Hans Rotenburg, who never has to think twice about buying whatever strikes his eye in a store window or stopping in for refreshments at the Metropole whenever he is in the mood. You probably don't even know how much money you have in your wallet right now, do you? The rich never bother counting it up before leaving home because they take for granted that there'll always be enough. But people like me can tell you to the last penny the total sum in their pockets, their savings books, and their pension funds! I am sure you have your own table kept ready for you at our fanciest hotels and that everything is just put on your account, so if you don't feel like it, you needn't bring along something as sordid as real coins. Well, for someone in my position, the world is a rather different kind of place, so if we are going to continue being friends and enjoy a nice, intimate tête-à-tête, I'll have to ask you not to look quite so superior."

The idea of simply slapping Blumenthal, who was losing himself in his tirade like the worst kind of leading man in a provincial acting troupe, momentarily flashed through Hans's mind, but the physical intimacy required by the gesture was too distasteful. Instead he decided to amuse himself by testing the effect of different kinds of responses on such a person, beginning with a mildly reassuring nod in Blumenthal's general direction, accompanied by a genial, if somewhat indistinct, murmur of goodwill. To Hans's surprise, who had not expected so instantaneous a reversal, even that slight signal of interest was enough for Asher to modulate out of his aria of wounded dignity and revert back to the happier tones of his opening declamation.

"Of course everything's fine. I am sure you didn't mean to be rude, and that's all the apology I could ask for. And if I sounded a little harsh myself, I am not too proud to admit I am sorry too. It's been a rather hard few weeks on everyone, so I guess we're all a bit oversensitive. You know, it isn't easy for me to be sitting across from someone I have been dying to meet, who turns out to be as silent as a goy. It's a little hard for me to believe you are still really one of us, if you know what I mean. Here I am sharing all my thoughts with you, and you haven't really said a word to me about what you are feeling. But I am tremendously looking forward to my first drink at the Metropole and to hearing your reaction to an idea of mine on a very important matter. You see, I have come up with a plan that I am convinced can be of great benefit to us both."

· ◆ ·

This far to the east in Franz Josef's empire, the cultural prestige of Paris was a serious rival to that of Vienna, especially, perhaps, because by the term *culture*, the town understood primarily its eating establishments. The manager of the Metropole had never in fact spent time in Paris itself, but early in his career he had served a summer apprenticeship in Nice and ever since had dreamed of creating his own version of the grand establishments found along the Boulevard des Anglais. The result was one of the few places in town that disdained any attempt to resemble a Viennese coffeehouse and instead was determinedly formal and French-leaning in its architecture and furnishings. Although no one went so far as to expect the staff actually to know a word of French, they all were nonetheless carefully trained to imitate the supposed haughtiness of their Parisian counterparts, a task in which, under the autocratic rule of the formidable headwaiter, Anton, they succeeded admirably.

Every evening after eleven, though, a more relaxed atmosphere was tolerated, and the ornate central dining room, with its row of chandeliers and green silk hangings, reflected in four heavy gilt mirrors recessed in special niches in the side walls, was closed off. The kitchen shut down, the chef, along with Anton and the senior staff, retired home for the night, and only a small crew of younger aspirants stayed at their posts to serve guests who wanted to come in for a late-night drink or a bite of cold food in one of the smaller side rooms. It was a lucrative way to get rid of all the leftovers from the evening's dinners, and the manager, who had learned something useful from his time in France after all, correctly calculated that the clients who came at such an hour were even less likely to look closely at their bill than patrons who kept more conventional hours, and so inflated the already exorbitant prices of everything by an additional 15 percent. As a good Austrian, though, he was also thoroughly familiar with how to circumvent the bureaucratic regulations governing his trade, and he made sure that his extortions did not break any laws by printing at the head of the after-dinner menu a small notice, scarcely readable in the dim light of the side rooms, to the effect that there would be a "late-night surcharge" on all items consumed on the premises after hours.

It was into one of these small rooms that Hans and Asher were led, and after getting over his initial, and very visible, disappointment that he would not after all be eating in the Metropole's famous dining room, Asher carefully studied the menu, read the notice of the nighttime price increase, and settled into his seat with total contentment, the augmentation of an already unimaginable cost more than compensating for the slight falling off in the ornateness of the decor.

Hans, who was surprised by how hungry he felt, ordered enough food for both of them. He knew the menu by heart and quickly decided on some chicken à la gelée and cold smoked hare with red currant jelly, accompanied by a potato salad and an assortment of vegetables, pickled in the chef's own cellars. He also asked for a double serving of the restaurant's specialty, thin-sliced cold goose breast, which came to their table at the same time as a basket of poppy seed rolls and a half loaf of fragrant pumpernickel bread on its own small cutting board. Instead of wine, he chose a bottle of old Madeira, remembering that one of his father's English business associates always insisted there was nothing better for keeping out the cold. He tried a glass, satisfied himself that the man was right, and then started serving himself from whatever dish was within easy reach, concerned at first only to restore his strength without paying much attention to the taste of what he was eating. After a few minutes, though, he noticed that Asher hadn't touched any of the food and was being ostentatiously ignored by the young waiters, who continued to flurry around Hans. He quickly rectified that with a sharp glance and, feeling both warm and alert now, decided to see exactly what kind of conversation he had let himself in for.

Asher was clearly still brooding about his earlier outburst, and Hans was determined to forestall whatever apology Asher was on the verge of formulating. "Of course, Blumenthal, you do know I am not in the least still vexed by anything you might have said in the carriage. Far from it. Besides, I think it was very good of you to offer me a lift. I admit I am curious about whatever's on your mind, but frankly, I am not all that up-to-date about what's been happening at the club. Nobody asked you to come looking for me tonight, did they?" Asher's puzzlement at the question was too obviously sincere for Hans to doubt him, but he was still clearly relieved when Asher assured him that he had acted entirely on his own initiative. "Oh, I meant someone like my father, of course," Hans explained. "But I am glad to hear that he didn't. It was just a silly notion, don't pay it any mind. By the way, I am sure that if you prefer it, they have some first-rate slivovitz here. By all means, go ahead and order whatever you like. From what you have told me, it's probably been a while since you ate, so I ordered some of their best cold dishes for us to share. Please, just help yourself."

Stefan, the favorite of Anton's numerous cousins, had been entrusted with the supervision of the late-night staff and, sensing the prospect of a good tip, ordered away the other waiters and took it upon himself to serve Hans Rotenburg and his peculiar companion. He brought out a half-full bottle of the restaurant's oldest slivovitz and set it before Asher with a deep, formal bow that managed to combine a graceful apology for his earlier inattention and a look conveying that only in the company of a Roten-burg would a person like this dare come into the Metropole. Fortunately for Hans's nerves, Asher was sufficiently delighted, either by Stefan's def-erential near curtsy or by the sight of the bottle in his hand, that he paid no attention to the mockery in the waiter's expression. Instead he poured out as much of the slivovitz as the thin liqueur glass placed in front of him would hold and drained it in a single gulp. He repeated the gesture three or four more times, with an astonishing rapidity and single-mindedness, smacking his lips so loudly at the end of each gulp that Stefan's look changed from self-satisfied bemusement to something close to undis-guised alarm. But Asher was no longer paying any attention to the waiter. He looked contentedly over at Hans and, taking great care to enunciate each syllable clearly, said to him, "Um. Yes, this is exquisite. What a lovely room too. Just the place for two men of the world like us to discuss seri-ous questions, eh? This slivovitz really is better than anything I have ever had. I have to be careful not to get drunk. With my delicate constitution it probably wouldn't take much. Weak lungs. Hereditary, like my poor sister. Our ancestral curse. The poor and the Jews. Doubly so for poor Jews. But you wouldn't know about that, would you? No offense meant. It's just hard sometimes not to think about how unfair it all is. I'll probably never come back in here again, but for you this whole grand place is just your corner tavern."

"Maybe I understand better than you imagine. I think you are right to feel angry at so much injustice all around us. Only it seems to me you can't do much about it if you always look at everything in such personal terms. And I really don't see why you need to bring in being Jewish all the time, as if that were the key to everything. But let's leave that for another time. Here, I see there's just about enough in the bottle for another glass, so let me do the honors and freshen up your drink. It's starting to get re-ally late, and we're both going to need to go home and rest. So, tell me, what's this important matter you wanted to discuss?"

"All right." Asher agreed cheerfully enough. He didn't in the least mind being interrupted now since it gave him a chance to concentrate on the slivovitz in front of him. Occasionally he also took a few slices of the goose breast along with some bread, and only after having finished chewing both with immense concentration was he ready to go on talking. "But you have got to let me take my time. Here I am, after midnight, in the Metropole, drinking slivovitz and eating costly delicacies with Hans Rotenburg. You can't wonder if I am not in such a hurry as you to conclude matters. *You* get to eat with Hans Rotenburg all the time. That didn't come out right. I meant it as a little joke. A kind of compliment. I am not hopelessly tactless, you know, even if I have had a touch too much to drink."

"Of course not; in fact it's obvious how clever you are. I give you my word, I am planning to tell the friends I was with earlier tonight how interesting it was to meet up with you. It's high time they all got to know someone like you as well."

Immediately a look of shrewd, suspicious knowingness materialized on Asher's face, so incongruous with his expression only an instant earlier that it almost seemed as though he had simply borrowed it from some storehouse of ready-made looks and attitudes, kept available, like theatrical masks, for every new occasion and scene. "Why is that?" he asked. "Are they looking for a good accountant whose discretion they can rely on? I can't promise anything, you know, until I have studied all the documents, but I can tell you, without boasting, that I am very good at my job. Even if no one at Sobieski's seems to appreciate that," he added as a bitter afterthought.

For an instant Hans was genuinely baffled by this latest outburst. It took him a moment to work out what Asher must be thinking, but when he had done so, the absurdity of it made Hans laugh out loud for the first time all evening. "No, no, my dear Blumenthal, I wasn't thinking of your profession at all, although I certainly believe that you must be excellent at it. I just meant that my friends ought to get to know someone with your breadth of outlook and personal history. They have no idea about experiences like those you have been telling me about, and with your help, I want to correct that."

But strangely enough, the suspicious look was not exchanged for a different one from Asher's impressively varied repertoire of mistrust. On the contrary, if Asher had concluded one thing from his professional training, it was that when a rich man bothered giving his inferior a compliment, it could mean only that he needed some special service performed, and cheaply too. Otherwise he might simply hire someone to do the task at the prevailing wage and spare himself the need to be so polite. Something in Hans's tone seemed to confirm his intuition.

"That's very flattering, Rotenburg," he answered, "but after all, won't you be leaving for Vienna or somewhere like that soon? The moment you do, you are bound to forget the new acquaintances you have made here. That's one of the main things I intended to discuss with you."

"Go on, I am listening."

"Well, I was thinking, back at the club everyone was saying that you are going to go to work for your father, and it occurred to me that if you do, you'll no doubt be spending a lot of time in Vienna. But once you are there, it'll be only as Moritz Rotenburg's son that people will take you seriously. Oh, you'll still have all your father's money to spend, and the girls there are probably a lot readier for a good time than our homegrown variety, but won't you be just another Jewish arriviste with deep pockets? I have an idea of how you can establish yourself on your own terms and get the sort of name that carries weight with the right crowd, a name that has a kind of prestige that goes beyond money."

"Excuse me, but I really don't understand. Why do you suppose I am going to Vienna? I appreciate your trying to help, but I am honestly at a loss. How long have you been thinking about this? What if you hadn't run into me at all?"

"Well, to be perfectly honest, it all came to me in a rush when I recognized you there under the streetlight. It's true that I heard about your going to work for your father only this evening at the club, but somehow, as soon as our paths crossed, I knew exactly what I wanted to tell you. Seeing you tonight was just the inspiration I needed. Don't worry, there's something in it for me as well; it's not just benevolence on my part. But I will get to that after telling you my plan. Anyway, as I see it, what you need is a strategy to establish yourself in Vienna in a completely different sphere from your father's, and it so happens I have got just the way to do it. A friend of mine, Alexander Garber, who was at the Commercial College with me, left for the capital to become a playwright. He always dreamed about having a piece put on at the Burgtheater. Well, I don't know that there's been much progress in that direction, but in the meantime he wrote to tell me that he's become one of the editors of a small literary journal. It only has a tiny paid circulation, but Alexander says that its articles are read everywhere, and its reviews can help make or break a new artist. Even the Mendelssohn Club subscribes to it, so you can easily look through the latest issue there. Now I know journals like his are always desperately in need of capital, as well as on the lookout for promising new talent. And who, I suddenly realized when our paths crossed, could more

87

brilliantly fulfill both functions than Alexander's and my own fellow townsman Hans Rotenburg? Can't you see it yourself? You offer to underwrite the expenses of the paper, as a silent partner, at the same time as you become one of their regular contributors. Just like that, in almost no time, you go from being a complete unknown to a cultural force to be reckoned with!"

"Good heavens. Asher. Of course I am touched by your wanting to help me, but even you would have to agree that's a pretty extravagant scheme. Was this whole inspiration really triggered by our accidental run-in? I mean, here you have gone ahead and made all these calculations without asking if any of them had the slightest foundation in reality. Even assuming I did go to Vienna and that I wanted to make an independent name for myself there, what gives you the idea that I have any talent for literary journalism? Or that I'd be inclined to finance a magazine I have never heard of because it's run by someone from our town with whom you were at school years ago?"

By now all the food was gone, and the waiters had cleared away the dishes while the men were talking. Asher's bottle was quite empty, of course, but Hans was surprised to see that so was his own. He signaled Stefan to bring them two more bottles, only to have Asher shake his head to countermand the order and insist that he didn't want to drink anything more until he had finished explaining his ideas. Asher's tone became increasingly persistent as he felt his chance slipping away. "I know it may sound far-fetched," he conceded, "but just think of the opportunities. You say you are not interested in literary journalism, but surely there's something you'd like to write about for an audience a bit wider than the people in this dismal town. Who's to say that with your backing, *The New Order* would need to limit itself to the arts? Perhaps you are more interested in legal issues, or business, or maybe the Jewish problem. As a regular columnist you'd be free to develop any theme that struck your fancy. It seems to me that if we played our cards right—yes, I mean *we*, you'll see how in a few moments—it would be easy to redirect the whole focus of the magazine. At first, if you were hesitant, you could always turn to me for advice and help with editing your pieces, until you got your writer's legs, so to speak, and once you did get a reputation as someone with a new vision and a strong capital asset base, it wouldn't be too hard for Alexander and you to outmaneuver the other members of the board and take over the whole journal yourselves. You have no idea how compelling the combination of talent and money is to people who mostly lack either. As soon as your coup was successful, I could give up my wretched job here and join you to take care of the paper's financial and advertising sides. I wouldn't mind trying my hand at writing an occasional piece as well, and I am certain that the three of us together could expand the operation and take the whole city by storm. As a triumvirate we'd be irresistible, invited to all the salons and openings, and everyone would have to pay attention to whatever we said. People back here would never believe the success we were having. Just knowing how jealous they'll all be would satisfy me for a whole year."

"I am sorry for laughing"—Hans finally interrupted—"but you do need to catch your breath before you have us summoned out to Schönbrunn to advise the Emperor how to run the country and what operas to patronize. I would never have taken you for such an enthusiast, my dear Blumenthal. I am quite overwhelmed. Of course it's all hopeless nonsense, so please don't pretend to be offended, you must see that as clearly as I do. But you know, your plan is not without its interesting aspects either. And now I think we really do need those fresh drinks. You don't mind if I send the waiter for some ink and paper at the same time? I want to jot down a few things you have mentioned because I am sure I won't be able to remember much of this tomorrow. Now, you said that this journal . . . the what? that's right . . . *The New Order*, is almost bankrupt. Well, yes, of course you did, in so many words. Don't worry so much, no one here has ever heard of it, so to whom could I pass on the rumor, even if I were interested in doing so? I am just trying to get a sense of the real possibilities here. You won't be accused of betraying any confidences. A few minutes ago you were recklessly conquering Vienna, and now you look as nervous as if your employer might find out you'd been pilfering from the petty cash box. Oh, please, no. Don't take offense at my way of expressing things. It's much too late to start that all over again. Let's just work together to see if there's anything in what you have told me from which we could extract something useful. For both of us, I mean."

"But are you really not thinking of going to Vienna?" Asher asked in an appalled tone. "I can't believe you wouldn't leap at the chance to get away from here again, unless it's a question of some girl you are in love with? But you'd never let something like that stand in your way, not a man with your opportunities! So it must be something else. Wait just a minute now, you aren't thinking of using my suggestion all by yourself, are you? And leaving me out of it to rot away here forever?"

"No, of course not," Hans assured him. "No to both your questions. I am going home in a few minutes, but first I want to write down your address. I'll get in touch with you in a few days, and we can take these ideas of yours further then. In the meantime I want you to think about two things. In the first place, if we do work together at all, it is going to have to be done here, not in Vienna, and second, I am not about to finance anything that is under the control of others. Being a cultural patron appeals to me even less than becoming a writer, and I am not nearly as careless with my money as you seem to think. But some of what you have said about the journal is interesting to me, even if it needs a great deal more looking into. Right now, though, let me have them call you a carriage and I'll pay the driver to take you wherever you are heading. That's only fair. After all, you brought me here at your expense. Yes, what is it? There's really nothing else we can accomplish tonight, so why are you still so agitated?"

"But I haven't even gotten to one of the most important ways you might help me!"

"I am sorry. I thought the part about running the journal with Alexander and me was exactly that."

"That was mostly to help *you*! I think it's pretty obvious that any advantages coming to me from the plan would take a long time to materialize. I have already admitted that I improvised a lot of it as we were speaking, and of course I still think it's a wonderful scheme, but my original hope was much more modest. You remember about the dreadful landlady who wouldn't let me invite even someone like you to my flat for a late-night drink? Well, it doesn't matter, but that's what she's like. Anyway, you can imagine how impossible it is for me to entertain a young lady properly under such constraints. I don't like the kinds of hotels where one rents rooms by the hour; I have been in one only a few times and then always felt too afraid of being robbed and beaten to be at ease. I am not ashamed to admit that in such surroundings I am not really able to, well, you know what I mean, respond the way a man should. So I have nowhere at all to go late at night for an intimate rendezvous. What I was hoping, you see, is that you might occasionally let me use your flat in the Josef Quarter."

90

When Hans started asking how Asher had found out about his apartment, the accountant just looked at him with a superior expression and answered, "Oh, come, who's being absurd now? Of course everyone in the district knew about your wanting a 'secret' apartment from the moment you began to look around for one. It became the talk of the whole neighborhood. People were terrified that their rents would go up! But there must be many evenings you don't go there, and if I could just know that I might use it on one or two of those nights, it would transform my whole social life. Well, yes, maybe I am overstating things again, but I don't know how else to convince you what a difference it would make to me if I knew that I had a discreet, cozy apartment to which I could invite lady guests. It goes without saying that I'd be extremely careful not to compromise you in any way, and it seems to me that having someone respectable occasionally look in at your flat might be helpful as a safety measure."

At this Hans looked up with annoyance and, in a sharper tone than he had used before, muttered that he didn't think the police were likely to break into his apartment, even if it was located in the Josef Quarter.

"No, I do not mean vis-à-vis the police." Asher went on, too wrapped up in his own story to give much thought to Hans's interruption. "Why would they care? It's just that I could make sure the place was kept clean and that there was always enough fresh linen and coal or wood plus whatever provisions you wanted kept on hand for whenever you dropped in. I don't expect you to agree right away, but please at least promise me you'll think about it and let me know your decision in person. You can't imagine how much all this means to me."

Hans stayed silent and just let Asher keep on talking until he had worn himself out on the topic. Then he promised to consider Asher's offer seriously but said that he was much too tired to do so now. Hans signaled for Stefan to bring him the bill, and Asher, realizing that he had gotten everything he could out of the encounter, stood up to leave, letting one of the other waiters help him into his coat, oblivious of the obvious distaste with which the man held the garment.

"This has been wonderful!" Asher said once he was fully enveloped again. "I'll just borrow one of these excellent cigarettes for the drive home and get going. I'll barely have time to shave and change my shirt before I have to go back in to work, but I wouldn't have missed talking to you for anything. Yes, good night, Herr Rotenburg. Or rather, good morning. Don't forget to let me know what you think about my suggestions. And please remember to give my respects to your distinguished father. I will be waiting eagerly to hear from you. Good-bye."

• ◆ •

Had Asher turned back to glance around the room one last time before stepping out in the snow, he would have been astonished at the loathing with which Hans watched him depart through the Metropole's glass-paneled front door. Stefan, who did catch Hans's expression, thought it might be directed at him and instinctively retreated back into the closed kitchen, expecting to forgo the large tip to which he had looked forward all night. But Hans's anger had nothing to do with the restaurant's service, and had Batya been there, she could have explained his mood from her own experience. It was simply that nothing is more irritating to a rich man than to be taken for a fool merely on account of his wealth. Yet such miscalculations occur all the time, and purely in self-defense the sensibilities of the rich have become extraordinarily prickly about their intellectual or artistic gifts. The extravagant respect paid to a great fortune by the larger portion of humanity is balanced by the stubbornness with which a smaller part thinks it is being particularly high-minded by showing its indifference to mere material advantages. When the rich man in question also likes to imagine himself an original thinker or artist, the problem of how his less wealthy associates react to him becomes painfully acute. They of course have their sights set on his capacity to alleviate their daily anxieties with a single, strategically placed signature on a loan; he, on the other hand, is concerned to obtain their recognition of his gifts in realms remote from checkbooks and bank balances. This mutual incomprehension is likely to end in recriminations, whether actually uttered or not, and it might almost be best, before any harm occurs, if both parties were forced to hear the warning Austrian nursemaids used to cry out to their young charges when their games became especially boisterous: "Be careful, this is going to end badly!"

Fortunately, Hans was not in the least artistically inclined, nor, for all his reading in radical literature, did he delude himself that his few short essays had made an important contribution to revolutionary theory. But at least in comparison with others of his own age, nothing had happened to make him doubt his general intellectual gifts. With much less reason, he also prided himself on a levelheaded discernment about human nature. Consequently, Asher's torrent of improbable schemes and presumptuous requests, all of which depended for their success on the palpable stupidity of their intended target, had succeeded in deeply irritating Hans. To have been taken for a spoiled fool by someone as overwrought as Asher Blumenthal was thoroughly offensive. His compensatory politeness to Asher was less a calculated ruse and more the manifestation of a need to think well of himself again. He needed time to suppress both his anger at Asher and his irritation with himself for being so exasperated by a nonentity like that. Contrary to Asher's assumption, Hans's promise to consider his proposals seriously was not motivated by any guilt at the disparity in their economic positions. Hans's expressions of goodwill were meant, instead, to display the trait he most admired, the ability coolly to put aside personal prejudices in order to extract from any situation the maximum advantage for his own long-term goals. Finding a way to convert their encounter to useful ends, in spite of his complete aversion to Asher, was Hans's way of restoring the always delicate mechanism of his pride. Hans could shrug off any direct attack on his privileged life since what he considered corrupting was his father's money, not his own, and in any case the economic theories in whose interests he was considering recruiting Asher had long ago dispensed with questions of individual responsibility for social injustice. Asher's desperate eagerness to change his situation, no matter how implausible the means, made him a potentially useful addition to Hans's cell. Not, of course, as an equal member, no matter what it might prove necessary to tell him, but Hans clearly needed someone to keep the apartment in order, and Asher was ideal for the position. Furthermore, none of the others in the cell had anything like the personal sense of grievance against the world that permeated Asher. From Marx, Hans had learned about the bourgeoisie's use of "the reserve army of the unemployed" to keep wages down. Why, then, shouldn't the revolution make use of the thronging "reserve army" of disaffected clerks to keep its safe houses well heated and clean?

The assumption of easy superiority in Hans's ruminations restored his good humor, and whenever in the following days he thought about ways in which Asher's schemes might be adapted to the needs of the movement, he was able to do so without letting his rancor cloud his judgment.

But if someone like Hans is unlikely to be as obtuse as the Ashers of this world imagine, it is just as true that the needy will scarcely appreciate having their indigence brought home to them with such casual disdain, as though differences they regarded as determined solely by the availability of a sufficient supply of money were actually a reflection of their character. Asher knew he had behaved extravagantly and was quite ready to despise himself accordingly. But in his mind Hans was far from blameless in the whole affair. In fact Asher saw his own excess of speech and gesture as an admittedly pathetic, but not unprovoked, attempt to break through the reserve of Hans's judgmental and bored generosity, an emotional reserve based, even if Hans didn't want to admit it, precisely on the serene expanse of his financial reserves. Far from cheering him up, the justice of Asher's case against Hans only provoked Asher to more caustic reflections, but at their core lay the indigestible, bitter clump that reminded him of how much easier it would be for Hans to forget their encounter than it would be for him. Hans was five years younger, yet simply because of his fortunate birth, he had already experienced so much more of the world than Asher was likely to know. In a curious way, though, it seemed to Asher as though Hans's condescension had pricked him on to some of his best ideas. In spite of enjoying the gossip from the capital provided by Alexander's letters, Asher had never before thought of their taking over the magazine together. He wasted little time regretting the need to involve someone as uncongenial as Hans in his scheme, in part because Asher had seen too much not to realize that in order to succeed, he would need to sell himself many times over and in part because he thought that whatever might happen, Hans's interest would flag quickly enough. Soon he would content himself with only the occasional, although no doubt galling, interference. For the moment what mattered was the sudden, sharp look of interest that Hans had directed at him as soon as Asher mentioned the journal. Why Hans would admit to at least some degree of curiosity about *The New Order*, while insisting that he didn't want to go to Vienna or become a writer, was a puzzle to which Asher had no key, but he knew one would soon be forthcoming if the project were to go any further. It was only to be expected that Hans would somehow try to use him, even if Asher still had no sense of how or to what purpose. But he registered Hans's discomfort at his emotional outbursts clearly enough, and Asher decided that staying in character as a touchy, overexcitable Jew, a role he knew was hardly alien to his repertoire, might give him unexpected advantages in the future. It was always a good idea to let others take one for a greater fool than perhaps one really was. All the same, to keep playing the fool to someone as callow and self-satisfied as the Rotenburg heir probably exceeded his own capacity for self-control, and Asher was afraid that in the future, just as in the restaurant tonight, his outbursts of wounded feeling were likely to be more authentic than staged. Practically, though, things were looking far more promising than he had imagined possible only a few hours ago. The real problem was how to determine if anything at all would result from their conversation.

When he tried to make a systematic inventory of useful impressions, Asher found that in spite of the care with which he had observed Hans, he had very little on which to build. But if Hans was clearly not as witless as Asher had at first assumed and, he had to admit, even hoped, neither was he as clever as he clearly estimated himself to be. And so Asher spent the next days using all his skill as an accountant to draw up elaborate columns in which he listed his own and Hans's qualities and motives, calculating from them how best to exploit whatever advantages he could discern in his position, until his notebook began to resemble the battle plans used in military colleges to instruct young recruits in the science of warfare. But armies, as we regularly witness, are taught only how to fight the previous war and are left pitifully unprepared for the one that is coming. Thus it is not too surprising that the only tangible result of Asher's feverish immersion in high strategy was a dreadful mix-up in the way he handled his firm's negotiations about the bars of soap the Sobieski Company wanted to import through Trieste until their Italian trading partners emerged with a much better contract than originally envisaged and Asher's employers became even more dubious about his suitability for a responsible position.

2

The first true luxury Moritz had permitted himself as soon as he could afford it was to install an enormous fireplace in the bedroom of the elegant house he had bought a few years before Hans's birth, and over the years, as his rise was marked by a series of ever more imposing residences, it was always the fireplace that he cared about most and to whose placement he paid the most attention, content to let Dina make all the other decisions. As a child, sleeping with half a dozen apprentices in an improvised dormitory in the foreman's attic, Moritz had woken up every morning from October until late April so stiff from the damp and cold that no matter how hectic the day's work, he never got completely warm, and now he ordered the fireplace in his room stacked nightly with enough wood to keep a steady fire burning from early evening until dawn, even during the summer months, when Dina, as well as his doctors, assured him that so much heat was not only unnecessary but actually bad for his health. These days, although he often felt unwell by the late afternoon, he continued, just as he had for many years, to stay awake much of the night, moving restlessly between the bed, propped high with pillows that were used to support a matched pair of small antique writing boxes originally intended for travelers—a birthday present from the Chief Rabbi in Vienna—and the simple desk, on which a stack of fresh paper was kept ready at all times. He would pore, seemingly at random, over his confidential correspondence, much of it written in a code based on Hebrew letters that he himself had devised years earlier. After a while Moritz stopped his reading to jot down some quick notes in one of the simple lined exercise books, identical to the ones used by generations of Austrian schoolboys, and then turned from these to glance through the pile of newly arrived pamphlets on Jewish history and mysticism that his numerous charitable donations kept streaming to his door. This was the world he had labored to build up, stone by stone and gold crown by gold crown, from nothing but his own indomitable will, intelligence, and self-discipline; it was a more variegated and wide-flung world than anyone from a childhood like his could have conceived, but when he looked around the room and saw the tangible fruit of so much effort, Moritz was certain that he could walk away from all of it tonight and not miss one thing.

A Jew, a father, a man of substance in his community and nation. He was all these things and would continue, for whatever time he had left, to do his best in each role, but none of his activities, nor any of the people he genuinely cared for and on whose behalf he was always ready to exert himself, reached him in his heart's depth. Dina was the last person, perhaps even the only one, for whom he had felt anything more, but lately, although her portrait hung on the wall over his desk and her photograph stood in its oval frame by the bed, he found himself having trouble recalling what she had looked like or what they had talked about. Moritz had an unsentimental awareness of his abilities and could draw up a ledger of his strengths and limitations as dispassionately as he would analyze the account books of a company in which he was thinking of investing. But he felt no special attachment to the enterprise of being Moritz Rotenburg, and neither the pleasure he took in his spectacular successes nor his frustration when his plans miscarried affected his sense of being somehow impersonal to himself. He knew that more than his wealth, it was this aura of what he heard one of his London associates call the notorious Rotenburg aloofness that separated him from others, and occasionally he allowed himself to wonder, with a touch of the self-pity he normally despised, if the most ordinary clerks in his employment were not more closely connected to their own lives than he was. Well, at least some of them anyway. Certainly not the hopeless nebbishes whose dues at the Mendelssohn Club he paid. These days he let the other members of the Governing Board decide who merited such support, but when he was still interviewing the applicants in person, it was clear to Moritz that most of them lived largely in their own fantastical schemes and anxieties.

Now Hans was suddenly taking an interest in one of them. Or at least pretending to, if only to irritate his father. The days immediately after the party had been singularly unpleasant. When Hans had finally come down to breakfast the next morning, he insisted on telling an absurd story about having been abducted by one of Moritz's "charity cases," who swore he knew the senior Herr Rotenburg from the club and who then proceeded to talk Hans's ears off for hours. "Ask the night waiters at the Metropole if you don't believe me," Hans insisted when Moritz looked doubtful. "Anton's cousin kept staring over at our table, clearly appalled at the speed with which your protégé drank and ate everything placed within his reach." The name Asher Blumenthal meant little to Moritz. He had a fond recollection of Eliezer, who had been one of the kinder souls in the community, but hopelessly impractical and always in debt. Moritz had paid for his funeral and willingly sponsored the son's club fees, but beyond that, he couldn't answer any of the strangely detailed questions about the family Hans pressed on him. From Hans's sketch, Asher sounded even more adrift than his father had been, but without the old man's good-natured optimism. To Moritz, though, there was little to choose between the delusions by which the town's poorer Jews tried to keep up their spirits and the petty intrigues by which an embittered failure like Gerhard Himmelfarb sought to compensate for his long history of miscalculations and near bankruptcies. The Himmelfarbs had once been the richest Jewish family in town, and Gerhard could never forgive those who had done better. At club meetings, whenever Gerhard opened his mouth to address the Governing Board, the resentment that festered in him like an abscess came out cloaked, as though by a law of cosmic balance, in tones of the most vapid sentimentality and benevolence. There was a whole litany of words that he was incapable of pronouncing without adding a prolonged tremolo, like a clumsy pianist trying to disguise his inadequate technique by keeping his foot on the sustain pedal for as long as possible. Simply hearing the way the man spoke the words *distinguished* or *a genuine Jewish soul*, each syllable more treacly than its predecessor, was enough to induce a twitch of repugnance that Moritz did his best to shrug off before it became evident to others. Maybe the strange wonder rebbe about whom Moritz had been hearing some alarming rumors lately was not so crazy after all, and the town really was full of lost souls whom only a cataclysm could save. But if so, Moritz hoped he wouldn't be alive to see it, and he was determined to do everything in his considerable power to have it also pass over his son and leave him unhurt.

Is it possible to love someone so entirely and irrevocably that it is less like an emotion than an involuntary physical function, as fundamental to one's daily existence as breathing, yet actually not like that person very much at all? Apparently so. If Hans's welfare had required it, Moritz would have laid down his own life with only the briefest hesitation, but he derived very little pleasure from his son's company and tried, without letting the boy realize it, to avoid spending time with him unless it was absolutely necessary. Except that it provided his enemies with a potentially dangerous weapon, Moritz was unable to take seriously Hans's mania for substituting political harangues for a real conversation. These days speaking normally to people seemed mostly just to enervate Hans. The moment any voice other than his own permitted itself more than two or three consecutive sentences, Hans unfurled a whole repertoire of gestures and looks that almost shouted out how hard it was for him to go on paying attention to such boring rubbish. Sometimes his eyes visibly glazed over and he slumped forward in his chair as though he were completely exhausted and unable to continue fighting off the need for sleep. At other moments his body started to fidget and tense up as though it were gathering strength to hurl itself into the next monologue, and then the frowns of exasperated impatience that played across his face the longer he felt constrained to listen to someone else became almost parodically exaggerated. It was astonishing to Moritz, who had always found it more useful to keep his opinions to himself and to learn what the people around him thought by encouraging them to dominate the conversation, how lecturing seemed to animate his son, almost, by Moritz's sour calculations, to the exact degree that actual dialogue fatigued him.

Moritz had observed his son's activities with increasing skepticism ever since the triumph of his exams, when Hans and Ernst von Alpsbach shared the top honors in the province and had been singled out together for special recognition by a visiting official from the Ministry of Education. Since then almost everything that he had heard either about Hans or from the boy directly irritated Moritz and made the effort of so much careful planning for Hans's future seem like a particularly unsound expenditure of his own emotional and intellectual capital. But Moritz also suspected that although they would probably never acknowledge it to each other, he and Hans shared a dynastic ambition to whose demands both were ready to sacrifice themselves. Everyone knew that out in Schönbrunn, the old Emperor was facing a similar dilemma with his own troublesome heirs, and some of the affection his subjects felt for Franz Josef was based on an obscure and, had it not been subtly encouraged by the Palace itself as part of its propaganda efforts, even slightly disrespectful sense of kinship with a father who had endured so many family disappointments. But at least the Habsburgs had a seemingly endless chain of official successors, and if one of them should fall away, the line itself remained unthreatened.

So why hadn't he and Dina succeeded in having more children? There was a time, years ago, when Moritz had been obliged to endure that question often enough from acquaintances sufficiently embittered by the sight of his prosperity to try to strike back at him for it. The query always came out with an unctuousness that barely disguised its malice, as though simply asking it were enough to point out that the heavens allowed no injustice to stay unpunished—and least of all the indecent abyss between Rotenburg's fortune and that of the speaker. To Moritz, though, it was a question with surprisingly little sting. The paltry wages Dina's parents earned had gone to feed the boys in the family, not the five girls, each of whose birth was treated as a calamity. Three of the sisters had died of tuberculosis before they reached adolescence, and Dina herself had barely survived into adulthood. Hans's birth came very close to killing her, and for several years afterward she and Moritz dreaded another pregnancy. But she never conceived again, and gradually her fears were replaced by a contrary sense of shame that her barrenness was hurting her husband. Such a thought hardly ever occurred to Moritz, whose attention was entirely consumed by a twenty-year-long series of carefully camouflaged moves, each more hazardous than its predecessor, to extend his financial interests into new industries. Moritz was convinced that entirely novel ways of manufacturing were on the way to becoming profitable. But since almost no one in Austria was ready to take a chance on their potential, Moritz had to keep bearing all the risks on his own. The return on these investments dwarfed anything available from more conventional enterprises, and in time they catapulted Moritz into an entirely different level of wealth from those businessmen whose equal he had been only twenty years before. By the end of the first decade of the new century Moritz was often the only Austrian financier invited to participate in secret negotiations about joint economic ventures by German industrialists like Rathenau and Oetker. He came back from those meetings only to leave again a few days later for a different financial center, and there were whole months when he never had dinner at home. Dina and Hans grew used to talking to him over breakfast while he looked through his morning mail or sitting on a chair outside the door of the large upstairs bathroom where he was busy shaving as one set of trunks was being unpacked and a second unscuffed set, identical in every way to the first, was being carefully filled with fresh linen for another trip. Neither of them doubted Moritz's love, but it was often hard for them to distinguish that feeling from benign absentminded-ness. Gradually Dina came to make the boy's welfare the center of her life, and from the time he was starting to speak, she transferred all her own ambition to Hans. For Moritz, it sometimes felt as though he had lost the best part of the only friend and partner of whose emotional fidelity he had been certain. Nothing had made that clearer than the sight of Dina and Hans walking arm in arm when the boy had just turned nine and they all went out together to watch the annual festival of some Polish or Lithuanian saint, Moritz could never remember his name, in whose honor red flowers and white candles were set afloat under the large bridge on a warm summer's night, and the local band in their military uniforms played an oddly disconcerting medley of cheerful waltzes and wistful Gypsy tunes. There was something in their intimacy, in the way Hans accepted his mother's hand straightening the collar on his blue sailor costume with its starched white shirt and shiny brass buttons, when he would have squirmed uncomfortably away had Moritz tried the same gesture, and in the concentration with which Dina made sure that the boy was happy with the vanilla and chocolate ice they bought for him from the stand temporarily set up in the square near the Cathedral that so plainly ex-cluded Moritz that he felt suddenly weighed down with a completely unexpected sense of bereavement. It was a momentary feeling he deliber-ately shrugged off without probing further, but a certain withdrawal took place in his heart that festival evening from whose imperceptible shadow he never entirely emerged.

Since Hans had come back from his travels, no matter what topic ei-ther of them brought up, the conversation quickly collapsed into mutual accusations. Moritz knew that he was as much to blame as Hans, yet he kept giving in to the impulse to say something he knew would irritate his son. But even when he tried to make common cause with Hans, the effort usually misfired. Fritz László from Koppensteiner's had sent a polite note of thanks at having been entrusted with furnishing Hans's apartment on the Maximilianstrasse, and when Moritz assured Hans that he understood why his son might want his own place for entertaining, Hans's only re-sponse was annoyance at being a subject of other people's speculations. "What an impressive circle of informants you have, Father," he snapped. "I'll bet stories about me get repeated to you regularly at that club you are so fond of. Asher Blumenthal told me that his crowd there gossips about me, but I didn't imagine it extended into your set as well. In case it makes any difference, up to now I actually haven't brought a woman to the apartment, although I may as well start since everyone, including you, takes it for granted that is why I rented it. The only reason I began to look for a place of my own is to have somewhere to go after mornings like this. Do you suppose it's easy to stay here and settle down to work after squabbling with you? Besides, doesn't anyone have something else to talk about except for my apartment? You are all so convinced I have set up a private bordello that this Blumenthal character actually had the cheek to ask me if he could use it to seduce shopgirls too."

To Hans's surprise, though, rather than retreat from the discussion in embarrassment, his father merely looked up and asked, "And what did you answer him?"

"I didn't say anything," Hans responded. "What do you expect me to do with a request like that? I am astonished you are not more outraged yourself."

Moritz ignored Hans's tone and went on, talking more to himself than to his son. "If you want my advice, Hans, then let him have it from time to time when you are certain of not needing it yourself. I know the type, poor nebbish. Don't forget that I didn't have more than a few pennies myself when I first arrived here. He's lonely and can't afford a place to meet his girlfriend. Helping him out may not be much, but I don't see it doing anyone any harm, and it may make two people happy for a while." Hans stared back at his father, suddenly aware of how long the two of them had lived alone together in this enormous house. He wasn't ready to concede anything directly, but his tone became less strident. He parodied a look of moral shock. "What a cynic you turn out to be, Father. I should have guessed as much. You are the libertine in the family, not I. Maybe it really is time you remarried. Or do you just want a set of keys too, so you can use the apartment for whatever wouldn't be appropriate here? Of course I am only joking. But I must admit, your broad-mindedness is really more than I counted on."

"I suppose that I just understand loneliness better each year." Moritz shrugged his shoulders. "But I don't really care. Do whatever you think wisest. At least this Blumenthal gave us something to smile about. I should have someone point him out to me when I go to the club. If he had the courage to make a request like that to you out of the blue, he can't be completely useless in other ways."

102

"That's exactly what I thought myself." Hans seized the chance to end the conversation on a friendly note. "You see, Father, we have been coming up with similar ideas all morning. I am even looking into finding some part-time work for Blumenthal."

Moritz felt Hans straining to make a good exit and did his best to help him along. He watched his son leave without regret, relieved that things had gone relatively well between them and content to be alone again. His business genius depended on an imaginative flexibility that let him project alternative and often contradictory outcomes from any situation; lamenting a condition that he was certain could not be amended was profoundly alien to his temperament, and he did his best to reconcile himself to the fact that he felt nearly as estranged in his own home as he did out in the world. He had always regarded the refusal to invest oneself in impossible projects as the beginning of wisdom, but since Dina's death even his most audacious stratagems had an element of unreality about them. Because their completion would only be triggered by his own death, he had to regard them as, in a sense, posthumous, and the fact of spending much of his inner life inhabiting a hypothetical world often made the present seem equally unreal. Late at night, when Nicholas had finally been sent to bed after checking the fire one more time and bringing Moritz a last cup of bouillon, the financier rallied his flagging energy and settled down at his desk to resume the correspondence that he could not entrust to anyone else. Mostly these letters dealt with the complex mechanism through which he was able to transfer large sums of money abroad in spite of the government's efforts to restrict the movement of capital out of the country. He knew that the Empire's economic development was lagging ever farther behind that of the other great powers and that the only way to preserve his fortune was to augment his partnerships with foreign industrialists. The interlocking directorships in which he now participated had an unmistakable dynastic element to them, and he watched as his associates groomed their children to take over their business interests when they would no longer be able to manage them. Hans's time abroad had been intended to prepare him for the same role, but the results had been dismaying. Rotenburg's partners in London and Zurich were at least as well informed about Hans's political activities as were the secret police, and Moritz found himself obliged to expend energy he did not have attempting to repair the damage Hans had done to his own prospects. It was clear that if Hans was ever going to be accepted by Rotenburg's foreign associates, he would have to return abroad for a more extended period and prove his reliability. For Moritz, sending Hans away again was not entirely unwelcome. It would be easier to keep him out of trouble in a country where Hans's contacts were limited and the laws against political activity more lenient. Although Moritz tried not to take Hans's revolutionary speechifying seriously, he knew that if Hans was ever to make good on his rhetoric in ways impossible for Moritz's wealth to smooth over, the consequences would be calamitous, not just for Hans personally but for the whole Jewish community.

Many of the same business associates who were shocked at Hans's political indiscretions were almost as puzzled by Moritz's insistence on staying in so insignificant a town, rather than establishing himself in one of the world's capitals. From their perspective, Moritz's choices were often scarcely less eccentric than his son's. But Moritz had no more wish to leave the town where he had lived with Dina than to abandon his Jewishness, and in his own mind the two actions were curiously linked. He had neither conventional patriotism nor religious belief, yet the idea of changing where he lived simply because another place was larger and more powerful was as unappealing as converting to an alien faith because its adherents were more numerous and better placed. He could manage his financial affairs equally well anywhere, and without Dina, he had no interest in the social pleasures a wider sphere could provide. If anything, he felt a slight distaste for men who had left the provinces for Vienna or London as soon as they had the means, and in his personal life, just as in his business negotiations, Moritz greatly preferred to underplay his worldliness. Contrary to the gossip of some members of the club, though, Rotenburg's desire to remain among them had nothing to do with his wanting to be the most powerful man in a small arena. His wealth and political contacts were easily sufficient to assure him a prominent place wherever he lived, and his influence was respected as much in London and Frankfurt as in Vienna. But the house he had built with Dina was where he intended to die, and though he suspected that Hans would almost certainly settle elsewhere, that thought was not sufficient to make Moritz do so as well.

Moritz had hoped to complete his financial arrangements before taking up the question of Hans's role in the company's international holdings, but the news about the boy's foolishness was forcing him to combine the two concerns much sooner than he had intended. Protecting his son from his own imprudence would have to take precedence over all of Moritz's other projects, and what made it all the more galling was that Dina was no longer there to get pleasure from knowing that their son was finally taking up so large a share of her husband's attention.

At the club, Moritz's problems with Hans fascinated the older members. For years now, none of them had dared oppose Moritz, and seeing him challenged, even if it took another Rotenburg to do so, promised to be immensely gratifying. Or at least it could have been, if they weren't facing similar problems in their own homes. The Pichlers, who had schemed ardently to match their Sophie with Hans, complained to anyone who would listen that they had completely lost control of their daughter. Even a basically easygoing, decent fellow like Viktor Demetz, who had accepted Elisabeth's rupture with Hans without making too much of his disappointment, admitted that her involvement with this von Alpsbach boy, an affair that was bound to end miserably as soon as he grew tired of her, deeply shocked both him and Rosa and that they had begun to quarrel all the time about who was more to blame for their daughter's behavior. The fierce clashes between fathers and sons that had provided such rich material for the writers of the previous generation now involved the cleverer daughters as well. At least in the eyes of the Mendelssohn Club, it was agreed that Jewish families were particularly susceptible to crises of this sort, and lacking the convents or father confessors of their Catholic neighbors, more than one set of distraught parents quietly took their daughters to Vienna in the hope that one of the newer sorts of mind doctors, most of whom were also Jews and thus, it was wrongly assumed, could be counted on not to reveal embarrassing secrets to the goyim, might exert a calming influence on their offspring. No doubt there was something laudably inclusive in the fact that all this turmoil now involved offspring of both sexes, but for the Jews to be both its main victims and the financial patrons of its supposed healers seemed to many of them to be fulfilling their role as the Empire's most open-minded subjects a bit too thoroughly. It was almost as bad as actually having to listen to some of the tuneless newer music simply because, out of a sense of cultural duty, one had subsidized the composer.

Moritz, whose mail began to include monographs in which these very doctors, far from exhibiting any discretion, itemized their patients' most indecent family scandals in lurid detail, felt no temptation to let such men meddle in his private life. The idea of appearing in their case histories was deeply repugnant to him, and although he had only a limited concern for what would be said about him after his death, so long as he was alive he was determined to use his power to control how his story would be told. What mattered more was trying to prevent Hans's life from taking a catastrophic turn. Neither Moritz nor Dina had felt any desire to mingle with the local aristocracy, most of whom, except for Count-Governor Wiladowski, were even more boring than the rich Jews of the Mendelssohn Club, but it was different watching Hans befriend young cadets like Chrissi von Hradl or the von Alpsbach heir, who was causing the Demetz family such grief these days. Although Moritz knew better than anyone how heavily mortgaged most of the province's noble estates were, he had come belatedly to share Dina's pleasure in their son's social success. It had been a long time, though, since Hans had returned home looking content from an evening with his friends, and the aggressive recitation of slogans about "the condition of the working classes," which now substituted as the boy's principal form of entertainment, was marked by a dreary joylessness that no amount of vehemence could quite disguise. Moritz suspected that parents and children inevitably end up disappointing each other, but he had never foreseen that his son would turn into someone able to learn only from listening to his own words. Since his return Hans's pontificating came out sounding embittered, and there was a new note that Moritz couldn't quite name, although if he hadn't known better, he would have been tempted to call desperation. A more forbearing man than Moritz might have been able to wait out the boy's first sarcastic flurries until the angry tones had dissipated sufficiently to permit a glimpse of whatever unhappiness really lay behind them. But Moritz, whose patience in business was legendary—like a venomous spider waiting for his prey, is how anti-Semitic pamphlets in Vienna portrayed him in their woodblock caricatures—could not sit attentively for a quarter of an hour during his son's harangues. There was simply too much crucial work to get done, and if the businessman in him couldn't help feeling something unpleasantly close to contempt for the carelessness with which Hans was ready to squander the opportunities he had been given, the animal part of Moritz that knew itself to be dying sometimes found its love for its own offspring riven by a shameful jealousy of the boy's strength and freedom from bodily pain. He still remembered how the waitress's breasts had felt brushing accidentally against his hand the night he invited the prizewinning students at the club for drinks after their exams, and he experienced a sour taste in his mouth at the thought that it was likely to have been the last time he would ever touch a young woman's body again. "I never knew dying was such an ignoble affair," he thought. "No wonder people put it off as long as possible. It's really too bad I can't hire someone to do it in my place. It can't be that much worse than traveling to Palestine to drain the swamps."

More self-mocking humor of the kind Zionists like his son's former girlfriend despised. To them, it was just another characteristic deformation of the Exile. Still, although it earned him no credit with Elisabeth Demetz and her set, Moritz was one of the few wealthy Jews in the Empire to support the Zionist cause. But he did so less out of any faith in the reestablishment of a Jewish homeland than as the best means of giving Jews something specific for which to strive. He had come to believe that passionate political feelings disconnected from any practical politics led only to theatrical self-dramatization, and all of Hans's actions these past eighteen months confirmed Moritz's belief. There were urgent questions between them that had to be settled before the scope of his foreign holdings became known to the government, but the longer he could avoid directly involving Hans, the safer it would be for them both. Fortunately, Hans's natural vanity convinced him that the opposite was the case, and whenever he left the house, he would tiptoe around his father's study, certain that if Moritz were to hear him, the old man would insist on their spending a tedious evening together. These past few days, especially, Hans's fear of being summoned in for a lengthy conversation was even more groundless than usual. The fact that Hans was taking up so large a share of Moritz's attention only strengthened the old man's desire not to wear himself out further by bickering with his son. In any case, it was vital that no one, not Hans, the Ministry in Vienna, and least of all the Count-Governor and his Jewish spymaster, should suspect that all of Moritz's resources were being redirected toward what had become a single aim, the practical businessman's version, as Moritz had started to regard it, of the Passover rite of shielding his firstborn from whatever perils their future might hold.

· ◆ ·

A few days later the first demonstration broke out in front of the Hollweg Timber Corporation gates. It was a hopeless affair, organized by men made desperate by hunger and fear, and none of the workers still employed by the company joined the protest. The local police politely declined Count-Governor Wiladowski's offer to call in the militia and in a quarter of an hour had succeeded in scattering the nearly frozen picketers. Because their orders included arresting "the ringleaders," the police seized half a dozen demonstrators who had appeared to be waving their arms with unusual energy and dragged them off to jail, although a longing to raise their body temperatures certainly sufficed to account for the prisoners' animation. Beyond curses and an occasional raised fist, neither these supposed organizers nor their companions offered the police any serious resistance. No doubt it is hard for men with threadbare clothes and empty stomachs to hold their ground against a company of gendarmes, who arrive in their thick regulation loden coats and steel-tipped boots, ready to enforce the ban on all unauthorized public gatherings with their truncheons. But since it was largely impossible for Austrians to believe that any threat to the peacefulness of the Empire was more than a momentary aberration, no charges were pressed against any of the arrested men, who were released with merciful speed after paying only token fines that wiped out whatever financial resources their families and friends still possessed. The wisdom shown by the government in maintaining the morale of its provincial constabularies, by a generous allowance of both food and equipment, even in the harshest months of the recession, was duly admired by loyal citizens throughout the Empire. Nowhere did even a single new recruit disgrace his uniform by showing any untoward sympathy with the mobs he was called upon to repress. Even more disturbing from the perspective of the radical circles was the absence of solidarity between the recently fired and those still clinging to their jobs. The fear of losing the little they had and a disheartening awareness of their vulnerability compelled the workers to a sullen identification with the policies of their employers, no matter how drastically downward their working conditions were revised. Soon enough one of the few beliefs still uniting the various camps of laborers was anger at the inexplicable economic breakdown and a compensatory certainty that the current crisis was the fault of outside troublemakers, whether these were identified as the rich speculators of Vienna and London or as the clamorous hordes of job seekers from the Empire's eastern borders. Since Jews were regarded as a prominent element in both groups, they were viewed with growing suspicion, and that Christmas season saw the first widespread success in town of the kind of anti-

Semitic pamphlet that had previously been regarded with indifference and even distaste by most of the population.

At the Mendelssohn Club, opinions were divided about how to react to these increasingly blatant racial provocations. For the older members, wild accusations in a nationalist tract or a stream of insults by an occasional rabble-rouser were momentary setbacks, not to be blown out of proportion or allowed to disturb the inevitable, if sometimes frustratingly tardy, progress toward universal tolerance. The anti-Semitism of the half educated was, for them, a social given: distasteful, but ultimately incapable of causing serious damage. They knew that the Emperor himself despised troublemakers who wanted to drive a wedge between one group of his subjects and the rest, less out of any fondness for Jews, it must be admitted, than out of an instinctive, patrician disdain for the opinions of the mob. "Properly regarded"—by which the Court simply meant "events as seen from the viewpoint of the Imperial and Royal dynasty"—there were few discernible differences among the various lower orders, and certainly none that justified such impertinent clamor. The undistinguished birth of the agitators made ludicrous their pretension to superiority over anyone, even Jews, and it was impossible for a member of the ruling house to take seriously racial differences that were not also accompanied by genealogical ones.

But since the middle-class Jews knew nothing of the reasons for His Majesty's outspoken condemnation of the anti-Semitic provocateurs, their loyalty to the Imperial house only increased, and it was never voiced so passionately as the day after a more than usually scurrilous pronouncement on "the Jewish question" came to their attention. Moreover, many of the Mendelssohn Club's wealthier members had themselves suffered serious financial losses during the ongoing slump, and their anxiety was directed more at keeping their businesses intact until the financial markets improved than at the idiocies that always arose out of the gutter at such moments. Moritz Rotenburg, whose investments now included a significant stake in a Manchester manufacturing company and a Dutch banking concern, was one of the few who actually benefited from the slump, since whatever business he lost within Austria was more than compensated for by the relative gain in the value of his foreign earnings. But as with so many of his decisions, it was impossible to estimate the proportion attributable to shrewdness rather than to luck, since he never explained, and often seemed not to have, a general strategy. Indeed the terse accounts he occasionally gave that might have implied an overall analysis of the situation were themselves so contradictory as to confuse anyone trying to understand, let alone anticipate, Moritz's next move. His devotion to the elected government and the ruling dynasty remained unparalleled, and it was accompanied by generous donations to the treasuries of the main centrist political parties, as well as to the charities patronized by members of the royal household. The various yeshivas, Talmud Torah Hebrew schools, and rabbinically administered communal aid societies also saw their requests for funds met without complaint, and Rotenburg's reputation for benevolence and financial solidity soon spread throughout both the commercial centers and the impoverished shtetls of the Empire. Even the famous *Rabbinerseminar* in Vienna was now heavily sustained by Rotenburg's gifts, and increasingly the volumes of Jewish scholarship that came from its presses bore fulsome dedications to the profound Jewish sagacity of such an inspired benefactor. At the same time, his contributions to the Zionist cause, and especially to the Jewish National Fund, increased by a large percentage every year, thus seeming to confirm the joke current in skeptical Viennese Jewish circles that defined a Zionist as "a Jew who wants to send another Jew to Palestine, using the money donated by a third Jew." Had they known the extent and diversity of Rotenburg's largesse, the same Viennese cynics might have been still more amused at so blatant a transposition into the private realm of the well-known stock market principle of risk diversification, with each donation constituting a separate kind of insurance policy for a calamity not fully protected against by any single form of coverage. When he began to place a disproportionate percentage of his investment capital in foreign concerns, acquiring, along with his expanding British partnerships, a significant stake in such uncharted ventures as American heavy industry, his maneuvers might easily have been seen as a double betrayal, demonstrating, as they did, a lack of commitment to the very causes he publicly championed, the Habsburg Imperium and the Zionist struggle for a Jewish homeland.

The poorer Jews in town, however, had other worries. If they had jobs, they felt caught between the hostility of their fellow workers and their desire to make common cause with them against the ever-stricter demands of their employers. If unemployed, they were quickly made to feel that the job crisis was due largely to their presence in town. In the long line of anxious job seekers who huddled each morning in front of any factory rumored to be offering a few hours of shift labor, Jews were pushed aside and told to go back home—wherever that might be—and stop trying to take food out of the mouths of good Austrians. Socialists and Communists, whose quarrels had previously turned on the finer points of economic theory, now found themselves drawing on a lavish repertoire of dialectic racial insults, so that it became a matter of considerable polemical prestige to convict one's opponent of advocating "a Jewish science" instead of a real proletarian ideology. Frequently both combatants in these disputes were themselves Jews, but of course this did nothing to lessen their vehemence. Each was certain of having history on his side.

Yet the town was no more consistent in its prejudices than in any of its other passions. So, in spite of his being employed by a company that even in the most prosperous times had maintained a strict Jewish quota, Asher's notorious bungling of the Trieste contract was not used, contrary to everyone's expectation, as grounds for his dismissal. For two weeks his stomach was an acid bath of nervous fear, and even the coldest day of the year did not stop him from walking around like a posthumous apparition, his face coated with a constantly renewed film of sweat. By the time of the annual Christmas party Asher felt close to a complete nervous collapse and was seriously afraid that he might break out into uncontrolled fits of sobbing if anyone asked him about his plans for the New Year. Although only a few weeks had gone by, the meeting with Hans Rotenburg seemed further away than Asher's graduation exams, and if he let himself think of them at all, the hopes that he had built on the encounter only tormented him with their absurdity. Of course he had heard nothing from Rotenburg in the interval, and when Asher tried to write an aggrieved letter reminding Hans of the promise to respond quickly, and in person no less, the tones that he found himself unable to control, of injured vanity, supplication, false pride, and cringing entreaty, were too distasteful for him to post it. So it was all the more astonishing that not only did the company not fire Asher, but his section chief even smiled at him at the annual party and wished him well over the brief vacation. The shrewder among his fellow clerks immediately speculated that the director, who prided himself on having never allowed a Jew to rise above divisional manager, had decided, in loyal imitation of the Emperor, to pick exactly this time to show his superiority to vulgar nationalists of all stripes by ordering a general amnesty for any Jews still in his employ. Its adoption by the riffraff had given anti-Semitism the wrong tone entirely, and men like Herr Director Hehemann were willing to forgo their oldest prejudices rather than be seen to share the opinions of hoi polloi. As a result, Asher's paycheck for the month actually contained the Christmas bonus that had always been withheld before because, as the payroll officer explained, such bonuses were really meant to help pay for the offerings at the Christmas and New Year's masses and not just to supplement one's wages.

But Asher had scarcely finished counting his salary when the fear, which he had experienced like a fist clenching and unclenching somewhere in his chest, turned, as it so often did, to rage. He was furious with his employer for having the power to inflict such anxiety on him, with Hans Rotenburg for having forgotten his promise and leaving him desperate for some other source of rescue from a miserable situation, and with himself for being so shamefully vulnerable to the whims of other people. Now, whenever he quickly walked past the Metropole, having to will his eyes not to stare into the room in which he had sat so recently, he felt such a surge of humiliation that he winced.

The immediate result of these feelings was his decision to avoid any place he might be forced to see the Rotenburgs. Asher stayed away from the club as much as possible, preferring to hurry home after work and take his meals in the shabby restaurants of his own district rather than linger anywhere near the town center. As a result, he never knew that for several nights in a row Hans Rotenburg had left word with the porter that he wanted to be informed if Asher Blumenthal came into the building.

When Asher changed where he ate, so of course did the composition of his dinner companions. At first he avoided talking to anyone in the dreary, half-lit room where he tried, as much as possible, to keep his spoon and fork from touching the greasy wooden tabletop on which the stains, and often the chunks of gristle and potato left behind by his predecessors, were all too visible. Yet if there was something degrading to Asher in seeing how quickly he was accepted as a "regular" in so run-down an eating house, he was partially consoled by the fantasy that his superiority to the other customers was immediately apparent. In the Josef Quarter, one was as likely to hear Yiddish, Polish, or Russian as German, and Asher made a point of enunciating his order with great care, avoiding the singsong inflections and vowel changes associated with the poorer sorts of Jews. He did so, not from any embarrassment about his race, which, in any case, made up the majority both of the quarter as a whole and of the restaurant's guests, but as an audible manifestation of his education and professional status. Asher was relieved, rather than troubled, that no one seemed to pay any attention to these signals, and he began to take the general indifference to him as a welcome easing of the burden he usually felt to make a public performance out of the disparate fragments of his own identity. And so, over the next few nights, Asher began to relax sufficiently to listen to the conversations around him for their own sake and not just to overhear if anyone might be talking about him. All around him, whether conducted in soft, quick syllables accompanied by an anxious look over the speaker's shoulders, or in louder, more guttural and defiant outbursts, the expressions of shock from the neighboring tables worked both to calm Asher and to heighten his sense of detached sympathy. Their hurried phrases were simultaneously poignant and faintly annoying, the way an acute distress, voiced in a few repetitive formulas, can strike a dispassionate listener who knows that he can do nothing to help.

It was only slowly that Asher noticed how closely the words around him echoed his own predicament. As the ranks of even the most militant workers, who only recently had found an anchoring pride in thinking of themselves as members of a worldwide proletariat, splintered along just those lines of race and nationality that their class consciousness had taught them to consider empty shells, many of the Jewish activists were left feeling doubly abandoned. Increasingly unwelcome either at the public meetings or on the secret committees formed to plan a unified response to the Confederation of Industrial Employers, they reacted with numbed confusion and hurt rather than anger. Along with the daily strain of simply surviving and keeping their families intact through the next two or three months—and everyone agreed the situation was bound to improve before too long—the worst part was being rejected by the movement in which they had placed all their hopes. It was easy for Asher to believe he understood them, even from the disconnected talk to which he paid attention, in part because the conversations went over the same ground for hours every night, but mostly because he was surprised to find himself so sympathetic to their dilemma. If his self-absorption made politics seem like a frivolous diversion from the overriding issue of his day— namely, the securing of Asher Blumenthal's personal well-being—it had the compensatory merit of triggering a quick, even if shallow, rush of sympathy for anyone with whose plight he was able to identify. More sharply than just their words, the way they sat, hunched down on their benches, looking up with haunted eyes each time the door swung open for a moment, brought home their bewilderment. It was as though he were witnessing them all being inexorably mastered by a shame that would never leave them again. At its extreme there was the despair of his immediate neighbor on the right, who kept turning to anyone who would listen, asking for reassurance that he would not be laid off and have to watch his three children go hungry. But more often what Asher heard was the humiliation of men whose miserable jobs kept them alive but paid too little for them to think of starting families. They lived alone, in one of the filthy rooms without plumbing or heat that made up most of the Josef Quarter's housing, and were forced each day to endure the condescension of their landlords and the abuse of their foremen. All this Asher could recognize and feel. The mixture of fear and shame in the room gave off a smell that is unmistakable to someone who knows it from his own body, and Asher had the unwelcome sensation of finding more of himself in the atmosphere here than when he had eaten at the Metropole or even, if he were keeping a strict account, at the Mendelssohn Club.

But sympathy with others is often thoroughly enervating, especially when one can do nothing to help, and Asher was soon ready to check the diversion of his energy along such unaccustomed channels and return it to its proper course. "The labor question" had always engaged him much less than the other two banner issues of the day—"the woman" and "the Jewish question"—since in these, at least, he could foresee the promise for an immediate change in his own circumstances, and up to now the clearest statements about society as a whole that anyone had ever heard from Asher, beyond a violent loathing for his immediate superiors at work, was his complete support of female emancipation, especially in the sexual sphere.

Because Asher also liked to think of himself as a connoisseur of ideologies to which he himself remained indifferent, he was surprised that none of the voices around him seemed drawn to one of the parties that united specifically Jewish with socialist or Marxist programs. The subtle differences in the platforms among the various factions were the subject of intense debate for the younger members of the Mendelssohn Club, especially those who were also enrolled in its Hebrew classes. Since Asher was likeliest to stay and listen to these debates after an especially satisfying dinner, he couldn't help linking the clash of theories with the diligent rumbling of his own digestion. Tonight, looking down at the last bits of the suspiciously colored lamb stew on his plate, Asher kept thinking that he was missing the annual Chanukah dinner provided free by the club's Governing Board. The sight of the food he had just swallowed made him regret with painful clarity the roast goose, fried potatoes, and delicious red cabbage that was always his favorite part of the Chanukah feast, and he remembered that it was exactly two years ago, after just such a banquet, that Leo Drobizky had tried to interest him in joining one of these oddly named movements. It was Drobizky's gratingly insistent tone, the way he made his voice almost break with feeling when he spoke about combining a commitment to "the dignity of labor" with the creation of a Jewish homeland, that had especially repelled Asher, and when he thought about it alone the next day, Asher was unable to give any concrete meaning to the slogans that seemed to inflame self-important nitwits like Drobizky. Asher thought it ludicrous to associate the concept of "dignity" with any labor he had ever performed, and draining swamps in the Galilee or harvesting oranges before sunrise somehow failed to conjure up the requisite counterimage. But it was clear to Asher that at least in At the Five Hussars, the splendidly inappropriate name Isaac Meir had given his squalid restaurant, Drobizky would not have been very successful as a recruiting agent either. The Jewish workers to whose conversations Asher was intermittently paying attention were not looking for a new political faith; they were trying, however they could, to come to terms with a series of catastrophes that had wrecked the lives they had spent the past decade constructing. It was hard to imagine any of them in Palestine, hard for Asher and obviously even more difficult for them. But when it came down to it, it was impossible for Asher to visualize Palestine at all, except as an entirely abstract place populated by fervently socialist vintners who expended an unimaginable effort to produce completely undrinkable wines, bombastic nationalist ideologues, who, in his fantasy, celebrated the redemptive power of manual labor in voices horribly reminiscent of his father at his most moralistic, reading out secular Sabbath sermons from the dreary writings of Moses Mendelssohn, and downright cranks who insisted that Jews would never be respected until they learned to ride through the countryside dressed like Berbers and armed to the teeth like highway cutthroats, the whole lot suspiciously watched over by an unctuous Turkish effendi with his hand out for the mandatory bribe. Asher knew that his description was nothing but a compendium of vulgar clichés, but he was certain that the Palestine invoked by the Austrian Zionists was itself little more than a mawkish fantasy too, and he saw no

115

reason to reject the deliberate crassness of his picture in favor of the sentimental exhortations of men like Leo Drobizky.

Perhaps we should admit that emotions and ideas, just as much as physical sounds, each have their own specific resonance and that a person can hear only those tones to which he is already predisposed. The rest is disregarded, as an animal pays no attention to sounds it identifies as unthreatening or that fall outside its auditory range. So Asher did not so much ignore as simply not take in everything that was fundamentally alien to him in At the Five Hussars. As a result, he probably failed to notice many of the most characteristic incidents going on around him. But that is hardly surprising, since the question is never merely "Revelatory of what?" but also "Revelatory to whom?" When Asher decided a few days later, after a spectacularly depressing and badly cooked New Year's dinner, that his exile had lasted long enough and it was time to return to the club, he was thrilled to find Hans's letter awaiting him. Nonetheless, in spite of being asked repeatedly, he was unable to give people at the club any information about the itinerant religious teachers from the east who had appeared on the outskirts of town and were starting to attract a sizable following from among the worst-off Jews in the Josef Quarter. Whether any of these preachers were actually trained rabbis or not, they all insisted on the title and were obviously hoping to find new students among a Jewish proletariat demoralized by the anti-Semitism of their fellow workers. The men who came out from the Josef Quarter to hear their sermons had just been purged from the labor movements and were motivated more by a need for simple companionship and a restoration of their lost sense of community than by any thirst for religious instruction. Most of the rabbis must have misunderstood this, since they tended to move on after a short time, disappointed by the lack of a sustained commitment, but a few found lodgings in town and stayed on, and cumulatively their influence was greater than anyone would have predicted.

Although he lived in the district from which these preachers drew most of their audience, Asher had no curiosity about them and paid scant attention when several of Meir's customers began to talk enthusiastically about having gone to hear a strange new teacher who seemed to know Marx and the Torah equally well. Even before any of these preachers had mixed politics into their sermons, though, their popularity had disturbed both the secret police and the socialist workers' councils, each of which sent its own secret agents to report what was going on. But few of the preachers were fluent in German, and they spoke to their followers in a constantly varying mixture of Yiddish, Russian, and Polish that was incomprehensible, not merely to the government spies but also to the informants from the now largely aryanized trade unions. Had Asher been in the audience, he probably would have fared only a little better at explaining what was being said. But it is also possible that if he had joined in the nightly debates at Meir's tables, as he later boasted of doing to Hans and the other conspirators, or if his perceptions as a listener had only been alert to a wider range of frequencies, he might have been invited to come hear the most scandalous of these rebbes. This one, Asher would have been told, spoke in High German as readily as in dialect, and his followers included several unattached, beautiful women, a prospect that would almost surely have been enough to tempt Asher to come along and might have kept him from returning to the Mendelssohn Club ever again.

PART TWO

January 1913–April 1913

1

No, let him finish. I want all of us to hear what Nathan thinks." Brugger raised his hand from the makeshift pulpit on which he was leaning and smiled toward Nathan Kaplansky, encouraging him to go on with his questions. The hostile murmurs in the room subsided, and the group of the rebbe's disciples who were starting to advance toward Kaplansky, their short wooden batons just visible inside their coats, returned to their positions where they stood guard by the back door. "In any case"—Brugger went on, looking out into the small basement room, whose low ceiling and uneven, buckling walls gave the impression of crowding everyone together into a single mass—"what he is saying is true. I never claimed to have worked in a factory like most of you did—before they fired you all, that is. But that doesn't mean I can't understand your suffering. Pain isn't a private possession. It belongs to all of us: to you, to your wives and children, and certainly to someone like Nathan, who worked alongside you for twenty years before the union he himself helped start threw him out. Don't turn your anger on one of our own. Didn't you feel the same way the first time you came to hear me? Most of you probably haven't set foot inside a shul since you were children, and I am sure a year ago the idea of going to see a rabbi would have seemed something only fools and superstitious old women do. I weep when I think of the desperation that brought you to my door, but some of you have returned every week, and you've started bringing your friends, although you know I can't find work for you or make the bosses give you more than a beggar's crust when they finally start hiring again. If you trudged all the way down these steps to hear a man like me, with only a thin wall between you and the frozen river outside, it's because you are looking for something that the rich can't give you, not even if they opened up their coffers like Joseph doling out wheat from Pharaoh's granaries. But tonight I am sure you don't need a pious sermon either. Instead let me tell you a story about what I see happening to Jews in this city, and then judge if I have understood you or if a scoffer like our friend Nathan, here, is right about me."

Kaplansky was about to protest that Brugger had promised to let him finish speaking, then cut him off more effectively than Sonnenschön and his gang of hooligans could have done. But he knew from running union meetings how useless any protest would be, so he sat down again, astonished at being outmaneuvered by this preacher in front of his own former comrades.

Brugger paused, glancing down at Kaplansky. Later Kaplansky swore that when their eyes locked, the man had a mocking, lightly quizzical expression, as though the two were engaged in a private game that Brugger was faintly disappointed to be winning so handily. But the moment passed, and Kaplansky could never be sure if his impression wasn't an illusion caused by the flickering oil lamps that had been set up behind Brugger to provide the room's only source of light.

Brugger abruptly turned away from Kaplansky and resumed speaking to the rest of the audience. He talked in a normal, conversational tone, with none of the usual rhetorical flourishes of a religious teacher. "What I see," he told them, "is a long line of men who've been standing in the cold at the factory gates since well before sunrise, but the sun isn't coming up, and the only difference between when people began to arrive at half past four in the morning and the start of the regular workday is that by dawn you can make out a little better how gaunt and threadbare everyone looks. And then, at six-thirty, the foreman really does come out to announce that the company is probably going to hire a few extra bodies, but seeing so many are already assembled, he doesn't want to waste anyone's time or encourage false hopes. So he tells all the Jews they might as well go home right away because there is no work for them. The Jews look around, shocked at the matter-of-fact way in which they've just been talked to, as though they were a different species from everyone else in line, and when none of the Christian workers object, they have no choice but to shrug their shoulders and leave in silence. The day keeps getting colder, and after a while a fresh storm begins to sweep through the streets. At noon the foreman reappears and says he still hopes to take on some new hands, but only those who can prove they've completed their military service should bother staying. More men leave, this time with a jealous look back at those still in line. By three o'clock those left look more like a column of spindly snowmen frozen in place than job seekers, and when the foreman opens the gates and repeats his earlier promise, this time dismissing all those who aren't parishioners of the nearby Congregation of St. Katharina, those turned away are barely able to walk home. Now there are scarcely a dozen souls left, shivering, but sure that their merits will get them a job at last. Finally, at nightfall, the foreman emerges for the last time, full of regret, to say that the management has concluded they're not in a position to hire extra help after all. As the news slowly sinks in, one of the remaining men shakes his fist in the air and, turning to the fellow behind him, spits out, 'You see, those damned Jews have all the luck!' "

Kaplansky was not aware of having any particular expression, but he must have shown his surprise at the effectiveness of the story—one he thought he had heard in a slightly different form before—because now Brugger was clearly looking at him. "Don't be so astonished, Nathan," Brugger said, his voice singling out Kaplansky with what sounded like genuine goodwill. "It's just a foolish little story. But yes, I do know how injustice feels. I know how it scalds your guts, how it makes the scraps of food you put in your mouth taste like sawdust and infects your dreams when you try to sleep. In everything you say, I hear a collective scream that you can't go on like this much longer. You are afraid that soon you won't be able to hold back your anger, and don't dare think about it, because you fear that whatever you do will only make things worse. Maybe you were expecting me to tell you the same thing as the other rabbis, but I haven't come here to give you a lesson in the ways of patience. You have heard enough of those a thousand times over. No, I have come here to tell you that you are right to be angry. It is time to throw down the tyrants who oppress you and shake their thrones until it is they, not you, who cry out for mercy."

As he continued speaking, Brugger's demeanor seemed to change. Rather than become more passionate, his voice grew colder and more clipped, as though he were no longer talking to a group of careworn, dispirited Jews, but issuing commands to an army at the gates of a city under siege. "Soon our meetings will be full of traitors and spies. But they have not yet found their way to our door, and I can still speak freely to you. Listen carefully, because there will not be many more such nights.

"I said that I have not come to preach patience to you but to tell you that if you are only strong enough, the Last Days are within your grasp. The Apocalypse isn't simply bestowed from heaven; it must be earned by those daring enough to demand it and ready to do anything to bring it about. But before we can be free, we need to lop off everything poisonous that has festered among us since we were driven into exile. Every taskmaster who has added to our suffering and every coward who has held back our deliverance are our enemies and must be treated as such. Hasn't that always been our greatest weakness, the hope to find a painless way to freedom? But pain is good when it is part of a great healing, and sharp knives are nothing to recoil from when an infection must be purged. Murder is not murder in a holy war. Soon there will come a day mongrel dogs in the streets grow sick from licking the putrefaction we have lopped off like so many gangrenous limbs. But whom among you can I trust to pledge himself to our cause? Whose eyes burn with the wish to see the new day?

"Before you go home tonight, I want to ask all of you a simple question, What is the truest way to evaluate an event? Well, Nathan, what do you think? What would be your gauge?"

"Its effect on the lives of the people."

"Well, that's certainly a wise answer, but tell me, how can anyone know what all the effects of his actions are going to be? Sometimes a man needs to act first and trust to God and the new morning to bring about the right results."

"All right, then. The justice of the cause."

"Bravo!" Brugger nodded derisively. "I am sure we all believe that along with you. Only people have many different ways of deciding what is just, and sometimes a great cause requires what look like unjust actions to help it triumph. What wrong did the Egyptian firstborn ever do to the Jews that the Angel of Death should come for them at Passover? Who was ever more innocent than those babies? But their death was necessary, and so it was just. The next time, perhaps, it will be not only the firstborn who must die but their fathers as well. That's why I want to give a different answer. You may not agree with me tonight, but the next time you are sent away from the gates of a factory or are barred from running for the workers' council, remember what I said here to you: Throughout history the one true measure of an event is the quantity of blood that has been spilled for its sake."

◆

Most of the others had long since filed out. Brugger, as usual after one of his sermons, paced restlessly up and down the room, waiting for the streets outside to be empty again so he could return without being further disturbed to the tenement house he and his closest followers shared. Sonnenschön and a few disciples stood quietly at the back, knowing better than to interrupt their teacher at such a time but unwilling to leave him unattended. They kept glancing suspiciously at Kaplansky, who, alone of all the visitors, was still sitting in his seat, apparently lost in thought, wordlessly watching Brugger's movements. Although he thought of Kaplansky as already dead, an empty husk whose soullessness Brugger had taught them to recognize, Sonnenschön felt jealous of the attention the rebbe paid this onetime union organizer. Along with his job, the man had lost his authority over the other workers, and Sonnenschön couldn't understand why Brugger still seemed to take him seriously. Several times he wanted to walk over to Kaplansky and shove him back out into the snow, but he knew that in spite of his distracted air, Brugger was aware of everything happening in the room, and Sonnenschön would never take such a step without a direct order.

Whatever the rebbe intended, he was clearly not yet done with Kaplansky. With surprising suddenness, Brugger was no longer at the other side of the room but standing directly in front of Kaplansky, inviting him to come back to the house with them to break the long night's fast. Brugger gestured to Linnetchen to join them and whispered a few words to her. There was something in the playful, brash way she then leaned forward to take Kaplansky's hand and second the rebbe's invitation that made the blood rush to Sonnenschön's face. Her pose reminded Robert of the night she had brought him to meet Brugger, and it seemed to hold the same sexual promise that had overcome his hesitation. To Sonnenschön's relief, Kaplansky refused, inventing some other obligation, but the confusion with which he did so made plainer than any direct acknowledgment how troubled he was by everything he had just witnessed. "Then we'll all walk together to the end of the next street," Brugger announced, helping Kaplansky to his feet and signaling to the others to lock up and join them as soon as they were done. By the time Sonnenschön caught up with the two men, they were deep in conversation only a few yards down the street, impervious to the gusting wind. Kaplansky must finally have gotten out some of his objections, though Sonnenschön arrived too late to hear them. But he did make out a good deal of what the two said and afterward tried his best to write an accurate description of their words for his sister in Russia. "It was moments like this," he confessed to Sonia, "seeing him standing in the snow with no more than three or four people around him, indifferent to whether any of us listened or understood what he was saying, that bound me to this man forever as though I had taken a wedding vow."

Brugger was speaking in a disarmingly everyday voice that Sonnenschön knew from experience often preceded a particularly intense outburst.

"True enough, Nathan," Brugger was saying. "It was wrong of me not to include the quality of the blood spilled. But are you really starting to doubt that everyone's blood is equal? You probably don't know it yet, but if so, you have just taken your first step out of the darkness. Believe me, this breathing universe knows everything except equality. Nothing that lives is ever equal to another life. Souls can't be exchanged, or bought, or made equal; each one has its own secret place in an order that links together all of creation, and it will never find happiness until it recognizes where it belongs in the hierarchy. And to save you the shame of asking, yes, it is true I know that secret place."

Brugger paused, and when he resumed again, it was with an urgency Sonnenschön rarely heard from him. "There are people among us who could help our cause, but instead they use their strength to cripple every healthy impulse we still retain. Would you really regret their removal? You were one of the first men expelled from the workers' council, weren't you? The other Jews used to look up to you, but inside, you feel more helpless than any of them. This is the fifth time you have come to my lessons, and you still can't make up your mind if I am a charlatan or the real thing. You are even afraid to come home and break bread with us or admit your desire for Linnetchen."

Kaplansky appeared as oblivious of the elements as Brugger, but he seemed to flinch away from the rebbe's words as though he were being slapped. When he tried to murmur a protest to the last accusations, Brugger swept aside his objections. "That's all right, don't bother telling me something different. The affliction is inside you, Nathan, not in what you think about me."

Kaplansky stayed quiet for a few moments and then, speaking with enormous strain, as though he were dragging up the words from within like iron weights, managed to reply. "I am afraid of you. Of what you can tempt our people to do. I don't know if I could stand seeing Jewish blood spilled on still another row of dirty streets because they believed their redemption was at hand."

Now Brugger pounced, as Sonnenschön knew he would. "You are afraid of what I might tempt our people to do? Not of what I might ask of you? Are you being honest with yourself, Nathan? What if those who sacrificed themselves were right and died in vain because a man like you refused to join them? Listen, the only question that matters is how you will ever be able to decide one way or the other. Why do you always deal with your own soul as though it were that of another? A person who drinks water knows for himself whether it is fresh or stale. But you? If you keep waiting for a sign, I am afraid you'll have to wait forever. Think carefully about what I told everyone back in the shul. I did not come to predict the future, but to make it happen. Come back when you realize where your own heart lies. And until then, my friend, good night."

· ◆ ·

Before the latest round of firings Friday mornings had always been the busiest time of the week. Even in the middle of the winter, when it was impossible to find fresh vegetables, the town's Catholic and Jewish housewives spent the hours until midafternoon rushing from stall to stall in the covered market, looking for the fattest carp and the tastiest pickled cucumbers and cabbage to bring home. The two groups patronized different merchants, but otherwise there was little to differentiate them as they carried their heavy baskets back across the Nepomuk Bridge from the shops near the Cathedral Square, eager to complete their errands and return to their stoves to finish cooking the evening meal before sundown. This year, though, the women tended to stay inside more, and in their place the streets were crowded with bands of unemployed men who lingered in isolated groups, barely moving all day from the gathering places they had established in front of the main post office and the Franciscan hospital. Their presence discouraged the few shoppers who still had money to spend, and more and more stores were boarded up, either out of fear of looters or because the merchants themselves had gone bankrupt and were unable to pay off their creditors. The tradesmen's guild sent a delegation to the Count-Governor to protest the presence of so many "potentially dangerous elements" on the very doorsteps of their places of business. From Count Wiladowski's perspective, there was a certain presumption in such citizens having political opinions at all. He disliked having to placate these merchants, whom he regarded, in the long run, as a greater threat to his authority than the workers against whom they were seeking his protection, and it was with some reluctance that he agreed to a stricter enforcement of the laws against vagrancy in public places.

Count Wiladowski read through the daily police reports specially prepared for him more attentively than he did the official government bulletins from Vienna. Lately he had taken to stationing a heavily armed guard in front of his bedroom door. Even so, his dreams were far from peaceful. Often he lay semiawake for hours, his sheets soaked with night sweat, watching himself as though he were a character in a scene set amid the explosion of assassins' bombs, the crash of glass windows shattering in his study or carriage, and the sight of his wife and adjutant covered in blood and dying at his feet, he himself barely escaping alive.

Following the debates in Parliament was, no doubt, part of his professional responsibility, but Count Wiladowski found doing so only made his nightmares worse. In his opinion, the moment people organized themselves into political parties, it became impossible for them not to assume their opponents were either thoroughly stupid or fiendishly cunning, and often, with an exhilarating defiance of logic, both at the same time. Throughout Europe, men with influence over the masses seemed to regard people advocating a policy different from their own as though they were little better than rapacious beasts, whom it was only logical, as the latest dismal jargon put it, to "liquidate." Apparently the satisfaction of butchering people whose names one had heard since childhood was at least as great as slaughtering complete strangers in a foreign war.

As long as their adversaries had come from the same caste, the aristocrats, who, at least in Franz Josef's Empire, fortunately still filled most of the important government posts, found it much easier than did their middle-class successors to suppress the opposition without first needing to vilify its members. It is awkward after all to join a man for the autumn stag hunts in Bad Ischl after having, so to speak, banished him from the fellowship of common humanity in an election pamphlet. These days, although their country boasted some of the finest political minds in Europe, even they had to admit that as far as its own governance was concerned, the Empire seemed to abhor clear definitions altogether. If it was far from democratic, it could no longer be described as entirely aristocratic either, and as each class became less certain about the boundaries of its power, the areas of friction between them increased. But so too, it was often affirmed, did the areas of cooperative contact, contradictions that only meant that the administration of the Empire had now joined theology as one of the unfathomable mysteries about which more and more impenetrable studies were being written. That there was now a vogue for political speculation could hardly be denied, so much so that even hereditary titleholders like Count Wiladowski, of whose impeccable pedigree and well-bred aversion to disputes of any kind there could be no doubt, had begun to exhibit mild symptoms of the general mania. Of course an important Imperial official could scarcely be expected to find time for academic treatises. Furthermore, Wiladowski continued to believe that it was somehow in bad taste for journalists and professors to raise political questions at all, except, as was happening more and more, when they were hired by the government itself to discredit one of the many movements hostile to the dynasty. In principle, Wiladowski thought it absurd to be instructed in his hereditary vocation by some middle-class scribbler. "For one of our kind to read a book on politics," he said in a bon mot that won sufficient favor to be repeated in the presence of the Emperor himself, "is like expecting a bird to learn about flying from a booklet on ornithology."

Happily, Matthias Pfister, the Count-Governor's First Secretary, hit upon the idea of preparing brief excerpts of the most famous political treatises from the Castle library for his master's evening reading. He tried to guarantee the acceptability of his selections by ensuring that all the chosen authors satisfied three criteria: that they had been dead for at least two hundred years, the passage of time having lent them, as it were, a sort of posthumous patent of nobility; that they were all good Catholics, or at least not open heretics; and that nothing in their writings could be interpreted as a criticism of the way society was governed today. But in this the First Secretary underestimated his employer's curiosity. Like most men forced to work their whole lives for people whose intelligence they wrongly assumed was second-rate, Pfister was unable to recognize the Count-Governor's originality of mind. Wiladowski was vitally concerned to preserve both his own position and the privileges of his caste, but he did so without any illusions about the intrinsic merits of either one.

Indeed his First Secretary would have been quite astonished had he known that late one evening, finding himself unable to sleep because of another dream of being trapped in a fiery explosion, Wiladowski had gone into the library to take down one of these books himself, an action virtually unprecedented in the memory of his staff. Even more surprising was that his choice fell on Niccolò Machiavelli's *The Prince*, a title that had long since become a byword for the kind of overintellectualized immoralism Wiladowski considered especially grating. What had stayed in his mind with the stubbornness of a popular tune one never really liked but still finds oneself humming at the most inopportune moments was an idea from the dedicatory epistle to Lorenzo de' Medici, with whom, Wiladowski seemed to recall, his family could claim an indirect kinship through one of its innumerable well-married female ancestors. Wiladowski had retained enough Italian from his service as a young aide-de-camp in Habsburg Trieste and his posting, years later, as the Emperor's ranking attaché in Rome to puzzle out the passage. Force alone, Machiavelli argued, can never guarantee a Prince's safety. To be secure in his position, a ruler must comprehend fully the nature of the people over whom he is placed and be prepared to gain that knowledge by any means at his disposal.

During the following week something in those words must have continued to affect the Count-Governor, because he decided to become better informed about what the town's different ethnic groups were saying about him. The reports from the small team of police agents, all of whom were good Catholics inherited from his predecessors, were frustratingly sketchy in this regard, and in his dispatches to Vienna, Wiladowski now regularly requested funds for an unprecedented increase in the number of informers available to go among the population and keep him apprised of people's states of mind. In the ministry these requests were attributed solely to Wiladowski's well-known fear of assassination, and his comment about needing "to comprehend fully the nature of the people over whom he had to rule"—he put the phrase in quotation marks but left it unattributed—was regarded as nothing more than a flimsy rationalization for his cowardice. But the repeated official rebuffs of his request discouraged Wiladowski only briefly, and he decided to find other means to gather the necessary knowledge. Although he was not prepared to draw upon his own considerable fortune for such a purpose, he was confident that a discreet inquiry to the richest manufacturers—and an even more discreet request for their financial contribution—about how best to ensure "the maintenance of public tranquillity" would soon raise the necessary funds. To the amazement of the few members of his staff allowed to know about the plan, Wiladowski's expectations were, if anything, far too modest. The donations so far exceeded his immediate requirements that in addition to the dozen new spies he was able to put on his payroll, Wiladowski had enough money left over to present his wife with a lovely set of earrings, to compensate her, as he put it to himself, for all the disturbances to her sleep caused by the pressure of his official duties.

By far the largest contribution came from Moritz Rotenburg, and as though indirectly to show his appreciation for such public-mindedness, Wiladowski hired a specialist, fluent in both Yiddish and Hebrew, to read through the mail sent by the town's worrisomely voluble Jews. To Wiladowski, they were the most opaque of all the peoples under his supervision, and the Count-Governor's orders to his new spymaster made clear that he expected to be kept informed about the social ideas and habits of "his Jews" in substantial detail. And so, sometimes as often as twice a week, Wiladowski received a précis of the dense and multifarious correspondence steamed open by the new recruits to the security force and translated by their leader, Jakob Tausk, a former religious student expelled from a Jewish seminary famous for its scholarly rigor. Beyond assuring himself that politics was not involved, Wiladowski did not inquire into the reasons for Tausk's banishment, certain, in any case, that his spymaster would never tell him the truth and wishing to save them both the embarrassment of a transparent fiction. Pfister insisted that some kind of sexual dereliction had to be at the root, since licentiousness was simply in these people's blood, but Wiladowski ignored his First Secretary's theories about Tausk, as he did on most matters not directly related to court etiquette. For his part, though, the Count-Governor never mentioned to Tausk, who only found out for himself several months later, that the spymaster's salary, as well as that of the people under his command, was, in effect, being paid from money contributed by Moritz Rotenburg, a name Tausk knew well as the chief benefactor of the yeshiva where his promising rabbinical career had foundered.

As a result of his new arrangement, Count-Governor Wiladowski, who had never sat down to an official dinner at which a Jew was present without feeling slightly self-conscious for himself as well as for the Jew, intuitively sensing that his guest's ancestors, as well as his own, would have found such promiscuous intermingling in bad taste, began to know more about what mattered to the region's Jews than did many of that community's official leaders. Although knowledge acquired by spying scarcely seems like a solid basis for philo-Semitism, the relative absence of unpatriotic, let alone violent, tendencies in the letters summarized for him made Wiladowski feel a paternal benevolence toward a people who presented no threat to his safety and was always so prompt in its subsidies of his favorite causes.

Unlike some of His Majesty's other subject peoples, the Jews did not seem obsessed with the vulgar business of carving up the Empire into a set of separate countries of their own, and the few who did make mention of such longings seemed to have fixed on Palestine for their putative homeland, a decision that pleased Wiladowski since it took the matter out of his hands entirely. Although the Emperor entertained a distant claim to the throne of Jerusalem, the place was not presently a Habsburg domain, and as Wiladowski once noted to his colleagues in Vienna, if the realization of the Jews' longings were not so patently absurd, the dynasty actually might be well served having Palestine governed by a group of amply funded, German-speaking Semites who could be counted on to retain a sentimental attachment to the woods and rivers of the Danube lands.

Once, when he was musing aloud on these questions to Tausk, his new spymaster pleased him by replying that obviously His Excellency had decided to become not only the embodiment of Imperial authority in the province but also its most distinguished Zionist. In this, Tausk hastened to add, the Count was only echoing the first apostle himself, who, as the Scriptures said, asked the resurrected Christ, "Lord, wilt thou at this time restore again the kingdom to Israel?" It was regrettable, Tausk went on, that the official impartiality on all ethnic matters required these days by someone in the Count-Governor's position prevented Wiladowski from openly informing the Jews of his sympathy, thereby costing him the title of *pater Iudeorum*, or father of the Jews, which they would doubtless have sought to add to the long list of honors that already followed his name.

While Wiladowski occasionally resented Tausk's habit of quoting as glibly from the New Testament as from his own Jewish holy books, especially since his voice imparted a slightly ironic undercurrent to everything he mentioned, the Count-Governor was growing to value the man's advice. Now Tausk pointed out to his master that the richest Jews had their own avenues of communication to which it was impossible to gain access and that consequently, the information he could glean from opened mail and overheard public conversation was largely useless as far as they were concerned. Because of Hans Rotenburg's carelessness in not always using his father's private couriers, Tausk's men had found out almost immediately about his interest in *The New Order*, but an hour spent going through back numbers of that journal made clear its harmlessness, and the agents who now included the Josef Quarter apartment in their normal rounds reported that nothing going on there was cause for alarm. They assured Tausk that they had the situation under control and advised not interfering with young Rotenburg and his friends until more dangerous elements from the radical movement came out of hiding to work with them—an unlikely development, in everyone's view, given Hans's reputation for frivolity.

Far more worrisome to the Governor and his superiors in Vienna than anything Hans Rotenburg might be up to were his father's plans, which remained impenetrable to everyone. Although the man had always shown himself loyal to the dynasty, the power of Rotenburg's wealth was itself adequate grounds for vigilance, all the more so since there were rumors that he had succeeded in investing a significant proportion of it outside the Empire. Wiladowski contemplated asking Rotenburg to increase his monthly donation to the government's emergency fund and then using the money to bribe financial experts in London to find out more about Rotenburg's secret investments. But the Count-Governor's inborn sense of caution resisted so crass—and, in all likelihood, futile—a step, and he contented himself with the thought that after all, these questions were hardly germane to his already sufficiently burdensome responsibilities. No doubt Rotenburg had disguised his maneuvers far too well for anyone to unravel, and in the long run it was too risky to ask the financier to pay for his own surveillance abroad as well as at home. The Count-Governor's colleagues might still talk in tones of scandalized respect about a book like *The Prince*, but to Wiladowski, a political treatise that had no advice about dealing with a subject who was considerably richer than his ruler was sadly out-of-date.

Rather than be discouraged, though, Wiladowski found a certain melancholy satisfaction in that realization. Tausk's methods of gathering information were not the only ones available to the Count-Governor. It would be interesting, as well as potentially enlightening, he thought, to watch Rotenburg, who was rarely seen in public these days, directly engage with some of the Empire's leading nobles, and toward that end Wiladowski decided to honor a few of the town's leading Jews by including them in the official ceremonies planned for the three hundredth anniversary of the rededication of the Cathedral Bell Tower. In 1614 the great Bell Tower had been among the first buildings restored after a devastating fire had gutted much of the town, and the commemoration of its rededication had become the most important holiday in the district, combining civic and religious motifs in a way the dynasty particularly encouraged. This year a large delegation of important visitors from the capital was expected for the festivities, and since the group was likely to include Clemens Zichy-Ferraris, a notorious anti-Semite whom Wiladowski detested, the Count-Governor was delighted to institute a daring emendation in protocol that would show him as politically tolerant and ecumenically broad-minded—all to Zichy-Ferraris's acute discomfort. Naturally, Wiladowski would need to check the plan first with the Ministry, but he was confident it would be approved since it concerned Moritz Rotenburg, and the Count-Governor intended to make it very clear to the other Jews invited along with him that this token of Imperial favor did not constitute a precedent as far as future ceremonial occasions were concerned.

Matthias Pfister was too well trained to manifest any surprise as he was drafting the invitation to the Rotenburgs, Demetzes, and Pichlers a few days later, but sensing his First Secretary's unspoken puzzlement, Wiladowski felt the gratification that comes whenever we see ourselves capable of surprising those with whom we have worked for a long time. At such moments the Count-Governor reckoned himself closer than he usually did to the Italian branch of his ancestors, most of whom, he reminded himself so as to complete his newly restored sense of well-being, had died peacefully of old age and in their own beds.

• ◆ •

Perhaps the long row of barren trees and the expanse of fresh snow, unmarked by any footsteps, was distorting his sense of distance, but to Nathan Kaplansky, the garden in which the Rotenburg villa had been built appeared as large as the town's public park. In spite of all his years as a union militant, he had never let himself picture what it meant for one man to own so much land without using it for anything except a barrier between himself and the street. Kaplansky's disgust at such profligacy came close to making him turn around and head back to his own district, but Brugger had terrified him enough so that he felt he had no choice but to accept Rotenburg's carefully worded invitation.

He had never expected to set foot inside a house like this except at the head of a workers' delegation or under police guard, so when Rotenburg's

134

English butler politely opened the door for him and led him straight into the financier's study, Kaplansky took his reception as proof that the preacher's reputation was beginning to extend beyond the Josef Quarter. He had been too ill at ease to let the butler take his heavy coat in the hallway, and now, although it was stiflingly hot in the room, there was no place for him to hang it. Kaplansky had to content himself with bundling it awkwardly on top of a chair, while feeling himself observed by the drawn face of the figure sitting in a large armchair near the fireplace. Before today he had only seen Rotenburg from a distance and was astonished at how frail the financier looked up close. There was something shocking about the disparity between the man's power and his physical infirmity, and it galled Kaplansky to think that all this wealth should be in the hands of someone who had so little life left in him.

And yet, when Rotenburg began to speak, there was no hint of weakness in his voice. His tone was clear and attentive, as though Kaplansky's visit were a long-delayed pleasure for them both. Nicholas poured them each a strong cup of coffee from a simple dark red and gold china service and, at a signal from his master, set the cups on a small side table and discreetly withdrew. Rotenburg gestured for Kaplansky to sit down near him and waved off, as though it were a formality quite unnecessary between them, his guest's nervous explanation about how reluctant he had been to come. "No, not at all, Herr Kaplansky." Rotenburg interrupted him. "Your calling on me this afternoon took real selflessness, and I am grateful for it. If this preacher continues to gain support, it won't be long before the authorities hear about it, and then we are all at risk."

"I simply didn't know where else to turn," Kaplansky admitted. Rotenburg had to understand just how dangerous the situation in the Josef Quarter was becoming. Nothing else could have induced Kaplansky to solicit this conversation. "I am more scared of this rabbi than I have been of anyone for years. I know how strange that must sound to you, in a grand house like this, and right now I am not sure myself anymore if I haven't made a mistake coming to you. You are the sort of capitalist I have spent my whole life fighting. But my comrades tell me you actually care about what happens to the Jews in this town, and I am willing to trust their instincts over my own."

Out of habit, as much as anything else, Kaplansky had hoped to strike a defiant tone, but even to his own ears, his attempt sounded forced. He braced himself for Rotenburg's mockery and was grateful when the financier ignored his rudeness altogether. Instead Rotenburg looked down thoughtfully for a moment, and then went on. "Socialist, capitalist . . ." His face screwed up with distaste at the words. "When the people with the titles and brocade uniforms look at someone like you or me, it's not our political beliefs they see. If serious trouble breaks out, and there is any way it can be blamed on the Jews, we all are going to pay for it, no matter what kinds of roofs we have over our heads or whom we support in Parliament."

Kaplansky had been prepared for almost anything, but not this spontaneous acknowledgment of mutual interest. "I swear I will never understand a man like you." He burst out much too loudly. "You control the economic life of the whole region, everyone knows you give money to that overstuffed pig of a Governor for his thugs to break strikes and spy on us workers, your son spends his time hobnobbing with all the Christian aristocrats in the province and debauching working-class girls in the Josef Quarter, and then you tell me that you and I are basically on the same side! I'd be crazy to believe a word you say."

"Come now, Herr Kaplansky, be reasonable. Why isn't it just as crazy for me to trust you? You want to take away my property and divide it among a bunch of schnorrers who would leave it bankrupt in six months. And most of them are more anti-Semitic than the Governor and the Archbishop put together. Of course I have a certain appreciation for a government with its own interest in preventing the mob from threatening our safety—especially when those wonderful proletarians of yours keep voting for one anti-Semite after another. Only I'm not naive enough to think the Habsburgs have suddenly adopted us Jews as their particular favorites. The moment they conclude we've become too much of a problem, it will be a good anti-Semitic mob favorite, not the Jew Rotenburg, they will call on to restore order. Look, I know your reputation for honesty. That is something I respect, and what is more important, so do a lot of the Jewish workers. From what I have heard, though, it doesn't look like Jews are welcome anymore at union gatherings. Have all of you really been asked to resign from your positions on the executive?"

"So you do send spies to our meetings." Kaplansky flared up, not certain if he should be more angry at the fact itself or at Rotenburg's casual way of admitting it. "I thought as much. I just wonder if you have hired your own agents or are relying on the Governor's."

"Both, actually, if you really want to know." Rotenburg's avowal was accompanied by a rueful smile. He shrugged his shoulders as though conceding a disagreeable, but hardly very important, detail and continued to look directly into Kaplansky's flushed face with an untroubled expression.

To Kaplansky, the financier's cynicism was repellent, and he made up his mind not to let himself be disarmed again by any conciliatory phrasemaking. "This may surprise someone like you," he said, "but listening to talk like that disgusts me. I can't believe I ever let myself hope we had any interests in common."

"I was only trying to answer your question honestly." Rotenburg went on as calmly as before. "Would you prefer I lied to you? We both know it's only self-preservation on my part, just as it is on the Governor's, to infiltrate your meetings. So what? That's the way it has always been, and your side and mine both have survived. But this rabbi who has you so worried is causing serious mischief. To me, that's enough to put us on the same side, even if just temporarily. Think of it this way. Unlike a lot of others with your politics, you didn't stop calling yourself a Jew the day you became a socialist. I'm really not so different. I have never been tempted to change what I am or stop caring about what happens to our people. Now, what exactly can you tell me about this Brugger?"

Before Kaplansky could reply, there was a soft knock on the door, and when Rotenburg called out, "Yes, go ahead," a young servant came in carrying an armful of firewood. Although the room was already overheated, the boy headed directly for the fireplace and arranged the fresh logs so that they would catch immediately. The presence of another person made Kaplansky feel momentarily embarrassed at being found in such a setting, and he walked toward the window as though to see what the garden looked like from inside the house. It was still only late afternoon, but there was already too little light to make out anything except for a few shadows on the snow and a faint line of smoke from the other chimneys in the neighborhood.

As soon as the servant was gone again, Kaplansky went back to his chair and tried to shrug off his feeling of being somehow in the wrong. "It's not really possible to be certain about anything where Brugger is concerned," he said, "except that I am sure he is dangerous and possibly mad as well. He already has a small cadre of followers ready to do anything he asks, and the number is only going to increase."

"What do you mean, 'do anything'?" Rotenburg asked. "Give him their possessions, steal for him?"

"I can't be sure, but I don't think they would stop there. In fact I get the sense that the more extreme his demand, the more eager their obedience. There is something horribly perverse going on in that shul. I think he is training a kind of private army to do his bidding. In any case, he already has a group of women willing to let themselves be offered to anyone Brugger wants to recruit. But I am not just worried about his seducing a few young hotheads away from the trade union movement. Brugger wants to subvert for subversion's sake. There isn't any higher cause that I can make out, except his own vanity. And above all, there is this clamor for violence, for blood. It's as though he knows how to draw on every humiliation the Jews have endured and turn it into a desire for revenge. Do you know what he said to me once when I asked him if he wasn't afraid of leading his congregation to destruction? He just shook his head at me as if I were a child and answered, 'To save these people from themselves, it would take a greater terror than the earth has ever seen.' Sometimes I think he fully intends to be the instrument of that terror. But even if it is just his craziness speaking, he is starting to feed the same messianic delusions that have not changed the life of a single Jew in over five hundred years except to bring us total ruin."

"What exactly is he planning?" Moritz asked. "Do you have any idea of his specific intentions?"

"I don't know, and I suspect Brugger himself doesn't know yet either. But unless he is stopped, there will be violence—of that much I am absolutely convinced."

"Is he like that all the time? What do you know about his background? Does he have any education?" Moritz threw out his questions in a rush, making no attempt to hide how disturbing he found Kaplansky's story.

"No, not at all. He isn't any one thing consistently. And to me, that only makes him more alarming. He is perfectly capable of acting as though all that apocalyptic talk were just an elaborate charade he never expected anyone to take seriously. He has laughed openly at the notion of a Jewish Messiah and called it a shameful trick to defraud poor Jews of their savings. But the next moment he will turn around, gather his disciples together, and say, 'But if he does come, the Messiah will not arrive like a poor man riding on a donkey into Jerusalem. He will appear among us like a man of our century, riding in an armored car with a gun in his hand and a military escort clearing his way.' And before you have a chance to react, Brugger will look up with an amused smile, so there is no way of knowing how seriously he means it.

"I have heard that although he doesn't appear to have a single penny to his name, his parents were very well off and gave him a first-class education. To judge by his accent in shul, he must have come from somewhere in the Ukraine. But he can just as well talk perfect High German. Sometimes he gives the impression of having spent his whole life among the most pious shtetl Hasidim, and a few hours later he will talk to a room full of young workers and sound as emancipated as any of them. Instead of stories about the Ba'al Shem Tov or Rabbi Nachman, he starts quoting passages from Marx and Engels. But when he is with the followers he trusts most, he keeps returning to the idea that everyone is trying to save a way of life that died long ago and that he has come to bury it once and for all."

Rotenburg's distress was obvious. He had picked up a small writing box from his desk and sat opening and closing it, staring into the fireplace. "Whether he means it or not," he snapped, "those are exactly the kinds of speeches to feed Wiladowski's nightmares and send all of you directly to prison. I am surprised the police haven't raided your meetings yet. How long has this been going on?"

"I think Brugger only came to town a few months ago, and of course it took him a while to attract anybody to his meetings. Besides, there are a lot of types like that around these days, trying to take advantage of the situation to make some money. When people are desperate, they will spend what little they have left on dreams of a better life. We Jews don't get drunk all that much, so I suppose we make up for it by longing for miracles. Anyway, I remember that I first went out to hear him a day or two after the police arrested a bunch of us in front of Hollweg's yard."

"You were in that demonstration?" Rotenburg's astonishment was too palpable to be feigned. "I never realized that you would take part in a pointless gesture like that."

"Well, that only shows that your friends in the police don't tell you everything that goes on in town. I really only showed up there to lend moral support since the timber workers have always been loyal union men. But when the square was raided, I don't imagine the police looked very closely at whom they were carting off. Anyway, they vaguely recognized my face from an earlier strike, and so, of course, they concluded I must have organized this one as well. It wasn't too bad, except for a few bruised ribs and the obscenely large fine, but while I was in the holding cell, I heard about Brugger from one of the other men locked up with me, and as soon as I was released, I decided to go see for myself."

"Does Brugger believe in God? Is he really a rabbi at all?"

Kaplansky was surprised by the question. He hadn't kept track of how long their conversation had gone on, but in spite of all the coffee he had drunk, he was starting to feel light-headed. The heat was becoming unbearable, and he was eager to be back outside in the fresh air. Rotenburg, though, was sitting up without the least sign of fatigue and seemed to be growing only stronger.

"I have no way of knowing what Brugger believes, if he believes the same thing from one day to the next, or if he believes anything at all. It is impossible to piece together a coherent story of his life. A number of us have tried, but we've gotten nothing except a string of separate adventures that seem to have taken place all over the map. I have written for information to my comrades in the east, but they don't have much contact with the Orthodox Jews."

"I can help you there." Rotenburg nodded. "I know people at a number of the yeshivas on both sides of the border who might be able to tell us more."

"But in the meantime what do we do?"

"I think the first thing is for me to talk to Brugger himself," Rotenburg replied. "I need to find out what he really wants before deciding how to deal with him. Right now it is crucial to stop him from making any more provocative speeches. Let him say whatever he wants about strictly Jewish matters, but nothing that sounds even vaguely like a threat to the government. He probably has no idea how jumpy everyone at the Castle is these days and how quickly he could end up locked away forever in some jail cell in Lower Austria. I don't want to bring him into my house, so do you think you could overcome your aversion to the Mendelssohn Club enough to persuade him to come see me there? Shall we try for a week from today, at three in the afternoon?" Rotenburg jotted down the details in the large notebook open on his desk, as though he were concluding a business meeting. "Let me know as soon as Brugger has agreed. And whatever else you do, make sure he understands the likelihood of police agents in his audience. No more seditious talk about terror or an armed Messiah—for everyone's sake."

Kaplansky had risen from his chair and was already buttoning his coat to leave. "Brugger strikes me as pretty hard to scare, but I have no doubt that he can control himself when it serves his purpose. And no doubt he would go out of his way to win the trust of someone as powerful as you."

But Rotenburg was not finished yet and indicated as much to Kaplansky. "One last thing before you go. You mentioned my giving the Governor money. It's true that I do, both for the reasons I have explained to you and for others that are strictly my own business. But for some time now I have wanted to find a discreet way of helping those of our people who've lost their jobs, and talking to you today has given me a solution. What would you say if I arranged to give you a monthly sum exactly equal to what I contribute to Wiladowski for you to distribute where it would do the most good?"

"With no conditions?" Kaplansky had conducted too many bargaining sessions for his union to accept any offer from a plutocrat like Rotenburg without asking to know all the details.

"Of course there are a few conditions." Rotenburg was not in the least offended by the question. "But they are straightforward enough, I think you will agree. Only please understand that they all are linked, and it is either yes or no to the proposal as a whole. First, the money is to go only for the relief of the poor and out of work, not for political activity of any kind; second, it all will be distributed exclusively by you, without my name's being mentioned in any way; and last, you are to take out for yourself a fixed amount matching the salary you would have drawn if you had a full-time job on the leadership committee of your party."

For a moment Kaplansky was too shocked to speak. He felt almost as trapped as when Sonnenschön and his thugs had surrounded him in the shul and were starting to push him into a corner. The sense of helplessness, of being like the boy lost in a forest when the animals have eaten all the breadcrumbs that were supposed to show him the way back home, was slow to subside. He wiped his face, which he only now realized was covered with sweat, and forced himself to wait several more heartbeats before letting himself consider Rotenburg's proposal. But he knew what his response had to be. He looked up and saw Rotenburg still sitting patiently at his desk, in no hurry to force an answer from him.

"All right," Kaplansky heard himself saying. "What else can I do? Almost every day I have to watch people dying of hunger in the Josef Quarter and hate myself for having nothing to offer them. But your third condition is unbearable. You are making me your employee."

"It is only a short-term arrangement, Nathan." Rotenburg refused to treat the matter as anything of great consequence. "Just until the slump is over and our people have work again. In the meantime we each have good reasons to make sure no one will ever know about our understanding. And if you are still so uncomfortable with my offer, just think of how furious the Governor and the other business leaders would be if they suspected me of helping you. If I were you, I would be comforted by that and by the knowledge of all the good you will be doing."

· ◆ ·

In the years before Tausk entered his service, the Count-Governor had never bothered to reflect how curious it is that the most plausible-sounding maxims are so often completely misleading as guides to human behavior. But his practical experience had begun to convince Wiladowski that none of the resources his senior colleagues were still recommending—neither the two centuries of political dispatches and espionage reports, carefully bound and shelved in the secret archives of the Ministries, nor the rules of statecraft formulated in celebrated manuals like *The Prince*—provided the advice he needed to administer his province without getting blown up or forced to resign in disgrace. Not even self-interest and ambition could be relied upon in the way that any orderly bureaucracy prefers. Only a year ago family duty had forced him to spend a dismal number of hours examining police photographs of one of his cousins, savagely gutted to death in his own hunting lodge in Bukovina. Of course the killers had vanished long before the body was discovered, and so beyond hanging a few inept local smugglers and sentencing a young anarchist who taught algebra in the village school to a decade at hard labor, the provincial prosecutor had no adequate way to demonstrate his zeal. For Wiladowski, who had always considered his cousin an utter fool, the only part that truly unsettled him was the uncertainty about the killers' motives. Drunk peasants and thieves he could understand, but not men capable of eviscerating a human being and then covering the walls where the corpse lay with bizarre apocalyptic slogans. The chief inspector assigned to the case permitted himself to point out that since the deceased had been stripped of all his clothing and valuables, and the house systematically looted, perhaps the strange writing was a false clue, deliberately left to make a simple robbery look like a political crime. Wiladowski didn't bother arguing with the man, but by the time he returned home on the night train, he had been certain that poor Cousin Max, who had spent his happiest hours hunting and drinking among well-meaning, deferential idiots, had now wound up with one of them to investigate his own murder.

Unfortunately, Wiladowski's impressive equanimity at his cousin's fate had no influence on the constantly growing anxiety he felt for his own safety. Fear began to dictate his reactions to even the most benign domestic rituals. On his sixty-third birthday Marie-Luise celebrated the occasion with a party during which he could not help detecting a faint but disconcerting note of satisfaction in her newly melancholy demeanor, as though she were already testing out in her imagination what tones would be most appropriate to a widow of an assassinated statesman. Actually, Marie-Luise was so nervous about how the new pastry cook's desserts would turn out that she was unable to concentrate on anything else, and only Wiladowski's self-pity made him interpret his wife's absentmindedness as further proof that everyone around him was already resigned to the likelihood of his violent death. He was too well bred to allow his vexation to mar the placid smile with which he greeted his guests and too indifferent to his wife's inevitable denials to bother mentioning his suspicion to her. But even to himself, the extent of his grievance against his wife became apparent only the next day, while listening to Tausk's weekly report. To his own amazement, the Count-Governor interrupted his habitual series of peremptory questions to slip in what amounted to the briefest hint of an apology at having been unable to persuade his wife to invite Tausk, whom she made no secret of detesting, to the party. But then, as though embarrassed at such a breach of their respective roles, Wiladowski impatiently shrugged off the Jew's effusive birthday wishes for a long and successful future with a brusque declaration that his ambition was not to win new honors but merely to continue staying alive. In this, it is true, he was just echoing, in the minor key of his own life, his Emperor's semiacknowledged official policy. But as both an Austrian and a hereditary nobleman he found it almost physically painful to admit that assumptions crystallized over centuries in the axioms of his caste were unlikely to help him accomplish even the modest goal of physical survival.

Wiladowski was too little given to naming his moods and dwelling on their nuances—an activity he regarded as suitable only for bluestocking women and middle-class Jews of either sex—to describe his feeling as one of abandonment. Yet it is as common to find oneself deserted by one's own earlier ideas and feelings as by one's first lovers, and the experience of an unrecoverable distance between one's present outlook and long-since cast-off states of mind, in which one had once dwelled as securely as in a childhood home, is as painful as any separation from another human being. More painful, perhaps, since it is from oneself that one is now divorced and to one's own earlier self that one goes on being increasingly unfaithful. Wiladowski allowed himself to think none of this very clearly, but a sense of exile from the effortless confidence he had felt looking out on the golden Triestine harbor during his first posting was unmistakable and, considering his disposition, subtly humiliating as well.

Perhaps it was this same feeling that prompted his occasional tones of near intimacy with someone who should have been so far beneath his personal notice as Tausk, a familiarity that afterward nearly always succeeded in puzzling Wiladowski himself as much as it irritated the rest of the Castle staff. Although it manifested itself in profoundly different ways, both men at times gave the impression of performing their duties as though they had just been abruptly recalled from some other realm and had to struggle against an initial inner disengagement in order to take seriously the tasks at hand. But since neither man was ready to admit this about himself, each took the other's occasionally preoccupied looks and gestures as the involuntary expression of a feeling with which he himself was almost, but not entirely, familiar. And because of its very incompleteness, this never-achieved moment of identification let an unacknowledged and almost subterranean intimacy develop between two people who, for the most part, continued to regard each other with all the inherited suspiciousness of their antithetical upbringings. Every other human emotion, whether its existence could be inferred plausibly or not, had recently become the subject of the most intensive study in the capital, but there were no Viennese specialists in the sensation of infidelity to oneself, even though a lucrative practice probably awaited anyone who set himself up as an expert in its treatment. Had such a man existed, there is a chance that Tausk and Wiladowski might have found themselves in the awkward predicament of one day running into each other in the doctor's waiting room, thereby destroying any likelihood of ever being able to talk more or less openly to each other again.

Tausk had taught himself to study the world with the single-minded coldness of someone both brilliant and desperately poor, and because all his resources were focused on triumphing over the privation he had endured since being expelled from the yeshiva, his ambition left him no more leisure for extensive self-scrutiny than, from the opposite side, did Wiladowski's patrician disdain for emotional self-display. Nonetheless, an awareness of having lost something that had once been fundamental to his existence could sometimes be heard in Tausk's gratingly sarcastic tones, a sudden change of timbre as though he were momentarily surprised by a twinge from an old injury that he had thought completely healed. Tausk did not delude himself that he had made all his choices deliberately—his unexpected position at the Castle was sufficient evidence to the contrary—he simply recognized that nostalgia was beyond his means, spiritually as well as materially. Perhaps those he served could afford the luxury of such distracting emotions; he could not. In this sternness toward himself, Tausk embodied the austere discipline of the chivalric ideal better than a hereditary great nobleman like Wiladowski, who was quite unashamed of exhibiting a limitless compassion for his own circumstances. Of course this was balanced in the Count-Governor's consciousness by his habit of regarding the rest of humankind, including his own family and supposed intimates, with a dispassionate lucidity every bit as glacial as Tausk's.

In games of power, the ability to play a part without at least to some extent believing it oneself is much rarer than amateurs think, and in spite of popular belief, thoroughgoing, calculated hypocrisy is among the most infrequently mastered, because among the most difficult, of skills. Wiladowski, whose gift in this domain was sufficiently developed to have impressed his Roman friends in the College of Cardinals, enjoyed insisting that it was fundamentally a matter of class and breeding. "No matter how intelligent they are, shopkeepers first need to convince themselves of the value of the goods they are selling before they feel right peddling them at a profit to their customers" was how he explained himself to Tausk on one of those nights when his fears prevented him from sleeping and he summoned his spymaster to keep him company. They were talking in the smaller, private salon across the hallway from the Count-Governor's dressing room, and except for the guards posted in front of every door, no one else on the floor was still awake. The Count-Governor knew he could rely on Tausk to be an engaging conversational partner, but he was surprised by the passion with which Tausk took up the theme. Tausk politely disagreed with his master about the middle class, which seemed to him to differ very little from the aristocrats he had met so far, but he completely shared the Count-Governor's idea that most people need to dupe themselves first before cheating others. "What I learned, even before I came to work for Your Excellency, is that people want to think well of themselves more than anything else," Tausk elaborated, "and that to have a clean conscience there is no vileness they won't commit. The really dangerous people are those who have given up the illusion of innocence." Although he disliked on principle hearing about anyone dangerous enough to concern the man charged with his security, conversations like this enabled the Count-Governor to return contentedly to bed, where he, unlike Tausk, could now fall asleep until midday if he were so inclined.

On Tausk, though, the effect of their last exchange was entirely different. Even if he were not awaiting the morning reports from his spies in town, Tausk knew that he would be unable to fall asleep until he had shaken off the memories his own words had raised. When he was finally alone, back in the low-ceilinged room he had been given in the Castle's north wing, he spent hours reliving his spectacular fall. He had gone from being the rabbi's all-indulged favorite to a banished and homeless reprobate without any hope of a pardon. The difference between the world he now inhabited and that of the yeshiva could not be greater, yet these strange late-night colloquies with Wiladowski threw Tausk back to questions he thought he had left behind forever. From the day he arrived at the seminary, Tausk had marveled at Rabbi Pelz's union of intense inwardness and absolute control over everything that went on in his school, and he determined to win his teacher's love through the only accomplishment Pelz valued: an intense, single-minded dedication to the study of the holy texts. But the first time he had gone in alone to the rabbi's study, instead of asking Tausk for his interpretation of a disputed passage in the rabbinic commentaries, Pelz had invited him to share a cup of tea and tell him about what Tausk hoped to learn studying with a group of students so evidently inferior to him in intellectual promise. Though he tried many times, Tausk could never reconstruct exactly what he had answered. The intensity of his desire to see himself acknowledged in Pelz's eyes was like a fever, burning the words from his consciousness even as he was speaking them. The only thing of which Tausk was certain was that he had revealed himself more nakedly in that half hour than he had imagined possible and that he had left the study in a daze, bewildered about whether he had won over the rabbi or had shamed himself irretrievably.

Pelz never referred to their conversation again, and within a short time Tausk's gifts were conceded throughout the seminary. The gulf between him and the others was too great to arouse the usual jealousies, which were confined instead to fierce contests for who would be the rabbi's second-best student. But for Tausk, the more praise his exegetical mastery won from his peers, the more disconnected he felt from his triumphs. He was entirely at home in the yeshiva and adapted to its rhythms more naturally than to any other place he had ever lived, but something he could not clearly name barred him from responding with the same rapt passion as everyone else. His brilliance existed in isolation, a mental facility unconnected to anything else inside himself. Years later he would compare his early self to one of the musical prodigies who were regularly being discovered in the shtetls and sent out to earn their—and their families'—fortunes in the capitals of Europe. Only in his case, that virtuosity coexisted with a fundamental lack of pleasure in music itself. Against his will, the thought slowly took shape that if Rabbi Pelz's teachings had real substance, Tausk's indifference to the question of their truth or falsity must surely reveal itself in the work Tausk submitted to him. If he could continue to succeed so brilliantly, there had to be something grievously wrong, Tausk thought, not merely with him but with Rabbi Pelz himself. Without diminishing the wide-ranging learning that buttressed everything he said, Tausk deliberately began to make his answers more provocative, as though to force Rabbi Pelz to hear his pupil's inner discord. It was not himself, but Rabbi Pelz, whom Tausk wanted to safeguard from the unspoken taunt of his prize pupil's ingenuity, or rather, Tausk wanted to compel the rabbi to rescue him from his own arid virtuosity. To love Rabbi Pelz and, as his pupil, to exceed all his expectations without feeling any love for what Pelz himself revered, was turning everything into a perverse and poisonous farce.

Once or twice, in spite of the fear Avraham Pelz inspired even in those who cared for him the most, Tausk tried to find a way to speak directly to him about his distress. He had braced himself for either compassion or anger but not for the glacial impassivity with which the *rav* heard him out. For Pelz, it was not part of a Jew's task to monitor the depth of his belief. Christians might agonize over their loss of faith, he explained, as though discussing a disease from which he was determined to keep his distance, but for Jews, study and obedience were all that was asked. "The gentiles want to make themselves *interesting* with their spiritual crises," Pelz said, his voice suffused with contempt, "but that is just idolatry and self-regard." He dismissed Tausk with a curt nod and returned to his books without saying another word.

Tausk was unable to decide whether the *rav* cared too little for him to offer any help, or whether feelings like his were really so alien to Pelz that he was incapable of recognizing their danger. From that day on, though, Tausk sensed that the erosion of his trust in his teacher was merely the first of a succession of renunciations that were far from over. He still worked hard to win Rabbi Pelz's familiar nod of approval when he said something especially thoughtful and sometimes daydreamed about exercising a similar sway over pupils of his own one day. Yet without being fully aware of it at first, Tausk found himself taking ever-greater risks in the audacity of his views. A note of sly mockery crept into his discussion of biblical stories, never in Rabbi Pelz's hearing, but among his fellow students, and especially when he was doing lessons with the youngest pupils, who were starting to look up to him as a sage only a few degrees below the *rav* himself. After Rabbi Pelz's derisive comment about Christian self-worship, Tausk secretly sought out their writings, and although he found them even more implausible than those of his own tradition, he knew instantly that in them he had found the weapon with which to shake Rabbi Pelz's serenity.

Tausk never said anything critical of Rabbi Pelz, but in the evening conversations among the students, he began, indirectly at first and then more boldly, to suggest that as far as he was concerned, at least as a thought experiment, the possibility of Christ's divinity need not be categorically excluded. As a legend, Tausk said, it was just as profound as any of the ones in their own Scriptures, and surely, Rabbi Pelz himself had taught them that something of value could be extracted from anything that moves people to religious devotion. Tausk was far from trying to incite anyone to convert, and as soon as he finished talking and saw the alarmed looks on the boys' faces, he found himself worried that Rabbi Pelz would hear about the episode. He swore the students to secrecy and joked that learning how to dispute against proselytizers sent out by the Christian religious orders was always worthwhile. But even if Pelz should come to hear of what he had said, Tausk was more curious than fearful of the consequences. He imagined some kind of great theological debate in which he would be required to defend his position against various challengers from the school, including, in the end, perhaps even Rabbi Pelz himself, who—and this was crucial to the whole fantasy—would ultimately vanquish him. It would be Tausk's first significant public performance, and he intended it to be a masterpiece.

The next morning before breakfast little Benny Perelemutter brought him Rabbi Pelz's letter of banishment. Its tone made clear the uselessness of any appeal, and Tausk knew better than to try. No one talked to him as he packed his cardboard suitcase, and when he walked out the door, not one of the pupils among whom he had lived so much as looked up to wish him farewell.

By comparison, the hostility that Tausk sensed walking through the hallways of the Castle seemed mild. There was a constant traffic in rumors to account for the Count-Governor's unfathomable trust in "his little Jew." No one guessed that both men knew the desolation of having left behind something that had once been vital to their self-understanding and shared a certain chagrin at their vulnerability to such feelings. Tausk felt himself move into what he only half-mockingly called the bleakness of his acts with a contempt for his cleverest schemes that was exceeded only by the still-greater contempt he felt for anyone defenseless enough to be ensnared by them. The shock of his expulsion from the yeshiva made Tausk regard his present good fortune with the skeptical gaze of a man who has received an early and near-lethal lesson in his own vulnerability, but it did nothing to diminish his scorn for the people among whom he now worked. He certainly coveted all that the goyim he now served could give him; but these desires never engaged more than a small part of his soul, and he often felt quite indifferent to the rewards that his intelligence was starting to bring within reach. Very soon his power would be able to touch most of the town's population, and with that authority would come a marked increase in the bribes that the Castle officials regarded as wholly normal supplements to their salaries. But seeing the fear he inspired in those summoned to his office, whether they were there as subordinates whose reports required amplification or as citizens brought in for questioning, thrilled him in a way that counting the growing pile of gold crowns in his strongbox never would. To Wiladowski's formulaic question of what he liked best about his new responsibilities, Tausk replied with the expected banalities about duty and public service. But his own silent answer was considerably simpler: "I like to watch them squirm."

As the circle of those vulnerable to his intimidation widened, Tausk had to recognize that for him, power was not a means to some further goal but something deeply satisfying in itself. In his own eyes, the value of his new life was confirmed by the degree of dread he was able to arouse, and he would have sacrificed any reward, including promotion to a higher post, if it required giving up direct intervention in people's lives. In this, he differed completely from someone like Matthias Pfister, who used every possible occasion to proclaim himself an idealist of the most conservative Catholic hue, but whose actions, especially his divulging of confidential government documents in return for stock market tips, revealed him to be eminently at home in his own pragmatic century, eager to oblige the wishes of the new industrialist classes, whether these were represented by his fellow Catholics, by Lutherans, or, if absolutely unavoidable, even by suitably baptized Jews. It was not that Tausk always refused a bribe, but without fully admitting it to himself, he regarded such perks as secondary, and he pocketed the offerings almost as an afterthought, with the kind of distracted nonchalance that, were the term not so absurdly out of place, one would have been tempted to call aristocratic.

Wiladowski, whose private fortune, particularly since his marriage to one of the wealthiest heiresses in the Empire, was more than sufficient to make his own flamboyant corruption a matter of professional reflex, not genuine need, called the Jewish spymaster the sole inflexible moralist on his staff, a charge that infuriated Tausk because he recognized both its accuracy and its implicit derision. No one in the Castle, especially not Wiladowski, could have guessed how hard Tausk struggled to leave behind the intellectual habits acquired in his years as a rabbinical student. Yet the inability to break completely with one's past, even when it has no place in one's present life, was another and perhaps the deepest of the strands connecting Tausk and his patron. Though each privately found the other's pride in his lineage absurd, both men honored their ancestries as essential parts of themselves. And like all acts of homage to an idealized aspect of one's own being, their racial and dynastic pride carried with it unexpected pangs of self-denigration. Both had been raised in strict regimens, according to clear and uncompromising codes, and they were bound to experience the immense distances they had crossed to arrive at their present attitudes not merely as a self-betrayal but as a severing from the only histories they found meaningful. The realization that the most vital prompting of their heritages was precisely what they needed to ignore in order to survive was a source of intense, if intermittent, anguish and helped account for the mood of unexplained tension in which all of the Castle's business was carried out.

To men of Wiladowski's caste, whose loyalties were based on a constantly recalibrated conjunction of family tradition, practical opportunity, and personal impulse, infidelity to one's earlier self was a familiar predicament. But to most of the Empire's Jews, the very possibility of such a betrayal had been unimaginable only a generation and a half earlier, when their choices were strictly limited by both law and custom. For them, the exhilaration of their new possibilities was often accompanied by a sense of remorse at everything they had abandoned along the way. Still, returning to the life from which they had so recently freed themselves made no more sense than it would have for Wiladowski to look forward to dying in battle for his Emperor because his ancestors had done so since the Middle Ages. No doubt the alarming rise in nervous disorders and melancholia among both the nobility and the newly assimilated Jews was due in part to both groups' finding it impossible to live according to tribal customs that had endured for centuries. Even for a man like Moritz Rotenburg, only the concentration required to administer his labyrinthine business interests helped keep at bay a growing tendency to melancholy. Lately there were many days when he emerged from his study, having just gone over the correspondence from his associates abroad, to find himself struggling to shake off a sense of lingering depression. Choosing to sit down to lunch alone, in a silence unbroken except for the discreet sounds of the head butler directing the household staff, was more a symptom than a cause of his mood, but there were times he actually welcomed being interrupted at the table by old Katinka, the first maid Dina and he had ever engaged, although she rarely spoke an intelligible sentence and looked more funereal each month. The firm's senior employees were convinced it must be his son's political sympathies that worried Rotenburg, but in this, as in most of their guesses about him, they were quite wrong. He took for granted that a young man with an independent income and the consequent expectation of having his every whim carefully listened to might proclaim himself a socialist and was quietly amused to notice how sharp Hans was when it came to calculating the dividends due on the shares he had inherited from his mother. Whenever the yield dipped more than a few points from the previous quarter, Hans politely, but with an impressive folder of company reports from prior years, asked for an explanation of the drop in his profits. As he did any sign of astuteness about money, Moritz viewed Hans's concern as entirely positive, and since the boy was his sole heir, he hoped that it was simply a matter of time before his demand for information would extend to asking for a larger voice in the day-to-day management of the whole enterprise.

Moritz knew better than to look for companionship in someone of his son's age and temperament, and his sense of isolation had little to do with the entirely predictable differences between them. What he had not expected, though, was how his own success would end up distancing him from his former ways of experiencing the world. He was still fluent in the Yiddish he had spoken with his parents and then with Dina in the years before Hans was born, but now he used it largely as a source of a few piquant expressions for which German had no equivalent or as a sign of ethnic solidarity when Jews from the shtetls visited him soliciting financial assistance. As though to disguise a gulf he thought was in danger of becoming unbridgeable, Rotenburg steadily increased his contributions to the most prominent yeshivas throughout the east and labored to convince himself that the pamphlets on Jewish history and customs to which he subscribed in great number spoke to an undiminished feeling of identification with the traditions of his people. But sometimes, after meetings like the one with Nathan Kaplansky, he allowed himself to measure just how far he felt from identifying with anyone at all.

Before his illness Moritz had spent many hours at the Mendelssohn Club, in his capacity as chairman of both its Executive and Finance committees, and in order to be seen socializing on equal terms with the other successful Jews in town. In reality, though, he felt he had little in common with any of them. It was not merely his wealth that separated him from acquaintances of twenty years' standing like poor Rudi Pichler, who was so relentless in the courtroom and so henpecked at home, or envious gossips like Gerhard Himmelfarb. But years of dealing with financiers and senior government officials in half a dozen countries, and being required by the diversification of his holdings to react to global developments with dispassionate self-interest, had transformed him in ways he was not prepared to let anyone see. Unlike Wiladowski, Moritz had never been received by His Imperial Majesty himself, let alone been invited to one of the Empress

Elisabeth's spectacular hunts, but in the Ministries charged with stabilizing the Empire's precarious finances, the advice of this provincial Jew, who had never fought a duel or learned to sit on horseback without visible nervousness, was solicited much more frequently than the Count-Governor's.

Money and power, in spite of their negative resonance in the minds of most litterateurs, are profoundly imaginative qualities, as capable of effecting a metamorphosis in someone's character as is the experience, in a differently constituted soul, of a great work of art or a beautiful woman. And since every transformation necessarily entails discarding a prior way of being, there are perhaps more people than we think for whom even the most longed-for changes are accompanied by a sense of unease at finding they have sloughed off traits they once considered essential to their whole character. An outside observer would have found it difficult to point to any real alteration in the routines Rotenburg had followed for the past thirty years, but inwardly his attitude toward everything had changed, and, in his own uncomfortable self-assessment, not always for the more humane. It was as though he no longer completely identified with himself, as though the person he had become had hollowed out, without entirely displacing, the person he had been, so that now the two coexisted, making it difficult for him to take entirely seriously the local responsibilities that had devolved upon him and that he made sure to fulfill more scrupulously than ever. He realized that his acceptance of one office after another was widely interpreted as a desire for dominance, but he preferred accusations of ambition to the charge of indifference to the honors the community had in its power to bestow.

Like a great novelist who spends so much time living among his characters that in the end he begins to find their company more compelling than that of the people actually around him, Rotenburg had joined in the conversation conducted among the best-informed men in the world's financial capitals for so long that in his thoughts, he had begun to address all his serious remarks to their ears alone. When the full board of the Mendelssohn Club was called to order, Moritz noticed that it took an act of deliberate self-narrowing before he could attend to the preoccupations of his immediate circle with the requisite show of zeal. He knew how passionately an embittered man like Himmelfarb, who had twice avoided bankruptcy court only because of a secret loan from one of the Rotenburg holding companies, would seize upon any sign that Moritz was allowing his wider interests to distract him from the town's concerns. There was, though, no one to whom Rotenburg could admit these feelings. Moreover, since it is unfortunately impossible to converse with one's financial portfolio, no matter how artfully diversified, Rotenburg had little choice except to spend his evenings alone or to linger in the club reading room, politely enduring Rudi Pichler's inane chatter or, if he was luckier, the condescension of a beautiful young firebrand like the Demetz girl.

In his own way, each of the three men would have been appalled to hear himself compared with either of the others. A shtetl prodigy like Tausk had been brought up to regard his mental gifts as the sign of a quasi-divine election, and his whole turbulent career, from talmudic wunderkind to de facto master of the Castle's security apparatus, only corroborated his belief that such uniqueness had to be paid for by sacrificing any chance at ordinary human intimacy. But the conviction that intelligence was necessarily accompanied by loneliness, an idea that a century earlier would have struck most of the country's foremost thinkers as the delusion of a crank, was now so widespread that even a sensible man like Moritz Rotenburg accepted his emotional isolation as inevitable, while Wiladowski saw it as confirmation of his superiority over those he would otherwise have had to acknowledge as his equals in rank or social influence.

It is doubtful, though, that it would have occurred to many of their fellow citizens to connect figures as different as Wiladowski, Rotenburg, and Tausk, except for the much-discussed fact that together they effectively controlled the affairs of the whole province. What underground pamphleteers liked to unmask as "the iron alliance of government ministry, private capital, and secret police" was already common knowledge, and public gossip linked the three men just as intimately as did revolutionary journalists. Perhaps too, their more oblique affinities could become visible only through the contrast provided by an outsider like Brugger. Nothing had prepared the Jews of the town for Brugger's recklessness. His joy in the sheer effrontery of his transformations sanctioned whatever his listeners secretly longed to experience themselves. Brugger gave the impression of traversing enormous inner distances without suffering a moment's dizziness, and for those among his followers who felt themselves twisted by the force of irreconcilable longings, there was something thrilling in the dismissal of nostalgia or regret in his demand that they change their lives at once and entirely.

"He's the first Jew I have ever met who really doesn't give a damn about proving to everyone how innocent he is" was what Sonnenschön wrote his sister, urging her to come join them instead of continuing with her studies. "I know you are laughing at me, Sonia, but can you imagine what it means to have as our teacher a man who has freed himself completely of the need to please others? It makes no difference to him whether anyone likes him or not, and I sometimes think he would be just as happy without a single follower instead of the crowd that he now has around him all the time. Do you remember, when we were little, how Father always used to take his hat off on the street whenever an officer walked by and how ashamed we were for him and swore we'd never be like that? But were we any different, parroting whatever nonsense adults asked for, just so we wouldn't damage our chances of getting into the right high school? How often did *you* repeat to yourself our father's pet speech about one black mark on our records and we'd never be admitted to a decent school and how Jews had to be at least three times as good as any Christian just to be considered for a place in one of *their* colleges? I know that it rang in my ears every time I wanted to open my mouth and protest some stupid rule or other. I could never admit this to anyone but you, Sonia, but do you know that there was a time when I was so worried about doing well that before I handed in an important test, I used to say a quick Hebrew prayer over it, and then, just in case that might not be enough, I usually also traced a little cross on the first page with my fingertips, in case their God had more power than ours with the examiners? I never told you any of this when we were going to school together, but the way you used to look at me, sitting there at my desk, petrified of not getting every single problem right, made me think you knew what I was going through. And now that you have matriculated at the university, how many people are you being careful not to offend?

"I am not mocking you, Sonia, I am just trying to answer all the questions you and Mother asked me the last time I came to see you. I admit that at first I was put off by Brugger's self-dramatization, it seemed so, well, you know what I mean, so typically Jewish, but then I began to understand that he was doing it on purpose to make people like me see how wonderful it feels to stop censoring ourselves all the time. It's as though he were making himself coarse and melodramatic for *us*, and if you only knew, the way I do, how delicate a man he really is, you'd understand what an amazing gift he is bestowing on us. You have always known how I used to cringe inside if somebody I was with still talked with a Yiddish accent or was vulgar enough to wave his hands around while he was speaking, especially if there were any gentiles around. Before Brugger taught me to revel in our instinct for excess, I think I was more afraid of seeming vulgar than of humiliating all my friends. And if you are honest with yourself, Sonia, you'll admit that the self-restraint we prided ourselves on was just our more circumspect way of doffing our hats to the goyim, and our flawless diction was how people of our generation continued to step into the muddy streets and leave *them* the sidewalk—not out of cowardice, oh, good heavens, no, but so that they'd finally have to admit how well mannered we Jews had become. Do you have any idea how freeing it is just to let oneself become hysterical, to talk as loudly as one feels like, and to shout for attention in a coffeehouse without wondering what people at the next table will think of you? To shrug off all that suffocating caution is the best thing that could happen to a Jew today, even if she is about to become a Doctor of Medicine like my wonderful sister."

But no matter how much mockery Sonnenschön thought he had endured before joining Brugger, it is unlikely to have matched the contempt in Tausk's voice when he steamed open the enormous packet of letters Sonnenschön had sent back to Russia. Tausk called in Roublev, his second-in-command, to read out various choice sentences, and afterward Roublev swore that it had been a long time since he had seen the spymaster's talent for mimicry exercised with so much glee. But there was one paragraph that particularly caught Tausk's attention and made him look through the whole parcel again more slowly. It was a sentiment Sonnenschön had kept out of the letter to his sister but used twice, even underlining it once with thick pen strokes, in writing to some friends from a Jewish hiking fraternity in which it seemed he had been active as an adolescent. To them, Sonnenschön wrote in the tones of a man who had undergone a decisive illumination. He became openly rapturous about what he called his teacher's didactic savagery. Nothing had torn him more cleanly away from the cowardice and hesitation of his years at home than Brugger's consecration of every one of his most extreme desires and the permission he gave to act on them, whatever the consequences. Brugger had shown him that Jews too could taste the voluptuousness of destruction without guilt, and when they all were out on a mission together, he felt himself completely free, soaring above history and race on a path no bird of prey had ever known. It was true, Sonnenschön admitted, that in the world Brugger opened for his disciples, comfort and horror had an equal share, but even in the midst of devastation he felt nearer to the great Redemption than at any time before. The books they all had grown up reading had deliberately deceived them; it was not by following prohibitions that they could regain innocence, but only by learning from within their own hearts how to sanctify that which is forbidden. But he knew this was the wrong way to put it, because to the man whose understanding has been opened, everything is already holy, and even to speak of the forbidden is to fall back into the old divisions. He understood now that whatever he might do was already pure in the crystalline light of his new consciousness. Sonnenschön kept repeating that it was his duty to urge his old friends to leave their careers and families behind and join him at Brugger's side while there was still time to free themselves from the customs of a dying world and be written into the book of the new kingdom. Once the final gathering had begun, no one would be able to choose whether he was to be numbered among the redeemed or discarded like an empty husk.

Even to Tausk's professional eye, there was something unnerving in Sonnenschön's haphazard stringing together of personal confession, hints at serious breaches of the law, and messianic proselytizing. Tausk found it uncharacteristically difficult to decide how to use the letters, and he wasted several hours cross-referencing dates and timetables from the growing dossier on what he was beginning to call his lumpen heresiarchs, trying to see if there might be any link between Sonnenschön's wanderings through the province and the killing at the Bukovina hunting lodge. But if a connection did exist, it was too vague to act on legally, and Tausk's instincts told him that a man who was so proud of beating up a gentile in a tavern brawl was likely to find his desire for transgression satisfied well short of sacrificial murder. On his own, Sonnenschön was insignificant. Whatever he did would depend entirely on the will of the man whose instrument he had now become.

Since leaving the yeshiva, Tausk had continued to read some of the more celebrated Christian Church Fathers. He did so less out of interest in their dogmas than as his own strange way of continuing the quarrel with Rabbi Pelz and also, in part, because he clung to the odd notion that to understand the people among whom he was now living, a knowledge of their theology was indispensable. His reading did little to revise the generally low opinion he held of Christian intellectual rigor, but there was a pleasure, which the Count-Governor appeared to encourage, in annoying a pompous fool like Matthias Pfister by suddenly interjecting some grim quotation by St. Augustine into a discussion of police tactics. Now, after putting away his surveyor's maps of Bukovina, with the train lines and roads going near the Wiladowski country estate carefully inked in, and filing away in his private safe the copies he had made of Sonnenschön's letters, Tausk couldn't stop himself from comparing his life at the Castle with what it had been at the yeshiva, where a thug like Robert Sonnenschön would never have had a claim on anyone's attention. Although Tausk rarely allowed himself to think about whether he still missed any part of his former existence, he was struck, and in a way even relieved, that it was a religious text that immediately suggested itself as the aptest commentary on his changed state. Even more appropriate, in his eyes, was that the phrase came not from one of the famous rabbis whom he used to cite with limitless facility but from St. Jerome, the great Jew-hating ascetic, who wrote: "Then the desert held me: would that it had never let me go."

Tausk liked the line so much he thought he might try it out on Wiladowski, perhaps at the end of that same week's report, and he already looked forward to his master's tolerant amusement at having to put up with hearing what he would probably mistake for still another Hebraic sage from Spain or Morocco, quoted at him alongside the political advice that he had grown to value above anyone else's—in direct proportion, so the Count-Governor's critics in both Vienna and the Provincial Council were already emphasizing, as his own judgment was becoming increasingly more eccentric and unsound.

2

Elisabeth Demetz—he still found it hard to think of her as Batya—was the last person Hans Rotenburg had expected to run into in the Josef Quarter. He recognized her first, coming out of one of the tenement buildings near his flat, dressed more simply than he remembered and carrying a large basket under her arm. She was looking down as she walked, treading carefully in order not to fall on the icy front steps, but a moment later she had caught sight of him as well, and it was impossible for them not to stop and acknowledge each other. They had managed to avoid being alone together since Hans's return, and in spite of the forced naturalness with which they greeted each other, their discomfort was apparent. But alongside Hans's ill ease was an unexpected rush of surprise at how desirable Batya looked in the dull midafternoon light. He hadn't remembered her going out without a hat before, and her hair, which she normally wore in elegant curls, was loose today and hung straight to her shoulders. Her face appeared slightly flushed from the cold and the exertion of climbing up and down several flights of stairs. Hans was unaware that she came here regularly to distribute warm clothing and food to needy families she knew from the Zionist Youth Movement, and she told him that she had just finished her last visit of the day. Largely as a reflex, Hans asked her if she wanted to join him for something warm to drink on such a chilly day. He was certain she would politely decline and plead other obligations; instead she quickly accepted his offer. It was only when he saw her looking up at him with an amused smile that he realized there was no place in the neighborhood to which he could bring a woman like Batya. They would have to go upstairs to his apartment, and though she clearly knew all about it—was there anyone in town who didn't? he was starting to wonder!—Hans felt vexed at the idea. Considering his flat's unsavory reputation, it was embarrassing that the first woman he actually brought here should be a former girlfriend who, by all accounts, was quite happy with his successor and showed no interest in renewing their intimacy.

László had done his best with the place. A faint smell of moldy newspapers and wet ceiling plaster would probably linger until spring, when the apartment could be given a thorough airing, but at least it was now possible to spend one's time there in reasonable comfort. The old stove had been replaced by a larger one, powerful enough to spread an agreeable warmth within a short time of being lit, and the dark brocade curtains, full-length floor lamps, and heavy oak bookshelves had completely transformed the rooms. Batya looked around with unashamed curiosity and wondered who had picked out such uninteresting pieces for Hans, many of which struck her as much too ponderous for the size of the apartment. To her, it resembled a prosperous doctor's consulting room more than a secret love nest, and although she had long since stopped thinking of Hans with any desire, Batya found herself inwardly pleased by her comparison.

They had just sat down in the stolid oak and leather chairs arranged about the room by László's staff when Batya realized from Hans's expression that he had no idea how to prepare the snack to which he had invited her. She quickly got up and walked over to the cupboard, which, except for fresh bread, was amply stocked with everything necessary. On one of the upper shelves, she found an assortment of expensive English tea biscuits and shortbread in an unopened tin, which she brought to the table, along with a large pot of coffee and some different jams. She had been running around the Josef Quarter since early morning without a chance to stop for a meal, and although it was getting near dinnertime, she was glad of the refreshment before returning home. Ever since Rina Fischbein, one of the mothers in the district whom Batya was trying to help, had pointed out Hans's flat to her in a tone of scandalized disapproval, Batya had been eager to see what it looked like from inside. Now that she had done so, though, and finished her coffee and biscuits, Batya had no wish to prolong the visit. Hans had barely said a word to her the whole time they were eating, and Batya began to find their mutual awkwardness absurd. She thought to herself that perhaps ex-lovers who haven't faded into vague friends ought to have the courtesy to leave town permanently to avoid embarrassing each other. But just as she was preparing to get up and make her way back downstairs, Hans suddenly asked her whether any of Ernst's old friends had been talking out of turn about him lately. He was smiling as he said it, but Batya knew Hans well enough to recognize how charged the question was for him. His voice had an edginess that she remembered only too well from their quarrels, and he sat watching her face with a concentration that belied his casual tone.

More than anything else, the fact that the first serious words he had spoken to her in almost two years should be about other people offended Batya. "That's simply outrageous." She bristled in reply. "Ernst and his friends do not talk 'out of turn' to me. How can you let yourself say something so offensive? Whatever we discuss is our concern, and I don't see that we need your approval. Besides, what makes you think that anyone bothers gossiping about you at all?" For several minutes Hans said nothing more, annoyed with himself at his clumsiness. With Christoph and Leo, he could always count on steering the conversation in whatever direction he wanted. But he should have foreseen that Batya wouldn't put up with being interrogated. Seeing her out there on the Maximilianstrasse, especially today, had alarmed him sufficiently that he had no choice. If Asher had received Hans's message, then in less than an hour and a half he would be arriving at the front door, just ahead of the rest of the group. Hans intended to present Asher to them tonight, and nothing was more disconcerting than the possibility that Ernst was already plotting against him. Batya's appearance in the neighborhood was probably just a coincidence, but not one he could risk letting pass without further probing.

But even as he was telling himself all this, Hans was aware of responding to Batya with a tension that had no connection to anything they were saying. As it grew warmer, her body gave off a subtle perfume, intensified by the closeness of the room. She sat there, absently stroking the nails of one hand with the fingertips of the other and continued to avoid looking at him. When he first made up his mind to break with Batya and go abroad, Hans had been convinced that he no longer cared for her. He had thought that having her out of his life forever was precisely what he desired. But the loneliness that tormented him during his first months in London had shown him how wrong he had been; now that it was too late, he realized that his indifference had as its necessary condition his belief that she would never consent to their rupture. When that belief disappeared, so too did his feeling of indifference. Slowly, though, the lack of any direct contact with her and the exhilaration of his double life—learning during the day how large business concerns were run and at night how revolutionary parties were organized—accomplished the detachment from Batya that he thought he had reached when he left Austria. New habits and a series of casual love affairs did the rest, and by the time Hans returned home he mostly had stopped thinking about her. But Batya's relationship with Ernst jeopardized all his plans. Her presence in the Josef Quarter felt like the violation of an implicit compact between them, and whether it was deliberate or not ultimately mattered less than her reemergence into his history. Hans felt an almost sensual excitement at the complications this entanglement was bound to bring.

Through their silence they could hear the quarreling voices of the family upstairs. Batya had gone over to the window while Hans was collecting himself and pressed her head against the pane. Outside, the new snow was shifting in the evening wind. Hans got up and stood beside her, so that they were looking out together into the ice blue January twilight. As simply as he could, he leaned toward her and said, "I am truly sorry, Batya. I had no business using a phrase like that. I was just worried you were getting the wrong impression about a lot of things from Ernst. You know that he used to be my closest friend, so naturally I feel a little touchy on the topic."

Although her tone made it clear that Batya was still far from mollified, Hans was relieved that at least she didn't withdraw completely. "And you think I have had something to do with your estrangement?" she asked. "Isn't that a convenient explanation? Whenever two men differ, there must be a woman behind it. If it is any consolation, Ernst seems quite troubled by how differently you two now look at everything, but when I asked him if that had anything to do with me, he said no, not at all, that you weren't the type to get pettily jealous." Then, after another interval, during which she finally turned her gaze from the street outside to look directly at Hans, Batya went on, less forcefully than before. "This is all a little mortifying. At the beginning I often reproached Ernst that he and I spent far too much time talking about you, and now you and I are sitting together for the first time in ages, and we are deep in conversation about Ernst. Aren't either of you ever going to talk to *me* without always needing to bring up something the other one said? I sometimes get the impression that I am the one who ought to be jealous, you two are more involved with each other than either of you ever has been with me."

Hans found the idea of Ernst and Batya talking about him at all acutely disagreeable, but he had learned enough from his earlier misstep not to let her see his annoyance. The wind outside was getting stronger, and the thin glass windowpanes scarcely provided any barrier. Batya shivered slightly from a sudden gust, and Hans drew the thick curtains together and led her back to their chairs near the stove. He did not have enough time for the maneuvers such a delicate situation required, but anything was preferable to letting Batya and Asher Blumenthal meet in his apartment. He pretended that she had meant her comment about being jealous merely as idle banter and began to tell her about his time abroad. More than anything, he said, he had missed talking to her and sharing his new discoveries with her and, yes, he had to confess, with Ernst as well. But ever since he had returned, both had made it clear they wanted nothing more to do with him. It was as though he had become a pariah, deserted by the very people on whom he had counted most. As a result, he felt more alone now than he had in London or Zurich.

He knew he was taking a chance by being so direct, but this time Batya didn't seem offended at a word like *desertion*. Instead she stirred the remains of her coffee and appeared to be studying the richly colored patterns in the carpet at her feet. It occurred to her that whoever had installed these thick Persian rugs for Hans had ensured that anything said here would be inaudible from outside. She was suddenly struck by the idea that while privacy had always been necessary to Hans, it was somehow never entirely personal for him, not even when they had been a couple. Oddly enough, as soon as Batya put it that way to herself, it became important to her that Hans understood what she was thinking. She and Ernst had not deserted Hans; they had simply renounced the place in history that he saw as a birthright. "Ever since I have known you," she said abruptly, "you have had this powerful conviction of being destined to become a historical figure, and it comes through in the way you talk about everything you are doing. It is part of what I found so attractive about you, that's true, but toward the end, whenever I thought about it seriously, it made me want to get as far away as possible. I don't know how I could ever convince you—or even if you'll try to understand what I mean—but for me, it is the body's marks, not history's, that are indelible. Listening to you today and seeing what you have done with this apartment, I realize how unsettling it must be to experience yourself . . . and the world . . . from inside like that. I used to think that maybe every rich boy, especially if he is an only child, adored by his parents, grows up with this sense that whatever he does is immediately part of history. But I have never seen it pushed as far. No disagreement is ever just a private quarrel with Hans Rotenburg; to oppose you in anything is equivalent to criticizing the general interest of mankind. You feel every difference of opinion like treason against the future, and I suppose that puts an unbearable pressure on you to make all the right decisions. But you have to understand how exhausting that is to be around after a while. Forgive me, if I am sounding harsh. It is not at all my intention. But I want to answer you honestly about why we aren't with you anymore."

Hans was startled by the frankness of Batya's attack. "But it isn't only me." He shrugged his shoulders with assumed resignation, trying hard to keep his tone as measured as she had hers. "Don't you think Ernst feels the same way? Otherwise, why wouldn't he simply live on his father's estate, with nothing to do except wait until the title and lands all belong to him? And what about you, Batya? Are you really all that different? Isn't everything you Zionists do justified by the same principle? What else is all that noise about draining some malarial swamp in Palestine about if you don't believe you are changing history? Every time someone moves there and writes you back a letter describing a new settlement, you treat it like a turning point in the course of the world. And the more romantic-sounding a Hebrew name they can give their collection of huts, the more it thrills all of you. The difference is that I believe sentimental gestures like that belong only in novels, not in the real world. At least not if you are serious about wanting to change it."

"By murdering people, I suppose?" she interrupted, with her face flushed, not from the cold now but with exasperation. "Is that how you are planning to change the political realities in this country?"

Hans drew his breath in sharply and, although they were alone, couldn't stop himself from quickly scanning the room before saying anything else. He would hardly have been more shocked if Batya had pulled a police warrant from her coat pocket. "Are you playing a game with me, Batya?" he asked. "Is that what it all seems like to you? Obviously I was right, and Ernst and his friends have been babbling after all. I suppose it is pointless to ask you what they have said exactly. That would just be more of my high-handedness. Please, just look at me, Batya. I haven't raised my voice, and I am not trying to browbeat you. But don't you understand that I am the one who is vulnerable here, not you? One word about this could land me, and everybody else involved, in jail for the rest of our lives. Even Ernst would certainly be punished for not reporting what he has heard to the authorities. So if anyone ought to feel threatened, surely you can see that it's me."

This time it was Batya whose eyes widened with astonishment. Hans's reaction caught her off guard, and her instinct was to make light of it as quickly as possible. "Don't be so melodramatic, Hans," she said in what she hoped sounded like her familiar bantering tone. "You know that I couldn't denounce you to anyone, and not just because of the risk to Ernst. For one thing, I refuse to believe you would be stupid enough to try any of the horrible things you seem to like talking about in these meetings of yours. It's just too ridiculous. I have told Christoph and Leo the same thing I said to Ernst when we began seeing each other. They're all dead inside, anyway, the people you hate. They and their Empire along with them. Let it go, Hans; it's not worth consuming your life with plots and fantasies. I won't betray you, but you can be sure that eventually someone will or that the authorities will find out some other way. They always do. And you will have thrown away your life for nothing—for some crazy threats no one except Wiladowski's spies take seriously anyway."

"And what about Ernst?" Hans asked, quite calmly now. "Does he agree with you that it is all crazy fantasies?"

"I am not sure I understand all the different things he has been feeling since you came back." Batya's voice, like Hans's, had resumed its normal timbre, but her unhappiness at the turn the conversation had taken was apparent in the way her limbs were hunched together as though to take up the least possible space in the room. "My guess"—she went on—"is that although he would never admit it, Ernst is mostly just confused by everything that has been happening. He hasn't told me anything specific about your ideas; all he knows is that what you are involved in isn't right for him, and even if it is mostly just talk, you and I agree he is correct about that, don't we, Hans? I am asking you, please, now that he is out of it, let him be without making things more difficult. He is no risk to you, and you know how hard it is for him to turn his back on you."

"And you don't think it's difficult for me?" Hans thought he sensed a yielding in Batya's tone and pushed his chair closer. "To see you and Ernst reject everything I stand for? You two are the best friends I ever had, and your opinions are still the only ones that really matter to me. If you choose to think what I am doing is just a vicious game, how can that not hurt me? Don't look away like that, Batya; I haven't suddenly become some kind of monster just because my ways of fighting for what is right are different from yours. Yes, I do believe that revolutionaries have to learn to hate, and I suspect the prospect of having to feel such an ignoble emotion is what finally made Ernst decide to oppose me—apart of course from his love for you. I don't imagine for a moment that Ernst is too squeamish to kill—under the right circumstances, that is—but for him, it would have to be done with the proper ceremony. I have gone hunting with him. It is not the idea of taking a life he finds repugnant; it is doing so with loathing in his heart, using sly tricks, and in the company of lower-class types who have never fought a duel or learned to ride a high-spirited horse. And I am not criticizing Ernst either. On the contrary, I am just repeating what he himself as much as admitted: that for all his revulsion at the injustice of our system, he is too much of an aristocrat not to be equally disgusted by the methods necessary to bring it down."

"The methods *you* have decided are necessary," Batya interjected. "You are right to see they aren't his, so why are you surprised at his withdrawing?"

"It's not a question of my being surprised," Hans continued. "I only want to clarify in my own mind what Ernst's and your decision says about me. About what I believe in. Because you see, Batya, I *know* that you are wrong about me. You want to see me as a poseur who enjoys wallowing in sordid plots. But that just makes it easier for you two to go your own way with a clean conscience. As far as I can tell, what our differences really come down to is that you and Ernst have chosen to value your innocence above the welfare of others. Have you ever walked along the river at night and listened to the sound of children too weak to beg, coughing their lungs out, with no food or medicine? Once you have heard it, it is a sound you can never forget. You and Ernst should go see them for yourselves, down under the stone embankments, trying to keep a small fire going out of old newspapers or huddled in front of the Cathedral on Sunday morning, begging for charity—at least until the police drive them away so they won't upset the good worshipers going to mass. Well, when I hear those children and see their parents' anguish, I would risk anything to punish whoever permits such misery to continue. I want the men who govern us to feel some of the same fear and helplessness as those wretched families we have almost stopped noticing anymore. Of course our benevolent rulers don't want to alleviate the situation; after all, they directly benefit from the suffering because it keeps wages low and the workers docile. I can't believe anyone could call *us*, rather than the government, terrorists and murderers. What puzzles me is how a person with a sense of shame can continue living peaceably in a country that brutalizes so many of its own people. I am not talking only about this winter either. Look around, and you'll see that most of our population suffer from hunger and fear every day of their lives. The hatred you and Ernst reject gives a man the strength to fight back. I hate because what I see around me deserves to be hated, whether it's already dying or not. We have been raised to think of our rulers as superior beings, almost like gods, with their elegant carriages and armed guards, so of course the idea of resistance appears unthinkable. But if people can be shown that the Wiladowskis and Zichy-Ferrarises of this world are just as weak and vulnerable as anyone else, that they feel the same fear of dying and flinch from a blow as quickly as the most abject peasant, it might give them the courage to protest the next time their wages are cut. I am not deluded enough to believe terror will alter the government's policies, but if it convinces the workers that they don't need to cower before everyone who wears a uniform or a waistcoat, it could inspire them to change their whole way of thinking about what is possible."

Hans paused to see the effect his words were having, but it was impossible to tell from Batya's expression what she was thinking. She made no move to reply and just sat there staring straight ahead, withdrawn into herself. He felt sure she intended her silence as a reproach to his own insistent fluency, but having gone this far, Hans was no longer able to give up until he had worn out both of them with his arguments. He was starting to find the sound of his own voice exasperating. But it was not a question of winning her over anymore.

"Look"—he began again—"it's true that I have always thought of myself as able to make a difference in the world. But don't you see that everything we used to talk about is coming true? That society is changing faster than ever before, even here in Austria? Helping to speed up those changes, not how large a role I'll end up playing, is what I really care about. I know that the path I have chosen will make me an undesirable to our so-called decent people, but I never expected to find you and Ernst among them. I have to accept the fact that even if our movement is successful, the leaders who come after me will have to disown what we did; no government likes admitting what it owes to the people history calls fanatics and zealots. Today's tame trade unionists like Nathan Kaplansky are appalled by people with my beliefs, but it took decades of revolutionaries willing to break the law before the government was forced to legalize even his milksop version of social reform. Contented slaves are always the most relentless enemies of freedom. Without the threat of class warfare, we still wouldn't have voting rights for anyone but the nobility, and unless we overcome our aversion to violence, it will be another half century before they let women vote at all. Those acts you find so unsavory will demonstrate that if the ruling classes continue to refuse to deal with mild reformers like Kaplansky, there will be more and more revolutionaries like me ready to make them pay a terrible price for their stubbornness. If any of the gentlemen who talk about social justice all day in Parliament ever get to form a government, it will be on the backs of men and women who didn't mind getting their hands dirty doing the shabby back-alley work. And when they feel secure enough to discard us like a ladder that isn't needed anymore, it will only show how indispensable we really were."

The knock on the door was much too timid to be a policeman's, but it reverberated through the room like an explosion. Hans and Batya momentarily froze as though they had been interrupted in something illicit, and when neither of them replied to it, the knock was repeated, slightly more insistently. Hans finally pulled out his pocket watch and, when he saw the time, let out an exasperated groan. "Just a moment, Asher." His voice rose by almost a full octave as he shouted loudly enough to be heard out in the hallway. "I am afraid you will have to wait a few minutes while I finish some urgent business." He shrugged apologetically to Batya and was starting to explain about his visitor, but she was already putting on her coat and waved off his remarks.

"No, Hans, it is quite all right," she told him quietly. "It is high time I got back home. Mother will be worried by now. She doesn't like me coming to this part of town alone, and I don't want to have a quarrel with her tonight. Not after a day like this." She had a slight smile as she said it, but her eyes looked exhausted. "Besides, it is rude to keep your guest waiting out there in the cold." She went on, walking slowly toward the door. "Thank you for being so candid. I wish I had the strength to answer all the things you said, but I wouldn't know how to begin so that it meant anything to you. You certainly aren't interested in contributing to the supplies we bring here to get the families through another night," she said, showing him her empty basket, "and I have another collection drive to organize at the club tomorrow." By now she was reaching for the door handle, and as she pulled open the door, Hans's visitor, who must have been pressing himself against it, nearly tumbled into the room. For an instant Hans looked at both of them blankly, then gathered himself together, and, with obvious reluctance, mumbled, "Fräulein Demetz. Herr Blumenthal." But Batya had already extended her hand to the startled accountant, and after a quick handshake she walked briskly down the steps and out into the street. Asher tried to linger in the stairwell to watch her retreating figure as long as possible, but Hans drew him inside and bolted the door shut behind them.

· ◆ ·

Hans had not seen Asher since their dinner at the Metropole and was surprised at how much worse he was looking after the holidays. Blumenthal had let his sand-colored hair grow long and, in an attempt to appear more thoughtful, now parted it straight down the center. But the decision only encouraged his new tick of constantly straightening his hair with both his hands, giving him the appearance of a man clutching the sides of his head in panic. He seemed unsteady on his feet, and his eyes were red with fatigue and excitement. Asher was even more openly curious about the apartment than Batya had been and, not content with just looking around, went slowly through it, scrutinizing the contents and making appreciative noises every time he came across an object that was recognizably both new and expensive.

Ordinarily, Hans would have found Asher's inquisitiveness offensive, but at that moment he was glad of it since it gave him a chance to settle his nerves after the fiasco with Batya. He was left feeling equally frustrated and embarrassed at the ambiguous role he had just played, unsure how much of his conversation with Batya he could excuse to himself as a performance and how much was the expression of an overpowering need. As long as it served what he thought of as "objective political necessity," playing a part to obtain his ends was completely acceptable, even if the role involved a spurious show of tenderness or jealousy. But it was profoundly disturbing to sense that far from manipulating the whole scene, he had let himself be overwhelmed by it and that a momentary flare-up of his desire for Batya had led him into a whole series of inexcusable blunders, culminating in the near confession that his plans included political murder. The one thing of which he was certain was that Ernst had become his enemy. It was far from clear to him, however, just how much of a threat he represented. And now, rather than be able to focus on what had just happened, he had to compose himself so that neither Asher nor the other members of the cell would suspect how shaky he was feeling. Hans had seen the fascination with which Asher stared at Batya, and there was no doubt about what Asher imagined had been going on in the apartment before his arrival. Asher might have recognized Batya from the Mendelssohn Club, but if so, that was all to the good, since it could only help confirm Hans's reputation as an incorrigible womanizer. At the very least, it gave Hans an immediate way out of his inner turmoil, and it was with the tone of a slightly harassed man of the world that he called out to Asher, who had not yet finished his tour of inspection.

"I don't want to hurry you," he said, gesturing to a chair near the bookshelves, as far away as possible from the one Batya had recently occupied, "and I'll be glad to show you around later. But the people I want you to meet will be here in about half an hour, and it is important that we talk together first. I am sorry about the confusion at the door, but I am grateful that you were so punctual."

Asher looked up at Hans with greater respect than he had shown at the Metropole. Being kept waiting while Hans finished with such a beautiful woman was itself thrilling and fed his hope of being able to use the apartment for the same purpose. A phrase he had overheard in one of the neighborhood taverns suddenly sprang into his mind—"what I love are the really hot ones who copulate like cockroaches on a sofa"—and he felt himself flush with excitement at the prospect of being able to talk like that about his own experiences. But he knew that for it to happen he would have to persuade Hans of his usefulness, and the strain of guessing what he could possibly offer a Rotenburg was excruciating. "Being on time is a professional reflex of mine," he said, trying for a tone that was at the same time both serious and obliging. "Complete dependability is something on which I have always prided myself. But whatever made you write to me at work in the first place? Not that I mind in the least, you understand. In fact, having a letter on Rotenburg stationery delivered to me there boosted my reputation with the section chief enormously."

"I am glad it worked out well for you, but I really didn't have much choice in the matter." Hans was relieved that Asher made no direct mention of the scene in the stairwell and, for the first time since he had seen Batya out on the street, felt fully in command of the situation. "I am sure you gave me your address that night at the restaurant"—he went on—"but I must have lost it going home. Then, when you suddenly stopped coming to the club, I had no way to reach you until the holidays were over and I could send you a note at work."

Asher's excitement was starting to override the prudence he had cautioned himself to maintain ever since receiving Hans's invitation, and he found himself unable not to interrupt. "Well, if what you called me for has anything to do with business, I am your man. I can make your books come out whatever way you want, and no one will be able to prove anything. And if it is for your father, I won't charge him much at all. It's an honor to work for a man like him."

"I am afraid not." Hans shrugged impatiently. "Anyway, after what you told me over dinner, I thought your ambitions were aimed in a completely different direction."

"Well, in the meantime I do still have to eat and pay my rent, you know. Of course I would love to go to work for your father. Just walking in to tell my boss that he would have to find someone else to abuse because I'd been offered a position by Moritz Rotenburg would be worth a month's salary. I can't believe you wouldn't understand that from everything I told you about my life." Asher had the sickening sensation of hearing all his hopes casually brushed aside, just after they had seemed on the verge of being realized. His mouth started to feel horribly dry, and he patted down his hair more frequently. Even as he was trying to convince himself the idea was ridiculous, he couldn't help suspecting that Hans had brought him there only to make a fool out of him. All at once the tension of maintaining his self-control became too much, and though he already knew how much he would regret it later, there was something unspeakably delicious about letting himself go in front of this spoiled boy who had been given everything at birth. "My ambitions?" Asher felt the words cascade out of him like a shameful declaration. "Why even bring them up? Do you have any idea what it was like for me after our dinner, waiting day after day, no, hour after hour, for you to get in touch with me? Being made to feel like some insignificant insect by a man I trusted, for whom I felt the beginnings of a real friendship? Do you know that I was so humiliated it took me ages to dare show my face again in town, where I was sure everyone would be laughing at me? The poor nebbish who deluded himself that he could really interest a rich playboy! What about our great dreams? Don't you remember how we were going to conquer literary Vienna together? I won't even mention my hope that you might lend me this wonderful apartment so that my landlady wouldn't always be shaming me in front of my few friends! Think of how it must feel for me to come rushing over like some lackey in response to your note, just so I'll be able to remember what a real gentleman's flat looks like after I am dismissed to crawl back to my hovel."

After their first encounter Hans thought he was prepared for anything from Asher, but not an outburst like this. Before he could think of a way to calm him, Asher stood up, his face utterly drained of color, and lurched toward Hans with his hand outstretched. "Oh, my God, Herr Rotenburg, I am sorry." He was almost crying as he spoke. "I didn't mean to carry on so shamefully. In fact on my way here I swore to myself a dozen times not to lose control. A strictly professional attitude, that's what I was going to stick to, no matter what. I even stopped in at a tavern and had a double brandy to steady my nerves. It's the first time I have ever been inside a place like that during the day, I swear it! And now I see that's exactly why I am talking like this without being able to stop myself. It's that accursed alcohol. Oh, God, why did I ever have that drink? Why does everything always have to end up in such a hopeless muddle?" Just as quickly as he had gotten up, Asher lowered his arms, fell back into his chair, and went on in a melancholy, resigned voice. "But I am not the only one at fault here. Surely you have got to admit that part of the reason for my distress is the heartless way you have treated me. Really, you do. And it's not fair for you to just sit there and look away with that embarrassed expression. I know I am sweating too much. I can feel and smell it myself, but that just makes me feel worse. If you prefer, I am ready to walk out of here right now and never show my face again. Just tell me honestly what it is you want from me."

Far from being disturbed, Hans was relieved by Asher's confession that he had been drinking. It gave him an excuse to ignore the tirade. "To tell you the truth, Asher," he said, "right now having a double brandy sounds like a fine idea to me. I am sure the only problem is that they served you something ghastly in that tavern, and that is why you are feeling unwell. My prescription is to correct their mistake with a drinkable brand!" Hans went over to the liquor cabinet and was relieved that Herr László had stocked it with everything necessary. He picked out a bottle and some glasses and brought them over to his guest. "Here, Asher, let me pour us both a glass of something that will clear our heads. Let's just forget any misunderstanding and concentrate on our common interests. As you can see, I did remember you liked my cigarettes back at the restaurant, and I had a supply brought in especially for your visit. Just help yourself from the case there on the table."

Asher nodded appreciatively but was clearly feeling worse by the moment. He excused himself and went to find the toilet, from which he emerged, after what seemed to Hans like an interminable amount of time, looking queasier than ever. When he had finally regained his seat, he saw Hans take out a set of papers from the desk drawer and invite him to look them over. "I will, gladly," Asher answered, "only let me have one of these cigarettes first, to finish settling my stomach." He struck a match, inhaled deeply a few times, and then, quickly draining his brandy as well, went on. "There. That's better. Now this really does restore one's spirits. Sorry that rotgut threw me off the way it did. You know how it is. Well, I suppose in theory anyway. I ought to report the tavern keeper to the police. I'll bet he never paid excise tax on that keg of fermented poison. But yes, I do feel quite well again, thank you. Now, let me take a closer look at these documents."

The instant Asher's eyes fell on the papers, he let out a howl as though someone had slapped him across the face. "You have done what?" he cried out. "Without even asking me? And Alexander has already answered you? Here, let me see for myself." He grabbed the first sheet from the table and held it up toward the light as though testing a forged banknote.

"I don't really see why you are so shocked." Hans willed himself to remain calm and not contribute to the scene Asher was eager to provoke. "I thought you would be happy that I took your suggestion so much to heart. I am sure Garber has already written to you himself explaining everything in detail, only you know how slow the mail is over the holidays."

"I notice your letters reached their destination without any delay." Asher had switched from loud outrage to a sulky whine. "And you obviously had no problem remembering Alexander's Vienna address, although you couldn't get a single note to my lodgings over the holidays."

"In fact," Hans said, "I had one of our business agents in Vienna forward Garber's note by special courier, and if you remember, you yourself made a point of having me jot down your friend's whereabouts."

"Really?" Asher sounded dubious. "I don't remember that at all. But, Herr Rotenburg, it is important for me to know if your father is involved in any of this or not. Is it some stock market scheme? But, then, why bother

173

with such an insignificant art review? Wouldn't it make more sense for him to buy a stake in one of the major dailies? I am more confused than ever. Can't you just tell me how all this fits together?"

"Look, Blumenthal"—Hans had begun to check his watch every few minutes—"time really is getting very short, and I do not want any of our, well, let's just call them unusually intense conversations to derail the meeting I have set up."

At this, Asher's face brightened with understanding, and he looked thoroughly pleased with himself at having grasped the real reason for Hans's concern. "So the rest are all goyim," he blurted out. "That is why you are worried about my making a good impression. I understand now. I'll be perfectly restrained, you needn't worry. You forget I work among them all day. Please, go on. There is no way I would embarrass you in front of your gentile friends."

"What's their religion got to do with it?" Hans answered, unable any longer to keep the annoyance out of his tone. "That is not what I meant at all. I just don't want you to get overwrought again, especially around complete strangers."

But Asher was suddenly all business. He went through each of the pages on the table, muttering to himself the whole time he was reading, and only when he had finished did he look up at Hans to say, "I see that Alexander has managed to get you a pretty detailed account of *The New Order*'s balance sheet. I don't know how he did it so quickly, but if these figures are accurate, it is obvious that the journal has very little time left to attract fresh capital before it is forced into bankruptcy. I would wager that if his colleagues knew Alexander was distributing information like this, they wouldn't be very happy with him. So, do you want me to go over these numbers with you now? Have you really decided to take over the journal with Alexander and me? Is this what the whole meeting is about?"

"Yes and no," Hans replied. "I'll come to that presently. Garber's journal is not the sole reason we all are getting together this evening, and I plan to talk about it to everyone else only if the atmosphere seems right. But try to be patient, and I'll fill you in as fully as I can." At that moment they both heard the heavy downstairs door bang open, followed by the muffled sound of men's voices on the stairwell. Hans was noticeably vexed at being cut off. "Damn," he let out. "There's the clatter of Christoph's boots on the steps. He always stomps as if he's on parade. They'll be knocking on the door in a moment. Please, Blumenthal, even if what I say sounds strange to you at first, just be patient. If you have any suggestions, or don't agree with the way I explain certain details, you can tell me once we are alone again, but not in front of the others. All right?"

"Of course, my dear Rotenburg. Don't look so worried. I already promised not to embarrass you in front of your important friends, didn't I? Go on, open the door and don't be anxious on my account. I'll just have another small taste of this outstanding brandy and get myself ready to meet your guests."

· ◆ ·

As bad as Hans's day had been up until then, the meeting with the other conspirators quickly deteriorated into something still worse. When they got to the door, it turned out that Christoph, Joachim, and Manfred had just come from the von Arnstein town house, where Leo lay ill in bed with flu. Without everyone present, there was little they could settle. Hans made no attempt to disguise his frustration, and although he tried his best to keep their discussion moving forward, it was quickly apparent that the assignment of specific tasks would have to wait.

The next day his friends returned to report to Leo what had taken place. He was already feeling better and received them in a small salon off his bedroom. Although it was almost noon, Leo was still wearing pajamas and sat wrapped in a voluminous red silk dressing gown, slightly frayed along the cuffs. Instead of tea or coffee, he was drinking a large cup of hot chocolate into which he dunked a freshly baked sweet roll. Even to his friends, Leo looked more like a cadet at home for the holidays than a political revolutionary, and they were relieved Hans was not there to see him. They could scarcely wait to describe what had happened at the Josef Quarter flat and waved aside Leo's offer of refreshments. Christoph began by telling how comfortable the place now appeared and how Hans had succeeded at last in getting it warm enough for them to take off their coats. "But then," he said, "just as we were settling in, Hans announced that he had someone new to present to the group. We all were surprised, but before we could say anything, from the kitchen or the study, I can't be sure which, he dragged in this impossibly dressed man, who stared at us for the longest time with a completely blank expression on his face, saying absolutely nothing. His forehead quickly became covered with sweat, and since he didn't seem able to move enough to dry himself, it continued to trickle down his face with all of us watching in horrified fascination. The whole thing was becoming acutely painful, like at a play when an actor forgets his lines and stands there looking lost, and everyone in the audience cringes inside for the poor fellow. Another moment of this seemed unendurable, and just when I had made up my mind to begin talking about anything at all to ease the situation, his face broke into a ghastly grin, and he started jabbering at us with superhuman rapidity. I just wish I could do his voice properly.

" 'Ah, I see you have already come in. Excellent, gentlemen, excellent. It's really freezing out there, especially if your coat is getting a bit ratty. Not that anyone would ever think such a thing about your lovely coats, gentlemen, not at all; everyone can tell right away that they are of the highest quality, I give you my word. How wonderful that you all have made yourselves comfortable. We're delighted you could come today, Rotenburg and I. I mean Herr Rotenburg and I. Herr Rotenburg the younger, of course, not Herr Moritz Rotenburg. But you already know that, gentlemen, how absurd of me to tell you that when he is standing right here himself. Yes, do take your coats off, and don't bother drying off your boots. There's no need to worry about staining the carpets, just walk directly in, it's an honor for us to receive you. At least it certainly is for me. For him too, I am sure, I hope I am not being impolite, only he is more used to it than me. And the cognac, gentlemen, the cognac, I assure you, is beyond reproach in this house. You won't go home and be sick tonight, I can vouch for that. I am eager for us to get to know one another better and have a long, cozy chat together. It's wonderful to be among friends, isn't it?' And then he collapsed into a chair but missed it entirely and landed on the floor instead. There was a dreadful silence, and the next sound we heard was Hans's strange guest producing a whole series of noises that we took for giggling but might as easily have been groans. And I have got to give credit to Hans, who was standing there, completely white and rigid throughout this scene but otherwise quite unreadable and making no effort to interfere. But as soon as the poor man seemed sufficiently calmed down, Hans went over to help lead him safely off to the bathroom and then into the small bedroom at the back of the apartment. That is where he must have slept off his stupor the rest of the evening because he certainly never showed himself to us again."

Leo was laughing out loud by now and spilling bits of hot chocolate mixed with soggy bread crumbs onto his dressing gown. "You're making it up, Christoph," he said, "just to help me feel better. But I assure you, I am completely recovered and ready for serious work."

"No, it really happened more or less the way I have described it," Christoph said, looking toward Joachim and Manfred for support. Both nodded vigorously in unison, and Christoph went on. "But Hans had more surprises for us, Leo. You do have to admire his self-possession. When he joined us again, there was no hint of apology for subjecting everyone to such a bizarre spectacle. If anything, he looked more serious than ever. Although it did feel a little strange to have a brandy after what we had just seen, everyone was glad of a drink, and after a few minutes of catching up on small details and gossip, Hans began to tell us that the man we'd just met, whom he described as high-strung and somewhat inclined to hysteria, which I think we were all able to figure out by ourselves at this point, was basically quite shrewd and represented first-class 'revolutionary material,' which was definitely not the description that sprang into anyone else's mind. It even seems that Hans has decided to engage him for the group as a kind of paid assistant, bookkeeper, and go-between."

"Does he have a name, this fellow?" Leo asked.

"Asher Blumenthal, I think," Christoph answered. "He looked positively on his deathbed for the short time I had the pleasure of seeing him, so it was hard to judge his age, but Hans said he's only five or six years older than we are. He's been working since he was seventeen, and of course that is entirely to his credit. I suppose if this Blumenthal fellow had been sober, Hans might have given us a more complete picture, but so far what I have gathered is that Hans wants to use him to get hold of some bankrupt literary journal in Vienna that we can turn into a propaganda organ. Since none of us has the slightest idea about how to manage a press, I suppose it makes sense to take over one that is already in operation if we can continue to use some of its staff. Anyway, that is only part of Blumenthal's supposed usefulness to us."

"And what is the other part?" Leo's laughter had been replaced by something close to fascination.

"The only thing Hans was willing to tell us right then," Christoph concluded, "was that this man has a rare quality of loathing that the rest of us evidently lack. He sees a potential for violence in Blumenthal's hysteria that seems to impress him to no end. Apparently, he believes he can direct it away from purely personal grievances and focus it on political targets. I got the impression, in fact, that the more degraded Blumenthal seemed to become, the more Hans was convinced that he had found the right man for our purpose."

· ◆ ·

My dear Alexander,

By the time you get this, I am sure you'll have long since heard all about the fiasco at Rotenburg's apartment. Given the speed with which the two of you seem to be in touch these days, I practically have the feeling you were there to witness my disgrace yourself. Almost the only thing about which I am in doubt is which of his limited repertoire of tones Rotenburg drew on to tell you the story. Was it his amused and tolerant "man of the world" air, which he seems especially to like putting on whenever he's just spent a few hours with his aristocratic friends? Personally, I find it the most insufferable of all, that imitation goyish clubman pose, as though the camaraderie of boarding schools and barracks were something worth aping. But I can imagine he might find it irresistible in a letter to someone he thinks of as moving in the world of sophisticated Viennese culture, someone, I hope you don't mind my reminding you, about whom he only heard from me in the first place.

So, were you treated to a story about a slightly awkward but basically comic misadventure in which poor, ridiculous Asher Blumenthal nearly ruined a perfectly civilized evening by his impossible behavior, only to be prevented from doing so by the good-natured forbearance of as fine a group of fellows as anyone could imagine? Or did Hans at least admit that he was exasperated to the point of rage by my shameful performance and that after everyone had left, he blustered at me for what felt like several hours although I was too sick to take most of it in? Seeing him lose his self-possession like that comes close to redeeming the day for me, but considering the pay I am likely to be docked for having spent this whole week in bed, it's probably too costly a pleasure for someone in my position.

If you weren't my oldest friend, I could never tell you this, but you know what I can't get out of my ears? Not Rotenburg's pompous lecture, that's for sure! No, it's the memory of such frightened whimpers, such horrible inside sounds that came out of me in that wretched little back bedroom, while they all went on merrily chatting and enjoying themselves. There can't be any-

178

thing as repellent as being forced to hear how squalid the noises produced by one's own physical misery really are. I remember that when I was little and the doctors thought I might be catching tuberculosis, my parents borrowed enough money to send me to the mountains for two weeks. I knew what it had meant for them and was determined to spend all day doing nothing but concentrating on breathing as much mountain air in and out of my lungs as possible, making sure to do it just the way the doctor had ordered: in through the nose, out through the mouth, at exactly the same regular rate all day long. It was a maddening exercise, and by the end of the first hour I thought I would go crazy from the strain of concentrating so hard. That night, though, as I was lying in bed, I felt myself slowly starting to suffocate again. It didn't happen all at once. At first I only realized that I had trouble falling asleep. Then I noticed that instead of the deep breaths I'd been ordered to draw in, I was panting more and more shallowly and quickly, trying, in any way I could, to make up for the lack of air reaching my lungs. I was completely bathed in sweat, which still happens to me whenever I get seriously ill, and was certain that any moment I was going to faint and never wake up again. Imagine drowning, only instead of being in the water, you are drowning in air, and nothing you do is of any use because there is no other element to reach for. Well, that night, in between the sounds of my gasping, I suddenly heard myself whimpering like some injured and terrified animal. It was a sound I never thought I would hear again, and until a week ago I hadn't.

Of course, within a few days, I became acclimated to the altitude and the mountain air and started being able to sleep again. When I got back to town, a different doctor—you remember him, the Jew who used to examine us free at school once a term—told me that I'd never had tuberculosis at all and that my parents had wasted their money on the cure.

But as far as the evening at Rotenburg's is concerned, as I write about it to you now, it occurs to me that I might as well have been stumbling around onstage in one of your still-unproduced plays, the drunken buffoon collapsing ignominiously in front of the town bluebloods. And the fact that the buffoon is a Jew might just give it that final, piquant touch of exoticism the critics seem to applaud these days. Playing against type, you might say: a Semite who undermines his own pecuniary interests because he's in the grip of a degrading vice. At least no one could accuse the author of having made his Jew too sly and calculating. But of course that's all nonsense, and you probably think my ignominy isn't worth even a momentary interlude in a comic operetta, let alone in one of your own satiric pieces. Although I am afraid that if you go along with Hans's plans for all of us, you may not have enough time for your real writing anymore, and I can't think of a more tragic loss to Austrian literature.

You know, Alexander, if only I had really been wildly, extravagantly drunk, it might not have seemed so shameful. These days it is much less embarrassing to make an ass of oneself because of alcohol than because one is acutely sick. We all think the blond ruffian calling for more champagne and insulting everyone is actually quite dashing compared to the poor nebbish who is burning up with a high fever and doesn't know what he is saying anymore. Of course I am not used to brandy in the middle of the afternoon! Where in my entire life would I have acquired the tolerance for it? I'd like you to tell me. Knowing him the way I do now, I am sure Hans told you about my stopping at a bar on the way to see him and then having a few more brandies while we were waiting for the others. But I wonder if he bothered mentioning that the doctor he finally called in, when it was clear that I couldn't stand up on my own, let alone walk home, diagnosed a debilitating parasite in my stomach? I must have picked it up in one of the greasy restaurants near my flat where I have taken to eating lately to save a little bit of money. Anyway, according to this doctor, who must be reasonably competent since his name was in Rotenburg's address book, it seems that whatever malignancy this bug secretes becomes many times more toxic when it interacts with even a modest amount of alcohol and that my whole system was already going into shock by the time I arrived at the apartment. So when Hans urged me to have another drink with him, he was actually poisoning me, although probably—to give him the benefit of the doubt—quite innocently. But the truth is, as soon as he saw the condition I was in, he should have had me lie down and immediately sent for that doctor, not kept talking about his momentous plans and offering more drinks to a man who was quickly approaching a total physical collapse. But our generous patron was so intent upon his stratagems that I don't think he noticed how I was feeling until my seizure shamed him in front of his important guests.

By the way, whatever high purpose Hans says he has in mind doesn't interfere with his spending most of his time chasing women. Sick as I already was, he kept me waiting forever in the freezing hallway while he and one of his girlfriends finished their little midafternoon session and got dressed. Since she's also a Jew herself and her father is one of Moritz Rotenburg's dependents, she must be an especially easy target. I am not telling you all this just to counteract whatever impression you may have gotten about me from Hans.

I know we have been friends much too long for you to pay attention to gossip about me, whether from Hans Rotenburg or anyone else around here. Actually, I am much more worried about your own position, especially since you don't really know the way things are shaping up. You may be walking into a situation that is stickier than it looks. For example, did you suspect that Hans would show me all the financial statements you sent him about The New Order's deficits? Imagine if anyone else knew that you were providing confidential information like that to a person interested in taking over the journal. I don't need to tell you what that would do to your reputation! Consequences like that would never occur to Hans, who lacks the imagination to realize how precarious the world can be for people not born into his circumstances. I know all about his famous sense of "social justice." Believe me, Alexander, I have had to listen to him expound on the nature of "wage slavery" and "class exploitation" often enough not to admit that he's a veritable Solomon on those topics, although considering that he learned the laws of capital accumulation in his father's court, maybe Absalom would be a better comparison. What I can't understand is why he's persuaded himself that any of this revolutionary chattering should matter to him in the first place. As far as I can tell, he doesn't have an ounce of feeling for other people. What's more, he seems completely devoid of interest in higher ideas, and he has no sense of humor either. I am at a loss to think of what else I could offer him. Being a troublemaker may give a rich boy with nothing to do a bit of a racy reputation, but it doesn't help you or me. What really irritates me is that he's also not in the least ashamed of being so rich; in fact it's obvious that he enjoys all the advantages of his position and is thoroughly ruthless about enforcing those advantages whenever he thinks it's called for. Just as with your journal, for instance. It's galling to think that the rest of us are put on earth so that our problems can provide a leisure time activity for the offspring of the rich.

It's not just Hans's carelessness in passing around the documents you sent him that makes me so nervous. I happen to believe in you as a writer and think you are much too talented to sacrifice your gifts to serve Hans Rotenburg's ambitions. And believe me, Alexander, that is what you would be doing the moment the journal came into his control. I still haven't gotten a clear answer from him about what he's really after with The New Order, but it has nothing to do with a love for literature, that's for sure! He told me many times that he has no interest in what he calls fine writing, and I don't see how you could be employed by someone like that and still create the works I know you are capable of. What I feel worst about is that I told him about you and the

181

journal only in order to get you the freedom you need for your writing. I wanted Rotenburg to bring me to Vienna to look after the business end of the paper so that you could finally concentrate entirely on your art, and now it looks as though all I have done is jeopardize your present position. The whole shabby affair is my fault, Alexander. I admit it without any reservations and only hope you can forgive my misjudgment.

I am sure you were tempted by the idea of working alongside people like Rotenburg and the aristocrats in his crowd. Heaven knows, I felt a certain thrill when I first began to associate with them myself, but believe me, in person they're very far from inspirational. Among other things, their condescension never lets up for a single moment, and the more careful of one's feelings they think they are being, the more patronizing and superior they get. Do you want to know how Hans offered me a job when he finally looked in on me where I live to see if I had recovered from the poisoning? Well, what he said was that his political discussion group would welcome the contribution my ideas and perspectives would bring, especially since, as he so delicately put it, none of the present members had much direct experience with the problems of the educated urban petty bourgeoisie. At this point I had a violent stomach cramp, but I am sure he took my groan as a sign of how flattered I felt by his offer. You remember how dismal my room is from your last visit, so I needn't tell you what it's like trying to survive in it during the coldest winter in decades. I am sure Hans had never set foot in anything as wretched. I don't know if he had come already prepared to offer me money or if the sight of how the "educated urban petty bourgeoisie" really exists gave him the idea, but if I hadn't already been so weak, I think I would have collapsed anyway from laughing at the way he explained himself.

It's rare that one gets to hear so clearly the inner tensions in the words of a rich man who is used to buying and selling people like so much merchandise when he is also trying to sound like a sympathetic ally in life's struggles. As a connoisseur of human types, I am sure you can appreciate the whole situation, and if my delirium is too paltry a theme for one of your pieces, then maybe Hans's little recruiting scene is more promising. Right after making it abundantly clear that I would function mostly as a kind of secretary and general underling in his group, Hans assured me: "I know how busy you are and how much this work will take away from time you need for other activities, and of course, since we're all equal in the group, there's no question of direct payment from the organization as such, but in recognition of all the extra time you'll be putting in, I hope you won't mind if I help subsidize you for the losses you'll be incurring through your commitment."

I don't have your ear for dialogue, Alexander, so I may have gotten a few phrases wrong, but these were Hans's actual words as close as I can reconstruct them. Can you believe it? Me offended by an offer of money from a Rotenburg! Now tell me yourself, who is the drunk: Hans, who made such preposterous speeches, or I, who lay there trying not to look too smug while counting up the returns that all my preparations were finally going to bring in? But I am also starting to feel a little uncertain with all this talk about a "group" and an "organization." Since it's obvious my entire salary will be paid directly by Hans, why the pretense that anyone else is really involved? When Hans wrote to you, did he mention anyone else, or did he approach you in his own name? The nonentities he invited to his apartment the other day clearly don't figure in his calculations in any serious way, and my own guess is that he wants to use them as shabbes goyim the better to hide his real intentions. Somewhere behind all this I detect the old fox himself. I am certain Moritz has decided to work through his son, who will be working through hirelings like me and a handful of snobs whose dissolute habits probably put them in his debt. Subterfuges within subterfuges—my God, I admire that man! If only his son were half as subtle as his father, I'd consider it a privilege to let myself be used by him. If you were able to tell me exactly what Hans asked you about the journal, I might be able to figure out what he's after. To me, he's only spouted book talk about the class struggle and how I ought to see that my enemy is the economic system as a whole, not the imbecilic section chief who insults me every day and keeps me from advancing in the company. I'd like to see him work for a swine like Galatowski for a week and then talk so dispassionately about how it's "the whole economic system," not any particular individual, that's rotten. But of course I don't believe a word of all this revolutionary gibberish. If a Rotenburg is involved, there's money in it for him somewhere, I'd stake my life on that. Right now my instincts tell me that he wants to encourage troublemakers in order to drive down the shares of our big industries. Then he could buy them up for nothing, and as soon as the police finished off the poor fools who listened to him, the companies' stocks would rise, and he'd have realized another colossal profit. On that topic, by the way, when Hans finally got around to specifics with me, the sum he mentioned for "all the extra time you'll be putting in" was much less than I'd hoped for. But I have learned by now that it's pointless to try to get more out of him than he's

183

ready to pay, and I must say that I can't help admiring him for that. I hope you'll succeed better with him than I have in the financial department if you do come back here to work for him.

That is the part that puzzles me the most. If he does want to use the paper to encourage radicals and strikebreakers, I would have thought Vienna was a better place than the provinces. But probably his father wants to separate his activities on the Vienna bourse from any possible connection with the content of the paper, in case his son's ownership of it is discovered. I am assuming of course that he's told you his intention of moving the paper down here in toto, equipment and all, changing its name, and letting you run it for him. But strictly along the lines he decides are worthwhile. You can imagine how delighted I feel at the chance of our being together again and seeing each other every day, but I can't help wishing we could do it in Vienna, rather than here, and certainly not just to enrich the Rotenburgs still further. But maybe I am being too hasty in urging you to refuse Hans's offer. After all, I know so little about what he's promised you, what your alternatives are if the paper goes bankrupt and he doesn't intervene, how you feel about leaving Vienna, etc. etc. But, Alexander, whose fault is that? If you'd kept me informed from the beginning, rather than writing only to Hans, I'd have had a clearer picture of the whole situation, and together we'd have been able to devise a sound strategy for dealing with it. But that's all in the past, my old friend, and it is not too late to try to make the best out of our opportunities. We have to be clever, though, and not make any more mistakes. So do write me quickly and in as much detail as possible about everything that Hans or any of his agents have been telling you. And especially, make sure you send me a copy of anything that he's put in writing to you, since that may help us legally if things don't go so well. In the meantime remember that the only really important question in all these tedious machinations is to secure your future as a writer. Austria's preeminent Jewish man of letters. That's how I see you, and that's why I will do everything in my power to help you realize your destiny.

Your devoted friend,
Asher

· ◆ ·

Although the Count-Governor had made certain his police knew every detail of young Rotenburg's movements, they were never able to learn what was said during Hans's meeting with Elisabeth Demetz. The agents Tausk had stationed outside Hans's apartment building recorded only the times of Batya's arrival and departure, and consequently, it never occurred to anyone that the conversation between the former lovers might have brought a useful perspective to the midnight speculations between the Count and Tausk in the Castle library. In any case, Wiladowski had become so accustomed to considering every question solely from its bearing on high politics that he would have been unable to see the pertinence to his own interests of an argument between two young people, unless of course they came from one of the Empire's governing families. But, as Marie-Luise could have told her husband had he shown the slightest inclination to consult her on anything beyond the menu for official receptions, it is through the intimate diplomacy of the bedroom and nursery, whether as children confronting the world and will of our parents or, soon after, as adolescents venturing into the initial, tentative alliances and rebuffs of sexual desire, that we learn that the first prerogative of power is to surprise those over whom it is exercised. It is always to unexpected music that we respond with our most ingenious steps, and the capacity to astonish is a gift equally potent in the bedroom, on the battlefield, or across the negotiating table.

Had such a description been offered in Tausk's hearing, he would have found himself in the curious position of understanding exactly what the Countess meant, even though all her examples were utterly alien to his experience. Separate nurseries and bedrooms were unknown where he had grown up, sleeping, eating, and working alongside his seven siblings, numerous other more or less immediate family members, and a constantly changing contingent of visiting relatives and itinerant peddlers with whom his father carried on an illegal and, to judge by the results, mostly unprofitable business in petty smuggling. But the claustrophobic setting only intensified the sharpness of the lessons in domestic diplomacy that Marie-Luise had acquired from her more spacious viewpoint. Later, after the young Tausk's outstanding memory and precocious intelligence had secured him the sponsorship of a rich townsman to study at the yeshiva of the famous *rav* Avraham Pelz, his fellow students' constant jockeying for their teacher's favor, their ruthless competition for recognition as promising scholars, which exceeded even their daily battles for the tastiest morsels at the communal meals, and their still more fanciful schemes to attract the attention of wealthy potential fathers-in-law were conducted with a ferocity and shrewdness in comparison with which the bitterest rivalries at the Foreign Ministry or Imperial Staff College were serene exercises in mutual assistance. Shortly before his expulsion Tausk had formulated a general rule that Marie-Luise would certainly have corroborated if the two had ever exchanged more than a rare, accidental sentence. Tausk's experiences both at home and at the yeshiva led him to conclude that the more symbolic and abstract the reward, the sharper the competition for it and that even among those who have the least, it is prestige, not just material improvement of their condition, that motivates people. Between greed and envy, it was clear to him that envy was by far the more potent social force. He was convinced that given a choice between obtaining some desirable prize, but with the knowledge that their enemies would be given an equivalent reward, and receiving nothing tangible except the certainty that their opponents would never know any advancement, even the most avaricious men would pick ruining their foes over augmenting their own fortunes. Still, any exchange of observations along these lines, although it might have been enlightening to both parties and perhaps helped confirm Marie-Luise's always wavering trust in her own powers of observation, was an impossibility, since if her husband often politely forgot that his wife was actually in residence with him and not away visiting one of her innumerable cousins, she in turn thought that any personal observation in front of a paid servant, let alone a Jew, was in exceedingly bad taste.

The impossibility of a dialogue with Marie-Luise did nothing to damage Tausk's position since the relationship between Wiladowski and his wife was such that neither would have dreamed of sharing a confidant with the other. In any event, Tausk's attention was soon absorbed by a peculiar confrontation that had occurred under the eyes of the whole town but on whose meaning no two witnesses could agree.

The scene took place a week after Batya's visit to Hans's flat and was played out directly across the street from the Mendelssohn Club, in plain sight of the Metropole's front entrance. To the surprise of Tausk's spies, they noticed Nathan Kaplansky, the notorious socialist agitator, who almost never visited this district, hurrying down the Mariahilferstrasse toward the intersection at the Radetzkyplatz. He was accompanied by a recent arrival in town named Brugger, a rabbi from one of the eastern shtetls, who was almost certainly a fugitive from Russia traveling on forged papers. As the two men got closer to the restaurant, they were accosted by one of the numerous beggars who always loitered in front of the better establishments in spite of repeated attempts by the police to enforce the laws against street mendicants. The beggar sat leaning against the base of the Schwarzenberg statue, showing everyone his heavily swollen and bleeding feet, crying out as loudly as possible that he was near death from starvation. But when any of the passersby bent down to toss him a coin, he tried to take advantage of their generosity by pleading for shoes or at least for additional money to buy himself some sort of covering for his suppurating feet. He complained that he couldn't even go into a tavern to get warm because as soon as the other patrons saw the condition of his feet, they threw him back out into the street. The instant he realized that instead of just rushing off after dropping something into his outstretched hat, Kaplansky and Brugger were actually listening to his story, the man's wailing became still louder, until a number of the hotel's guests, as well as some members of the nearby Jewish social club, rushed outside to learn the cause of such commotion.

A large group of bystanders, especially the contingent from the Jewish club, remained in the square, in spite of the cold, to see how Kaplansky and Brugger would handle the situation. Almost everyone began to argue against giving the beggar any money. According to a few well-known street agitators, who were arrested later the same day, individual charity accomplished nothing. What was needed was to abolish the whole social structure that allowed such misery to exist. But just as they were getting well launched into their declamation, one of lawyer Pichler's daughters came over from the crowd on the other side of the street. She made it clear right away that although she agreed one should refuse to give the beggar anything, she thought no one had given the most important reasons why.

"If you look closely at the fellow"—she began to harangue the others— "he is clearly a Slav, probably an anti-Semite as well, not to mention a wife and child beater. As soon as he gets any money, he'll rush off to spend it on alcohol, and after taking out his drunkenness on his family, he'll be back here just as hungry and shoeless as before. What I can't understand is why we Jews always help others and do so little for our own people. Why can't we look after our own kind first, the way the Catholics dispense their charity to their own parishioners? I'd like to see a hungry Jew show up and beg for a meal at the soup kitchen the nuns set up in front of St. Katharina on Sundays!"

Just then she was joined by another one of the crowd from the Mendelssohn Club, who eagerly seconded everything she had just said.

"Of course he's a drunk; anyone can see that. I agree completely with the young lady. He would only squander every penny we gave him on alcohol. And may I say that it is truly inspiring to hear such passionate Jewish sentiments from one of our own community. You have taken the words right out of my own mouth, miss, and I would welcome the chance to hear more of your ideas on these crucial questions, perhaps over coffee, when you have the time. My name is Asher Blumenthal, and I often come to the Hebrew classes at the club. I know I have seen you there as well, and perhaps you'll recall my leading the applause for the Zionist speaker last year." Blumenthal said he was sure that someone like the beggar had many friends among his own kind. How lucky they all really were, Blumenthal added, to need nothing more than a bottle of cheap brandy to feel better. But inner sorrow like his own, brought about by too many long nights spent studying how to improve the fate of the Jewish people, was a much bleaker fate. Yet no one, he sighed, pitied solitary thinkers like him or gave any thought to alleviating their loneliness.

The whole time the shrill debate was going on around him, the rebbe stayed completely silent. Gradually everyone, including even Blumenthal and the Pichler girl, ran out of words and turned toward Brugger. At that moment he reached into his shabby coat and pulled out a purse, which he emptied into the beggar's hat. He made no effort to count the amount he poured out, and several gold pieces were clearly visible in the winter sun. For a moment it seemed Blumenthal was going to throw himself on top of the beggar and wrench the money away from him. Somehow, Blumenthal stopped himself from doing so, but not from crying out, "But why *him*?"

Brugger was already walking away, but when he heard the cry, he stopped again and looked at Blumenthal with a friendly smile. Then he spoke to him as though they were alone together, somewhere warm and comfortable, with all the time in the world. Although Brugger was talking much more quietly than Blumenthal had done when he blurted out his question, everyone in the square heard him as clearly as if he were speaking into his ears alone. He told Blumenthal, "What you said is true, even though you didn't believe it completely yourself. You *are* lonelier than this man here, and neither the brandy you have been drinking nor the gifts you have started to depend on have made you feel better. All the arguments that this lady and the others came up with are also right, each in its own way. But no matter how it strikes you, believe me, my giving the man money is not intended to rebuke you. If I haven't come here to judge the justice of this beggar's claims, how much less so to judge yours. Yet if I am not here to judge others, then it must be to help them in whatever way I can. I have no illusion that what I give him will improve the man's life for more than a minute, only I have to consider that perhaps this single minute is the circumference of all my duty in the world and already contains all the permanence my soul requires. There are days the heart pleads its case with the advocacy of desire, even when it knows it is helpless to do so by cold reason. Let this be one of those days." Then he crossed the street, walked up to the door of the Mendelssohn Club, and said to the porter, "My name is Moses Elch Brugger. I believe Herr Moritz Rotenburg is expecting me. Please be so kind as to take me to him."

Reading through his spies' reports of the episode disturbed Tausk more than the descriptions themselves justified. There was certainly nothing in the story he could take to Wiladowski to obtain an arrest warrant, but everything about this Brugger struck Tausk as worrisome. He was dismayed that a rebbe, about whom he knew next to nothing, could arrive in town and, within a short time, appear to have turned Nathan Kaplansky into his personal attendant. Not only did Brugger have enough money to give a purseful of coins to a stray beggar, but he was able to improvise a speech that silenced a whole crowd of contentious personalities without incurring their hostility. The suggestion of a connection, no matter how tenuous, linking Kaplansky, Brugger, and Moritz Rotenburg was too astonishing to ignore, and Tausk made it the basis for a formal request to his master for additional resources to look into the situation. When Tausk finally drew up his own account for the Count-Governor, he concluded by saying only that in his judgment, anyone able to exercise that kind of power in the middle of the day on the Radetzkyplatz could use it in quite different ways when he felt himself unobserved. And if Moritz Rotenburg really had sent for Brugger, then it was vital for the security services to find out about the man as quickly as possible. "I think the state ought not to be less well informed than our leading capitalist," Tausk concluded, only to be interrupted by a brisk laugh from his master.

"Don't be absurd." Wiladowski brushed aside Tausk's misgivings. "Since Rotenburg is involved, of course you should find out everything you can, just don't let yourself get too hopeful. Don't forget that the state is *always* less well informed than its leading capitalist."

3

O n a desert island a single Jew, all alone and stranded, will build two synagogues: one to go to and one to stay away from." The familiar saying ran through Moritz Rotenburg's mind as he stood at the window, sourly watching the scene unfold on the square below. He didn't like what he was seeing, and wished there were some way to interrupt it. For once it was not snowing. The midwinter sun was sending sparks of icy brilliance off the Cathedral roof, and from his vantage point on the second floor of the Mendelssohn Club, Moritz could clearly make out all the people clustered together around the base of the Schwarzenberg statue. Even Rudi Pichler's daughter had gone running out of the club, along with more than a half dozen others, to talk to Nathan Kaplansky and the man with him, who, Moritz assumed, had to be the wonder rebbe himself. It was still too cold to open the thick windows, so Moritz couldn't hear what anyone was saying, but there was no doubt the stranger had already succeeded in making himself the center of attention. The whole scene looked so perfectly orchestrated that Moritz wondered if Brugger hadn't hired the beggar ahead of time to be part of the performance. "Just what Wiladowski's spies need to make their master even more frightened than he is already," Moritz thought, walking away from the window in disgust to sit down at the head of the large conference table and await his visitor.

It had been hard enough to persuade the other members of the Governing Board to let him deal with Brugger entirely on his own, and no doubt, after what had just taken place on the club's very doorstep, they were already regretting it. But his promise to take full legal and financial responsibility for anything concerning Brugger would be enough to overcome their eagerness to participate, especially if Moritz made clear how high the cost of the necessary bribes was likely to run. A soft tap on the door told him that Geza, the senior porter, on whose loyalty Moritz relied to keep the corridor clear, had brought Brugger upstairs and was ready to let him in. Moritz signaled his consent by gently sounding the small silver bell that lay on the table beside him. Soon afterward, when he and Brugger had finished shaking hands and were sitting down across from each other, he was struck by how young the rebbe looked. Somehow, he had forgotten to ask Kaplansky the man's age and simply assumed he would be dealing with someone close to his own years. But Brugger looked to be only in his early thirties. The rest of his appearance, especially the fine European clothes, matched Kaplansky's description. Brugger's gaze, though, had none of the seductive warmth Moritz expected. Even when he smiled, Brugger's eyes looked coldly metallic, like finely hammered steel with no specks of another color to soften the effect.

After a few more seconds, during which they sat silently sizing each other up, Moritz adopted his heartiest tone and began what he suspected would be a long and difficult afternoon. "I hope Kaplansky wasn't offended when I asked him to wait downstairs in the reading room. I wanted to talk to you alone, and in any case, it is probably better for him not to be seen up here in the executive offices. That was an impressive performance you just put on out there. Even the older members looked on in wonder. But you must be worn out. I wish you had accepted my offer to send my carriage for you; it is a long walk from where you live. Can I at least offer you a drink, or something to eat, before we start?"

Brugger's eyes never swerved from Moritz. He ignored the sideboard, on which a variety of dishes had been set out, and in an intimate tone, as though he were speaking to an old acquaintance in his own living room, asked, "Why are you so nervous, Moritz Rotenburg? Someone like you, who has sat across the table from the most powerful men in this country? Nothing bad will happen to you and yours as a result of my being here; you have my word on that. Your son is young and will make many grievous mistakes, but you need not worry on his account. When he dies, he will still call himself a Jew and be older than you are today."

In his business negotiations Moritz placed a great deal of weight on his adversary's opening gambit, and although this conversation had only begun, Moritz was already certain it was going to prove extraordinarily burdensome. "I am not sure what you have heard about me, Brugger," he said, deciding to allow his impatience to register right away, "but I don't care for mystifications of this sort. My donating money to the yeshivas may have given you the idea that I am a superstitious dupe looking for another holy man to support, but I dislike being taken for a fool who reaches into his pocket at the first clever words he is told. Every father in my position worries about his son, and if he is an Austrian Jew, he worries especially about whether his son will convert, so I am not impressed by your prophecy. It sounds a great deal like telling a widow she is about to meet a new suitor who is richer and better-looking than her late husband. Of course she will be delighted at the news. But I am not that widow, and I have no intention of crossing your palms with silver for telling me what you know I want to hear."

Moritz had gone on longer than he normally did at the outset, but he was hoping to goad Brugger into defending himself at least with a look or gesture, if not actual speech. But the rebbe stayed disconcertingly unruffled. "First nervousness and now anger." Brugger continued in the same even tone with which he had begun. "I am sorry my presence raises such disturbing feelings. Please remember, though, that I was not the one to solicit this meeting. You asked to see me, and I was glad for the chance to talk with you. If I were to take you for less than you are, I would be the simpleton, not you. But I have not come looking for alms either. Unlike the beggars at your front door, my feet have carried me this far without becoming infected, and I am ready to walk home on them whenever you have satisfied your curiosity."

"What makes you think I am curious about you?" Moritz asked with a dismissive shrug. He was determined to strike a spark from this strange man, even if it meant making himself appear the more touchy of the two. "Just because I suggested that Nathan bring you to me? I admit I have been hearing strange rumors about you and wanted to find out for myself if you really are a danger to our community. But believe me, I am far from taking a personal interest in your little charades."

Brugger replied as though he were reflecting on a knotty philosophical problem. "I am impressed by how easily you make all these distinctions," he said thoughtfully. "If I suspected someone were a threat to our people, I would certainly be interested in the man—even quite personally interested. But in what way could I possibly be a menace, I, a foreigner who arrived here only a little while ago without friends or contacts? If you don't mind my echoing you, I am not sure what you have heard about me either, but I dislike being taken for a pious fraud out to swindle everyone I come across. I can't imagine traveling all this way for so banal a role! Anyway,

Moritz—you don't mind if I use your 'Christian' name, do you?—for a confidence man, I must be remarkably thick-witted, since here I am, preaching to a crowd of unemployed debtors and vagabonds in the Josef Quarter. What a waste for someone with the intentions you attribute to me! But you know better than anyone that it is never wise to pay too much heed to rumors. Especially when they are spread by the *erev rav*, the mixed multitude you call Jews in this town. How could I be a threat when the best of you are just reverse Marranos, pretending to be Jews on the outside but no different from your gentile neighbors within? How could anything I say touch you?"

It had been decades since anyone except his oldest acquaintances had dared call Moritz by his first name, but he was determined not to react to Brugger's provocation. He looked up at the bookshelves along the wall of the wood-paneled room and scanned the solemn rows of all the major German authors, identically bound in uniform editions, shelved alongside the club's extensive collection of Judaica, cased in the same ornate leather design. Although the downstairs library was used extensively, especially by the poorer members, the books in this room, restricted to the elected executives and community leaders, were hardly ever opened. Inwardly Moritz couldn't help acknowledging the justice of Brugger's description of the town's Jews, and against his instincts, he was finding himself intrigued. At least the rebbe wasn't entirely predictable, and in this setting, hearing anything unexpected was a rarity. "You may be right about that, Brugger. But if so, what is it you really want here? Money? A position? Or did you just come to take advantage of people's desperation? Even if it means alarming the authorities and turning them against the Jews?"

"Pardon me"—Brugger permitted himself a slight laugh—"but even in the little time I have been here, it doesn't seem as though the authorities need much encouragement to turn on the Jews, especially on those without enough money to make their presence less offensive to Christian sensibilities." Unexpectedly Brugger got up, went over to the window, and looked out onto the square as though trying to visualize exactly what Moritz must have seen when he was standing there half an hour earlier. Moritz found it oddly disconcerting that Brugger positioned himself in the very stance that he himself always took up: leaning against the windowpane just where Moritz did, with his arms extended at the identical angle that Moritz instinctively used to support himself. Brugger's shoulders were bent in the way Moritz knew his own to be whenever he was standing in one place, lost in thought. Except for the difference in their coloring, viewed from the back, it would almost be possible to confuse the two. Brugger stood there a long time, without speaking, but then shook his head, as though in reaction to what he saw in the streets below, and, without turning around, said, "You really needn't be so anxious about my influence, Moritz. On the contrary, ever since I arrived here, I have felt ashamed about how little I can do to help any of you."

"Help us?" Moritz was still troubled by the uncanny glimpse of Brugger at the window, looking almost like his younger twin, and raised his voice in order to force the rebbe to turn around and break the illusion. "What do you mean, 'help us'? I asked you before not to play games with me. And I do wish you would sit down again and have the courtesy to look at me when we talk. You ought to know that there has been mention of forcing you to leave town, even if it means hiring some nasty types to help persuade you. So far I have opposed anything like that. No matter what is considered permissible where you come from, it is not how we do things on this side of the border. But if I am to go on protecting you, I have to know what you are after, and you need to convince me you won't keep putting all of us at risk."

"I see," Brugger answered quietly without moving from his position by the window. "You feel threatened by the government, and in order to cover your shame, you summon someone like me here to threaten in turn. If this were a witty comedy by one of your Burgtheater playwrights, I suppose I would now go out and yell at some poor servant, who would pick on someone else still more helpless, and so on, until all the lower-class characters had been properly browbeaten and the fine audience sent home thoroughly amused. But I have no interest in performing in such a piece. I am sure no end of crazy schemes have been proposed to get rid of me, but we both know there are more than enough out-of-work men ready to protect me. You must suspect how much they hate all you rich Jews out in the Josef Quarter." He finally turned around and looked directly at Moritz, but only to draw the financier's attention to the rows of squalid houses between the river and the municipal cemetery whose gates were just visible in the window's upper quadrant. "How long has it been since you yourself walked anywhere near the Maximilianstrasse, where your son keeps his famous secret apartment? Things are becoming more desperate there every day, and it wouldn't take much to spark a conflagration. I would hate to see a careless misjudgment set off a wildfire that would require calling in the army to stamp it out. Try to understand that so far, simply by being there and continuing my lessons, I am helping to maintain the peace, not disturb it."

He swept his arm along the length of the window like a puppet master indicating an elaborate miniature set and then, as though suddenly weary of the whole effort, returned to his chair.

"Is that what you mean by helping us?" Moritz asked him once Brugger was seated again. "To whom are you offering your services? To the workers or to me? And what is it you want in return?"

"I am not offering anyone my services in the way you mean." Brugger shook his head. "Certainly not the way poor Nathan has offered himself to you. I want to work together with you, not have us on different sides. I have never cared what class a Jew thinks he belongs to, or how much money he has. Since the Exile began, none of those differences have ever lasted very long among us anyway."

"What do you mean by that?" Moritz was displeased with the direction the discussion was taking but didn't want to cut it short. "But, please, no long sermons this time," he told him. "I still have a lot of work to do and want to finish with you before the whole day is wasted."

"Be patient, Moritz, and I will be glad to explain. I am sure you have sat and listened tranquilly to someone like your provincial Governor going on about his hunting dogs and his wine cellar, but a few words about Jewish history and you become irritated. What I mean is that no real Jew can take all this talk about social classes as seriously as the goyim. How could we? We have been driven out of every country at one time or another and are likely to be so again. Tedium, apprehension, humiliation, and remorse: It is from that cycle I came here to free you. Not by what I can do or what I know, but by recalling you to yourself. Yet what I teach you aren't ready to hear, and the questions you are driven to ask can be answered only by someone who has lost all respect both for himself and for you."

In spite of the man's grating theatricality, some of what he said was too shrewd to be dismissed as empty posturing. Moritz reflected that if the rebbe had agreed to see him at a place like the Mendelssohn Club, it could only be because, for all his reluctance to come to the point, he must want something material, something only Moritz could give him, and the real question was how long it would take until the stakes of the conversation became clear. "Look, Brugger"—Moritz tried to press him—"I don't have the time or the temperament for all this metaphysical shadowboxing.

I can't understand half of what you are saying, and I am not at all convinced you do yourself. What worries me are more practical matters like where you got the money you gave to that beggar. Your congregation out in the Josef Quarter couldn't raise what you had in your purse today if they turned over all their worldly goods to you. Is someone paying you to cause trouble? There are people in the club suggesting you were sent here by a foreign intelligence service to set the government and the Jews against one another and weaken our loyalty to the Emperor in case of war."

Brugger made no effort to hide his disdain. "And these are the people whose opinions you pretend to take seriously? It must take enormous self-control for you not to tell them what you really think. If you are truthful, Moritz, you will have to admit that you are the actor here, not I! For myself, I don't know how you endure the strain." He got up and went over to the sideboard to look at the food being kept warm in different size chafing dishes but, after piling some baked chicken and stewed sweetbreads on a plate, ended up leaving it there without tasting anything. Instead he poured himself a large glass of cold mineral water and kept drinking from it while he talked. "There is no need to fantasize about plots hatched in some foreign capital." He went on. "For the people among whom I live and work, men of your kind are the only masters they have ever known. They don't see any difference among a rich Jewish businessman, a local Austrian judge who fines them whenever they try to open their mouths, and a Russian anti-Semite with Slavophile plots in his head. Believe me, when men are starving, their anger doesn't need stoking by outside agitators. I may be new in town, but it is you who need to hire spies and informers to know what is happening among your own people. Sitting in rooms like this, how can you be certain who has been coming to hear me and how much they donate? I believe that the heart of every person remains as unknowable as that of his Creator. In any case, I gave the beggar what I had. I don't remember where it came from, and I refuse to believe that it really makes a difference to you. Haven't you understood yet that you yourself are worse off than that injured wretch out there in the snow? I wish I could help you as easily as him. Everyone I have met in this town seems more spiritually destitute than the poorest Jews I preached to in the east."

"If this is what they teach in the yeshivas, my son is right to tell me I am wasting my money subsidizing them. Not one of us has to endure the kinds of humiliations that are routine in your country. At least not regularly."

"What a wonderful qualification!" Brugger made a dumb show of clapping his hands together. " 'Not regularly.' Believe me, the eastern Jews you look down on may not have your political rights, but at least they haven't traded in their heritage for an empty legal formula. Every day you make certain the government knows what loyal and devoted citizens you are. Of course you are Jews, but only 'privately,' where it makes no difference to the state. 'Austrian citizens of the Mosaic persuasion.' Isn't that how you put it? In everything that matters, none of you can rush fast enough to cast away any sign of your Jewishness for a few crumbs of toleration—I won't say equality because that is something no one seriously believes in anymore, at least no one on their side, and only a few fools on ours. Even the most deluded of them knows that to have an official career, a formal conversion will always be indispensable."

"What do you care about official careers?" Moritz asked. "I thought your interest was in stirring up unemployed workers with messianic fantasies, not in protesting restrictions on Jewish advancement in the Empire. What you are saying now doesn't sound very different from the Zionist whom we allow to recruit among the members downstairs, and if that is all you have been preaching out there in the Josef Quarter, I don't understand why people are so upset."

"You see, Moritz"—Brugger looked at him with amusement—"I told you not to trust rumors, not even when they are brought to you by someone as honest as Nathan Kaplansky. We have a saying that a single coin in a box causes a noisy rattle, and it seems made to describe poor Nathan's powers of perception. Incidentally, I hope you are paying him well for whatever he has been telling you, because if any of his associates found out he was working for you, I doubt they would be very pleased. You needn't frown at me like that. I would never give him away. Haven't I already promised not to bring any harm to you and yours, and haven't you made him one of yours as surely as if he were living in your own household? I find the situation quite instructive: He fears and distrusts me, yet it is you who persuaded him to betray his beliefs. Only he doesn't even realize it. That shows me how gifted a man you are and how much we could do for our people by collaborating."

Moritz pursed his lips disapprovingly but contented himself with telling Brugger that to suggest someone as idealistic as Kaplansky could simply be bribed revealed how little the rebbe understood about winning over people whose opinions differed from one's own. Brugger listened politely but made no attempt to hide his skepticism. "I am afraid Nathan has grasped one thing more clearly than you," he told Moritz. "My welcome among his comrades signifies the rejection of every one of his hopes. What he dreams about is a brotherhood of man in which all our differences will be dissolved and no questions of race or belief will trouble humanity again. A deadly dream for Jews. Either religious differences do have an inner meaning or our history is one long, macabre joke."

"And that is what you have been telling the workers?" Moritz asked. "I can understand why he sees you as a threat. Fair enough. But what about your sermon that when the Messiah arrives, it will be in an armored car with a military escort and a gun in his hand? I haven't heard anything like that from the other Zionists who have come through here before, and I am quite sure the police haven't either."

"What would you have him do, Moritz?" Brugger replied. "Come mounted upon a donkey and carrying palm leaves? Why should things of the spirit always need to be presented as something quaint like a festival where everyone dresses in so-called native costumes? It is not folklore we are talking about but the breath of the Living God. When has violence not been part of His creation? I set no timetable for our Redemption, but surely when it arrives, it will not find gunpowder and the internal-combustion engine insuperable obstacles."

Moritz, who had been suffering from throat and stomach pains for several months, winced as a spasm went through him and, with a slight nod of apology, got up to pour himself a glass of chamomile tea. The only food his doctor allowed him when his condition was this serious was a small bowl of warm cream of wheat and some bland white toast. He took his food and drink back to his place at the conference table and with some difficulty finished both. Brugger watched him the whole time with no discernible expression of either sympathy or scorn. He seemed to have halted in mid-sentence, waiting for a signal to resume, and as soon as Moritz put down his empty teacup, Brugger continued as though he had never been interrupted. "But you should understand one thing," he said emphatically. "I am no more interested in the Zionist's fairy tales than in Nathan's socialist fantasies. Ever since Herzl organized them, his followers have gone around telling the world that Jews merely want to be 'normalized' in a country of their own. Another deadly dream. *I* certainly do not want us to try to be like other people. Not so long ago Jews of that sort yearned only to make this a country in which they could become Jewish professors, Jewish members of academies, Jewish officers in the army, Jewish civil servants, and Jewish trade unionists, identical to every other European citizen. The trivial, cosmopolitan humanism of the coffeehouse at its most soulless! When some of them finally realized they would never get even that, they just transferred the same childish fantasies to Palestine, although there the land itself mocks the idea of its inhabitants' being 'like everyone else'! I know. I have been there. I have walked out alone into the harshness of a sun utterly unlike ours and watched it set hill after hill on fire, and I tell you, Moritz, we did not wait two thousand years just to build a second Ringstrasse in Jerusalem so that the Jews can finally get the best seats in the restaurants."

"When were you in Palestine?" Moritz looked genuinely surprised. "No one I have talked to mentioned that you had gone there."

Brugger refused to consider Moritz's question seriously. "I don't necessarily tell the same stories everywhere I go. Just imagine how bored I would be. In any case, nothing I have told you is as void of truth as that dossier you are assembling about me. I know you have been busy writing everywhere to gather information, and two days ago you sent one of your flunkies to bribe my students to inform on me. What a colossal waste of money. Whatever you could learn from all your inquiries, I would willingly tell you myself for nothing."

"What about the story I heard that in Armenia you were ordered flogged by an officer of the rabbinic court, who gave you forty stripes and forbade your company to all Jews? That hardly seems like an insignificant piece of gossip."

"Yes, I was flogged." Brugger nodded agreeably as though he were describing a weekend invitation to a country house. "Only it was ten strokes, not the canonic forty. It is so easy to guess how your informants interpret the little they have heard about me. What value can there be in reports by men who never understood anything of what they had witnessed? Every word is going to be shaped by something they have already come across in some book of legends. When you finish assembling your dossier, it will read like the biography of every dangerous heretic and schismatic we Jews have ever produced. They have no other lenses with which to see. But I am not a heathen, nor have my teachings anything in common with Sabbatai Zevi's or Jacob Frank's. I am only a Jew who has walked with his eyes wide open where the people you have asked to betray me do not dare look themselves, and I have returned from the abyss with my faith stronger than their weakness imagines possible. I have already told you that I know you have sat across the table from the powerful men of this Empire, and I respect you for it. It should never be forgotten how much we owe to strong men like you who have built a rock in the land of the heathen. But in the deserts I have crossed, I too have dined with kings and been offered more treasures than your vaults contain and have never been impressed enough to turn aside from my path. As for your famous 'report,' well, in reality, I was beaten many times before I ever began my wandering. So I was used to it, and treatment like that never broke my spirit. Were you also told that when I was a boy, I was considered the local child prodigy because I had memorized so much of the Talmud and the great rabbinic commentators? But every Saturday afternoon my father would call me into his study to question me on my reading, and no matter how carefully I had prepared, he would find enough errors to beat me until neither of us could stand straight. After that, the punishments of the most severe Jewish courts seemed inconsequential."

"And your mother?" Moritz forced himself to banish a picture of Hans enduring such pain while he and Dina watched helplessly. "Where was she while you were growing up? Didn't she try to placate your father's anger?"

"At the beginning"—Brugger went on—"when I would still cry out and beg him to stop, I think my screams did bother her. But that didn't last very long, and soon I stopped showing any reaction at all. Besides, of the two she was by far the more vain, and she cared so much about my impressing the important adults in their circle that she was willing to have me beaten if it would make me study even harder."

"Where are they today?" Moritz felt hesitant about probing further, but Brugger's demeanor made it clear that he welcomed the questions. "Do they know what has become of you since you left home?"

"They both died in the blaze that destroyed their house." Brugger looked into Moritz's eyes with an expression of boundless inner tranquillity. "Apparently some madman set fire to it after mutilating their bodies. Or maybe it was a convict on the run; the case was never solved. After some neighbors denounced me for supposedly having threatened my father during a quarrel a few months earlier, the police briefly arrested me.

Fortunately, a few of my students came forward to testify that I was leading a study session in another town when the fire broke out. So I was released almost immediately, although still under suspicion. I am sure that story will make its way into your files eventually. If you are going to waste money paying for idiotic gossip, you at least ought to get the most picturesque version."

Moritz scarcely knew which he found more sinister, the news about Brugger's parents or the casual way in which he told the story. He remembered newspaper reports about a notorious series of brutal killings in Bukovina, some of whose details sounded similar, but he had never connected them with Brugger and didn't know if the rebbe intended him to do so now. "Why are you telling me all this?" Moritz asked, pouring himself another cup of chamomile tea. "I thought we were discussing your pronouncements about what the Jewish Messiah's coming will be like?"

"What other Messiah's coming could I talk about?" Brugger's equanimity had given way to a mocking smile. "The goyim have already had theirs."

Moritz's cramps were coming more frequently now, and he was beginning to feel worn out. Worse, though, was his sense that Brugger knew about his pain and was deliberately prolonging the conversation to test what effect his suffering would have on the financier.

"I admit I don't trust noble sentiments when they go around unarmed, hoping to be admired for their purity of heart," Brugger continued. "You can care about survival or about innocence, but not about both. At least not at the same time, not if you are a Jew. I once told Nathan the only thing that really matters is what a person would die for rather than give up; the rest is just anecdotes. But tell me, Moritz, since you have set yourself up as both chief investigator and sole magistrate, exactly *what* am I supposed to have said to make you keep bringing up the Messiah? You are the one who can't go five minutes without mentioning him, not I. The only time I referred to him at all today was in direct response to one of your questions. You seem obsessed by one sentence of mine from a few weeks ago—a hypothetical sentence at that—about the transportation the Messiah would be likely to choose if he came in our lifetime. Speculating that he would probably pick an armored car instead of the traditional white donkey is hardly the incitement to violence you make it out to be. But of course you know what the country's rulers think, so I am ready to believe you if you tell me that my simple conjecture is enough to unleash dreadful consequences on our whole community. In that case things are worse here than I thought, and even someone as well connected as you might be better off with the Zionist pioneers on some work detail, transforming yourself into another one of their fabled new Jews by the sweat of your labor. If your health would permit it, of course."

"You can leave my health out of it, Brugger." Moritz rallied himself sufficiently to speak to the rebbe as coldly as he would to any business colleague whose presumption needed to be checked. "It would never occur to anyone at the Castle that what the workers are being offered is—what did you call it?—a hypothetical speculation by an itinerant preacher."

"Call it whatever you like, Moritz. When the time is ripe, labels like this won't matter anymore. I am sorry, though, for my cruel remark about your affliction. It was heartless of me, and I always regret causing unnecessary hurt. I wish I could heal your illness, but I came here too late for that."

Moritz was suddenly seized by a desperate urge to ask Brugger how long he still had to live. Although he was furious for being weak enough to think such a thing, very little in his life had required as much self-control as swallowing this question unasked. At that moment Brugger abruptly got up and brought a soft-boiled egg with a thin slice of cold veal and a small glass of port from the sideboard. He set them gently in front of Moritz, saying, "I know these are prohibited dishes, but today your doctor can be safely disobeyed. It is a small transgression, and you will feel stronger for it." For some reason, Moritz believed him and found himself enjoying the food without any pain. He was uncertain what to say to Brugger now, but as soon as the rebbe had seen the change in Moritz, he reverted back to his former manner. "What I have seen since coming to this town is a gulf not only between people but within each of you as well. You divide yourselves in more ways than I can count, and you move from studying business ledgers to books on Jewish law without the two ever contaminating each other. Everything is kept chastely in its own sphere. But what if that kind of chastity left us barren forever? What if indiscretion and audacity are exactly what is needed? When men like Moritz Rotenburg use the same word for their heart's yearning and their mind's cunning, only then, perhaps, is there a chance we shall see—I won't mention messianic days, since those syllables make you so nervous—but let us say a radiance that comes from being fully alive for the first time ever."

Far from winning Moritz over, Brugger's bringing him forbidden nourishment intensified Moritz's ill ease to an almost unendurable pitch. Although he had hoped to force Brugger to declare his real intentions without being asked directly, Moritz knew that he could not stand another moment of uncertainty. "What is it you want from me, Brugger?" he asked simply, and in a voice that left no doubt of his unhappiness.

"Even if I wanted to, I could not tell you," Brugger replied. "Searching your heart for what is demanded of you is your responsibility alone. No one is permitted to lift that burden from you. Come see me in my shul when you know, and tell me your yes or no. No matter what your word to me will be, you can go back to your other affairs certain that I will keep my promises to you—every one of them, without omitting anything."

"You already know what I believe, Brugger. The same way you know what Nathan believes. Aren't you at all worried that you are casting your pearls before swine?"

"As far as that goes, Moritz, my faith in our people is limitless, and I believe the swine are only proved such when they actually trample the pearls. I hope you rest peacefully tonight, and I wish you easy dreams."

· ◆ ·

Among Count Wiladowski's many gifts, the one that had proved most useful to him throughout his career was his ability to listen to people with apparently total attentiveness, and even to repeat back precisely what he had heard, with his mind completely blank. In reality, he had stopped being able to take in almost anyone else's feelings, words, or ideas long ago, but everything in his demeanor suggested the exact opposite. So Marie-Luise was just as mistaken in her certainty that she was the only person in the world to whom her husband was completely indifferent, as, from the contrary side, were his friends from the Ministry in their confidence that Wiladowski shared their absorption in the political intrigues at Court. For a long time already, Wiladowski had been intent exclusively on his own state of mind, but rather than become clearer as a result of so much attention, his thoughts grew paradoxically more formless and inchoate with each year. Outwardly the only visible signs of the transformation in the Count-Governor's consciousness were his by now proverbial terror of being assassinated and a greed for money that had become so fervent it was beginning to assume legendary status throughout the province. Both obsessions, and especially his covetousness, had overtaken him gradually, and reports of their intensity were greeted with surprise, as well as a certain distaste, by those who had known the ambitious young aide-de-camp decades earlier in Vienna and Rome. But these traits were more profoundly linked than Wiladowski's oldest friends, most of whose imaginative energies were still transfixed by the allure of Imperial honors and ministerial portfolios, wanted to understand.

"My damned lack of imagination" was the diagnosis that after much reflection, Wiladowski had finally seized upon to explain to himself what divided him from both his professional colleagues and his former self. He had become convinced that it was the increasing atrophy of that quality in his response to the world that made him feel so isolated whenever he heard colleagues buzzing with curiosity about some shift in government policy or rumored change in foreign postings. To most such news he had no inward reaction at all. It was as though the people among whom he had grown up had formed a family with its own private interests and distinctive ways of conversing. They all shared an extensive anthology of familiar histories and intimate jokes whose references would be lost on outsiders—indeed their unintelligibility to the rest of the world was the chief pleasure of most of the stories in the first place—but Wiladowski, somewhat to his surprise, found that these conversations no longer interested him. When he was asked how he felt about the latest "dramatic development" from the Ballhausplatz or Hofburg, Wiladowski found himself quite empty of any emotion, except for an irritable astonishment that people of his own class, well on in years, seemingly intelligent, and with comfortable estates and incomes, should still be so stirred by happenings from which they could derive no concrete benefits. All in all, he had come to conclude, nothing requires quite as vivid an imagination as to believe in the significance of issues that neither extend our lives nor promise us any increase in our physical well-being. To Wiladowski, the subtle shifts in power that formed the constant theme of his friends' speculations had begun to seem more like theological mysteries than matters of personal concern, and he was no longer able to marshal the energy to care about such abstruse questions. Even spending all of one's time hunting, like his late dim-witted cousin, now struck Wiladowski as no more senseless a way to go through life than analyzing budgets and receiving delegations in the perpetually underheated state rooms favored by His Majesty's senior Ministers in imitation of their Emperor's famously austere taste. Yet as Wiladowski had recently seen for himself, even a debauched old cynic like Count Károlyi grew tender-eyed at the prospect of a private audience with

His Imperial Majesty, although no one ever recalled Franz Josef's uttering a single significant phrase on such occasions. Wiladowski accepted as self-evident the principle that dynastic rulers like the Habsburgs had no need of personal magnetism, or even of intelligence, to awe their subjects, and he knew that their cultivated dullness was an almost ostentatious reminder that they could leave garish qualities like talent to plebeian upstarts who had to work to win the obedience that was the birthright of hereditary monarchs. The craving to make oneself interesting was no doubt a disagreeably parvenu trait, long since bred out of a family accustomed for generations to the fascinated attention of its subjects. But the ardor with which even otherwise skeptical members of the Empire's leading families scrutinized the slightest rearrangement in the Imperial household's daily schedule and guest list now struck the Count-Governor as an amiable superstition, no different from the fervor with which peasants abased themselves in front of the sacred pictures placed in some quaint roadside shrine.

Wiladowski took for granted that all deeply felt veneration requires endowing something inherently without meaning to the nonbeliever with an aureole of mystery and power, but he himself no longer possessed the inner elasticity required to do so except at rare intervals and with wavering conviction. Far from arriving at any new convictions to replace those he had absorbed, first as a child from his tutors and then as an adolescent, from the strict regimen imposed by his teachers, Wiladowski simply began to do without fixed principles altogether. He had slowly evolved into that most uncharacteristic of beings for the new century, an aristocratic materialist *without* a philosophy, and as an experienced gambler in the salons and casinos of Europe he calculated that the odds of someone like him surviving with his titles, income, and physical health intact for many more years were unappealingly slender.

The inner consequences of his lack of faith showed Wiladowski how similar were the demands both throne and altar placed upon their worshipers and how much imaginative energy the whole population expended in order to sustain these twin pillars of the regime. For himself, the Count-Governor had no regrets about having spent his life serving the interests of the Court, which until recently he had regarded as largely identical to his own. But unless it was completely unavoidable, he also had no intention of carrying his devotion to the point of actually putting his life at risk. The trouble was, as Tausk unkindly permitted himself to point out, that the socialists were unlikely to care much about the Count-Governor's private change of mind and would surely continue viewing him as an ideal target for their anger at the present order. Wiladowski reluctantly agreed that there was a certain insurmountable difficulty in his hope of continuing to exercise his post, which meant, among other things, to go on collecting all the revenue, both authorized and illicit, that were an Imperial Governor's perquisite, while somehow convincing the regime's enemies not to hold him accountable for his actions simply because he now believed as little as did they in the theoretical principles underpinning his authority. But even Tausk, who had come to anticipate the curious turnings of his employer's mind with uncanny accuracy, was unprepared for the Count-Governor's insistence that the very flagrance of his corruption ought to have demonstrated to the revolutionaries how little stock he still placed in the aristocratic code of disinterested public service and how entirely he had adapted his behavior to the modern insistence on the primacy of economic motivation in human nature. Instead of hating him for his venality, the radicals ought to applaud him for so publicly enacting their model of man as a creature driven purely by economic self-interest, and indeed, if they would only think hard about it, they would soon realize that logically, killing him was a kind of self-refutation unworthy of their ideological seriousness.

Tausk had little faith that such an argument was likely to prolong his employer's life, even if it reached the right ears, and suggested instead that he try to arrange a secret and, as it were, strictly personal truce between the Count and the socialists—say, a quid pro quo, in which they were guaranteed immunity from arrest in return for a promise never to make an attempt on the life of either the Governor or his Chief of Security. But as there were not just one or two but a good half dozen underground organizations, each with different aims and conflicting tactics, it would be impossible to conduct negotiations without its becoming known to mischief-makers in both the Imperial bureaucracy and the other radical cells. If the authorities in Vienna required midnight raids and regular convoys of prisoners as evidence of the Governor's official zeal, the revolutionaries were dependent on similarly predictable theatrics of rigged trials and exemplary martyrs to keep their adherents' passions properly inflamed. So Tausk reluctantly had to admit that his practical tactics offered not much more hope of success than the Count-Governor's fantasy of being applauded by the terrorists for the very flamboyance with which he incarnated the materialism they held sacred.

Among all these true believers, whether they spoke for the court or the militant factory workers, Wiladowski regarded himself as the only remaining authentic Austrian—the only one, that is, who valued survival higher than being in the right—and it struck him as curious that he should have remained faithful to what had been the millennial political practice of his country while entirely discarding the belief system that gave those practices their inner dignity. Although no one would ever dare say so to his face, Wiladowski often thought that without the Church to understand and forgive him and without the principle of legitimacy to justify his vast holdings, his behavior amounted to little more than swinishness and fear. And yet during the long, sleepless nights he spent pacing in his study, rather than feel shame when he tried out those words on himself, the Count found a certain mordant pleasure in the way they tasted in his mouth.

As it turned out, except for some of the gloomy and embittered priests, who compensated for their despondency at being relegated to an impoverished, backwater parish by a ferocious Augustinianism, there was no one except Tausk to whom Wiladowski was able to talk about the subtle gratification a man could feel contemplating his own ignominy. Everyone else he had tried to consult, from the members of his own staff to the approved thinkers whose works were carefully indexed by theme in the Imperial Staff Library, simply did not include any term resembling *swinishness* in their catalog of decisive human motivations. But perhaps it was his race's incomprehensible abhorrence of pig meat that had prepared the spymaster to speculate so lucidly about human piggishness in general. If so, then Wiladowski couldn't help wondering if Tausk, with typical Jewish argumentativeness, were not simply inverting a quite common trait, according to which everything that is deeply unpalatable as a metaphor becomes deliciously enticing as soon as it is understood literally. "It is just like kissing someone's behind" was the image he tried out on Tausk to illustrate this principle. "Think of how nobody is willing to admit he would ever do such a thing metaphorically to advance his career, yet how many of the most fastidious men are eager to enumerate all the lovely behinds they have kissed—especially if the lady in question is married and her husband is out of town. You Jews, on the other hand, seem to be as terrified by the lit-eral as you are unembarrassed by the metaphoric. I am sure that is why you had so much trouble with our Savior back then"—here he waved his hands in delicate semicircles to indicate, by the spatial ripples he produced, a vague stretch of centuries—"and why so many of you still balk at such an advantageous and obviously meaningless step as a simple act of conversion." When Tausk pleaded a former religious student's ignorance of which parts of a married woman were most suitable for lip service and confessed his inability to see the relationship between that act and converting to Christianity, Wiladowski, far from being irritated, felt subtly flattered by the suggestion that there were numerous domains where his worldly experience would always surpass Tausk's. "Well, then, to return to the metaphoric, where you are clearly more comfortable, wouldn't you agree that swinishness, malice, and fear have been greatly underrated by our political theorists? Can you name any better candidates to explain why people act so disgracefully even when they could easily afford not to? How many people stand in front of your desk every week to denounce someone they have known for years, who has done them no harm, and from whose troubles they have no way at all of benefiting? A department like yours needs its quotient of ordinary, unprompted human swinishness to do its job, that much is obvious, but I am convinced that so do the Foreign Office and all the cultural Ministries. Right now, in decent circles, only the Church talks openly about such matters, and that is why it is likely to survive even when no one pays any more attention to the rest of its teachings. We need *somebody* to tell us what pigs we are, if only to save us the annoyance of having to do so ourselves! When you show me those illegal pamphlets with their endless drivel about how naturally good everyone is, except of course for a few wicked people like me who can afford to wear clean collars, I start feeling quite cheerful because I just can't believe they will ever be taken seriously."

Wiladowski did not limit himself to Tausk as a conversational partner by choice or without a good deal of inner vexation at finding his options so circumscribed. But the few times he permitted himself an observation along these lines to someone whose intelligence he had once respected, he saw that his protests of indifference to even the most minor political skirmishes of the day were immediately interpreted as conventional opening gambits by an acknowledged master of diplomatic indirection. The more he insisted that he really had stopped caring who would be awarded the Leopold Cross in the Emperor's birthday honors list or who would be appointed to the delegation entrusted with negotiating a mutual defense alliance with Germany, the more he was credited with exercising a sinister influence on the government's decisions. Although Wiladowski had never been a Freemason, nor, as far as people knew, had any of the Imperial family, frustrated voices began to fantasize the existence of a vast network of interrelated Masonic lodges over which the Count-Governor and his accomplices ruled, secretly pulling the strings behind every important state decision. The rumors went on to explain that it could only be their common Masonic allegiance that joined a conservative aristocrat like Wiladowski to an odious creature like his new Jewish familiar, whose advice was sure to have terrible consequences for respectable, God-fearing citizens. Indeed, among those for whom Wiladowski's putative Masonic connections had been accepted as self-evident, a new skein of suppositions began to emerge that hinted at an ancestral mésalliance, perhaps even an intermingling with a shade of insufficiently baptized Jewish blood, somewhere in the family ancestry—possibly in the Italian branch, where such matters were less strictly regulated—until it was remembered that Marie-Luise's parents, whose anti-Semitism was beyond reproach, would never have permitted their daughter to marry someone about whose racial purity there could be any doubt.

Early one evening, immediately after the Count-Governor's return from a short trip to the capital to consult with the Ministry about conditions in the province, he summoned his spymaster to deliver his report at once, rather than wait for the regular morning conference with the rest of the Castle's senior staff. The tension of the past few months had begun to affect Wiladowski's usually voracious appetite, and the jolting of the express train had ruined the prospect of dinner for him entirely. As soon as Tausk came into the library, Wiladowski's spirits lifted somewhat, and after glancing through the thick file of papers Tausk handed him, the Count-Governor poured himself a large brandy, nodded at Tausk's obligatory refusal of his invitation to join him in a drink, and set about describing the expected effects of the government's latest policies. Soon, though, he swerved from official business to the theme that had become his latest obsession. "I am sorry I could not take you with me to Vienna," he said. "It would have been much more amusing to have you there, but your work here was too important for me to interrupt it. Still, I do wish you could have met people like my Colloredo nephews. They would have helped you understand right away what I am talking about. You see, they are lifelong, ferocious Imperial careerists, and so, to my way of thinking, their whole existence is one long exercise in abstract idealism. They get everything completely backward, of course, and think I am being particularly subtle the more crassly I express myself. I am the only one of that whole lot who has stopped worshiping phantoms and started taking care of his own skin first and last."

Tausk, who knew perfectly well that the people his master visited in Vienna would never exchange a single syllable with someone like him, tried not to show his skepticism about the pedagogic benefits of accompanying the Count-Governor. In any case, he knew that at moments like this, his employer did not want to be interrupted and so kept his expression attentively neutral. To Wiladowski, though, who had gone a whole week without feeling himself free to talk unchecked to someone who might actually understand him, Tausk's reticence was simply another welcome provocation. "There is no reason to look so theatrically over my shoulder while you try to make your face expressionless." The Count-Governor leaned in toward his spymaster and made a show of studying him closely. "I don't know what is going on inside that cunning Jewish brain of yours, but in your own way you are as much an idolater as any of those highborn imbeciles in Vienna. No matter what you tell me, I know you did not become a spy only for the pay, any more than my uncle became a Cardinal because of the cuisine in Rome. You both believe in power as something wonderful in itself, you both would sacrifice anything, including yourselves, to hold on to it, and secretly, you both take someone like me, who no longer feels the same way, for a fool."

Although Tausk had no interest in fine cooking, he was beginning to feel weak from a day in which he had been too busy to eat, and he found the Count-Governor's mention of food a torment. Dinner was about to be served downstairs, but it was unthinkable for him to bring that up, so Tausk did his best to rally himself and get through the conversation as best he could. "Your Excellency certainly should not go to Vienna so often if it puts you in that frame of mind," he said. "I would never presume to compare myself to His Eminence the Cardinal and still less permit myself to pass any judgment on my employer and benefactor. Besides, if I may speak freely without causing offense, haven't you yourself always taught me that the fundamental principle of statecraft is to sacrifice *others* but never oneself? That seems an admirable principle, which both idealists and men of prudential wisdom can happily endorse. But if I can redirect your attention to the dossier I brought in, Your Excellency will see that I have recently got hold of some information that might help us anticipate where trouble will come from next and perhaps even let us have a say in directing the socialists' plans without their knowing it."

"So that is why you appear so pleased with yourself today." Wiladowski smiled delightedly at his spymaster, whose exhaustion was visible in his eyes and whose appearance suggested anything but pleasure. "If you do have any information, it could not come at a better time, especially since it seems as though in spite of all my discouraging noises, the Minister is determined to go ahead and send Zichy-Ferraris to represent him at the rededication of the Bell Tower." Abruptly Wiladowski's face darkened. "Just what we need. A state visit with parades and full uniforms. Why don't we just put up a sign asking Messieurs les Assassins please to present themselves in front of the Cathedral steps, where His Imperial Majesty's government will provide them with plenty of chances to exercise their craft. 'Target practice courtesy of the Governor and his distinguished visitors!' I only hope your plan is a good one. I could do with some cheering up!"

"You may perhaps remember my report about a strange scene in front of the Mendelssohn Club the other day? The one involving Kaplansky and a rabbi who was unknown to me before." Tausk had given up any hope of a warm dinner and decided instead to take advantage of his tête-à-tête with the Count-Governor to advance his plans without interference from his enemies in the Castle bureaucracy. "Well, one of the people who came out of the club to talk to the rabbi was a certain Asher Blumenthal, an accountant employed by Sobieski but generally thought to be one of Rotenburg's creatures. Well, what I learned from keeping Blumenthal under close observation confirms the Rotenburg connection in a most unexpected way. I have prepared a brief file about it for you, based on a series of letters we have intercepted and copied from Blumenthal to an old friend of his who originally came from here and is now living in the capital as an aspiring writer."

As soon as he had heard that there was something in Tausk's report that concerned Moritz Rotenburg, the Count-Governor sat down at his large desk, put on his spectacles, and carefully went over the dossier. When he finished, he pushed aside the last pages, looked up at his spymaster, and in a tone of genuine admiration told Tausk: "But this is brilliant! Quite humbling in its subtlety. I understand now. Of course

Rotenburg is not going to want us to crush the troublemakers *yet*—not until he has milked the situation for everything he can. It is the sheer simplicity of his scheme that so enchants me; it is positively Mozartian! Really, if there were more of you, I don't know how any country could keep the Jews from taking over completely."

This time Tausk really did not understand what his employer meant. He had never found business interesting for its own sake and was quite willing to believe that the Count-Governor had grasped something in the file that he himself had overlooked. But when he said as much, the Count-Governor refused to believe him.

"Don't pretend to be so naive, Tausk," Wiladowski replied. "It hardly suits you. Even you have to agree that Rotenburg has devised a masterstroke. Look, here in your transcription of the accountant's letter, where he explains that Rotenburg is behind all the unrest. Since Rotenburg is obviously counting on using the Imperial army to manipulate business conditions for his private benefit, it is not surprising that he turns out to be the one secretly directing your mysterious preacher, and no doubt Kaplansky too. I sometimes wonder if even our poor Emperor is not being tricked into acting as one of your tribe's secret agents! We simply need to make clear to Rotenburg that keeping me alive will ultimately cost him less than dealing with my successor. That will ensure my safety all by itself." Wiladowski put his spectacles back in their case and, after first signaling that he wanted no written record of any of this, issued a set of new instructions. "From now on," he continued, "I do *not* want you to ask Rotenburg for additional contributions, no matter what the purpose. Is that understood? Just the regular payments should be perfectly adequate; anything extra we can raise by doubling the fines on the next lot of strikers and charging the smaller merchants more for police overtime. That way nobody can say we are favoring either side. And there is no more need to go easy on those we do arrest, is there? I am sure Rotenburg won't care what happens to his underlings, especially since we always seem to catch more Christians than Jews anyway."

Tausk ticked off each of the Count-Governor's sentences on his smoke-stained fingertips to show that he understood perfectly what was required. But he was unable to look as delighted by the new state of affairs as Wiladowski evidently expected, and when his master asked Tausk the reason for his air of concern, the spymaster allowed himself to state: "The makeup of the strikers may still change, Your Excellency. For the moment the picketers have forbidden Jews to march alongside them, so we aren't likely to encounter many in our raids. But I am not convinced it would be prudent to rely for Your Excellency's safety on nothing more than some information gleaned from a few letters by an insignificant creature like Asher Blumenthal. A man like Rotenburg would never have admitted Blumenthal into his full confidence. I think we have to treat this as un-proved speculation and continue working on several fronts simultaneously. In any case, we need to maintain some consistency in our strategy—if only to disguise the fact that we have figured out what is really going on."

The Count-Governor's disappointment was immediately apparent. Wiladowski slumped back into his chair and poured himself a fresh brandy, this time not even going through the ritual charade of inquiring if Tausk cared to join him. But after several deep sighs, and a nervous look at the library door, guarded from outside by two armed sentries, Wila-dowski nodded his head toward Tausk in reluctant agreement. Then, as though he had now devoted enough time to gloomy thoughts, Wiladowski reflected that even if it was not absolutely confirmed, there was no evi-dence Blumenthal's theory was wrong either. He liked Tausk's phrase *working on several fronts simultaneously,* since it kept open the possibility of spectacularly enriching himself while also safeguarding his life. On bal-ance, Wiladowski concluded, the news was still heartening, especially af-ter the futility of the recent meetings in Vienna. "You are right to be prudent," he told Tausk, "but your accountant has given us an opening we would be foolish not to use. The immediate business with Blumenthal, I leave in your hands. You should also send a few words over my signature to the Chief of Police in Vienna, requesting that he assist us in any way he can. It might be useful to have someone in the capital talk to that writer fellow as well. But be careful how much you give away to von Kirchmayr. I do not want any details of what we have talked about to get out, espe-cially not to anyone with influence in Vienna. If I am right about what they signify, these letters of yours are not only going to save my life—they are going to double my fortune! All I need to do is find out which factories Rotenburg is planning to buy and step in ahead of him with an offer of my own or, if that is too risky, secure enough of their shares so that at the least I will participate in Rotenburg's profits after the recovery. This is all very promising, Tausk! Very promising."

Tausk, who had been looking forward to returning to his quarters and asking for a cold meal to be sent up from the kitchen, was hoping his em-

ployer was getting ready to dismiss him. But Wiladowski had become intrigued by Tausk's dossier and was enjoying his own speculation about
what it signified.

"And what about this preacher?" the Count-Governor asked. "I would
not be at all surprised if he were higher up in Rotenburg's organization
than it appears. You were right to caution me about him, Tausk. What
have you learned about him since your first report?"

"Almost nothing useful, I am embarrassed to admit." Tausk's distress at
having to acknowledge his failure was allayed by the sheer relief of finally
arousing his master's interest in the rebbe. "He seems to have kept mostly
to himself lately," Tausk went on. "Although there is a regular stream of
visitors to his rooms, he is not admitting any of them. The people who
come to hear him are mostly just poor laborers anyway, and except for Kaplansky, no one of importance has been in touch with him since the
episode in the square. He has been getting some mail that we have gone
through, of course, but we've found nothing except a few innocuous
books."

"What kinds of books?" Wiladowski asked. "If they were on the prohibited list, why weren't they confiscated?"

"At this stage," Tausk said, hoping he had not made a tactical mistake
that would displease the Count-Governor, "it seemed wiser not to let him
know for certain that we are reading all his correspondence. But if Your
Excellency prefers a different approach, we can implement it right away.
My thought had been that if Brugger feels safe, he may get careless and
give away something useful. But so far the only thing that is really suspicious is that absolutely nothing he has received is forbidden. *Everybody*
who orders books from abroad gets sent at least some prohibited works,
but Brugger's package contained mostly well-thumbed studies in philosophy and mathematics. All of them completely respectable and even a bit
old-fashioned, according to some of the experts I consulted. It is true that
there were also a few treatises on biblical numerology and some volumes
of poetry, but nothing political at all, as far as I could make out. I even
went over an anthology of poems in Hebrew that looked as though they
had been marked up heavily, in case any of the verses were in code, but
they were just the usual lamentations for the fall of the Temple and the
hopes that the Messiah would come soon to restore his people to their
land."

Wiladowski had recovered his good spirits and wanted to let Tausk share in them by joking with him, almost without letting consideration of rank intrude. "To judge by the latest municipal elections in Vienna and Linz," he told his spymaster cheerfully, "it certainly looks as though every year more of our population shares the wish that *somebody* would send your people back to wherever it is you came from. Personally, though, I would find things dreadfully boring without a few Jews to provide the leaven we Austrians need. At least on that score His Imperial Majesty and I agree completely, even if his reasons are not exactly the same as mine. I don't suppose you know that before her horrible murder, the Empress herself stayed with Julie de Rothschild in Paris—and this in the middle of all that stupid fuss over Dreyfus."

When Tausk, to whom the anecdote about the late Empress meant nothing, tried to think of something pertinent to say, he could think of nothing but to ask whether news of Her Majesty's graciousness had been widely heralded in the newspapers.

"No, of course not!" Wiladowski stared at him in surprise. "She traveled strictly incognito. But still, what a tribute to her broad-mindedness! Not that her instinctive goodness toward her inferiors helped her in the end, poor woman. Well, let us try to make sure nothing similar happens to me. The thought of Countess Wiladowski's surviving another twenty years as my grieving widow is truly appalling. Maybe because she would be so perfect in the role, even if black is a particularly unsuitable color for her."

This time Tausk's blank look was entirely on purpose. There was no comment he could make that was not potentially dangerous to his career, and he stayed as imperturbable as a first-class diplomat overhearing a juicy scandal at an embassy ball. Wiladowski looked over at his spymaster and nodded approvingly at the dispassionate gaze he received back. The Count-Governor was pleased to find that Tausk really was a first-rate pupil, and it was in his role as teacher that Wiladowski went on to caution Tausk. "You do know that my wife would blame my assassination completely on your incompetence and see it as her sacred mission to punish you for it?" he said. "And believe me, without my protection, all the confidential information on us that I am sure you have managed to store away would not be nearly enough to protect you. What is it the French are so fond of advising their young? *Enrichissez-vous!*—'Get rich!'? Well, that's exactly what we are going to do with these letters: make me rich enough to continue living as luxuriously as a Jewish financier after I resign this post and move to where nobody is interested in killing me. And I won't forget

215

to include you when it comes time to cash in on the spoils. If everything works out, you will have the kind of private income to let you climb over all the virtuous Pfisters who stand in your way. Think of what a splendid coup it will be, how utterly fitting for this absurd century. Good work, Tausk. Even Zichy-Ferraris's coming is not going to bother me now. For the first time in weeks I feel positively famished. Literally and metaphorically, just ravenous. I was worried our little talk might run late, so I had the cook set my dinner aside and keep it nice and hot for me. I think I will have it now in my bedroom while I go through the rest of these papers from Vienna. You can tell them to bring it up now as you leave. And do try not to quarrel too much with Pfister at the meeting tomorrow."

· ◆ ·

It had required numerous such conversations, far more, actually, than he was happy to admit to himself, before Tausk recognized that in spite of the supercilious look his master habitually adopted when discussing anything not immediately related to his own practical welfare, Wiladowski possessed both a subtler and a more speculative mind than any of his subordinates. He was also far better read than he let most of the people around him see. Perhaps the years of recurrent childhood illness, before military service had forced the young Count to harden his nerves, had encouraged him, for a while at least, to explore his family's capacious library with a curiosity that extended beyond the famous leather bindings, each bearing the family crest, with which the sanctioned masterpieces of world literature stared out, symmetrically arrayed according to the book's size and thickness. There was something happily reassuring about such uniformity of appearance, and like their peers, the Wiladowskis were happy to think that by reclothing the mostly middle-class authors in calfskin and gilt, they had somehow rendered them socially acceptable—*Salonfähig*, or worthy of being admitted into distinguished company, to echo his mother's favorite phrase. Such a transformation in the physical appearance of the volumes before they were permanently enshrined in the library corresponded exactly to the discreet but detailed instructions about what to wear that accompanied invitations sent out to those especially favored bourgeois writers invited to join the nobility for after-dinner champagne and dessert on some of their larger semipublic receptions. Before they could be publicly seen, that is, both authors and texts were expected to put on a kind of costly livery, and the elegant symmetry in the way the aristocracy treated printed works and living artists was so entirely instinctive it had never occurred to any of them to put the principle governing their conduct into words. Wiladowski himself, who was thrilled the first few times his father had allowed him to stay up late and participate in these parties, found himself first astonished but then, within a few months, openly impatient at the discrepancy between the self-assured, graceful paragraphs he had read a few hours earlier in the library and the pompous banalities the same writers now exchanged with one another and their hosts. What grated most on Wiladowski was the odd combination of limitless vanity and anxious self-doubt with which these men conducted themselves. Like all Austrians, irrespective of class, Wiladowski had grown up immediately recognizing the various accents and expressions that distinguished domestic servants from factory laborers, middle-class tradespeople, or officials and bureaucrats of all ranks. Also like most members of his own caste, he was thoroughly trained in adjusting his expectations and demands to the capacities, as defined by his status, of the person he was addressing.

But the new generation of artists and intellectuals that began to go into society during Wiladowski's late adolescence was so awkwardly uncertain about its position that it required a continuous effort not to injure its self-esteem. For the possessors of hereditary titles, the whole idea of this uncertainty about one's place was not so much seditious as plainly nonsensical. Living artists, for example, were simply the elite of the servant class—clearly superior to, but belonging to the same general order as, the tutors who raised their children. If a malicious soul had wanted to vex a woman like the Princess von Magdeburg, Wiladowski's godmother, with a tricky question of social precedence, he might have asked her to distinguish the precise degree of respect that ought to be accorded a celebrated artist from that owed to a member of the lower clergy when he was not performing some impressive mystery like dispensing the Savior's body to her at mass. But apart from such delicate conundrums, there was very little uncertainty about everyone's rightful station. Lately, though, some of the younger geniuses, their titles freshly bestowed by one of the new monthly reviews, seemed to have lost all sense of their place, but rather than feeling freed from social constraints by this elevation, their misgivings about how much respect was actually due to them left them all absurdly skittish. Now that their articles had been published somewhere or other, or their plays produced in some small theater, silence about their success from even the most casual acquaintances was like a deliberate slight, and suddenly everyone, from an aloof headwaiter at a fashionable coffeehouse to an indifferent neighbor, was a potential source of injury. And so, if their unrecognized talent had been a constant torment, their acceptance into the world of official journals, art galleries, and stage troupes opened up surprising new grievances as well, if only because the disparity between being utterly unknown and attaining a measure of fame was not nearly as all-transforming as they had fantasized. Neither their wallets nor their public acclaim had swollen to anything like the extent they had dreamed about, yet it was not entirely insignificant either; some vital transformation in their situation must have occurred, or else what were they doing here, awkwardly balancing a champagne goblet and a plate heaped with Demel's fussily complicated miniature cakes in the billiard room of the Wiladowski townhouse? Just to be permitted past the liveried doorkeepers had seemed quite impossible only a year ago, and the envy it was raising at that very moment among all their uninvited rivals was more gratifying than anything else that their hosts could offer them. But if there was no doubt that their lives *had* changed, for how long and to what effect were maddeningly unclear. No one had ever given them advice on the most crucial questions of salon etiquette. Foremost among these was whether it was incumbent on a great talent like theirs to condescend to the undoubtedly fatuous aristocrats whose dessert wines and pastries they were avidly sampling, or to flatter them in the hope of securing a second invitation, and there were many minutes when the antithetical appeal of both options, even more than the borrowed evening clothes, made them excruciatingly uncomfortable. Unable to settle on one tone, they usually tried both, either in rapid succession or even at the same time, so that a single sentence testified both to indifferent hauteur and to the compulsion to make a favorable impression, a complexity that usually exceeded anything they had thus far attempted in their art.

Wiladowski was far too polite to show how keenly he felt the banality of both these options. He had grown up more like his Italian cousins than any of his Germanic relatives in considering intelligence a supremely entertaining quality, and since his principal ambition at that time consisted largely in being amused, he had looked forward to such evenings as an antidote to the tedium of conversations with his aristocratic friends. As a result, it was Wiladowski, not the rest of his family, who had never expected anything better, whom the crassness of these artists left disappointed and irritable. For a few more months, he still continued his afternoon reading sessions in the pleasantly quiet library, but at the parties it was the best-looking young ladies to whom he now paid attention, not the writers and musicians who had intrigued him only a little while before. Gradually his taste for women and his enthusiasm for books began to feed into each other, and an intense erotomania, in which the devouring of rare, obscene novels and the obsessive pursuit of constantly newer and more extravagant sexual experiences so took him over that he had little energy left for secondary pleasures. But this phase too ended abruptly, although hardly with the same indifferent boredom that had marked his withdrawal from the cultural chattering of the capital's famous salons.

One night, in a filthy lodging house in the Ottakring district, a proletarian part of town few of his friends would visit during the daylight, let alone at night in search of pleasure, the woman Wiladowski had bought suddenly attacked him with an open razor. If there had been any warning that she was unstable or even distraught in any way, he had been too absorbed in his own internal images to notice, and even long afterward, when he tried to reconstruct the whole episode, from the quickly concluded bargaining downstairs to the instant she emerged from the minuscule toilet with her clothes on the floor and her arms crossed provocatively behind her, there was nothing he could recall as in any way out of the ordinary. Since the beds in such places filled him with disgust, he was, as usual, sitting naked in a chair, fully aroused and tense with curiosity how her sex would feel when she lowered herself down on him, and the only detail he could remember with certainty was how repulsive he had found the sight of a few small hairs and hint of shaving soap clinging to the edge of the blade as it grazed him. At first he couldn't feel the actual injury at all, but even when he saw the blood start to trickle out of him, slowly at first and then with more rapid pulsations, his mind mechanically kept on speculating whether the light black stubble he had just glimpsed was from the girl's own pubic hair or a residue left by her pimp's mustache. Three weeks later, when he finally removed the last bandages, the doctor Wiladowski's set went to for the kinds of emergencies it was impossible to mention to their family physicians assured him that the thin scar on his abdomen would in time become almost invisible. The man's tone of avuncular worldliness was especially grating because it accompanied a litany of predictable phrases about how lucky the young Count was to have escaped with only a flesh wound and how easily he might have been permanently injured had the cut been a few centimeters higher or lower. But Wiladowski's displeasure had less to do with his doctor's commonplace mind—that was, after all, one of the reasons it had been advisable to consult him in the first place—than with the realization that in addition to the ugly physical reminder across his belly, the episode had left Wiladowski with a new sentiment that both men, patient and doctor, would have been shocked to hear verbalized, a permanent sense of the fragility of his flesh and a creeping fear of unexpected attacks on his life.

Wiladowski's fastidiousness about filthy bed linen had never before affected the excitement he felt touching the skin of the women who slept on such sheets, and their availability to every passerby was no more disturbing than the faintly disagreeable sensation that sometimes overcame him as he settled himself down into his seat on a train, knowing that he was about to spend several hours in intimate contact with a headrest and cushion that a total stranger's body had just occupied and left disagreeably warm to the touch. He certainly had no desire to become personally acquainted with his predecessors in either place, train or brothel, but he accepted the fact of their existence as part of the way the world was arranged: admittedly unsanitary, but also, so he had always taken for granted, convenient and unthreatening. Now, though, in spite of several attempts to resume his old habits, he found that since the attack his nervousness made it impossible to obtain gratification from a paid woman. He remained too alert and wary to yield to his own arousal, and all the familiar gestures of an experienced streetwalker, intended to signal her readiness to please him, became subject to sinister new interpretations. Even as he shrugged off these fantasies, the very effort required to do so reminded him of his vulnerability. Shopgirls were scarcely more reassuring than licensed prostitutes, and if his friends wished all such women could be forced by law to carry a medical certificate vouching for their health, Wiladowski was much more concerned about their state of mind. Had such a thing been available, and had he believed in the reliability of psychological diagnoses, it was a certificate of sanity, not freedom from venereal disease, that would have done the most to reassure him. Since no such document was forthcoming, Wiladowski began to modify his tastes once more, and he concentrated on finding something appealing in the well-bred, dull girls whom he knew his parents considered suitable matches. Their conversation might be inane, but this was compensated for by the no longer insignificant guarantee that their underwear and hairbrushes were free of stains from potentially diseased male interlopers and that they were unlikely to come at him with hidden razors.

In all these categories Marie-Luise proved exemplary. The reputation of her devout mother, as well as the strictness of the nuns who had educated the girl, was sufficient guarantee that her silk undergarments, like her mind, were utterly immaculate. The fact that she was widely regarded as the loveliest of the marriageable girls whose homes he and his friends visited, that she had every prospect of being even wealthier than he, and that her family and his own were so closely related that anything nearer would have required a costly papal dispensation, convinced him that it was senseless to look further. Thus, since such an alliance suited both sets of parents, as well as the group of powerful uncles and cousins who were involved, as a matter of course, in anything that centrally affected the whole family, Wiladowski went from sexual predator to zealous suitor to tolerably devoted husband in little more than a single social season. But the consolations of his library accompanied him in his marriage and career from Trieste to Rome, and he made certain that his favorite volumes were included in his suitcases that were packed for their holidays in the grand hotels of Biarritz and San Sebastian or in the hideously drafty rooms of his father-in-law's vacation lodge near Bad Aussee. It was in his books that the Count's libertinism found a permanent sanctuary. In time he began to return to some of the more serious writers who had attracted him as an adolescent, and if Marie-Luise had stayed awake long enough to scrutinize the titles on which her husband was soon spending most of his nights, she would almost certainly have been as distressed by the irreverence of the volumes of political theory on his nightstand as by the shameless indecency of his extensive collection of pornography. Indeed Wiladowski had let his reading influence him in unexpected ways. For one thing, unlike his wife or First Secretary, Wiladowski was less and less inclined to an automatic caste snobbism; he felt so little inner link to anyone around him that he actually welcomed the great levelers, as he liked to call them, of desire and fear, because they bore witness that he was somehow still connected to others. Just recently, for example, when Wiladowski took down a preposterously costly illustrated edition of *Grushenka's Enslavement* to signal that their meeting was at an end, he felt quite charmed upon hear-

221

ing Tausk confess to having spent many secretive nights in the seminary rapturously poring over cheap printings of the very same erotic classics that, decked out and aestheticized in exquisitely bound first editions, now provided the Count-Governor's chief consolation for the dreariness of his provincial posting. A snob like Pfister would no doubt have found repellent the suggestion of intimacy implicit in having yielded to the same seductive images as a filthy Jewish schemer, but then again, it was hard to imagine which stories beyond the fantasies of his own future career could possibly arouse Pfister in the first place. "The wonderful thing is," Wiladowski thought, "I am quite sure Tausk already possesses a complete list of the books Pfister has so much as leafed through during the past year. I will have to make him describe them to me in detail, especially if any of them are obscene. Perhaps afterward I will ask Pfister to lend me one of them—on Tausk's recommendation, of course!"

That the competitiveness between his First Secretary and his spymaster amused, rather than irritated, Wiladowski was well known throughout the Castle, especially since the Count-Governor so often goaded them into embarrassing demonstrations of their mutual loathing. As with many of his other personal eccentricities, everyone from Marie-Luise to senior department heads wrongly assumed that some cunning strategy had to lie behind Wiladowski's fostering of this rivalry. Deliberately to sabotage the smoothly impersonal functioning of his own bureaucracy by having his two most powerful subordinates constantly preoccupied with each other to the detriment, even, of their official duties must be part, so the widely accepted theory ran, of a larger plan to retain control of all administrative initiatives in his own hands. Initially Tausk had accepted this interpretation and believed that the more he proved his superior reliability and competence, the quicker Wiladowski would stop wasting such a valuable asset to check the ambitions of a second-rate personality like Matthias Pfister. Soon enough, though, Tausk had to confront the unsettling possibility that Wiladowski had no such plan in mind at all. The whole complex affair, all the slights and provocations he endured every day, might be no more than a whim, a game with which the Count-Governor entertained himself during the daily round of reports and memoranda in which he had long since ceased taking any interest except when they concerned his own private welfare. In a way, this knowledge felt more degrading than actual insults. To be a pawn in some elaborate maneuver was one thing, but here there was no subtle purpose at work, only the boredom of an idly powerful man whose consciousness found nothing worth its attention and had begun to seek relief in sheer malice.

• ◆ •

Subsequently, when each of the pertinent government agencies was asked for its evaluation of what the First Minister, with characteristic insistence on the need for a protective vagueness, refused to call anything more definite than "those unpleasant events at the rededication ceremony," the clearest point of unanimity in all the conflicting analyses was their lack of attention to the collapse of the province's economy and the ensuing pauperization of thousands of its inhabitants. No one was crass enough actually to quote the Lord's saying "For you have the poor always with you," but the truth of that observation was so thoroughly taken for granted that it made any further inquiry along such lines theologically, as well as politically, in dubious taste. But even Tausk, had his opinion been solicited, an unthinkable step considering his compromised status as the local functionary most directly at fault for failing to prevent the "unpleasantness," would have been skeptical of any attempt to link political terrorism to the misery rampant throughout the district. Yet he certainly knew how real that misery was. Tausk had spent endless frigid hours walking alone through the town, loitering on the street corners near the rows of dilapidated tenements close to the river, or drinking heavily sweetened mocha in some of the less elegant coffeehouses near the main square, listening to people's conversation and trying to form a clearer sense of their mood than his agents were able to provide in their reports. Contrary to his own expectations, Tausk had been forced to recognize that his familiarity with the poverty of the squalid Galician villages of his adolescence had done little to prepare him for the scope of the wretchedness in a city like this.

If Pfister had his way, Tausk's men would spend their days investigating every minor infraction, from petty smuggling to repeated attempts by Jewish artisans and storekeepers to work on Sundays, in spite of strict prohibitions against doing so. But whatever dangers the present situation harbored, Tausk was certain it would not come directly from the Josef Quarter's miserable specters, too caught up in the struggle to get through each day to plot an uprising. The Nepomuk Bridge, which spanned the river separating the army barracks from some of the worst districts, had been widened a century before by a prudent administration, and at the first sign of an emergency a whole squadron of cavalry could charge into any attempt at a riot before it got properly started. Against a mob, the will to strike first, swiftly and ruthlessly, was all-important, and although Tausk, unlike others in the provincial government, acknowledged that the population's suffering was reaching appalling proportions, he was just as ready as his superiors to have the army crush the slightest public unruliness. Out his office window, Tausk could often see dozens of hungry families awaiting the distribution of alms, huddled in front of one of the charitable institutions like pieces of battered luggage on a train platform. From a distance the long straggling queues, made up of lank, emaciated forms with their pale, cadaverous faces, looked more like an army of phantoms than living beings, and Tausk took for granted that if they could ever muster sufficient strength, their hatred would make them a terrible force. But so long as the army maintained its devotion to the Emperor, there was little to fear beyond a few broken windows and some trivial looting.

Walking amid the crowd in the once-thriving great market one Friday in the late afternoon, shortly before the Jews began to hurry home to light the Sabbath candles, Tausk carefully took in the casual brutality with which the police pushed aside all those who lingered too long in front of a display but were obviously too poor to buy anything. Often the men would flinch in anticipation of a blow before they were touched. Tausk understood, as though from deep within his own skin, their sense of shameful defeat. But his acute imaginative capacity to place himself in another's situation was severed from any forgiveness or love, and Roublev, his assistant, who had the best chance to observe him at work, was certain it was because Tausk refused to identify fully with his own unhappiness that he was unlikely to be stirred by anyone else's.

It was precisely this disjuncture between Tausk's imagination and the emotional indifference of his soul that Wiladowski valued, both because of its professional utility and because he could not help viewing it as a curious Jewish version of the inner aloofness from oneself and one's world that his instructors had held up, half a century ago, as a virtue unique to Catholic aristocrats who entered holy orders. Spying was certainly an odd kind of monastic discipline, Wiladowski reflected, but the more closely he observed Tausk at work, the more the parallel suggested itself to him. To most of humanity, informing on one's coreligionists might seem profoundly repugnant, but to the Count-Governor, who felt himself hedged in by innumerable contradictory desires and fears, for all of which he had

224

only contempt, there was something rather pure, and even enviable, in Tausk's lack of any discernible human fellow feeling.

Since Wiladowski now required his spymaster to be on hand for a late-night summons whenever his nightmares prevented him from falling asleep, Tausk had to return to the Castle much earlier than he thought prudent. He pleaded to be allowed to stay in town to continue his surveillance at least two or three nights a week, but more and more, Wiladowski's fear of terrorists took second place to his need for intelligent conversation to distract him from the loneliness of his bedchamber. Although Tausk understood how flattering the Count-Governor's desire for his company was, nothing had made him so uneasy since he began working at the Castle. Tausk was certain that so long as he knew what was going on, he could forestall serious trouble, but his confidence depended upon possessing enough reliable information to guide his decisions. Like many men with turbulent inner lives who succeed in the world only after they learn to subject their own first impulses to strict discipline, Tausk feared losing control of a situation by having nothing to dwell on except the proliferation of his own fantasies. He needed the resistance of a real world the way softer temperaments needed its acquiescence. If his own bleak childhood had not already done so, years of theological studies had shown him how quickly ingenuity could populate a cosmos with purely imaginary titanic forces, and in his exposed position, he was determined to rein in the inclination to spin webs of intrigue unjustified by objective evidence. The men he had personally trained were more afraid of him than of any street violence, and no doubt they would do a competent job reporting back to him the night's events, but to find his peace of mind dependent upon their powers of observation was excruciating. When Wiladowski, his nerves finally calmed by talking to his spymaster through much of the night, went peacefully back to bed, Tausk began the anxious wait until the first reports from his senior agents began to arrive. Before he had thoroughly digested all the dossiers, Tausk was unable to stay seated at his desk, let alone seek a few hours' sleep. Instead he paced his rooms, smoking one cigarette after another until the pads of his fingers were calloused with heat and nicotine. Since the formalization of his duties now required his presence at a series of midmorning budgetary meetings with the other departmental heads, Tausk often had to wait until the afternoon before he could lie down for a quick rest on the military cot he had ordered brought into his office.

Over the following weeks the ensuing exhaustion began to take its toll even on a man of his inflexible will. He grew increasingly short-tempered and found himself forced to expend ever larger amounts of self-control not to break out in rage at the professional incompetence and calculated slights of his enemies in the Castle bureaucracy. No matter how high the wood fire burned in the conference rooms, his hands and temples throbbed with a chill worse than two winters ago, when he had been awakened before sunrise for the day's first prayers. The permanent rings under his greenish gray eyes grew still more somber, and a rasping cough contorted his wiry body as though he were tubercular. The few times Marie-Luise, on her way to consult the Count-Governor about a domestic matter, encountered Tausk, she shied away from him as though he were a macabre apparition. She began to avoid crossing Tausk's path with the same aversion that made her pick a circuitous route into town in order not to drive past the foul-smelling tannery close to the river, and when she invited Pfister to one of her afternoon teas, she gave him the immense pleasure of comparing his rival to a venomous spider who had corrupted her husband and turned him against both of them.

Since the day he had entered the Count-Governor's service, no one except Tausk's most trusted lieutenants had ever seen him flustered by anything said in his presence. One morning in late February, though, when he was brought a report of a secret meeting at which Brugger was expected to appear, the agitation in Tausk's voice so unsettled the duty officer outside the door that the man applied for a different posting as soon as his shift was over. This mysterious wonder rebbe troubled Tausk far more than the mutterings of unemployed laborers in the Josef Quarter. The thinness of the information accumulated about Brugger so far made it impossible to gauge his motives for coming into the district, but Sonnenschön's letters left no doubt about the preacher's power over his followers. For all Tausk knew, Brugger might already have created a whole network of disciples on both sides of the border who could move about unnoticed by the police and whom Brugger had trained to act on their own. What Sonnenschön called Brugger's "liberating embrace of destruction" could easily be turned to political ends. Robert's urgent pleas to his sister to come join Brugger and to bring the worthiest of their childhood friends with her, an appeal echoed in the letters of the other disciples, sounded more like the gathering of a secret army than the pious exhortations Tausk was used to reading from followers of other wonder rabbis. It was impossible to exclude the idea that Brugger intended to incite an uprising among the poor Jews as part of his apocalyptic mission. Such an insurrection could spread wildly before being crushed. The dreams of some divinely sent rescuer regularly scorched the Empire's eastern provinces like a brushwood fire, and in the impoverished little market towns where Tausk had grown up, a holy man intent on mischief could do terrible damage before he was stopped. There was no reason to think something similar could not happen here, and with far bloodier consequences. If the army had to be called in to quell the disturbances, the only beneficiaries would be the Empire's enemies, and it occurred to Tausk that they might even be abetting Brugger—with or without his active knowledge—to foment a crisis along the border. But whether Brugger was acting entirely on his own or at someone else's behest, arresting him without knowing his intentions or the number of his adherents would solve nothing and itself could precipitate the violence Tausk was determined to prevent, especially if his followers were well trained enough to have no need of a direct order to carry out Brugger's wishes. Right now, in any case, Tausk had little to go on beyond his own instincts, and he knew that if he continued to press his argument about Brugger at the Castle, Pfister would accuse him of wanting to use the police to settle a quarrel for preeminence among a pack of disputatious Jews. Tausk's job, the First Secretary would enjoy reminding him, was to ferret out traitors and terrorists, not to set himself up as the arbiter of Jewish affairs. The Count-Governor's reaction to Tausk's first report about the wonder rabbi, immediately after the incident in front of the Mendelssohn Club, showed the spymaster that without tangible evidence, his master was unlikely to take Tausk's anxiety seriously either. Wiladowski, who was deathly afraid of known agitators like Nathan Kaplansky, lacked the capacity to recognize a threat from an entirely different source and would no doubt regard Tausk's dread of the rabbi as a parochial aberration.

To himself, Tausk had to admit that such an accusation might not be altogether wrong. Perhaps he had not entirely shed his religious training after all. In place of the rigorous faith that he had abandoned with relative ease precisely because it made claims on, and so was refutable by, his intelligence, he had never fully shaken off a cast of mind that manifested itself too obliquely to be recognized and thus expunged. Rabbi Pelz had been the only human being to have inspired in Tausk a combination of fear mixed with reluctant awe, and perhaps there was something about Brugger that reawakened his vestigial dread of holy men. But even if that were so, there was nothing mystical about Tausk's apprehension. He knew how deep the hatred against anyone with power ran throughout the province. It had already motivated a number of brutal crimes of which the still-unsolved butchery at the Bukovina hunting lodge was only the most flagrant example. More recently, one of Tausk's men had found a dog hung upside down from one of the broken streetlamps near the Nepomuk Bridge, with its belly carved open and Wiladowski's name on a piece of paper attached in place of a collar around the animal's neck. For the Count-Governor, these atrocities could only be the work of trained political terrorists, inspired by the latest seditious doctrines from Zurich and London, and Tausk knew better than to jeopardize his own position by trying to persuade Wiladowski otherwise. The Count-Governor wanted his spy force to concentrate its full attention on the militant socialists, and Tausk had a difficult time obtaining his agreement to keep the rabbi and his disciples under constant surveillance. But the trust Tausk had built up was sufficient to overcome the Count-Governor's reservations, and although Wiladowski refused to allow any further allocation of resources to the Brugger case, he decided, for the moment, not to interfere with Tausk's use of the agents already designated for the purpose.

Tausk understood Wiladowski's reasons for treating his disquiet about Brugger with dismissive amusement, but he regarded such easy psychologizing as fatuous, especially from a man whose shrewdness he had been forced, almost against himself, to acknowledge. Tausk saw no reason to take for granted, as Wiladowski, with his eighteenth-century sensibility did, that religious passions were dwindling as a political force. Tausk was ready to concede that his reaction to Brugger was shaped in part by memories of Avraham Pelz, but unlike the Count-Governor, he considered this a providential advance warning, not a misleading anachronism. He had experienced firsthand how unshakable a rabbi's rule over his disciples could be. A single word from Pelz was enough to settle everything, from whom his followers should marry to what professions they could pursue, and neither their parents' wishes nor the authority of the state counted for anything in their eyes once their teacher had spoken. The prospect of a man with this kind of power, unchecked by any inner compunctions or respect for the law, worried Tausk more than the sullen desperation of the crowd in the food lines. Whether Brugger really was such a man would be impossible to know for certain until it was too late, especially since Wiladowski's refusal to take the matter at all seriously was leaving Tausk dangerously isolated.

PART THREE

April 1913–May 1914

1

Perhaps because they had begun to spend so much of their time in the countryside at Brunnenberg, the von Alpsbach summer home, Ernst and Batya scarcely registered the feverishness gripping the town. And yet just as the muffled echoes of rifle shots from a party of hunters miles away will jangle the nerves of even the most cheerful picnickers, so the tensions the two brought with them from the outside world kept breaching the tranquillity of the vast estate.

Sometimes, after they made love, when she was sure Ernst had fallen asleep, Batya would slip on the Japanese-style dressing gown he had given her for her birthday, go out into the hallway, open the massive, freestanding wooden closet that had been built during his great-grandfather's time, and simply stand there, staring at the rows of Imperial uniforms hanging in a long double row. Although she couldn't identify the regimental markings, she knew that each uniform was the legacy of a firstborn son and that these uniforms had been worn by successive generations of von Alpsbachs ever since the Thirty Years War. She had once caught sight of Ernst doing the same thing, and in spite of her curiosity, a growing sense of discretion had stopped her from asking out loud what he was thinking as he took out first one and then another of the uniforms, held them up against his chest, and looked at himself in the large gilt mirror across the hallway. Many of the uniforms were far too short on Ernst, but that didn't seem to provoke a smile when he saw the comical figure reflected back at him, and there was something both moving and slightly irritating to Batya in the way he posed there, so serious and pensive about parts of his life from which she felt herself totally excluded. Two or three times since that afternoon she had found herself drawn to the same spot, as though the imitation of his gestures might bring her closer to understanding what he had been feeling. Against her own better instincts, she had spun out countless contradictory stories about what it was like for Ernst to see himself in these familiar ancestral costumes that had been waiting for him since childhood but that he would never wear except in private masquerades like these. She knew, though, that all these stories came out of her own imaginative repertoire, not his, and the sense of difference that knowledge brought with it caused her more pain than any of their frequent and increasingly sharp quarrels.

At least the fact that they were now openly together, even out here in Brunnenberg, had become less straining of late, since almost everyone of significance in the family hierarchy had left for Bohemia to watch Ernst's younger brother, Karl Gustav, at the spring maneuvers. Even Ernst's father, whose spirits had deteriorated precipitously since his early retirement from the service, and who was now usually too dejected to do much around the estate, cheerfully ordered his old military trunks packed in order to be present when the Emperor himself reviewed his troops at the all-day march-past that traditionally concluded the three-week military exercises. The large stone house, freshly painted in the dusty yellow that all the provincial nobility had copied from pictures of the Imperial residence at Bad Ischl, stood semideserted now, except for a stone-deaf aunt who had not come downstairs since Franz Josef's Great Jubilee of 1898 and a much-reduced staff of servants who adored Ernst and, to Batya's amusement, still insisted on referring to him as the young master. But no matter how the servants might have felt, for the family it was clearly Karl Gustav, three years younger than Ernst, but already possessing the inflexibility and self-satisfaction of a junior career officer destined for the General Staff, who had become the real inheritor of the von Alpsbach traditions.

It was impossible for Batya to guess how much Ernst minded this kind of relegation. Before they had ever met, Ernst had already made it clear to everyone that he would not take up a commission in the Imperial army and preferred spending his evenings with compromising types like young Rotenburg than with his own relatives. At first Karl Gustav had been scandalized by the way his brother, whom he had grown up passionately admiring, now turned the few family gatherings he still bothered to attend into a platform for seditious political lectures, but after a while the shock had given way to a bored impatience; like the rest of the family, he decided that Ernst's moralizing was simply tedious and, as he put it after one acrimonious dinner, "in the worst possible taste." Batya knew that Ernst would never be so unfair as to blame her for his having rejected a way of life on which he had turned his back long before they had met, but she was afraid that if he ever began seriously to regret that decision, he might link their love to his apostasy from family customs and so feel inwardly obliged to discard her as part of reclaiming his birthright. She knew as well that the suspicion was unjust to Ernst, but that didn't stop her from feeling aggrieved by her own fantasies. What made it all even more unfair, as she often told herself, as though deliberately to intensify her sense of being wronged, was that it was largely due to her urging that Ernst had begun to treat his family less belligerently in the first place.

From the first time Ernst brought her to a small luncheon at the Metropole with his mother, his two sisters, and a visiting cousin, everyone had been ostentatiously courteous to Batya, but their exaggerated politeness made clear, in a way no deliberate snub could have done, just how appalled they were at his inviting a middle-class Jewess to such intimate family occasions. For once the food really was superb. Everything was prepared exactly the way Ernst liked it: The cook's renowned clear beef consommé was followed by a perfectly poached freshwater trout, accompanied by delicate pitchers of rendered butter, boiled potatoes with a mild dill sauce, and a cucumber and tomato salad, all served with a chilled bottle of his favorite Grüner Veltliner. The women chattered away to one another in a series of breathless bursts that left no one time to complete a whole phrase and showed Batya why Ernst described the rule at his mother's parties as "Whoever stops talking to take in oxygen has already lost the match." No one was ever mentioned by anything Batya recognized as a plausible name. Instead, the conversation raced through the latest doings of various Putzis, Lilliputs, and Puckhes. The more famous the family name, the more its bearer seemed to prefer being called by something akin to the noises a baby makes. There was no way for Batya to participate without everyone's slowing down to explain the family shorthand to her, and she felt herself start to flush from the combination of strain and irritation trying to follow what was being said. But whenever one of them addressed her, it was with a peculiarly mollifying tone that showed the speaker so certain of her own superiority, and so certain that her listener knew how unbridgeable the social gulf between them was, that she was glad to make a special effort to spare Batya from feeling too intimidated by the disparity. Worst of all was the enthusiasm with which the more liberal younger women like Gretel von Wallderdorf, Ernst's cousin from Salzburg, tried to make clear the depth of their philo-Semitism. Gretel insisted upon mixing up her already grammatically shaky German with as many Yiddishisms as she could approximate, each one whispered to Batya with a conspiratorially friendly smile, as though she and Batya were allies in a setting that was rife with danger for both. "She must think that I am from some other species," Batya reflected, "and hopes that by trying to imitate the sounds we make, she can keep me calm enough not to jump up and knock over all the dishes on the table. It is the kind of noise people make at the zoo to show they aren't afraid of the large animals they have come to study, but since there aren't any protective bars here, poor Gretel needs to keep one eye fixed on the door." Gretel was starting to look positively cross-eyed with anxiety, and even Ernst wondered what could be the matter with her. What made it all the more absurd was that Batya knew no more Yiddish than the Wallderdorf girl. At home she had never heard anything but pure German spoken, and her own commitment to the revival of Hebrew made her regard Yiddish with more contempt than did any of the Catholic aristocrats at the table, for whom it was just one more of the numerous quaint dialects used by the Empire's subject races.

Of course she herself would never mention it to them directly, but Batya couldn't help being annoyed that none of Ernst's relatives ever suspected how many unpleasant hours it had taken her to persuade him to show up at his nephew's christening at Schladming or how she had tried repeatedly to get him to join his parents in Bohemia for at least a few days during the maneuvers. She had failed in that attempt, but at least Ernst didn't seem to resent her for having made the effort. There were times he showed something like gratitude for the ways she was trying to help him build a bridge back to his family. She passionately wished, though, that he would realize how much less awkward her position would be if he simply took the trouble to let his mother know that Batya had never pressured him for an introduction into the von Alpsbach circle. Initially, she had to admit, she felt flattered at the image of herself sitting in her prettiest green spring dress with her serious, wide-set eyes, which Ernst had described as looking like petrified wood, set off by the Loebner earrings he had given her, enjoying lunch in a window seat at the Metropole as an intimate of the family of one of the province's leading landowners. But the inanity of the conversation and the vexation of seeing herself being treated as an object of charitable condescension dissipated that pleasure quickly enough. Still, even that first time Batya was a little ashamed of herself for whatever flashes of vanity were being gratified by finding herself in such glamorous company. She knew that she would blush like a schoolgirl if Hans or, worse yet, his father were to see her there, leaning forward with an attentive expression while Magdi von Alpsbach talked loudly away, oblivious of the bits of cake and whipped cream clinging to her formidable upper lip. Except for special occasions, her own parents rarely went into the Metropole, so she was not worried about accidentally running into them, but she knew how much her liaison with Ernst troubled both of them, and although she didn't take seriously her mother's warnings that Ernst was merely using her as an exotic distraction until he found one of his own kind to marry, it was obvious that she would never be able to bring him into her own home without causing her parents, as well as him, intense embarrassment. Things would no doubt have been even worse had she known that Alfred ("Alfi" to all his intimates) and Magdi von Alpsbach entirely shared Rosa Demetz's expectations about the natural course the affair between their respective offspring would run, but with the crucial difference that for them, Ernst's temporary dalliance with a pretty Jewess was fundamentally reassuring. Though they never talked about it directly with each other, they both saw the affair as one of the few signs Ernst had given them, since becoming an adult, of an instinctive fidelity to the time-honored traditions of his caste. That a young man like Ernst had to sow his wild oats before making a satisfactory marriage was only natural, and an obviously healthy and halfway presentable Jewess was, all things considered, a safer choice than one of those potentially diseased and almost certainly money-grubbing females whom he might have been foolish enough to take up with before choosing an appropriate wife. Ernst's parents had heard enough horrifying stories about how a rapacious mistress could go through larger fortunes than even the von Alpsbachs possessed. Only last year Alfi had read Ernst's mother a long letter from one of his old regimental friends lamenting the necessity to sell off a choice tract of timber forest, and at a shockingly deflated price, in order to extract his son from a careless liaison of that sort. Besides, Batya's father was a doctor after all, and so, should any unfortunate accidents occur, no doubt the father could be relied upon to take care of the situation promptly and with a minimum of awkwardness. Weren't Jewish surgeons, who were not bound by the Church's scruples, always reliable for just such emergencies? Perhaps that was part of the reason why God, in His inscrutable wisdom, let them flourish in such unseemly numbers in the Empire's best medical schools.

Batya knew that the von Alpsbachs were unlikely ever to regard her as a suitable match for their son, but it never occurred to her to interpret their tolerance of the affair not as the first steps of a gradual inner accommodation but as a sign that for them it was impossible to imagine that it could go any further. They showed Batya the same degree of cautious politesse they would have extended to an agreeable stranger encountered at a summer resort whom they certainly never expected to meet again once the vacation had ended. The whole situation put Alfi in mind of one of old von Hradl's typically scabrous anecdotes. At least once every quarter the Count-Governor invited the provincial nobility to a dinner at the Castle, and after the women had retired upstairs with Marie-Luise, Wiladowski passed around his exquisite cigars and cognac—provided for him, according to a malicious and, one could only hope, unjustified rumor, by the rich Jew Moritz Rotenburg—and made a halfhearted attempt to sound out the men about conditions in the province. Wiladowski made no effort to disguise the fact that he was doing so only in obedience to a decree from Vienna, yet no one seemed to mind his obvious distaste for even this absolutely minimum gesture of consulting them about his decisions. As long as there was peace in the countryside and nothing interfered with their arbitrary rule on their own estates, they were glad to leave larger questions of policy entirely in the hands of the Governor. The really agreeable part of the evening for most of the men came when their host dropped any pretense of soliciting their political opinions, and emboldened by the Count-Governor's amused encouragement, the more self-assured among them took turns reminiscing about a colorful episode from earlier in their careers. If he was in an exceptionally cheerful mood, the Count-Governor might bring in one of his own famous engraved erotic volumes and leave it open on a special small lectern, designed originally for a family Bible, for them to admire as an illustration of whatever story he had found especially titillating. There was one anecdote, in particular, that Alfi regretted he could never tell his wife since it might have given her a reassuring glimpse of how men of the world handled the always delicate question of what to do when importuned by the wrong kind of woman.

Once, years ago, when he was finishing his first tour of duty in the army, Philip von Hradl had met a delicious young girl working in her father's millinery shop. He had gone in originally to buy a pair of gloves for the wife of one of his senior officers with whom he, as well as at least two other second lieutenants from a different regiment, was having the expected love affair. He had long ago forgotten the shopgirl's features but not her look of complacent sensuality or the way her breasts shifted in her loose-fitting white blouse when she bent down to retrieve the samples he had asked to see. He didn't linger overly long in the store that first day and kept his tone distantly courteous. He did make certain, though, that the gloves he settled on were the most expensive in the store, and by the time he left, he had added several items of a more intimate nature to his purchases. He found himself returning to see her almost daily and was charmed by the way their flirtation faithfully followed the verbal formulas prescribed by an insipid, sentimental novel long after their actual behavior had begun to resemble an inspired series of pornographic tableaux. As long as nothing indecent was ever spoken out loud, she was the most naturally eager sexual partner von Hradl had ever found, and he never ceased being fascinated by the discrepancy between her conventionally chaste speech and her body's capacity for almost instantaneous and feverish self-abandonment. Of course she expected the normal tribute of expensive little trinkets, but she kept her exactions within moderate bounds, and he was glad that he could buy them for her without straining his generous allowance. Being with her made him happy in a way he had not known before. That happiness had the unexpected benefit of endearing him all the more to his captain's wife, who dramatically renounced her other suitors to give herself exclusively to von Hradl, along with—since he was by general consent a truly kind man—her unsuspecting husband. Although von Hradl was far from overwhelmed by her sacrifice, he thought he owed it to his reputation as a gentleman to continue the adultery and so went regularly from one bed to another without, he was proud to remember, missing more than four or five morning parades because of exhaustion the entire time. Gradually, without his fully realizing it, the time von Hradl spent with his beautiful milliner had become indispensable to him, and he was astonished at the sharpness of his grief the day he heard that the regiment had been ordered to leave for a distant posting. Of course they exchanged promises to stay in touch, which neither believed—at least he assumed that she knew the conventions of a permanent break as well as she did the rituals of washing and perfuming herself before going to bed—and although he dreamed about her often in the weeks after he had left the area and sometimes found himself superimposing her features onto the most improbable women he saw in the store windows of his new town, it took only about six months longer than he had expected before she vanished entirely as an active presence in his mind.

So completely had he relegated her to a vague memory that two years later, when he was back at his parents' home in Vienna, he needed a few seconds before fully taking in that it really was her name on the letter the servant brought in late one afternoon as he was dressing to go to dinner. She was now an apprentice at a fashion house in the capital, managed by one of her father's business friends, and she hoped that they might start seeing each other again. She said that it was out of the question for her to entertain visitors in the room she had been given with her employer's family, but that she would be overjoyed if he were to invite her to visit him at the splendid house that she had passed several times in her first wanderings through the city without realizing it belonged to him. It wasn't easy for von Hradl to resist her offer. He was sure the gentlemen hearing the story would realize that; none of the women of whom he occasionally availed himself now came close to matching the milliner's freshness or sexual enthusiasm, but he had only recently begun to yield to his parents' entreaties to set about finding a rich wife before commencing his career, and an affair with a woman like that could undermine his resolve to regulate a life that was beginning to arouse adverse comments in the circles upon which his professional future as well as his marriage prospects depended. He answered her politely by return courier and gave a series of vague reasons, couched in all the acceptable phrases, for deciding—for both their sakes, of course—that it was best not to reopen old wounds now that at long last they had begun to heal. Remembering her former tastes, he enclosed, along with the letter, a lovely silver and gold powder case that he had bought as a going-away present for his sister and forgotten to give her last winter. More letters from her soon followed, not precisely forward in tone, but giving clear signs that her time in Vienna had already begun subtly to corrupt the girl's former innate modesty—unless that too had been only a youthful fantasy of his. But if she had grown more worldly, her progress was trivial compared with the miles that von Hradl had descended—that was not his own term for it, although Wiladowski subsequently used it to describe what charmed him about the story—along the path of self-betrayal. Von Hradl knew, no doubt before the idea occurred to her, that sooner or later she was bound to come to see him, even against his specific wishes, and he was determined that the first

238

time would be the only one. So when the day arrived, two weeks or so later, that the girl knocked at the great doorway, the porter already had his instructions. The uniformed old man listened patiently to her story of why she had come and the importance of her errand. Then, without raising his voice, or showing any sign of anger, he firmly pushed her back into the street, telling her before bolting shut the door, "Excuse me, dear lady, but a few barracks room fucks in Carinthia are not sufficient for a social introduction in Vienna." Von Hradl never heard from her again.

Batya, however, interpreted the courtesy shown to her as proof that her position at Brunnenberg was slowly but unmistakably becoming more secure and sometimes, when she was certain no one was observing her, began to speculate about how she would redesign the way the gardens had been laid out if she were ever to be the mistress of the house rather than simply the lover of its firstborn son. But if her intuition about how Ernst's parents felt about her was wildly misconceived, she was beginning to accumulate enough firsthand evidence to realize that it was pointless to look to Ernst's ideological convictions for any kind of guide to how he would behave toward others. Karl Gustav might make fun of his brother's "democratic mania," but in Batya's experience, Ernst's willingness to set aside the prerogatives of his rank was remarkable mostly for being so intermittent. With people he didn't know well, and sometimes even with those he did, Ernst could switch in an instant from the thoughtful naturalness Batya loved to a dismissive, patrician aloofness that made staying in the same room with him painful to her. Hans had once told her that a nobleman like Ernst was a revolutionary only at moments that suited his own convenience, and sometimes Batya felt that was equally true of Ernst as a lover and friend. In public, his radical political views allowed him to have a clean conscience while being just as rude to social inferiors as any of the arrogant cadets from the school at Mährisch-Weisskirchen. If Batya tried to remonstrate with him about his behavior, he often turned on her as well and insisted that it was exactly because he did *not* consider himself superior to others by birth that he felt entitled to insult them. "You do see that the poor clerk may not immediately realize that your bullying him is really a sign of equality?" Batya asked him, and as he often and winningly did, Ernst broke out into a wide, cheerfully appreciative smile and agreed that she was no doubt right. But if his accord was completely sincere, it did not seem to have any lasting effect on his behavior. Only a few days later, when they were on their way back to his apartment in town, Ernst flew into a violent rage with a cabdriver he insisted had been disrespectful to her. Batya had not even registered whatever Ernst found so offensive and tried to reassure him that it didn't matter in the least. But instead of calming him down, her composure seemed only to exacerbate the crisis. She had never seen anyone as furious as Ernst, standing there on the street, his clothes visibly drenched by the continuous heavy rain, oblivious of the alarmed looks of passersby who rushed as quickly as possible past the spectacle of this elegantly dressed, huge man waving a gloved fist threateningly over their heads. Batya was not afraid for herself, and certainly not for Ernst, who, if it came to a fight, was easily capable of cracking open the driver's skull, but it was terrifying to be in the presence of rage like this, unleashed, as far as she could tell, for no reason at all. It was as though the Ernst she knew had disappeared to be replaced by a stranger who was half insane with murderous urges. "It's horrible," Batya thought. "He looks exactly like that famous portrait of the von Alpsbach general who slaughtered all the Hussites three hundred years ago." But a little while later, when she had finally succeeded in paying off the terrorized cabdriver and had dragged Ernst inside, he seemed bewildered by his own outburst. He slumped down into the nearest chair as though recovering from a lengthy, exhausting journey. At first he tried to justify himself to her by insisting that what the man had said was so unspeakable that simple human self-respect made it impossible to let those kinds of insults go unanswered, and for a moment it almost seemed that he might suddenly transfer his rage to her. She saw the flush of anger flicker momentarily, like a fever, across his face, only to be extinguished with a quick shaking of his head. Then he asked her to get him a lukewarm compress, folded it over his eyes, stretched out fully dressed on the leather sofa, and almost immediately fell into a peaceful sleep that lasted well into morning.

Batya intended to sit beside him in the dimmed light throughout the night, hoping he might wake up after a while and help her make sense of what had just happened. She was too nervous to rest at first, but hearing her lover's untroubled breathing gradually calmed her agitation. Slowly, as the lassitude of her own exhausted spirit began to penetrate her body, she fell into a dream in which she and Ernst were engrossed in an enormously intricate and subtle conversation that had already gone' on for innumerable hours yet felt as though it was still in its initial rhythms. They had never spoken so naturally or completely before; not only was every word taken in and understood exactly as it was intended, but she felt that they each were able for the first time to find a language for who they were and whom they wanted to become without any sense of distance between the words they used and the inner ideas and feelings that prompted them. The awareness of harmony was so powerful and reassuring that Batya was barely surprised when she looked around and noticed that instead of being anywhere that she could recognize, they were sitting alone at a watering hole in an immense, radiant desert in which Ernst had chosen to live. All the uncertainties that often paralyzed her feelings for him were dissolving without leaving any residue, and she thought it was right that in the glare of the midday sun over the dunes, he should no longer look to her like an ordinary man, but like some shimmering desert creature, only partially human, with just his face still entirely unchanged.

Later, when Batya recalled her dream, she was struck by the realization that for the whole time it lasted, neither of them ever spoke directly about their love for the other or, as they sometimes tentatively enjoyed doing in moments of intimacy, made any plans for their future. All those questions seemed to have been settled long ago, and the certainty they felt was like seeing a gatekeeper open a path for them into an ancient clearing, trusting them to build a habitable dwelling place there. Words that had always sounded like nothing more than bloodless abstractions felt as palpable and real to her as the wheeling birds overhead or the freshness of the bright water in the pool where she periodically dipped her wrists. "Have we often been permitted to come here?" she asked Ernst, as though she had forgotten a crucial part of their common story but was no longer troubled by that forgetting. But Ernst, or rather the semistrange, semifamiliar creature that he had become, did not answer her directly but only stretched his massive limbs and scanned the horizon for the first tremors of an approaching sandstorm. Since even in the midst of her dream, Batya clung to the belief that she was only lightly asleep and retained the conscious willpower to take in and store everything she saw, she was surprised by how little of it remained with her after she was fully awake. But for the rest of her life she was certain that it really was Ernst, transformed into some new kind of being, and not a purely imaginary dream creation summoned out of her own exhaustion and bewilderment, who had told her his story and thereby made it hers as well. And although she could not recreate his exact words or the fierce legends that accompanied them, she knew that he had shown her how people all held, hived in the cells of their bodies and the blood that coursed through them, the stored-up traits

241

of all their ancestors. The fragmentary deeds and desires of men and women whose names had been obliterated in cemeteries for generations were as much part of the living person who emerged into the ambiguous brightness of every new day as were his own birth parents. Ernst told her how bewildered he had been the first time he was forced to recognize that his strongest emotions had never belonged only to him but were also the portals the dead made use of as their opening back into the world. For years he had suffered agonies of self-reproach each time he felt himself defeated in the struggle to shield his consciousness from their insistent clamor. He had read voluminously about demonic possession and, without telling anyone, even made a pilgrimage to consult a celebrated religious healer at the Benedictine Abbey of Melk. He rode away again after only two interviews, convinced that the Church had nothing useful to say on what was tormenting him. Only out here, in the desert, had he begun to learn how to summon and blend the voices inside him like separate instruments in a single musical score whose performance was his life's task, just as it had been that of each of his predecessors. In this place of safety he was finally able to welcome all of them without fear of being flooded or taken over. He had gone into the the wilderness to find a different kind of teacher, but the best one he met only shrugged his shoulders and sent Ernst on his way, saying that there were already enough heresiarchs inside Ernst to start a dozen new sects. "Why me then," Batya asked him, "or why anyone?" And he pointed toward the clearing that she thought had been only a momentary image in her mind, and she understood that it was their shared place of safety, not his or hers alone, that he was looking for and that it was her promise to make a garden for him, spoken once, weeks earlier, in reconciliation, that had brought both of them there. She wondered if her body too would start to change like his, and she felt the beginning of desire and curiosity. Only slowly did she grow aware of losing the dream to the numbness in her arm where it had curled around her head to keep out the morning noises from the street.

It took her several more minutes to distinguish the muted sounds in the next room from those coming in through the dark green curtains, but once she raised herself up and began to focus on Ernst fumbling with the breakfast tray, she thought that no matter how many ancestors might have left him their experiences to draw on, clearly not one of them had ever prepared his own meals. The clumsiness of the man trying to arrange something as simple as a morning tea with warm rolls and the imported,

242

slightly bitter orange marmalade he loved and always assumed, quite incorrectly, that she must as well was disconcertingly unrelated to the fluid grace with which he had cared for all her needs in the desert. To Batya, holding on to her dream seemed incomparably important, and she brushed aside all his attempts at ordinary morning chatter in an increasingly desperate effort to pick up their conversation at the watering hole which they had left off only moments ago. Perhaps no part of our dream is harder to surrender than the belief that the words and feelings addressed to us while we were sleeping must have left some echo, a resonance, no matter how attenuated, in whoever had appeared with us in our dream, and it was almost with anger that Batya kept on giving Ernst the outline of what he had told her in the desert in order to jog his memory and confirm her sense that something enormously important had happened between them. "Don't you see how this changes everything"—she kept hammering at him—"how far we went together tonight, and how terribly sad it would be to lose it all just because I am the only one who believes it? It is not just *my* dream you would be denying; it is also what I have started to understand about *you!*" But the more she pressed, the more she felt Ernst retreating, until his amused reassurances that it was no doubt a lovely dream and that he was glad for her that the night, which had begun so badly, had redeemed itself, and, he hoped, him as well, began to take on a slightly impatient and even edgy tone to match hers, as though he were being asked to honor a promise he was certain he had never made. Turning their attention to the meal seemed to offer the best chance to sidestep what was quickly becoming a rancorous dispute, and fortunately, as soon as they began to devour the rolls Ernst had brought in, they both realized how famished they were. But even the pleasure of finding themselves together on a fresh, clear day, alert and physically quick with hunger, was slowly being dissipated by the effort to shake off their disappointment at having come to that common morning from such incompatible directions. The apartment was starting to feel oppressive, and both were relieved to notice that the servants, who had assumed Ernst was staying at Brunnenberg, had neglected to lay in anything substantial for them to eat so that they would have to go out to a coffeehouse to appease their craving for more sandwiches and morning pastries.

Throughout their long breakfast, which was beginning to merge into that wonderful Austrian custom of the midday snack, Batya tried to take stock of her position. She needed to balance the intensity of her dream not with Ernst's frivolous dismissal of it but with a clearer picture of what she wanted for herself. But the more she tried to fix her thoughts, the more equivocal they became. It was as though she were looking down at the table and taking in the large silver creamer beside her steaming cup of Indian tea, the half-eaten golden brown crescent pastry filled with dark poppy seeds, and the stack of newspapers, each on its own awkward wooden rack, piled up next to Ernst, but somehow not being able to identify the scene as breakfast in a restaurant with her lover. All the individual details were unnaturally sharp, but the composition as a whole was losing coherence every time she looked at it more closely. It was a feeling that was becoming unnervingly familiar of late and matched nothing that had ever happened to her before this year. Batya sometimes felt that her whole world was disintegrating into separate scenes into which she was suddenly thrust—into which, in truth, she deliberately thrust herself—without being able to form any sense of connection among them. She kept on breaking off pieces of different pastries and sharing them with Ernst long after she was full, not just out of nervousness but as the only physical way she had of confirming their intimacy without the risk of a conversation that might show how fragile it actually was. Wherever she looked these days, it was as though Batya perceived vultures hovering nearby that no one else seemed to notice.

She and Ernst had eaten together in a similarly tense mood a few days after she had run into Hans and had coffee in his flat in the Josef Quarter. When she tried to tell Ernst about the encounter, it had gone far worse at first than she had anticipated. Whatever feelings had once made Ernst and Hans see themselves as brothers-in-arms had been replaced by undisguised contempt. Ernst had nothing but abhorrence for Hans's politics, and although Batya shared Ernst's judgment, it was unnerving to hear him lash out at Hans's fascination with violence in a tone that was itself a knot of rage. She saw Ernst make an enormous effort to calm himself, and when he finally succeeded, he explained that it was her safety, not anyone else's, he could not forgive Hans for jeopardizing. "You know," he told her, "we all have followed your wishes and called you Batya for so long I had almost forgotten you were originally named Elisabeth, after the late Empress, weren't you? So your nickname could have been Sissi too? I met her once at Schönbrunn when I was a very little boy, and of course, like everyone else, I fell madly in love with her. Less than two years later that madman from the Regicide Squad stabbed her in Geneva. I know it has nothing to do with you, or me, or Hans, but I refuse to lose you to another fanatic's deluded fantasies." Hearing him like this, Batya reached her arm across the table and gently ran her hand along his arm. She saw in Ernst's eyes how her gesture only seemed to heighten his nervousness, but he mastered himself sufficiently to go on in his familiar ironic tone. "Just pick up any of the Viennese journals," he said, "and you will see right away that in our politics, in our dreams—at least according to the latest experts in that field—and certainly in our fashionable plays and novellas, all we talk about is murder. If you haven't at least committed a few killings in your imagination, you are considered a hopeless reactionary. Did you know, by the way, that the man who murdered Sissi actually wanted to kill King Umberto of Italy but couldn't afford the train fare from Geneva to Rome? At least that is one logistical difficulty no one working with Hans needs to worry about. It makes a splendid argument for having only wealthy terrorists; at least one can be confident they are able to travel to wherever their preferred targets live and not have to settle for second choices. It really is true, Batya; your namesake died because an anarchist had the nerve to stab a woman through the heart but not to board a train without a proper ticket. Now why hasn't someone made a play about that? I wonder."

Ernst was sure the police were already keeping Hans under surveillance. It occurred to Batya now, thinking back on their earlier conversation, that perhaps Ernst had taken the cabdriver for a police spy and that his rage had been triggered by a combination of fear for her safety and anger that she had put herself at risk by going into Hans's apartment. Nothing in the cabdriver's attitude matched her conception of a police informer, but she knew better than to trust such impressions, and in any case, what really mattered was how Ernst had perceived him. It was revolting to Batya to recognize that her world now included the real possibility that the man driving her home might be reporting to the authorities what she and her lover had talked about. Her whole being felt dirtied, and she recoiled back into herself as though she had suddenly felt something foul dragging itself across her skin. For the rest of the meal she had a desperate urge simply to run away from all of them, from Ernst as much as from Hans, from her parents, from the Rotenburgs and the von Alpsbachs, from everyone she knew in this dreadful province. She was so startled by the chain of ideas set in motion by her thoughts that she reached across the small restaurant table a second time and tenderly held Ernst's palm between both her hands. The promptness with which his smile answered her immediately made her feel better and allowed her not to ask Ernst to confirm her suspicions about the cabdriver, lest in talking about them, she might also give away how far she had wandered from Ernst in her musings.

They both agreed that it was better to return to Brunnenberg at once and forgo a second evening in town. The ride helped restore their equanimity, and they enjoyed pointing out to each other how the countryside was beginning its slow modulation into the first faint colors of spring. Over the stubble fields, the afternoon shadows were pearl and blue-gray as though still awaiting the snow that had covered them for so long. As one entered the nearby woods, though, the air around the birch trees seemed already to have picked up subtle hints of the coming thaw. Batya loved the taste at the back of her throat of different seasons mixing together like two kinds of apple, sweet and a little tart at the same time. Whenever they came out together for a few days, she felt herself start to smile with contentment the moment she caught sight of the white-columned gates, and what had seemed so unwelcoming to her only a short while ago now felt almost too comfortable. As soon as they had alighted from the carriage and gone inside, Ernst, satiated and sleepy, lay down for a nap, joking to her that he was doing so to try to take up in his own dreams the discussions he had begun in Batya's the night before. Batya sat reading for a while; but then her mind and limbs grew restless together, and she found herself wandering back into the hallway with its oppressive accumulation of von Alpsbach heirlooms. This time, when she opened the old wardrobe, the pungent, familiar odor of naphthalene and camphor with which the uniforms had been treated against moths suddenly made her terribly homesick for the smells of her parents' house. Every spring her mother's fur coat and her father's heavy woolen suits were put into storage, and she remembered helping her mother stuff mothballs drenched with exactly the same smell into all the pockets. Then, right after the grape harvest, a month before the first autumn storms were expected, all the clothes were brought out of storage, the pockets emptied, and everything given a thorough shaking out in the backyard. Although the start of the school year would be almost three weeks away, Batya remembered being afraid that the smell of naphthalene would still be clinging to her when classes began, and for her final year at school she had firmly refused to help with the annual chore.

As she lifted the heavy uniforms out of their protective covering, she noticed again how even the oldest of them were kept impeccably clean and ready for wear, the sword blades still sharp enough to cut through flesh as easily as through the bit of fabric on which she tested several of them. Everything hung there as though the long-dead cavalry officers would return, like phantoms from a childhood fairy tale, to answer the summons of their Emperor in his hour of need. It was something Ernst could never talk about with her, and he must have felt that she regarded all these relics as absurd idols, meaningless except to flatter their possessor with tangible evidence of the family's antiquity. And probably she *had* once made a careless joke to that effect; it was one of the things she found most annoying about herself, her inability to let a clever phrase pass unspoken, but it was also foolish of him to assume right away that she would be unable to understand what his heritage meant to him. She needed his words to feel her way into how the world must look to someone like him, and by never speaking about that part of his life, Ernst was only widening the distance between them. He seemed helpless to do otherwise, with a stubborn, injured brittleness that quickly exhausted her never overlarge storehouse of patience and only made everything worse. Their mutual incomprehension often left them both feeling bruised, and the intensity of their desire for each other now seemed to exist in a separate realm from the rest of their being. Lately many of her own emotions had begun to perplex Batya, but none so much as her awareness of a continually widening abyss, not just between herself and Ernst but within herself as well, as though the different parts of her own personality were simply no longer able to communicate with one another. She told herself, "I don't feel diminished by the life ahead. But who is the 'I' in these sentences? Sometimes I no longer know who is speaking when I talk. These days when I wake up at night, I don't know who is inhabiting this body." When Ernst came to her for sex, she was often as eager and hungry for it as he was, but the shock of her always renewed craving for him made her feel that her body, for all the pleasure it was giving her, had become, in a sense, more strange to her, not less. Once in a letter she wrote to him but tore up before it was halfway completed, she asked Ernst if he didn't think their physical merging was being paid for by a kind of psychic disintegration. She had begun to think of passion as subject to some implacable law that regulated outpouring and withdrawal, intimacy and isolation, according to a rhythm she could never fathom. The more they desired each other, and the more happiness they found in being together, the less of themselves they could actually share. It made no sense to her, and if her frustration sometimes found an outlet in provoking meaningless quarrels, it more often left her unnaturally silent, trying to comprehend a growing sense of dread to which she could not give any name, except that it was as though she were losing her physical substance and that as long as she stayed with Ernst, she would never take up enough space in the world.

Because most of her girlfriends kept complaining about the weight they gained when they were contentedly in the middle stages of a love affair—the regular afternoon rendezvous for hot chocolate and whipped cream–covered cakes almost guaranteed such a result—Batya could be amused at her worry that love was robbing her of her physical solidity. But she was also bewildered by a fear of becoming, if only in her own eyes, too insubstantial to take seriously. She could not turn the events of their affair or even the shifting course of her emotions into any kind of story, not even to herself, and felt a sense of emptiness that none of Ernst's reassurances could reach. There were hours when she deliberately made herself catalog everything from which she had walked away during the past few months and was always freshly astonished at how easily she had done so. In her harsher moments that struck her as a moral failing, but there was nothing she could truthfully claim to miss from her previous life, except, in a way that was useless to herself now, the fact of having had a previous life at all.

The next day, when she came back inside from a long walk across the gardens that stretched out behind the glass-domed hothouse, her shoes clotted with mud from the puddles that made crossing even the carefully laid-out gravel pathways an adventure, she again realized how much she had grown to love this place. Lately Ernst too was starting to take a greater interest in Brunnenberg and often spent hours going over the accounts with Franzi Potoscheck, the estate manager, while Batya had gotten into the habit of using that time to retreat into the library and browse among the rows of maple shelves lined with perfectly dusted, black and gold leather–bound books. Although she enjoyed being in the warm room with its heavy dark curtains and invitation to lose oneself in random daydreams, Batya was rarely tempted enough by any of the titles to disturb their placidity. There were too many things she needed to clarify in her own mind before she could regain the concentration to give herself over to anyone else's story.

It was neither her intelligence nor her sympathy that Ernst mistrusted, Batya was sure of that. But there was some fundamental quality of imagination, either his own or hers, in which he seemed unable to believe. In spite of her mother's warnings, she was certain that her being Jewish had very little to do with it. Hans had treated her the same way, and when she thought back on her discussions with him, she could not help recalling all his comments about Ernst's lack of inner depth or resolution. The fact that *inwardness* and *resolve* were two of Hans's favorite terms and that he used them freely to browbeat anyone with whom he disagreed did not stop them from sometimes being applicable. There was something grating, as in a too neatly structured theater piece, about the way the two men's disparaging comments about each other were so perfectly symmetrical. Hans cautioned her about the moral hollowness of the born nobleman, Ernst about the natural self-indulgence of the irresponsibly rich. For all their antagonism and jealousy, though, Batya was pained by the realization that even now, after their break, Ernst and Hans would continue to take each other seriously in a way that neither of them had regarded her so far.

· ◆ ·

"Treason is simply a question of dates." How smugly the wits in the Foreign Ministry loved quoting that fifty-year-old aphorism of Talleyrand's as though it crystallized some profound wisdom. The philosophy of a lackey out to impress everyone with his worldliness was how Wiladowski characterized the idea to his First Secretary, who, the Count-Governor knew, secretly studied the French statesman's writings like Holy Writ and referred to his maxims whenever he thought it advantageous—most frequently when Marie-Luise was nearby, eager to be impressed by the political sagacity of her protégé. Now that his wife had taken up Pfister as her counterweight to Tausk's growing influence in the Castle, the boredom the man inspired in Wiladowski was turning into active dislike.

The Count-Governor knew it was pointless trying to make someone like Pfister understand that every treason that really matters also involves an act of self-betrayal. To betray one's Emperor, lover, or friend requires first abandoning the man who has pledged himself to them. And if his embittered nights of self-scrutiny had taught Wiladowski anything, it was that the men coming to blow him up would find that he himself had already done a good part of their work for them. The paralyzing fear of dying that sometimes made every slight ache something to be fretted over for hours was not based, as Marie-Luise and most of his staff suspected, on an absurdly exorbitant self-love. Quite the contrary; it is, if anything, easier for a man who has learned to regard himself with fastidious distaste to dread the end of his life than for someone who still has faith in the integrity of his passions. The innumerable acts of betrayal that he had committed; the lengthening shadow of the betrayals he had suffered: Far from canceling one another out, they seemed rather to merge into a single story in which if there were no clear villains or heroes left, there were also painfully few unpolluted moments to hold on to. At most, time might muffle the pain of injuries he had suffered at the hands of men and women whose appearance he could scarcely remember, but it did nothing to assuage the knowledge of the self-betrayals that punctuated the decades of his life more decisively than any birthdays. There were whole weeks now when, instead of concentrating on governmental matters, he found his mind rummaging through an inner ledger book of faithlessness and equivocations like some overscrupulous archivist hired to bring order to a jumbled heap of carelessly amassed records. He knew that although their remedies would differ, his private doctor and the Castle's official chaplain both would point out how unhealthy such morbid thoughts were, but he had long ceased being interested in such advice. What astonished him was not his own state of mind but that hardly any of the people he knew were troubled by similar thoughts. He was not misunderstood, far from it; but to his colleagues, what Wiladowski called betrayal was simply the way of the world, and to them it made no more sense to become agitated about it than about the inevitable August rainstorms that could be counted on to disrupt a certain percentage of vacation days in the lake district outside Salzburg. Besides, didn't both their professional and personal lives depend on dispensing with anything as inconvenient as a too finicky scrupulousness about out-of-date loyalties? As diplomats, as well as men with expensive mistresses and inquisitive wives, if betrayal were not an elastic concept, amenable to constant reinterpretation, life would quickly become impossible to manage, and both the nation and most of its leading families would find themselves embroiled in unending warfare. But in spite of his position and wealth, Wiladowski was surprisingly immune to such perfectly reasonable considerations. At the Foreign Ministry his advice was regarded as a baffling mix of cynicism and moralistic priggishness. Once, when Wiladowski was being considered for an important mission to St. Petersburg, his superior, Prince von Aehrenthal, complained that "the problem with employing Wiladowski has nothing to do with the man's intelligence. He is easily clever enough for any job, but one can never be sure whether he will decide to respond like Machiavelli or Savonarola. In either case, it is bound to be one of those Italian heretics he is so fond of quoting at us, never an honest Austrian. Whenever his advice is solicited on a new diplomatic overture, he seems to enjoy pointing out every departure from our proclaimed principles in the proposal and in the next breath suggests another tack that is so dishonorable it is simply indecent to acknowledge even having thought of it."

Domestically his reactions were, if anything, still more difficult to predict. A libertine who refuses to take a lover because there aren't any women of quality sufficiently depraved for his tastes: That was how his friends in Vienna explained the almost scandalous absence of an official mistress. But for once, the explanation was much simpler. Wiladowski was too deeply engrossed in his own brooding to summon the curiosity about another person that is indispensable, at least at the start of a love affair. While sex remained as compelling as ever, it could no longer compensate for the enervation he experienced whenever he had to spend several consecutive hours with the same person, and since even the most ritualized and mechanical liaison requires a certain show of interest in the conversation that surrounds the act of lovemaking, it was to his extensive and constantly growing collection of rare pornography that the Count-Governor was happy to turn for his pleasure. He was still regarded as an attractive catch by many of the most desirable hostesses looking to add another lover to their collection, but as he told a colleague, he knew it was merely his indifference that tempted them. Such women, he had come to realize, were like political alliances. Both come to one easily only when one is no longer certain they are really necessary or even desirable. Unlike many of his relatives, though, especially his murdered cousin Max, the memory of whose bad temper could still make his widow cringe three years after his burial, Wiladowski rarely quarreled with Marie-Luise, and when he did so, his tone barely changed from the weary politeness with which he tried to get through some bothersome official duty. The constant presence of the Castle servants and a shared aversion to displays of any kind made the idea of domestic bickering extraordinarily distasteful to them both. But on nearly every important question they had begun, almost without noticing it, to take opposing positions, as though the distance between them could find expression only by political rather than merely personal antagonism. In his dreams, though, Wiladowski often saw his First Secretary advising a black-clad Marie-Luise about how to arrange the funeral for the assassinated Count-Governor, but somewhat to his own surprise, even when Pfister's consolations became more lewdly carnal, and Marie-Luise's elegant mourning dress suddenly metamorphosed into the kind of sluttish undergarments the Venetian whores used to wear for him decades ago, the image raised no jealousy, only surprise, tempered with an undeniable satisfaction that she seemed unable to find someone at least a bit more prepossessing. That both Marie-Luise and Matthias Pfister should have survived him is what really distressed Wiladowski, and since his nightmares forced him to occupy simultaneously the roles of mangled corpse and posthumous witness to their ungainly mutual seduction, what the two did with the life they were so obviously reveling in was far less important than their not dying beside, or, better yet, instead of, him in the first place.

But interminably repeating a question is no guarantee of any precision in analyzing it. Of course Wiladowski confided nothing of his disturbing dreams about Pfister and his wife to his spymaster, but he saw no reason to deny himself the morbid pleasure of drawing out Tausk's views of perfidy. After all, the man had been hired precisely for his expertise in such matters, and it was no more compromising to solicit his opinion than it would be to consult an expert dentist should one be suffering from a toothache or a urologist if one were afraid of having caught some unpleasant venereal infection.

Fortunately for the Count-Governor, the increasingly rare pleasure of being interested in the people he encountered was not the only form of distraction available. Just as many of the Empire's notable thinkers, including several of its leading philosophers and political economists, were avid connoisseurs of the most formulaic stage farces, so Wiladowski often walked through the routines of his day as though he were a character in a commedia dell'arte skit who should scarcely be surprised at finding himself meeting only the other stock types of the genre. There is an involuntary, utterly instinctual pleasure in seeing how thoroughly the people one knows fulfill the conventions of their role. Wiladowski liked his officials to be as officious as possible, for the local nobility to be as provincial and self-satisfied as a mediocre writer would have imagined them, for the Jews to be as colorfully Jewish in dress, accent, and manner as though they were appearing in some historical pageant, and for the farm laborers on the estates he visited to exude a distillation of what he pictured as the fundamental traits of a timeless peasantry. Wiladowski sometimes wondered if at the end of the day everyone did not go home, take off their costumes and makeup, look at themselves in the mirror, and say, "Well, I certainly played the pompous bureaucrat, or cunning merchant, or court lackey to perfection today. I am totally exhausted, but there can be no doubt that the performance was everything it should be, and I have earned the right to sleep with a clean conscience tonight." The one obvious failure that grated on Wiladowski and came close to ruining the harmony of the whole spectacle the way a single bad actor can throw off an otherwise first-rate repertory company was his own undistinguished effort as Governor. He had his moments, no doubt, but they were intermittent at best and then only in scenes that sparked his personal interest rather than the requirements of the drama as a whole. Perhaps the inability to concentrate on one's acting when one no longer had any faith in the script was just another consequence of a mediocre imagination, and Wiladowski, who liked describing himself as radically devoid of any creative impulses, found himself, as so often, far more fascinated by his self-perceived limitations than he was concerned to rectify them.

The Emperor, the army, and the Imperial Civil Service. Every schoolboy learned that it was upon those three solid pillars that the state was based and from which it derived its enviable stability. Cardinal Archbishop von Salis would no doubt have liked to add the name of Holy Mother Church to this list, but both Wiladowski and Tausk were dubious about any such claim, since many of the dynasty's implacable enemies in France and Belgium also went to confession with pure consciences and received communion from good Catholic priests who regarded the Habsburg territorial exactions with no more sympathy than they felt for the ranks of godless atheists. This discouraging fact of political life presented no small problem to Wiladowski's pet notion of proceeding as though he were cast in a thoroughly hackneyed theater piece, since even if the aristocrats, Jews, and government officers could be relied upon to look and act their parts so as to be immediately recognizable, assassins and traitors might not always be so obliging. Besides, he had ample evidence in his own circle that no one is so adept at refashioning himself to suit a new part that he can completely shed all the characteristics acquired in a lifetime of playing other roles. Even Tausk, who had changed his entire existence with spectacular success, continued to smoke only the abominably cheap cigarettes he had become addicted to in Rabbi Pelz's seminary. In spite of his now-substantial salary, not to mention Wiladowski's repeated offer of the finest Montecristos from the Governor's private stock, the spymaster insisted on polluting every room he entered with the most noxious odor Wiladowski had ever smelled. Even in the most seedy Triestine coffeehouses that he had sometimes frequented as a young man looking for illicit pleasures, Wiladowski had encountered nothing comparably cloying. In fact, if it were not for Pfister's barely controlled outrage every time he was forced to enter a room clotted with fumes from Tausk's tobacco—if the brand contained any tobacco at all—Wiladowski, who also found the stench repellent, would probably have forbidden its consumption anywhere in the Castle. Self-transformation is always partially an illusion, if only because, as Wiladowski and Tausk both bore rueful witness, there is inevitably a residue, a stubborn remainder that stays in the soul and will resist being absorbed into the new identity. If nothing of one's past really stayed vivid and alive, betrayal would be far less painful.

Without the Count-Governor's ever needing to make his wishes explicit, Tausk instinctively understood that his function was to wait until his employer himself raised these questions and then to listen with an air of intense interest mingled with an understated yet deeply flattered surprise at being chosen as a confidant for such intimacies. The look of faint surprise was always the hardest to maintain, especially after he had been summoned to the library for weeks on end for no better reason than to hear out Wiladowski's elaborate self-descriptions and nightmares. Tausk had heard the Count-Governor's eccentric theories often enough not to let his lack of enthusiasm for them come out, and when Wiladowski made a genuine, if brief, effort to get Tausk to draw on his own experiences for corroboration, it was usually easy enough to deflect him. Once though, when Wiladowski asked the spymaster what would happen if duty required him to arrest and extract information from people he actually respected if not now, then at least at some time in his prior life, the sudden tightening in Tausk's voice was unmistakable. Something fugitive, like a half-forgotten pain, flickered for the briefest moment behind Tausk's eyes, but just as quickly his expression resumed its habitual veiled and slightly malicious look, and he began mechanically fumbling for another one of his cigarettes, which he lit before the one he was holding had been fully extinguished. Both men knew that a nerve had been struck, and Wiladowski returned to bed not a little proud of himself for having made his self-possessed Chief of Intelligence give away something of his emotional core. The Count-Governor liked collecting what he thought of as "revelatory moments," and although he trusted Tausk with the job of protecting his life, he also thought there was no harm in accumulating a small mental inventory of such moments against an unforeseeable future.

At Wiladowski's command, Tausk had prepared an elaborate dossier of all the political murders committed in the Empire during the past decade and tried to group the suspects—whether they had been successfully convicted or not—by whatever categories might prove statistically significant. Profession, city of origin, race, sex, age, degree of education, and field of study: All these were carefully correlated in an elaborate series of charts by Roublev, whose brilliance as a mathematician Tausk had often had occasion to find useful. Had Roublev not been a Jew, or had he learned to disguise his abrasive sense of superiority, he eventually might have secured a position at the university where his promise was still talked about years later, but all of Roublev's ingenuity could not make the information yield patterns that helped predict from where the next attack might come. The only generalizable conclusion in fact was a negative one—namely, that in Franz Josef's Empire, unlike in Czar Alexander's Russia, there were almost no Jewish terrorists. Jews were indeed notable in various illegal organizations, as well as in those semi-tolerated trade unions that were not programmatically anti-Semitic, but their almost complete absence from any groups suspected of terrorist activities was too palpable to ignore. "Perhaps the Galut simply weighs on Jews less here than in Russia, so they can stay true to their time-honored abhorrence of bloodshed." Tausk deliberately threw in the Hebrew term for the "Exile" because he knew the pleasure the Count-Governor would derive from questioning him about what the Jews understood by living in permanent exile and how it fitted into their wildly self-aggrandizing way of understanding world history. But this time Wiladowski showed no such curiosity and simply asked if it might not be truer to say that Austrian Jews were more adept than their Russian coreligionists at avoiding military conscription and thus missed one of the best chances of learning how to use firearms, a skill in which too many monarchies were shortsighted enough to educate their contumacious subjects.

Finally alone again in his room, Tausk let himself collapse into the large armchair that stood with its back against the wall near the simple infantry cot on which he slept. These days, no matter how close he sat to a blazing fireplace, it took all his willpower not to shiver continuously with a sense of cold that seemed to have taken root in his bones. In front of the Governor, Tausk was able not to let his fever show, a task made easier by

Wiladowski's conspicuous lack of interest in anyone's health but his own. But now, as Tausk passed his hand nervously over his chest and thighs, he felt an exhausted, futile distaste at the clamminess of his own stale sweat and at the body that produced it. More and more he smelled to himself like one of the prisoners he was interrogating, but at least his cigarettes were strong enough to prevent anyone else from noticing the similarity. He had never wished more ardently for a scientific detachment like Roublev's. Well before his expulsion from the yeshiva, Tausk had known that he lacked the true biblical scholar's enthrallment with divine enigmas, but the struggle of his whole system to adapt itself to his new function forced him to acknowledge just how far he was from feeling at home in this world either. Unlike his master, the one thing Tausk could not permit himself, especially not now, when there was so much he still needed to do before the Zichy-Ferraris visit, was to let himself be caught up in Wiladowski's obsession with the inevitability of betrayal. Just to be able to *have* a theory about it was to be more comfortable than Tausk believed possible for himself. So, as on every other anemic morning these past few weeks, Tausk forced himself to shrug off the insistent pressure throbbing within his temples, wrapped an enormous gray army field blanket around his shoulders, and tried to use the half hour or so of alertness that he knew he could still muster to catch up on the backlog of reports from his agents.

When he finally succeeded in falling asleep, his dreams were too feverish and intermittent to cohere into any story. But had they done so, the link among the different images that traversed his sleeping consciousness might easily have been taken from the story of Joseph in Egypt, a tale with which Tausk had felt an instinctive kinship ever since his interpretation of it had awed—and angered—his fellow students in Rabbi Pelz's class years ago. Now, though, if he was still performing, it was for himself alone, and instead of spinning out an elegant, multilayered allegory that ascended in meaning by precise degrees, Tausk was himself nothing but a baffled cry asking anyone who would listen for a solution. What felt most uncanny of all was that rather than being stranded in some abandoned, sinister place, Tausk found himself back at the seminary in the main study room. Only *he* was Rabbi Pelz, and when he asked his questions, he felt himself utterly devoid not just of the correct answer but of any reply whatsoever. His listeners, though, only smiled at him with a horrifically vacant cheerfulness. He stared out at a roomful of faces struck dumb with hideous, congenital imbecility, and it was to the hopeless, unending repetition of his questions sent out to drown in the blank, infinite immobility of the audience that Tausk awoke, more terrified and unhappy than if he had spent the night wrestling demons with horns, gnashing teeth, hooves, and all the other trite paraphernalia of the Christian imagination.

◆

If there was one thing that never failed to distress Marie-Luise, it was any sign of impertinence on the part of the lower orders. It was vexing enough to put up with their effrontery in Vienna, where radical journalists, most of whom no longer had the decency to be embarrassed by their unpronounceable Jewish names, were constantly at work abusing the Emperor's lenience by trying to poison the minds of the working class, but to have to endure the same insolence out here in the provinces, without any of the capital's pleasures as compensation, was simply intolerable. Almost daily now, even in her own Palace, she was forced to suffer the most ghastly headaches because Otto would not forbid that repulsive little guttersnipe of whom he had become so fond from polluting every room with his poisonous cigarettes. Still worse was the shameless way the creature looked at her when they passed each other in the corridors: inquisitive, amused, and appraising all at once. She had never been stared at like that before, not even when her coachman was forced to pass through streets inhabited by the most degenerate specimens in Vienna, and the shock of it sent her hurrying to her rooms, flushed and out of breath, hoping no one would notice her agitation. She had made no secret of her loathing for the man, and by all rights *he* should have been the one to lower his eyes and slink away when their paths crossed. Instead she could feel him deliberately hold his ground and follow her retreating figure with his coarse gaze. To be looked at like that was almost like being handled, and there were times she longed to strike out at Tausk with her riding crop just to redress the imbalance between them and remind him of who she was. Otto could wear himself out assuring her that his new minion was indispensable to her welfare, but it was obvious that Tausk had been hired solely to allay her husband's terror of assassins and that Otto had not given a moment's thought to anyone's safety but his own. Initially, Marie-Luise had been prepared to tolerate the spymaster on those terms, but she quickly concluded that there was nothing at all reassuring about him; rather than looking like her potential protector, he struck her more like an executioner deliberately and carefully measuring her neck for the scaffold.

In spite of her husband's baffling reliance on him, she was certain that if there were anyone whom people of her kind should fear, it was types like this Jakob Tausk. In more than thirty years she had never known her husband to trust another human being, beginning, she suspected, with herself, yet now, when he was convinced that his life was in constant danger, he was suddenly willing to stake his very survival on the loyalty of a renegade Jew. There was something profoundly unnatural in such a relationship, Pfister was certainly right about that, but she dismissed the widespread rumor that it had to be a question of blackmail. According to Pfister, the Castle officials were evenly divided on the question of whether their master had been delivered into Tausk's hands by the Freemasons or by a still more shadowy cabal controlled by international Jewry. Her husband's eccentricities were so widely known, both at the Ministry in Vienna and in all the chancelleries of Europe, and his contempt for the judgment of others so undisguised that it was impossible for Marie-Luise to imagine his being vulnerable to threats of public exposure irrespective of his supposed misdeeds. What could a blackmailer reveal about the Count-Governor that he had not already made a point of saying aloud in front of at least a dozen highly placed witnesses? The more he suspected his listeners of hostility, the more provocative he became, and during the first years of their marriage Marie-Luise had spent many exhausting afternoons making social calls designed to undo the damage Otto had inflicted on his professional prospects the evening before. At that time some of Otto's most ambitious rivals speculated that the couple had carefully mapped out their respective parts ahead of time, following a crafty script Wiladowski had himself composed: In it, he would take on the role of the mocking, critical voice whose audacious sarcasm was all the more effective precisely because it only seemed to be reckless; behind it, as everyone well knew, lay the steadying counterbalance of Marie-Luise's exquisite manners and unimpeachably orthodox opinions. Thus the young pair acquired a reputation for being interesting and just a bit "modern," but without actually offending anyone, and since Viennese society loved nothing more than the appearance of hearing something shocking, so long as it could be quite certain that it was just a more subtle form of flattery, there was soon no more successful couple on the capital's social circuit.

But like all such schemes, this entirely hypothetical one eventually shattered against one adamantine obstacle. Unlike his more worldly subjects, the Emperor detested being shocked, even in jest. He regarded wit as insolence if applied to one's betters, as blasphemous if it dared address religious questions, and as a sign of ill breeding if directed at one's social peers. Privately the most modest of men—on the exceedingly rare moments he allowed himself a private emotion—Franz Josef expected his flattery to be unadulterated by any impurities and applied with the same lavishness as the whipped cream with which the pastry chef smothered his favorite Hungarian chocolate hazelnut cake. To him, the most florid terms of praise were, in a sense, quite impersonal; it was in the name of the Habsburg dynasty that he accepted the obeisance that was its due, not for any personal merit of his own. And so, even had Otto and Marie-Luise concocted the elaborate charade attributed to them by their enemies, it would surely have miscarried since the methodical transcription of Wiladowski's witticisms included in the regular reports submitted by the secret police to the Emperor on the doings of the younger nobility guaranteed that he would never attain a permanent ministerial rank. An important provincial governorship and occasional special diplomatic missions were as high as someone so gifted, but fundamentally unsound, would be allowed to rise, no matter what his wife might do to mitigate his offenses, and the very same young men who had once been afraid that the combination of Otto's mind and Marie-Luise's virtue would guarantee their ascendancy soon found themselves promoted over him. They naturally attributed their advancement to their own merits and seeing Wiladowski's career lag behind their own, quite forgot ever having regarded him as cleverer than they. In reality, of course, no such compact had ever existed between Wiladowski and his wife. Indeed anything resembling it was inconceivable for a woman of Marie-Luise's rectitude, and by the time he took up his first post in Trieste, she had begun to find his contemptuous tone as trying as did his superiors at Court. But the very fact that she had endured decades witnessing how little Otto cared about the consequences of his behavior forced her to dismiss Pfister's blackmail theory. No, whatever lay behind the demeaning intimacy between her husband and Tausk was quite different, she was sure of that much. But she was becoming resigned to the fact that none of the people in the Castle who were loyal to her were subtle enough to intuit what men like the Count-Governor and Tausk were up to. Marie-Luise had long known that her husband was an abject coward, but even after he had begun to shower Tausk with official favors, against the unanimous advice of his own administrative personnel, she was unable to agree with the unspoken speculation that the Count-Governor might be turning into a gullible fool as well.

Pfister, who was far stupider than Marie-Luise, had no such hesitation and concluded that his employer's reliance on Tausk was sufficient proof that Count Wiladowski had lost the mental agility for which he had once been famous. Whether simple old age or fear was responsible for his employer's deterioration mattered less to Pfister than trying to extract some advantage, or at least not to incur too great a loss, from the situation. He was confident that he could count on Marie-Luise's support, but in this he entirely overestimated both her personal feelings toward him and her influence over her husband. Marie-Luise found Pfister a flattering attendant and a useful source of information about what was happening in the Castle. She approved of his slight tinge of prudishness, his respectable family, and his agreeable features, and she shared his revulsion against the lax, Judaizing liberalism that was spreading even among the upper classes. However, in the course of his career her husband had been served by numerous First Secretaries, and although she had enjoyed patronizing—and, in some cases, graciously befriending—the most attractive of them, she had trouble differentiating them from one another in her memory. She and the Count-Governor had long ago given up trying to explain themselves to each other, and their conversation had gradually been pared down to the shared goal of successfully managing their complex social and political obligations. But although she suspected that Otto was unaware of it, the relative intimacy of their first, simpler years together, when he would still think out loud in front of her and pretend to pause with interest for her response, had opened her eyes to the difference between a first-class mind and a commonplace one. A nonentity like Matthias Pfister, for all the elegance with which he could hold his teacup, kiss her fingertips, or genuflect at Sunday mass, was not likely to make her forget that. Her support for Pfister was based on an assessment of his character and abilities that he was no doubt fortunate in never suspecting. Marie-Luise's instincts were deeply consonant with those that had guided the Empire's rulers for centuries, and like the dynasty she venerated, she far preferred a reliable dullard to a potentially troublesome genius. Had it not been repeatedly proved that unless genius was kept in the strictest check, it was likely to be disruptive of the social order whose preservation she regarded as a sacred duty? In any event, all this fuss about intelligence was absurdly short-sighted. To judge by the men who were being credited with exceptional cleverness these days, it was becoming a thoroughly plebeian quality, and she saw no reason why it should merit any more regard than such more obviously useful traits as family piety and respect for one's betters. All these thinkers were taking themselves far too seriously, and the musicians and actors were, if anything, even worse. The trouble with the mob was how much it would adore anyone who flattered it. That clearly was why there were so many geniuses being discovered by the press every day. Lumpen sentimentality cheered on by the newspapers for their own profit, all of it tasteless, exaggerated, and horribly vulgar, even at the Imperial Opera House, where the most impossible people now strutted about in the great foyer loudly arguing about their opinions as though they were in an Asiatic temple. There ought to be a service medal or official decoration for loyal subjects who demonstrated lifelong contentment with their station in life; that was what the Empire needed nowadays, not more so-called geniuses convinced of the importance of their latest scribblings.

Nothing vexed her more than the daily proof that her husband, who, she had no doubt, understood quite well what he was setting in motion, seemed ready to jettison the most basic principles of aristocratic rule for some cynical amusement of his own. She suspected that it was his horror of being bored, a condition he dreaded almost as much as he feared a fire-bomb or bullet, that made him introduce a disruptive presence like Tausk into their household. Although Marie-Luise and the Count-Governor had never directly compared the two men except to voice puzzlement at each other's choice of favorites, their private estimation of Pfister and Tausk was actually quite similar. But the very qualities that recommended the First Secretary to Marie-Luise made her husband detest spending more than a few minutes in his company. Tausk, on the other hand, was obviously too clever by half—Marie-Luise had realized that after ten minutes—and she supposed that from a jaded point of view like Otto's, there probably was something fascinating about him. But that only made it all the more important to keep him subordinate to a conscientious Catholic mediocrity like Pfister for as long as possible. The rabble's time would come soon enough; it was impossible to misunderstand the muttered curses she overheard in the streets or the growing defiance in the looks cast at her when she and her husband rode through town. But that was no reason why those entrusted by Providence with the governance of the

Empire should help speed along their own demise by freely opening their doors to their godless enemies.

At least the other Jew, the financier Rotenbaum or something similar, whom her husband also insisted on favoring with his attention, was rich enough to have some claim on official recognition. Even in Vienna, his readiness to contribute whatever was needed for the government's semi-clandestine operations had been warmly spoken of at her dinner table by a Minister who was known to be in the special confidence of His Majesty himself, and Marie-Luise had felt a proprietary pleasure in hearing that one of her husband's Jews was acquitting himself so well in official eyes. She did think that there was altogether too much speculation about just how rich the man was on the part of people whose birth ought to have made such questions secondary—curiosity like that showed a lack of self-respect astonishing in a member of a family like the Minister's, which had produced three Archbishops and a slew of generals—but she had to agree that at least the Jew's money did not seem to have made him impossibly overfamiliar in the typical way so many of his race behaved as soon as they achieved any commercial success. So far he had made no effort to force himself upon her socially, and at the few large-scale receptions to which it had been impossible not to invite him—the obviousness of a snub would only have singled him out in an excessive way—he had restricted himself to a polite bow followed by a few formulaic phrases before retreating to join the others of his sort near the back of the room.

Marie-Luise was in her own right one of the richest women in the Empire, a position that allowed her to be almost as suspicious of great wealth in the hands of the middle class as she was apprehensive of an original intelligence in anyone who was not devoted to the cause of the aristocracy. Admittedly too many of the best people were becoming alarmingly short of both brains and money; nonetheless, it was absurd to make an inordinate fuss about social inferiors who happened to have a surplus of either one. She was clearsighted enough to recognize how infrequently wealth and intelligence coincided in her own milieu and was visibly relieved when the Minister, citing a host of deliciously absurd legal, as well as political, gaffes culled from the secret police files, assured her that a similar divergence between mind and money could increasingly also be found in the merchant classes. However, perhaps it was different among Jews. It was hard for an outsider to be certain about anything when it came to so secretive a race, but Marie-Luise would never be persuaded that their motives could be anything but pernicious. In this view, she found an unexpected and, in truth, unwelcome ally in Aurelia von Margutti, a notorious bluestocking who had spent the last five years in Paris at the legation being ignored by society and had returned home determined to reclaim her social footing in Vienna. The woman immediately took advantage of this turn in the conversation to try to redirect the table's attention away from Marie-Luise and onto her gloomy prognosis for the future of France, a country, she assured everyone, now entirely under the heels of Jewish financiers. Marie-Luise smiled benevolently at her would-be rival and, in her most sympathetic voice, reminded her of the folly of trying to appear interesting. "At least the Jews there seem to have left you quite alone, my dear Aurelia, even though Otto told me that you sent invitations by the handful to the Comte de Rothschild and that ghastly old *mater Iudeorum*, Clara de Hirsch. But then, considering the wine you served at the embassy, it is a wonder you could persuade even our provincial Prussian cousins to come to your state dinners." That was clumsy. Although everyone laughed and the interloper spent the rest of the evening staring morosely at her plate, Marie-Luise knew that Otto would have phrased it better, and the thought depressed her more than her momentary triumph gave her pleasure. It was vexing always to judge a conversation according to what she imagined her husband might say about it, especially now, when his quizzical smile from the far end of the table made it clear that he thought she had deployed heavy field artillery against a dormouse. But the Minister, no doubt attributing it all to his own charm, seemed cheerfully flattered by the sudden antagonism between the two women and continued his explanation with a marked increase in enthusiasm and, in a spirit of true Imperial politesse, accompanied his words with numerous intense looks directed alternately into Marie-Luise's and Aurelia's eyes. At one point Marie-Luise noticed her husband quietly parodying the way the Minister's whole upper torso shuttled gracefully back and forth between the two ladies with the precision of a Swiss timepiece, and Otto's mockery struck her as very nearly insufferable. But for now there was nothing she could do to retaliate, and gradually she allowed her curiosity about what the Minister was saying to dissipate her annoyance. Not long afterward the dinner party broke up, and as the guests made their way to the row of carriages waiting in the courtyard, she admitted that the evening had left her deeply uneasy about this Moritz Rotenburg in whom everyone was so interested. Not just her husband, whose propensity to overpraise Jews made her mistrust his descriptions of their qualities, but even confirmed anti-Semites like the Minister seemed unpleasantly eager to talk about the man's shrewdness and the subtlety of his financial schemes. Ever since rumors that he was suffering from some mysterious illness had started circulating, it seemed that everyone she knew, from the capital's leading political figures to the senior members of her husband's staff, was speculating about what would happen if he were to be incapacitated while the Empire's general financial situation was still so unsettled. Since no one was sure of either the full extent or the specific disposition of his holdings, every kind of wild conjecture found an echoing voice. If certain whispered suggestions were to be believed, any precipitous liquidation of his assets might seriously upset the course of some delicate three-way negotiations, just now nearing the critical stage, among Vienna, St. Petersburg, and the Quai d'Orsay. At the very least, it was clear to Marie-Luise that she now had not just one worrisome Jew to reckon with but two, and this sudden doubling of the forces massed against her felt extraordinarily discomfiting.

Marie-Luise's suffering would only have been intensified if she had been able to guess how fully Moritz Rotenburg had been apprised of what the Minister had said about him that night. Rotenburg's business dealings had created a private network of informants in all the European capitals, and they made certain that he was kept up-to-date on the nervousness caused by the rumors of his illness. Decades ago, when he was just starting his financial ascent, he had encouraged himself with vivid fantasies of how envious everyone he knew would be when he had become as rich as his first partner, Ludwig Ginzburg. But by the time his fortune grew far beyond what he had then imagined possible, nothing at all had remained of those daydreams. Now, when he thought about those years, it was mostly to calculate that he was already eleven years older than Ginzburg the day he accompanied the man's widow to the small plot in the Jewish cemetery. Finally, two summers ago, the influenza carried her off as well, and the two Ginzburgs now lay together, largely forgotten by most of the town, who, if they ever mentioned them at all, did so only as the helpless couple outmaneuvered by Rotenburg in his first major business triumph. "At least the man was lucky enough to die before his wife" was what Moritz told himself, as though it were somehow necessary to him to regard his old partner as forever the better off of the two. The conjunction of absolute confidence in his business intuitions and a lifelong habit of shrewd observation had inured Moritz against the need to hear himself praised, even by his own inner consciousness. But it did not spare him from the sense of isolation that nothing was able to break through anymore; he had long since simply grown to accept that no other part of his life would ever seem as familiar or trustworthy.

What was worse was that somehow Brugger had so insinuated himself into Moritz's reveries that it was often his face, not Dina's or Hans's, that Moritz now saw when he let himself drift along the margins between dreaming and wakefulness. For a moment Moritz again remembered the eerie sense he had had standing at the window, watching the strange scene between Brugger and the beggar unfold in the square. Viewed from below, Moritz could not have been more than a vague figure outlined against a half-drawn curtain, yet he could have sworn that Brugger was deliberately orchestrating the whole spectacle in order to give Moritz a glimpse of his power. Several times he sensed Brugger look up toward where he stood, and the sensation of suddenly no longer being the watcher but rather the object of someone else's scrutiny made him jump back into the safety of the room. He could not shake the feeling that Brugger, this Jewish rabble-rouser who had come from nowhere and could have heard nothing of importance about his private affairs, nonetheless knew exactly what Moritz was planning. In their confrontation Moritz had intended to treat Brugger like a mountebank, hardly worth his attention, but at the end it was all he could do to disguise how thoroughly he had been rattled. No doubt, Brugger, like confidence men the world over, spoke in such broad generalities that his listeners could scarcely fail to find something personally applicable in his words. But where was it written that it would always be easy to distinguish the bearer of the truth from an impostor? Although he would never say so to the community leaders when they asked Rotenburg to tell them about the conversation with Brugger, to himself Moritz admitted that he had never experienced a more unnerving performance. Everything Brugger said came out somehow doubled. Sometimes he spoke his lines like someone deliberately impersonating a bad actor because it was beneath him to imitate a better one. The more predictable his words, the more his eyes showed an epicure's delight in their staginess, like certain debauched old men Moritz had known who, after a lifetime of eating only the most subtle dishes, had learned to derive their satisfaction from food that was visibly rotten. Brugger gave the impression that he was mocking himself for talking in such a fashion, mocking Moritz for having expected him to do just that, and then mocking both of them for seeing through the charade but not daring to put anything better and more honest in its place.

What was it that Brugger had told him about Hans? "When he dies, he will still call himself a Jew and be older than you are today." A safe enough prophecy since Moritz would not be alive to verify its accuracy. But it galled Moritz's pride that this man, whom it should have been easy to despise, could be so certain he knew the only words that Moritz was desperate to hear. Brugger spoke about Hans's future with such casual, almost lazy confidence in the effect his words would produce that Moritz had the sense Brugger was showing him how playing on his heart required no more skill than the simplest conjuring trick. For the first time in many decades Moritz felt the beginnings of fear of another human being, and with fear came hatred and nights of violent fantasies whose exactions on his nervous system his body spent the following days vainly trying to repair. Sufficient rest, though, was the only thing Moritz could not afford right now. Early in his business deals, he had almost always found a way to disguise his vulnerability and convert actual weakness into at least the public semblance of strength. But with Brugger there was no way to know what would work. Simply to wrestle a man like that to a standstill would require a constant drain on the diminishing reserve of Moritz's inner resources at the very time he had the most need of them. He knew he could not risk a prolonged division of attention, and just as his most important investment decisions always emerged from the inchoate swarm of contradictory possibilities with a crystalline self-evidence, whether almost immediately or only after several tense nights of rumination, this time too he abruptly got up from his bed, splashed some cool water on his inflamed eyes, wrapped his dressing gown more tightly around him, and sat down to write his first brief note to Jakob Tausk.

2

Vienna, Wednesday, April 2, 1913

Dear Asher, my cherished friend and ally,

I don't think I will have Hans Rotenburg's private courier service available much longer, and I wanted to use it at least one more time to let you know what has been happening here. Yes, the rumors are really true: The Burgtheater is going to put on my comedy The Jew's Misfortune—*an ironic title, as I am sure you can guess*—next season. I was suddenly summoned to a meeting with the director, and less than an hour later found myself walking down the Graben with the signed contract in my pockets. Actually, walking doesn't come close to describing it: I felt wildly exultant and was striding through the crowd like a triumphant hero taking possession of a city he has just conquered. I kept pulling out the document and looking at the Imperial seal with my name right there on the second line as "AUTHOR," and I couldn't wait to rush over to the Café Central and wave it under everyone's nose. I, Alexander Garber, the provincial upstart whose accent is enough to raise smirks every time he opens his mouth and who still doesn't know how to tie a cravat properly, am now an official Burgtheater playwright! It's impossible to tell you just how much this means, Asher. In less than three years here I have accomplished more than a lot of the so-called distinguished figures who walk into the Café Central as though they were conferring an enormous honor on all of us by taking their afternoon coffee in the same room. A few weeks ago I heard one of them muse aloud across the billiard table whether history would judge him among the five major writers of his era or if he would have to settle for ranking only in the top dozen, and this in spite of the fact that no one has ever managed to get through more than a few pages of the little he has published without eyeball-clawing boredom setting in! I am not exaggerating. You wouldn't believe what a bunch of daydreaming nonentities most of the scribblers here really are. Hacks and parasites, the whole lot of

267

*them! Pretentious as anything too just because they were born and educated
in Vienna, not in some festering outhouse like you and me. Every one of these
gentlemen seems to think it is enough to have grown up in sight of St.
Stephan's Cathedral and have heard his first concert in a room Schubert once
played in to be assured of possessing perfect taste. And to think that I used to
look up to them! Do you remember my writing you how thrilled I was the first
time I went through the doors of the Café Central? I had barely gotten off the
train and stored the canvas bag with all my books at my cousin Rina's before
I rushed over to the Herrengasse to find the café I'd dreamed about so often while I was supposed to be working at some stupid school assignment
back home. It was like completing a pilgrimage. Just seeing all those people
crowded together happily chattering to one another or reading their newspapers and eating enormous slices of Gugelhupf with their mochas was like
stepping into the most glamorous stage set imaginable, and for ages all I ever
wanted to achieve in this city was to be welcomed there as one of their own.
But you know that even though I kept going back whenever I had a few pennies to spare, no one ever bothered to ask me my name or what I did. Not
once! Month after month, unless the place was almost completely empty,
Wellisz, the malignant headwaiter who always has such a welcoming, deferential smile for the better-known patrons and could barely spare a glance for
anyone else, deliberately kept seating me off in the corner by the kitchen door.
Back there it is like being exiled to the provinces all over again. You are completely excluded from all the lively conversation, and your main intellectual
activity is making sure your feet aren't mutilated by the waiters rushing by
with their trays. You try writing anything while looking anxiously over your
shoulders for a cup of scalding coffee to come streaming down all over you!
Do you still remember how old Herr Ignatz, the one who was too "elevated" to
notice the boys giggling at the permanent ink stains on his cuffs, used to walk
up and down the classroom, hypnotizing himself with his anecdotes about the
defunct old Café Griensteidl's illustrious history: how, when he was a student
in the capital, all the most daring young minds of the Empire could be found
there every afternoon, debating the radical innovations in art and politics that
were going to shape the life of this new century just the way spirited young
Viennese had done at those identical tables since "the glorious days of '48"!
And how melancholy he used to get telling the story of its demolition in '97 as
though he were mourning the fall of the Temple in Jerusalem. It was like bad
Chekhov with a Jewish accent, all that impotent, melancholic longing to be
somewhere else. Probably you and I were the only ones in the class gullible*

enough to take him seriously, but I have to confess that to me, his words sounded like the fulfillment of everything I had been fantasizing about without even realizing it. Ignatz actually had me believing that a magical room existed where anyone with real talent was welcomed and put at his ease without regard to rank or prestige—and not in some unreachable place like Paris or London but right here, in our own capital! The names of the coffeehouses Ignatz talked about were like incantations to me: the Imperial, the Sperl, the Café Museum, but most of all, to hear Ignatz tell it, the Café Central, where he swore he felt the atmosphere of the old Griensteidl triumphantly resurrected. To me, they all sounded equally wonderful. The one thing I knew for sure was that nothing remotely similar could be found in our shithole of a town; two visits to that pathetic Jewish club you are always going on about convinced me of that! Well, I don't know about you, but if I saw Ignatz today, I would happily throw the lying fool down the nearest stairwell. I give you my word, no one is as punctilious about the smallest specks of public reputation as our liberal Viennese coffeehouse literati. They all pretend to be terribly cynical and knowing, but that is just a way of disguising what slimy little toadies they are. One almost has to applaud the ingenuity with which they have cloaked the most abject conventionality as independence of spirit. If only they could do it unobserved, they would like nothing better than to go around all day looking for someone with influence and then to set about licking his hindquarters with rapturous devotion. But since open servility is not fashionable these days, they are forced to do it covertly. Iconoclasts with their eyes fixed firmly on fat government pensions and their rear ends glued cheerfully to Thonet chairs. I have begun to think that is the one truly flourishing new species we have spawned in our famous coffeehouses. In a hundred years all the history books will have to have a chapter on the pervasive influence of state-salaried revolutionaries!

Until the word got around that I had landed a job writing for The New Order, *I can't recall a single comment ever being addressed to me, but of course, as soon as it was known that I regularly published my work in a real journal—even in one as small as ours—and might be in a position to help them get their dreck into print, it is amazing how many people remembered a witty observation I once made or just had to let me know how much they enjoyed a piece I wrote six months earlier that no one at the time had shown the slightest sign of noticing. At first I was so taken aback by the unexpected attention I really believed they were sincere, and if I couldn't talk any editors into actually taking their stuff, I at least did my best to get reviewer's passes to* the theater for everyone who asked. Of course, when it turned out that I could get free tickets only for the most obscure performances, and then just on off nights, and that our whole readership never included a single prominent name, I was relegated quickly enough to being just a sliver above a nonentity. Four whole tables in from the kitchen door, that is where I had the honor of being seated now, and for a while Wellisz kept looking over toward me dubiously, as if he were not quite sure I deserved the promotion. But a play in the repertoire at the Burgtheater! Now that is a different story altogether. From now on I really am someone to reckon with, and they all had damn well better get used to it. Just watching everyone see Wellisz try to ingratiate himself by the absurd flourishes with which he will usher me to the choicest table will be revenge enough for all the slights I have had to endure in that place!

You simply could not have believed how courteous Herr Director von Bruck was to me. A real gentleman born and bred, yet after just one sentence it was clear that above everything else he is a true connoisseur and cares about nothing except furthering Austrian literature. He has the kind of flair you can't learn from books, and I am slowly finding out that when it is developed to a sufficient degree, discernment of that high an order is itself a sort of genius! Without men like that there would be no great art, and it is wrong not to recognize how vital their support is for really creative souls to realize their full potential. No doubt the dilettantes at the Café Central would be horrified by my saying so. I can't count the number of times I have heard one of them pronounce, as though it were some daring new insight he had just come up with, that the true artist creates his own audience and cares only for the judgment of the posterity his own works help to shape. As though we all had not heard that slogan held up to us a million times since grammar school. All that high-mindedness comes so damn easily to wellborn sons with rich fathers and good connections. They can afford to polish their writings while Franz, the butler, is getting dinner ready and Gaby, their maid, is making herself pretty for the young master. As far as I am concerned, faith in posterity is just one more luxury item the rich can buy for themselves. In my position, von Bruck's approval and the applause of a real, live audience are worth a lot more than any amount of posthumous acclaim.

That is why I am ashamed to remember all the nasty things I said about the man in the past. It is true that for months he never answered a single one of the letters I sent him begging for a minute of his time, but you know, someone as busy as he is . . . I can see why it might take him a while until he had *a chance to convince himself of the merits of brand-new work like mine. Of course it certainly helps to have patrons who move in the highest spheres and care enough about improving the public's taste to make sure the right sort of talent finds preferment. But enough of that, they already know how profoundly I value their encouragement and how unwavering my gratitude will always be. Although you know that no one abhors sycophants more than I do, I am afraid that if I go on too long here telling you how I feel, the men whom I am proud to think of as my benefactors might make the mistake of suspecting me of trying to flatter them.*

I know I owe you an apology too, at least in my own mind, for all the curses I showered on you after I left the Chief of Police's office. I wouldn't be surprised if your ears burned all the way back home from the abuse, but I am sure you would have reacted the same way. I still feel myself getting queasy when I remember my landlady handing me the morning mail with the order to present myself at 11:00 A.M. in three days' time to the Baron von Kirchmayr himself. I don't know what horrors she imagined I had committed when she saw me look so distraught, but who cares now, since I will soon be packing up to move into better rooms. The only thing that has ever thrived in Frau Reichle's lodging house are the bedbugs that torture me all night, and if I never set foot in such a dismal cell again, for as long as I live I will still loathe the memory of having been forced to exist in this kind of squalor.

Have you noticed how often the people with whom we get most angry are just the ones who turn out to have our best interests at heart? I ought to write a little feuilleton sketch developing that theme and take it over to Benedikt at The Weekly Review. *Now that I have found favor with men who really count, why not use the opportunity to get more of my work placed in all the best journals? Encouragement makes such a difference to us artists, Asher; it is like being given the confidence to bring out what one always had inside but that shyness, or fear, or simply lack of opportunity kept from ever getting expressed. Just to know that there is really an audience out there ready to listen to one's words, that one isn't just alone in one's room with a headful of ideas and stories that no one will ever hear, is enough to transform a man. There is always something misshapen about a completely imaginary world in which no outside voices are ever heard; believe me, no matter what they tell you about the joys of solitary work, it is gruesome to hear only your own thoughts rattling around day after day without evoking any response from another human soul. No one can endure living like that forever without going crazy. I am sure that is why I spent so much of my miserable salary on the whores out in Ottakring, not just to have sex with them but to have someone there who had to listen to me talk and pretend to look interested! It is certainly more than I ever got from going to the Café Central! The more confident we are of being heard, the less we need to chatter to everyone around us anyway, and now, for the first time in my life, it is becoming easier for me to sit still during the weekly editorial meetings at the paper and listen to everyone else's opinions without getting fidgety waiting for my turn to speak. And no one knows better than you how important it is, with all that is going on these days, for me to keep a firm check on myself and give nothing away of what is being planned for the journal!*

Frankly, although I owe everything to it, I am still amazed that so many important people took an interest in our correspondence about The New Order. *At first I suspected that you had simply lost your head completely and passed my letters around to anyone who might be impressed by hearing literary gossip firsthand from the capital, but when von Kirchmayr made it clear that he also knew every detail of your letters to me, which I am positive no one else could have seen (unless that bitch Frau Reichle rifled through the papers on my desk when I was out), well, I was too amazed and, I don't mind admitting, too terrified to have any theories left. One thing is certain, though: I will remember that interview for the rest of my life, and if I was ever foolish enough to doubt how far the reach of our Imperial security organs extends, the first five minutes in there disabused me of that error. In fact I am not at all certain that the famous Rotenburg courier service is as secure as you and Hans believe. From what I have seen of his power, it wouldn't surprise me if Herr von Kirchmayr will be reading every word we write to each other. Well, if he does, I certainly have nothing to hide from his eyes, and I know he will understand that I am just a loyal subject, lucky enough to have been saved from making a terrible mistake. Of course a writer like me enjoys telling his friend back home the story of what it was like to meet a great man, and I can't imagine he could be offended by my account. At least I fervently hope not, but if I am wrong, I apologize in advance for my blunder.*

I have been told that quick, vivid descriptions of people and settings are supposed to be my specialty, but after two hours waiting on a bench in the freezing hallway outside the Police Chief's office, by the time the officer on guard called out my name and opened the enormous wooden doors, I was so shaky inside that nothing really penetrated my brain at all except to wonder whether I would be going home that afternoon or straight to prison. In all the time since I arrived in Vienna, that was the one and only moment I ever found myself hoping I could be back in my room at Frau Reichle's again as soon as possible. I am not even sure how von Kirchmayr really looked, except that when I first saw him standing at the window behind his desk, I had the impression that he was inordinately tall, more like one of the full-length dynastic portraits from the last century that were hung along the walls in the corridor than like a real person. If I were inventing the scene for one of my plays, I know exactly how I would want it to look. I would have the stage designer create one of those flickering, somber Rembrandt-style rooms they do so well at the Burgtheater, maybe like something out of a production of Don Carlos. There would be two main figures visible when the curtain opened, one all in drab, contemporary street clothes, leaning forward slightly in a supplicant's pose, and the other, standing a few feet behind him downstage, holding himself stiffly erect in a formal, ceremonial uniform suggestive of some earlier time, almost like a Renaissance painting, mostly black velvet but with touches of gold and white fur to draw the audience's gaze to his thin, elegant hands and the dazzling Imperial decoration on his chest. At first you would think the two men were alone in the room, but after a few minutes, once your eyes had grown accustomed to the half-light, you would catch a glimpse of a third figure, a shadowy, malevolent creature leaning against the elaborately curved library ladder, his features almost completely obscured by the thick sheaf of files he was holding up. Even before there was any dialogue, the setting and the disposition of the figures would make it clear to the audience how perilous a situation was about to unfold.

Thank heavens my literary fantasies were completely contradicted by reality. Von Kirchmayr's office was nothing like the gloomy council chambers with which the theater has made us familiar. On the contrary, although it did little to diminish the unremitting cold, at least the sun had come out for the first time in weeks, and by the time I was admitted inside, the curtains that opened to the inner courtyard had been drawn most of the way back and the whole office was flooded with a brilliantly clear and shadowless midday light. There was nothing ostentatious or intimidating about the room, except for its scale; in fact the dense smell of cigar smoke and the half-empty coffee cups left carelessly standing on a small table near the main desk came closer to suggesting a casually elegant private apartment than the antechamber of an inquisitor.

If I hadn't been so petrified, I think I would have been thrilled just to stand in a room where so many decisions are made that affect the whole Empire. The man at the center of so much mysterious power was also nothing like the sinister interrogators we have watched onstage a thousand times. After a few minutes I realized that rather than being immensely tall, he was actually slightly shorter than I am, with a light, friendly voice, and dressed in a simple green-gray uniform without any signs of rank that I could recognize and certainly with none of the antique lace and gold decorations any competent set designer would have considered indispensable. Everything was conducted in the most normal of tones, as though I had just dropped in to continue a discussion we had started somewhere else a few days ago. Yet all that deliberate ordinariness only made my bafflement about why I was there much more unnerving. Courtesy from someone who can make you disappear forever is enough to reduce anyone to panic. I knew after the first sentence that I would tell him anything he might ask me about or obey any orders he might have for me without reservation.

There were just three of us in the room, and after I had caught my breath a bit, the absence of armed guards struck me as odd, especially with everything one hears about terrorists these days, but of course His Excellency knew very well with whom he was dealing. Still, I didn't comprehend anything at all about what was going on, least of all why I had been summoned. Was I under arrest or had I just been called in as a witness in a case about which I had some knowledge without realizing it? None of my articles has ever been seditious, but perhaps there was something in one of the many unsigned pieces we regularly publish in the journal that had offended the government and they wanted my help in tracing the author? Or maybe it was me that someone had falsely accused of a crime serious enough to concern the Chief of Police himself? I sensed the best thing was to keep a respectful silence and wait attentively until it suited the Baron to inform me of my position, and to my own surprise, I more or less managed it. At least he didn't keep me standing there waiting to be spoken to while he pretended to be absorbed in other matters, the way policemen do with their suspects in bad novels. On the contrary, after thanking me for coming to see him, "especially on such a beautiful day, so rare at this time of year and yet so characteristic of our beautiful city, don't you think?" was how he put it—as though I had any choice in the matter!—he asked me in the most natural way possible why a writer from whom "so much was expected by all of us"(!) had allowed himself to become "ensnared" by a group of absurd would-be revolutionaries from the provinces on whom the authorities had been keeping an eye for months. Did you know that this is what your precious Hans Rotenburg is to these men, a harmless nuisance, nothing more? If he has been allowed to go free so far, it is only because no one is worried enough about him to bother pressing charges. I think the police hope he will lead them to the real leaders higher up. And this is the person you wanted to put in control of The New Order? By now, though, even you must realize that although the Rotenburg brat isn't going to go to jail anytime soon, I, on the other hand, came very close to doing so thanks to your crazy schemes. According to the menacing little man with the dossiers, who seemed to join the conversation only when it was time to interject something really unpleasant, just by showing Rotenburg my letter about the magazine's financial plight and suggesting that we use his money to assume control of it, you left me vulnerable to charges of "fiduciary impropriety," "trafficking in confidential company documents," and "conspiracy to take over a legitimate, registered business by manipulating the value of its assets." Its assets! The whole magazine couldn't raise enough money to take its staff to a decent coffeehouse for pastry and hot chocolate on a Friday afternoon. But apparently that makes no legal difference, and the punishment for my "betrayal of company secrets" could be as much as five years in jail, not to mention the complete and permanent closing to me of every newspaper, literary journal, and publishing house in the country. And then, before so ghastly a picture could sink in, von Kirchmayr interrupted in the same easygoing, courteous tone as before to say that of course his office was not really concerned with financial improprieties, which were really the province of his colleague over there (he waved his hand vaguely in the other man's direction, and I had the impression he did so with a slight air of distaste at having to include someone so coarse into our little chat) but that when the scheme began to involve "disreputable elements," well, I could surely understand that the Ministry had no choice but to become directly involved.

I must have looked utterly cretinized the whole time von Kirchmayr was explaining the situation to me. For three whole days I had done nothing but rack my brain fantasizing about what I could have done to attract the attention of the police. Not once, though, did it cross my mind that their interest in me had something to do with our letters about finding a backer to help us take over the journal. I felt myself gaping at the Baron as though I could not quite understand what he was getting at and kept hoping he would repeat himself just to help me make sense of it. All the terror I had gone through had to have been for something more important! I began to suspect him of trying to trick me and racked my brain, looking for some polite way of letting him know that there was no need for any subterfuge with me; I was totally at his service and wished only that I were in possession of some dreadful, really

275

compromising secrets just so I could betray them to him. If only I could have made him happy with me by pouring out my soul to him! There was nothing I would not gladly have confessed to, nothing I wanted to keep back; the more complete and shameful my confession, the better. I might as well have been a character in one of those preposterous, overwritten Russian stories that everyone in Vienna is reading these days and that I have made it a point of pride never to let influence my work. To top it all, the whole time that I was standing there explaining myself, I was inwardly mortified both by having such ignoble urges and by the certainty that I had nothing at all to offer up that von Kirchmayr didn't already know. In any case, he was much too much a Viennese gentleman not to have found emotional extravagance ridiculous, and so instead of provoking his irritation by an outpouring of sentiment, I made a real effort to phrase my replies in short declarative sentences and only let my look and tone of voice testify to the sincerity of my devotion and my complete repentance for any errors into which I might have fallen. I once heard one of the bluestockings at the Café Central complaining to Wellisz about the way I was staring at her "with those enormous frog eyes," and I felt myself blushing with shame that a similar image might be occurring to von Kirchmayr. But luckily for me, our "interview" took place in the offices of one of the principal guardians of our cherished Empire rather than in a piece of dubious literature, and von Kirchmayr made it very clear he wasn't in the least interested in watching me abase myself. He let me see right away that he had no desire whatsoever for an inventory of all my derelictions, and I made no attempt to deny any of the specifics he brought up. But what he did want was much more astonishing. He waved aside my protestations as though they were quite out of place now that we understood each other so well and asked the other official if he had the memorandum in question ready. The man produced several thin sheets from the mass of files lying spread out in front of him and proceeded to read them out loud as though what he was saying were the most natural thing in the world. Well, not to me it wasn't, but I tried my best not to gape at him too much. The whole reading could not have taken more than five minutes, although he drew out each sentence as though he were trying to fix an important lesson in the mind of a dim-witted schoolboy who would otherwise forget some crucial point and embarrass both himself and his instructors when it came time to take his final exams. And what lessons in subtlety they were! But as artful as these orders seem to me now, when I heard them enunciated one after another, I thought I had suddenly stepped over into a pure fantasy, that the playbill must have been misprinted and instead of being ensnared in a dangerous political drama, I was being given one of the lead roles in a fairy-tale operetta. I didn't put it to myself very clearly right then, but part of me instinctively grasped that what I saw at work in that office was something like the true political genius of our Empire. What a shame that I will never be allowed to write about it directly! Where else would a great official like von Kirchmayr take so many different tones to a nobody he had just summoned into his office and manage all of them with such sovereign playfulness? It is as though he governed like an author who is not afraid to shift from one genre to another in less than a sentence, and all so quickly you can barely register the transition. In spite of the enormous distance in rank that separated us, at that moment I had an almost physical urge to rush forward and applaud him. I thought that if anyone could know enough about the world to compose a human comedy for the new century, it would have to be a man with the experience of power like that. You know, Asher, that is probably the most valuable thing I have learned from living in our capital, where it seems as if everything important were presented as though it were just an amusing sketch, and it turns out that the Chief of Police can orchestrate a scene more effectively than any professional dramatist. I am sure none of our neighbors in France or Germany will admit it, but our absurd theatricality is the most up-to-date thing about us. You will see that not one of the foreign critics will understand how much of these thoughts I have put into the comic elements of The Jew's Misfortune, but I am confident all the Viennese, even those who will hate the play, won't deny that mixed modes where tragedy and farce keep running into each other are what suit us best because they are the only ones that reflect how we really live. And anyhow, the better elements in the audience will end up finding my writing wonderful because the reviews in the court papers will tell them that doing so is the patriotic thing to think, and no one except you and I and, of course, the Baron and his staff will ever know just how comic that is!

So that's it then. Instead of your rich acquaintance, it is the government that is going to buy The New Order through one of its intermediaries and make me chief writer. I can't imagine why they should want it, and when I asked von Kirchmayr, he would not tell me any more than that his department intended to keep a discreet eye on the more "bohemian" and "artistic" circles in the city and that a magazine like ours, with no imaginable connection to the authorities, was admirably suited to the purpose. We are even supposed to start printing the occasional political essay critical of the government, just to encourage contributors with unreliable tendencies to come to us with their work. And since we are now going to be able to pay for all the work we publish, I suppose that means the government is going to finance the very articles attacking it. Where else but in our Vienna could so civilized an arrangement exist? Can you imagine a Prussian coming up with this subtle a way to run the German police department? But between the vanity of our radicals, who are even more eager than our littérateurs to see their names in print, and the wittiness of a Chief of Police who has decided to become their main publisher, we have a perfect example of true Austrian cooperation—and one that is absolutely modern at that.

The casual way the Baron mentioned that he would also put in a good word for me with some friends of his at the Burgtheater impressed me enormously. There was not a hint of anything as sordid as offering a reward for services rendered; it was a great aristocrat helping a young artist, not a policeman bribing some squalid informant. You know, it never occurred to me that von Kirchmayr meant he would speak to the director of the theater himself, and of course, when I saw Herr von Bruck a week later, he was far too discreet to mention any intervention on my behalf. Our conversation was all theater business with no reference at all to my recent interrogation at Police Headquarters. But without my having realized it at the time, it is clear to me now how much I learned from talking to von Kirchmayr. There are nuances of tone I simply couldn't hear before that are now transparent to me. It is as if I had learned a foreign language just by being forced to spend time among dangerous natives whom I had to appease at all costs. For example, I knew the director intended to conclude our meeting when I saw his eyes turn momentarily toward the window overlooking the Ring, and he asked me if I'd ever noticed how soft the early-afternoon light was at that time of year. As a dismissal it was certainly oblique enough, but since I recognized the similarity between that little scene and the way the Baron had signaled that he was done with me, I was able to take the hint and make my withdrawal without needing a more direct cue. What an odd world I seem to have landed in, Asher! Even now that I have had a glimpse of how things are managed here, I keep wondering if they all really understand one another as completely as they pretend or if they aren't sometimes just as puzzled about what is being said as any of us outsiders. How in heaven's name people like that manage to carry on a courtship, let alone produce their heirs, seems to me unfathomable, but I am sure there must be some pretty droll misunderstandings along the way.

At any rate, I have acquired sufficient discretion during these past few *days to resist asking what our masters have in mind for you. My best advice is if they haven't already called you in, then simply wait for their instructions and try to make yourself as useful as possible to them when they get around to you. Of course I am sorry that it doesn't look as though you will be joining me in Vienna anytime soon, but who knows, once this business with The New Order is fully under way, maybe they will want us to work together here after all. I would love to take you to the Café Central and make Wellisz dance attendance on both of us. In a few weeks, when I get my first advance on the play and find new lodgings, I intend to ask the bluestocking from the table right by the door if she wants to come with me to a rehearsal at the theater; somehow, I doubt that my large eyes will still seem so unappealing to her then! I will write to you again as soon as there is any real news, but in the meantime please be careful what you say to anyone in town, and try not to get both of us into more trouble.*

Affectionately,
Alexander

· ◆ ·

"Who else knows about your note to me?" That was Tausk's first question when he let himself into the ground-floor study that served as Moritz Rotenburg's informal reception room. In that same moment Moritz knew he had made the right decision. Outside, the blue of the late-afternoon sky had taken on an almost metallic sheen from the last chilly rays of the early-spring sun as it set, but Tausk's chalky face showed no trace of color from his walk. He was utterly without physical grace or manners, but rather than making him seem clumsy, there was something predatory in his awkwardness. Each of Tausk's movements confirmed this impression, from the way he shut the door and threw off his dirty overcoat without being asked, to the continual, rapid hand gestures that made his cigarette slash the space around him like a conductor's baton keeping time not so much with his conversation as with some irregular and overpowering inner rhythm that he alone could hear. He looked almost as worn out as Moritz, but only the shocking redness in his eyes and the nearly constant slight twitching of his legs betrayed any sign of the struggle between exhaustion and nervous tension that was coursing through him. The first five minutes would be crucial, they both sensed that, and although Tausk looked as though he might collapse before the end of the day, Moritz knew better than to underestimate such a man. What he did instead would have delighted, in its utterly calculated straightforwardness, no less a connoisseur of delicate negotiations than Count-Governor Wiladowski himself. Moritz simply answered Tausk's belligerent question as if they had already been conversing for hours, had long since gotten past all the customary opening exchange of courtesies and established a working level of mutual confidence. He spoke as if they were now merely mapping out the specific details of a routine transaction on whose outcome they had already agreed in principle: "Only Asher Blumenthal, the accountant, who brought the note to you, and he would never dare open the envelope. Besides, you already own him, don't you? As do I, of course. In any case, he is quite useful for these sorts of errands. Let's just agree, then, that making use of Herr Blumenthal's limited gifts is the first and, I hope, soon the least important of the joint ventures in which you and I will be partners." As much as anything else that afternoon, it was Tausk's smile, which he now saw for the first time in response to his description of Asher, that astonished Moritz. He had expected a thin, unpleasant smirk, but instead Tausk broke out into a boyishly wide and open smile that made him suddenly look as though he were barely fourteen. He even smoked like a boy enjoying something prohibited, lighting what were all too unmistakably the cheapest cigarettes available, one right after the other, from the stub of its predecessor, completely careless of both his own yellowed and singed fingers and of his host's exquisite Persian carpets. Instinctively, Moritz knew better than to offer Tausk one of the aged Havanas he kept on hand for important visitors, and he saw in Tausk's slight head tilt of acknowledgment that his avoidance of the conventional gesture had been recognized and appreciated. Moritz felt as though in Tausk's mind, he had just passed some important test, and against Moritz's own expectations, the adolescent aggressiveness of it all was somehow faintly touching.

"This man needs me, or I wouldn't be here." No matter where their negotiations might lead, Tausk had entered the Rotenburg mansion determined to cling to that thought, but when he looked closely at this man about whom even his teacher, Rabbi Pelz, used to speak with a tinge of respect, Tausk quickly reminded himself, "but not at any price." For the first time since he had been put in charge of the Governor's network of secret agents, Tausk was face-to-face with someone, possibly an antagonist, whose sources of information utterly dwarfed his own. It was also, Tausk realized with a growing sense of excitement, the first time he had felt fully alert since his expulsion from the yeshiva. Perhaps because he had had no way of guessing how much depended on the interview, or perhaps because he had grown up unable to take any gentile, no matter how powerful, completely seriously, not even his first meeting with Count Wiladowski had filled Tausk with the same heady sense of promise and danger. As weapons the shreds of data he had accumulated about Rotenburg's affairs were farcical, and it was impossible to discount the possibility that the financier himself had carefully selected the information he was prepared to see fall into the government's hands. Tausk had only one card to counterpose against the vastness of Rotenburg's wealth and power, and there was something thrilling in not being certain of its value. The shrewd move, the one he had already decided *not* to take, was to hold off revealing anything until he had a better sense of how much his sole tangible resource was worth. When he finally stopped moving about the room, sat down, and leaned in close enough to Rotenburg to smell the faint, sweet odor of the man's sick flesh, Tausk realized that he had faced similar choices countless times during interrogations at the Castle. Upon entering a prisoner's cell, Tausk listened to the suspect more intensely than the man had ever imagined possible. Tausk's mind and attention were riveted to every syllable the prisoner uttered and even to the way he drew his breath. Tausk would lean forward, his eyes utterly focused on the man's lips as well as his eyes, and the sheer concentration of Tausk's listening made the suspect increasingly anxious. Tausk exhausted people, wore them down, not by threats or promises but just by the way he listened to them. They felt increasingly guilty the whole time they were speaking, probably from incurring such profound scrutiny without deserving it except by their derelictions. A more theatrical temperament, even one with as subtle an intellect as Roublev's, was always waiting for what he called the psychologically propitious moment to spring forward with some especially damning fact from the prisoner's dossier in order to confound the man and break his resistance. But Tausk had no patience for such stock set pieces. Although he was uninterested in formulating any general principles on which he based his technique, not even when pressed repeatedly to explain the methods that produced his unmatched record of extracting confessions, he knew that when he and a suspect sat down across from each other, he wanted to reach something radically different from what Roublev meant by the man's psychology. Tausk did not care if it was a deeper layer or merely another one entirely, but if he had to name it,

Rabbi Pelz's cherished word *soul* was as good as any he had come across. It was the soul of the miserable prisoners who ended up crying to him in his cells that he went after, and to Tausk, they were *his* cells, not the government's in Vienna and not even those of the Count-Governor, who was much too squeamish to set foot anywhere near the prison. Whatever information he extracted meant nothing to him personally; it was the coin with which he paid his employer and that made him indispensable to Wiladowski; but politics interested Tausk even less than psychology, and he never entirely overcame his surprise that anyone was willing to risk himself for such transient goals as replacing one set of overseers with another. To him, all this political agitation was just a modern form of the same idolatry Rabbi Pelz had taught him to despise, and although Tausk had turned away inwardly from devoting his life to sacred texts, nothing tempted him to replace them with the thin utopian fantasies on which his prisoners nourished their sense of mission. Still, he had learned something important from all those desperate confessions, whether they were blurted out in one breathless cascade or emerged slowly over hours and days in trickles like the runoff from an enormous ice floe that was breaking apart and melting at different speeds. Men could be as promiscuous with their souls as with their bodies and were ready to sacrifice their lives for fatuous reasons in which even they themselves did not fully believe. It was as simple as that, although perhaps Rabbi Pelz, for all his dark insight into human nature, was too sheltered by his disciples' veneration to recognize how all-encompassing the sway of that promiscuity was. But not in this house. There was a ferocity of concentration in Rotenburg that rivaled anything Tausk could summon from within himself, and he shook his head rapidly from side to side like an animal emerging out of the rain, in order to focus entirely on the financier's slightest cues in reaction to the offer he had decided to make.

Before plunging ahead, Tausk could not help smiling to himself as he imagined the shocked expression of all his assistants had they been privy to his unorthodox tactics. But why not? The idea of possessing a useful strategic reserve against a man like Rotenburg was, in all likelihood, a stupid delusion, so there was less risk than there might appear in Tausk's coming right out and saying, "I know that a man with your influence has many ways of saving his son from the consequences of his mistakes, but I can do it more discreetly than anyone else and with less risk of the details ever coming out."

Rotenburg said nothing until Tausk had completely finished outlining his offer. If he was at all irritated by the direction Tausk had imposed on their conversation—and to some degree he must have been, if only by the spymaster's ill-founded notion that he knew why he had been summoned in the first place—the financier's fabled patience was easily adequate, even in his weakened state, to the task of suspending any reaction. When it came time for him to reclaim his position as the story's controlling voice, it would happen, so his attitude of tolerant curiosity announced, without requiring any special exertion, as though for Moritz Rotenburg being obeyed were simply part of the natural order. Count Wiladowski would have recognized the performance immediately. He had sacrificed enough hours to watching Franz Josef adopt precisely the same stance with his advisers, to whose competing briefs the Emperor would listen with exquisite courtesy for several hours only to dismiss all their suggestions out of hand and inform them, with an unchanged, slightly abstract politesse, of exactly what he wanted done. But even Wiladowski, for all the rumors about his preferring the company of Hebrews and freethinkers to men of his own class, could hardly have failed to find something distasteful in the spectacle of these two Jews, one of whom was his own employee, and the other a mere commoner in the province over which he was in charge, mimicking so perfectly a scene the Count-Governor had always thought unique to the Imperial residence in Vienna. Yet Wiladowski was peculiar enough that it was just possible he might also have reacted by becoming more convinced than ever of his sagacity in making a strategic alliance with such men. Since no one is ever truly offended by something that flatters his self-judgment or from which he believes he can profit, this descendant of great cardinals and princes might have been only too ready to overlook the presumption of the two Jews in exchange for a percentage of whatever their plotting would yield.

But anyone who had ever watched Tausk at work and learned to recognize the signs of growing tension in the way the constant motion of his cigarette hand began to diverge more and more eccentrically from the rhythm of what he was saying would realize how different he was from the ineffectual courtiers Wiladowski encountered at the Palace in Vienna. For all his respect for Rotenburg's power, Tausk was not ready simply to give his speech and retire with a graceful bow into the wings to await his final instructions. By the time he finished his third sentence Tausk had realized that he had erred. The only thing unclear was by how much. The man must care enough about his son to want him out of danger. All the information Tausk had gathered emphasized Rotenburg's extraordinary generosity to Hans, and in Tausk's experience, no one, least of all a brilliant businessman, trusted anyone, even his own son, with such large amounts of money unless he meant to make him a partner in his enterprises. Only the slightest shadow of frustration had passed across Moritz's eyes—more like a momentary slippage of attention than any tangible indication of impatience—but it was enough to tell Tausk that he had arrived at the meeting without knowing nearly as much as he had hoped about Rotenburg's intentions. But since he had no secure lines of retreat, Tausk was determined to press forward and see how far his hand might carry him. With an absence of ostentation that he himself realized was a shade too stagey for so canny an observer as Rotenburg, Tausk went over to his coat and from its inner pocket took out the précis he had made of Hans's extensive police dossier. He gave the dozen or so pages, written on the thinnest government-issue paper in his own precise, almost femininely small hand, to Rotenburg and waited while the financier went over to his desk and read each page through with a careful scrutiny that seemed more like a gesture of courtesy to his guest's offering than any overpowering curiosity about the document itself. When Rotenburg finished his reading and carefully refolded the papers along their original crease, he asked simply, "You must be wondering how much of this I have already been shown by other sources? Well, most of it, yes, but I have never read a document entirely in your own words before, and it is *your* phrases that give the report its value. I thank you for it. You have trained your men well, and since my son is monumentally careless, the only surprising thing is that he has not yet committed a crime sufficiently serious to worry anyone of importance. Those absurd meetings in the Maximilianstrasse apartment are barely worth spying on, and I doubt that even our dear Count-Governor, with all his terror of being killed, would be too worried about what a few overwrought young men were saying to impress one another."

Tausk allowed himself a slight sound of demurral. "Really? I am sure you know best, but in my experience, I have never seen Count Wiladowski disregard any potential threat to his well-being, no matter how far-fetched. Not to mention all that business with the literary journal. It's been taken care of by the Ministry of the Interior, and so far they all seem quite pleased with their acquisition—of Garber, I mean, more than of *The New Order*—but your son's name did figure in the seized correspondence in a compromising way, and it is never a good idea to bring oneself to the attention of those gentlemen in the Viennese security forces, even if one is a Rotenburg. Or would it be fairer to say *especially* if one is a Rotenburg."

"Oh, that." Rotenburg was entirely untroubled by Tausk's revelations. "Von Kirchmayr told me how delighted he was, especially when I advanced the money to put on *The Jew's Misfortune*. None of us expected it to be such a success with the public, and my share of the royalties has already helped complete the subscription for the new wing of the Imperial War Veterans' Hospital at Hütteldorf. I think what pleased them most at the Ministry was their satisfaction at having turned to their own purposes what they all were convinced was another plot to further my influence over the stock market. According to von Kirchmayr, his staff is quite sure I must have intended to plant a series of rumors about certain new railway bonds in *The New Order*. That money is at the bottom of it all is self-evident to everyone in the Ministry; the only puzzle is why I picked so insignificant a magazine. That is what is so wonderful about the police in general, even our brilliant Austrian one: With certain rare exceptions, like yourself, my dear Tausk, they will always turn up conclusive proof for whatever theory they already believe in. If a Hungarian is involved in anything suspicious, at some point the story has to contain a passionate mistress, an injured husband, and a secret duel; if it is a rich Jew, it has to be about money, that is obvious, isn't it? In any case, no one in Vienna takes Hans or Asher Blumenthal to be anything more than my proxies in the negotiations with Garber. I did think, though, that it was an inspired stroke of yours to summon poor, defenseless Asher for a formal interrogation and threaten him with immediate conscription into the army unless he told you everything he knew about Hans. How he must have trembled to see himself so completely at your mercy. My guess is that it took less than five minutes before he offered to betray everyone with whom he had ever come into contact. At least that is how long it took him, standing practically where you are right now, to begin wringing his hands and confessing how what he called your savage and inhumane methods forced him to reveal all his secrets to you in spite of his heroic attempts to resist. Of course you understand that I am glad things turned out so equitably; that is in part why I said we can go ahead and use Asher as our go-between in the full confidence that we both shall stay informed about everything he hears. Complete venality can be just as reliable as the sternest integrity, don't you think? Especially when it is combined with fear."

For a moment Rotenburg looked away as though to catch his breath, but Tausk saw his lips twitch with the effort to control what was evidently a painful attack. But he recovered almost immediately and proceeded as though nothing had happened. Tausk had heard all the rumors about Rotenburg's illness but until now had never known whether to believe them or not. Now he was certain that they were true and that Rotenburg's health was even more precarious than people suspected. Rather than assume this gave him an advantage, though, Tausk decided only to be still more prudent.

Rotenburg continued speaking without noticeable discomfort, but there was a contained anger in his voice that Tausk had not heard at the beginning. "I give you sufficient credit," he told Tausk, "to realize I would have defused Hans's blunder in being linked, no matter how indirectly, with crazy schemes to take over a bankrupt journal well before you hauled in poor Blumenthal to show him his correspondence with Garber. So what does that leave? A few midnight gatherings at an apartment that everyone knows is being used for sexual liaisons. Hardly a cause for serious alarm, even in our province. Our Count-Governor may *say* he wants you to check out every compromising sentence whispered anywhere in the whole province, but he hired you because he can trust you, unlike the other people around him, to make a sound decision about where to allocate your resources. It is your flair that he is buying, not just your diligence."

"Actually"—Tausk allowed himself to interrupt—"he hired me because I can read Hebrew and Yiddish, and without them it is impossible to decipher a large part of the mail that enters and leaves the province. He is firmly convinced that no greater menace exists among us than Nathan Kaplansky. Count Wiladowski has me read every one of Kaplansky's letters at least half a dozen times to look for secret codes about an attempt on his life, and my agents have been through the man's lodgings so many times searching for hidden weapons that his landlady has gotten to know them all quite well and developed the embarrassing habit of cheerfully waving to them on the stairway outside Kaplansky's front door."

"I am impressed by how easily you speak for Wiladowski. Are you really so much at one with the Castle officials? Perhaps my information to the contrary is out-of-date, in which case I can only offer you my genuine congratulations and conclude that I must have erred thinking we had certain interests in common." This time the sarcasm in Rotenburg's tone was unmistakable, and if it was strategically assumed, rather than genuine, it stood out, so Tausk thought, as the most persuasive enactment he had ever witnessed. For an excruciatingly long moment during which time the financier's eyes never moved from the play of the flames in the great fireplace, Tausk was sure that he was about to be dismissed with no more chance of appealing Rotenburg's decision than Rabbi Pelz had given him. Unlike that morning at the yeshiva, though, now Tausk felt prepared for whatever happened next. Overwrought and often anxious though he was, he had come to believe that in a crisis he could count on being sustained by his own nerves. His equanimity was a consequence of a certain inner distance from everything around him—what the other Castle officials referred to among themselves as Tausk's unpleasant "postmortem" way of looking at them—and it had been intensified by passing through and surviving his own emotional disintegration in the months after leaving the yeshiva. Instead of sending him on his way, though, Moritz stepped back from the fireplace, signaled Tausk to draw his own chair closer to him, and almost in mid-reflection, as though he were speaking from an exhaustion whose grip made absurd their preliminary banter, told him the following curious anecdote:

"You see, I thought of asking you to come see me for many reasons, but what finally convinced me to make the effort happened only a little while ago. It is so minor that I am not sure you will understand why I attached any weight to it at all. Although I have tried not to let it be generally known, during the past year, as my illness has forced me to go out less and less, I have found it harder to resist reminiscing about all the years I was constantly rushing around Europe, establishing my business. One thing I remember with pleasure is that whenever I came back here from one of my trips, I would immediately take Hans and his mother to the public gardens just across from the Workmen's Insurance Institute building. That whole part of town has hardly changed at all since I was a young man myself; that is why going there was so relaxing after a trip to a city like Paris or Berlin where whole districts are constantly being torn down and rebuilt. Even the small wooden bandstand in the middle of the lawn looks as though it has only been repainted two or three times in the past thirty years. My late wife and Hans loved listening to the military band there play the latest popular marches and waltz tunes every summer evening just before the gardens were closed for the night, and I loved watching their pleasure in doing something so much like other, normal families. On the way home I would always buy each of us a colorful Italian ice and a slice of chocolate and hazelnut cake from the old army veteran who ran the concession stand right in front of the exhibition pavilion. By tradition, when the license holder became too old to operate the concession, it passed on to another ex-soldier, and even though the man selling us the sweets might be quite different in height from his predecessors, somehow they all seemed to resemble one another enough to give the reassuring impression that it was the same fellow contentedly serving his customers year after year. I am sure you know that a few months ago, for the first time in the town's memory, the license was granted to Julius Goldschagg, a Jew who had never put on a uniform in his life. Everyone howled with anger at the decision: not just the usual anti-Semitic rabble but many of the province's outspoken liberals as well. Of course what provoked the loudest outrage in both camps was the certainty that it was *you*, the Count-Governor's new spymaster, who had been bribed to help a fellow Jew. For the sake of better relations with the gentiles, I was asked to make sure that the decision would be reversed and the refreshment stand turned back over to one of the veterans from the Fourteenth Hussars who had come home to retire in the area. What I found out almost immediately is that it was the Count-Governor's First Secretary, Matthias Pfister, whom Goldschagg had bought off and that Pfister took the money with glee because he knew that all the blame would fall on you anyway, thereby accomplishing two agreeable objectives with one venal act."

Tausk's attention did not waver for a moment during Moritz's story, but the look of intense concentration on his face gradually gave way to an expression of frank bewilderment when the financier abruptly ended it on such an oddly inconclusive detail. "Well, of course I appreciate the warning, and the thoroughness of your information about what goes on in the Castle always astonishes me," he told Rotenburg cautiously. "But I have to say that it is hard to believe there is much to worry about from that source. Pfister is not a serious threat to anyone, not even to your son. He is certainly an anti-Semite through and through, but I am quite sure that he could never imagine that a person with Hans Rotenburg's income— Jew or not—would be anything but completely reliable politically. That is to say, as long as he pays his taxes on time and does not expect the same signs of Imperial favor as a loyal Catholic from a good family." The whole time he was speaking like this, Tausk felt embarrassed at how clumsy he sounded. Whatever Rotenburg might intend by his story, alerting Tausk to danger from a man like Pfister was certainly not the entirety of his meaning, and it was galling for Tausk to be so thoroughly at a loss for a plausible interpretation. Irrelevant fragments of rabbinical exegesis insisted on emerging unbidden into his consciousness, and he found himself viewing the story of the ice-and-pastry license not as anything immediately connected with him but as a parable of blame unjustly assigned, something like a skewed retelling of Joseph and Potiphar's wife. But that was absurd, not only because Rotenburg did not speak in allegories but because although Tausk knew himself blameless of the charge of taking Goldschagg's bribe, innocence was hardly a quality to which he could, or even wished to, lay a claim. So what was being communicated? Perhaps the rumors were true after all, and Rotenburg was simply getting old and indulging himself in sentimental reveries about happier days. But nothing in their earlier conversation suggested a man who was losing his acuity, so the problem of what Rotenburg really wanted was both real and apparently, until he felt like revealing it himself, unsolvable.

"Do you remember the strange man Kaplansky accompanied into town sometime ago?" Rotenburg's question, coming as it did from a train of thought that seemed to have nothing to do with the anecdote he had just been telling, momentarily compounded Tausk's confusion. Only later, when he was alone again on his simple army cot, carefully going over their whole conversation in his mind, did Tausk register that this must have been the moment Moritz decided to shift the conversation decisively away from the spymaster's misguided focus on Hans. At least that was the first time Tausk sensed a new sharpness in Rotenburg's voice, nothing so obvious as to be noticeable to a casual listener, but to a man like Tausk, who had trained himself to pounce on the slightest alterations in tone or speech rhythm, it was unmistakable, almost as urgent as though Rotenburg had suddenly banged the surface of his desk with his fist. It was also then that Tausk must have begun to grasp just how badly Rotenburg needed to talk to him about the strange wonder rebbe. It was impossible to overlook the transformation in the financier's bearing as soon as he referred to Brugger. Rotenburg briskly stood up and moved away from the fireplace toward the window with a decisiveness that suggested he had simply shaken off all his weariness after a long nap. His pupils, which had seemed clouded over with an opaque, milky film, now scanned Tausk's face for a reaction with the fierce clarity of a man decades younger.

"How long he must have debated inside himself before sending for me! But no one in the government, not even von Kirchmayr's whole staff, could have accumulated this information on Brugger so quickly." These were Tausk's first thoughts when he saw the massive dossier Rotenburg pulled out of his desk and handed over to him. By comparison, Hans's police file, which Tausk had counted on to produce at least some effect when he brought it with him to Rotenburg's house, was shamefully thin. Yet the more he read about Brugger in Rotenburg's folders, each item carefully dated and annotated in the shorthand based on the Hebrew alphabet that Tausk already knew from opening every piece of the financier's correspondence that did not travel by private courier, the less clear an image of the rebbe emerged. How could Rotenburg have amassed so much information only to have it yield such imprecise results? Simply at the level of professional tradecraft, such vagueness was unnerving. The annoyance Tausk had felt at being denied extra funds to investigate Brugger was replaced by the still more unwelcome thought that even if the Count-Governor had shared his concern about the rebbe, the proposed investigation would have turned out largely futile. By the time Tausk made his way through half the dossier, which he read standing upright, leaning slightly against one of the room's wood-paneled walls and swaying back and forth on his heels while turning over the pages, he was completely out of cigarettes, and a thin dust of gray ash covered the carpet in a circle where he was standing. But as he was nearing the end of the last folder, Tausk became aware that something about the dossier was troubling him. Or rather, he realized that there were serious omissions in it, and with that realization came a rush of excitement.

"Does the name Robert Sonnenschön mean anything to you?" Tausk quietly asked his host while returning the papers to him and accepting, without noticing that he was doing so, a plateful of biscuits, along with a glass of brandy. Tausk would have preferred strong coffee but was glad of the chance for any nourishment. Although Tausk occasionally drank alcohol when his work required it, the fumes from Rotenburg's brandy reminded him too much of the dense, fetid stench that had saturated his father's tavern, and he refused the offer of a second glass.

"I mention Sonnenschön"—Tausk went on, with his mouth unpleasantly dry from the biscuits—"because I was surprised to find so little about him anywhere in your files. It looks as though no one thought him worth bringing to your attention. That might be a dangerous oversight. He is a young Jew from Odessa, who has a reputation as something of an athlete. Ever since hearing Brugger speak, Sonnenschön has devoted his life to the rebbe, and he writes his sister in St. Petersburg lengthy, violent hymns of praise to the man. I have copies of several of Sonnenschön's letters and will be glad to provide you with a set." This time Moritz did not even pretend to disguise his curiosity and simply urged Tausk to tell him right away whatever he could recall from the correspondence. Tausk's mnemonic training as a rabbinical student made it easy for him to quote the documents with nearly verbatim accuracy, and as he recited Sonnenschön's ecstatic accounts, Tausk noticed how seriously Rotenburg was taking in every word. When Tausk first read the letters aloud to Roublev in the Castle, their fervor had aroused more contempt than worry, but as his anxiety about Brugger grew, that reaction had given way to a deep sense of misgiving about how the rebbe might use Sonnenschön's limitless devotion. Rotenburg too was clearly perturbed both by the content of the letters and by the fact that his own investigation had not turned up the same information. If Sonnenschön had somehow slipped through the net of Rotenburg's numerous correspondents, who was to say that there were not many more like him about whom Tausk in turn was also ignorant?

Yet seeing Rotenburg share his worry was also reassuring to Tausk. He had watched Wiladowski brush aside his warnings about the rebbe enough times so that he no longer bothered bringing them up at the Castle, and he welcomed having someone with Rotenburg's worldly acumen confirm that there was nothing laughable about his anxiety. Perhaps in Rotenburg, the spymaster thought, he had finally found if not exactly an ally, then at least a collaborator with whom he could talk about what should be done with Brugger. For all of Tausk's apparent power, his own options on that score were frustratingly limited. His instinct was to arrest the man and intimidate his followers so that they would not dare strike back, but to do so effectively, Tausk needed the Count-Governor's consent and the backing of the civil administration. Even then the famously liberalized new legal code greatly limited the police's right to hold a prisoner without a speedy trial, and the last thing Tausk wanted was to hand Brugger the leading role in a public spectacle. Tausk could not help reflecting how much easier a job like his would be in a government that gave him adequate means of repression, but somehow he would have to ensure Wiladowski's safety without them.

The only certain way to handle Brugger and his followers would be to have the army take them all into custody and charge them in a closed military tribunal with plotting against officials of the state. But that would require a declaration of martial law. After all the labor unrest of the past few months, elements in the army were looking for an excuse to suspend civilian rule, and only Count Wiladowski's distaste for such extreme measures—"provocations to useless violence in the present and an incitement to continuing hostility in the future" were what he called them in letters to his superiors in Vienna—had forestalled immediate steps in that direction. But if anything else were to threaten the maintenance of public order in an area so close to the Russian frontier, the government would override his objections. In such circumstances, though, both the Count-Governor and Tausk would lose their authority since the entire provincial administration would be placed temporarily in the hands of the senior army officer assigned to pacify the district.

After their disconcerting meeting at the Mendelssohn Club, Moritz was as certain as the spymaster that the rebbe intended to incite his disciples to violence and could not be stopped by any kind of appeal. He seemed equally indifferent to bribes or threats, and to Rotenburg, that made him truly dangerous. Kaplansky's description of Brugger's sermons and the reports Rotenburg had gathered from the eastern shtetls showed a man enthralled by murder as though it were a holy rite. Everywhere Brugger had passed, unexplained fires had broken out in the synagogues, often with heavy fatalities, and prominent officials from the local Jewish communities had been killed or badly injured in a series of supposed accidents that were clearly acts of ruthless terror. In almost every case, however, the savagery occurred after Brugger had already left the area, so it was impossible to prove him responsible. His followers, though, had remained behind to pack up and dispose of their possessions, and Rotenburg's correspondents were sure that the destruction visited on their towns was Brugger's revenge for their having rejected his messianic summons.

It was evident to Rotenburg that Tausk's intense involvement in the case meant he regarded Wiladowski as Brugger's probable target. Moritz, though, was not at all sure. Judging by what had happened on the other side of the border, Rotenburg suspected that the rebbe's anger was more likely to be aimed not at a gentile but at someone like him, a rich Jew with wide influence, who had refused a direct appeal from Brugger himself. Rotenburg was not worried about his personal safety, but how much assurance could he take from Brugger's promise that nothing bad would happen to Hans as a result of the rebbe's appearance among them? If Brugger intended to strike at Moritz through his son, all the talk about the boy's future might have been a diversion so that Moritz would leave Hans unprotected. Hans now spent most of his time in the Josef Quarter, and the house Brugger shared with his followers was only a few blocks away from Hans's flat. But no matter who his target might be, Rotenburg was certain that unless Brugger was stopped, something terrible would happen from which none of the Jews in the town, and perhaps throughout the Empire, would recover without lasting damage.

Neither man ever spoke the word *murder* out loud, either that evening or in any of their subsequent conversations. Part of what made their collaboration so unfathomable to outsiders was how little they needed to make explicit to each other. Some of this was due to a common quickness of intuition that made lengthy explanations superfluous; some, to a shared reluctance to commit certain thoughts to either air or paper; and some, to what must have been a finely honed awareness about just how much, and no more, it was necessary to tell each other so that there would be a sufficiency of information without adding the lies that must inevitably follow if the issue were pressed by so much as an extra syllable. There was something almost domestic about the way they stood together by the fireplace, having settled the main details through an improvised conversational shorthand, looking for all the world like a couple of old friends who have known each other for so many years, and have shared so many experiences, that neither feels the need for more words. Each seemed ready to enjoy the solitude of his own quiet musings, sheltered in the knowledge of the other's undemanding proximity. The one thing Moritz truly regretted about the whole affair was the necessity of sacrificing poor Kaplansky, but he had to admit that Tausk was right: There was no better way to deflect any official inquiry from the Castle beyond what the spymaster's report would contain. Who would concern himself with a simple case of two overambitious Jews quarreling for leadership of the poorest of their race? The Count-Governor's delight in being rid of a man of whom he was terrified would make him countersign whatever legal sentence Tausk recommended, and the Christian trade union leaders would probably welcome any strictly personal accusations against Kaplansky as belated justification for their shabby treatment of him. "It is a pity, because Kaplansky really is a decent fellow," Moritz thought, "and it won't be easy co-opting another man with such good connections among the workers. But Wiladowski is going to have him arrested sooner or later anyway on a trumped-up political charge, and at least like this, I can make sure he is treated well in prison and that his family gets a substantial monthly allowance."

About the decision to plot Brugger's liquidation, Rotenburg never had any regrets, not even on his deathbed, when he tallied the list of his merits and sins with the scrupulous exactitude of his head bookkeeper calculating the year's gains and losses. Working with Tausk, who seemed to have no special regard for human life and death, no doubt made it easier, but only in a limited, tactical sense. The meeting with Brugger at the Mendelssohn Club had confirmed everything both Kaplansky's and Rotenburg's correspondents in the east had told him. The only choices were to join Brugger or eliminate him. All the rest felt secondary. Sonnenschön's letters made the matter still more urgent since the more recruits the rebbe gathered, the harder it would be to catch him alone, and the greater his capacity to do harm.

As much as possible, Rotenburg avoided thinking about the nearly overwhelming urge he had felt that day at the club to ask Brugger how long he still had to live. The taste of the solid food the rebbe had brought him, and the mystery of how he had given him the strength to swallow it without pain, lingered in his memory longer than whatever words they had exchanged on the subject. It was enough that Rotenburg had witnessed for himself that the rebbe's power did not depend solely on having armed men at his command. "My thoughts light fires in your cities." Moritz no longer remembered if Kaplansky had quoted that sentence from Brugger's sermons or if it was in one of Sonnenschön's letters home, but during the following weeks the words haunted the financier until he felt as though a terrible conflagration had already been started and would soon be visible to everyone.

· ◆ ·

When Tausk let himself out of Rotenburg's mansion shortly afterward, by the same inconspicuous back entrance through which he had come in, he was surprised by how few hours he had actually spent there. Although it was well past the legal closing hour for taverns, there were still plenty of places close to the river where he was certain of being able to buy a fresh supply of his cigarettes and perhaps something warm to eat before returning to the Castle. A sharp rain was starting up again, striking the rooftops like a string of small glass beads rolling across a countertop, and as Tausk ducked into a cheap tavern where no one would recognize him, he finally let himself uncoil sufficiently to take stock of how things had turned out.

Even for this district, Löffner's Bar was notoriously squalid, and the contrast between such a place and the elegant house he had recently left appealed to Tausk. Instead of a proper door on hinges, only a thick oilskin curtain separated the inside from the street, and as soon as Tausk pushed through it, the dense miasma of grease, alcohol, and kerosene saturating the whole room left him momentarily dizzy. Tausk quickly gave up any idea of eating here and sat down with a glass of heavily sweetened coffee at one of the unoccupied tables, looking around with an expression of such morose hostility that even the owner was not about to press him to buy anything further. What mattered right now was to be alone, away from Roublev and his all too solicitous curiosity. Tausk needed to decide for himself what he intended to gain from the whole affair. So far that was the question to which he had given the least thought, though he suspected that none of the people working for him would believe him on that score. Yet if there was one thing of which Tausk had been certain from the outset, it was that keeping the issue of recompense fluid for as long as possible was crucial to his dealings with the financier. Rotenburg was accustomed to paying immense sums to get whatever he wanted without the cost's meaning anything to him, and in consequence, he devalued both what he wished for and all those who provided it for him. Tausk, however, was in a unique position to render Rotenburg a service he passionately wanted. What Rotenburg had asked of him would create an obligation directly proportional not just to the gravity of the act but to the intensity of his need to see the deed done. There were some debts for which the slate could never be wiped entirely clean, and Tausk intended this to be among them. He had no doubt that the day the Count-Governor left office or withdrew his favor, his own position at the Castle would collapse, and he would be lucky only to be shown the door like any dismissed lackey. Just as likely, he might end up spending some distinctly unpleasant hours being questioned in one of his own interrogation cells. Rotenburg's obligation to him was Tausk's best safeguard against the future, and he decided to let it accumulate interest for as long as possible before drawing on it. The financier was obviously unwell, but it would be a mistake to press his claims prematurely. Men like that often held out much longer than their doctors thought possible, and Rotenburg had just shown a determination that suggested reserves of still-untapped inner strength. Tausk knew that everyone looked forward to presenting his bill to Rotenburg at the first opportunity. By not asking for anything right away, the spymaster would underline that what he had done had nothing in common with the usual services rendered by Rotenburg's paid retainers. Perhaps that was part of what Rotenburg had meant to tell him with the strange story about Goldschagg's bribe: that a thick dossier of Tausk's transgressions was being compiled to which his enemies were adding new pages every day, even if they themselves were committing the crimes for which Tausk would be accused later, and that it was high time for Tausk, in so isolated a position, to find another patron besides the Count-Governor.

All in all, Tausk concluded, it had been a remarkably successful night, especially considering how inept his approach had been at the start. He was still surprised by how little Rotenburg seemed to care that Tausk had so badly misjudged the financier's purpose in sending for him. Unlike Count Wiladowski, who enjoyed speculating out loud in front of his spymaster, Rotenburg had no real desire to be understood by Tausk. Whatever the financier might pretend, it was evident that the explanations he offered were not intended to win over his listener; they were meant simply to ensure that his wishes were carried out to the letter. Rather than being offended, Tausk was relieved at not being the recipient of more elaborate confidences; Rotenburg's attitude exempted Tausk from any need to adopt as his own whatever personal justifications Moritz was constructing for himself. Tausk felt free to concentrate on the task, even if his reasons for agreeing to it were not identical to Rotenburg's. But he could not help wondering if Rotenburg and Brugger had ever tried to explain themselves to each other. Tausk's attempts to find out what the two men had talked about the day Brugger went to the Mendelssohn Club had proved futile since Rotenburg's protection made it impossible to suborn any of the club's employees. But whatever threat Rotenburg saw in the rebbe must have been formidable since it helped seal his decision to have Brugger killed, and the alarm Brugger was able to inspire in a man as confident as Rotenburg sharply heightened Tausk's awareness of how cautiously he would have to proceed with any plan to liquidate the preacher.

The rain had let up again. The only sound from across the narrow bridge leading to the Castle gate was the regular clanking of the nightguards, whom Count Wiladowski had ordered to call out their stations every three minutes in order to show any lurking terrorists how carefully his residence was being protected. As he walked past the bored soldiers into the central courtyard and continued up to his room, Tausk remembered how Rabbi Pelz, to the astonishment of visitors who had come to see him because of his reputation for sanctity, enjoyed scandalizing them by finding something edifying in everything that happened, even if it was culled from the newspapers that circulated only among the most corrupt of the goyim. One such event had fascinated all of them at the yeshiva for a whole month, and the story came back to Tausk so vividly that he was only sorry it was too late to go back and see how Rotenburg would react to it as well. It seemed that early in Franz Josef's reign, in one of the poorest villages in Galicia, a foreign preacher, dressed in rags like any other vagabond, was standing in the town square, declaring himself the Messiah come to lift the curse of exile from God's Chosen People. The man was completely lost in his own passionate testimony and paid no attention to a group of uniformed riders, headed by the local magistrate, who were passing through town to consult with the district military commissioner about where to put up the new army barracks. In the official entourage there happened to be a Jewish doctor who knew Yiddish and had just been assigned to the regiment as its assistant surgeon. The others asked their Jew to translate the preacher's words, and he did with an obvious expression of distaste. But as soon as the magistrate understood what was being proclaimed in his own town, he indignantly ordered the preacher arrested on charges of blasphemy. At dinner the next night, though, when the case of the crazy preacher was brought up as another example of the kind of rural idiocy to which one had to become accustomed in such postings, the provincial chief judge pointed out that if they brought the preacher to trial, they would have to prove that the man was not who he claimed to be. According to the law, he had every right, as part of his defense, to show that he was indeed the Redeemer. If such a trial ever took place, and the Viennese press somehow found out about it, the entire provincial administration would be the laughingstock of the capital, and their careers blighted forever. In the end, after a discreet exchange of letters with more experienced ecclesiastical and political officials in the government, they decided to lock up the man in a madhouse and not press any charges against him at all. After a half dozen years he died in the asylum, still proclaiming his messianic calling to all the inmates, apparently having succeeded in converting several of them, including a number of the guards, who themselves were promptly incarcerated as madmen after they had attempted to help him escape.

3

The next morning, nothing in Tausk's manner gave any hint that his attention might be wavering from the detailed political reports he and Matthias Pfister were supposed to prepare for the Count-Governor. Everyone on the Castle staff had long since become accustomed to the look of irritable exhaustion with which Tausk hurried along the corridors, especially on days he was obliged to drag himself out of bed after only two or three hours of fitful rest. Like many insomniacs, for whom sleep comes only with the first, faint sounds that signal the start of a new day, Tausk was chronically worried about being late for morning functions, and by way of compensation, he made a point of trying to arrive at such meetings before anyone else. This time too he virtually hurled himself into the empty conference room a few steps ahead of Pfister and Count Wiladowski, whose treads he could clearly make out approaching from different directions a dozen or so steps behind him. Tausk was relieved to hear that at least they were not walking together and, in the same instant, felt unpleasantly surprised at his own relief. Perhaps he had been more rattled than he had realized by Rotenburg's warnings about the secret dossier being prepared against him. Usually he was indifferent to his surroundings, but today the conference room, with its overlarge central table on which the servants had already carefully stacked three separate piles of the purest-quality writing paper, each sheet embossed with the Imperial crest, filled Tausk with repugnance, and he looked around unhappily at the half dozen massive chairs with their rigid backs and green silk coverings, not one of which gave the slightest promise of comfort to his aching back and neck. But since he knew that Pfister had enthusiastically seconded Marie-Luise's loathing for his cigarettes, Tausk quickly lit his first one of the day and began to smoke it more energetically than he really wanted to, so that the air would be as saturated as possible when the First Secretary came in. When Pfister did so, he ostentatiously avoided exchanging glances with Tausk and remained standing near the entrance with a disgusted expression. Then, as though afraid that a purely silent enactment of his feelings might be insufficient, he also began to cough aloud in the exaggerated way people do when they want to make a point to an observer and not just relieve an itching in their throat. Since Count Wiladowski had chosen just then to linger in the hallway for a few more moments to give further instructions to the two guards on duty outside the room, Pfister was obliged to prolong his stage cough until doing so became embarrassing, even to him; that was precisely when the Count-Governor finally stepped into the room with a cheerful smile, designed to show that of course he understood that the little charade was being performed for his benefit and quite approved of it—not because it was especially well done but because the zeal with which it was performed was itself reassuring. A province whose senior functionaries had time for such histrionic demonstrations of their rivalry might be mistaken for the backdrop of some boulevard farce, but, so Wiladowski told himself, surely it was quite unsuitable a setting for any serious outbreak of revolutionary terror. He refused to abandon the notion that even in his own day, politics retained an internal logic of its own that, like the elaborately scripted rites that had governed his world for centuries, could be relied upon to thwart the more extreme violations of decorum for which the radicals were clamoring.

To Tausk, trained on rabbinical texts full of far wilder dialectics and more precipitous transitions, the Count-Governor's assumption that the same gradualism that had marked the Empire's slow growth could be relied upon to regulate the rhythm of its decline only confirmed his suspicion that even the subtlest goy was, at bottom, amazingly frivolous. Tausk knew his employer well enough not to risk seriously disagreeing with him in front of others, especially not within earshot of Pfister, who would immediately spread the story of a rift between the Count-Governor and his Jewish spymaster throughout the Castle. Rumors like that easily took on a life of their own and often ended up creating the facts they pretended only to report. In addition to the officially scheduled meetings, though, when protocol made Pfister's presence unavoidable, the Count-Governor regularly consulted Tausk in private about what he had learned by spying on the town's Jews, and Tausk used those occasions to try to impress on Wiladowski that the conspirators under interrogation in the prison cells only a few floors below the conference room never exhibited the slightest respect for artistic parallelism in their plots. Once he went so far as to suggest that it was perhaps a touch capricious of the Count-Governor to stake his safety on the aesthetic sensibility of his would-be murderers. Here Wiladowski corrected him: He was terrified of being killed by someone very much like one of Tausk's prisoners but regarded this as a strictly personal calamity, not as part of any larger political conflagration about whose outcome he ought to care. There was nothing symbolic or representative about his physical well-being. He intended to avoid assassination not because he feared being succeeded in his public offices by a fanatical thug but because it would certainly hurt dreadfully and end his enjoyment of what was, all in all, a thoroughly agreeable existence. Unlike his colleagues at the Ministry and the conservative journalists in their pay who wrung their hands and lamented what they called the creeping degradation of the continent's politics, Wiladowski was entirely unsentimental about the future of his class as a whole. He took it as axiomatic that men of his breed were already in the process of being pushed aside for good, but he was equally certain that the beneficiaries would be the virtuosi of the stock market, ruthless industrialists and financiers like Rathenau in Germany or his country's own homegrown Moritz Rotenburg, not a pack of embittered ex-students with a few pistols and several suitcases full of wretched pamphlets. Yet when he tried to explain his reasoning to Tausk, the too studiously noncommittal, almost expressionless look he got in return made Wiladowski, who was not at all inclined to doubt himself, wonder if he was risking a potentially lethal misjudgment. Although there was more than a whiff of impertinence in his spymaster's manner, if having his theory disregarded helped keep Wiladowski alive, then the Count-Governor was willing to overlook a great deal of what his wife called that intolerable Jewish impudence.

In fact, though, Tausk had come much closer to Wiladowski's position than the Count-Governor could have imagined, and in the hours since his unexpected pact with Rotenburg, Tausk was nervously revising all his own calculations about the distribution of power in the province. Until recently doing so had seemed easy compared with the rigors of the yeshiva, but Tausk was no longer so sure. The last time he had gravely miscalculated the forces arrayed around him, he had found himself cast out into the world like some infected animal; he could not make the same mistake here. His services were now pledged both to the Count-Governor and to

Rotenburg. Maybe in one of the cheerful, lightly scabrous Italian comedies Wiladowski so enjoyed, a cunning servant could negotiate the difficulties of serving several masters without stumbling. But looking out from
the Castle's high leaded windows onto a gray, rain-soaked landscape that
even its hereditary owners found too depressing to inhabit for very long,
Tausk was acutely aware that the odds were heavily against his long-term
success. Simply by remaining silent about last night, he had already betrayed Count Wiladowski, and Tausk suspected that sooner or later his
own survival might require his betraying Rotenburg as well. Both men
probably expected a certain amount of duplicity from him, much as a prudent storekeeper always makes an allowance for items lost to theft in
determining the final cost of his goods. But Tausk doubted that their
tolerance extended very far. Balancing the financier's demands on him
against those of the Count-Governor was difficult enough without including Brugger's elimination in his tally. If Tausk had been one of the semi-
literate, superstitious Jews whose drunken stories had been fueled by the
contraband vodka in his father's inn, he might easily start believing he had
fallen into some diabolical trap from which there was no escape. For all
his cynicism, Tausk was still close enough to the world of those tales that
on days like this, when he was so utterly worn out that even the simplest
tasks took an immense effort of will, he could visualize these figures of
power suddenly throwing off their human disguises to reveal themselves
as malignant demons intent on ensnaring his soul. The madness of these
momentary, scarcely acknowledged phantasmagoric images was what
made the beefy solidity of Matthias Pfister's broad blond forehead and
vexed expression so entirely, and quite unexpectedly, welcome a sight.
Tausk already knew that the combination of nervousness and exhaustion
left his mind vulnerable to the eruption of grotesque fantasies in which
reality became shamefully permeable to his hallucinations—it had happened to him like that several times at the yeshiva—but he was certain
there was no way his imagination would ever invent someone as mediocre
as Matthias Pfister. "What nonsense this all is. I am just worn out, that's
all. Even the most minor devil could not have that characterless a face"
was what Tausk mumbled to himself as he looked up and smiled at the
First Secretary through a new cloud of cigarette smoke.

Although all the windows were fitted with thick curtains whose color
perfectly matched the backing on the chairs, a grimy March light flowed
into the room in broad swaths wherever the drapery had not been pulled

tightly together. At the Count-Governor's command, Tausk and Pfister seated themselves at their customary places across the table from him and spread out their reports. As usual, Pfister spoke first, and just as he would do immediately afterward over midmorning coffee and pastries with Marie-Luise, he read out an account of a province all of whose subjects were thoroughly content with their lot and, except for a handful of unreliable Jews of no great influence, desired only to serve their Governor and, through him, their beloved Emperor with unassuming respect and gratitude for all the favors his rule had brought them. Like many men dependent on the arbitrary favor of his superiors for advancement, Pfister thought the securest route to success lay in enabling these people, who already had enormous self-regard, to admire themselves and their positions in the world even more. The sole recommendation Pfister now permitted himself to put forward was that perhaps the funds currently allocated to the new spy service—funds for which no one in the Castle's Finance Department had ever seen a proper accounting—might be better used for charitable donations to augment the good work the Church was already doing to assist the deserving poor through their temporary hardships. Although Count Wiladowski had long ago stopped making the slightest show of listening, that did not inhibit the evident satisfaction with which Pfister finished his little speech. In fact each time he delivered it, it seemed to please him more, as though like some great poem, it required multiple recitations for the richness of the words to be fully graspable, and if his audience did not appear to be taking in the entire significance of what he was saying, no doubt the next time it would all become clear.

When his turn came, Tausk, as he had done for the past few months, declined to answer a single one of Pfister's gibes and proceeded as though no one at all had spoken before him, a tactic he knew would irritate the First Secretary more than any direct rejoinder. Instead, and without any emotion in his tone, Tausk simply read out a list of every politically motivated crime and seditious utterance committed in the province during the past thirty days, sometimes adding choice tidbits that Roublev had copied out for him from the more sensationalistic papers in Vienna, Trieste, St. Petersburg, and Berlin. Over the previous two months alone, in a nearby region not hitherto considered especially infected with antigovernment tendencies, the authorities had recorded more than 120 cases of violent confrontations between unemployed factory workers and the police, with more than 30 workers killed and a larger number wounded as a result.

Damage to the police and the army was reckoned as 9 killed and 15 badly injured—not a large total, but twice the figure of government losses from similar grievances only a year earlier. Moreover, seditious pamphlets had been discovered in the homes of the ringleaders of some of the most violent clashes, writing identical to what Tausk's spies had seen in the hands of the local agitator Nathan Kaplansky. Although their province had been spared from serious violence so far, the same printed incitements to bloodshed that had corrupted weak minds elsewhere in the Empire were already being distributed here as well.

While Wiladowski did not doubt the factual accuracy of Tausk's catalog of horrors, he also knew that its recitation was every bit as calculated and polemical as Pfister's blandly reassuring one. This is how they always divided the news: Pfister was certain that the Count-Governor's fear made him long to hear only positive and uplifting reports, whereas Tausk instinctively chose to feed his master's anxiety. To judge by the abrupt change in the Count-Governor's posture, Tausk was right in his decision. Wiladowski could not stop himself from leaning forward to listen with rapt attention for the slightest variation in the incidence or location of revolutionary violence. Cowardice as vivid as his was itself a form of desire, and it worked on him as compellingly as any of the erotic stories he collected. Since his official brief was simply to gather information, not to make policy unless directly asked, Tausk never permitted himself to offer any specific recommendations at these meetings. Besides, it was much more revealing to hear what Wiladowski himself would suggest. Although Tausk had watched his master closely for months now, had spent numerous hours in intimate conversation with him, and flattered himself that he knew the man reasonably well, he had no illusions about being able to predict the direction in which the Count-Governor's thoughts might run. But this morning the abyss between what they had been discussing and the Count-Governor's reaction perplexed Tausk just as much as Pfister. Wiladowski first drew the two reports to his side of the table and leafed through them in such a way as to make clear that the act was an inbred gesture of polite acknowledgment for work done more or less satisfactorily, not a prelude to any perusal of their content. Then, after dropping the pages into his large red leather portfolio for his personal servant to file away later, he got up and, from the smaller revolving bookcase that stood near the back of the room, pulled out one of the sumptuously illustrated volumes with which he usually relaxed after concluding any disagreeable official duty. To Tausk and Pfister, who were still waiting to be dismissed, he said in his familiar tone of faintly aggrieved disappointment, "Of course I appreciate your efforts, gentlemen, but you know, your reports confirm how pointless it is to look anywhere except in my own library for guidance about my future. And even among the best of my authors, there is a great deal more nonsense than real understanding. I don't know if you have bothered with the French novelists, Tausk, but I am sure that Pfister here has, if only because my dear wife has developed quite a taste for them lately and needs someone besides her confessor and maid with whom she can chatter about what she has been reading. Now just look at this beautiful edition. Not the kind of novel you would find on the Countess's night table, I am afraid. Of course mine is all about magnificent whores because really, that is all these scribblers are good for. The minute one of them sits down to describe what people in my position are like, well, they are hopelessly out of their depth. Most of them have never gotten close enough to real power to have any idea what they are talking about. Everything gets so banally romanticized and exaggerated. Even your reports, Pfister, stupefyingly sunny though they invariably are, would depress any sane man. Don't look so aggrieved, being sunny is not at all bad—especially around me, who can use being cheered up from time to time. We certainly know that cheerfulness is not exactly Tausk's forte. All that heavy Jewish pessimism can be a bit hard on one's digestion so early in the day. What I really regret is that it's impossible to close every high school in the Empire for a few years. That would be the best way to keep me safe. I am convinced that in any country with a lot of political fanatics, the taverns are much less dangerous than the high schools and universities. But I suppose if we did close the schools, all the troublemakers would just run off to study in Switzerland, and then, by the time we arrested them on their return, they would have started talking with that dreadful Swiss accent, so that not even Tausk here could understand their confessions. Well, then, what am I supposed to read to become wiser? More ministerial briefs. That is just death by slow torture instead of by a firebomb. I would rather retire and spend vacations in Trieste with my little library, admiring the illustrations and watching the fishing boats come back into the cove below Miramar at sunset. Anyway, thank you both, gentlemen. I will take my coffee alone now, so please have Aloïs send it into my study right away."

For one of the only times since the morning reports had been instituted, Tausk and Pfister walked out of the room together. Usually the

First Secretary left before the spymaster, bowing formally to the Count-Governor and using his two-inch height advantage to look right over Tausk's head in the direction of the family quarters, where Marie-Luise was waiting to be briefed about what had gone on at her husband's meeting. Now, though, his eyes looked genuinely alarmed as though for the first time he thought that the stories about Count Wiladowski's slide into lunacy, stories he himself had done nothing to check, might actually be true. A wicked superior was certainly distressing, but a mad one was something altogether worse. As soon as the guards had again closed the heavy doors to the conference room and taken up their positions in front of it, Pfister stopped and leaned against the stone wall, looking quizzically at Tausk for some explanation of what they both had just witnessed. But just as Pfister's obtuse solidity had calmed Tausk's fears about his own mental balance at the start of the meeting, so now the man's confusion had a marvelously bracing effect on him. Before Pfister could say anything, Tausk joined him by the wall and offered him a cigarette to, as he said, "steady your nerves." Pfister's expression of repugnance struggling against the temptation to try the vile remedy almost redeemed the whole exhausting morning for Tausk. There was no point trying to build even the frailest bridge between them. The instant Pfister felt restored, all his resentment would surface again, so Tausk treated himself to the pleasure of seeing his enemy visibly discomfited. Before Pfister could say a word, Tausk began to talk at him with the breathless singsong rapidity he knew men like that expected from lower-class Jews: "You will have to excuse me now, but I have urgent work down there." He accompanied these words with a sinister glance to the immense winding staircase at whose bottom lay the Castle's prison cells and interrogation rooms. "I do wish I had your culture, though. Frankly, I did not fully understand what our dear master meant there at the end, but as he himself was gracious enough to point out, that is no doubt due to my woeful ignorance of the sort of book he was showing us. I am sure you had no trouble following what he was saying, and I only wish I had the time right now to impose on your courtesy for clarification. But perhaps later in the week, if your busy schedule permits, you would help me in this matter. In the meantime it is clear that I will have to procure a copy of that novel in order to learn what the Count-Governor expects of us. I do hope the local booksellers have a less costly edition in stock since I would not want to add such a high-priced item to my professional expenses unless I had no choice in the matter." Then, without looking back, Tausk hurried down the staircase to find his room, where, after a brief and, he suspected, probably futile attempt at a nap, he would try to make sense of the morning's strange scene.

That it all had been an improvised but nonetheless deliberately staged scene, Tausk had no doubt. Last night's experience with Moritz Rotenburg had enlarged his awareness of how various and complicated the motives for such performances might be and sharpened his antennae for their implications. The Count-Governor was mocking both Pfister's and Tausk's ritual set pieces at the morning's meetings, even if Pfister remained blind to the fact. But there was a sting to Wiladowski's game as well, a warning that fear, like lust, could become satiated. The indifference that would succeed it might spring from entirely different sources than real courage, but it was not always easy to tell the two apart. If Wiladowski were now playing at being terrified of assassination, rather than really living in constant fear of his own murder, in much the same way, and with the same control, as he had long played at his other vices, Tausk would need to be very careful indeed. Yet nothing in Wiladowski's tone gave Tausk the feeling he was being pushed away. On the contrary, there was almost an appeal to him, a gesture, through the strict formality of their scripted roles, toward other registers of feeling. But, Tausk cautioned himself, to trust such impressions was the height of folly, especially in his present, overwrought state. Later, when he himself was feeling less shaky, he could reflect more on the plausibility of his interpretations.

As it turned out, though, Tausk never had the chance to lie down at all. In spite of strict orders forbidding anyone to enter his room without permission, from the doorway the spymaster already saw Roublev sprawled out, barefoot, with his clumsy-looking, dirt-encrusted walking boots propped on top of the faded gray wool blankets Tausk always slept on. Although he had enormous respect for his assistant's intelligence, he sometimes had to overcome something like a twinge of nausea at the first sight of the man's scruffiness. Tausk himself might prowl around the Castle half shaved and with more than one soup stain faintly visible on his trousers, but he was markedly fastidious about others. Wiladowski, who was the only one to have noticed this, understood immediately that far from being a contradiction, Tausk's disregard for his own appearance was intimately connected to his visceral distaste for physical slovenliness in anyone else. Any too strong reminder of the body's needs and weaknesses repelled Tausk, and if he did not change his own linen as often as Castle propriety required, it was because he preferred to forget entirely that he was a creature who was dependent upon taking in food and whose internal organs were subject to the same digestive processes and decay as everyone else's. He could never understand how his mother could be so matter-of-fact about scrubbing the night's thick layer of stale alcohol and filth from the tavern floor every morning, and later, at the yeshiva, when one of the other students picked his teeth too near Tausk, he would edge away with disgust lest one of the dislodged particles of food might fall on him. Now, simply the knowledge that his own bedding had come into contact with Roublev's permanently sweat-stained clothes made Tausk feel queasy, and he wondered if this was not how people like Marie-Luise and Pfister felt when they caught sight of him. "I suppose I am their Roublev," was what Tausk told himself, and for a moment he found himself close to sympathizing with their reactions. But the moment passed, and instead of compassion, the knowledge that he probably elicited the same response in Marie-Luise as Roublev did in him just left him more bitter than ever at his vulnerability to such judgments. The only one of them who never showed any traces of squeamishness around him was the Count-Governor himself, but then Wiladowski, as Tausk had witnessed for himself many times, would find the repulsion his Jew evoked in his wife and First Secretary sufficient reason not to let himself be bothered by any of Tausk's habits. His master's combination of vanity and aristocratic self-control seemed as helpful a model as any to get Tausk through the rest of the day. From strictly within himself, Tausk doubted he had sufficient resources left to invent a better solution. From the moment he had taken Rotenburg's summons out of Blumenthal's hands, so much had happened that Tausk was certain his fever had begun to worsen sufficiently to affect his judgment, and the shudder of near delirium upstairs had done nothing to reassure him otherwise. Roublev's presence in his bedroom could only mean another urgent message, and that in turn guaranteed it would be hours before Tausk could lock himself in and find a few hours' rest. He had no ally except Roublev for the maneuvering that lay ahead, so when he strode into the bedroom, it was with as friendly a smile as he could manage that he kicked Roublev's feet off his blankets and asked him what the devil he was doing there.

Instead of the summons from the Count-Governor with which he had been expecting Roublev to justify the intrusion, what awaited Tausk was the one thing for which he felt completely unprepared, the need to make an immediate decision about the Rotenburgs. There had not been any time yet to evaluate his options. Unlike Wiladowski, who moved from bored indifference to a swiftness of decision without any apparent interval, Tausk worked best by laying out multiple, divergent contingencies. When playing chess, he would use as much of the available time as he could, tracing out in his mind all the fields of force radiating across the board, whereas someone with his master's limitlessly renewable resources could trust himself to glance at the same board and quickly push the right piece forward as though he were a prodigy delighting in his skill at some high-speed tournament. The fact that such prodigies were mostly Jews, while the slower, more tactical players whom Tausk emulated were not, only compounded the oddness of his predicament. Just now, though, Tausk had no choice but to plunge ahead and hope that his intuition, like the Count-Governor's, was also accompanied by a healthy measure of good luck. The cheerless reflection that nothing in his life so far seemed to indicate the presence of any such providential gift was quickly confirmed when Roublev, after pulling his shoes back on, tying up the muddy laces, and locking the door behind Tausk, drew out a thick sheaf of fresh surveillance reports, all of which, he announced with pride, gave clear proof of Hans Rotenburg's involvement in treason. And treason of the clumsiest kind, as Roublev was delighted to emphasize. Not only had the amateurish code taken less than an hour to break, but Hans had sent some of the most compromising letters through the regular post rather than use his family's impenetrable network of private couriers. Throughout his meticulous summary of the information, with the full, page-by-page proof ready for Tausk's detailed perusal later, Roublev, whose usual manner tended toward a dour inexpressiveness, looked as though he were in danger of breaking into howls of joy at any moment. Since he could not allow himself to do so here, Roublev had to content himself with signaling his elation by a sort of feral grimace that served as his best approximation of a silent laugh. He seemed as pleased with himself as though he already had Hans manacled and ready for interrogation in one of the cells a few feet away, and it was Roublev's reaction, more than anything specific he had yet heard, that showed Tausk just how deep the resentment of Rotenburg's son ran.

If Hans had wished deliberately to offer himself up in sacrifice to his enemies as an act of atonement for everything he possessed and they lacked, and nothing in his words or actions to date suggested such an urge, he would have found it hard to improve on this latest folly. The letters between Asher Blumenthal and his friend the Viennese playwright implicated Hans only indirectly, and then solely in the kind of shady financial transaction that was of no interest to the security services. But this was something altogether different. What Roublev had collected were inflammatory exhortations to an act of political provocation, possibly even involving murder. There seemed to be several alternative plans for carrying out what Hans called an exemplary act of revolutionary justice, the majority apparently set down in his own handwriting and, if that were not careless enough, with his naked signature visible at the bottom of several different sets of pages. "Hasn't the damn fool ever heard of pseudonyms?" Tausk whispered aloud in annoyance. "I thought that part of the pleasure of playing at being a revolutionary is that you get to pick a heroic new name for yourself." The urge not to let Roublev see the extent of his agitation, along with a fear of being overheard, even in as relatively secure a location as his own bedroom, forced Tausk to swallow the rest of his words. But reading through the précis made the spymaster, who cared too little about money to feel jealous of Hans, grow incensed at the recklessness of someone so secure in his wealth that it simply never occurred to him to take any precautions because he was confident nothing really bad could ever happen to him. Most galling of all was that last night, by securing Tausk's services, Moritz Rotenburg had gone a long way toward confirming the truth of his son's assumption. Tausk could not help asking himself what he might have done had information this incendiary been put into his hands forty-eight hours ago. Would he have taken it straight to the Count-Governor? Or would he first have sought to approach Moritz Rotenburg with it anyway? If so, what else would he have wanted for his silence? His hand in their negotiations would have been much stronger if he had gone to the Rotenburg villa with more than a copy of Asher Blumenthal's letters in his pocket. Perhaps some revision of their arrangement was still possible, although having seen Rotenburg's reaction to the threat Brugger posed, Tausk had little inclination to press the old man for additional favors.

With a quick gesture, Tausk signaled that he wanted to continue the briefing elsewhere, and a moment later, if anyone had been looking out of an upper-story window, he would have seen two gaunt figures wrapped in heavy, plain service cloaks, walking together along the muddy embankment, their bodies leaning toward each other seemingly in intense conversation. But only one of the men was actually speaking. Roublev had marveled at Tausk's tradecraft for so long that he had started to wonder if he would ever have a single idea Tausk had not already thought of and improved upon. His respect for Tausk was at times close to worshipful, but it also made him determined to show what he could do entirely on his own. That was why he had waited until he could bring Tausk a complete archive and not just a few random snippets of information. Tausk could not begin to imagine how much self-control it had taken Roublev not to reveal anything until he had succeeded, but now the story of how he had come by the information burst out of Roublev in one long, breathless torrent, propelled in equal measure by the intensity of his need for Tausk's admiration and the agonizing delay he had made himself endure until he could claim it in full.

They had been opening all of Hans Rotenburg's mail for a long time now, just as Tausk had instructed, but without any positive results. Recently, though, several of the letters contained sections written in code. These all were addressed to sons of the provincial nobility, and the amateurish encryption barely slowed Roublev down. The letters dealt mainly with questions about what hunting equipment was kept in working order by the gamekeepers on the large estates and whether their cadet training had taught them anything useful about how to use light ordnance. Hans was also keen on confirming the dates of any upcoming receptions for important state visitors at the Castle to which the Count-Governor might have invited their fathers. The intent of such questions was clear, especially since Hans had gone to the trouble of trying to disguise them, but Roublev knew that they were not unambiguously compromising enough to guarantee a court would convict someone defended by the Rotenburg lawyers. At least the letters confirmed that Roublev was not wasting his time spying on Hans. No matter what the general opinion, the boy was definitely not spending all his time chasing women and acting as factotum for his father's stock market manipulations. No, the problem was only how to fill in the picture so tantalizingly outlined in the letters.

The solution came when Hans accepted Christoph von Hradl's invitation to join him out at Weidenau for a week, in order, as the note said, "to enjoy the country air and talk more about their common project." Roublev quickly confirmed that the elder von Hradls were indeed expected to go to Vienna on business matters right after the spring maneuvers in Bohemia and that Christoph had sent similar invitations to most of the young aristocrats with whom he and Hans corresponded regularly. As far as Roublev could tell, everyone in Hans's inner circle would be there, except for the von Alpsbach heir, whose mail, also closely monitored, contained no such invitation. In fact none of the group had written anything to either Brunnenberg or the von Alpsbach townhouse for some time now. But that of course proved nothing, since any of them could easily have run into Ernst in town and arranged matters then. Roublev hoped so, because he would have loved nothing more than to take a detachment of soldiers from the Castle and show up unexpectedly at Weidenau with a warrant authorizing him to put the whole pack of them in leg irons and handcuffs. He kept picturing to himself the look, first of indignant surprise and then of rapidly growing fear, on the faces of these spoiled young dilettantes, each of whom probably spent more in a month on keeping their horses well groomed than he was likely to earn in several years. The streak of personal bitterness that had troubled Tausk before in his assistant marked Roublev's whole approach to the case, and although Tausk said nothing and let Roublev pour out his story without interruption, he had to look away to hide his annoyance. Tausk turned his head for a moment toward the far bank, trying to make out from this distance in which of the rows of rickety houses bunched together over there Brugger had his lodgings. Soon everything below the second story would be at risk of being inundated by spring floods, which would render all the basement rooms uninhabitable. Not that the families living in them had anywhere to which they could flee, except to beg temporary shelter from relatives or friends. Half distracted, Tausk still took in how thrilled Roublev was by his own report. The man's excessive personal investment in the case was just one more problem to take into account, and right now Tausk had no patience for further complications. In his agitation, Roublev was starting to talk much too loudly and wave his arms about almost as though he were drawing lengthy formulas on a blackboard with one hand and simultaneously erasing them with the other. Tausk was certain that they were out of earshot, but Roublev's agitation would be visible to anyone who caught a glimpse of him, and that in itself could lead to awkward questions when they got back to the Castle. More sharply than he intended, Tausk snapped at Roublev to stop jumping about so much and finish his report as though he were delivering it in his room with regular duty-officers standing nearby.

To his credit, Roublev responded immediately and, without giving any sign of how difficult he must have found it, checked one of his exuberant arm flourishes in mid-flight. He explained that once Rotenburg had fixed the date of his departure for Weidenau, the rest of his plan fell into place almost by itself. He would have several undisturbed days to go through the apartment on the Maximilianstrasse. The front door would present no problem since more than a few of the best professional burglars in the province owed Tausk a favor and would be delighted to discharge their debt by exercising their skills on behalf of the government. No, the only real risk could come from sympathetic neighbors telling Hans that the police had been in his flat while he was away. Fortunately, most of the families on the street regarded Hans with unmixed dislike and did their best to avoid any contact with him. In their eyes, his notorious dissipation had turned their district into an embarrassing public joke, and they resented the fact that he was happy to use the Josef Quarter for indecencies he would never have dared perpetrate in his own neighborhood. Roublev decided that his best move would be to take advantage of Hans's bad reputation. If anyone should notice him loitering in the building, he would just present himself as a pimp come to talk to the young gentleman, who was one of his best customers, about how many girls he wanted sent over for the Easter party he was planning. That would shut everyone up quickly enough and guarantee that Hans would not hear about the strange visitor. As it turned out, though, no one took any notice of Roublev, and he was inside the flat about an hour and a half after he saw Hans ride off for Weidenau. He waited that long only to make sure Hans had not forgotten anything that might make him return unexpectedly to retrieve it. As soon as Roublev was inside, it was child's play to go through everything and gather every single scrap of paper Hans kept in his apartment. Although one of Roublev's expert thieves would no doubt have made short work of any strongbox or safe, Roublev was relieved not to require such professional aid. It took several thorough searches, but finally Roublev was certain that Hans had not bothered with even minimum security precautions. Rotenburg's utter carelessness with such incriminating documents was completely baffling to someone like Roublev, whose obsession with secrecy was as intense as Tausk's. Many of the papers that Roublev expected would be carefully hidden were simply bunched together loosely in a stained brown leather folder, in clear sight on one of the custom-built bookshelves, while the rest were locked away in the double row of drawers running down both sides of the large desk that took up most of the rear bedroom. These locks sprang open with the slightest turn from one of the crude master keys Roublev always carried, but he suspected a simple penknife would have worked just as easily. "What could he have been thinking! That is what kept running through my mind while I went around carefully marking where each sheet of paper came from so that I could replace it in the exact same spot. I can't believe the rest of the group could choose someone like that as their leader, no matter how rich his father is. What must the crowd out there in Weidenau be like? At least Rotenburg's carelessness meant I didn't have to spend a long time making sure that I had found everything I came for. I just wrapped up the whole bundle, posted young Boris Morros across the street with strict orders to keep an eye on the building, and then rushed back to my own room, where I spent the next day and a half making a clean copy of every word. After I finished my copying, returning the pages exactly where I had found them was as easy as removing them had been, except that my hands were aching from all that writing. Rotenburg didn't return for several more days, and so far he shows no sign of having noticed anything wrong."

For once, Tausk was grateful that Roublev's skill at deciphering people's feelings was in inverse proportion to his gift for solving complex equations. In spite of Tausk's worry that his nervousness might betray him, Roublev's contented expression made clear that he had no inkling of how his success complicated matters. The two men continued walking along the embankment toward the Nepomuk Bridge, which loomed just ahead of them where the river curved sharply away from the remains of the medieval walls that marked the town's original perimeter. But as they were slowly going up the bridge's stone steps, still slippery with morning cold, on their way to Roublev's lodgings in town, Tausk could not get rid of the idea that someone who was much more alert to any signs of agitation than Roublev was watching them the whole time from one of the distant tenement windows. There was nothing unusual about that. Only in books was there anything alarming about a spy's discovering himself under surveillance. Tausk expected to be spied upon, certainly by Pfister's minions and now, perhaps, by Moritz Rotenburg's agents as well. But if his premonition was right, the eyes trained on him belonged to someone else altogether, and the eerie feeling that Brugger, or one of his disciples, might have become as interested in him as he was in the wonder rebbe only added to his discomfort. The sole piece of reassuring information was Roublev's guarantee that he had not carried any of Hans Rotenburg's documents into the Castle with him, where they might have been seen by someone else. He had kept the copies carefully hidden in the safe house that Tausk had arranged for him shortly after taking him on. Roublev slept there whenever he was on field duty, and both he and Tausk often used it to question informers who were too nervous about being seen talking to the police to present themselves at the Castle. In spite of his weariness, Tausk began to walk more quickly, his rapid strides forcing Roublev to stop talking and speed up his own pace.

The cache of documents, when Roublev had taken them out of a cunningly disguised wall safe and spread them out on the rickety wooden table, was almost as bad as Tausk had feared. In addition to the actual letters, there were a number of detailed street maps with the different approaches to both the Castle and to the Cathedral Square carefully marked out in red ink. All the main intersections along the way were circled in black, as were the army barracks and the three police stations that controlled the main roads into and out of town as well as the access points to the two bridges spanning the river. Any decent investigator would have had no problem knowing immediately what such maps were intended for, but without a specific target clearly identified, it might just be possible for suspects with important names like von Hradl, von Werburg, Rotenburg, and von Alpsbach to claim it was all a mad misunderstanding. Proving states of mind was always problematic, and since the revised legal code now required proof positive of a criminal conspiracy, not just of criminal thoughts, political convictions had become much harder to secure. The accompanying correspondence, though, was almost too bizarre to be credible. Outbursts of frustration at the obtuseness of parents and the prudish philistinism of various girlfriends, identified only by monosyllabic nicknames, were interspersed with page-long declarations of loyalty to what was always called "our cause." Everything, in fact, from the identity of their mistresses to the actual scope of their plot, was constantly chattered about yet left without an identifiable name, according to what seemed like a collective principle of well-bred vagueness. That the vagueness was a matter of coterie shorthand, not prudence, was made clear by the expansive fervor by which each of them kept vowing his readiness to sacrifice everything, "including my possessions, my family honor, and even my life, to bring about the transformation whose necessity only becomes more apparent with every passing day." Tausk cared nothing about literary style, but he found it impossible to read such phrases without repugnance, and to his own surprised amusement, as he leaned forward in that chilly room with an invented name on the door and several different forged passports in the desk at which he was sitting, he felt a stab of sympathy that a man like Count Wiladowski should be in danger from such children. Let them kill Pfister, who expressed himself in a similar way at the morning meetings; that would have a certain formal parallelism that everyone, including perhaps even Wiladowski, as a connoisseur of hidden symmetries, could appreciate. It was frustrating to read all this material in Roublev's familiar, punctilious hand, which resembled printing rather than cursive script. Of course Roublev had not tried to imitate the conspirators' actual handwriting, and Tausk missed seeing how the individual letters looked on the page when the man who formed them was certain they expressed something of immense significance. The only one who seemed to avoid the high Romantic tone entirely was Hans Rotenburg, who went out of his way to correct his friends' effusions. In one such passage Hans cautioned von Hradl, "Our movement is a cool and totally rational approach to a fundamental social problem, and it is based upon the highest development of scientific knowledge and its practical realization. Above all, our beliefs are the expression of the iron law of history itself and under no circumstances to be understood as merely the convictions of another political party. Insofar as the enlightenment and awakening of the working classes demand the use of certain harsh methods, sometimes even distasteful ones, these methods are rooted in practical experience and were arrived at by exclusively pragmatic considerations. Hence it will be necessary to make these methods part of any new government dedicated to completing the task of social transformation until circumstances no longer require their application. The entire basis of our work must be the fulfillment of our historical obligation, and our mission must be pursued ruthlessly, without regard for temporary setbacks, and with complete indifference to any short-term gains."

If the other letters made Tausk squirm with irritation, Hans's actually alarmed him. The unwelcome glimpse they gave of the family resemblance between the two Rotenburgs had never presented itself so palpably. Moritz and his son were entirely ready to sacrifice not just their own but, equally, everyone else's welfare in order to realize their plans, and not for the first time that day, the idea of being caught between them struck Tausk as a decidedly unhealthy prospect. But for now, at least, the boy was mostly still just trying on the role. From the police files Tausk knew that except for what was contained in these letters themselves and the moot issue of possible financial irregularities with *The New Order*, Hans had never done anything illegal in his entire life. Everything about the tone he took with his friends, from the way he boasted that he shared none of their qualms about shedding blood to his tic of aligning every one of his opinions with the inevitable course of history, showed Tausk how far Hans was from his father's contained self-sufficiency. Hans needed an audience to give substance to the picture of himself in which he wanted to believe. Compared with his father, he still stumbled in his role, trying out different inflections and gestures like an understudy, not yet ready to play a leading part, but already with the capacity to cause enormous damage behind the scenes to everyone else in the troupe. However, even a Rotenburg in training had the resources to be truly dangerous. Tausk found it frustrating that with all the information Roublev had gathered, it was not clear if the conspirators had settled upon one particular victim. So far as Tausk could determine, the dossier contained a reasonably complete list of every significant official visitor expected in the province for the next six months, compiled from announcements to the local nobility as well as from regimental honor lists. But since more than half a dozen of these names had been circled by Hans, there was no way to be sure when or against whom an attack was being planned.

It was the kind of dull grayish day in which the sky scarcely changed from midmorning until the onset of darkness, and when Tausk finally raised his head from the pages now scattered everywhere around him, stretched his arms above his head to ease the soreness in his shoulders, and got up to look out the window, it was impossible to tell how many hours had passed. Behind him, Roublev, who knew that Tausk would want to read everything through once without any comments from him, was curled up in one of the stuffed chairs propped against the far wall, engrossed in an account of the great 1912 St. Petersburg chess tournament. As soon as he sensed Tausk begin to stir, Roublev put down his book and leaned forward to signal his readiness to be of use. His loyalty was so visible in the way his gaze followed Tausk around the small room it was as though he had finally sensed the spymaster's uncertainty and were trying to let Tausk know that he could be relied upon for anything. Tausk had no idea how he had managed to inspire such fidelity in a man notorious, even in his own circle, for his prickliness, but he was as grateful for it as though it were something he had deliberately cultivated. It was a quality he would need to draw upon in the days ahead. He turned around and, pointing to the mass of papers, opened his eyes wide and nodded his head in a dumb show meant to signal his approbation for Roublev's hard work. Then, to give himself a little more time alone, and because he felt light-headed with hunger, he sent Roublev to fetch lunch for them from one of the nearby taverns. As Roublev quietly opened the door to let himself out, Tausk called out to him to make sure he brought enough food and coffee and, most important, more cigarettes to last them through several hours of hard work, even using Roublev's first name as a marked sign of favor. Then, with Roublev safely out of the room, Tausk lit his last remaining cigarette from the stub of the one still burning on the small saucer he had been using as an ashtray and tried to make up his mind what to do. There was no way he could leave Roublev out of his plans now. He knew too much to be shunted aside and was much too intelligent to be placated with a simple cover story. In spite of his exhaustion, Tausk easily conjured up the amused, slightly malicious smile and pleasantly distracted air with which Count Wiladowski conducted his most important conversations, especially about illicit plans, but he knew that he himself was too worn out to imitate his employer successfully. Relying on the truth was always the riskiest strategy. Because it cost one so much, there was a strong temptation to overestimate its effectiveness. Tausk believed it should be used as cautiously as possible and with no greater faith in its potency than any other story's. All Tausk had was the first fragment of a plan, as inchoate and wild, he had to admit, as anything he had just been reading in the conspirators' letters, and Roublev's dispassionate analysis of its viability was nearly as important right now as his help implementing it would be later. And so, with the relief that always accompanies any decision, no matter how reluctantly reached, Tausk stubbed out the last cigarette, gathered all the spent ends and loose ashes so they could be thrown away far from the flat, and patiently awaited his assistant's return.

By the time he heard the tread of Roublev's heavy boots on the outer stairwell and the familiar, odd noise, somewhere between a slight groan and a sigh, that Roublev always emitted when he was carrying something, Tausk had nearly finished arranging the letters into separate piles according to his estimation of their importance. How a man who made so much noise could manage to conduct a successful surveillance regularly astonished Tausk, but it was part of Roublev's disconcerting combination of delicacy and grossness, and his record showed that far from jeopardizing his work, Roublev had been able to use it to advantage to blend into a crowd in a way Tausk was never comfortable doing. At least this time the groans were understandable since Roublev staggered into the room loaded down with enough food to treat all of the Castle's security agents to a feast. At Tausk's astonished expression, he quickly explained that he always had trouble deciding among different items, and rather than waste vital time debating the choices, he had simply opted to buy some of everything and continue eating it slowly over the next week. Together, they cleared enough space on the wooden board next to the small stove to spread out the enormous lunch: a loaf of black peasant bread; a sampling of several different kinds of salami, thinly sliced and separately wrapped in waxy brown paper; a block of goose liver pâté; a few large pickles, still chilled and moist from the barrel out of which they had been drawn; a small amount of smoked whitefish; and several pieces of apple strudel, along with an ample supply of cigarettes and coffee beans. Tausk didn't know whether to be amused or appalled at realizing that in spite of Roublev's thin, almost gaunt frame and hollow cheekbones, the man was evidently something of a glutton. Tausk was usually oblivious of what he ate and never ordered more food than he thought sufficient to stave off hunger. But he was also pleased that Roublev knew enough not to have bought any cheese since Tausk was strongly allergic to it and became queasy simply smelling it anywhere nearby, a fact he never talked about out of concern the information would reach the ears of Matthias Pfister, who thereby would learn a sure way to retaliate for Tausk's cigarettes. First-rate, strong coffee was the only thing he could make in a kitchen, Roublev said with a certain pride, and soon the two were sitting down in silence, rapidly finishing more of the meal than Tausk had imagined possible. Although neither was still observant, they ate with the nervous, mechanical briskness of the Orthodox Jews in the easternmost villages of the Empire, who were unwilling to be seen relishing so worldly an activity and who had learned from their history never to take for granted that they would have enough time to finish their food before someone snatched it away.

Before Roublev had finished clearing away the remains of their meal, Tausk was already back on his feet, walking over to their worktable, precariously balancing a cup of coffee and a lit cigarette in one hand and pulling a fresh sheet of paper toward himself with the other. He intended to begin by drawing up a preliminary list, as preparation for a more elaborate battle plan, of what facts they could be sure of, which ones were highly probable, and which had too many variables to be settled with certainty. Anything to make it look as though he were proceeding in a methodical way. But after tracing three broad columns with thick pencil strokes and writing down a few sketchy details, Tausk impatiently crumpled up the sheet, threw it on the floor, and looked up at Roublev, who was just now closing up the cupboards and coming over to join him. "Well, what are we going to do now?" Tausk angrily demanded. "We have landed in a total shit heap, you and I. Without more evidence, these idiots haven't done enough yet for us to risk arresting them. Their parents would run screaming to the Castle for our jobs the minute they heard the news. They would telegraph every important Minister they knew in Vienna, and I doubt that the Count-Governor could back us for very long against that much pressure. Of course, if he were actually killed, it would be our fault for not having prevented it." Tausk rarely let himself look flustered or curse out loud around his subordinates, and although it alarmed Roublev to see him like this, it also gave him a thrilling feeling that Tausk and he were not just master and hireling but comrades, fighting alone together against a whole contingent of powerful enemies. At least that was how Tausk intended Roublev to respond, and to judge by the happily determined look in Roublev's face, it seemed to be working. Tausk was inwardly embarrassed at his own blatant theatricality, yet the more serious he was about putting his counterconspiracy into motion, the more he felt obliged to act out the role of conspirator with a stagey exaggeration, as though only by first trying it out as a parody could he endow it with sufficient reality to inspire an actual deed. According to Wiladowski, the same pattern appeared to be the way events were taking shape in the Empire as a whole these days, where everything seemed to be doubled, occurring, as it were, twice: the first time as light comedy in the salons and onstage, the second time as a kind of imitative tragedy in the streets. In the same mode, Tausk stealthily walked over to the front door, pulled it open in a single motion, and looked around a few times to show Roublev that he was making sure no one was out there listening to them. But that was the last flutter of a charade that Tausk sensed had exhausted its usefulness, and so, after quietly closing the door again, he leaned against the windowsill and, in a completely normal tone of voice, began outlining his plan.

Roublev never knew how much of the whole scheme Tausk had conjured up in a single burst that day in the safe house and how much he had improvised later, as events unfolded. But his faith in Tausk was unwavering, even when Tausk made it clear that he considered both Wiladowski and Rotenburg his superiors in strategic skill and foresight, as well as in resources. According to Tausk, his only chance for success depended on exploiting the rival potency of these two powerful men, the way a smuggler seeks out the narrow trough formed where two opposing currents meet, calming the water and making a safe passage for a swimmer and his cargo to get across. Somehow, Tausk said, they had to ensure the safety of all these men, and that included Hans Rotenburg, whose father would destroy anyone who put his sole heir into danger.

Although the cold afternoon wind was starting to penetrate into the room from the nearby river, neither Tausk nor Roublev had moved from their places near the window throughout Tausk's deliberately circuitous analysis, and as Roublev freely admitted, he still had no idea what Tausk wanted from him. So the shock was enough to leave Roublev inwardly dazed when Tausk abruptly stopped and, shivering slightly, asked him to throw some more wood into the stove and then to think of the surest way to get Hans Rotenburg safely out of the area before he could compromise himself further. At first Roublev was certain that he must have misheard, but when Tausk calmly repeated his request in its entirety, in exactly the same order and matter-of-fact tone, Roublev stood frozen in place, staring straight ahead as though he had been tagged in a children's game and had to maintain whatever posture he had been in at that moment. It was not until he felt the stove tiles against which he was leaning for support start to singe his wrist and elbow that he recovered enough to ask Tausk to explain the point of the joke. "But what could be more logical?" Tausk went on with perfect equanimity, helping Roublev stoke the fire and put on more water for another batch of coffee. "You are the mathematician. If you can come up with a different solution that has a higher probability of success, by all means, tell me, and we will use it instead. But just look at it dispassionately, and you will see that the situation is quite straightforward. Think of it as an elementary four-step equation. Condition one, we need to keep the Count-Governor from harm; condition two, if anything were to happen to Hans Rotenburg, sooner or later his father would find a way to destroy us. But if we save his brat, the old man will be in our debt forever. Condition three, Hans Rotenburg intends to kill either the Count-Governor or someone else in his immediate vicinity. Condition four, so far you and I are the only ones to know about the plot, but considering their carelessness, it is likely these conspirators will betray themselves to someone else, who will then use that discovery against us, as well as against both Rotenburgs. Conclusion, we have to get Hans away from here as quickly as possible and destroy the evidence against him before he can do any more damage. But that is the simple part of our predicament. It is the next stage that gets tricky."

Roublev continued to stare blankly back at Tausk, his mobility seemingly reduced to moving his scorched arm back and forth to cool it down. Tausk was worried that he had overestimated his assistant's adaptability in the face of a crisis. To Roublev's credit, though, after pouring himself a glass of water, drinking half of it, and wetting his handkerchief with the rest to hold against his temples, he looked as though he were recovering his equilibrium. Perhaps Tausk had misjudged him on their walk, and Roublev's exuberance had less to do with hatred of Hans and his friends and more with a desire to please his patron. Since he had left the university, Roublev's sense of grievance against the world had become only more intense, and his resentment at all the accumulated slights simultaneously blinkered his imagination and gave it a remarkable plasticity. Like a beast in some fairy tale, he required a constant supply of targets to hunt down, but these were completely interchangeable. That one's trusted comrades and blood enemies today should, by the next morning, have switched roles struck Roublev as deeply consonant with human nature, and if Tausk were to order him to arrest all the other spies and have their interrogations conducted by newly released prisoners, Roublev would have seen nothing unusual in that beyond a certain acceleration in an inevitable process. All his life Roublev had looked for someone to tell him who, among the limitless, ever-fluid legion of potential adversaries, should be his prey, and from the moment he met Tausk, Roublev's instinct told him that he had found a commander who would never disappoint him. His devotion to Tausk was as unqualified as his pleasure in finally being able to make others afraid. He knew the spymaster had no idea how deeply he had pledged himself to serve Tausk's needs, and he had been almost physically pained by the flicker of uncertainty in the man's voice. That was what had immobilized him just now. Not the change of plans, just the idea that Tausk could be unsure of his loyalty. Whether Hans Rotenburg lived or died was a matter of indifference to Roublev, and he felt surprisingly little regret at the hours he had spent assembling the dossier Tausk was now planning to destroy. He had enjoyed the work, and more important, Roublev considered spying, like mathematics, a highly specialized skill that required mastering an enormous foundation of separate discoveries and building on them to advance the discipline. He knew the value of what he had accomplished here and had seen his work recognized by Tausk; whether or not it had any immediate, practical application was beside the point. In any case, the advantage of a permanent war was that no weapon was likely to go to waste forever.

Tausk nodded with relief when he saw Roublev set about grinding the last of the beans and pour boiling water over them with a steady, calm hand. When they sat down again, chairs pulled close enough to each other that Roublev's eyes were soon stinging from cigarette smoke, Roublev said that technically, the only indispensable factor was Moritz Rotenburg's active help. "Since we can't use any of the Castle resources, we are going to have to rely on him, more than I would like, but it is his son we are saving, after all, so I don't imagine he will object." As often with those Tausk had trained, Roublev's straightforward observations hid a host of deeper questions. Tausk had been prepared for them since before they came into the room, and he had already decided there was nothing to gain in not answering more or less accurately. But it took much less time than he expected to describe the long evening at the Rotenburg villa. Strange, how something that was redirecting his life could be summarized in so few words. Rabbi Pelz taught that a man's life could be told properly either in three sentences or in the infinite pages of the holy Book of Life but that anything in between was an exaggeration or a simplification. "And what about that sentence, Rav? Which is it, an exaggeration or a simplification?" Tausk had asked, proud of his dialectical wit. Only now, sitting here in this wretched town, scheming together with a man whose soul was perhaps even bleaker than his own, did Tausk realize that it was just the simple truth. That such words should suddenly surface in his mind at this moment, and in such a place, was like a painful wrenching that Tausk did his best to ignore until the memory vanished of its own accord. Words from a world that was less than a day and a half's train ride away but that might more easily belong to a different continent and century. Tausk wondered what had made them surface in his mind, unbidden and distinctly unwelcome. Brugger? He was just getting ready to talk about him with Roublev, and perhaps that was enough to drag the other thoughts along, like a shadow that distorts as much as it precedes the shape of a man walking toward one in the late-afternoon sun. How to bring up Rotenburg's orders regarding Brugger worried Tausk more than anything else he needed to reveal to Roublev. Roublev relied on clarity from him, but there was no clarity here to share, just a story in which Tausk's and hence Roublev's roles were no doubt crucial but also, in any deeper sense, secondary. Tausk repeated, as dryly as possible, what Moritz Rotenburg had said about killing the wonder rebbe and his own idea of placing the blame for the murder on Nathan Kaplansky. Tausk felt that the simpler he could keep his account and the more straightforward the words he used, the less his own uncertainty would leak out. In the end this was just another urgent assignment, different, admittedly, from earlier ones, since their work had not yet included surreptitiously taking a life, but different only in degree. Nonetheless, it was turning out harder than Tausk had imagined. His mouth and lips felt unpleasantly dry in spite of the coffee he kept drinking, and rather than becoming increasingly plain, his sentences began to show an alarming tendency to unravel as he was formulating them. Tausk was about to tell Roublev that he was simply too tired to continue anymore and that with so much first-rate work already accomplished, it was a good time to stop for the day. But the exuberance that began to light up Roublev's face arrested Tausk in mid-phrase and told him that his hesitation was unnecessary. Roublev could barely stay seated with the rush of new energy that Tausk's half-finished story had given him. Far from requiring any justification from his superior, Roublev looked as if he had been waiting for precisely this turn of events and felt only joy that his wait was over at last. Before Tausk could say much more, Roublev reached forward, and if Tausk hadn't pushed his own chair back and gotten up first, Roublev would have demonstrated his enthusiasm by grasping Tausk's shoulders with his large, hairy hands, still greasy from their lunch. "This is what he has been looking forward to since taking the job with me," Tausk realized. "He has been longing to kill someone for years and doesn't care about who or why, so long as it is sanctioned by the authority of a man he respects."

"Brugger deserves to die." Roublev almost chanted the words. "Ever since I saw him dazzle the crowd across the square from the Mendelssohn Club, I suspected that eventually someone would want to put a stop to him. I am glad we will be taking care of the job ourselves, and whether the Count-Governor or Moritz Rotenburg gives us the commission makes no difference. The important thing is that we do the job quickly before he gets more followers. But as for some specific proposals about how to proceed, it is best if I don't try to answer you right away. I understand what you need and want to think on it before offering my recommendations. You can count on my total support no matter what plan you finally adopt." As he said these words, Roublev succeeded in getting hold of Tausk's hands and, in spite of his superior's visible discomfort, not only shook them vigorously several times but accompanied this with a prolonged, fixed look directly into Tausk's face, locking eyes with an intensity that was as close to a declaration of love as Tausk had ever experienced and left him feeling squeamish and eager to change the subject.

In Tausk's experience, Roublev had never talked for so long to anyone, and having received such a flood of personal confidences made Tausk conclude that it was high time for him to return to the Castle. Before doing so, he asked Roublev to rewrite all the letters, but in a new code of his own invention that no one else could crack. He should then carefully destroy all the original transcriptions and dispose of the ashes, as well as any remaining evidence of their lunch, in the river. Then, before Roublev could be seized by a second fit of enthusiasm, Tausk gathered his coat, pulled on his galoshes, and walked out, looking over his shoulder as he reached the door and telling Roublev, in a tone he tried carefully to calibrate falling between professional approbation and personal warmth, that he was glad of his help. He had to hurry back now to make sure Count Wiladowski had not summoned him in the meantime. With another friendly nod, Tausk shut the door and, without turning around again, walked rapidly toward the bridge.

◆ ◆ ◆

"It is truly strange what even the brightest people seem unable to learn if they have not been brought up to do so." Count Wiladowski leaned back in the immense leather chair that dominated the center of his private library and permitted Aloïs to pour him a homemade pear brandy from near the Attersee, where his family kept a small country house to which he occasionally vowed—in vain, as it turned out—to return for a visit one of these summers. Aloïs's people came from there, at least that is what the Count-Governor remembered his saying once, but if so, the fellow had been in his service for so many years now that he too would probably have only the vaguest recollection of the place. Over the years this had become Wiladowski's favorite hour: The last bells for the evening mass had finished ringing, the watchlights had been lit everywhere, and in their half shadow, a lilac grayish twilight enfolded the Castle gardens and nearby bridge. As he looked outward across the river, even the dreary town took on a silvery sheen that was deceptively inviting. Within the Castle there were no more official meetings to attend, and the Count-Governor finally had some time to himself before having to dress and join Marie-Luise for dinner. Tausk, in whose company he frequently enjoyed musing at the end of the day, was nowhere to be found, but in a way it was just as pleasant to have no one present except for Aloïs, who could be counted on not to interrupt his master's reflections with any words of his own or repeat elsewhere anything he overheard here. Wiladowski supposed the man must have a last name, but fortunately, no one, least of all Aloïs, expected him to remember it. Even Marie-Luise approved of his taciturn loyalty, and if two decades as his personal servant had not cemented the man's total fidelity to the Count-Governor, she would no doubt have wanted to "borrow" him for her own staff. "Take Tausk, for example," the Count-Governor went on, lighting a Montecristo. "I know most of you don't care for him, but he has qualities that are extraordinarily useful to a man like me in these times. There are only two brilliant police minds in the whole Empire: Rudi von Kirchmayr in Vienna and my own Jakob Tausk. I am sure the Emperor has no idea how lucky he is to have someone as gifted as von Kirchmayr so close at hand. But if it is true, as everyone keeps whispering, that von Kirchmayr's desire to join his mistress in Italy is beginning to overcome his sense of duty, who knows how long the Emperor will be able to persuade him to continue? Tausk is the only person I am certain could replace him and do as good a job, but it is out of the question to propose him as a candidate. Not because he is a Jew—a few drops of holy water would cure that disability quickly enough—but because baptized or not, he will always be socially impossible. It is really a question of his incredible vanity. For instance, he refuses to learn that someone who wants to appear in decent society cannot wear the same shoes several days in a row. After each time it is worn, the leather needs to rest for at least twenty-four hours around some good cedar shoe trees, or it will begin to smell of stale sweat, no matter how thoroughly you clean it on the outside. Now a fool like Pfister was brought up to know that, but Tausk wasn't, and when I tell him these kinds of details, he only looks amused—which is to say, offended but unable to show it except by ignoring my advice. Of course his cigarettes cloak the odor effectively enough, but I can see the look my wife's crowd gives him whenever he comes into the room, and I know they have already judged and condemned him before he opens his mouth. It is all trivial nonsense, agreed"—and at this, Wiladowski nodded in the general direction of his servant, whose own expression had not changed throughout his master's ruminations and who maintained the same placid demeanor, standing unobtrusively behind the small two-tiered table holding the various bottles of alcohol on the upper shelf, in case another drink was called for—"but why give your enemies any more weapons against you than they already possess? And it is not just my wife's set who react like this. Zichy-Ferraris just wrote me, demanding that when he comes for the dedication ceremony at Easter, if I have to have that odious little spy nearby, he be kept as far away from the delegation as possible. Apparently, he has never forgotten how unpleasant it was the last time he was stuck in a room with me when I had brought Tausk along. If there is one thing Court life consists of, it is confusing the trivial with the dreadful, and sometimes I think half the Archdukes would rather go into exile than have their survival depend on a man who did not look completely at home in an aristocratic salon." When he heard Aloïs's soft cough behind him, Wiladowski knew his servant well enough to be sure that the man was not yielding to some physical need of his own but only giving a discreet signal that it was getting near the time for him to lay out his master's dinner clothes. He took out his watch and saw that it was indeed later than he had thought. The seasons must be changing at last, since only a few weeks ago by this time it was already pitch-dark outside. Wiladowski stretched lazily in his chair and thanked Aloïs for the reminder, sent him on ahead into his rooms, and promised to be there soon.

Now that Wiladowski was alone in the library, it momentarily felt too large to be completely comfortable, as though Aloïs's silent presence had been part of what had made it such a hospitable refuge. He got up to pour himself another small pear brandy and looked idly around at the books lining three of the walls. Unlike even the richest and most influential of his subjects, like Moritz Rotenburg, the Count-Governor was resigned to figuring in history books that would look very much like the unread tomes shelved in this library. As a nobleman connected to most of the ancient dynasties in Europe, Wiladowski had always regarded narrative histories as little more than extended versions of a great family tree, a kind of discursive *Almanach de Gotha* in which the list of his titles took up several closely printed pages. But he treated his inevitable appearance in such volumes not as an achievement but as a family duty, like showing up at the afternoon reception of a boring aunt or going to a dress ball at the embassy, knowing in advance that not a single pretty woman had been invited. Appearing every night at dinner in the large main hall with his wife and senior staff fell into the same category for him, and Wiladowski, for all his complaints, rarely failed in his formal duties. "Like the damned cedarwood shoe trees. In that way I am no freer of my upbringing than Marie-Luise or Zichy-Ferraris." He smiled faintly at his own thoughts, always ready to extend a generous tolerance to the weaknesses he discerned in himself. But he knew that the absence of such tolerance was just what confirmed how wrong Matthias Pfister was about Tausk when he described the spymaster as a shameless cynic. On the contrary, Wiladowski had hired him precisely because he saw in Tausk the one strict idealist he had found who was prepared to work for him. To the Count-Governor, there was something fascinating in Tausk's fervent belief in the sovereignty of the mind, and the fact that such faith could coexist with no discernible scruples whatsoever made it only more interesting. He slowly walked across the hall from the library to his dressing room, where Aloïs had already finished brushing the dark jacket and trousers the Count-Governor would wear to dinner, and let his servant dress him while his mind continued to amuse itself wondering how his relationship with the Jewish spymaster would be described in the histories. For once, though, his prediction about the future turned out to be quite wrong. So far, at least, the newer generation of historians have not found Wiladowski's career sufficiently compelling to merit even a slender monograph. But it is doubtful whether such a fate, had he known of it, would have bothered the Count-Governor or whether he would not have found a pleasing way to interpret that neglect as a subtle, if indirect, proof of his larger political sagacity.

· ◆ ·

Wiladowski's assumption about the place awaiting him in the history books was not his only misjudgment that evening. Although he came down to dinner thinking that he was in a fine mood, almost as soon as he had finished greeting his wife and guests, he realized that on the contrary, he was feeling unusually brittle. As the meal progressed, he became increasingly frustrated with everyone present, including, perhaps even especially, himself. The general conversation was no more banal or self-preening than usual, and as a rule, the impeccable quality of his wine cellar and kitchen was sufficient to keep at bay a growing tendency to an irritable melancholy. But not tonight. Although numerous members of his family had been subject to fits of acute gloom, and more than a few had died in circumstances that might have barred a less distinguished corpse from being buried in consecrated soil, the Count-Governor strongly disapproved of such traits and was determined not to yield to them. In company he adopted a tone that gave the impression of an easy, carefree loquaciousness. His sentences spun out with a self-amused formality that reminded his listeners of conversations they had heard on the stage of the Court theater in plays from a prior century: aphoristic, polished, and speculative, the attitude always slightly detached, ironic, or licentious. Behind such a mask Wiladowski himself remained permanently elusive. But for several years now the Count-Governor had been careful to maintain the same way of speaking to himself, even when he was alone. He had fallen into the habit of treating himself as though he were a polite but not overly familiar acquaintance, in front of whom any emotional extravagance would be in bad taste. At the legation in Italy such a strategy had worked perfectly, since it immediately enlisted the active and intelligent collaboration of half his friends there, many of whom seemed to have settled upon the same tactics for reasons of their own, about which he in turn was too delicate to probe. But out here, amid the immense distances of wet, chilly fog and early dusks of the Empire's outermost boundary, his improvisations began to feel like a solo performance that was developing a noticeably overemphatic quality, not because the performance itself had changed in any way but because, by dint of being carried on alone and in an alien setting, it could not help sounding somewhat histrionic. So Wiladowski found himself in the vexing position of talking and acting exactly the way he always had, but hearing himself sound not only different but almost exactly the inverse of how he wanted to. Probably all these unfathomable Jews had something to do with it as well. At any rate, there certainly was nothing amusing about the fact that not only was he beginning to sound like his idea of an ill-at-ease old Jew, but that if Lieutenant von Sulzbach, seated there on his left, made one more idiotic comment about the Viennese municipal election, or the spring hunting season, to the fat provincial landowner's widow placed next to him, he would need to exert an unreasonable amount of willpower not to order both of them picked up where they were sitting and thrown into the river.

To cloak his inner discomfort, he turned to the lieutenant, a particularly unappetizing specimen, with a splotched, fair-haired countenance and the dulled eyes of a steamed carp, and engaged him in a friendly discussion of how he was enjoying his new posting in their province. Von Sulzbach, who had been completely ignored by his host until now and had been conscientiously drinking himself into a stupor in order to get through a dinner in such appallingly rude company, was positively alarmed by this sudden interest in his well-being and grew even paler as he responded, through a slight, lifelong stutter, with what he hoped were the correct formulas for such occasions. He need not have worried about offending the Count-Governor with some inappropriate phrase that might be reported back to Vienna and ruin his chances for a speedy promotion out of this backwater. Nor, for that matter, need his table partner, the rich widow Traudl Nahowska, from whose vast, puddinglike bosom regular clouds of powder floated upward in unmistakable testimony to her distress at the interruption of her delicious tête-à-tête, have quaked at the prospect of losing the most tempting male to have been put in her proximity for many months. In reality, Wiladowski was not taking in a word the lieutenant was making such valiant efforts to pronounce. Instead, after a prolonged, dubious stare in their direction that quite belied the courteous tone of his "Ah, yes, I quite see, yes, of course," the Count-Governor turned away, fully content to leave the pair to each other. But it was not a different guest who had seized Wiladowski's attention. Quite the contrary. Something in von Sulzbach's way of speaking, not exactly the stutter, although that was part of it, but more like the man's momentary hesitation, almost a slight intake of breath before any long vowel, suddenly reminded Wiladowski of a lazy mid-autumn afternoon when he was a student at the Theresianum in Vienna, and the teacher, Markus Potiorek, a brilliant man, whose words came out sounding uncannily like this dim army lout's, had asked the whole class to write on a piece of paper what they wished for their future. Wiladowski had shocked everyone by putting down, "My real work, I suppose, is to become an anonymous man." To his schoolmates, this was the rankest hypocrisy, its obvious desire to shock surprisingly transparent for someone hitherto renowned, and often deeply distrusted, for his indirection and arrogance. Even those who most detested him recognized not only that Wiladowski was easily the most brilliant of them but that his ambition was nourished with an intensity that made their own fantasies of worldly success seem like pale daydreams. Wiladowski himself had no clear idea why he had answered so out of character, except that the phrase appealed to him without much regard for its content. But he saw by Potiorek's expression that the reply had succeeded in catching his teacher off guard in a decidedly unfavorable way. After a few days, during which he was teased about his love for mystification by the other boys, everyone, including Wiladowski himself, forgot the matter. Tonight, looking around at the dining room with its overdressed, sweating company and constant, steady hum that was as bad as the noise at the Northern Railway Station in Vienna, Wiladowski had the unpleasant thought that maybe some malignant fairy had heard him that afternoon and granted his wish after all and that evenings like this were nothing less than its fulfillment. Like all the fairies in the stories he had grown up hearing, this one too had bestowed its gift with a perverse variation: Wiladowski's name might be known to every Court and Foreign Office in Europe, but he had no doubt that in the eyes of the young boy from the Theresianum, and, increasingly, in his own adult ones as well, the person he had become was so unfamiliar that it was hard to come up with an apter term for him than that he was just another anonymous man in a well-cut suit with lapis lazuli cuff links, looking out unhappily from his seat at the head of a well-set table.

Wiladowski did his best to banish the image from his mind, but it was more persistent than he would have thought possible. For someone with his training, there was something deeply shameful in allowing private emotional disturbances to intrude into the performance of his social duties. But everything about this dinner was turning out wretchedly. Even the veal roast with onions, usually one of his favorite dishes, tasted just the slightest touch overcooked, and only the liver dumpling soup and the wine, a superb Léoville Las Cases, which he noticed the lieutenant was going through as though it were a cheap local product, palatable only if drunk in huge mouthfuls and at breakneck speed, lived up to his hopes. Solely by making it a deliberate test of his self-control did the Count-Governor succeed in recovering at least a surface equilibrium, at least enough to get him through the rest of the dinner without any more lapses of attention and with sufficient presence of mind to tell Traudl Nahowska that she had surely lost weight lately and should be careful not to let herself get too thin, a mockery so blatant that Marie-Luise, who overheard the end of it, looked up at him, half entertained and half repulsed by the way her husband combined apparent flattery with casual malice in a single phrase, leaving everyone amused at the insult except its victim, who felt

only delight at being complimented. Since his wife despised the Nahowska woman and resented the obligation to invite her more than Wiladowski himself did, Marie-Luise's displeasure was not really motivated by
any compassion for the unsuspecting widow. But years of having been the
target of her husband's sarcasm, and possessing sufficient intelligence to
have registered every sting, Marie-Luise had come to identify with whoever was his latest victim. It was impossible for her to be present when the
Count-Governor ridiculed someone without its arousing a defensive reaction. Her sympathy for Matthias Pfister, a man who, had she met him
under other circumstances, she would almost certainly have dismissed as
commonplace in much the same way as Wiladowski did, was no doubt
motivated in part by an obscure sense that in her husband's mind she and
Pfister were linked as similarly tiresome. If he preferred spending time
with his seedy Court Jews, not one of whom had any sense of the larger
social world that was her birthright, it could only be to underline the fact
that in his eyes even they were more interesting than her company. Well,
at least when he retired from his public offices, he would have to leave all
these Jews behind. For now she could do no more than forbid them her
table and insist they eat downstairs with the lesser staff, all in anticipation
of the day she would finally be able to deny them her front door as well.
Even at this moment, as everyone was rising from the table, she saw her
husband call over one of the guards with instructions to deliver what she
was certain was an order for Tausk to join his master in the billiard room
where he always took his after-dinner digestif. As usual, unless they were
entertaining especially important visitors, it fell to her to complete the tedious business of bidding farewell to their guests and excusing the Count-
Governor, who, in the ritual phrase she somehow still managed to endow
with a ring of sincerity, "was unfortunately obliged to return to his duties."
For a moment she was tempted to wave Pfister over to her side from his
place near the bottom of the table and suggest he accompany the Count-
Governor with an offer to play a round of billiards with him. But that was
too transparent. Their game of mutual provocations, as formal in its structure as a gymnastic competition, required something more unexpected,
especially after the gibe at poor Traudl, which had made Marie-Luise
worry about the amount of dessert she herself had just eaten. The new
lieutenant, though, was another matter. She had seen how much he had
irritated her husband during dinner, and his continued presence would
certainly spoil any intimate conversation between Wiladowski and his

Jewish spy. The prospect delighted her, and she silently dedicated her plan as an offering to all the pudgy widows the world over, too dim-witted or vain to know when they were being held up to ridicule. It took all of Marie-Luise's charm to cajole von Sulzbach, who was plainly horrified at the idea of spending a further half hour with the Count-Governor and tried to plead an early-morning regimental inspection for which he needed to be well rested. But in the end he agreed, as they both knew he would, and he dragged himself after his host, all the while looking back toward the door to the outside with the resigned melancholy of a conscripted sailor who, after six months at sea, has glimpsed a friendly harbor only to be denied shore leave by a capricious first mate.

To make matters worse, when he caught up with Wiladowski, he found the Count-Governor, with his cue stick idly propped against the billiard table, deep in conversation with an altogether impossible-looking little man. The fellow appeared utterly haggard with exhaustion and gave off an unpleasant odor of fatigue and sweat. His clothes looked as though they had not been changed in weeks and had served him as both street and sleepwear throughout the whole period. Whatever the fellow's role at the Castle, he was lucky that it let him keep his civilian status, because if any-one in His Majesty's army had appeared in public like that, he would have risked imprisonment for bringing disgrace to his regiment and uniform. Wiladowski glanced up, clearly as unhappy to see the lieutenant as the man was to be there, and he made the introductions in the clipped tone of an irritable commanding officer barking out orders on the parade ground. "Jakob Tausk. Lieutenant Erich von Sulzbach." The lieutenant did not know what was more surprising: that Count Wiladowski had remembered his first name or that his duties really included spending time after dinner with, as was clear from his name, some Jew or other, no doubt come to wheedle a favor from the province's Governor. Perhaps the rumors he had been hearing about Wiladowski ever since he arrived were true after all. Instead of shaking hands in the civilian mode, von Sulzbach clicked his heels together and bent his neck as few millimeters as was permitted within the bounds of protocol, in the general direction of this Herr Tausk. Then, to his immense relief, he saw that the billiard room was graced by a large sideboard, toward which he glanced with such fixed longing that the Count-Governor mercifully cut short the awkward introductions and in-vited him to help himself to a drink. Although he had already consumed more alcohol than was advisable, considering that he was in unfamiliar and probably hostile territory, the glimmer of a bottle of Fernet-Branca was irresistible. Von Sulzbach nearly leaped over the furniture separating him from the bar and, with a rapidly muttered "To your health," poured himself a generous shot of the familiar bitter liqueur. He stayed at the bar, watching the two continue their strange colloquy while refilling his glass two or three more times, when the Count-Governor interrupted what was becoming a quite agreeable waking nap of the kind he had learned on maneuvers, sitting with his eyes wide open on his horse, but with his mind peacefully asleep. Would he care to play billiards? Count Wiladowski inquired, thus summoning him to one of the few real skills he possessed that did not involve the active collaboration of a well-trained thoroughbred. Since the Jew was no doubt incompetent at billiards, and the Count-Governor was in the mood for a game, von Sulzbach was glad to oblige, thinking how pleased the gracious Countess would be to find out later that her inspiration had been right after all and that in spite of his initial coldness, her husband had ended up being glad of his company.

The Count-Governor, who expected things to arrange themselves according to his whims without giving the matter any further thought, was probably less grateful than Tausk for the lieutenant's availability. Von Sulzbach's presence excused Tausk from any further involvement in the game, and the officer's deliberate rudeness during the introductions was so exaggerated and clumsily executed that Tausk was able to let it pass with a shrug. More important, Tausk truly loathed billiards, cards, and all such games not, as his employer, and even Roublev, were inclined to suspect, because of a lingering residue of his yeshiva training but because they reminded him so powerfully of the seedy all-night gambling at his father's inn. There were few duties Tausk found as disagreeable as being obliged to stand there in the billiard room, trying to carry on a serious conversation with his employer, while the Count-Governor lined up the angle for his next shot. Such moments reduced the Castle, and his own role in it, to just a more refined version of his home, a place to which Tausk had sworn never to return, not even when his expulsion by Rabbi Pelz left him without any shelter or prospect of a job. All these games struck Tausk as so debased a way to spend one's time that he took for granted that no one as intelligent as the Count-Governor could actually enjoy them. Surely men like Wiladowski only pretended to like gambling because it was a necessary part of any diplomat's social repertoire. But Tausk was wrong, the way even clever men often are, in not understanding that their equally clever fellow creatures are likely to find pleasure in utterly dissimilar ways. Wiladowski enjoyed many kinds of games, especially billiards, and valued them precisely for their similarity, but in what he himself called a frivolous key, to his political activities. The sense of timing, capacity for rapid, accurate calculation, and sangfroid under pressure that were necessary for playing billiards and skat, especially for high stakes, drew on skills similar to the ones that had made him a legend in diplomatic circles, and in the eyes of the Court, Wiladowski's success at the tables compensated for the fact that he had always been a mediocre horseman and hunter. Even thick-skulled Cousin Max, who, before his horrible murder at the hunting lodge, had gone on numerous shoots with the Emperor, had to admit that someone as gifted with a cue in his hand as Otto Wiladowski could not be written off completely, for all that he was suspiciously bookish. Now, just to amuse himself, the Count-Governor made a plausible estimation of how much the lieutenant's wine consumption had cost him and decided to set the wager high enough to win back the evening's expenses. To this, he decided to add an additional 125 percent, levied as a secret fine for the man's impertinence to someone presented to him in the home of his host, who, he had clearly forgotten to keep in mind, outranked him in every conceivable way. The insult, though it would be decades before von Sulzbach had matured enough to realize it, was not to a familyless Jew of no importance but to the man who had chosen to employ such a person, the Imperial Count-Governor and holder of the Grand Cross of the Leopold Order, who counted the Minister of War among his closest childhood friends. Wiladowski wondered if years from now, when the aging officer, who for all his early promise never rose beyond the rank of captain, reflected back on his inexplicably blighted career, marked by a series of lateral assignments to distant outposts, rather than the ascending promotions of which he had once dreamed, he would finally understand that a careless moment in a billiard room long ago had set his steps on the downward slide for which, since there was never any official reprimand or word of explanation, there could never be a pardon either.

Tausk happily took advantage of Wiladowski's being occupied for what looked as if it might be several hours, to curl up in one of the comfortable chairs placed all along the side walls to accommodate spectators. He welcomed any chance to resume the nap that he had barely started before being awakened by an urgent summons to attend the Count-Governor, and whether he owed it to the lieutenant or the devil himself made no difference. The regular clicking of the billiard balls against one another was soothing in a way Tausk had never experienced before, and since there was none of the drunken swearing that had so terrified him as a child, he fell asleep almost immediately. Unexpectedly it was one of the few totally dreamless nights he had been granted in months, and coming at the end of such a day, it was a gift that, when he woke up, almost made him mouth a silent prayer of gratitude. As soon as he had cleared his head enough to sit up and look around, Tausk noticed the Count-Governor was alone in the room with him, contentedly smoking a cigar and pouring himself a glass of a dense amber-gold liquid from a large bottle of Château d'Y quem that Tausk was certain had been nowhere in sight when he had first come in. Out of habit, Tausk quickly scanned the room. There were no windows, so it was impossible to tell from the changing light outside how many hours had passed, but a glance at the fussy ormolu clock on one of the side tables showed him it was already after five in the morning. He remembered having come into the billiard room shortly after eleven on what was now the day before, but he had no idea when the game between the lieutenant and the Count-Governor had ended. When he tried to apologize to his master for what was, in effect, falling asleep on duty, Wiladowski waved him off and said that all in all, it had been one of the more amusing evenings he had passed lately. It was a shame, he added, that Tausk did not ride since he had just won a fine gray stallion from the lieutenant and, having no use for it himself, would have gladly given it to Tausk as a present. In any event, Wiladowski hoped the thought of this von Sulzbach's turning up on foot at the morning inspection would gratify Tausk. For the second time in less than twenty-four hours, the spymaster was baffled by the Count-Governor's behavior. First, the bewildering speech at the end of yesterday's morning conference and now this unprecedented decision to avenge a slight that Tausk himself had barely registered. Pfister was at least as rude to him several times a day, often in Wiladowski's presence. As far as Tausk knew, Wiladowski had never shown any desire to take on the role of his champion before, and for him to do so now, upon so trivial a provocation, was more disconcerting than anything about the encounter itself. Tausk felt the weight of an immense weariness, deeper than just physical exhaustion, at yet another proof that he was likely to spend his entire life being the object of great men's capricious benevolence and equally abrupt anger. None of his fellows at the yeshiva, or at the Castle either, would believe him if he told them that the change from serving Rabbi Pelz to working for the Count-Governor, and now, if he wanted to give the full picture, he would be obliged to add Moritz Rotenburg as well, was much smaller than they imagined. No matter how careful his calculations, at the end of the day it was always their decisions that counted, and their wishes came to him out of nowhere with all the arbitrariness of an authority that never needed to explain itself. More and more Tausk believed that someone with his own miserable experience of the world was much better suited than a great sage like Rabbi Pelz to expound on the relationship between the Jewish people and their moody, unfathomable God.

With the intuition that often made him positively alarming to the people around him, Wiladowski turned in his chair, pushed a large ashtray over to Tausk, and asked him in a tone that hovered between amused skepticism and intense concern what his holy books had to say on the topic of betrayal. The question came at Tausk so unexpectedly that he sat bolt upright, instantly wide-awake, with his senses sharpened to the point he thought he could hear one of the guards on sentry duty try to suppress a cough outside the heavy wood-paneled door. He quickly lit a cigarette and took a while to finish his first puffs so that he could be sure, when he did speak, that his voice would give away less of the confusion he felt. But nothing at all occurred to him, and with something like baffled despair, he reverted to the feeblest of the defenses in his arsenal, hoping to gain another few moments by answering the Count-Governor with a question of his own about why such a recondite topic should interest him just now, when it was surely far too early in the morning for theology. "Because, my dear Tausk, it is the only question left that people with our experience can take seriously. I have made countless lists of every vice and passion, studied them all, and watched them pass in front of me striking familiar poses, like carnival figures going to a seedy ball. Exclude betrayal and they don't amount to much, do they? Just small, childish self-indulgences, like stuffing candy in your mouth before going in to the confessional. I don't know where you Jews are inclined to put the blame, but my Church is always pointing its finger at pride. The odd thing about that, though, is that while I have certainly come across a great deal of vanity in my life, I have seen so little real pride that I can still repeat the name of the three or four human beings who had more than a smidgen of it. Everyone else just wanted more applause, more love, more recognition—always something from outside himself. I don't see how that can count as pride at all! I am no longer even sure about Lucifer. To me, all that complaining about a demotion sounds more like injured vanity, not to mention the tastelessness of brooding forever about what you have lost, like one of those pathetic ruined noblemen outside the casino at Monte Carlo, always wanting to tell everyone about the fortune they squandered at the tables just when they were so close to breaking the bank. I wonder if it is different down there in your cells with all the hotheads you do such a splendid job interrogating. What makes them hate everything so much they are happy to risk execution just for a chance to kill someone like me? Is it vanity or pride that makes them traitors? You must have learned enough about betrayal down there to teach me more than you put in your reports, haven't you? Or what about a man like Moritz Rotenburg? Do you think he has pride, or is it just the vanity of someone with more money than his neighbors?"

Wiladowski's casual acknowledgment that he actually read Tausk's reports carefully enough to form an opinion about what the spymaster excluded was sufficiently dismaying, but as soon as he heard the question about Moritz Rotenburg, Tausk was convinced that rather than stifle a cough, the guard at the door was preparing himself for a prearranged signal to burst into the billiard room to arrest him. A dozen crazy, contradictory thoughts flooded his brain. He could throw himself at Wiladowski's feet, confess everything, and beg for mercy. But how to do it so it had the best chance of working? Tearfully, with loud sobs and hand gestures, or with an attitude of frozen, devastated contrition? Perhaps he could still make a bargain and save his own neck by offering to sacrifice both the Rotenburgs. The various possibilities refused to stay still long enough for Tausk to focus on any one of them, melting into one another with a speed that made him afraid he was about to faint. Soon the only thing stopping him from actually doing so was the loud pounding in his brain that replaced any thinking at all and kept him staring straight ahead, silent and immobile as surely as if he had already been handcuffed and gagged. Sounds reached him now as though from far away, or as if they first had to travel through a thick layer of water, and it took him a few minutes to register a shift in the Count-Governor's train of thought that seemed to imply—but who could be certain with such a man?—that he was momentarily out of danger. He could tell by the patient but slightly puzzled way the Count-Governor was looking at him that a response of some kind was expected, but since Tausk had no recollection of the last question, he forced himself to beg Wiladowski for permission to fetch himself a glass of water before answering, since the air in the room was very dry and his throat completely parched from his nap.

Tausk's grasp of court etiquette was uncertain at best, but even he knew that bringing up a personal need while his master was speaking to him must rank as a serious violation. By now, though, he no longer entirely believed in what was happening to him. It was as though he had stumbled into one of the legendary villages from his childhood storybooks, populated by fools, demons, and holy men, where the laws of nature were regularly suspended. Rabbi Pelz had been deeply suspicious of such tales, linking them to an unhealthy fascination with miracles and the still more dangerous, because so seductive, excesses of the Hasidim. He must have been right because even at his own yeshiva the taste for these legends flourished surreptitiously among the younger students until Rabbi Pelz had shamed them out of it and taught them to regard even the most pious of these tales as inimical to the Law. Tausk himself had put away his old books easily enough and felt no lingering attachment to any of them, but now it seemed to him that in this elegant game room, cunningly designed to shut out any intrusion from the outside world, imitating the behavior of the characters in the forbidden stories who accepted the oddest happenings as though they made perfect sense, or as though the very category of making sense was just a particular way of being crazy, was the best way to get through whatever lay ahead. At least the Count-Governor's face did not show any sign of irritation at having been interrupted, and he waved Tausk over toward the sideboard. Wiladowski seemed content to wait until Tausk had brought his glass back to the chair, but as soon as he sat down again, the Count-Governor immediately resumed his strange musings. Unusually for him, Wiladowski seemed to have fallen into the habit of phrasing his thoughts in direct questions, but Tausk was beginning to grasp that although he was free to intervene with an answer, should one occur to him, his master was just as glad to go on without any contribution from another voice.

"He is not interested in entrapping me at all!" The realization came on Tausk so swiftly and with so little connection to what Wiladowski was saying at that moment that he almost forgot to feel relieved. Wiladowski's curiosity about his own consciousness was perhaps the only emotion that outweighed his fear of assassination, and Tausk reproached himself for not having realized much more quickly that it was only the question of self-betrayal Wiladowski wanted to talk about, not his servant's possible treachery. Tausk's faithlessness was shielded by the immense shadow of the Count-Governor's egotism—was that based on pride or vanity? Tausk allowed himself to wonder—and a stricter moralist than either of these two men would have found an elegant justice in the fact that only Wiladowski's complete absorption in his theories of betrayal blinded him to the signals of a troubled conscience that Tausk was unable to stop himself from giving off. Gradually, though, the certainty that he was not in immediate danger of being dragged off to one of his own cells calmed Tausk enough to make him attempt at least a show of participating in the conversation. For the most part he welcomed these moments with the Count-Governor. But less than forty-eight hours ago he had agreed to work for Moritz Rotenburg, even when that meant acting against Wiladowski's best interests, and he had spent much of the previous day destroying evidence directly identifying Hans Rotenburg as the leader of a revolutionary terrorist cell. And yet he continued to feel something like real affection for the Count-Governor. There are men who, once they have decided to injure someone, need to blacken that person in their own minds as much as possible, as though the discovery of their victim's iniquities would justify their own baseness. Tausk was not like that. He had few illusions about himself and so did not require any fabricated self-justification to disguise the nature of his actions. In spite of everything, Wiladowski was perhaps right, after all, to turn to Tausk as the only man with whom he could talk on the topic of self-betrayal, almost as though to an equal.

"Your Excellency once told me that every significant act of treason involves a prior self-betrayal. If I remember correctly, what you said was that betraying someone else means first betraying the self who had pledged his fidelity to him. Since our conversation that morning I have thought a great deal about your idea without being any surer how much I agree with it. The longer I have been in your service, the more uncertain I have grown. Maybe hearing so many different confessions down in the prisons has given me too intimate a glimpse of treason for any one explanation to be convincing. People seem to betray in much the same way they fall in love, and every story I have heard lately sounds either very similar to the one before or absolutely singular, depending on how one listens to it. If I have been of any use to Your Excellency, it is probably because my training at the yeshiva has taught me how to hear the differences between what suspects tell me more sharply than someone who has come to you directly from the Police Academy." Tausk had barely said a word until now, and

Wiladowski was unprepared for this sudden burst of loquacity. But after a moment's vexation at being interrupted in mid-thought, during which the Count-Governor found himself missing Aloïs's wonderfully attentive way of being silent, Wiladowski changed his mind and decided to be glad his spymaster was sufficiently awake for them to have a real discussion after all. Poor Aloïs, for all his virtues, could hardly be counted on to understand his master's favorite theories, let alone comment on them intelligently, and Tausk's courtesy in beginning with a nearly exact rendering of Wiladowski's words from weeks earlier showed an almost aristocratic flair for politesse that was as pleasing as it was unexpected. Moreover, Wiladowski's questions had not been purely rhetorical: He really was curious about what someone who had been trained, first as a student of the Jewish God and then as a spy in His Apostolic Majesty's service, might have learned about duplicity. But watching Tausk warm to his topic made Wiladowski wonder if he might not soon swerve back to regretting Aloïs's absence. Already the ashes were forming in haphazard circles around Tausk's chair, and the Count-Governor could see that at any moment the spymaster would be on his feet again, walking around the room, picking up whatever objects were within his hand's reach, and, without really taking in what they were, begin fingering them in the same distracting way a pious Catholic might tell the beads on a rosary as an aid to reflection.

Wiladowski hated all involuntary nervous gestures and could never understand how a man of Tausk's intelligence could be so unaware of what his body was doing. Not wanting to embarrass Tausk by staring at him too obviously, the Count-Governor got up and went to fetch a fresh cigar from the inlaid humidor near the cue rack. The last thing he expected to hear while he was cutting open the end of his cigar was the sudden sharpness in Tausk's voice as he put down the white billiard ball he had started rolling back and forth along the outer rim of the table and asked, "But why assume a person has just one basic nature? If that is true, then of course he can only be faithful to it or betray himself, but I have trouble seeing sufficient reason for such an assumption." Tausk must have realized that his tone was badly out of place because he abruptly stopped talking and looked over to the Count-Governor with something like a self-deprecating smile, as though to mitigate by his manner any offense he might have given through his undue vehemence. But Wiladowski was both too interested in what Tausk had to say and too aware of the difference in their stations to register his servant's no doubt atavistic zeal for debate as personal rudeness, and he encouraged Tausk to go on. Tausk retreated back to the sideboard and stood there rapidly gulping down another mineral water while he organized his thoughts. He too found himself drawn deeply into the conversation for its own sake, but unlike the Count-Governor, Tausk had to be careful not to let his enthusiasm betray him into an inadvertent admission. The urge to buttress his ideas with compelling personal examples, of which the past several days had given him all too many, would obviously have to be resisted, but even though it was his own neck that hung in the balance, Tausk found a mordant amusement at thinking to himself how much more he knew about betrayal now than when Wiladowski had first started talking to him about it months earlier. "We Jews do believe that our God is One and repeat that daily in our prayers. But none of our texts say the same thing about human beings. The souls I have come across are mostly driven less by either pride or vanity than by the pull of irreconcilable desires. Is not whatever one does, whatever vow one makes, or fidelity one pledges, already a betrayal of the opposite longing, which, in one's heart of hearts, feels nearly as compelling? It seems to me that the only sure way to avoid self-betrayal is to do nothing at all. Your Excellency's theory of self-betrayal strikes me as grounded on an admirably biblical principle of monotheism, but with a particular image of your inner self, not God, as the subject, and even for a Catholic, is that not just a touch heretical? With regard to women, it is easy to understand that one can fear equally being possessed or being abandoned by them. For certain men, I think the same fear exists—only still more strongly—about their own soul. Think of the unfathomable inner distances we have each had to traverse from how our lives started in order to be talking together like this. Who is to say if we have betrayed ourselves along the way or, instead, have begun to come into our own as more than just the boys we were? To waste one's strength gazing backward, paralyzed with regret for who we once were, sounds very much like trying to usurp God's role and live outside time."

Although he felt more sentences along the same lines welling up inside him and saw, by Wiladowski's alert, expectant expression, that he had captured the Count-Governor's attention, Tausk forced himself to stop before he said any more. He felt genuinely alarmed by his own words. They bore little resemblance to what he had intended to say. It was not that he misrepresented his ideas, but everything came out in a way that sounded alien to Tausk's own ears. The last time he had experienced such a loss of self-possession was back in Rabbi Pelz's study, but although this feeling was similar, it was also subtly different and more sinister. Involuntarily some of the stories about dybbuks and evil angels came into Tausk's mind, and he decided that if anything, Rabbi Pelz's warning against such nonsense had not been nearly strong enough. Tausk had only contempt for the salon and silver tea service mysticism that was one of the favorite indulgences of the Empire's upper classes—Marie-Luise and Pfister had tried to organize several evening séances with a spirit table, although up to now the Count-Governor had mocked them out of it—but another episode like this, and Tausk was worried he might begin to take their gibberish seriously. For the moment he was determined not to think further about why he had begun to talk so peculiarly and to concentrate on finding the kind of indirect, slightly disrespectful, but pertinent anecdote he had intended to produce in the first place. None occurred to him, and he recognized that the Count-Governor was showing clear signs of disappointment at Tausk's unexpected retreat into silence. Wiladowski suspected that Tausk had been stricken with an attack of nerves about revealing Jewish mystical secrets to an outsider, and since it was precisely those mysteries about which his interests had been piqued, the whole conversation was in danger of dwindling from a promising beginning to a mediocre anticlimax. The absurd secretiveness of these Jews was really too vexing, especially after all that he had done for them. They wrote down their tribal stories and then set about worshiping them as the laws of a universal god. At every turn you came across another set of taboos and prohibitions. Even the oldest aristocratic dynasties in Europe did not treat their family histories with such proud reverence. But there was no point in trying to push things further with Tausk, who, for the first time since Wiladowski had begun to take a personal interest in him, seemed genuinely at a loss for words. Except for the regular movement of the ormolu clock, which had just chimed the three-quarter hour, the room was entirely still. It would soon be six, and outside the billiard room, the Castle's daily routine was already in full motion. The morning inspection at the military barracks was long over, and the horseless lieutenant had no doubt been confined to his quarters until his commanding officer decided how to handle such a case. There was a disagreeably sour taste in Wiladowski's mouth from all the cigars and alcohol he had consumed, and he realized that he was simply too tired to stay annoyed with Tausk. It was clear from his half-closed, bloodshot eyes and drawn features that the spymaster was even more worn out than his employer. There would of course be no meetings this morning, he reassured Tausk, whose transparent relief at being spoken to in Wiladowski's normal tone of voice gratified the Count-Governor's vanity and soothed his pride. "After all," he said to Tausk as they left the room together, "the conspirators from whom you are supposed to keep me safe probably do all of their plotting late at night, and for once our rhythms can correspond more closely to theirs. No self-respecting terrorist would think of getting up on such a miserable morning, and that should assure both of us of a few hours' peaceful sleep."

4

By now nothing could shake Asher Blumenthal's faith that Rotenburg was behind all the disturbances unsettling the town during the past year. It was obvious to anyone able to look beneath the surface that from his sickbed—and who could be certain that he was even really ill?—the old man controlled everything that happened in the province. When Asher scanned the local newspaper, the report that another business had gone under thrilled him as though he himself would soon be profiting from its purchase and rehabilitation. Every bankruptcy increased Asher's admiration, and even if the company wasn't immediately taken over by Rotenburg, that could only mean he was waiting until the purchase price had sunk still lower and the owners were compelled to accept whatever pitiful offer he chose to make. If, for once, Asher felt no jealousy at hearing about someone else's triumphs, it was not solely because the abyss between his means and Rotenburg's made any comparison too incongruous, even for him. On the contrary, Asher's pride was so gratified at understanding the secret pattern behind events that by a strange excess of identification he could revel in the success of Rotenburg's schemes without feeling himself diminished. To be among the few people who really understood what was going on was a source of intense pleasure almost sufficient in itself, diluted only somewhat by the fact that there was no one he knew who would be properly dazzled at having such precious knowledge revealed to him. That Rotenburg had the tacit support of the government in his schemes was clear from the sealed messages Asher was occasionally ordered to carry back and forth between the financier and the Governor's terrifying chief spy, who, he had no doubt, was acting as Count Wiladowski's intermediary in these matters. So the Count-Governor was involved with Rotenburg as well, no doubt as a kind of powerful "silent partner." There was no telling how much higher the lines of involvement went, and sometimes, when Asher's glance happened to take in the innumerable identical pictures of the Emperor hanging in every store and public building, he caught himself looking at them a bit more carefully, half expecting to see an image of Moritz Rotenburg standing there at attention alongside the Imperial ruler. Whenever that happened, Asher came close to trembling with devotion at his private vision of the secret conjunction of State and Capital, a mystical marriage before which the world was already kneeling without being aware of it.

He could not wait for the day that the whole weight of potency represented by the irresistible combination of Rotenburg money and Habsburg state power came crashing down on the heads of the spoiled fools with whom he was forced to spend so much of his time and for whom he was expected to run errands as though he were still a mere junior accountant rather than someone who himself now had direct access to the loftiest circles. Thus far he had spoken to Moritz only a few times, but there were nights when Asher looked around at the smug, unformed faces of Hans's cronies, poring over their maps and pamphlets, and felt himself to be every bit as much Moritz's son as was Hans, in whom, if the truth be told, he had yet to see any spark of the Rotenburg brilliance. Perhaps the old man had been a bit of a rake in his younger years and quietly paid off Eliezer Blumenthal to raise the boy his wife had conceived when Moritz had seduced her. Or more likely, Eliezer had been tricked into doing so without knowing the child was not his; Asher had always suspected his mother was by far the more worldly-wise of the two and cunning enough to persuade her husband of anything that was to her advantage. It was delicious to think how differently everyone would treat him the day his real parentage was revealed and he could cheerfully send the whole pack of von Arnsteins, von Hradls, and all the rest of the damn vons to the devil without fear of the consequences.

Asher had grown to loathe these young aristocrats even more than his former superiors at the Sobieski Import-Export Company or the prosperous Jews of the Mendelssohn Club, who had demanded a ten-page application before agreeing to sponsor him for a few useless Hebrew lessons. As different as they were from one another, at least men like his old Jew-hating section chief, Galatowski, or Rudi Pichler and Gerhard Himmelfarb from the club's Executive Committee, had quickly sensed Asher's real feelings about them and kept him at arm's length, making it clear that anyone's company was preferable to his, a sentiment that Asher found easy enough to understand and heartily reciprocated as far as they were concerned. But the gaggle of titled blockheads whom he had met at Hans Rotenburg's flat that ghastly night when he became so ill were prodigies of obtuseness. If there was one thing at which Asher knew himself to be thoroughly inept, it was disguising his aversions, but there was no need to try with any of these noblemen because nothing he said or did could shake their assurance that a nonentity like him must feel himself inestimably flattered merely at being allowed to participate in a conspiracy with men of their rank. Perhaps the wealthy and the wellborn really were different from the rest of humanity, even down to their physiological makeup, since not one of them was in the least disconcerted by Asher's resentful looks and virtually continuous stream of muttered complaints. They obviously assumed that this was just what lower-class Jews were like the instant they went off duty. It was as though the bodily senses of these conspirators still operated according to all the aristocratic principles their political convictions condemned to the dust bin of history, and while they were quite prepared to commit murder on behalf of the lower classes, actually noticing what one of their social inferiors was thinking was a different matter altogether. They were simply incapable of registering what torture Asher endured listening to them talk. No one bothered to look up and ask him what was wrong, not even when his persistent teeth grinding grew loud enough to interfere with the general conversation. In midwinter, when he suffered horribly from a cold for a whole month and spent his evenings on Hans's couch, coughing violently and leaking fluids from his nose into a waterlogged swath of cotton, not one of the bluebloods had thought it worth interrupting himself for a moment to commiserate with the sick comrade or offer to buy him a proper linen handkerchief to replace the obviously disintegrating rag that he was forced to keep using and that he draped over the tile stove as often as possible, less to give it a chance to dry than in the hope of infecting all of them with his illness.

The worst of it was that Asher never really got a chance to test if having Hans's apartment available would help him with the women living in the Josef Quarter. Asher began to spend most of his free evenings following different groups of girls as they trudged home along the riverbank, the unpaved path barely visible through the twilight, returning from some wretched job as cleaning women or laundresses in the better districts. They were, of course, never employed in the finest houses, where only girls fresh from the country, unspoiled by ideas and expectations above their station, were hired. But many of the poorer women from town found temporary work in the middle-class homes whose mistresses were less choosy and were willing to take on the wives and daughters of unemployed laborers so long as they could pay them only the meagerest day wages, supplemented by some leftover scraps from the family dinners to take back to their lodgings. There was one in particular to whom Asher longed to talk, a plump, exuberantly large-breasted girl who could not have been more than seventeen or eighteen but who walked with a self-confident air that Asher was sure could only come from an extensive repertoire of sexual experience. She had a slightly flared, freckled little nose, wide hips, and reddish blond hair that looked cheaply dyed. Once Asher followed her into the corner tobacconist, and coming up close behind her in the narrow space in front of the counter, he felt himself grow flushed with embarrassment and arousal at the sharp smell of sweat from her underarms as she reached over to pay for the cigarette paper. There was something thrillingly shameless in how the sudden, accidental intimacy between their bodies let him take in her most private odors. The way she surrendered to her craving for cigarettes, unconcerned whether this stranger standing directly behind her noticed her indifference to decencies like clean underwear and soap, promised a similar casualness about her other desires.

Poverty worse than his own had always acted as a potent aphrodisiac on Asher. On weekends, when he was still a student at the Commercial College, although he had been terrified of being beaten up by the street hooligans against whom his perpetually anxious father cautioned him, Asher had deliberately loitered in the seediest neighborhoods, staring up at the tiny, grime-smeared tenement windows. To his frustration, he never managed to see anything truly indecent, but just the thought of what sordid acts were surely taking place at that very moment in the rooms above him would overwhelm him with waves of desire. When he was older and had started work, he recognized how eagerly he would commit almost any vileness for the right sum and took it for granted that a woman whose circumstances were even more abject than his own would think nothing of giving her body to any man for a handful of small coins. Unfortunately, in spite of the generous tips he was now secretly getting from Moritz and the more modest, but regular, payments he had persuaded an obviously skeptical Hans to give him as compensation for the wages he had sacrificed by quitting his job—"in order to be available whenever you should need me" was how he had put it to Hans—Asher hated the idea of offering a woman enough money to make his proposal persuasive, and he was afraid that if he mentioned the actual amount with which he was willing to part, he risked being insulted by her for his stinginess or even threatened with violence from an irate male relative who would surely have known how to vanish discreetly for a more spendthrift customer. Hans of course faced no such limitations on his pleasure, and Asher was certain that by now he had worked his way through every attractive female in the district, no doubt including the strawberry blonde with the craving for cigarettes and the sensual beads of sweat on her arm. She—and all her good-looking friends—probably adored Hans, or at least his money, which, in Hans's case, was the same thing, and that thought so irritated Asher that just as he was debating actually increasing the amount he was ready to spend on a girl this mesmerizing, he lost heart, abruptly turned around, and left the tobacconist without looking at her further.

So far, to his frustration, the apartment had never been available to Asher long enough to use as a base of operations for the erotic conquests on which he had counted. Whenever Hans left town, he insisted on locking it up and simply deflected Asher's pleas to be allowed to look after it until Hans's return. He never even bothered to come up with an acceptable excuse for his refusal. That, more than any direct rudeness, made plain precisely where each of them stood. He might just as well have announced, "A Rotenburg does not explain himself to the Asher Blumenthals of this world. He simply does whatever he feels like without wasting time wondering what the other fellow will make of it." Asher was tempted to get a duplicate copy of the house key made to use when Hans left for visits to the country estates of the other fine gentlemen, no doubt for hunting and drinking parties to which there was no question of inviting him. But the risk of being found out and possibly losing his place with both Rotenburgs was too great. Hans was clearly acting as his father's secret agent in these sham political conspiracies, and from the scattered clues he had picked up, Asher had worked out a shrewd guess at Hans's exact role. Whether or not Asher's secret hope that he might be the old man's illegitimate son was true, this was no time to test the supposition by doing anything to interfere with the family's schemes. Occasionally Hans decided to sleep in his rooms in the Rotenburg townhouse and would tell Asher he could use the apartment for the night—needless to say, only after first asking him to change all the linen and towels and make sure the cupboards were restocked with food and drinks for the next group meeting—but even this happened too irregularly for Asher to turn it to his advantage. When the chance did present itself, Asher was desperate enough to be tempted by any possibility and even considered trying to seduce the fierce-looking Slovene waitress who served him his double brandies in the disreputable local tavern he had taken to frequenting. In the few seconds it took her to bend down and replace his empty glass with a freshly filled one, he could perhaps whisper to her about his warm, carpeted flat with a porcelain bathtub only a short walk away and invite her to go back there with him after her shift ended. But somehow, he was never able to steer their brief exchange of monosyllables in the right direction for such a suggestion. Probably all to the good too. Asher certainly did not look as though he possessed a place of his own, not even in this district, and she didn't seem like the kind of woman to whom it was safe to lie. Perhaps if he drank a bit less, he might divert some of the savings to augmenting what he was able to offer for a woman. But ever since his first visit to Hans's apartment, Asher had begun to find himself increasingly drawn to seedy taverns like Löffner's, where he felt safe from being recognized and could drink as much as he wanted without worrying about attracting attention. No matter how sullen or gloomy he felt or how much alcohol he drank, compared with the other customers, Asher was certain he looked like a model of respectability. The gulf between him and the desperate wrecks who seemed to have taken up permanent residence at Löffner's stopped him from feeling too bad about himself when he tried to steady his spinning head to verify the evening's bill and saw with shock the number of double brandies he had consumed. More worrisome than the amount he was now drinking was how thoroughly at home Asher felt in this unappetizing place and how often during the course of a day he found himself looking forward eagerly to the hour he would be free of all his duties and be able to push his way through the oilcloth curtain into that dank cellar. Only a few months earlier, sitting down to eat at one of Isaac Meir's greasy tables in At the Five Hussars had made Asher physically queasy, but judged against Löffner's, a workers' restaurant like Meir's was as clean as Moritz Rotenburg's own kitchen. Most of the time, though, Asher looked back on the day he first stumbled into Löffner's as a godsend, and he had no doubt that drinking there, rather than in one of the more respectable bars in the area, was proof that his good judgment had not been affected by all that was happening to him. The truly fancy places like the Metropole, into whose opaque windows he used to peer with longing whenever he found himself walking past them, as though the ornate wood-paneled rooms with their plush stuffed chairs and marble countertops belonged to some inaccessible, magical kingdom, had lost all their appeal once Hans had invited him there two or three times. Even if he could have afforded the outrageous prices on his own, just sitting at one of those marble tables made Asher hideously uncomfortable. Everyone there, from the smirking headwaiter to the people at the other tables, knew Asher was there only as a poor guest of someone who really belonged, and the contrast between the condescension with which he was treated and the deference shown to Hans, who was treated as though he were at least a Grand Duke, took away all of Asher's pleasure at finally entering such an imposing setting.

There was something especially offensive in the nasty looks Anton, the Metropole's headwaiter, obviously worried this interloper from the town's Jewish rabble would leave an unsightly stain on the pale green cushions for which the restaurant was famous, cast toward Asher. Simply knowing Anton's name was a sign of belonging to the circle of privileged regulars, but although Asher had often watched Hans summoning him over to plan out a luncheon menu as casually as if speaking to one of the domestics in his father's house, he himself never dared use the man's first name, and since he refused to abase himself by saying Herr Prigl, Asher had to avoid addressing him altogether. Unless he was occupied serving one of the select guests, Anton always loomed right by the entrance, tall and very pale, his thin hair combed flat across his forehead, scanning everyone who walked into the Metropole to make sure he merited admission. He showed his more distinguished visitors to their tables with all the solemnity of a nobleman's private chaplain performing some mysterious religious service, and Asher was certain that he must be even more hateful than Garber's notorious Wellisz from the Café Central. Since his life had taken such an odd turn, Asher especially missed being able to talk over his ideas with his only friend. Garber would surely have applauded the acuity of his insight into the old man's financial strategy and helped advise him how to profit from his position with Moritz, but of course any letters between them would be immediately read by the police, so it was safer not to write at all. He did hear reports from time to time that Garber's career as a dramatist and short-story writer was beginning to succeed beyond anyone's expectations. Although Asher was glad for his friend, he found the extent of Garber's triumph a bit grating as well. Not only the government newspapers but even some of the liberal journals were giving his pieces extravagant reviews. One article he had seen rated Garber above Schnitzler, and almost in the same league as Hofmannsthal, when it came to capturing "the essence of the Viennese melancholy charm," a description that thoroughly depressed Asher until he consoled himself by imagining the political pressure placed on the unfortunate reviewer to make him produce such a brazen exaggeration. It did seem unfair that the seizure of their harmless correspondence about *The New Order* should have catapulted Garber to fame as the police-backed darling of Vienna's Burgtheater while sentencing Asher to the role of provincial go-between and informant. It was just the kind of capriciousness of fate that Garber used to write about in his early plays, long before either of them had experienced it firsthand, and if Asher had found nothing very droll about the theme back in their student days, he was even less inclined to do so now. There is damn little to laugh about at finding one's circumstances anticipated in a popular farce, least of all when that farce is by one's only real friend.

But his chagrin did not stop Asher from wondering what Garber would have made of the crowd of titled would-be saboteurs at Hans's flat. How would he have represented them onstage? Would the censor insist that he disguise the actual people involved, or would he let Garber teach his actors to mimic their features, even if this would mean lampooning some of the Empire's most prominent families? It would be wonderful to hear some comic actor, maybe even a converted Jew born in the Viennese slums, perfectly capture the slight, hereditary lisp that undercut the ferocity that Leo von Arnstein, the group's latest recruit, fresh from boarding school at Mährisch-Weisskirchen, tried so hard to give his vows of loyalty to "our great cause." Asher had overheard enough stories from von Hradl about the disgusting kinds of relationships between the best-looking novice students and the more senior boys that took place in the dormitories after lights out had been called to form his own theory about why many of these fellows tended to blush so readily, even years later. But he supposed that none of that could ever be mentioned in a play. Still, a bold enough actor could do a lot with hints and suggestions. Now if Garber had the courage to base his next comedy on Asher's stories about the political goings-on in their town—say, as a goyish pendant to the runaway success of *The Jew's Misfortune*—and call it *The Cadet's Disgrace*, then Asher would willingly concede that no one had captured the national temperament more satisfyingly than Alexander Garber. As far as Asher could tell, these aristocrats treated everything as a kind of fancy dress-up party anyway, so what was the harm in portraying them accurately? But then, such a play would have to succeed without the heavy hand of the Imperial bureaucracy to help it along, and by now, Asher was certain, Alexander had become far too prudent in the ways of the capital to run the risk of falling afoul of his patrons. Unlike Hans's crowd, these men were quite capable of being offended by a single out-of-place expression from a subordinate and, what was worse, were more than ready to act on their vexation. Asher could afford to stagger into Hans's apartment, his clothes stinking of the mixture of cheap alcohol and tobacco that clung to anyone who had spent the previous four hours at Löffner's without washing up in between and tell everyone in the room how fed up he was with the whole charade since nothing important to him would ever change until someone found a girlfriend for him and instructed the Governing Board of the Mendelssohn Club that Herr Blumenthal was hereby appointed their permanent president to make up for all their past injustices. "What's the use of your revolution if I still have to go to bed alone and everyone I hate is walking around as prosperous as ever?" That is what he longed to yell in their faces, and though he never phrased it quite like that, he came close enough on more than a few occasions to have left them with no doubt of his feelings. But except for a bored shrug, no one, not even Hans, from whom he might have expected some sign of fellowship, paid any attention. He might as well never have spoken a single word. Considering how things always worked out for him, Asher felt certain his being ignored like this in real life corresponded precisely to what would have been his role onstage in Garber's never-to-be-written dramatization of the conspiracy.

Artistically the main challenge for Garber would be in how to treat Hans. This was something about which Asher himself was far from clear. On his own there was nothing especially interesting about Hans, Asher could certainly vouch for that; but as the chief instrument of his father's plans Hans would have to be given a more prominent role than pleased Asher, and it would be impossible to deny him a certain subtlety. Just the duplicity required to carry out his assignment meant Hans possessed a depth that could not help worrying Asher. And what a plan it was too, the culminating masterpiece of the greatest man Asher had ever met. Moritz could manipulate the stock market to drive the town's manufacturers to their knees and then use the strikers, spurred on by that naive clown Nathan Kaplansky, who did not even realize he was just doing Moritz's work for him, to complete their ruin. But that clearly was not enough for a man of Moritz Rotenburg's stupendous ambition since it left the provincial aristocracy, very little of whose wealth depended on the stock market, relatively untouched. That was where Hans came in. By seducing their sons into a ridiculous criminal conspiracy designed from the outset to end in their betrayal and utter ruin, Hans would leave these families completely dishonored. In the aftermath of their public disgrace, many of them would be desperate to quit the area entirely—and maybe even the country—leaving Moritz as the only possible purchaser of their estates. At best, they would have to turn to him for the ready cash to finance their sons' legal defense, thereby putting themselves heavily into his debt and postponing, but only temporarily, the inevitable forced sale of their lands to repay his loans. The Rotenburgs were clearly aiming at nothing less than control of every desirable property in the whole province, and had found a marvelous way to trap all their prey in a single net. The letters Asher carried between Moritz and Jakob Tausk must be full of strategic discussions about the right moment to spring the trap, and Asher fervently hoped he would be allowed to see it happen in person. Who could say what Moritz Rotenburg might not yet ask of Asher in the aftermath of the decisive day? To play for such stakes meant a certain amount of risk. Anything could happen in the confusion of the arrest, and it was impossible to guarantee completely Hans's safety. Should something unfortunate happen to Hans, Asher was determined to be a comfort to the old man and let him see that his dynasty would continue in spite of his great loss, as surely as that of the Imperial house had continued after the double suicide of the Crown Prince and his lover at Mayerling a quarter century ago.

• ◆ •

For once, though, Asher had seriously underestimated his effect on others. From their immediate visceral distaste the first time he greeted them at the door of Hans's flat, the conspirators soon grew to despise Asher unreservedly. Just being in the same room with him became a physical ordeal, like brushing against something dank and malignant while on cadet maneuvers in the fetid marshes near Brody. They had been trained since

353

childhood not to display their feelings to anyone who was not an intimate, and even with those closest to them they relied on a certain indispensable, and mutually protective, veil of courteous detachment. But even their strict upbringing, which had taught them how to use politesse to keep unwelcome types at a distance, was unequal to the task of staying pleasantly impersonal toward Asher. Their experience had never included conversing with someone who thrust his boorishness forward as though it were an especially commendable accomplishment with which everyone should be as charmed as he himself clearly was. They all had known rude servants who had to be dismissed if they presumed too much, but far from Asher's gratefully accepting the role of a privileged hireling to which his incessant sponging should have kept him confined, his whole demeanor emphasized his insistence on being regarded as one of them, and they reluctantly had to admit his claim had some merit. It was all Hans's fault, really. What could he have been thinking to bring a man like that into their circle, thereby subjecting them all to someone so unredeemably repugnant? Not to mention that the man was about as trustworthy as Judas Iscariot and undoubtedly would jump at the chance to betray them the instant there was more profit in selling them out to the authorities than in continuing to scrounge off them. As long as Asher was around, they carefully avoided saying anything specific about their plans, so that even if he ran to the police, he would have nothing to report beyond the predictable criticisms of the Empire's out-of-date social policies that everyone under thirty was making these days—except, as Hans morosely observed, for that toy soldier Karl Gustav von Alpsbach and, for all any of them knew, maybe his brother Ernst as well. In any case, people of their sort were not hauled off to jail for just mouthing a few complaints about the social order, of which they themselves ranked among the main beneficiaries, and certainly not on the evidence of a creature like Blumenthal. Fortunately too, the Count-Governor had been eccentric enough to appoint as his chief spy a Jew even more unsavory than Asher, and if this Tausk fellow was half as clever as his reputation suggested, he surely knew that every magistrate and jury in the region would be ill disposed toward him. He would never dare touch them without the kind of evidence that, as Christoph put it to them during a meditative, predinner walk in the enclosed park behind Moritz's townhouse, would become available only after they had acted and it was already too late.

Nonetheless, Asher's regular presence in the Josef Quarter flat had made them shift their center of operations elsewhere. Mostly they used Hans's spacious rooms upstairs in the Rotenburg villa, which was, they quickly agreed, a far more congenial setting than this depressing part of town, and, when the weather began to improve, arranged to meet out in the country, either at Hirschwang, the von Arnstein estate, or at Weidenau, whichever promised them more privacy. Hirschwang had been granted to Baron Johann Alexander von Arnstein in 1772, the year the province had been annexed into the Empire, as his reward for fifty years of exemplary service making life miserable for Lutherans, Jews, Russian and Greek Orthodox, and all other manner of heretics and schismatics. Unlike many of the large estates of that era, Hirschwang had nothing of the expensive rusticity that was still so much in fashion. Rather than follow his peers and build, at great cost and to an elephantine scale, an imitation farmhouse or hunting lodge, thereby ending up with a counterfeit that lacked either the charm of genuine simplicity or the serenity of attained elegance, Johann Alexander finally gave vent to his hitherto submerged impulsiveness by going entirely in the other direction and ordering his bewildered architect to design nothing less than a rigorously formal country retreat in the style of a Spanish grandee, something like the Royal Palace and gardens at La Granja outside Segovia, where he had spent many contented hours as a member of the Austrian legation. Some of his laxer neighbors, for whom von Arnstein's religious zealotry came close to being in bad taste, at least for an Austrian, quipped that he had built an imitation Spanish palace out of frustration at not being able to take home from his years in the Iberian peninsula the commendable traditions of the Holy Inquisition. Instead what he did manage was to saddle his descendants with an awkwardly miniaturized Royal Palace and formal gardens that cost a fortune to maintain—heating it in winter was virtually impossible, and no one could inhabit it during the coldest months without regarding every day spent there as a form of religious penance—and that looked as unlike its original model in Spain as the overbuilt farmhouses of the other provincial noblemen resembled anything in which a real farmer could ever imagine living.

It was in the late afternoon on the terraced gardens at Hirschwang, near a decorously chaste statue of the sleeping Ariadne, that his friends decided to confront Hans openly about having brought Asher into their midst. The large windows of the music room directly on the ground floor behind them blazed with the early-spring sunset, and as they leaned outward over the terrace's edge so that they would no longer be facing the house, their eyes followed the immensity of a reddish golden sky igniting the numberless acres of tilled fields and woodlands that flowed all the way from this easternmost outpost of the Empire to the Asian steppes. Instead of preparing himself inwardly for the sharp quarrel that he knew lay just ahead, Hans, to his surprise, found himself remembering the time he and Batya had gone out together for a ride to a country inn to taste the first new potatoes of the season. Although it was a chilly day, they wanted to be alone and asked the landlord to set up a table for them out in the small, fenced-in wine garden. Hans had often heard his father lament that nothing was harder for him to recollect than a particular taste or sensation, but the savor of those wonderfully hot, thin-skinned, small potatoes, still redolent of the nearby field from which they had been harvested that same morning and scarcely needing the sweet butter and parsley with which they were served, and the chilled, slightly acidic local white wine that accompanied the meal was as vivid in his mouth there, on the terrace at Hirschwang, as though he had just gotten up from the table and walked back into the inn with his fingertips gently tracing the lines of Batya's veins from the heart of her palm up to her elbow. Although he himself was vaguely troubled at finding no connection between the thoughts that seemed to be flooding through him as swiftly as the successive waves of light flashing over the countryside, now tinged with the first shades of the approaching darkness, Hans remembered how at the climax of one of the petty, spiteful arguments that had marked the last days of their intimacy, Batya had suddenly turned to him and in a new, almost puzzled voice said, "But I still don't feel anything of all these words we are both shouting." They had been to the theater earlier that evening, mostly out of curiosity to see a one-act curtain raiser by a rising young dramatist from Vienna. Moritz had been a major contributor to the stately new German-language theater, erected a few steps from the stock exchange by the same architect who had designed the famous theaters in Graz and Odessa. Although the Rotenburgs maintained a box there for the entire season, neither of them used it very much, preferring to give away their seats to senior employees of the firm or one of the numerous literarily inclined, but insolvent, members of the Mendelssohn Club. Hans was generally indifferent to imaginative works of any kind, especially comedy, and could not remember the piece five minutes after the final curtain, but Batya had loathed it and insisted on itemizing everything about it that she found annoying, from the vulgarity of its female characters to its fawning celebration of aristocratic behavior. Over a late dinner at the Metropole, a restaurant she disliked but had agreed to go to only because the right guest could get a full meal there at almost any hour, she had gone on dissecting the performance, and although Hans did not doubt that her reaction was genuine, both of them also recognized that she was seizing on an apparently neutral topic as a way to voice a growing frustration with her role in Hans's life. She spoke more passionately than any of the actors had done onstage, and once or twice, when her voice grew particularly loud, Anton, tortured by the conflict between his veneration for the Rotenburg money and an almost equally powerful urge to go over and ask the young lady please to speak more softly so as not to disturb the other diners, cast a look of pure misery in her direction. In the end, the fear of losing Hans's tips won out, and Anton stayed paralyzed in his customary post near the door, but for a few minutes the two impulses hung in perfect equilibrium, and in its speechless inner violence, the struggle within Anton was perhaps the most intense drama played out anywhere in town that evening. When he looked around to order another mocha, Hans noticed that Anton's posture was even more rigid than usual and guessed that something must be bothering his favorite headwaiter. But knowing Anton's punctiliousness as well as he did, Hans decided not to increase the man's embarrassment by inquiring what the problem was. In any case, Batya, who had developed a strong dislike of Anton, would have been furious at such clear evidence of Hans's wandering attention, and he dreaded another misunderstanding while there was still some hope of getting her to spend the night with him. He found it hard to follow most of her polemic, except for one bizarre outburst that kept returning to him afterward at unexpected moments. He never did get a clear idea of what the larger issue was supposed to be, but Batya evidently regarded that night's performance as an especially irksome manifestation of some fundamental national malaise. Toward the end of the meal, when they had already been served coffee and the small chocolates that, for her, were the Metropole's only redeeming feature, Batya leaned forward in her chair as though determined, by her own surplus of energy, to throw off the torpor infecting everyone in the room and demanded to know, "Why do people move their arms so clumsily onstage? Why don't they know what to do with their arms? It is the little details that make them seem so graceless. Why can't they move their arms like people who care about what they feel?"

Hans had no memory of how that conversation ended. All he recalled was that shortly afterward she insisted on returning alone to her parents' house and that by then he was more relieved than disappointed by her decision. And now she and Ernst were probably together out at Brunnenberg, which, on a good horse, was less than forty-five minutes away. The day before, when he and Leo were in the library, studying the detailed maps of the district collected by the older von Arnstein, Hans had not been able to stop himself from carefully noting the exact disposition of the roads between Hirschwang and Brunnenberg. The next morning, when they all went out for target practice into the thicket of birch trees beyond the formal English park, the first thing Hans did was to confirm that the direct route to Brunnenberg really did begin on the far side of the small private path leading up to the elaborate wrought-iron gates at the entrance to the von Arnstein estate. But the longer Hans stared at the empty road, the more he found himself thinking of Batya and Ernst as inhabiting some foreign country more remote from him than any of his family's business associates abroad. It was as though they all had lost touch years ago, and if he was sometimes able to remember them now without rancor, it was because at those moments they inspired only the equivocal sadness we feel hearing about a former close companion toward whom we already had grown emotionally indifferent long before we broke off contact. Yet just a short while ago he had received a letter from Batya, the first in many months, begging him not to go through with his "mad idea" and hinting, between the lines, that things with Ernst were not going as well as before. Reading it through, Hans had the odd sensation that what was being awakened in him was not a renewed desire for Batya but only for the person he himself had been when they first became lovers. Hans knew he had little talent for phrasemaking, but even so, he wished he had been able to find a better way of replying than the hastily scribbled note he ended up sending her: "You make me miss myself, Batya, but even I know that is a terrible reason to reenter someone's life. You always wanted to leave this country. I hope you succeed and persuade Ernst to go away with you. He is probably the best of any of us, and maybe you two can find happiness away from all this muck. Try to think well of me. Hans."

A brisk evening chill was beginning to rise up to the main buildings from the small pond with its imported Neptune fountain, around which the principal section of the garden had been designed. One by one, the young men made their way back through the large French doors into the house, where a hot buffet had been prepared for them in the smaller dining room. Leo had dismissed the servants for the night, and the dinner was neatly arranged in a row of platters, each kept warm by its own chafing dish, up on a sideboard at the far end of the room. The silverware and specially commissioned pale blue and white Meissen china were identically engraved with the von Arnstein crest and, in a circle of laurel leaves, the date the family acquired Hirschwang. Christoph, whose family had been ennobled a century and a half before the von Arnsteins, looked over the display with an expression of quizzical amusement. Leo of course saw his friend's eyebrows rise in von Hradl's characteristically stagey pantomime gesture—as indeed he was intended to—and blushed furiously. No doubt his lisp would be especially pronounced tonight should the debate grow heated and he and Christoph find themselves on opposing sides. But for the moment no one except Hans thought about what lay ahead since they all were eager to start eating and rushed to fill their plates as though they were still students coming into the refectory after too many hours in the classroom. This time, though, their hunger came from the day spent outdoors practicing with different-caliber firearms, from small pistols that could be easily hidden on one's person to larger hunting rifles, specially equipped with the latest high-powered Zeiss telescopic sights. With one of these, a skilled marksman could hit his target from a good distance. For all of the school's faults, every graduate of Mährisch-Weisskirchen was proficient in riflery. Hans, though, had never been a cadet, and his father's position had secured him an indefinite postponement from the obligatory army reserve duty. From the War Department's point of view, Hans represented a difficult administrative, racial, and ethical conundrum. The army had no interest in safeguarding the young man from the rigors of active duty, since the sons of the Empire's oldest and most powerful families all served as a matter of course and considered it an indispensable part of their education. No, the problem was that as a Jew, Hans could not be posted to one of the fashionable regiments, nor could he be advanced to the rank of officer in the reserve corps, without immediately arousing heated opposition. And of course it was utterly unthinkable to assign an Israelite to the General Staff. But as a Rotenburg, and his father's sole heir, he could hardly be placed anywhere else without causing anxiety at both the Foreign and the Finance Ministries. Even within the War Department itself, no one wanted to risk offending one of the most generous contributors to all the various charitable campaigns for discharged veterans. More important, Moritz Rotenburg was a principal shareholder in two of the heavy armament manufacturing plants with which the army was negotiating new contracts, and the General Staff was counting on his influence to help secure favorable terms. So, in the best traditions of the Empire, which, when in doubt, had always preferred strategic delay to the perils of excessive haste, it was quietly decided that since no satisfactory solution to the question of Hans Rotenburg's military assignment could be devised, the whole matter should be deferred until next year's army draft. Once such a judicious policy had been arrived at, and the appropriate memorandum attached to Hans's dossier, there was no reason the deferral could not be renewed indefinitely until Hans was too old for active duty and his case formally closed.

An unintended consequence of all this intricate planning on his behalf was that Hans became one of the few physically sound young men in the Empire with no military training whatsoever. Since he also found hunting completely unappealing, Hans lacked even a minimum proficiency with firearms, a limitation that was of no consequence for the inheritor of an international business Empire but that did present certain obstacles to someone contemplating a political murder. On the outdoor range they had set up, Hans's results were consistently below those of the others, and his shots were often so far from the bull's-eye that he was starting to wonder if he might not need to start wearing eyeglasses. Even Langer was more reliable with a weapon than Hans. Although Hans found any form of clumsiness irritating, whether in himself or in others, and avoided being seen doing anything at which he looked awkward, being revealed as a mediocre shot was too trivial a failing to distress him. Still, right now, when he sensed his authority over the group was shakier than it had been since Ernst's defection, the danger of any visible weakness was far in excess of its objective significance.

As Hans bent over his steaming bowl of oxtail soup, he looked up and down the long table at which they all were seated and wondered from whom the first attack would come. He felt entirely calm now that the moment of open conflict was imminent. Without Ernst to rally around, none of them had the self-confidence or willpower to challenge Hans's leadership successfully. Had Ernst stayed, the outcome would have been unpredictable, and there was a chance they might have settled for the kind of tepid social reformism Ernst and Batya seemed to favor these days. Indistinguishable, really, from the rubbish Nathan Kaplansky or Viktor Adler spouted in front of every closed factory without making the slightest difference to anyone out of a job. Hans knew that his father owned Kaplansky, although the man himself probably managed not to realize just how much. In Vienna, no doubt, the Prime Minister secretly paid the whole trade union leadership a regular stipend to keep antigovernment agitation within easily manageable levels, and if Moritz were to open all his books to Hans, including the private ledgers he kept locked in the hidden safe in his study, it would probably turn out that the Rotenburg firm was a heavy contributor to this subsidy as well. Everyone in this country was bought and paid for several times over, and the fact that his own family's money did much of that buying and selling filled Hans with an often bewildering synthesis of revulsion and pride. Short of killing someone close to the Imperial Family, there was probably nothing he could do that a generous enough bribe from his father would not smooth over, and if Hans had ever been tempted to waver in his plan, the evidence of Kaplansky's corruption, combined with the sentimental cant Ernst and Batya invoked to gloss over their faithlessness, drove any such notion out of his mind.

But about one thing Hans was almost immediately proved wrong. He had been certain that Christoph would be the one to launch the attempted coup, but instead the first volley came from Gerling, whose voice, when it was raised in dispute, turned out to be much shriller than one would have guessed from the tone of his infrequent attempts to engage anyone in an ordinary conversation. Gerling's father was some kind of academic much favored by the government—Hans could not recall his exact field but remembered seeing his name on the list of experts called before one of the Imperial Commissions dealing with the unemployment crisis—and Joachim gave the impression that his only notion of speaking in front of others on a serious subject was to do a perfect imitation of his father's lecturing style. The whole time he was speaking, the younger Gerling, as though himself at a rostrum, kept his gaze fixed somewhere just over Hans's left shoulder and gave every appearance of a man in acute discomfort. But whatever he said must have been collectively rehearsed, since the nods of agreement from the others came before his phrases had been completed. It took Hans only a few sentences to understand the gist of the accusation, and as soon as he had done so, the whole predictable charade filled him with irritable impatience. Arguing with Ernst had been altogether different, but tonight nothing was at stake except the wounded vanity of some second-rate temperaments that lacked the inner authority needed to lead or the self-recognition to accept their subordinate roles without grumbling. When he went to a concert or play, Hans often found himself briefly falling asleep at arbitrary points during the performance, even if it was a piece he especially enjoyed. At first he had felt abashed at his inability to stay awake and tried in vain to fight it by drinking countless cups of strong black coffee before the curtain went up. Nothing worked, though, and after a while he gave up struggling and simply accepted that enforced passivity of any kind induced in him a kind of drifting somnolence. Now too he suddenly became aware that although he had been staring with increasing displeasure in Gerling's direction, he must have missed a whole series of the fellow's carefully rehearsed sentences. Somehow, during Hans's fit of inattention, the complaint had progressed from his general high-handedness to the specific example of Asher Blumenthal, whom Joachim was now denouncing with the self-righteousness of a born pedant: "The man is so absolutely, irredeemably despicable that just having had his company forced on us for all these weeks is an offense to everything we stand for. He doesn't have a grain of revolutionary consciousness, and now that he has become a drunkard as well, and completely unable to keep his mouth shut, he is even more dangerous to us than before. I wouldn't be surprised if half the tavern keepers in the Josef Quarter know all about us, thanks to your new recruit. Not to mention the customers in such places, where we know the police like keeping a spy or two posted to identify potential troublemakers. Heaven knows what he is going around saying about us in whatever pigsties he has found to hole up in and get soused. The only thing he does the rest of the time is hang around your apartment pestering us for money and introductions to any easy women of whom we might have grown tired. Do you have any idea how besmirched his constant stream of indecency makes us feel? To be talked to that way by a guttersnipe like Blumenthal, when the right of women to be saved from exploitation is part of what we are fighting for in the first place! None of us can understand what use you imagined he would be to us, Hans, and we have a right to a fuller explanation. Whatever happened to the principle of collective decision making? We all admit that you are the one who has done the bulk of the work so far; but we did not join together just to become junior partners in another Rotenburg enterprise, and we certainly aren't ready to let you commit us to whatever plan you have thought up when none of us is given any voice in shaping it."

The ascending rhythm of Gerling's speech made it clear that he was nowhere near done. On the contrary, from the way he was starting to shift from one leg to the other behind the high-backed chair against which he had been leaning up to now, there was every chance he intended either to go on lecturing in place for a long time yet or, worse still, to begin to walk up and down the length of the whole dinner table to add the punctuation of physical display to what he clearly regarded as the irresistible eloquence of his words. The self-enchantment that, to his own ears at least, had transformed a tongue-tied, desperately shy underling into the Danton of this dining-room rebellion was far too thrilling for Gerling to pay any attention to the effect his words were having on his listeners. Hans, though, had been trained by his father to make use of every slight shift in the disposition of power in a business negotiation and immediately noticed that the others, especially Christoph, were showing clear signs of restlessness at Gerling's performance. They had long since stopped nodding at his sallies, and the more impassioned Gerling sounded, the more displeased Christoph and Leo looked. "I was right the first time," Hans thought. "It was von Hradl who intended to take over from me tonight, with Leo as his lieutenant. That's why this whole weekend was arranged with all that shooting at which they knew I would come off badly. In a day or two they probably plan to go crawling on their knees all the way over to Brunnenberg and beg von Alpsbach to rejoin them as their lost leader. Ernst, the knight errant with his pure soul and impeccable pedigree. Gerling was supposed to be their stalking horse, that is all. Only now the supporting actor has found out how much he enjoys the lead role and obviously does not want to give up center stage for anyone. It is wonderful to see Leo squirm in his chair every time Gerling waves his hands in the air and comes close to knocking over the tureen behind him. For them to be led by a Rotenburg is one thing, not exactly what they have been brought up to expect, but having watched their parents swallow their pride to ask my father for help, it has become part of their experience of the world. But to be lectured about collective decision making by some bourgeois professor's son is turning out to be more than they can stomach, even for an hour."

Just before he heard the noise of the crash, Hans saw Leo's eyes widen in horror and immediately guessed the cause. The large soup bowl that had been a present to Johann Alexander von Arnstein from Their Royal Majesties in Madrid on the occasion of his leaving their country to return home forever tottered on the sideboard for a few seconds, and then, before anyone could get there to steady it, the dish lay in pieces on the hardwood floor, except for one thin section that now dangled incongruously from Gerling's soaked sleeve. Hans had a good idea how heavily mortgaged Hirschwang and the surrounding forestlands were and how little ready cash the von Arnsteins had to replace far less costly items than this ghastly-looking antique. When the rest of Leo's family came back, being held incommunicado in one of the Emperor's prisons might seem like a welcome alternative to facing their collective fury. Right now, though, to everyone's amazement, the most annoyed countenance in the room belonged to Joachim Gerling, who was visibly incensed that something as trivial as a piece of breaking pottery should have interrupted him in midsentence. He kept shaking his arm to dislodge the sliver that had been caught there, spraying bits of soup and meat particles everywhere, and threatening the safety of several other dishes still within reach of his long torso. Moreover, since he was certain that the rest of the group was fully as eager to hear him continue his speech as he was to oblige them, Gerling nodded reassuringly to the room at large to show that he had every intention of resuming as soon as he had freed himself of the last bits of porcelain still attached to him, and indeed the moment the final shard joined all the others on the floor he returned to his original position behind his chair and, as though nothing at all had occurred, continued with "What we have all agreed has to happen, Hans—"

"Is for you to sit down, shut your damn mouth, and stop waving your arms around like a lunatic while there is still one plate left unbroken." They had never heard Christoph so angry before. His face was contorted with the same nearly hysterical fury that the elder von Hradl's tenants were forced to endure when they dared plead for postponements in their quarterly rents. Gerling just stood there immobilized, staring around blankly as though unable to take in what Christoph was saying. For several seconds nothing whatsoever registered within him except surprise that his friend would interrupt him in what sounded, even through the paralysis numbing his mind, like an enraged tone. But Gerling could not have repeated back a single syllable, any more than if he had suddenly been turned into a deaf-mute. It was as though a set of random sounds were reaching him from very far away and he needed time before they could be decoded into a comprehensible utterance. Then slowly, as his numbness began to give way to the realization that something was going badly wrong, Gerling strained forward to look into each of the other men's eyes for support, but when he saw only the contemptuous absence of any sympathy, he collapsed into his chair like a puppet when the wires holding it upright have been suddenly severed. He seemed no longer able to raise his head and just sat there mumbling in the general direction of von Arnstein, "I am so dreadfully sorry, Leo, I can't tell you how sorry."

No one bothered looking over at Gerling, who was left sitting there as though he were invisible, like an inept servant who had been dismissed and with whom any further dealing would be embarrassing for everyone concerned. That was exactly when Hans walked over to him and, as though it were the most natural thing, tapped him in a friendly way on his slumped shoulders, gave him a quick, sympathetic smile, and, without any undue fuss, sat down in the empty chair beside him. None of them heard what he then whispered into Gerling's ear, but the look of total adoration with which Gerling gazed back up at Hans made it clear that Rotenburg had just won an adherent whose loyalty nothing would ever shake again. Next, Hans carefully unscrewed the cap of his oversize black lacquer and gold fountain pen, took out the small leather notebook from his inner jacket pocket, set both down on the table in front of him, and only then looked up coldly at the others. His expression was impossible to decipher, but there was no mistaking the contained, lethal quality of his anger. They all had braced themselves to be shouted at and were prepared to argue back, but when Hans finally began to speak, he did so without raising his voice at all. He stayed quite still in his chair while addressing them. None of his words received any special emphasis or stress, and since he talked in a tone that was almost too soft for such a high-ceilinged room, everyone had to lean forward and strain in order not to miss half his words.

"So, which of you really believes this counterrevolutionary nonsense? Tell me, please, because I am sure the party leaders would love to know how far the rot has spread, and I will be glad to forward the list of your complaints. What a shabby little antiparty faction you have organized here. When a soup bowl breaks, you all gasp with shock, but violating party discipline and spreading dissension on the eve of our most ambitious and dangerous venture, well, that is nothing, a mere trifle for you gentlemen. Because that is all you are: gentlemen with a grievance against your parents and teachers, not revolutionaries, and certainly not the kind the party needs to carry out its historic mission. Who are you to talk about revolutionary consciousness at all? Has anyone taken a step to clean up the mess on the floor? No, of course not. The servants will take care of that in the morning. We have better things to do. Like plot against one another and turn everything into a high-toned debating society as though we were still at school. But that won't do anymore, and just so there is no chance for another mistake, let me tell you exactly why not.

"Do you really believe that ours is the only town in the Empire for which an exemplary action has been decided? Don't any of you suspect that something bigger is at stake than a little playacting at subversion in what everyone knows is the most backward province of the second most backward Empire in Europe? All this ladylike hand wringing about Asher Blumenthal? Can't you hear how pathetic you sound? 'Oh, dear. The man drinks too much and makes lewd comments. If only Ernst were still here, he would never countenance someone who doesn't respect women.' Well, Ernst is not here, and you can be sure that no one in the leadership regrets that. If you only knew how much I had to plead in certain quarters for him to be allowed to walk away without facing extremely unpleasant consequences for his desertion! And as far as Blumenthal is concerned, if the party needs to use someone like him, the only thing that matters is how well he completes his assignment! Whether he wants to fuck all the women in the Josef Quarter or sacrifice himself to 'save them from exploitation' is completely insignificant except for how it affects the task he's been given.

"We've all had to listen to Ernst prattle on about why he rejects violence as a political instrument. Well, the party also knows about his position, and as far as the leadership is concerned, Ernst's opinions are sentimental drivel. The sermonizing of a Sunday school teacher, that's what his politics amounts to these days. The only people to whom such verbiage could sound persuasive are the most reactionary elements in our ruling class—if they don't make themselves ill laughing about it first. If the oppressed actually renounced armed struggle, the ruling classes could sleep securely forever. Walking away from violence is just an excuse for not fighting evil at all. Not to act, not to do everything possible—whatever that entails—to overthrow the whole corrupt social system, is just criminal complicity with the police and the government. No class has ever abdicated power voluntarily, and I doubt our rulers are likely to start doing so now because it would help noble souls like Ernst von Alpsbach and Elisabeth Demetz enjoy their little idyll in Brunnenberg with a clean conscience. Because that's really what all these high-minded ideals are intended to accomplish. A way for sensitive rich people to continue with their lives without needing to feel guilty. But we pledged ourselves to more than that, and fortunately, there is a whole network of comrades-in-arms ready to do whatever is necessary to keep the revolution on a true course.

"I probably should not be telling you any of this, and I would be in serious trouble if anyone finds out that I have done so. Although you may not know it, I am sometimes just as puzzled as you about the reasons for a particular directive, but I know that my duty as a revolutionary is not to waste precious time quibbling about every order. If you think that I am making all the decisions for us, well, I give you my word, you could not be more mistaken. I am just one of the channels the party leaders have chosen to transmit their instructions for this region, and I do not have more influence on what they decide than anyone else in this room. What I have been told, in strictest secrecy, is that there are dozens of cells like ours throughout Europe, preparing right now to strike a blow against the ruling classes from which they will never recover. The idea is to launch all the attacks on the same day and as close to the same time as possible—noon, this very Easter—to make it clear that we are an organized and disciplined revolutionary army from whose reach no one is safe. None of us knows the names of our fellow militants in other towns or the identity of the targets that have been selected, so that if one group is compromised, the others won't be endangered. Because so much is at stake for the party, it has created a corps of mobile disciplinary squads with orders to root out and liquidate any backsliders who, out of cowardice or ideological vacillation, are jeopardizing the cause. I have seen one or two of these revolutionary tribunals at work, and believe me, I would hate to end up in their bad graces. We are in a state of war right now, and in the middle of a battle, proletarian justice does not have time for all the legal niceties of the bourgeoisie. So if I tell you that I have used up whatever limited influence I had with the leadership to shield Ernst—and maybe even that only temporarily—from a visit by these men and that after seeing one of this cell's founding members walk out on it, the party is not going to tolerate any more defections from among us, it is *your* safety, not my position, I am worried about. My orders were very explicit on this score: The party suspects that there are counterrevolutionary elements in every cell and wants me to send them a list of anyone I think is unreliable—with what results, I leave up to you to imagine. So, I ask you for the last time: Who is willing to go on record as questioning the leadership's decisions, and who wants to forget all the nonsense we have fallen into this weekend and return to our revolutionary tasks without any more dissension?"

All traces of anger had long since vanished from Hans's face. After he finished speaking, he leaned forward in his chair, lightly holding on to his pen, and began to write a few words on the blank sheet in front of him. Whether deliberately, or simply because of how he was sitting, his arm blocked the paper from view, and in spite of what looked like a conscious effort not to let their curiosity overwhelm them, the other men kept glancing over toward Hans, straining to watch the movement of his hand in order to decipher what he was jotting down from the way his pen progressed across the page. Except for the faint scratching sound of his gold nib on the paper, the silence in the room was absolute. None of the men looked at one another, and only the seemingly irresistible attraction exerted on their eyes by Hans's pen and notebook gave any sign that he was not completely alone. It was as though each of them had been trapped in a narrow blanket of ice and, as the cold spread through his limbs, had lost the ability to take in the presence of another body only a few feet away.

At first none of them, not even Hans, was sure of the source of the clear, repeated thudding sound that punctured the silence. Then, as if responding in unison to a common cue, they all looked to the seat beside Hans and saw Joachim Gerling softly striking the edge of the table with his closed fist in the familiar student gesture of approbation. When he had satisfied himself that they all were finally looking at him, Gerling began to increase the volume and pace of his one-handed applause and accompanied it by a defiant glance at each of the other men in turn. One by one, they lowered their eyes away from Gerling's, folded their right hands into fists, and joined together in banging the table until the whole room resounded with the thundering clang. Hans had maintained his air of mild impassivity throughout, but when the noise reached a crescendo and then sustained itself without any diminution because no one was willing to be the first to stop clapping, he smiled faintly, closed his notebook, returned his pen to his jacket pocket, and shook his head slightly as though to dispel any remaining tension. When he signaled his wish to resume their conversation, he did so with marked politeness, as though carefully soliciting their goodwill, but even so, the banging still continued for another few moments, as if it had acquired a life independent of the hands that were producing it, until it finally faded out with a few last vibrations lingering in the air like the report of a rifle fired repeatedly in a closed space.

"Now, as for Asher," Hans said in his most businesslike tone, moving on to the next unresolved item on the agenda as though he were running a routine board meeting of one of the numerous companies in which his father was the majority shareholder, "I can't imagine anyone, myself included, spending a quarter of an hour in his company who would not emerge with the same impression as Joachim and Christoph." As Hans said this, the muscles on von Hradl's neck visibly tightened, and it was apparent that he was bracing himself for an oblique critique of what he had been saying about Hans's supposed blindness to his protégé's failings. Leo too leaned forward and tried to nod even more enthusiastically than before at Hans's characterization. But Hans didn't glance at either man and maintained the same friendly but slightly time-pressed air that he had adopted throughout, concerned more to include everyone at the table in his report than to dwell on earlier, and no longer pertinent, areas of friction.

"He is mercenary scum. Utterly unreliable and with no loyalty to any cause larger than himself. That is precisely why he is indispensable to our plan. The man keeps a running tally of everything he lusts for that he has been denied so far, and I am convinced he became an accountant mostly in order to keep the record as up-to-date as possible. What makes all of you find him so odious—his greed and self-absorption—is what keeps him from complete disintegration, no matter how paralyzed with alcohol poisoning he might be. There is something almost transcendent about a focus so blinkered and selfish it makes a man ready to sacrifice everyone around him to gratify it. Before this evening, though, I never suspected how contagious petty individualism like his must be. Because it is obvious that our earlier problems drew inspiration not just from Ernst's example but also from the surreptitious spread of Blumenthalism among us. If we had the time, we could probably write a collective pamphlet about our experience as a warning to others and call it *Against Blumenthalism: The Anti-Party Deviation from Below*.

"Of course Blumenthal has no revolutionary consciousness. When has the petty bourgeoisie ever manifested real solidarity with the working class? On the contrary. They make themselves sick with longing to live like their betters. What the party can do, though, is direct that sickness toward

369

useful ends. These past months I was ordered to spend hours, some of the most painful and tedious hours of my life, listening to Asher's endless catalog of frustrated ambitions so that the party would know how best to motivate him when the right moment came, and doing that has taught me how important even the most personally distasteful assignment can turn out to be."

Hans stopped himself abruptly, less to catch his breath than to make sure that everyone's concentration was as riveted as when he began. Fear is a great focuser of attention, so there was little risk of anyone's interest wandering. But in spite of Hans's confidence that no one would dare question him now, he knew better than to go beyond a certain point in forcing his confederates to acknowledge the extent of his dominance. His father had taught him the long-term benefits of leaving one's junior partners the illusion of being consulted, a tactic all the more valuable because it costs nothing except the self-discipline not to flaunt one's power. According to Moritz, it was surprising how few men could restrain the urge to remind everyone around them of their importance, even when it was in their own interest not to do so. Apparently, Count Wiladowski was one of the rare examples Moritz had come across of a figure of undoubted intelligence whose family had spent the last three and a half centuries helping to administer the Empire yet who was quite willing to be taken for much less than he really was. From his schooldays on, Hans had grown used to hearing the province's Count-Governor dismissed as an affected, insignificant nobleman by everyone who wanted to be regarded as up-to-date. But Hans's experience at his father's side in business meetings had given him good reason to trust Moritz's judgment about people, and he developed a wary respect for a man his father regarded so highly. Almost alone among the group, Hans saw him as an ideal target for assassination. But whether the Count-Governor should be the conspirators' primary target or just one of the possibilities was less important right now than ensuring that everyone felt directly involved in making that determination. So Hans deliberately left the question open, even in his own mind, while he waited for Christoph to steady his nerves sufficiently to intervene in the discussion.

When Christoph finally did so, it was only after he had put his body through a whole ballet of awkward twitches and contortions, choreographed according to some complex inner music only he could hear, and watching him fidget in his seat, Hans wondered, quite without sympathy, what luck one of the new kind of expensive alienist from Vienna might have in treating the affliction. Like the others in the group, Christoph seemed, from now on, to address his words solely to Hans, without ever turning his head to look directly at anyone else, so that although Hans made sure to engage each of them in conversation, they in turn spoke only to him and communicated with one another largely through what they said to Hans. Hans himself had long ago concluded that there was no rational basis for preferring loyalty freely given to a fidelity enforced by self-interest and fear. On the contrary, there was every reason to assume the latter would last longer and prove less fickle, and he was fully prepared to welcome back Christoph and the others so long as they compromised themselves sufficiently along the way. Christoph, who was the cleverest of the group, understood quickest what was demanded of him and surprised even Hans by the alacrity with which he threw himself into his expected role. It was certainly an exemplary performance that Christoph now gave, one that all the others, especially Leo, envied for coming first and that Hans was certain they would try to emulate when their own turn came.

Not only did Christoph denounce Ernst's desertion in the most abusive terms imaginable, but he strongly implied that he had never really been able to trust Ernst and had put up with his masquerade for so long out of a shortsighted loyalty to a former school fellow whom he had known his entire life. The potential usefulness to the cause of the von Alpsbach family ties to the Imperial General Staff had also made a strong impression on Christoph, and he felt only gratitude to Hans for letting them all see that ideological reliability and revolutionary dedication mattered far more than any external attributes. As for the disciplinary squads, well, Christoph felt sure he was speaking for everyone present in wholeheartedly endorsing the idea. The need for strong measures was obvious to anyone who analyzed the objective situation from the correct perspective. Moreover, while it was certainly noble of Hans to expend his own store of accumulated goodwill to shield his former friend from the revolutionary justice to which his antiparty activities had left him vulnerable, Christoph could not help wondering if by doing so, Hans had not fallen into a similar error to that of Christoph himself and let personal feelings cloud his judgment of the bigger issues at stake. While saying this, Christoph stood up on his tiptoes to smile broadly at Hans, so that there could be no mistaking that he meant his observation merely as a shared pleasantry to underline how much the two had in common and certainly not as a serious criticism. But his smile, which normally had a leering, feral quality, looked hopelessly stricken as it contended against the nervous tics that were still coursing, although at slower intervals, along his facial muscles and jaw-bone. While Christoph struggled to bring his features back under control, Hans gave him an approving smile, chuckling with apparent pleasure at his cleverness in implicating both of them in a similar act of weakness. Then he looked around the table to encourage the others to join in and follow Christoph's lead. With trained precision worthy of the Imperial Opera House orchestra a few years earlier, when Mahler was principal conductor, they all began to speak in rapid but strictly hierarchic succession, the order and decibel level of their entrances determined by their family's seniority in the *Almanach de Gotha*, until the tumult of their blended words seemed nearly as loud as their former pounding of the table. Soon the only issue in doubt was whose suspicion of Ernst had been awakened first and who was the most unforgiving in his judgment. On that score they were quite willing to compete with one another, each passionately asserting that his own distrust of Ernst was at least the equal of Christoph's and had never been tempered by schoolboy sentimentalism. Their unanimity was everything for which a skeptical adherent to the rule of collective decision making could have wished since as a gesture of good faith, formally moved by Gerling and immediately seconded by Christoph, who was visibly vexed at not having thought of the motion himself, the whole cell voted to support Hans's plan even before he had explained it. "It is inconceivable for us not to show you our trust from the outset, Hans." So Gerling solemnly declared on everyone's behalf, and since his voice was close to breaking with the intensity of his feelings, it was fortunate that so few words were required to complete his speech.

To Hans, what was striking amid all these avowals of fidelity was how careful everyone had been to avoid mentioning Asher at all, even though—or, rather, so he silently corrected himself, exactly because—it was by associating him with the man's degeneracy that they originally planned to justify their coup. Even his deliberately tantalizing hint about Asher's central role in the conspiracy had not been enough to provoke a single question, as though once they had absorbed the idea of the party's identifying Blumenthalism as a dangerous petty bourgeois deviation, just taking Asher's name into one's mouth had suddenly become too hazardous. But Hans had no intention of letting his name drop, and irrespective of how much he was relying on improvisation in presenting his plan, the one element from which he had no intention of swerving was to stress that Asher would be vital to its success.

Only a few hours earlier it would have been impossible for even the most acute observer to anticipate how carefully attuned all the men in the room could become to Hans's slightest signals. He had barely started pushing his chair away from the table when everyone instantly fell silent and waited for him to start talking again. Unlike the others, though, Hans made no move to get up before speaking. He took a few moments to refill his water glass and then resumed exactly where he had left off, not ignoring what anyone else had said in the interval but treating their words like a necessary but strictly preliminary precondition for his continuing. He talked to them the whole time without getting up from his seat, but although he maintained nearly the same amiable, uninflected manner as before, what he said sounded like a formal speech at a party congress, composed before he had ever agreed to spend the weekend at Hirschwang and not necessarily by Hans alone. He was deliberately speechifying, not just talking, and the way he discarded even the external form of a conversation was more intimidating than any actual menace in his words. There was no more question of a dialogue. He spoke without notes, quoting from memory like someone delivering a set text who knows his listeners will hurry to learn it by heart.

"What we need to keep in mind," Hans told them, "is that the first successful killing will ultimately gather thousands of supporters to our cause. Even if we should somehow fail and our target survive, just the fact that we dared attack an important public official will provoke the authorities to a general repression, which can only mobilize public sympathy for the whole opposition movement. If the repression is severe enough, scores of liberals, including men like our former comrade Ernst who lack the courage for direct action, will come to acknowledge an ethical and a social obligation to provide the armed combatants with their tacit support. Eventually we will be able to shame them into providing shelter, money, proper travel documents, and even their homes to conceal our weapons. If they refuse, that of course will mark them as accomplices of the police, and then they can expect to meet the same fate as any uniformed enemy of the people. A few carefully placed sticks of dynamite in one of those houses, accompanied by a clear public explanation of why such a step was necessary, and I am sure we won't encounter many further refusals. Our immediate goal quite simply must be to provoke, and keep on provoking, the government, no matter the cost, until it lashes out against even the mildest agitation for reform, so that in all the good liberal circles, including university professors, schoolteachers, engineers, journalists, lawyers, and doctors, at least some level of sympathy for our militants becomes required as proof of a 'clean conscience.' From there it is just a question of increasing the pressure until we are in a position to demand active assistance as well. Once someone helps us in any tangible way, no matter how slight, we own that person forever, since just the threat of an anonymous denunciation to the police will be enough to bring him to heel.

"Now it is obvious that if we want our action to have more than local repercussions, bombing the police station in town or shooting a few strikebreakers won't be enough. Probably not even an isolated attack on Wiladowski would ensure the kind of overreaction the party is counting on. That is why it's so perfect that the Interior Ministry has decided to make all this fuss about the Bell Tower anniversary. The authorities in Vienna must be hoping that a little bit of Imperial pageantry will distract people's minds from their misery. A chance like this comes along too rarely for us not to take full advantage of what our enemies have handed us. 'Luck is a residue of design.' You all know the phrase from party conferences; now is the time to make those words reality.

"Most of our families have already received their invitations to the festivities the Castle is organizing, and I will do my best to get extra ones from my father for anyone not on the guest list. Enough important names are coming here from Vienna to attract the attention of the whole Empire to our town. There will be the usual round of balls in the evening, but it is the public ceremonies on Easter Sunday, when all the dignitaries will be packed closely together, that give us our best chance. So far, from what I have seen on the official schedule, the most promising moments are during the speeches planned for noon in the Cathedral Square, where they are already setting up the wooden platform and canopy for the chief participants, and earlier in the day, when the procession through town makes its prearranged 'surprise' stops for an inspection at the army barracks, followed by a short visit to the Mendelssohn Club and the Greek Orthodox church. It is obvious that they have singled out the last two in order to demonstrate our famous Austrian tolerance. I am not sure exactly what kind of ceremony they have in mind at the church, but I know the directors of the Mendelssohn Club have been given permission by the Count-

Governor himself to present a petition respectfully asking for an easing of the Jewish quota at the university. I am sure that if I ask him, my father can arrange for Blumenthal to be part of the delegation, especially since for years now, Blumenthal has told everyone at the club that if it hadn't been for the Jewish quota, he might have had a chance at an academic career.

"Of course Wiladowski will expect a handsome gift for honoring the club with his visit, and the Governing Board will be delighted if I offer to provide one at my own expense. When I say it is to make amends for having missed the party they threw for me, they'll be still more pleased. Now, what I propose to give Wiladowski is an extremely rare seventeenth-century table clock, signed by Margraf, the Imperial clockmaker in Prague. I have managed to track down a dealer in the capital who specializes in pieces like that, and as a noted connoisseur Wiladowski will immediately recognize the value of the present. I am sure he will want to keep it safely in sight as much as possible. As soon as the clock arrives from the antiquarian dealer, I will take it to the club and show it off to everyone, so all can satisfy their curiosity. No doubt they will feel obliged to offer me the honor of presenting the gift myself, but I will suggest that it might look best if one of the humbler petitioners, someone like Asher Blumenthal, is entrusted with actually handing the Count-Governor his memento. It is the kind of idea that will delight the committee members since it will spare them endless wrangling about who would get to do so in my place. Then I will take the clock home with me for safekeeping until the day of the ceremony and use that time to replace part of the mechanism with a powerful bomb set to go off half an hour after Wiladowski is scheduled to receive it. Blumenthal will be overjoyed at being given such an important role in the ceremony and play his part to perfection. The clock itself is too heavy to be placed anywhere except in one of the carriages—given its value, almost certainly Wiladowski's own—and when it goes off, it will take him and everyone nearby with it. There is always a slight risk carrying the bomb from my house to the club, and I will be accompanying Blumenthal all the way, but if everything goes according to plan, we both should be far away when it detonates. If not, well, it is as good a way to die as any, I suppose. But for us to have a chance to succeed, everything depends on the arrival of the expert in explosives whom the party is sending us from Geneva. He goes by the nickname Botho, and I have been told he is a brilliant chemist who has been in charge of more than a dozen successful bombings organized by the party. I have been instructed to work closely with him and make sure he gets all the materials necessary for the job. No one else will be permitted to meet with him or know what he looks like; I am sorry about that, by the way, but the orders were very explicit on that score. I will make sure, though, that everyone stays informed about his progress. In case the plan miscarries, we can still fall back on firing directly at the enemy. Two of you—I would suggest whoever had the best score at target practice today—will take up positions at opposite corners of the Cathedral Square near the front of the crowd, and if the procession makes it that far, you will know the bomb has failed, and it will be up to you to make use of the skill that you showed so impressively on the practice range. At that distance even I would have a chance to get off several successful shots and hit my target before vanishing back into the crowd, and the party certainly expects you to do much better than that, especially after the glowing report I will be sending in about your prowess as marksmen. In the confusion there is a reasonable chance for the shooters to get away cleanly, and if so, there will be false passports and train tickets out of the country waiting for everyone at the Josef Quarter flat. I know that there are a great many specific details that need to be worked out, and I'll be relying on your ingenuity to improve what is still only a rough sketch, but since Easter falls on April twelfth this year, we do not have a great deal of time. So I suggest we clean up the mess on the floor together now to save the servants from doing all the work in the morning, after which we should try to get a few hours' sleep before returning to town separately and setting about our duties. But first, I suppose, I should ask if there are any questions you need to have answered right away and, more important, if anyone here is reluctant to go forward with the plan."

· ◆ ·

Although every room in the enormous villa had its own separate fireplace, each one carefully tended by the staff, whether it was occupied or not, just the heat from Moritz's bedroom was strong enough to penetrate the entire building. Hans normally found the house unbearably stifling and ordered the windows in his suite to be left open at all times, but after Hirschwang, where he had been forced to wear a thick winter sweater even into bed, Hans was grateful for his father's obsession with keeping warm. He rushed upstairs, past his father's bedroom door, relieved by the absence of any noise from there, which could only mean that Moritz was resting and hence unlikely to call his son in to ask where he had been lately. As soon as he closed the door of his own room securely behind him, Hans threw himself, fully dressed, on top of his bed, too weary to ask the servants to run a bath for him, although he had been looking forward to one the entire ride back into town. Now that the actual tension was over, all the accumulated fatigue and nervous energy of the weekend that he had kept in check at Hirschwang without any apparent strain came flooding back. He had never felt so drained of energy and was sure that he would fall asleep for at least a dozen hours the moment his head touched the pillow. Instead he just lay there for what seemed an endless stretch of hours, too exhausted to fall asleep and too agitated to let his mind drift off to a relaxing topic. Ever since he could remember, Hans had been able to stay almost preternaturally calm in the midst of a crisis, no matter how threatening the situation or how long it took to resolve, but once the problem was safely behind him, his whole system often collapsed under the weight of deferred pressure. Now that he was alone, rather than admire his performance with the other conspirators, Hans found that the futility of the whole bizarre exercise kept running through his mind. It had all gone so much more easily than he could have imagined beforehand, but why had he pushed things so far? He had kept the group together in spite of Ernst's desertion and greatly strengthened his dominance over it, in spite of Christoph's and Leo's ambition to replace him. But to what purpose? Outside of proving to himself that he could do so, Hans found it difficult to see that his triumph had gained him anything, except the pressure to stay in character from now on, like a young actor whose early success in a certain role condemns him to play variations on that part for the rest of his career.

Only slowly, as he was lying there, endlessly replaying the dining-room scene in his mind, did Hans let himself spin out some of the likely consequences of what he had set in motion. That he was doing so only now was one of the irritating differences between himself and his father, whose tactics Hans had instinctively adopted to orchestrate his victory at Hirschwang. Moritz Rotenburg had shown Hans how to change the whole dynamics of a negotiation just when your opponents think they have you in their power, and Hans had been amazed at how easily he could adopt his father's techniques to the plot against him at Hirschwang. No wonder Christoph, Leo, and the others were so easily routed; they never had a chance against the ruthless willpower and concentration Moritz had bequeathed to Hans, more by example than by formal instruction. It came down to one's intuition about what would make the other side buckle and the imaginative capacity to make that scenario plausible and vivid to them. Although most of the famous writers his teachers and friends held up for admiration seemed to have only contempt for businessmen (if they represented them in their works at all), Hans was far from convinced that the difference between a man like his father and a serious novelist was nearly so absolute. Perhaps too it was always more their intellectual readers than the authors themselves who felt only scorn for great financial minds. Hans had watched his father make men of considerable will and self-confidence see exactly and only what he wanted them to see and take as absolutely real the imaginary scenarios in which he needed them to believe, in each case using just his own words to do so. It is true that these words were never written down and that their intended audience was always merely a few other men from the same world as Moritz, but the imaginative force required struck Hans as similar to the kind of power a strong writer could exercise over someone like Batya. On the whole, Hans himself did not much care for either writers or businessmen and was perfectly ready to despise both, but he saw no reason to denigrate one at the expense of the other. In a more rational future, Hans was certain, both would occupy a far lower place in the social hierarchy than they did at present, but he had to admit that he was grateful for how much he had learned from Moritz about ensnaring one's antagonists.

The problem, though, was that for Moritz, "novelizing" was a tactic strictly subordinated to a general strategy, whereas Hans had to admit that he badly lacked an overall plan. His tactics had become ends in themselves, and that was always an error. He had felt himself under threat and responded with the most effective weapons at his disposal, but in doing so, he had let himself be caught up in the excitement of the part he was inventing without including any exit lines. It was a mistake his father would never have made, and it smacked all too much of a certain bent toward the theatricality that Hans despised in himself. Everything about the episode at Hirschwang now stank to him of the second-rate and derivative. He had no wish to go to prison or, really, to see the others jeopardize themselves for a plan whose chances of accomplishing anything positive were so remote. Even his best stroke, the invention of the punitive disciplinary squads with which he had so thoroughly intimidated everyone, he owed to one of Batya's absurdly overwritten books from which she had once read aloud to him as he was falling asleep. Until the instant that trying out the idea to see its effect had suddenly sprung into his mind, Hans was unaware that he had taken in the episode at all, and even now he could not recall the name of the book from which Batya had been reading. But that was how ideas usually came to him, in fragments from the most diverse origins, linked by nothing except his need for them at that moment. He rarely managed to find a genuine inner necessity among them or to create a new one himself beyond their short-term purpose. So far his gift for brilliant improvisation, and his last name, had gotten him whatever he wanted, but without satisfying his need for confirmation that he was anything more than a talented mediocrity. Years ago, after passing his exams with the highest score the school had ever awarded, he had asked one of the younger teachers, Herr Portatius, whether his work had showed any signs of genius, explaining that if it was certain that he could never be one, he was prepared to go home and blow his brains out that very afternoon. In the friendliest way possible, the man had just laughed out loud at him, and rightly so. But Hans never forgot what followed. For a high school teacher, Portatius came from a relatively well-off family, with connections among the Empire's permanent administrative class. He was a prominent figure in local liberal circles who prided himself on despising vulgarities like the anti-Semitism of the radical parties. After he had stopped laughing, Portatius invited Hans into his office and, as a sign of special favor, as well as to show his disdain for conventions, made as though he were offering Hans one of his own cigarettes, although smoking by a student within a block of the building was strictly against school rules. Hans knew enough to decline the invitation, while making clear how much he valued the gesture. Portatius looked over his desk at Hans with genuine affection and assured him that he was unquestionably a shrewd boy and, like his father, would someday be a great success in business, but that of course it was simply self-deluding for him, as a Jew and the son of a businessman, to aim at anything higher. Except in the religious sphere, true creativity was not something Jews possessed, not because of any moral failing but because their basic nature was to be expositors and analysts of other people's ideas. Even their noblest invention, the God of the Old Testament, had largely been taken over and refashioned from Egyptian sources. They were too rational and analytic a race to be deeply creative, and although they often understood the original, but confused, ideas of a true genius better than that person understood them himself, the Jews' contribution was essentially limited to clarifying and building on the intuitions of simpler, more direct natures. "Your people excel as musicians and conductors, but not as composers, and though I admire many of the Israelite reviewers in our leading papers, you will have to agree that so far there has not been a single Jewish creative writer of the first rank in our German language." Hans rushed out of the room in a rage, as much for having left himself vulnerable to such poisonous nonsense by begging for approval as with the teacher, to whom he never addressed another word. Worse than his brief humiliation, though, was that he never entirely purged his mind of what Portatius had said, and sometimes, when he felt especially disgusted with himself for some failing, the man's theories returned to haunt him.

Hans never told his father what had happened, but for the next few months he watched Moritz more closely than before and, for the first time, began to listen with full attention to his explanations about the financial projects in which he was engaged. He even began to ask his father detailed questions about how he ran his affairs, all in an attempt to find out how much of Moritz's success was due to a gift for dispassionate analysis and how much to an inspired grasp of the deep principles governing international economic trends. Moritz was delighted at his son's newfound interest in the family business and not only answered Hans's questions with the seriousness that, as he put it jokingly, the heir to the Rotenburg fortune deserved, but began to invite Hans along to any meetings at which his presence would be acceptable to the other parties. Even as his politics grew increasingly radical, Hans never stopped attending most of the firm's major negotiations, and for all their differences and the frequent outbursts of mutual impatience and friction, Moritz developed a genuine respect for his son's acumen and was certain that if Hans were ever inclined to run the company after his father's death, he would do a better job than anyone else available for the task. For his part, though, Hans had no desire in that direction. All that really fascinated him, as he learned to understand the way his father constructed a complex new venture, was not the gain or loss that would result, but rather Moritz's absolute lack of self-doubt, either while he was still weighing his options before an important decision or after he had settled on a course of action. Hans saw no sign in his father of the endless self-cross-examination on which he himself wasted so many wearying hours. Moritz's assurance, unlike his son's, did not appear to fluctuate wildly with the outcome of every fresh undertaking, nor, at least since Dina's death, could it be shaken by what anyone else thought of him. Moritz's inner detachment from his public existence and even, as far as Hans could judge, from his private self was a trait his son both admired and envied but, most of all, saw as bafflingly alien. In one of their many quarrels about Hans's indifference to Judaism, the boy yelled out that *he*, not his father, whose character exhibited not a single authentic Jewish trait, was the real Jew. Moritz might subsidize half a dozen rabbinical schools and subscribe to all the Jewish charitable organizations and fund drives, but Hans saw, as no one else had, that none of this actually touched his father. What, if anything, did, Hans was unable to guess. He could only be sure that within himself Moritz identified with no one, least of all with an entire people, although he was perfectly ready to do everything he could for their benefit. But as he admitted to himself, Hans was really not so different. He felt the same way about the political causes on whose behalf he had just pledged himself to commit murder and quite possibly throw away his own life in the process. He genuinely detested the mendacity and corruption he saw everywhere but often felt himself estranged from the very politics in whose name he was ready to die. Only if Hans was right about his father's distance from his own acts, why did that not leave Moritz as restlessly self-divided as it did Hans? Like a gambler who throws more and more chips on the table, not because he cares about winning or losing but because he is afraid of how little the results really matter to him and hopes to revive a flagging interest in a game that has started to bore him, Hans could think of no way to jolt himself into feeling he was doing something important except to intensify the risk. The planned assassination was his way of staking everything on red, without much regard to the revolutionary theory he had made up to carry the others along with him. His position as Moritz Rotenburg's heir provided him with an automatic immunity from most of life's problems. It is difficult to get any satisfaction out of burning one's bridges when one's father can so easily build new ones. So when Asher, in one of his drunken rants, accused him of being only a poseur and dilettante, the reproach was mild compared with the charges Hans had been leveling at himself for years. Over time he had gradually come to believe that only a violent political crime like murder, especially against a Habsburg official, could not be washed away by his father's money. That the other human beings involved, including the targets of the attempted murder and whomever else

Hans snared into committing the killings along with him, might not place quite so high a value on confirming Hans's authenticity never seriously crossed his mind. Until the scene at Hirschwang, though, these feelings had stayed largely inchoate, and now that he had committed himself, almost by accident, to a specific plan, Hans realized how little it satisfied him.

At Hirschwang, Hans had found himself drawn so deeply into the story he was creating that he had committed the cardinal mistake of providing far too many specific details to retain the freedom he needed. Like a novelist who permits the publication of his opening chapters before completing the whole work and who, from then on, is constrained by character and plot choices he would have liked the option of entirely revising, Hans had built up a sufficiently thick description to be believable by the other conspirators, but at the cost of having to proceed along lines that could only be increasingly burdensome. He should have stopped with the threat of the disciplinary units. Their specter had been more than sufficient to scare the conspirators into giving up any challenge to his leadership. More impressively, it also seemed to have paralyzed their capacity for judgment and left them eager to believe in any invention he conjured up. Nothing else could explain their readiness to accept the reality of a figure like "Botho," who struck Hans, even while he was building his legend, as dangerously implausible. But now their belief had lent Botho a reality that was potentially ruinous for Hans, who knew next to nothing about bombs and had no way of designing anything like the device he described. Obviously none of the others did either, or they might have felt emboldened enough to question him, but it was clear that the mysterious Botho would have to meet with a fatal accident before completing his task. At least, so Hans grimly thought, staring out the open window at the early-spring buds emerging on the trees in his father's garden, he now knew the name of the first man he would ever liquidate, but it was decidedly odd that it should be a figure he had conjured into life just over a dozen hours ago. Well, perhaps he would think of a way to turn Botho's death to his own advantage. According to the mining books he had consulted these past weeks, the options of constructing a normal explosive device seemed fairly limited. Unless one used nitroglycerine, most of the explosives appeared to be relatively benign in their quiescent state and not excessively dangerous to transport. A particularly phlegmatic Swiss engineer assured his readers that one could jump up and down on a stick of dynamite without setting it off and that what he called a classic bomb, made up of six sticks of dynamite wired to a clock, would be safe to carry anywhere one wished—as long, of course, as the clock in question was of reliable Swiss make. Although he only realized the connection in retrospect, no doubt Hans's memory of that sentence was why he had Botho sent to them from Geneva in the first place. Still, the warning about nitroglycerine was worth bearing in mind when it came time to dispose of the imaginary Botho. Feeling more content with himself as his built-up nervousness gradually gave way to an agreeable fatigue, Hans decided that maybe the whole distinction between strategy and tactics was overrated. He was beginning to see a strategy emerge out of all his immediate, local decisions, not because he had started with a single overview in mind to which each individual detail was rigorously subordinated but because all his individual choices came together to produce just as coherent a result as if he had begun with a unified aim. Undoubtedly, as in any evolving project, numerous rough patches still remained—on that score he had been entirely forthright in confessing as much to the others last night—but the unresolved elements did not seem sufficient to jeopardize the whole undertaking. The conspiracy was safe, for the moment, from being derailed either by internal tensions or by the authorities. Even if the Count-Governor's famous spymaster was as relentless as everyone said, he would be too late to stop them. Now that they had fixed a date for their action, he would have to get rid of any incriminating evidence still at the Josef Quarter flat, but even if the apartment should be compromised, the danger was slight since it was unlikely that his code could be broken by the limited resources available to the police for such a task. Hans had been assured by one of the firm's employees in Vienna, who had invented the cipher for business secrets, that only a first-rate mathematician could break it. It suddenly occurred to Hans that there was still one crucial thing left to do before he could feel that he really had settled all his old scores this weekend. Tomorrow he would go back to the flat and make sure that he created at least a few documents clearly implicating Ernst as one of the co-leaders of the conspiracy. They would be left behind there with some of the other files intended to confuse the police about the dates; whether the authorities ever found them or not would be out of Hans's hands. That way, rather than take his revenge directly, he would leave it up to fate to determine if Ernst would be permitted to extricate himself and spend the rest of his life peacefully in Brunnenberg, with or without Batya. It was like making a final wager, only with Ernst's future as the stake. Hans felt extraordinarily comforted by the idea and finally drifted off to sleep, not thinking about the other conspirators any longer or about any plans for the future more complicated than the wonderful hot bath that he would step into the first thing upon awakening.

5

Somewhat to his surprise, Wiladowski had started sleeping more soundly ever since his triumph over Lieutenant von Sulzbach at billiards. He awoke early most mornings, refreshed and in a cheerful mood after only six hours in bed. As he sat sipping his first strong coffee of the day, watching his barber heat the soft towels he would use in shaving him, Wiladowski was quietly pleased with himself, remembering how completely he had routed an opponent thirty years his junior. In principle he was ready to concede that there was no connection between an easy victory in the billiard room and a prolonged run of good fortune in other domains, but it was an axiom in which he did not fully believe. Because his emotional range had narrowed until his immediate well-being was the only subject he was still able to take seriously, the Count-Governor's mind had become all self-generated turbulence and ennui. As a result, he had begun to regard everything happening to him as symbolically linked. He had turned into a believer in portents and omens, but only when these directly concerned him. The moment the story was about someone else, he dismissed any suggestion of hidden connections as unworthy of an adult intelligence.

His customary morning shave was one of the Count-Governor's favorite rituals. No one was permitted to interrupt it, and so it was not until the rest of the Castle was already buzzing with the news that it became possible to inform him that a brutally dismembered body had been found a few hours earlier near the Nepomuk Bridge. A servant girl, on her way to work, had stumbled across a headless trunk, naked, with its ribs smashed in, and all its extremities grotesquely mutilated. Just before she fainted, the girl's screams had roused the whole neighborhood, and when the local police rushed to the scene, they made such a mess of the initial investigation that Tausk's men were not optimistic about solving the case quickly.

For the moment there was no way to identify the corpse. So many people vanished these days, either out of despair or just to escape their debts, that most of the missing were never listed with the authorities. When the body was finally brought to the Castle for an autopsy, all that the medical examiner was able to say with certainty was that the victim was a middle-aged male, between forty and forty-five years old, and that he had been dead for less than sixteen hours. In all likelihood, the head had been severed with a heavy ax, but it was impossible to determine how many of the multiple injuries inflicted on the trunk, notably, the complete severing of the genitals, had preceded the poor fellow's death.

Tausk was struck by how calmly his master seemed to take the news. The Count-Governor betrayed no emotion except alert curiosity. He asked for a complete written report of everything known so far and to be informed immediately of any further developments. "Under the circumstances," he told his spymaster with deliberate politeness, "you have my permission to interrupt me, even when the barber is in attendance." When Tausk started to apologize for not having come in with the news right away, Wiladowski shook his head and, with a faint a smile, said, "Oh, no, not at all. This way I have had one more peaceful morning, and since there may not be many more for a while, I am grateful for it. Besides, there is nothing I could have done had I known an hour or two sooner, and the dead, I am afraid, have nothing if not patience and time." With that, he turned around and went back into his private salon adjoining the library to be alone until the preliminary report should be ready.

As soon as the door had closed behind him, and he was certain the armed sentries had taken up their posts again, Wiladowski went over to the window and drew the double curtains firmly shut. He turned on only one small amber-hooded lamp on the side table next to his favorite chair, so that the room was largely in shadow except for a single arc of softly diffused light. It was the first time for many years that he had performed such tasks himself, but right now he wanted no one, not even Aloïs, in the room with him. He resisted the urge to pour himself a brandy, thinking he could keep the panic already lodged within him at bay more successfully by ignoring it entirely. It was not the fact of another murder that alarmed him. The weekly police reports had accustomed him to a regular quota of killings, but even out here this degree of savagery was remarkable. No matter how he tried, Wiladowski was unable to stop himself from visualizing the mutilated corpse, except that in his imagination the missing head belonged to his cousin Max, whose body had also been mangled in similar ways. It was clear the murderers intended the corpse to be discovered; otherwise they would not have left it in so crowded a part of town. That fact, along with the violation of the dead man's body, told Wiladowski that the killers meant not just to butcher the victim himself but also to frighten others. But to what purpose? The walls of Max's vacation lodge, where he had been gutted like one of the deer he had gone there to hunt, had been covered with strange apocalyptic scribbling, but no one was ever able to offer a coherent interpretation of what it signified. So far nothing similar had turned up near the bridge, but Wiladowski nonetheless felt the two murders were connected. Almost like a young girl pulling apart the petals of a flower to discover whether or not she is loved, the Count-Governor slumped forward in his chair, his eyes fixed on his lap, calibrating on his fingertips the likelihood of his own survival. Everything depended on the still-undetermined identity of the corpse in the prison morgue several floors below. He decided that if the dead man turned out to be from the provincial nobility, the killers' political intentions would be as clear as if a note had been pinned to the victim's chest, and it would be a foregone conclusion that an attempt against his own life was imminent. But if the body were only that of a smuggler who had tried unsuccessfully to defraud his accomplices or of a lover caught in some adulterous affair, then there would be a good chance he himself was not in immediate danger. But unlike the flower game, which always yields a result, if not necessarily a satisfying one, Wiladowski's speculations quickly branched out in too many inconclusive directions. The dead man might just as well have been a union militant assassinated in a power struggle between rival factions or one of the religious fanatics who seemed to worry Tausk so much. But how could Wiladowski work out which possibility represented a greater threat? His official duties had brought the Count-Governor to numerous funerals, where he had been expected to speak to the mourners on behalf of the provincial administration, and it was an obligation he prided himself on fulfilling with just the right note of sympathetic gravitas. A respectful tone on such occasions came naturally to Wiladowski, whose deference for the bleak finality of death was based on the unpleasant thought that it was also bound to happen to him someday. But at the moment, the absence of any audience made him burst out in a harsh laugh, lift his hands from his lap, and exclaim, "It is damned hard to come to any conclusions when you are dealing with a man who shows up virtually at your doorstep without a head or a penis!"

Wiladowski did not realize how loudly he had voiced his thought until he glanced up and saw the astonished expression on Tausk's face as he came into the room, carrying the report Wiladowski had ordered. It was one of the few times the Count-Governor had ever seen Tausk visibly embarrassed, and the spymaster's attempt to look discreetly away only heightened Wiladowski's own momentary discomposure. But both men quickly recovered themselves, and when Tausk handed the dossier to his master, he did so with a visible air of relief. "I assume you have not yet succeeded in catching the killers," Wiladowski said testily, "and I find it hard to imagine what other news could make you look so cheerful." Before replying, the spymaster asked if he might turn on a few more lights and, as he always did, requested permission to smoke during their conversation. Wiladowski nodded his agreement without really listening, and Tausk immediately lit the cigarette that he was already holding between his fingers. Then he jabbed his cigarette nervously toward the concluding paragraphs of the dossier. "If Your Excellency will kindly glance down here"—Tausk spoke even more rapidly than usual—"you will see that we have been lucky enough to find the—how shall I put it?—missing parts of our victim. That did not really surprise me, since I was confident the rest of the body would turn up not too far from where the trunk had been tossed. If we had reached the site first and not had to work around the town police, I am sure we would have located the other remains much more quickly. But a short while ago we did have a stroke of real luck. When one of my men saw a drawing of the face, he thought he could identify the dead man, and I am only waiting for confirmation from the family to remove any doubt."

"And how does all this help me?" Wiladowski demanded. Rapid headway with the case was certainly welcome, but the Count-Governor had no intention of applauding any breakthrough before his own safety was categorically assured. But at least now that Tausk was with him, fouling the air with his cheap tobacco, there seemed no more reason for Wiladowski to deny himself his own pleasures, and he got up to light a cigar and pour himself a large brandy. The gratification that came from no longer resisting his craving also made Wiladowski less critical of Tausk's satisfaction with how the case was progressing. "So, in the past four hours our unfortunate body has regained both a head and a name," the Count-Governor commented, sounding in better spirits as he continued leafing through the report, his disquiet evident only in the way he kept turning over the pages without actually reading any of them. "And I suppose the other missing appendages have turned up as well?" he asked Tausk, coming closer to their usual shared tone. But when Tausk looked as though he were about to answer, Wiladowski waved him off, saying, "You can spare me the physical details, unless they are crucial to your investigation. I am glad that things appear to be moving forward, but all that really matters is to make sure there are no more such incidents."

Tausk's forehead was sticky with sweat as he leaned toward the Count-Governor. "Unfortunately, I am not sure there is any way to guarantee there won't be more killings." He spoke with uncharacteristic directness. "But knowing what we now do about the victim may help us to predict what the murderers will attempt next. That is why I think Your Excellency needs to be kept informed about the forensic evidence, as we piece it together, even if some of it is distasteful. As it happens, our first clue to the corpse's identity came when we found his severed genitals wrapped in an old handkerchief still sticky with blood and thrown into the bushes a few yards from the body."

"Tausk is enjoying himself telling me all this," Wiladowski thought. "Heaven knows, he has the temperament for it." But the Count-Governor was too concerned with what Tausk had discovered to care much about how the information was presented to him and steeled himself to let Tausk spin out as many grisly details as he wanted without showing any further signs of repugnance. "Yes, you already implied that you found all the severed parts," he said in a matter-of-fact tone. "But why is that important, except to his family, who, no doubt, would prefer to get him back complete? Is there anything especially noteworthy about the man's organ?"

"Only that he has been circumcised, Your Excellency."

The Count-Governor looked unimpressed. "But knowing the victim was a Jew hardly tells us much about him—especially not in this province."

"Not by itself, Your Excellency," Tausk immediately agreed, "but at least we are safe from dealing with any accusations of a ritual murder."

"Is *that* what worried you?" Wiladowski was beginning to understand Tausk's relief. Of course in times like these if the victim had turned out to be a Christian, it was impossible to discount the likelihood that some fanatics would start a rumor the Jews had killed him as part of their Passover celebration. In recent years the Crown Lands had seen an upsurge of such accusations, and once the denunciations began, it was hard to put a stop to them without a full-scale investigation. Tausk must have been extraordinarily nervous at the prospect of finding himself caught up in an affair that could easily turn bloody and in which his own position as a Jew working for the government might become untenable. Wiladowski, who considered the spreading of rumors the exclusive prerogative of the government, both despised and feared any outbreaks of mob rage. He had witnessed several such eruptions during his career—not always aimed at Jews either—and the participants always reminded him of rats emerging out of a drainpipe to vent their fury on whoever seemed most vulnerable. He had no wish either to see his resources depleted protecting the province's Jews or to lessen his authority by requesting special military assistance from Vienna, so his expressions of empathy for Tausk were entirely unfeigned. It was perhaps odd that he should congratulate his Jewish spymaster that the murder victim had been one of Tausk's own people, but there was no doubt it was the best possible outcome for everyone. Guessing that even the least parochial Jew was likely to be rather sensitive on the subject of ritual murder, Wiladowski took care to explain to Tausk his contempt for anyone who could take such legends seriously, and since he could not think of any other way to show his benevolence, he poured a glass of brandy for his spymaster at the same time as he refilled his own. "I propose a toast to a speedy resolution of this whole wretched business," he said, indicating to a thoroughly startled Tausk that he should pick up the second glass now sitting on the side table.

Except for the men he himself had hired, Tausk knew less about Castle decorum than anyone else in Wiladowski's service, but even he realized what an extraordinary sign of favor the Count-Governor was showing him. The last time Tausk had touched alcohol was when Moritz Rotenburg had poured him a brandy, and here he was, being offered the identical drink by Count Wiladowski. "In all likelihood," Tausk reflected, "Rotenburg paid for this bottle just as much as for the one in his own study." The fact that Tausk derived no pleasure from anything except coffee and often got a headache just from smelling alcohol fumes was impossible for these powerful men to imagine, and both took for granted that their underlings must be delighted to sample whatever they themselves enjoyed. But at least Tausk knew better than to let his distaste show, and he drained his glass in a single gulp with what he hoped was the proper expression of appreciation at his good fortune.

It took a few minutes for his stomach to settle itself, during which time Tausk lit a fresh cigarette and carefully placed two further sheets of paper containing a series of charcoal drawings of the dead man's head and body on top of the report. He drew the Count-Governor's attention to the sketches and explained that the medical examiner prided himself on his skill as a draftsman. Tausk said that he himself found the images repellent but felt duty-bound to bring them to his master. The victim's head had been crudely severed at the clavicle and then wrapped in a separate parcel made of thick packing paper and roughly stitched shut. It had taken so long to find because the twine sealing the package had come undone, and the head had rolled out into the dirt near the water's edge. In the brief time the skull was lying in the dirt, the skin from the face already had begun to peel away as various insects had gone to work gnawing at it. But enough remained from the clump of half-eaten skin and tissue for the doctor to produce his impressions—Tausk lifted the page so that Wiladowski was looking at the drawings on a level with his own eyes—both of the way the head looked when it had been found and a reconstruction of the man's face while he was still alive. It was from the doctor's sketch that one of Tausk's assistants recognized a certain Shmuel Kosch, who had come in over a month ago to complain about having been harassed by followers of the new wonder rebbe. It seemed that this Kosch was an ardent disciple of a rival holy man who held court in Buczacz and specialized in healing epileptics. When Kosch heard people praising Brugger above his own rebbe, he became incensed and went to confront the upstart. By his own admission, he interrupted one of Brugger's sermons and challenged him to match the Buczacz rabbi's miraculous powers, only to be thrown out of the room and beaten up for his impertinence. He immediately came to the police to complain, but since he had provoked the assault himself and the case seemed to have no political significance, Tausk's man had taken down Kosch's statement with a promise to look into the matter and then dismissed it from his mind. The report had been properly filed, of course, and Tausk located it straightaway; but it contained little more than Kosch's name and address and a brief description of his allegations. There were no witnesses to the beating, and Kosch was unable to name any of his assailants. He claimed to have been attacked by a gang of at least five of Brugger's disciples, armed with heavy cudgels, including, to his great horror and disgust, a female, who was easily the most vicious of the lot. After having been thrashed severely enough to require several stitches, he was warned never to show his face near the prayerhouse again. "To judge by the results," Tausk said sardonically, with his eyes on the doctor's drawings, "I should say poor Shmuel made a mistake ignoring the advice."

Wiladowski followed Tausk's gaze, but to him, the death's-head looked curiously like the crude drawings of martyred saints that he had seen in village churches throughout Austria. If he could just stop thinking about Cousin Max, the Count-Governor told himself, he might be able to find Tausk's news more reassuring. As long as these religious zealots limited their violence to one another, the matter was of no great concern to him. But Max had never believed in anything except hunting and horseback riding, yet whoever had broken into his lodge and cut him up had been inspired to do so as part of some holy mission. "What do you think, Tausk?" Wiladowski asked, pushing aside the whole pile of papers, including the doctor's sketches, in exasperation. "Was the man killed because he insulted the rabbi, or did that have nothing to do with it?" Without waiting for an answer, Wiladowski walked over to the window and opened the curtains, but after a few minutes standing there, looking out along the embankment road where Tausk and Roublev had taken their recent walk, he abruptly turned around and pulled them shut again. Tausk had been careful not to speak while his master was lost in his thoughts, grateful for the obligation to stay respectfully silent. Waving around those sketches had been stupid, and he felt lucky that the Count-Governor was too preoccupied to have taken offense. Tausk himself was riveted by the drawings, not only for what they showed about how far Brugger's followers were willing to go—if they were indeed the killers—but also for how much one could learn even from mutilated fragments of a body. The autopsy may have been unable to determine how many of the wounds had been inflicted postmortem, but the doctor's sketches of the face revealed a grimace of pain unlike any Tausk had ever seen. To have learned how much a man could be made to endure before dying was something Tausk would never forget, and he determined to keep the drawings close to him the way an expert geometer sometimes keeps his first copy of Euclid by his bedside, long after he has outgrown the need to look up any of its propositions. Still, it had been idiotic to think his employer would share what Tausk belatedly recognized were strictly technical interests.

Before Wiladowski could return to his question, Tausk was summoned back downstairs, where Kosch's family had arrived at last and were waiting to identify the body. Tausk had left strict orders that he wanted to be the first to talk to them, and he asked the Count-Governor's permission to come back and conclude their conversation after he had finished with the victim's relatives. When Tausk got there, Roublev was already waiting for him at the entrance to the morgue, and he explained that everyone who could claim a connection with Kosch had insisted on accompanying the police back to the Castle. Fortunately, Roublev had been on duty when a small wagonful of mourners had spilled through the gates, wailing hysterically and disturbing everyone in the courtyard. Through a combination of threats and entreaties, Roublev had managed to take them inside and isolate them in a separate room until Tausk could decide how to proceed. Until a few hours ago the family had assumed that Kosch was gone on one of his regular business trips, traveling around the province to peddle enamel household wares brought in from Germany. The visitors had not stopped weeping since being summoned by the police, but Tausk's sinister reputation and his coldly impatient tone with them quieted them almost immediately. He permitted only Kosch's wife, his twenty-five-year-old son, and a younger brother, who lived with them, to see the corpse. All the rest he ordered sent home as soon as they had provided a detailed account of everything they knew about Kosch's dealings with the Buczacz rabbi and Brugger. Tausk himself followed the three closest relatives into the morgue and watched their faces intently as Kosch's body was uncovered. The recognition was immediate and horrifying. A series of deep, but almost inaudible sobs, as though they suddenly lacked enough breath to scream, filled the room and removed the last possibility that the doctor's sketch had led to a misidentification. Kosch's wife lost consciousness before the sheet had been pulled down more than a few centimeters, and only the medical orderly's quick reflexes saved her from falling to the floor. Afterward Tausk stayed with the family for a few more minutes, but once he was certain that they had no additional information that might help him, he left them with the doctor and called Roublev over to accompany him back to his room.

Tausk knew that he had only a little time before having to return to the Count-Governor. Wiladowski wanted to be reassured that there would be no more such killings, but so far there was no way to determine whether the initial assault on Kosch was an isolated phenomenon or signaled the start of some larger turn toward violence by the wonder rebbe's followers. Talking to Kosch's family had only confused the issue. Although they all knew about the thrashing, and his wife, especially, had urged him to report it to the police, Kosch had never mentioned anything about wanting to confront Brugger again. Perhaps, along with peddling his enamel dishes and saucepans, Kosch trafficked in more lucrative, illegal materials and had been killed as a result. But although Tausk recognized the possibility, he did not believe it. Somehow, Brugger must be connected to the murder. No one knew better than Tausk how absolute the sway of such a man over his disciples could be. If Avraham Pelz had ordered his students to go out into the world and cut the throat of everyone they met on the road, man, woman, or child, the best of them would have obeyed him immediately, certain that they could not be committing a sin if Pelz had commanded it. Brugger's hold over his followers came close to matching Rabbi Pelz's, and that much control in another's hands, divorced from any prudential restraint, represented an intolerable threat. Tausk had already lost everything once because of a rabbi's unwavering moral rectitude. He was not prepared to let another rabbi's demonic criminality destroy the shelter he had built for himself out of the wreckage of his former life.

Tausk was so used to Roublev's presence that although physical familiarity of any kind repelled him, he had no hesitation in stripping off his sweat-soaked shirt and soaking his face and arms with cold water the moment they were back in his room. Then, while he put on fresh clothes, he sent Roublev to bring him some hot coffee and assemble every scrap of information they had about Brugger. Roublev hurried back with everything Tausk had asked for, and the two men sat side by side at the rough army table, looking over the files and extracting the most damaging details. There was not enough time for Tausk to rehearse what he would actually say to the Count-Governor, but in the private shorthand he and Roublev had developed for interrogating prisoners, Tausk was able to try out at least the core of his argument. Everything now depended on Wiladowski, and Tausk returned to the library upstairs profoundly uneasy about the mood in which he would find the Count-Governor.

When Tausk came into the room, he saw Aloïs clearing away a tray with the remains of a small meal. Although the windows were still tightly shut, the heavy curtains had been drawn aside, and Wiladowski was at his desk going through the morning's dispatches. Except for the half-empty bottle of cognac on the side table and the doubling of the guards in the hallway and on the staircase, it might almost have been a normal day. Tausk waited until Aloïs had finished his duties and closed the door behind him before presenting himself to Wiladowski to resume their conversation. Wiladowski noticed that Tausk had changed clothes and assumed the spymaster had done so out of courtesy to the victim's family. He asked how the identification of the body had gone, and Tausk quickly told his master everything that had happened downstairs. But to the question of whether the murderers posed a threat to Wiladowski himself, Tausk admitted that he still lacked enough information to predict their next move. "I am afraid that only the discovery of additional bodies would establish their intentions unambiguously," he said, "but in case they do decide to kill again, we cannot risk assuming they will always choose their victims from among their own."

"So are you suggesting that we need to strike first?" Wiladowski was irritated by Tausk's indirection. He wanted immediate action, applied with a firm hand. He remembered with sympathy Prince Schwarzenberg's fine phrase when urged to show mercy to some Hungarian rebels. "Yes, that is an excellent idea," the Prince was supposed to have replied, "but we will have a little hanging first." Well, Schwarzenberg had survived long enough to see his statue put up in every town throughout the Empire, and although Wiladowski had no such ambition, the sketch of Shmuel Kosch's severed head made a little hanging seem like a reasonable strategy.

When the Count-Governor told Tausk the story, the spymaster barely managed a pinched half smile. "I have no doubt that such a solution has much to recommend it," he told his master, "but if I may speak freely, it is unfortunately not all that helpful. The Hungarians had the thoughtfulness to identify themselves as open rebels, so the Prince knew exactly whom to hang. We do not have the same good fortune, and since the province is not under martial law, we have to go through the tedious formalities of arrests and public trials before we can get to the entertaining part of the whole process. I am confident that within twenty-four hours, I could extract a confession out of anyone I have locked up in our cells, but right now there are simply no legal grounds for moving against the suspects."

The Count-Governor had never known Tausk to be concerned with the legality of an important measure, and from his tone, he suspected that the spymaster was already working out a scheme to get around the problem. Tausk was walking around the room completely absorbed in his machinations, with a look of concentration that reminded Wiladowski of the way a skilled player at billiards circles the table lining up his next shot. "Whatever Brugger may have ordered," Tausk said carefully, "I am certain he was nowhere near Kosch when the murder took place. A man like Brugger whispers suggestions; he gives commands. But he does not bloody his own hands." Tausk spoke these last words lightly, with a quick look toward Wiladowski, who returned his gaze with a slight nod of acknowledgment. The spymaster paused a moment before going on. "If we arrested the rebbe, I have no doubt he would produce an unshakable alibi, and we would be forced to release him immediately. Any one of his disciples would gladly go to the scaffold in his place, and although I expect we will get around to hanging several of them before too long, right now we have no effective way to render Brugger himself harmless."

"Are you quite certain that he really is responsible for the murder?" Wiladowski asked. He deliberately sounded unconvinced, not because he doubted Tausk, but as a way of forcing the spymaster to reveal more of his thinking.

"No, Your Excellency," Tausk admitted. "We are dealing with probabilities here, not certainties. I cannot prove Brugger was responsible for Kosch's death, any more than I have been able to link him to the murder of your cousin in Bukovina. But the circumstances strongly point to such a connection, just as they suggest there will be more such killings. And with the Cathedral ceremony coming up so soon, doing nothing until every doubt has been laid to rest could prove catastrophic."

At the mention of the Easter festivities, Wiladowski's eyes fell on the invitations still awaiting his signature. He saw himself sitting on a platform in the Cathedral Square the entire afternoon, unable to leave until all the speeches were done. He would be a perfect target, with much less chance to defend himself than Cousin Max in his hunting lodge. Zichy-Ferraris, who would be seated beside him in the front row, would almost certainly choose to wear one of his preposterously ornate uniforms, and with luck, all that glitter might attract these maniacs more than his own comparatively subdued costume. But Wiladowski was not pleased at the idea of entrusting his survival to the aesthetic discrimination of a gang of religious fanatics. Anything Tausk proposed was preferable, so long as the plan had a reasonable chance of success and Wiladowski could not be compromised by it. But before committing himself irrevocably, Wiladowski wanted to understand more about these men, who, for no reason that he could comprehend, had gone from a life of prayer to random murder. Everything Tausk had told him up to now about Brugger was naggingly opaque, and Wiladowski suspected that there were tribal mysteries behind Tausk's reticence that he could not continue to permit in his most trusted subordinate.

When Wiladowski asked Tausk directly what the rebbe could hope to gain by encouraging his followers to commit such atrocities, Tausk took a long breath before explaining that in the world Brugger inhabited, murder was not important because of any functional value but as a magical power in its own right. "For religious Jews"—Tausk went on—"murder is the oldest prohibition of all, predating even the granting of the Ten Commandments. In Genesis, God categorically forbids the shedding of human blood. He says as much to Noah, right after the Flood, which wiped out everyone except for one surviving family, which is given this fundamental imperative, the interdiction against murder. Unlike other obligations, it is considered universally binding, not merely for Jews. So deliberately breaking it is an extreme gesture of defiance. There have been numerous false messiahs in our history, and most of them tried to show they were above the Law by indulging in daring transgressions like eating forbidden *cheleb*, or kidney fat, and changing the liturgical calendar. But Brugger has read Bakunin and Nietzsche, and for him, all those earlier profanations are evidently much too mild. He needs more violent gestures to rend the fabric of the world."

At the beginning Tausk's tone was flecked with his habitual irony, but as he continued talking, he seemed to be losing himself in his own exegesis. His speech became more excited, and his thin arms twitched as though having nothing else with which to gesture, he were in danger of setting himself on fire with his cigarette. "How much of this does Tausk himself believe?" Wiladowski wondered. "I know he was trained by these people. But still, Genesis and kidney fat and liturgical calendars? We may be living in the most benighted province of the whole Empire, but even out here it is the twentieth century, and we do have newspapers and the telegraph. Except for Moritz Rotenburg, Tausk is as intelligent a person as I have met since becoming Governor, and I refuse to believe he can find anything except the sheerest insanity in these ideas."

Although he noticed Wiladowski's quizzical look, Tausk was determined to finish his explanation. What had started as strategy had become something more. It was as though by the very intensity of his story, he hoped to leap the abyss between the utter strangeness of these categories to the Count-Governor and their uncanny intimacy to him. Rabbi Pelz had taught him to recognize Brugger's aspirations as the very voice of evil, but that familiarity also gave them a reality that had nothing to do with actual belief. Tausk had long ago emptied himself of anything that could be called religious faith, but for reasons that were as unfathomable to Tausk as to his master, nothing mattered more to him right now than to make Wiladowski glimpse the spiritual forces arrayed in combat everywhere around them. "Orthodox Jews"—he went on—"have a commandment called *tikkun olam,* or healing the world. It has many interpretations"— here, catching sight of Wiladowski's amused response, Tausk broke his own intense absorption to nod in acknowledgment—"as do most of our doctrines, Your Excellency is no doubt correct in thinking. But for a healing to be necessary, there must first have been an injury, and all the rabbis agree that the whole created universe bears witness to some fundamental wound. A rift between Creator and Creation. Otherwise there could not be so much suffering and pain. But Brugger's aim is not to heal the world but to heighten the injury, so that by a kind of demonic dialectic, the true nature of existence is revealed. Only a condition of permanent terror can bring about a new age because it is the final breakdown of the old one."

"I am puzzled, Tausk"—Wiladowski held up his hand to command attention, in a gesture that was not altogether different from the way he might attract a distracted waiter in a restaurant—"if this is all some arcane Jewish theological dispute, why should I concern myself? Aren't the murders likely to be kept within your own church, so to speak?"

"On the contrary, Your Excellency. Because the prohibition against shedding blood is universal, its violation must be as well. The murder cannot be linked to any race, class, or personal grievance, and the only way to ensure this is to select the target arbitrarily. A member of a family as well-born and distinguished as Your Excellency's or a nonentity like Shmuel Kosch is an equally legitimate choice. The killing is a purely symbolic act that has to be kept as free of unworthy motives as any ritual offering. Brugger believes that the house of Israel is on fire and that the blood he sheds is the only way to extinguish it. Who will be the butcher and who the sacrifice are an accident of place and history and nothing more."

As abruptly as he had begun, Tausk stopped. He carefully put out his cigarette in the ashtray on the Count-Governor's desk and drew himself together like an actor who has just come offstage and returned to his dressing room to greet his friends and family while still in full costume. "At least something like that is what I think Brugger and his disciples believe." He resumed speaking in his usual tone. "I apologize if my account was too vivid, but there was no other way to let Your Excellency see the danger this man poses."

Wiladowski looked at his spymaster with interest. Whether what he had just heard had been a performance or not, Wiladowski was convinced that Tausk's continued effectiveness on his behalf required that he be allowed to deal with the rebbe in his own way. "And so," he asked again, "what do you suggest we do if Brugger is as dangerous as all that?"

"We already know that Brugger and at least some of his disciples entered the country without valid documents." Tausk spoke as thoughtfully as during the regular briefings in the main library when Pfister would have been present, waiting to pounce on anything Tausk said that might be unsuitable. "But just sending them back across the border would not accomplish anything. They would simply wait a few days and then return. A radical threat requires radical measures. I propose that we arrest Brugger and the most loyal of his followers when they are alone together without anyone else nearby and charge them all with Kosch's murder. When they are safely in custody, I will offer them a straightforward exchange, their full confession to the killing in return for the rebbe's freedom. I am certain at least one or two of them will leap at the bargain, and then we can have the hanging Prince Schwarzenberg advocated. We will keep our word to the disciples and charge Brugger only with illegal entry into the Empire. A deportation order will be drawn up, and I and one of my assistants will take him directly from his prison cell to the frontier. But unless he can rise from the dead, he will never be heard from again."

The Count-Governor said nothing for a few moments. His face was turned slightly away from Tausk toward the closed door, through which one could just make out the footfall of the sentries pacing up and down the marble floor. Wiladowski appeared to be listening to the muffled sounds from the hallway, and while he was thinking over Tausk's story, he tapped his fingers on the desk in time to the soldiers' heavy tread. Then, having made up his mind, he briskly opened his desk drawer and took out a sheet of official stationery. He unscrewed the large black and gold fountain pen on his desk and began to write a few sentences. When he was done, he handed the page over to Tausk and, in the familiar tone he used to conclude meetings once a routine administrative decision had been reached, told his spymaster, "Yes, I thought that was the direction in which you were going. All in all, I suppose, it is our best option. Here is the order to arrest Brugger and whichever of his followers you think best.

You will notice that I have not filled in the exact details, so it is up to you to pick the right moment and people. How you arrange matters from here on is entirely your own affair. Only remember, I do not want any trouble in the Josef Quarter. A Jewish martyr is the last thing we need this Easter!"

Tausk took the signed warrant and put it away in his folder, along with the doctor's drawings of Kosch's head. He knew the Count-Governor would want him not to mention the matter again, and as he left the library, Tausk kept his gaze professionally neutral. Wiladowski watched him depart and gave him a preoccupied wave of his hand, saying only that both he and Pfister would be expected at the normal time tomorrow to begin the final preparations for the upcoming ceremony. But when he was alone again, Wiladowski found himself flooded by a memory that had been trying to surface ever since Tausk had begun his strange account.

He was on his honeymoon with Marie-Luise, and one of their first stops was in Venice, where they enjoyed two weeks of radiant sunlight in a small palazzo, from whose windows they could look out across the lagoon to the shimmering island of San Giorgio Maggiore. One afternoon Marie-Luise was too tired from a heavy lunch to go out again, so while his bride rested, Wiladowski decided to take a leisurely stroll through the city on his own. He lost his way in the narrow alleys several times without minding and felt the mild fatigue of his exertion as just another pleasure granted by this miraculous place made of water, marble, and light. He had never felt as thoroughly pagan as in this city of a thousand churches, and when he wandered into the great baroque structure of Santa Maria della Salute, it was with renewed astonishment that so much exuberant inventiveness should have been put to the service of a faith as hostile to the senses as Christianity. When Wiladowski and Marie-Luise had visited the Salute together a few days before, he had directed her attention principally to Tintoretto's *Marriage at Cana*, intending, by the picture's theme, a subtle compliment to his wife's gift for lavish hospitality. But now that he was alone, he was more interested in looking closely at the three altarpieces by Luca Giordano, the eccentric Neapolitan master whose violent *Fall of the Rebel Angels* he had often admired in the Kunsthistorisches Museum back in Vienna. First, though, he wanted to take in the whole of the Salute's immense octagonal structure, designed, so he thought, more like a grandiose theater than a place of worship, and all the more pleasing to him for that reason. He had just walked through one of the eight symmetrical archways leading from the center of the church to a side altar, wondering if it was impolite, in a place like this, to hum a cheerful little melody he had heard a young Venetian housewife singing near the Campo Santa Margherita, when he suddenly froze, broke into a clammy sweat, and then briefly stopped breathing altogether. There, hovering in midair a few feet from his own face, was the bloody body of Christ, brutally nailed to his cross and staring, with enormous, pain-filled eyes, directly at him. For a long instant Wiladowski was certain that he was about to lose consciousness from sheer panic. But he somehow managed to collapse onto a small bench and sat there trembling, with his head bent between his knees, forcing himself to breathe, all the while certain that the apparition, unfathomable and terrifying, was still there, waiting for him to raise his eyes. Like every Austrian, Wiladowski had grown up listening to sermons of miraculous visions, but by the time he reached adolescence, they had struck him as naive fables, composed in the worst possible taste. Now, though, confronted by the evidence of his own senses that such a thing could actually happen—even to someone like him!—he felt his mind totter like a building that collapses from a long-concealed fissure in its foundation. "None of this is real," Wiladowski tried to tell himself. "I must have caught a fever on the train down to Italy and am suffering from hallucinations. I am not responsible for what my delirium makes me see." Summoning his last shred of willpower, he forced himself to look up. There was a chance that having diagnosed the sight as merely a symptom of his illness, his brain would reject it altogether. To his horror, nothing had changed. The tortured figure was still there, gazing at him with unblinking sorrow. Somehow Wiladowski found the strength to continue looking around, and then, all at once, he was able to put together what had occurred. A life-size painted wood carving of the crucified Jesus had been taken down from one of the altars for repair and propped up against the wall across the aisle from a mirror. At just the right angle, and in the dim light of the church interior, the reflection of the statue looked as though it were materializing in the space between the half columns where Wiladowski was standing. Both the statue and the mirror had been invisible from Wiladowski's perspective, and not until he went forward a few steps did both come into view. As soon as he glimpsed the carving, Wiladowski's fear dissipated, replaced by embarrassment and relief, but it took a long time for his breathing to return to normal, and he never mentioned his experience to anyone or set foot unaccompanied into another church for the rest of the honeymoon.

Wiladowski was perplexed why that episode, which he had not thought about for decades, had returned so unexpectedly. He continued to feel himself having to resist being pulled back into a long-forgotten dream from which it had been difficult enough to awaken the first time, and although only a few minutes had passed since Tausk had left with the warrant, their conversation seemed to have taken place hours ago. Being alone suddenly felt impossible, but just now there was no one with whom the Count-Governor could bear to speak. He summoned Aloïs, asked him to stand quietly nearby in case he was needed for any urgent errands, and then resumed working, reassured by the silent presence of someone who had served him loyally since his first posting. Gradually the rhythm of his daily routine dispelled the last fragments of Wiladowski's lingering unease, and he managed to put the memory of the apparition in the Salute behind him completely. The rest of the day was crowded with obligations, and by the time he was ready to change for dinner, he had long since stopped giving the matter any thought. But that night, when, for the first time in over two weeks, he found himself unable to fall asleep, the realization struck him that no matter how much Tausk had convinced himself that he was being merely a good ventriloquist, the spymaster's description of Brugger's motives testified to an appeal of which Tausk himself was probably unaware. Tausk no more believed in the strange wonder rebbe than Wiladowski did in the Holy Trinity, but that had not stopped Wiladowski from nearly dying of terror in a Venetian church, nor could it prevent Tausk from fearing there might be something more than natural about Brugger's power.

Wiladowski did not summon Tausk to keep him company in the library that night. Instead he contented himself alone, occasionally leafing through one of his licentious novels but more often simply sitting for long stretches by the window, watching the thick early-spring mist curl around the rows of gas lamps near the Castle walls. Shortly before dawn, when he was finally tired enough to return to bed, the last thing still on his mind was an Easter story that Tausk had told him with great glee during one of their many all-night vigils. Now, though, Wiladowski was no longer so sure the story was originally intended to be entirely amusing. According to Tausk, a converted Jew meets an old friend, one of his former coreligionists, who asks him if his recent baptism was sincere or merely a way to advance professionally. The convert answers that not only does he believe completely in the teachings of the Church but that he came to do so with great reluctance and still feels remorse at having had to leave behind the faith of his childhood. "My own experience left me no choice but to accept the truth of their Scriptures," the man said, "but it gives me no joy to do so." Puzzled, his Jewish friend inquires, "So what are you going to do at Easter?" "What else can I do?" the new Christian answers. "I will mourn the Resurrection."

◆

There was no need to tell Brugger directly about the murder at the Nepomuk Bridge. Half the Josef Quarter had been awakened by Racheli Mayer's screams, and the rest found out soon afterward from the town police, as uniformed officers rushed from building to building, questioning everyone they came across. During the past year there had been numerous killings in the area, but none like this, and as the grisly details emerged over the next few days, Kosch's death acquired a sinister glamour. When someone started the rumor that he had been a police informer, the general revulsion inspired by the mutilation of Kosch's body diminished greatly, and his dismemberment was absorbed into the legend of a district that prided itself on settling its own accounts.

These days the early-morning wind was no longer so chilling, and the first rich smells of the coming spring were starting to be noticeable even in the town center. Brugger began to go for daylong solitary walks in the open fields beyond the cemetery, often continuing on into the thick forests that led all the way to the border. Although he normally went out without a skullcap, he made a point of always putting one on before entering the woodlands because, as he told Linnetchen, "it is one of the few undefiled places left around here." On rare occasions Brugger permitted some of his closest disciples to accompany him, and they treasured the privilege of being alone with him, away from the crowd that now regularly flocked to his sermons. One unusually clement morning, a week after Kosch's body was discovered, Brugger put on his thick-soled hiking boots, filled a small wicker basket with some bread and smoked meat, and invited Linnetchen, Robert, Leah Wissotzsky, the youngest daughter of a wealthy tea merchant, and Voytek Jakobi, a short, perpetually restless former music teacher who had joined the group soon after Robert, to walk with him. It was still far too early in the year to pick mushrooms, but Brugger led his disciples confidently along the narrow forest trails that only a week ago had still been invisible underneath a thick layer of snow and pointed out where dense clusters of cèpe mushrooms were just starting to be visible in the shelter of the fir trees. Robert, who had spent many months as a vagrant, often forced to survive by scavenging, was astonished at how much the rebbe seemed to know about living off the countryside. Except for occasional clipped warnings to be careful about straying too far from the footpath because of the animal traps set by hunters from the large estates nearby, Brugger walked along in silence, staring straight ahead, absorbed in his own thoughts. After about two hours they came to a small clearing, where even the thin sunlight of early spring felt unexpectedly warm on their skin, and the cloudless sky was as clear and fluent as if it were already midsummer. The trunks of several large trees, probably felled by the von Alpsbach foresters, lay at the edges of the clearing, and Brugger sat down on one of them and signaled to the others to gather around him in a small circle. Robert, who had carried the basket most of the way, set it down for everyone to reach, and for a while they busied themselves contentedly sharing their meal. Linnetchen was stretched out on the warm ground, her body delighting in the feel of the earth against her back, and Robert found himself hoping that the intimacy of their long walk together and her joy in being out-of-doors all day for the first time since last fall would sharpen her hunger for him in bed that night.

Without any indication that he intended to break his silence, Brugger suddenly turned to them and said, "If one could murder a person every night, things would be so much easier. Everyone would learn to be good." Over time they all had become aware that Brugger's moods were more visible in his lips than his eyes, and for anyone who imagined himself close to the rebbe, nothing was more frightening than the downward pursed twitch that occasionally distorted the imperturbable, ironic half smile into which he usually set his face. The slender fingernail-shaped cleft that formed a crescent midway between his lower lip and the tip of his chin stood out whenever he was tense, becoming noticeably elongated and deeper. At such moments Brugger often unwittingly caressed his lips and the cleft in his chin, and then his disciples knew better than to interrupt him. As they sat there in the clearing, Brugger's tone was as tranquil and meditative as if he were elucidating some abstruse rabbinic conundrum, but his hands kept tugging at his lip with a nervous insistence that left no doubt of his displeasure. Although all his disciples were concentrating with absolute attention on his words, careful not to irritate him further by making any noise, Brugger avoided their gaze and continued to stare past them to a line of pine trees that marked the edge of the clearing. He spoke as though thinking aloud, for himself alone, so softly that they needed to strain to catch what he was saying. "In the commentaries we are told about two twilights, called the raven's and the dove's, one fierce, the other gentle. At the time of the final purification whoever hopes to survive must learn to be at home in both, and neither pity nor the sword alone will be enough. But I know that what I believe is called heresy by those afraid to see beyond the darkness and that even while we sit here and speak together, there are men in town already plotting my death."

Robert tried to restrain himself, but Brugger's words were too much for him. He jumped to his feet and swore that as long as he had the strength to fight, no one would come close enough to hurt his teacher. If the rebbe knew who these men were, Robert begged, let him name them, and not one of them would survive the coming week. Brugger looked over at Robert, who had taken out his large double-edged hunting knife, and, with a weary expression, told him to put away his blade and stop being a fool. "And what if it was your loyalty that gave my enemies their excuse?" he asked Robert. "No matter who killed that scoffer the Buczacz rabbi sent, the blame will surely be cast on me." At this, Robert trembled as though he had been violently slapped, and the others, who had watched the exchange without making a sound, began to fidget and look away. Brugger turned his gaze from Robert to enfold all of them and continued as though there had been no reaction. "Once, before Robert joined us," he said to them, "I told Linnetchen one should never try to catch a falling knife. I was wrong, though, because there are times when that is all any of us are allowed to be. Because your motives were pure, none of you is to blame for what has happened. A sin performed with good intention is better than a commandment obeyed with an evil heart. I am not asking what you have done in my name, nor what you will do. I neither encourage nor forbid it. But understand that you reveal your own needs, not mine, by how you interpret my words. For myself, I know it is inside my own soul I must silence the voices of doubt. *My* war is against the demonic powers that have created this universe of pain in which we are imprisoned. But what are spiritual battles for some are material ones for others, and each of us must fight in the only way and place he can. Something savage and strange is seeping into the most familiar things. And if we are to be its messengers, it is a waste of breath to count the cost. In the end it always comes down to who is ready to sacrifice more. This morning I woke up with the dawn, and before deciding whether to come out here alone or seek your company, I sat by the casement window and brooded about the death of that small man Shmuel Kosch. Whether or not he was sent by the Buczacz rabbi as an unwitting sacrifice to encompass my ruin no longer matters. Already I hear the cries of mourning that will soon rend the air from the widows at every window and from every bereaved mother in the streets. A lust for murder is stalking the town like a beast of prey. Is it our mission to unlock the gates and let the thing begin?"

Not even Linnetchen knew whether Brugger expected them to answer. They had often heard him talk like this, but never with such urgency. Kosch was a man of no importance in the community; even at the court of the Buczacz rabbi his voice had carried no weight, yet for Brugger, his killing seemed to be the signal of something much greater than they had suspected when they left the body as a warning for everyone to see. Insolence like Kosch's had to be punished. Linnetchen was as convinced of that now as she had been on the night she brought Kosch to the riverbank where the others were waiting to butcher him. But she was furious with herself for not anticipating that in spite of their precautions, Brugger would be held responsible. They had been careful not to mention a word of anything they were doing the day of the killing, so that he could swear with a clear conscience that he knew nothing about the whole affair. Still, Robert had been right after all. They ought to have thrown the body into the river, weighted down with some heavy rocks, so that it wouldn't surface for several months. But it was the rebbe's reactions that absorbed Linnetchen. He had shown no surprise when the news was first brought to him, nor did he seem troubled by the crushing of an empty husk like Kosch. But there was a certain distance in the way he talked about it now, as though their enactment of his teachings were something for which he had not fully prepared himself and about whose significance he had not yet made up his mind. Linnetchen had no doubts about the justice of the act and did not feel the rebbe's wavering as a criticism of her or as a sign of timidity. He had already explained it best himself: His battles took place in a higher sphere, and there were often times when the necessities of daily survival were as foreign to him as they would be to a naked angel who had come directly from the gates of paradise to the slums of the Josef Quarter. She had known many days when he kept to his room, too weak to rise from his sickbed. Normally no one was allowed to see him at those times, but once or twice he had permitted her to bring him a cold compress for his temples and, since he was unable to keep down any food, some mild chamomile tea to stave off dehydration. At those times he became so dejected he lost the ability to read, and she sat for hours by his bedside, reading aloud to him from his favorite books. Now, although they had been outside all day in the gentle spring air, Brugger's face was as pale as during one of his attacks, and he no longer pulled at his lip with the same nervous energy. Instead he had cupped the palm of his right hand completely around his forehead and was using his fingers and thumb to massage both temples gently, the first sign that he feared succumbing to one of his crushing migraines. Bafflement, fury, and exhaustion were contending in his expression, but Linnetchen had no way to predict which would win out. She had the sense from the way he was still leaning forward, enclosing all of them with his presence, that Brugger had intended to say more about what lay ahead for them in the coming days, but with a muffled groan, he abruptly got up and wordlessly indicated that it was time to return to town.

On the way back, Brugger's tread seemed heavier and less sure, but he did not require any help walking, and once or twice, when Robert or Voytek offered him their support crossing a patch of ground that had become slippery with melted snow or climbing over a fallen branch that blocked their trail, he pushed their hands away and muttered that he was feeling better and would soon be all right again. Robert and Linnetchen stayed close by, a few feet behind the rebbe, so that they did not intrude into his solitude yet could be at his side in an instant if he called for them. Both felt only infinite grief at their teacher's pain and would gladly have borne it in his stead. They were certain that Brugger's suffering was the direct result of the Buczacz rabbi's malevolence. He had tricked them into murdering Kosch so that the civil authorities would rid him of a presence whose holiness exposed his own spiritual nullity. Robert thought it possible that along with his schemes and slanderous accusations, the Buczacz rabbi was also using dark arts to worsen Brugger's headaches. Evil was always stronger and more relentless the closer it came to its final defeat, and the very success of the plots against Brugger testified to the dread his mission inspired among the impure. Robert knew he had no head for theological subtleties and was content to have Linnetchen translate Brugger's lessons in terms he could grasp. In spite of the danger they were in, Robert felt freer and more at peace within himself than ever before. Linnetchen too seemed to flourish at the prospect of open warfare against their enemies. She instinctively matched her pace to Robert's, and the two walked together in a steady rhythm that was itself a kind of powerful physical intimacy. Occasionally their hands would touch as they swung them lightly side to side, and Robert was amazed to feel Linnetchen's skin so feverish with excitement. The more she explained their master's teachings, the more passionate she herself seemed to become, until her face took on an inner glow that left Robert ardent with admiration and desire. For most of the walk back, Brugger gave no sign that he heard any of their conversation, but as they were passing the old city walls before turning onto the long avenue that would take them home, he stopped and smiled at them with a look of pleasure they had not seen in his eyes for many weeks. "I feel almost restored," he told them, "in no small part thanks to your fidelity. If the light is truly sown on earth for the righteous, then it requires loyal harvesters like you. Part of me felt polluted by all the mockers who surround us, and I needed your faith to wash their words from my heart. If I have that still in the days ahead, nothing our enemies devise against us can make me waver again."

The rest of the walk home seemed to pass in a daze. Brugger's words filled his disciples with a boundless joy in comparison with which everything else felt empty. The people they passed on the streets seemed to them like slow-moving, mechanical puppets, imitating a life they could never know from within, and if the police had come at that moment to arrest all of them, they would have walked into prison content, certain it could hold them only as long as they themselves permitted it. When they reached the house, it was not yet evening, and for another hour they sat quietly watching the dusk eddy downward in slow bands from the great Bell Tower to the muddy streets of the Josef Quarter. No one felt like eating. Only after the other windows in the neighborhood were already reflecting the soft glow of candlelight and oil lamps did anyone notice that they themselves were now sitting in semidarkness. Instead of going off alone, as he usually did in the evening, Brugger stayed, leaning against the window in the large central room with all the disciples. But when the table lamp had finally been lit and someone had gone to fetch a bottle of wine from the kitchen, Brugger slowly got up, stretched out his arm to take Linnetchen by the hand, and, without another word, went directly into his bedroom with her.

Robert fell asleep hearing the sounds of their lovemaking through the thin walls. It was rare for Brugger to take a woman after his initial time with her was over, but Linnetchen's familiar, rasping cries of pleasure were impossible to mistake. Although it was unthinkable for him to feel jealous of the rebbe, Robert found himself saddened listening to the two, and he briefly thought about going to see if Leah Wissotzsky wanted his company in bed. But to his surprise, he felt much too tired to make the effort and sank back down with the pillow wrapped around his head to muffle the noises. The certainty that Linnetchen would be back with him tomorrow night was reassuring, and when the contentment he had felt on the walk home gradually returned and let him drift into his own dreams, he took it as a gift from Brugger, as welcome as the fulfillment he knew Linnetchen was feeling.

The next morning Robert and Linnetchen began to make their plans. It was easy to mingle among the poor artisans who formed most of the Buczacz rabbi's congregation, and twice in a row, only thinly disguised, both Robert and Voytek had attended one of his sermons. A week later the rabbi's house suddenly erupted in an immense ball of fire just when he and his family were sitting down to dinner. The flames spread so quickly that no one was able to get out, and the fire continued to smolder for several days after the whole structure had been reduced to ashes. Nothing was left of the building or its inhabitants. At least eight people in addition to the Buczacz rabbi were known to have burned to death in the house, but it was impossible to identify any of the bodies, and half a dozen more worshipers came forward to swear a relative of theirs had gone to see the rabbi to talk over a personal problem the evening of the conflagration and never returned.

The funeral was a somber affair. Most of Buczacz's Jews turned up for the event, but there was no body to inter in the plot that had long been reserved for the rabbi, and the well-meant suggestion by the local magistrate that some of the ashes from the house be gathered up and placed in a commemorative urn was rejected with abhorrence since it would lead to a promiscuous intermingling of the rabbi's remains with those of the others, including several women, who had been immolated with him. After several people reported detecting a distinct smell of kerosene, the authorities formally categorized the fire as the result of arson and sent a small contingent of uniformed police to act as guards during the funeral. In spite of a sizable reward for information about the fire, no witnesses appeared to assist the investigation, and even during the prayer service for the rabbi, members of his congregation kept looking around nervously, as though afraid that they were putting their own lives at risk simply by showing their last respects to the dead man.

. ◆ .

Acquiring a stockpile of weapons turned out to be less complicated than Hans had imagined. In a region famous for its hunting preserves, there was no shortage of able gunsmiths and merchants happy to supply the need for a wide variety of firearms. Many members of the provincial aristocracy prided themselves on their marksmanship, and it was still a source of great satisfaction throughout the region that twenty years ago old Baron Károlyi had won the pistol-shooting exhibition at Garmitsch-Partenkirchen in the presence of His Imperial Majesty himself. Koppensteiner's Department Store carried a notable selection of small arms, and when Leo von Arnstein and Chrissi von Hradl went in there one afternoon, loudly chatting to each other about their determination to equal Károlyi's great feat at next year's competition, Herr Lászny was glad to offer his assistance in making sure they had the best and most up-to-date weapons with which to practice. Joachim Gerling's father was in Vienna again, offering his expert advice to yet another government committee seeking a way out of the prolonged recession, and Hans decided to use that as an excuse for Joachim to go to the capital himself to buy additional equipment for the cell.

Like most of the houses on the Maximilianstrasse, Hans's building had a large, unfinished cellar used by all the tenants to store provisions for which their flats were too small or that required being kept cool throughout the year. Groups of families went out together in the summer during the two weeks when the cucumbers ripened overnight in the fields and bought them cheaply from the farmers and returned again to deal with the same farmers in October, when the cabbage was ready. Every housewife had her own recipes for preparing the food for the coming winter. Throughout the Josef Quarter part of every cellar was given over to storing large barrels full of pickled cucumbers and somewhat smaller ones containing roughly sliced cabbage, preserved in a mixture of salt, apple peelings, and vinegar. More recent immigrants to the city, who still clung to habits common on the farms they had left behind, also tried to keep potatoes, carrots, beetroots, and onions for the winter, piling them underneath a thick blanket of straw. In principle, space in the cellar was allocated according to the size of the tenant's flat, but up until now that had never presented a problem since there was more than enough room to hold everyone's things. Hans, though, quickly realized the utility of such a cellar for his own plans. The arsenal of guns and ammunition the cell was assembling would fit perfectly into empty cucumber barrels, and he was sure no one would ever think of looking there for weapons. Even more promising, the windowless cellar, with its massive stone walls, was an ideal place to store the necessary chemicals for his experiments in building an effective bomb. Hans, who never suspected how detested he already was by most of the neighborhood, was certain that the loss of a few vats of unappetizing food was a minor sacrifice in comparison with what he and his comrades were risking, and he had no compunction about leasing the entire cellar for himself. The delighted landlord immediately sent his agent to all the other tenants, ordering them to remove their possessions within forty-eight hours or see them thrown away. That there was no place to which the goods could be moved made no difference to him. Even if most of the apartments were not already overcrowded, the massive barrels were much too heavy to bring up the stairs. At risk were weeks of hard work laying in the vegetables on which people depended to supplement the meager diet they could afford to buy in town. Only the widespread fear of angering Moritz Rotenburg, whose name inspired a wary respect throughout the whole quarter and whose power was dreaded even by those who had no fear of the police, kept Hans from being assaulted by his outraged neighbors. One night Asher Blumenthal heard some of the customers in Löffner's Bar mutter that whoever was going around decapitating people had picked the wrong target in Shmuel Kosch when a much more deserving candidate was available. After spending several agonizing hours weighing where his own interest lay, Asher decided it was safest, after all, to warn Hans about the growing public resentment.

At first Hans was incredulous that anyone could think badly of him. Even if they had no way of knowing it yet, everything he was doing was solely for the benefit of the workers. The patrons in whatever sordid bars Asher frequented were obviously all idle drunkards, lumpen proletariat, and petty bourgeois opportunists. When Asher pointed out that some of the loudest threats had come from men arrested in the demonstration against the Hollweg Timber Corporation, who had been forced to pay heavy fines and so were even more dependent on foodstuff laid down earlier, Hans was unimpressed. "That is exactly the problem with a trade union mentality," he told Asher. "All these types care about is piecemeal improvements, and to get them, they are ready to give up pressing for real change. Gradualist reformers like that only dilute the revolutionary potential of the working class anyway." Although Asher himself had no great sympathy for the workers on whose behalf the cell claimed to be acting, he could not help reflecting that if the choice were between feeding one's family or seeing it go hungry, piecemeal improvements might not be so unwelcome. Even a brute like Asher's former section chief, Galatowski, was at least aware of the damage he was doing, but Hans simply acted however he pleased, without taking into account anyone else's reaction, the nobility of his motives apparently making such considerations irrelevant. Asher was afraid that he himself risked being beaten up if an open clash between Hans and his neighbors were to break out. Besides, if he could somehow become known as the man who had persuaded Hans to let everyone keep on storing their winter supplies in the cellar, his own prestige in the Josef Quarter could only benefit, and he might actually succeed in seducing the girl with the reddish blond hair and damp underarms, about whom he found himself thinking ever since walking up behind her at the tobacconist. Asher decided that the most effective way to deflect Hans was to speak to him as though the matter were entirely a question of tactics, and in spite of Hans's sour look, Asher went ahead and suggested that it might be useful, in the short term, to secure the goodwill of the other tenants. After all, if there were a disturbance, especially one involving a Rotenburg, the police would intervene right away, and surely nothing mattered more right now than attracting as little attention to themselves as possible. He was glad to see that in spite of himself, Hans seemed responsive to what he was saying. The apparent effectiveness of his argument made it easier for Asher not to add that in his eyes the whole idea of people as wealthy as Hans and the other conspirators deluding themselves into believing they could remain inconspicuous for a single moment in a district where more than half the men were unemployed was too ludicrous to take seriously. Asher was still convinced Moritz Rotenburg was secretly manipulating the entire situation, and he thought it a great pity that the financier was forced to rely upon as inept a tool as Hans, whose only claim for preferment was his birth certificate. Whatever the specifics of Moritz's plan, they could undoubtedly be carried out better by someone with a less blinkered view of the whole situation, someone very much like Asher himself, who, if the truth ever came out, might prove to have as much Rotenburg blood in his veins as Hans.

For once Asher's argument made sense to Hans. The last thing he could afford was to waste precious time in a confrontation with the other tenants. The news of Kosch's murder had shaken Hans profoundly, but not for the reasons Asher imagined. Hans had no doubt that the killing was the act of another underground cell whose existence he had never suspected. It was alarming to realize that it had established itself in his own town in complete secrecy, and though he had tried to find out who his rivals were, he still had no idea how many people were involved or what ideological faction they represented. They had managed to strike first, and that gave them a priority he might never be able to win back. Why they had chosen such an insignificant target was another puzzle, but perhaps eliminating a suspected police spy was their way of building broad-based support in the Josef Quarter for some larger action in the future. It was a shrewd idea, but Hans remained convinced that striking directly at a well-known figure from the ruling class would be much more effective. However, it would have to be done soon, no matter how incomplete the cell's preparations. To the others, Hans had always spoken in terms of the Bell Tower rededication ceremony, but inwardly he was far from certain they would be ready to act by Easter. Now he was sure they had no choice. To permit someone else to usurp what had been intended as his moment of revolutionary violence was unthinkable. Whatever their real objectives, Kosch's assassins had goaded Hans into taking his own plan more seriously than when he had proposed it at Hirschwang.

Hans managed to get rid of Asher surprisingly easily. The promise to rethink the plan to take over the whole basement appeared to delight Asher, who couldn't wait to rush off to Löffner's to celebrate his new prospects. To hurry him along, Hans agreed to let Asher represent him in whatever new arrangements he decided on and then went downstairs alone to look over the possibilities. He had already accumulated a significant cache of chemical explosives, including vials of mercury and bottles of ammonium nitrate, dimethylolurea, and sulfonic acid salt. Along with these, he had sufficient gunpowder, dynamite, simple fuses, and blasting caps to level two-thirds of the Josef Quarter, but he was still uncertain how to combine the components in the right way. Books on mining techniques were of some help, as were a few of the chemistry and civil engineering primers he had consulted, but it would be a while before he was competent enough to construct the kind of explosive device they needed. What a pity that in reality there was no Botho who could build the bombs for him, especially since the others were counting on the expert from Geneva.

At least there was no such problem with firearms. In addition to the hunting rifles and small-caliber pistols bought from Herr Lászny, they had obtained several powerful Roth-Steyr self-loading pistols, which had been taken into service by the cavalry in 1908, along with half a dozen eight-millimeter bolt-action Männlicher rifles, the army's main service weapon since 1895 but still far from outdated. Moritz Rotenburg was one of the principal investors in the Steyr-based company that manufactured both guns, and he had seen his shares rise tremendously when the army adopted them. For his own use, Hans preferred the German nine-millimeter Parabellum Luger pistol, which had the lethal look and heft he was looking for. There was something thrilling in handling such a weapon, especially for someone whose life had been spent entirely with books and ideas, but in spite of repeated practice sessions in the woodlands around Weidenau and Hirschwang, Hans was never able to become a proficient marksman. By general consent, it would be up to the others to be responsible for shooting whoever survived the detonation of the bomb, of which Hans would take sole charge. Standing there, in the center of the basement, looking at the cache of guns and explosives the cell had managed to assemble, he felt as pleased with his acquisitions as a connoisseur walking through his collection of rare art treasures. As soon as he found a new location, the arsenal itself would be relatively easy to move, but everything would have to be accelerated in order to ensure the effectiveness of their action.

When he had first taken the apartment on the Maximilianstrasse, Hans had been intrigued by a dilapidated structure on the far side of the street where it curved down toward the river embankment. Unlike the three- and four-story tenements that had been built in the Josef Quarter thirty years earlier to accommodate the influx of new workers from the countryside, this uninhabited squat shack dated from an earlier epoch in the district's history and was obviously being left to go to ruin. Only the drawn-out slump had prevented the owner from tearing the place down and replacing it with one of the standardized larger buildings. At one time Hans had considered it as a possible hiding place to which he and the others could flee if something went wrong. No one ever went in there anymore, and it might be possible to lie low there until it was safe to use their false passports to leave the country. Now, though, it occurred to him that if the place had a proper basement, it could be converted without much difficulty into a more secure storage depot and bomb factory than the publicly accessible tenement cellar. Buying the shack outright was probably the best way to have a free hand, and if Hans paid cash, the temptation to avoid the substantial tax imposed on all real estate transfers would give the owner good reason not to report the sale. Asher would be glad to look into the question tomorrow morning, and in exchange for whatever percentage he would no doubt manage to extract for himself from both parties, he could be relied on to conduct all the necessary negotiations with the speed required. Even in anticipation, Asher's pleasure in playing the capitalist was evident in the high spirits with which he had left the apartment. The expectation of a few gold pieces in his pockets made him walk more proudly, as though he himself were already an important property owner. His hand went repeatedly to touch his breast pocket, like a man making sure his ample wallet was safely tucked away, and his gait, as he continued along the Maximilianstrasse, was a perfect pantomime of a wealthy man judiciously surveying his holdings and debating within himself where to invest next. He smiled with contented benevolence at everyone he passed. So far he had put away more money running errands for Hans and the other cell members than he had gotten for informing on them to Moritz and Tausk, and this latest venture was likely to land him the largest sum yet. Perhaps only in Austria could working for revolutionaries be the speediest way for someone like Asher to become a man of property, but if so, he concluded cheerfully, it would be a kind of treason to the national spirit not to make the best of whatever chances came his way.

To Asher's exasperation, now that he finally had the courage, and, more crucially, the money, to speak to the Slovene waitress at Löffner's, it seemed that she had run away from the district with one of the other customers, a notorious thief and smuggler whose contraband goods she used to hide under her bed. They had managed to get away only a few hours before the police raided her room, apparently tipped off by someone in the force with whom she also regularly had sex in return for useful information about border patrols. Asher was furious with himself for having delayed seducing her until it was too late, especially after his third brandy, when a succession of vivid images of all the thrilling acts she and her lovers had performed on the sheets above the piled-up boxes of illicit merchandise refused to leave his brain. The next morning, with his head still throbbing from alcohol and frustration, Asher set about arranging for the purchase of the shack from Bernard Auer, an embittered old man who had seen most of his holdings in the quarter lose three-quarters of their value in the slump and was delighted to have found someone gullible enough to pay him for a property he had already written off as worthless. As Hans had expected, the promise of a cash payment prompted Auer himself to suggest to Asher that they not bother notarizing the sale with the District Commissioner and instead substitute a private, legally binding letter of ownership. When Asher appeared hesitant about whether he could really do that or, indeed, recommend the transaction to his principal at all, considering how unsafe the structure clearly was, Auer offered him a 5 percent middleman's fee, and after a few minutes' haggling, they settled for 7.5 percent, a sum Asher intended to supplement by adding 10 percent to what he would get Hans to pay. Before he went back to Hans's apartment to inform him that the deal had been concluded, Asher made sure to inform both Moritz and Tausk of Hans's latest plan, with the result that the shack was put under constant supervision by a team of Tausk's most loyal agents. Had Asher not volunteered the news to his two masters himself, omitting only the details of his own financial gain from the purchase, they would undoubtedly have heard the news almost at once from their other sources in the Josef Quarter. Within three or four days everyone knew who had bought the old ruin at the bottom of the Maximilianstrasse.

In spite of the improvement in Asher's finances, whenever Hans did not need him, he continued to take his dinner in Isaac Meir's At the Five Hussars before going on to Löffner's Bar, where, in between boasting to anyone who would listen about how he had negotiated one of the most complex business transactions in the quarter while saving a houseful of working families from hunger, he spent the rest of the night drinking and regretting the hot-blooded Slovene waitress. He would sit there, staring discontentedly at her replacement, a bulky widow whose unmistakable mustache and beefy, dark-veined arms and legs made her an impossible subject for erotic reverie, no matter how much one drank. A few days later Asher went from door to door in Hans's building, letting the other tenants know their stores were safe in the cellar and could stay there forever, thanks entirely to his timely intervention. Since he did so during the hours when the men were likely to be out, either at work for those fortunate enough to have a job or, if not, then on the street with the throng of fellow sufferers looking through the newspaper for any faint sign of improvement in the economy, Asher had imagined that at least one or two of the younger housewives, out of gratitude for his effort, or from simple loneliness, or, best of all, because his improved finances had transformed him into the kind of man who inspired a powerful sexual curiosity, might invite him in and, without any wasteful preliminaries, take him straight to bed. He was so aroused by these hopes that by the time he knocked on the door there was no question of his readiness for sex. Unfortunately for Asher, in spite of everything he had heard about such women, gratitude in the Josef Quarter did not seem to express itself in the ways he had hoped, and although his news was greeted with smiles of relief and appreciation, all he ever received back were a few quick syllables of thanks. No one even invited him inside for a glass of brandy to celebrate the tenants' collective good fortune. As soon as he delivered his message, the doors closed behind him, and on at least one of the landings, Asher was sure he heard suppressed giggling coming from the apartment he had just visited.

Instead of Asher, it was Hans whose reputation began to take on a new luster in the district. His buying the shack convinced everyone that he was more than just a spoiled pleasure seeker interested solely in using his money to prey on their women. The only conceivable reason why a Rotenburg would acquire such a run-down structure was to tear it down and replace it with a profitable modern building. Doing so would finally bring some money into the district and provide jobs for many of the workers in the neighborhood. Overnight Hans's behavior since arriving among them was reinterpreted as part of a long-range scheme, orchestrated by his father, to take advantage of the depressed prices in the Josef Quarter. Among those in the district who prided themselves on having shrewd heads for business, it was agreed that the old fox planned to buy up all the available buildings one by one, probably using a series of go-betweens, until he controlled enough of the area to be able to force the rest of the property owners to sell out to him on his own terms. Hans must have been ordered by his father to take an apartment in the quarter in order to evaluate the opportunities firsthand. He had come not because the girls were cheap but because the property was. The Rotenburgs had a stake in increasing the value of whatever they owned and so could not help being an improvement on the present landlords. The same people who had muttered curses whenever Hans passed them on the street now greeted him affably, and anyone who had spoken out against Hans only a week earlier was told that if he wanted to avoid trouble, he had better not do so again.

Hans became aware of the change in attitude toward him only when he was repeatedly asked by his neighbors if he wanted their help moving any of his stores from the common cellar to his new building. It was irritating that everyone seemed to know about his purchase and talked about it so openly, thanks, no doubt, to Asher's notorious garrulity and the general lack of self-discipline of workers who had dissipated their class consciousness in frivolous reform movements. It was futile to deny what was obviously common knowledge throughout the district, and he contented himself with brusquely declining their offers of aid. But with the practical streak he had inherited from his father, he put aside his annoyance enough to ask all those who volunteered assistance about their particular skills. Hans's opinion of people had never deterred him from using their services whenever it suited him. Whether others did his bidding freely or in expectation of a reward made little difference to him, and he felt neither gratitude for work done on his behalf out of goodwill nor surprise when he was presented with a clearly padded bill. As soon as he took formal possession of the shack, however, Hans saw how lucky he was to have a cadre of able workers at his disposal. The place required extensive repairs to be minimally useful, just as a storage facility, and if he was going to learn how to mix chemicals there, adequate lighting, a functional table, shelving, and workbench, and proper ventilation all would need to be installed. When Hans mentioned this to a few of the men who lived in the floor above his own apartment, keeping his tone as casual as if he were discussing some purely cosmetic alteration in his rooms at the Rotenburg villa, they promised to take care of everything for him, asking only for enough money to purchase the necessary materials. Hans was uncertain how reliable they would be, but to his surprise, they were as good as their word and set to work immediately. By the end of the week, without any architectural blueprints, and using only Hans's deliberately vague description of the place's intended function, all the repairs were done.

Out of the warren of cramped, narrow rooms they had managed to carve a single large space with ample illumination and air vents, furnished in exact accord with what he had told them he required. The rest of the building was not salvageable, they said, but by thickening the interior walls in a few strategically chosen places and using rough wooden supports to create a stable inner frame, they had secured a considerable area for his immediate needs. It was only a temporary solution, they admitted with some embarrassment, and without major structural repairs was unlikely to last through another winter, but by then Hans would surely have decided to tear down the whole shell and convert what was a potentially wonderful site into a model apartment house or office for himself. Although he was still vexed at all this bother because of a few ridiculous pickles and winter vegetables, Hans was impressed at how much the workmen had done in such a brief time and set about arranging the transfer of the weapons cache from the tenement cellar. Leo, Christoph, and Manfred dutifully reported to Hans's apartment after dinner the next evening, and taking great care to jostle the explosives as little as possible, they had succeeded in safely relocating everything by morning.

• ◆ •

For Tausk, Hans's latest folly was almost enough to make him despair of being able to keep his promise to the boy's father. Arranging to keep so many houses under observation simultaneously, without including any details in his official reports, risked arousing the suspicion of his numerous enemies at the Castle. Worse, the hovel Hans was now using looked as though it would collapse during the next powerful spring storm, and the prospect of having to inform Moritz Rotenburg that his only son had been buried alive in a broken-down shack in the Josef Quarter, amid a room piled high with illegal weapons and dangerous chemicals, was scarcely designed to reassure the spymaster. More than ever, Tausk was grateful he had taken Roublev into his confidence, and he remembered his assistant's prediction that before long they would need to use the financier's immense resources if they were going to protect his son. But in spite of several earlier suggestions by Roublev that it was high time to do so, Tausk had resisted approaching Moritz directly since the night of their long interview. Tausk had made a point of not asking Moritz for anything yet, either for himself personally or to help him with his work, and he told Roublev to think of Moritz as holding out a signed blank check to them, limitless in its theoretical worth but to be filled in and cashed once or twice at most, after which it would be permanently withdrawn. Now, however, he agreed the time had come for an initial installment. Tausk arranged for Moritz to set up an untraceable discretionary account out of which he would pay the full-time salary of fifteen additional men, whom

Roublev would personally select and supervise. Since Rotenburg already had a very similar arrangement with Count Wiladowski, to whose political as well as entertainment expenses he contributed a substantial monthly sum, the spymaster's suggestion amused Moritz with its symmetry. As he sat in his overheated study, filling out the necessary papers, he reflected that soon Marie-Luise, shielded by her private wealth and implacable anti-Semitism, would be the only figure of importance in the Castle whom he was not subsidizing.

Roublev's new team was divided into groups of three men, each team assigned to cover one of the secondary targets with the aim of freeing Tausk to concentrate on his two principal concerns, Hans Rotenburg and Brugger. Tausk knew he had very little time left before having to settle accounts with both men face-to-face, but the Count-Governor's anxiety about the Easter ceremony kept demanding his attention at the most inopportune moments. Wiladowski was becoming increasingly agitated as the day grew closer, and he had fallen back into the habit of summoning Tausk to keep him company all night while he tried to talk himself out of his fears. In order to leave their Russian neighbors with no doubt about the importance the Emperor attached to his easternmost province, Vienna had decided to make the most out of the Bell Tower celebration, a development that only increased everyone's already acute sense of strain. From a commemorative festival with purely local significance the celebration had become part of a complex diplomatic language whose intended audience resided as far away as St. Petersburg and London, and the revised guest list had been carefully constructed with that aim in mind. In addition to Zichy-Ferraris, the dynasty would now be represented by Eduard Trautmannsdorff, first cousin to the Emperor's own aide-de-camp, by Prince Konrad von Hohenlohe-Schillingsfurst, the former Lieutenant Governor of Trieste, and by Adrian von Kirchstein, grandson of the famous Minister of Justice, who had polemicized against granting Jews full civil rights, even if they had won medals of valor in the war against Prussia, with the widely admired bon mot "The assumption of their fundamental wickedness is not invalidated by acts of temporary bravery." Each of these men would be accompanied by his own staff and retinue of servants, and all of them, Wiladowski assured Tausk, could be counted on to squabble endlessly with one another and their host about the smallest questions of precedence. Moreover, these were only the principal guests. The list Wiladowski received from the capital also included a number of important

Church dignitaries and a few members of Parliament and General Staff officers who apparently came from the area but had not been back for so long that no one quite remembered what they looked like. There were nights when Wiladowski just stood at the side of his desk, staring down at the catalog of names with something like mute despair in his eyes and turned to his spymaster, muttering, "You really do have to save me from this, Tausk. The assassins won't even have to fire a shot to destroy me completely! These men will just bore me to death, and that will be the end of it!"

For the first time in his life Tausk was genuinely grateful for Matthias Pfister's presence in the provincial administration. If only he were left free to focus on the task, Tausk was reasonably confident that he could ensure the participants' physical security, but when Wiladowski began to involve him in questions that required diplomatic skills, the spymaster felt helpless. Who should be lodged in the Castle's guest suites, and who with one of the provincial noblemen, and whether a Trautmannsdorff or a von Kirchstein should ride in front of the other in the great procession through town to the Cathedral Square were mysteries that Tausk had neither the knowledge nor the inclination to solve. But apparently the peacefulness of the event depended almost as much on the right decision in these matters as it did on preventing any of these gentlemen from being blown to smithereens. Tausk found himself wondering whether genealogical expertise would be of any use if terrorists succeeded in exploding a bomb and the scattered body parts of the visitors needed to be identified, but he knew better than to risk a joke on that topic in front of the Count-Governor. With all these concerns, though, Pfister was truly in his element, and Tausk had the singular satisfaction of persuading the Count-Governor to order the night guard to awaken his First Secretary and summon him into the library at two in the morning for an urgent consultation.

Pfister had heard rumors about these all-night sessions between the Count-Governor and Tausk and entertained the darkest thoughts of what went on there. He had imagined everything from arcane Masonic rituals to unspeakable sexual debaucheries but had never allowed himself to hope that he would be invited to join them. Now, as he stepped cautiously into the library, bleary-eyed with fatigue but formally dressed, and even, as Tausk noticed with amazement, having taken the time to shave and perfume himself, Pfister looked about, surprised to see nothing unusual, neither strange implements of heathen worship nor traces of a recent orgy.

Pfister tried not to let his disappointment show, but something in his manner must have given away what he was thinking. His habitual self-control rattled by accumulated tension, Count Wiladowski unexpectedly broke out in a laugh loud enough to startle the guards on duty in front of his door. Four of them immediately rushed into the room with bayonets drawn and pushed poor Pfister against the wall before the Count-Governor waved them off and, apologizing to his terrified First Secretary, invited Pfister to take a seat and assist him in a crucial matter.

Once he had recovered from his alarm, Pfister quickly took in the full extent of the quandary. Unlike the spymaster, not only did he grasp the delicacy with which the ceremony itself needed to be stage-managed by the Castle, but he also understood, as though from within, the finickiness of the highborn visitors that their proper place in the hierarchy be respected. He permitted himself to look over at Tausk with a pitying expression, certain, even before he heard it confirmed by the man himself, that Tausk simply had no idea how such things were arranged. Pfister declared himself delighted to do everything in his power to ease the burden on the Count-Governor. Of course he would be glad to take charge of coordinating everyone's accommodations, and drawing on Marie-Luise's invaluable counsel, he would make sure the seating arrangements at the formal banquets were exactly as they should be. Along with his own not inconsiderable training in questions of protocol, he promised to comb the likely books in the Castle library for descriptions of Imperial festivals that might serve as models and to prepare a synopsis with specific recommendations for every step of the ceremony. Pfister was happily going on in the same vein when Tausk bowed his way out of the room with a relieved smile, leaving the triumphant First Secretary to savor what he interpreted as the complete rout of his enemy. Wiladowski noticed Tausk's expression and responded with a barely perceptible sigh, sinking into his chair to listen despondently to Pfister's increasingly elaborate proposals.

6

In the predawn hours of Saturday, March 28, when most of the Josef
Quarter was asleep, a tremendous explosion, apparently coming
from near the river, shook the whole district. A quaver ran through
the ground similar to the aftershock of a small earthquake. Immediately afterward there were three or four more rapid-fire blasts from
the same direction. Most people were too terrified to run out into the
street and see what was happening, but the few who did reported that the
detonations were coming from Auer's newly remodeled shack. Flames
were blowing out of the gaping holes that had once been ground-floor
windows. Plaster debris was scattered all over the street and down the embankment slope, and a large chunk of masonry was lodged grotesquely upright in the weeds at the water's edge. Where the building's front door had
been, there was a deep, incandescent glow, more terrifying than actual
flames, coming from somewhere far inside the house. In all the smoke
and chaos no one saw a lone man stagger out of the burning structure
with his arms badly scorched and his face singed. The explosion had
burned most of the clothes off his body. He stumbled forward in a daze,
covered with soot and ash, and barely avoided being hit by a large fragment of the roof that crashed to the street just inches from where he was
standing. He seemed oblivious of the falling masonry and just rocked back
and forth in the middle of the street, trembling with shock. At almost the
same moment a second figure, slightly built and unnaturally pale in the
glow of the burning timber, emerged from the shadows around the corner,
ignored the falling wreckage all around him, and, moving rapidly, but with
calm purpose, wrapped the disoriented burn victim in a thick blanket and
hustled him out of sight into a waiting carriage.

By now enough of the district's residents had gathered to try to stop
the flames from spreading. Soldiers from the nearby barracks, their

numbers reinforced during the past year by the Count-Governor in case of political trouble, also rushed out to help, and last of all, delayed by the distance between their station and the Josef Quarter, the municipal fire brigade arrived. Fortunately for everyone, it was a windless night, and since the shack was set apart from the larger tenements by a patch of barren ground, none of them caught fire in the explosion. The structure's proximity to the river made it easy to carry up enough water to continue dousing every nearby structure for several more hours until the flames were brought under control and the danger to the district as a whole was contained.

Hours before the fire was completely extinguished, a contingent of heavily armed men surrounded the still-smoldering ruin and prevented anyone from attempting to look inside. They were dressed in civilian clothes and took no part in the rescue operation. Although no one in the Josef Quarter recognized them, their demeanor made it clear that they had come directly from the Castle to take over the investigation. They forbade the firemen and town police from coming too near, and when Chief Sergeant Gruber tried to explain that duty required him to examine the site, their leader nodded indifferently and, with a sharp gesture to his troop to close ranks behind him, said that, unfortunately, security considerations rendered such a step impossible. Gruber, who had already received an official reprimand for tainting the crime scene in the Nepomuk Bridge murder, secretly felt relieved to have the whole affair taken out of his hands and withdrew with a characteristically Austrian threat to fill out an official memorandum objecting to the public undermining of his authority. The same taciturn agents, working in six-hour shifts, kept watch for the next day and a half, carefully controlling access to the site. They were observed cautiously sifting through the wreckage and removing all the contents in sealed boxes. At the end of the second day one of the agents let slip that a single body, hideously mangled by the powerful blast and burned beyond recognition, had been found inside. Everyone assumed that the remains were those of Hans Rotenburg, who was looking for suitable property in which to invest and had made the terrible mistake of starting with Auer's firetrap. No specific cause for the explosion was ever identified.

In public, Moritz Rotenburg tried to contain his grief, but it was plain that his spirit was broken by the calamity. He never went to the Mendelssohn Club anymore, declined all invitations, and sent his apologies for those he had already accepted earlier but would now have to forgo. He even refused the Count-Governor's personal request to join him at the Bell Tower rededication ceremony as the sole Jew among the guests of honor on the platform in the Cathedral Square. All that seemed right and understandable to the community, but then, to everyone's shock, he absolutely refused to countenance burying the victim beside Dina in the family mausoleum or to observe the ritual seven days of mourning. Moritz said that since the body had never been positively identified, he would not relinquish the hope that it was not his son. If Hans had been miraculously saved, it would be a provocation to God to inter someone else under his name and in his plot. Since no one else had any doubt about the boy's death, Rotenburg's behavior smacked of impiety, excusable only as the stubbornness of an old man too stricken in his heart to admit the truth. For the bitterest among his longtime enemies, like Gerhard Himmelfarb, it was a judgment on Rotenburg's pride that he not only had lost his only son but had become too unhinged to give him a proper burial. The man who had forged a financial Empire by using his unequaled ability to analyze events with dispassionate calculation now shut his eyes to the most basic truth and had become as self-deluding as the poorest daydreaming Jew in town.

Moritz made sure to be kept informed of what people were saying about him, but he did so purely out of habit, not real interest. Nothing he heard surprised him, except, perhaps, Himmelfarb's malice, which exceeded even Moritz's bleak expectations. His difficulty swallowing was growing progressively worse, and lately he barely managed to consume the beef bouillon and tepid cream of wheat that constituted his principal form of nourishment. He watched his body's deterioration as though it were that of a once intimate but now increasingly distant acquaintance from whom he would no doubt soon have to separate. By contrast, his immense disappointment in Hans felt nearly unbearable. The knowledge of how close the boy's folly had come to costing him his life had bent Moritz like a physical blow. The grief in his face was not feigned. To think of his son as having been spared by the sheerest luck from becoming either a suicide or a murderer was painful beyond anything Moritz had imagined. Only Dina's death had left him more emotionally destitute. When Tausk first brought him the news that Hans was alive and slowly recovering from his injuries in one of the spymaster's safe houses, Moritz was overjoyed, and nothing would ever diminish that sense of relief. But everything he heard subsequently from Tausk filled him with a debilitating mixture of heartache and anger. Lacking adequate knowledge or the most rudimentary safeguards, the boy had been trying to assemble a bomb entirely on his own. Tausk had gone over what little was left of the shack dozens of times, and as far as he could tell, Hans must have been standing behind one of the thick wooden supports when the explosion occurred. The force of the blast apparently hurled him forward, away from the workbench above which the chemicals were stored, and out into the street, where Tausk was able to intercept him and rush him to a doctor before anyone saw them. For the moment Hans was still too injured to be moved again, but as soon as it was safe to do so, he would have to be smuggled out of the country. He would be taken first to a clinic in Switzerland until he had recovered fully, and from there he could go on to England or the United States, where Moritz was among the few Central European financiers to have invested heavily. Returning to Austria, though, was almost certainly out of the question forever.

"Ruthless, puerile, and conceited" was how Moritz described his son to Tausk, and only after doing so did it occur to him that this was the first time for many years that he had told anyone else what he thought of Hans. Yet what he said to everyone at the Mendelssohn Club was also the strictest truth. In spite of Tausk's repeated urging that simply as a matter of tradecraft it would be best if Moritz held a funeral for Hans, he could not bring himself to agree. "I may be a superstitious fool," he answered the spymaster, "but I am not ready to tempt fate by pretending to bury my own son. The experience would be too much for me. Since no one actually died in the explosion, you can shovel all the ashes you want into a coffin and write whatever name you please on it—but not that of Hans Rotenburg."

Moritz's decision put his acquaintances in an unsolvable predicament. There was no way for them to offer words of consolation to the grief-stricken father for a loss he refused to acknowledge, yet not to say anything risked appearing both callous and rude. Most people retreated behind polite formulations that expressed very little directly but hinted at deeper feelings they could not express. The question of who would now inherit his wealth was palpable behind a large number of the letters Moritz received, and following the verbal contortions through which the writers tried to push their claims to be the worthiest recipients, while pretending they were doing nothing of the sort, was like watching a troupe of not particularly adroit circus acrobats perform precarious maneuvers on the high wire without a safety net. The strain left one queasy. Moritz read each of the notes as they were delivered to the Rotenburg villa and was struck by how few and formulaic even the phrases of genuine sadness were. "I suppose that this is the sort of thing they will be saying when I am really dead," he mused with the momentary self-pity that even the strongest old men who know that they have little time left permit themselves. He could tell that some of the writers, like the Demetzes, were sincere in their expressions of empathy and felt genuinely saddened by being unable to say so to him openly. Perhaps the fear that they were losing their daughter to a Christian aristocrat, who never once visited them in their own home, or invited them to his, gave them a measure of fellow feeling for Moritz's anguish. If so, it was a sad paradox that the most moving letter Moritz received turned out to be from their daughter and her friend Ernst von Alpsbach. Moritz remembered that they had been among Hans's closest companions before his trip abroad, and although he did not know what had caused the rupture, he was certain that his son's politics must have been at least partially to blame. But their letter, signed by them both and sent from the von Alpsbach country estate, where they were now living together, made no mention of any falling-out. They had sent it off as soon as the first report of Hans's death in the explosion began to circulate and so did not know about Moritz's insistence that nothing definitive about his son's fate had been established yet. Their words struck Moritz as the expression of an instinctive emotional generosity, saying neither too much nor sidestepping the grievousness of the occasion. Hans, they wrote, had marked their lives forever with his passion and courage, as he had that of all their school friends, and although they understood that their loss was nothing compared with a father's, they wanted Moritz to know how much Hans had meant to them. In his death, they concluded, they had seen their generation's finest hopes extinguished, and none of them would ever forget how much they owed to his example.

Reading Ernst's and Batya's words was among the most emotionally trying of the many exhausting experiences to which Moritz was subjected during the days immediately after the explosion. There was something uncanny in receiving such a condolence letter when Hans was very much alive, had acted like an utter fool, and, with each day, was more at risk of arrest than of permanent medical complications. Moritz's first thought, for which he reproached himself afterward, was to regret that Ernst was not his son instead of Hans. If the circumstances had been reversed, and a fire out at Brunnenberg had killed the young couple there, Moritz was sure Hans would have been incapable of writing the elder von Alpsbach a letter as affecting as the one he had just received. And yet, he told himself, what Ernst and Batya said must have been prompted at least in part by real qualities in his son, and if Hans had once been able to touch his contemporaries in that way, perhaps one need not despair of him altogether. It was the kind of hope at which he would have laughed in a business negotiation, but now, as he was completing the complex arrangements to take his son out of the country forever, Moritz had little else to which to cling.

The contrast between Ernst's and Batya's response and those of Hans's regular companions over the past months was striking. Although lately they had avoided meeting at the Rotenburg villa, Moritz remembered when they were constant visitors, and from Hans's scattered comments, he gathered that he had stayed on close terms with them throughout the spring. He knew their families well enough to be shocked at the silence from Leo von Arnstein and Chrissi von Hradl and could not help wondering whether their intimacy with his son had been counterfeit from the beginning, encouraged by their fathers in order to secure Moritz's consent when it came time to renew the extensive mortgages on their estates. When Hans was much younger, Dina often used to reproach Moritz for similar suspicions, especially because they seemed to upset their son so much. It was often difficult for Moritz not to regard expressions of interest in Hans, whether by his teachers or his friends, as entirely free of calculation, and it took a great many encounters before Moritz was ready to agree that someone was genuinely concerned for the boy without having any intention on his own wealth. Now, though, Moritz was willing to concede that perhaps his repeated warnings to Hans to be careful in case people were just using him to gain access to his father had helped push Hans along a path that led ultimately to the Josef Quarter and Auer's shack. But Moritz distrusted such theories, not only because they made him responsible for what Hans had become, but rather, because they explained too much. Being Hans's father had taught Moritz enough modesty not to overestimate his influence, and although he saw much of himself in his son's willfulness and inner distance from others, he also knew that his son's nature was still developing according to its own mysterious trajectory, which no one else could foresee.

Whether or not his distrust of Hans's acquaintances had ever been justified as far as the other conspirators were concerned, it could not have been more misdirected. Alone of anyone in town, they chose to take Moritz's steadfast refusal to acknowledge Hans's death as an example for themselves. In spite of being urged repeatedly to do so by their families, they were adamant about not writing him a letter of condolence. Like Moritz, they decided to go on as though Hans, for reasons of his own, had decided simply to absent himself from the area for a while. On the Monday after the explosion they all met at Weidenau, where Christoph immediately seized the lead in determining their next step. "I never thought I would admit it, but you know, the old man is right," he began. They were standing close to one another on the gravel path near his mother's glass-paneled summerhouse, looking out toward the broad avenue of walnut trees, and feeling chilled with fatigue and shock. The dark branches scored the hazy midmorning sky like lines of music waiting for someone to ink in the notes. The trees would not flower until late May, but a few short growths at the end of the stems were just starting to appear, giving the long double columns a less austere look than they had shown a few weeks ago when the conspirators had walked there with Hans. It was impossible for them not to think of that time now, and although they resented Christoph's bid for leadership, they were also glad that someone was prepared to take command. "If Hans really is dead"—he went on—"then the best way to honor his memory is to complete the task to which we all pledged ourselves, and if he is alive and the party ordered him to go underground before our action, that is all the more reason for us to maintain discipline and not desert at the last minute. The chemist sent to help with the explosives must have been stopped at the border before he ever reached Hans, so right now we are completely on our own. This is our chance to show what we can do in a crisis to make the party proud of us." His voice carried more conviction than he really felt, but simply by performing the role, Christoph had begun to give it a reality for himself. Somewhat to his surprise, he sensed how readily the others accepted him in it. Perhaps they had grown so used to following Hans's orders that, like any reflex, the habit of obedience was easily transferred to whoever made a strong claim on it.

"But what, exactly, can we do? All the material for making bombs went up in the explosion, along with most of our guns, and there is not nearly enough time to replace it by Easter." Anxiety made Leo's thin, schoolboy voice sound even more querulous than usual. But it was clear from his in-gratiating look that the question was less a challenge than an appeal for more precise instructions.

"Obviously we have to give up any idea of blowing up the procession, but that just means we need to improvise. I always suspected that at the end it would come down to looking our targets in the eyes and pulling the trigger ourselves. To me, it seems more honorable like that anyway." Christoph nodded encouragingly to the others. He was trying to imitate Hans's characteristic ways of rallying them to embrace his convictions as their own and felt pleased with himself at how easily the part came to him. "Besides, at least now we don't have to bring in Blumenthal," he said with an easy smile. "Hans's idea of getting him to carry the bomb was bril-liant—there is no doubt about that—but since we have no choice now ex-cept to use handguns, we can dispense with that odious creature entirely."

For all their talk of going on boldly without Hans, no one made a move to step away from the shelter of the summerhouse wall. The delicate layer of mist had burned off, and the rich blue of the sky hinted at the coming of summer. The day was turning markedly warmer, but they kept their lo-den coats buttoned and looked back with regret to the main house, where the servants were still clearing the table from the remains of their ample breakfast. With a shrug, Christoph said that until they had finished mak-ing their plans, they could not risk going back inside, where someone might overhear them. He pointed out that the pistol range at the far end of the large field behind the granary had been set up, and since they would soon need to be at their sharpest, he suggested they all take a few extra hours of target practice. As they slowly made their way across the path, Christoph watched his companions with a new skepticism and, for the first time, found himself wondering how Hans had ever managed to appear so confident in their abilities. He decided that the only way to be sure no one would get confused at the last minute and commit a major blunder was to retain as much of Hans's original plan as possible. In spite of what he regarded as its excessive intricacy, at least they all were famil-iar with it. In his own mind, Christoph was already starting to think of Hans as a distant precursor whom he would never criticize in front of the others but whose way of doing things he needed to start amending right away. The first step was to simplify everything and concentrate solely on the ceremony in the Cathedral Square itself. It was impossible to be sure of getting off a clean shot during the procession's brief stops in front of the

Greek Orthodox church or the Mendelssohn Club, where the sight lines would be hopelessly blocked. But during the celebration the Cathedral Square would be completely closed off on three sides, leaving only one way to get in and out. The police obviously assumed that by funneling access to the square through a single entrance, they could maintain strict control over who was permitted entry and eliminate potential troublemakers long before the procession arrived. But since none of the conspirators fell into the category of "suspicious types," they would have no trouble gaining admittance, and once inside, they could turn the security measures to their own advantage. In such a packed throng it would be much easier than out on the street to take careful aim at their targets, either when the procession entered the square or when its members had taken their seats on the elevated platform in front of the church. He and Leo would find a place as near as possible to the dais, and at that range, unless their pistols misfired or they lost their nerve, it would be impossible to miss. Joachim and Manfred would station themselves more toward the back, at opposite ends of the square, each in an outside row close to the street, from where they could fire on anyone in the procession who was trying to run away. They would also be perfectly placed to hinder the security detail rushing forward in the direction of the Count-Governor at the head of the column. With shots now coming from four separate locations, it would be hard for the police to estimate right away how many terrorists there were or to pick them out in the crowd. The resulting confusion might just give them all a chance to slip away. If they managed to drop their weapons the instant after firing them and merge back into the crowd without being identified, no one would suspect a young von Hradl or a von Arnstein, whose parents were themselves in places of honor in the procession, of being involved in an assassination. Joachim and Manfred both were from the middle class, but their fathers' long-established record of devotion to the established order placed them above suspicion as well. More important, the fact that they all continued to be at liberty could only signify that the plot had not been discovered as a result of the explosion, and so the arrangements Hans and the party had made for their escape must still be in place as well.

Christoph was intelligent enough to know how slight their chances of making it out of the country were, but he saw no reason to emphasize that to the others. Their need to believe in the possibility of getting away safely was palpable in the urgency with which they kept looking at him for reassurance, and he outlined his plan accordingly. Everything he said was accepted with the same unanimous enthusiasm with which they had greeted all of Hans's proposals, and by the time he finished explaining his strategy, the group was striding toward the target range with their spirits visibly lifted.

Their mood would have improved still further if they suspected how secure their position really was. Tausk continued to keep them under observation, but without clear proof he was helpless to bring charges against them, and since all his evidence named Hans Rotenburg as the ringleader, he was prevented from using it. Until they actually committed a crime, the conspirators were legally untouchable. Even if they had not been shielded from preventive arrest by their family connections, Tausk was content to let them dangle at liberty for now, watched by a team of secondary agents, while he concentrated his best-trained men on the imminent confrontation with Brugger. All the documents Tausk had intercepted convinced him that without Hans's leadership the conspirators were incapable of independent action, and he was certain there would be time to settle with them after Easter, when his own authority would have been strengthened by the success of the Cathedral Square ceremony. Tausk and Roublev had memorized every detail of Hans's plan and intended to flood the areas around the Mendelssohn Club and the Greek Orthodox church with enough police to thwart any attack on the procession. If the conspirators were nonetheless suicidal enough to try something, he would be glad to see them suffer the consequences of their folly, but he suspected that they had already abandoned any such idea. The real danger, he was certain, came from Brugger. Tausk had gone without a full night's sleep for so long he could scarcely remember what it felt like to stretch out in a bed without keeping his clothes and shoes on, but when he did seize a few moments to shut his eyes, he invariably got up more exhausted than before. Everywhere he turned in his dreams, he saw Brugger's face, or rather, he saw a constantly changing series of faces, each of which, through all its mocking disguises, he knew was Brugger. At times the figure appeared to him as gangly and clean-shaven, only to change, an instant later, into a much older man, stooped and with a full beard, but always smiling at Tausk, whether with gleaming white teeth or yellowed, rotten ones. Sometimes Brugger appeared to him sitting at a table laden with forbidden foods, on which he flung himself like an animal, eating everything with filthy hands and reaching over to touch Tausk with grease-stained, lascivious fingers. Worst of all was the night Brugger somehow managed to take on Rabbi Pelz's features and voice and began talking to Tausk with Pelz's customary, frightening attentiveness. In Pelz's immense, liquid eyes, shaded by heavy lids that did nothing to dim their intensity, Tausk saw reflected an eagle's-eye view of the accursed regions he had traversed since leaving the seminary. Tausk stuttered some reply to one of the rabbi's searching questions, only to see his teacher's pale face turn still paler as he began screaming in disgust, "You are even stupider than you are corrupt." When Tausk tried to excuse himself, Pelz grew angrier. He shouted out a string of the most hideous obscenities, culminating in a furious command: "Pack your bags and get out! Get out and never come back!" Then, to a completely flustered Tausk, he broke out into a raucous, nasty laugh that transformed his face back into Brugger's.

Tausk never told anyone the content of his dreams, but his distress on awakening was impossible to disguise. When Roublev tried to show some concern, Tausk kept him at bay with one of his typical formulations. "Don't worry yourself on my account," he said. "I found a perfectly good way to stop the nightmares."

"How?" Roublev asked.

To which Tausk replied simply, "I am giving up sleeping."

For the most part Tausk had little choice but to follow his own prescription. In addition to shuttling back and forth from the Castle to the Josef Quarter and from there to the city center to supervise the security arrangements along the procession route, he also had to make certain that Hans's injuries were healing sufficiently for him to be able to travel almost immediately. The delegation from Vienna would be accompanied by its own corps of security guards, responsible directly to the Interior Ministry, and with so many skilled agents in town not under Tausk's control, the risk of their detecting Hans was too high. Moritz had been urged repeatedly by his doctor to go to Switzerland to consult a specialist for the illness that was making it increasingly hard for him to breathe or swallow properly, and no one was surprised that he decided to leave before the Passover holidays. The more psychologically astute of his fellow townsmen were certain that Moritz's unacknowledged grief at the loss of his son contributed to his worsening condition and claimed to sympathize with his desire for a change of setting, where he would not be reminded of Hans by everything around him. For the first time in his life Moritz seemed to be listening to advice from others. He arranged for two private carriages to be attached to the midweek express train to Zurich and sent a note to Count Wiladowski explaining his decision. He wished the Count-Governor every success with the Bell Tower ceremony and enclosed a substantial check to help defray the cost of the function so that the entertainment could be appropriately lavish without straining the provincial treasury. Wiladowski had no qualms about pocketing a contribution he did not need, but as he told Tausk, he genuinely regretted the absence of one of the few men in town to whom he could speak and to whose company he had looked forward as a relief from the tedium of Zichy-Ferraris and Trautmannsdorff. He ordered Tausk to see Moritz off at the station on his behalf, and in recognition of Rotenburg's many acts of generosity to the community, he told the spymaster to place Wiladowski's official seal on the door to Moritz's carriage so that the old man could rest on the journey undisturbed by customs agents or border guards.

For Tausk, persuading Moritz to leave town was just as important as spiriting Hans away to safety. He was certain now that the financier's own life was in jeopardy. He had been dangerously mistaken in thinking Brugger ever intended to harm Count Wiladowski. Brugger was as contemptuous as Hans of conventional politics, but he too believed deeply in the power of symbolic actions. In the world Brugger inhabited, nothing would have a greater resonance than orchestrating the murder of the richest Jew in the Empire during Passover. Tausk had brooded for days about Brugger's next move and finally concluded that Rotenburg was the only target that made sense. Grasping the logic of the earlier killings had been difficult, but once Tausk had done so, the pattern was unmistakable. Strangely enough, it had nothing to do with revenge. Brugger had no idea that Moritz was plotting to have him killed, but even if he had, Tausk was certain the rebbe would never let that affect his plans. Messiahs are not concerned with mere reprisals. Tausk belatedly understood that Brugger was fashioning a ladder of death, a progression of victims in strictly hierarchical sequence. The first rung was Shmuel Kosch, a petty tradesman so insignificant as to be essentially anonymous. Kosch was followed by the Buczacz rabbi, a holy man venerated as a miracle worker by his followers. Now, to complete the pattern, a final offering must come from the realm of secular power and wealth. In these three sacrificial victims, Brugger would bring together the whole fallen world of the Jews and, by taking their lives, symbolically overcome it.

For all their internal coherence, Tausk still found himself wondering how many of these thoughts were really Brugger's and how many the crystallization of his own nightmares. His dreams had become sufficiently alarming to make him question his perceptions while awake. He had interrogated enough prisoners to know that prolonged sleeplessness could make a man believe anything, and he recognized in himself a similar depth of exhaustion. But he also knew that people in the grip of a hallucination rarely question the reality of their visions and hoped that his very uncertainty proved his intelligence was still functioning as lucidly as ever.

The spymaster would have been startled to know that just as he was no longer sure of his ability to understand Brugger, so Brugger himself was undergoing a terrible loss of faith in his own powers. For Brugger, the explosion in Auer's shack was devastating. It changed everything. If Hans had been his own son, Brugger could not have felt more abandoned. He remembered his exact words to Moritz and kept repeating them in his mind: "Your son is young and will make many grievous mistakes, but you need not worry on his account. When he dies, he will still call himself a Jew and be older than you are today." In Brugger's mind, when he told this to Moritz, he was simply informing him of a fact as incontrovertible as the report of an event that had already taken place. He saw Hans as clearly as if he were sitting in a room with him, an elderly man, busy writing someone a long letter, dressed in an exquisite suit of soft charcoal gray English wool. But if he had been that wrong about Hans, there was no reason to believe any of his other visions. Up until the hour when word of Hans's death first reached him, Brugger's greatest desolation had always come when he saw nothing, when an indifferent emptiness filled his consciousness and his prayers for a special understanding went unanswered. He had grown to recognize, and even to expect, although never without sorrow, the alternation within him of blindness and revelation. But never before had a moment of prescience later proved entirely delusional. His visions were already painfully incomplete; if they were actually false as well, he had nothing left to offer.

He began to spend all his time alone, either locked in his room or away from the house entirely. He stopped speaking to the disciples, except once, when, in a hoarse whisper, he told Robert to drive away the visitors crowding around the doorstep to seek an audience and then to go to the shul and announce that the rebbe would not be preaching there again. If Brugger ate and drank at all, it must have been by himself, somewhere on his walks, because when Linnetchen took advantage of his absence to go in and clean his room, there was not a single dirty plate or cup anywhere. His closest followers had started waiting up for him, and were heartbroken how often he did not return to the house until just before dawn, his clothes grass-stained and disheveled, and his face wet with tears. He shuffled past them to his room, not really seeing them on the staircase, with the look of a man emptying himself out from within until nothing remained.

One night, hoping to restore their teacher to himself, Linnetchen permitted herself to visit him in his room uninvited, something she had never dared before. She had carefully bathed and perfumed her body and lined her eyes with kohl, imitating, as closely as she was able, the erotic descriptions in the Andalusian songs Brugger had taught her the first time he took her to bed. But when he heard the noise of the door, he raised his head toward her with vacant horror, and she fled from the room, terrified not only by his baffled stare but by how he was slumped forward in the small seat by the window, his knees tucked up against his chest, looking out at her through a pair of thick eyeglasses.

· ◆ ·

Pfister's enthusiasm for his new duties as head of protocol for the Easter ceremony grew only stronger as he threw himself into the work. It was not just the title and additional prestige that appealed to him, although he welcomed both after having felt himself shunted aside by Tausk's pervasive influence over the Count-Governor. With the instinct of a natural bureaucrat, Pfister quickly realized there was no reason why the position need be temporary. At the most propitious moment—perhaps when he was being congratulated by a grateful Count-Governor on the triumphant success of the Easter festival—he intended to submit a formal proposal outlining his conviction that it would be much more efficient if one person were put in permanent charge of everything connected with public events and festivities in the province. The next few years would see a score of notable occasions, some of which, especially the seventieth anniversary of the Emperor's coronation in 1918, would far eclipse the Bell Tower rededication ceremony in importance. Officially, Pfister's rank as First Secretary was already higher than the new appointment, which he thought would certainly be offered to him, but combining the two portfolios would let him demonstrate his competence directly to Vienna and perhaps attract the favorable notice of the Minister himself. He already saw how uniting the two roles allowed him to make demands of every department in the Castle, from the kitchens to the security forces. Scarcely an hour went by without another memorandum from Pfister inquiring into the arrangement of the sleeping quarters for the highest-ranking visitors and the disposition of the guards around the platform in the Cathedral Square. He also kept his promise and sent both the Count-Governor and Marie-Luise a series of detailed transcriptions of the most famous state dinners chronicled in diplomatic histories so that the couple could select the dishes for the formal banquet with an eye to historical precedence. Even as dedicated a gourmand as the Count-Governor found himself losing his appetite contemplating page upon page of ill-matched menus, recommended only because they had once been served to someone of princely rank. Count Wiladowski took his copy into his wife's room and proceeded to read it aloud to her with mock earnestness. Marie-Luise, who had always defended Pfister from her husband's scorn, was furious that he had dared encroach into what she considered her exclusive domain. Her family had been entertaining the ruling houses of Europe for generations, and she needed no suggestions from a subordinate about how to fulfill her responsibilities as a hostess. In her eyes, Pfister had committed the unpardonable sin of presumption, and without directly admitting she might have erred in extending him her protection, Marie-Luise made it clear she was ready to abandon her former favorite whenever it suited Count Wiladowski to put him in his place. "Yes, there is no doubt that Pfister has become more insufferable than usual lately, but I think we should wait until after the ceremony before deciding what to do about him," Wiladowski said, smiling contentedly at having secured her consent in advance to whatever he should decide. If nothing else, his First Secretary's gaffe had provided one of the rare moments of accord between Marie-Luise and himself. Besides, for now Pfister's officiousness was useful to his master. Many of the unpleasant directives he issued were necessary for the ceremony to proceed smoothly, and it was always helpful to have an unpopular subordinate at hand whom one could sacrifice afterward to soothe everyone's ruffled feelings.

Without his realizing it, Pfister's interfering zeal had made him the most hated man in the Castle, displacing even the spymaster in that role. He had managed to turn everyone against him simply by insisting they do their jobs properly. Since an event like the Easter ceremony did not present many opportunities to collect bribes, poor Pfister found himself universally disliked at the very moment when circumstances were making him act with uncharacteristic rectitude. The only person whose opinion of the First Secretary improved during this time was Tausk, who felt enormous relief at not having to worry about any of the problems now under Pfister's sole authority. For the spymaster, this was his last chance to operate with a free hand in the Josef Quarter before the ceremony began. He still had the warrant for the arrest of Brugger and all his disciples in his pocket and had no intention of delaying its enforcement. Tausk had been watching Brugger's movements closely, trying to pick the right moment when to strike, and he knew every step of the rebbe's habitual route away from the house toward his favorite clearing in the von Alpsbach forest. Tausk was baffled that Brugger should choose the days before Passover, when his counsel would be sought by more people than ever, to stop teaching at the shul and remove himself from all his followers, but it was a gift of which he intended to make full use. It was crucial to avoid any large-scale disturbance in the Josef Quarter, and without their teacher nearby, Tausk was confident the disciples would offer little resistance to his well-armed men. Just as important, after the series of shocks—from the discovery of Kosch's body to the burning of the Buczacz rabbi and the explosion in Auer's shack—that had swept through the district and left its inhabitants anxious about what might occur next, it was unlikely any of the ordinary citizens would intervene to save the followers of a man who himself seemingly had abandoned them all. Still, Tausk intended to take as few risks as possible and, along with Roublev, spent hours drilling his men in how to conduct the raid. This year, the first night of Passover fell on a Friday, so that the regular Sabbath dinner would be sacred beyond all others, and no one, except the most defiantly secular Jews, would be out on the streets after sundown. If Brugger kept to his usual pattern of the past few days and went out alone early that Friday, Tausk and Roublev would secretly follow him and leave behind their men to keep watch over the house. Whether or not Brugger intended to return on time for the Passover meal, once he was safely away from the town, it would be easy to overpower him and make certain that no one ever saw him again. When Brugger did not appear that night, the blow to the disciples would be incalculable, and Tausk imagined them all sitting at the richly decked table, dispirited and confused. Around midnight Tausk's agents would burst into the house and arrest everyone there on charges of murder and arson. The prisoners were to be taken directly to the Castle and held incommunicado in the interrogation cells until Tausk arrived and obtained their confessions. If anyone resisted, either in the house or on the way to prison, Tausk ordered his men to shoot whoever it was without hesitation as a warning to the others.

· ◆ ·

Unusually for April, the gentle spring rain that had started falling in the early hours of Friday morning and continued intermittently until just before midday never turned blustery. There was no wind, and the forest paths were still easily traversable for anyone who knew the way. The trees at the edge of Brugger's favorite clearing were shimmering in the noon light, the droplets of water on their bark giving them a strange look of weightlessness, as though for all its depth, the whole forest was itself only a reflection of the sky overhead and could be scattered and rearranged by a simple shift in the clouds. The air was rich with the smell of recently wet soil and pine needles as Brugger, empty of any thought or feeling, sat against a felled trunk.

There was no surprise in his face when he looked up and saw Tausk and Roublev emerge from the woods to stand in front of him. If anything, he seemed relieved and merely asked Tausk bitterly, "Are you sure this is secluded enough? I have been expecting you for a long time, but I always thought we would meet when it still mattered." Although he had never talked to Tausk before, Brugger spoke as though they had long known each other and finally agreed to play out the last scenes of a drama whose outcome was a foregone conclusion.

In spite of Tausk's exhaustion and nervousness, he retained sufficient imaginative resilience to fall in with Brugger's tone. He sat down beside the rebbe and offered him one of his cigarettes. Brugger accepted with a nod of thanks, and for a few minutes both men sat looking out toward the horizon without exchanging another word. When they had finished, Brugger extinguished the cigarette underneath his hiking boots, gestured toward Roublev, and quietly asked Tausk, "Are you going to have him kill me now?"

When Tausk hesitated before answering, Brugger went on. "It has certainly taken you long enough to get here. I have been coming to this place by myself for nearly two weeks now expecting you and had almost given up waiting. By tomorrow I would have been gone from this district, out of your reach, and what would everyone have said then? Poor Tausk. You learned so much from Rabbi Pelz except what really matters."

It angered Tausk, as Brugger knew it would, to hear his teacher's name used so freely. But there was something in the rebbe's tone, beyond the baiting allusion to Pelz, that puzzled him. Not the note of resignation to his fate. Tausk had heard that before from men who knew they were about to be executed and had stopped struggling. This was different. There was no surrender in Brugger, no submission to those who had come to dispatch him. He was ready to die at Tausk's hand, but he spoke as though he thought of Tausk less as his executioner than as his instrument, summoned there to fulfill his self-chosen fate. To be Brugger's tool in anything, even his own death, rankled Tausk, but before he could say anything, Roublev, who had never interrupted an interrogation before, suddenly screamed out, "Don't listen to another word from him. He is not a holy man but a latrine!"

The whole clearing reverberated with the aftersounds of Roublev's outburst. As soon as he had recovered from his astonishment, Tausk spun around, glaring at Roublev, and prepared to give him a savage dressing-down. But then he saw Brugger nodding emphatically. "Your man is right," Brugger said. "You have no cause to rebuke him. That is exactly what I am. Anyone can see in his eyes how much he hates me and wants me dead. Even if his reasons are wrong, his judgment is not. He is cleaner in his simple hatred than either of us."

Tausk could feel the moment spinning out of control and was determined to rein it in. He was growing aware of having lost all sense of how long it had taken them to get there and how much time they had already spent talking. It was as though this place existed apart from the rest of the world and was only waiting for them all to be gone before it vanished completely from sight. High overhead, a few clouds were being drawn toward them by the first stirring of a fresh wind, but for the moment the light in the clearing was almost solid enough to touch. Only the ground cover seemed to be growing slowly deeper, the shadowy patches underneath the trees turning dark emerald in the changing air.

Brugger noticed Tausk straining to feel from which direction the wind was coming, and briefly his expression lost some of its bitterness. "Not that it makes any difference to you or the men who sent you, but the only person to whom I really have ever been a menace is myself," he told Tausk in a matter-of-fact voice. "Your Count-Governor and I do not inhabit the same world. What he does concerns only his kind, not ours. But Moritz Rotenburg is a different story. Together, he and I might have done much for our people. Perhaps everything. In the end I failed him much more than he failed me, and if he wants my blood for the error, that is his right. All I ask of you is that when you are done with me, you go back and tell him that I am sorry I was so mistaken."

By now Tausk was convinced that whatever Brugger's intentions, his attitude was not simply a desperate stratagem to cling to life for as long as possible. But rather than feel himself inclined to sympathy, the spymaster felt a growing frustration at finding himself in a dialogue whose meaning eluded him. The need to know everything around him drove Tausk more than the desire for power. Even now he could not enter someone else's room without picking up and examining whatever objects lay within reach, including, to their owner's consternation, obviously private letters and notes. In certain moods, he could understand and forgive almost any transgression, no matter how vile, but he could not endure the sense of helplessness, the feeling of being whispered about behind his back and of important decisions being made that concerned him, but on whose out-come he had no influence, that flooded him the instant he felt something was being kept from him.

"Mistaken about what?" he demanded of Brugger. "I am not in the habit of delivering messages from a man in your position. So far you have not given me a reason to do anything for you, let alone disturb someone like Moritz Rotenburg with your apologies."

"I permitted you to capture me." The entire time they had been speaking, Brugger had shown none of the flashes of temper his followers dreaded. Now, though, he brushed aside Tausk's gibe, and something of his old fierceness flickered in his eyes and in the downward pursed twitch of his lips. "I know that I am not what I once thought I was, but believe me, even today I still could have thwarted you with a word."

"Believe what you need to, Brugger." Tausk's sarcasm was palpable only in his voice, not in his eyes, which kept their wary attentiveness.

Brugger laughed derisively and gestured to the forest behind them. "I am talking about elementary tactics, not magic spells. You know some-thing of what my followers would do for me. These woods are as familiar to me as the Josef Quarter, and every time you followed me here you gave yourself away a thousand times over. Think how easily I could have hidden

441

half a dozen men anywhere along the way and the same number again in the trees at the edge of the clearing. Maybe even now a few of my people are nearby, ready to protect me. If they heard you admit you came to kill me, I would not want to be in your position."

Neither Tausk nor Roublev turned their eyes to where Brugger was pointing. If he had intended to ambush them, it would have happened already. But although he was not afraid, Tausk recognized that Brugger had told him the simple truth and was disgusted by his own blunder. If he and Roublev returned to town alive, it would only be because Brugger had decided that was what he wanted. From the beginning it had always been Brugger's choice. "Well," Tausk thought, "tonight, if the dead can still have any thoughts, Brugger will have a fine lesson in the limits of gratitude."

Brugger looked at Tausk with enormous weariness. He shook his head and sighed as though summoning the strength for a disagreeable task. "When I said that you learned much from Rabbi Pelz except what really matters, I was not trying to wound you, Tausk, only to force you to acknowledge what you already know. Your mind has become like a stagnant sea, renewing nothing, transforming everything that comes near you into itself. Long before you were expelled from the yeshiva, you had already failed its most important lessons. But not for any lack of brilliance. Far from it. It was common knowledge that no one as intelligent as Jakob Tausk had appeared in a generation. But you were never really there in the seminary except as a stranger and a spy. Your own brilliance and the power it could win you, that is all you have ever believed in. It is your nightmares to which you have given my face and now need to hunt down."

Tausk said nothing. He lit another cigarette from the still-glowing stub in his hand and stared at Brugger with his large, close-set eyes. In spite of Tausk's having been out-of-doors since before dawn, his pallor was even more marked, giving his skin an ashen translucence. Finally a slow trembling passed through him, and he put his hand out to steady himself, but encountering nothing except the empty air, he pulled it back to his side with a jerk and forced himself to stand straight by sheer willpower. "But they did die," he said softly, "Kosch and all the people in Buczacz. What were they? My nightmare or yours?"

"Why must it be one or the other?" Brugger challenged. "I stumble forward, sometimes guided by an irresistible clarity, sometimes lost in the dark. You discover a pattern in my actions where I was aware only of improvised steps, taken one at a time. Who am I to say that the connections

442

you find have no reality? It is the malice of your interpretations I shudder at, not your right to make them."

The air had started to turn colder. Brugger pulled his traveling cloak tightly over his shoulder. Then, articulating every syllable with pedantic care, as if lucidity were just another childish code, like schoolboy slang, at which he too could play, he said, "You live among Christians now, Tausk, so you must know that in their story, on a night exactly like this, their rebbe was abandoned by all his followers before he was arrested and brought to the Roman Count-Governor. One heretical version has it that if only a single disciple had proved steadfast and stayed awake with him, he would have been spared the cross. I will not say anything about the sentimentality of their tale. It has served them well. But I have come to accept that our God, unlike theirs, is a master of ironic dialectics. I am condemned to die because all my followers obeyed me too well; far from deserting me, they followed the part of me that sought out the darkness."

"Is that why you let us seize you? Because you think the murders have made you unclean?" Tausk could not stop himself from asking. In spite of himself, there was a familiarity to these ideas, a sense of urgency that nothing he had experienced at the Castle, not even his late-night colloquies with Wiladowski, had erased.

"Sins and errors hover about me like a swarm of flies," Brugger said bitterly. "I am amazed you cannot see them for yourself. Even if everything I believed was right, it was still wickedness to teach it. No one can bestow wisdom on another, and to give knowledge without wisdom is the activity of the devil. I thought all my transgressions were sanctified because my soul was righteous, but there was only vanity and the gleeful laughter of the unholy. I promised Rotenburg that his son would outlive him and die a Jew, old and respected among his people. I *saw* it, Tausk. I knew the cloth of his garments and the scent of his cologne. Instead he died stupidly and in shame, and with him, so did all my faith in myself." As he finished these words, Brugger slumped forward on the log, his face cadaverous in its withdrawal.

Tausk's quick gray eyes widened in amazement, but he said nothing. How could he be certain which would be more satisfying: to confound Brugger by telling him the truth when it was too late or to let him die convinced his visions were empty mirages? In the end it was not calculation that determined Tausk's decision as much as simple curiosity. He had to let Brugger know, if only to find out how the rebbe would react. Like many sudden revelations, the actual telling was simple and brief. Tausk was accustomed to the truth's always being more complicated than his lies, but now he found that only a few sentences were required, and even to these, Brugger seemed to listen with wavering attention. Once he had taken in the fact that Hans Rotenburg did not die in the explosion, he showed little interest in the additional details Tausk volunteered. His attention was fixed entirely inward, his lips forming a series of thanksgiving psalms of which Tausk could distinguish only every second or third line. When he was done, he opened his eyes, looked around with a clear gaze, and, in a tone as simple as if he were talking to a companion after a shared meal, said, "Thank you. You can't imagine the burden you have lifted from me."

Tausk thought he was prepared for almost any reaction, but Brugger's hymns left him at a loss. The spymaster did not discount the possibility that for all its apparent inwardness, some of Brugger's devotional rapture had been a performance intended to impress his captors. But whether aimed at him or not, Brugger's reaction was sufficiently perturbing to make Tausk waver in his intention for the first time since he and Roublev had set out that morning to trap the rebbe. It was not that he took Brugger's messianic dreams seriously—if indeed Brugger still had any such notions—but the thought of murdering this man on the eve of Passover suddenly troubled Tausk. And so he responded exactly the way he did when he found himself sitting in one of his cells across from a suspect about whose fate he had not entirely made up his mind: He asked the prisoner himself to tell him what he was doing there.

"Do you believe you are the Jewish Messiah?" he said to Brugger, keeping his own voice as neutral and unemphatic as he could.

Brugger turned and looked at him with calm curiosity. "I may have had a spark of that gift once," he answered, as though discussing some valued but by no means inconceivable faculty, "but neither I nor the age was ready, so I sent it away again. What does it matter whether I ever had such thoughts or not? They have departed from my heart, and their going has left me as broken as the most wretched Jew in this province." Rather than show any apprehension, Brugger seemed utterly serene, as though he had come to the resolution of some great crisis and the conversation with Tausk were just its placid aftermath. A stranger, listening to the two men, might have concluded that Brugger was the interrogator leading his prisoner inexorably to condemn himself by his own words.

Tausk realized that he should simply get up, walk away, and let Roublev finish what they had come to do. The wind had turned cold, and it chilled the thin layer of sweat soaking Tausk's body. Brugger was already at peace with himself. So too would Rotenburg be as soon as the rebbe was dead and Hans fully recovered. In three days, when the festivities were over and the dignitaries had returned safely to Vienna, Wiladowski would have everything he wanted as well. The image of all those contented faces grew more and more repugnant. All Tausk wanted was sleep. For once let the living bury their dead without him, and see what results that would bring. Without any warning, he lurched away from Brugger. "I cannot kill this man," he said to a startled Roublev. The look he gave his assistant froze any thought of argument. "Take him to the road leading to the border, and then come back for me. If he is ever seen again on this side, have him shot down on the spot like a rabid dog."

When Roublev returned alone, the sun had already set. In the shadows, the clearing looked empty, and Roublev was terrified his master had vanished. When he finally saw Tausk, he was lying unconscious on the ground, his body shaking with fever.

7

I have come to the conclusion that our national policy is made in three admirably synchronized steps: It is concocted at the various ministries in Vienna, approved at the Imperial Palace, and implemented nowhere." Wiladowski put down the latest set of dispatches from the capital in frustration. His mood could scarcely be worse, and it was only to stop himself from giving in completely to his displeasure that he tried to joke about it to Pfister, who was sitting across from him with an uneasy expression and an even thicker sheaf of papers in his hands for the Count-Governor to look at next. The visitors had started arriving the night before, and it seemed as if each group had brought along its own set of directives—phrased of course as polite recommendations—from whatever government interests they represented, often explicitly contradicting the proposals delivered only a few minutes earlier by a rival Department. Marie-Luise was still entertaining the early arrivals at one of her famous lunches, and Wiladowski had excused himself before everyone was finished so that he and his First Secretary could go over the final details of the ceremony. The man was absolutely indefatigable, Wiladowski had to grant him that, and now, with Tausk unaccountably laid up in the Castle infirmary, Pfister had taken charge of the entire event. Except that there seemed to be no immediate threat to his safety, it was all going as wretchedly as in Wiladowski's worst premonitions. The Castle was crowded with disagreeable guests, Pfister's officiousness had reached appalling proportions, and the weather had turned superb, thereby eliminating his last excuse to shorten the festivities. Marie-Luise was enjoying every moment of the attention that Zichy-Ferraris and Trautmannsdorff were lavishing on her, while Wiladowski had to maintain an appreciative smile as he was being complimented on how brilliantly his wife managed such affairs and how wasted her gifts were in such a backwater. And now Moritz Rotenburg's departure for Switzerland had spoiled Wiladowski's best chance at retaliation. Through skillful maneuvering, Wiladowski had persuaded the Finance Minister to request as a matter of urgent state interest that the Castle invite Rotenburg to all the private parties held in connection with the Bell Tower ceremony. But just when Wiladowski had an irreproachable excuse for doing what he knew would incense Marie-Luise and Zichy-Ferraris, his stratagems were frustrated by Rotenburg's need to go abroad for medical treatment. To Wiladowski, it seemed that doctors were sabotaging him at every turn. Rotenburg's flight to Zurich was bad enough, but to be obliged to forgo Tausk's services at the same time was an outrage. Wiladowski had sent his personal physician to attend the spymaster, in part as a gesture of great favor, but also to see if Tausk could not be encouraged to rally himself and resume his duties for just two more days before returning to bed. However, the doctor came back and assured the Count-Governor that the patient required complete rest if he was not to endanger his life. In Tausk's present condition he was much too weak to get up, and the doctor emphasized that until his fever broke, Tausk's judgment was likely to be as impaired as his physical strength.

Since nothing in his training had included advice on what to do when one's superior is disrespectful of the nation's leaders, Pfister made no reply to any of Wiladowski's sardonic comments about the mutually contradictory briefs he was being given. In any case, Pfister was preoccupied with pressing questions of his own. He had not found himself included on Marie-Luise's guest list for any but the largest parties at which his presence was virtually obligatory considering his position in the Castle administration. He knew how much the Count-Governor's wife enjoyed his company and found his sudden ostracism incomprehensible. Count Wiladowski had no fondness for him, Pfister knew that well enough, but he was unlikely to risk his domestic tranquillity by asking his wife to exclude her favorite protégé, and even if he did, it was far from certain she would obey. No, Pfister concluded, a conspiracy against him had been organized elsewhere. Almost certainly Tausk was at its center, driven to it out of jealousy over Pfister's brilliant management of the Easter ceremony. Everyone in the Castle was talking about how Roublev, the spymaster's sinister assistant, had come in late Friday night, carrying Tausk on his shoulders up to the infirmary in an advanced stage of delirium. Pfister's triumph must have completely unhinged Tausk, and with his race's notorious propensity toward hysteria, it was not really surprising that he had succumbed to his disappointment in so shameless a manner. But if Tausk was as ill as everyone reported, how was he still able to plot so effectively against an enemy whose augmented powers should have made him secure from attack? Since everyone in the Castle naturally would side with the First Secretary against the Jewish interloper, Tausk had no one through whom he could work, yet the guest list for that afternoon's coffee in Marie-Luise's private quarters again conspicuously excluded Pfister. The First Secretary was so perturbed trying to make sense of the plots being hatched against him that even Count Wiladowski, whose firm policy it was never to notice what his subordinates might be feeling, could not help acknowledging Pfister's distress. Reluctantly he asked what the matter was and, an instant later, already regretted that he had deviated from his principle of benign indifference. In a lifetime of watching courtiers scrape for advancement, Wiladowski had heard nothing quite as abject as Pfister's nearly tearful question about why he was no longer allowed the inestimable privilege of attending upon Countess Wiladowski during her receptions. Wiladowski had no idea what to reply and little inclination to do so. But good breeding required him to find a way out of the scene for both of them, so he mumbled something about how Pfister surely must realize he was needed elsewhere these days and could not be spared for minor social functions. As a last sop to his First Secretary, upon whose immediate dismissal, as soon as the last guest had departed, Wiladowski had now firmly decided, the Count-Governor offered to let Pfister stand at the back of the platform on the Cathedral Square, thus sharing the dais with all the principal dignitaries. Pfister's presence was not nearly as offensive to his wife or Zichy-Ferraris as Rotenburg's or Tausk's would have been, but it was the best Wiladowski could do, and when a grateful Pfister left the room, effusively proclaiming his gratitude, Wiladowski had the trivial but nonetheless real pleasure of satisfying two quite different impulses through a single gesture.

After being assured for at least the third time that Tausk's illness was not contagious, Wiladowski, accompanied by two guards, made his way across the Castle courtyard up to the north wing, where the infirmary was located. He needed some cheering up after the conversation with Pfister, and visiting Tausk seemed by far the best choice. It was probably kinder to let the man rest, but Wiladowski thought that lately he had made enough sacrifices of his own energy for others—though if pressed, he might find it hard to think of a specific instance—to feel justified in availing himself of some of his spymaster's companionship.

In addition to Tausk, who occupied a small private room, the infirmary held only a few soldiers, lying in long rows in the general ward, suffering from alcohol poisoning and various minor injuries sustained during their training exercises. Wiladowski went in with the day nurse and found Tausk half awake, propped up by a mass of pillows and looking more haggard than ever. His eyes were still clouded with fever, and he was badly in need of a shave and bath, but to the Count-Governor, who found being around anyone who was ill unsettling and who, out of egoism, not goodwill, was a firm optimist about people's health, Tausk seemed to be recovering admirably. The sickroom had the sweet, cloying smell of a confined space in which someone has been sweating with a high fever for many hours, and Wiladowski signaled for the nurse to open the window as widely as possible. The woman had never seen the Count-Governor except at a great distance and was visibly moved by the honor he was showing the hospital with his presence. She scurried around to air and tidy the room and, considering the visitor's august rank, tried to wash off the patient's face and as much of his upper torso as decency permitted. Tausk appeared awake enough to take in what was happening, although he shivered as though it were midwinter when the first warm breeze from the open window penetrated the room.

Wiladowski long ago had convinced himself that anyone ill enough to be laid up in bed, whether from a fatal malady or something easily curable, wanted only to be distracted from brooding about his condition and so, after a few formulaic phrases of encouragement, always talked about whatever was on his mind, quite sure that nothing could be better for the patient. Occasionally he was even right in that assumption. Certainly Tausk seemed to welcome the relief from his own thoughts and was visibly grateful that the Count-Governor's questions were vague enough to require no answer beyond a few general sounds of assent. He was fully awake now and able to swallow several spoonfuls of warm broth brought by the nurse, eager to demonstrate how well she looked after her charges. When Tausk finished eating, Wiladowski asked to be left alone with the patient and ordered his guards to take up their position outside the door to make sure they were not interrupted.

The nourishment seemed to have restored some of Tausk's strength. Although his speech was interrupted once or twice by waves of debilitating fatigue, during which he sank back helplessly into the pillows for several minutes before managing to rally himself, he nonetheless began by apologizing to his master for falling ill at such an inopportune moment. He explained that the damp night air in the Josef Quarter must have inflamed his always sensitive lungs and led to his present condition. He was starting to feel better, though, and even if he was unable to leave the ward, he would do what he could to be of service from there. Roublev, his second-in-command, whom the Count-Governor could trust absolutely, would stand in for him wherever possible and keep Tausk informed of everything happening in town. When Wiladowski asked how worried he should feel leading the procession on Sunday, especially since he would be without Tausk alongside him, the spymaster assured him that his men were already on duty along tomorrow's parade route and had secured the entire area. At the Count-Governor's urging, Nathan Kaplansky and a few of the other trade union agitators had been taken into custody for distributing banned leaflets during the last strike and would be released next week when the town was quiet again. Even the religious zealots he and the Count-Governor had talked about all were safely locked up. In sum, as far as Tausk could tell, everything possible had been done to ensure that the ceremony would pass without incident. The only area of concern was that Pfister, who insisted his position gave him sole charge of all the arrangements in the Cathedral Square itself, had rejected, as insulting to the provincial nobility, Tausk's suggestions to search everyone entering the square for weapons. In any case, Pfister said he intended to make sure that the whole square would be filled by the better families in town and had ordered the police to keep out anyone who looked unsuitable. More helpfully, though, since all the important visitors came with their own highly trained bodyguards, Tausk was confident there would be sufficient security personnel in the square. "Besides"—he managed to smile weakly to the Count-Governor—"from what Your Excellency has told me, I doubt that someone like von Kirchstein or Zichy-Ferraris would be prepared to overrule a good Catholic like your First Secretary at the behest of a Jew, so I did not press my idea."

"I notice you were polite enough not to include my wife in the list of your enemies." Wiladowski was surprised how delighted he felt bantering with Tausk again, even if it was in a hospital room. "In this case, your tact almost corresponds to the truth. Although I would never go so far as to say that she now prefers you to Pfister, she has taken such a dislike to my First Secretary that almost anything is conceivable. Well, perhaps not quite that," Wiladowski agreed with a smile, seeing his spymaster's skeptical expression. "But here, let me read you his latest notion." Wiladowski unfolded the thick sheet of paper he had removed from his breast pocket and waved it in the air while he summarized its contents. "Tomorrow evening, when we return to the Castle from the Cathedral Square for the evening ball, Pfister has arranged for exactly fifteen and a half meters of red carpet to be rolled out to greet the party. Don't ask me how he settled on that number, probably from a description of a similar festival under Maximilian the First or Maria Theresa. But his plan does not stop there. As the guests stride up the main hallway, he wants to station eighteen officers in full-dress uniform along their path, so that at a signal from their commander, thirty-six spurs can click simultaneously to herald the dignitaries' entrance. There is no sound in the world I loathe quite as much as clinking spurs, except for actual gunfire, and to my mind the two noises are intimately linked. I was going to veto the whole idea, of course, but then somehow Zichy-Ferraris got wind of it and swore it was the perfect way to begin the evening's festivities. As the host I had no choice but to agree. I can't tell you how much the whole lot of them get on my nerves."

Tausk's face arranged itself into what the Count-Governor took for an expression of sympathy, although just then he was convulsed by another trembling fit. Wiladowski noticed Tausk struggle to stop his teeth from chattering with fever and walked over to look out the window in order to save the spymaster the embarrassment of having anyone witness his ordeal. He stood staring out toward the river for a long time and then, as though they were chatting together comfortably in his study, asked Tausk, in a completely ordinary tone of voice, if he knew the famous saying by Prince Metternich "Asia begins outside my window." When Tausk shook his head, whether from ignorance of the quotation or from his illness, the Count-Governor explained that the great statesman and defender of aristocratic privilege, who had dominated the country after the wars against Napoleon, enjoyed thinking of himself as Europe's last bulwark against the hordes from the eastern steppes. "But the amazing thing, you see, is that Metternich said it in Vienna, on the balcony of his palace, thousands of kilometers from the border. Just imagine what he would say if he were standing in my place, almost in sight of the frontier. Between ourselves, Tausk, I think all these celebrated figures from history were guilty of shameless exaggeration."

Without replying directly to the Count-Governor, Tausk waited a moment and then inquired, "Has there been any important news from Vienna?" He had managed to recover from his latest attack and recognized that Wiladowski's irritation arose from something much more immediate and personal than a few overemphatic pronouncements by an illustrious predecessor.

Wiladowski turned his head back to the sickbed with an appreciative nod for being understood so quickly. "Well, yes, in a way," he said. "One of my aunts writes to tell me, in strict confidence, that on behalf of His Majesty, Trautmannsdorff is going to present me with the Order of the Golden Fleece at the end of the ceremony. It is the highest honor of all in the official table of precedence, and it is being brought to me along with a lengthy commendation from the Emperor himself about 'all my distinguished service on behalf of the dynasty.'"

Tausk was about to congratulate him when he noticed that the Count-Governor's face looked anything but pleased, so he decided to say nothing and wait for an explanation. Although the room was much smaller than any in which Wiladowski was used to holding a conversation, out of habit he continued to walk up and down while talking, and misjudging where he needed to turn, he terrified both the nurse and the soldiers outside by bumping into the two small end tables piled high with medical supplies and loudly scattering the contents all over the floor. "I do not know who first came up with the idea of giving the most distinguished decorations to the loser in the struggle for power," he explained to Tausk, entirely ignoring the wreckage at his feet, "but the man was clearly a political genius. Have you noticed that it is invariably the vanquished generals who are honored with a lavish parade and the gaudiest medals so that the population won't notice the country has been defeated once again because of inept leadership? That is what the Order of the Golden Fleece means, and I am not so obtuse as to misunderstand the message. Trautmannsdorff and the others have traveled all the way here not to gawk at some provincial Bell Tower but to let me know that there has been a change at the Foreign Ministry and my influence there is at an end." Wiladowski impatiently waved off Tausk's attempt to interject a comment. "And the truly infuriating aspect of the whole affair"—he went on—"is their assumption that I care in any way about my so-called influence behind the scenes or that if I did, I would be consoled by another colored ribbon for my collection."

Tausk had not heard his employer in this mood before and was tempted to respond to so unexpected a sign of confidence by offering up some personal revelation of his own, but almost immediately he managed to check the impulse. He knew the Count-Governor was far too absorbed by his own story to regard any disclosure from him as more than a pointless intrusion. But even if that were not so, Wiladowski could afford such gestures; Tausk could not. It was almost as simple as that. Yet Tausk was also afraid to give voice to what was haunting him. Earlier in the day, when Roublev had come in to check on him, his appearance had almost caused Tausk to go into convulsions again. Tausk was unable to listen to Roublev's report of what had happened after he and Brugger left the clearing together and sent him away after extracting a promise never to mention anything to him about that day again unless explicitly asked. Focusing on Wiladowski's situation was a wonderful way to banish his own nightmares, and Tausk was glad to give it as much of his concentration as his weakened condition permitted.

"How can I help, Your Excellency?" Tausk asked. There was nothing he himself could do about the political machinations in which the Count-Governor seemed enmeshed. It occurred to Tausk that on his return, Moritz Rotenburg might be able to intervene at the Ministry and help Wiladowski regain his position there, but for the moment it was more prudent not to mention his own connection to the financier. Instead Tausk brought the conversation back to Wiladowski's physical safety, a topic he knew would instantly absorb the Count-Governor's attention. Wiladowski complained that with his spymaster confined to bed, he would feel even more exposed throughout the daylong celebration, and he did not mind admitting that one of his reasons for coming to the infirmary was to seek Tausk's reassurance and advice.

Although he felt his strength starting to fail again and longed to be allowed to fall back asleep, Tausk did his best to provide both. He suggested that it might allay the Count-Governor's anxiety if someone new were found, preferably with military training and completely devoted to the government, to accompany Wiladowski as a combination adjutant and bodyguard until Tausk was on his feet again. None of the regular soldiers in the Castle would do since the man would have to be acceptable to the most fastidious of Wiladowski's guests. He would be expected to stay at the Count-Governor's side during the whole ceremony, from the public speeches to the most intimate receptions, and be equally adept in either sphere. Unfortunately, Tausk could not recommend anyone from his own staff, since the best of them were Jews, more experienced in infiltrating seditious gatherings in the Josef Quarter than in making themselves presentable at an aristocratic fête. "Perhaps one of the people invited by the Countess herself could be pressed into service," Tausk proposed. When Wiladowski looked dubious, Tausk readily amended his advice. "The guest list has been Pfister's responsibility," he said, "so I never familiarized myself with it completely, but I am sure that if Your Excellency were to look it over, a plausible choice would suggest itself quickly enough." Simply the notion of doing something concrete to protect himself appealed to Wiladowski, who suddenly realized it was high time he let Tausk rest. He ordered the nurse back into the room to look after her patient. As he was leaving, he watched her pick up the pile of broken glass and bandages on the floor and complimented her on a well-run ward. To Tausk, he shouted out in a voice meant to sound encouraging, but that came out much louder than necessary, that it was clear he was on his way to a full recovery and would be expected back on duty soon.

When he was back again in his study, looking over the names of his guests, Wiladowski congratulated himself on his shrewdness in visiting Tausk. "Who says good deeds are never rewarded?" he said to Aloïs contentedly. "This way I cheered up Tausk, who really does look dreadful, poor fellow, although I didn't let him notice that I thought so, and at the same time, I came away with an excellent suggestion." Although his master was not looking in his direction, Aloïs composed his face to accord with the mixture of gratification and concern in the Count-Governor's sentence. In his years of service, Aloïs's features had developed a remarkable plasticity that would have shamed a skilled actor. Since speech was hardly ever required of him, his physical expressiveness had blossomed over the years, much as a blind man's other senses are reputed to be compensatorily augmented. Indeed there were people in the Castle who had never heard him utter a single word and thought he might be one of those mute servants who often accompany heroes in old legends.

By contrast, unfortunately, whoever Wiladowski appointed as his temporary aide-de-camp would need to be minimally proficient at making conversation, and from his perspective, that eliminated most of the people invited to the ceremony. As he went through the files, Wiladowski found himself missing Tausk's ability to accommodate his tone to the Count-Governor's moods as much as he did the spymaster's professional competence. Almost imperceptibly, though, a new plan took form in Wiladowski's mind. It occurred to him that perhaps he could do more than just draft a socially competent protector for himself. Since he could no longer disconcert Zichy-Ferraris and the others by forcing them to consort with a Jew, why not go in the opposite direction and show that he still had first-rate contacts among the younger nobility with enviable prospects of their own in the capital? Everyone knew how much the Emperor cherished his young officer corps, and nothing would alarm Wiladowski's enemies as much as the thought that he was on intimate terms with a career soldier from a distinguished family, one clearly earmarked for the General Staff. With that as his criterion, the choice was suddenly clear. Von Alpsbach's younger son, Karl Gustav, had only just returned to the province on special leave from his unit to take part in the ceremony, and even if he were unlikely to be enchanted at the prospect of spending all his free time attending the Count-Governor, his well-known sense of duty would constrain him to accept the appointment. Besides, his family owed the Count-Governor a favor for not taking offense at the shocking rudeness of their firstborn, who had sent a personal note directly to Wiladowski and Marie-Luise declining their invitation to participate in the festivities ostensibly out of concern about the health of someone dear to him. What affectation! The whole provincial council was gossiping about Ernst von Alpsbach's tempestuous affair with his Jewish mistress, and now it seemed that she was ill out at Brunnenberg and causing no end of scurrying back and forth between the von Alpsbachs and her own family. Well, Viktor Demetz was reputed to be one of the best doctors in the area, with whom Wiladowski's own physician had consulted more than once, and no doubt he was sufficiently skilled to take care of his daughter's problem. Whatever the real reasons for Ernst's absence—and his dossier suggested an oversensitive pride and an unseemly desire to refuse the obligations incumbent on someone of his station—it put his father and brother in an awkward position and virtually guaranteed Karl Gustav's compliance. Wiladowski scribbled a quick note requesting that Lieutenant von Alpsbach come see him as soon as possible and gave it to the duty officer to deliver right away. Then, leaning back in his chair with deep satisfaction evident on his face, he allowed an equally gratified-looking Aloïs to hand him a large cigar and pour out a small glass of his favorite brandy. As he was finishing both, he remembered to have some tea and cake from Marie-Luise's reception sent up to the infirmary, thinking to himself how much pleasure the nurse, and perhaps Tausk as well, would derive from being remembered in this way.

· ◆ ·

Easter Sunday began with a triumphant peal of church bells from every spire in town. The steeples were glistening in the first light, and the rooftops of the villas glowed reddish gold as their metal and stone caught slivers of the morning radiance and reflected it downward into the streets in a thin, translucent stream. The rose-white columns of the stately German-language theater were just beginning to emerge from the surrounding darkness, while on the other side of the Elisabethplatz, the extravagant Jugendstil mosaics on the facade of the new Allianz Insurance Company headquarters gave an unexpected burst of color to a district otherwise dominated by the grayish walls of the older office buildings. All along the parade route, the balconies were strewn with lavish arrangements of milky blue spring gentians and early-blooming yellow primroses, and everywhere, from townhouse to tavern, fluttered the familiar black and yellow banners bearing the dynasty's heraldic double eagles. For weeks now the municipal authorities had made certain that the center of town looked like a colorful stage set on which a contented citizenry sought only to display its spontaneous love for its Emperor, and Pfister himself had ordered the police to apply pressure to any household that seemed stinting in its demonstration of ardor.

Fortunately for Pfister's state of mind, the procession was not scheduled to pass through the Josef Quarter. A low mist continued to hover over the river by the Nepomuk Bridge throughout the early morning, but finally, it too burned off, and the Josef Quarter was suffused with a brilliant spring sunshine that seemed simultaneously to emphasize and to temper its drabness. A few tenement owners, hoping to ingratiate themselves with the government, had put up wreaths in the Habsburg colors at the front entrance to their buildings, but as soon as it was nighttime, these were quickly vandalized by the ungrateful inhabitants. In order to ensure that at least along the main streets some signs of patriotic fervor were visible, large flags had been freely distributed to all the tenants, the shrewdest of whom worked out an arrangement by which they would earn a few days' remission of their rent in return for hanging the banners out their windows. But beyond forcibly taking down a scattering of seditious posters and removing the odd red flag from a lamppost, the police knew better than to interfere down here, and in spite of Pfister's repeated memoranda on the subject, no one tried to force the local population to exhibit the proper sentiments toward its rulers.

But if the workers in the Josef Quarter were not about to drape their district with Habsburg pennants, they were equally resistant to the idea of staging a counterdemonstration to disrupt the Bell Tower ceremony. At the last moment a contingent of mid-level labor organizers and radical journalists from Vienna slipped into a third-class carriage on the same train as the government dignitaries who filled all the first-class compartments. Last year's improvised strike against the Hollweg Timber Corporation had emboldened the socialist leadership in Vienna to hope that with a little persuasion, the same men could be roused to take to the streets and use the Easter festivities to protest working conditions throughout the Empire. But to their disgust, the organizers found few recruits willing to risk imprisonment in order to provide a stirring example for the rest of the country. The midnight raid on Brugger's house and the unexpected imprisonment of Nathan Kaplansky showed how far the government was willing to go to preserve order, and from his cell Kaplansky smuggled out a message that this was a time for caution, not unnecessary risk taking. Not that the more theoretically sophisticated writers on *The Voice of the Worker* were surprised by the mission's failure. As they pointed out in a series of stinging reports, had not Marx decisively proved that the farther east one traveled, the less the revolutionary potential of the masses?

But the dilemma of the Viennese radicals was minor compared with the spiritual quandary facing many of the district's observant Jews. The close conjunction of Passover and Easter this year had presented them with a serious theological dilemma. Card playing was of course strictly forbidden among them; indeed it served as the very archetype of *goyishe naches*, foolishness in which gentiles delight and on which they unaccountably waste so many precious hours. Twice a year, though, at Christmas always and at Easter, whenever it did not overlap with Passover, the rabbis not only permitted but actively encouraged their congregation to spend the entire night playing cards as a sign of disdain for the heretical religion that had sprung up from among them only to become their greatest persecutor. "But surely not this Passover?" the faithful asked one another, more uncertain than ever, now that they abruptly had lost two of their most powerful guides, Brugger and the Buczacz rabbi. Almost miraculously, the crisis forced a temporary armistice among the normally feuding religious leaders, who met to decide upon a uniform policy. After hours of heated debate, it was announced that this year, card playing would be strictly forbidden, primarily to honor the Passover but also as an expression of gratitude toward His Imperial Majesty, who protected his Jewish subjects from the terrible Easter pogroms that had broken out again on the other side of the border. As Rabbi Rechnitz, one of the gentlest and most learned of the council, said, "We are after all natives of Austria, where the Exile weighs less heavily on us than elsewhere and where our thoughts are naturally drawn to happier things." Sadly, though, no one in the government knew how deep a sign of loyalty the province's Jews had just offered their rulers. When morning broke, the Orthodox stayed at home in bed rather than walk through the streets to show by their exhaustion and haggard expressions how they had spent the night. But sitting in Marie-Luise's rooms over coffee, after they all had returned from morning mass, von Kirchstein turned to his hostess and complained that his servant had just come back from the Jewish quarter, where he had hurried to find a tailor for a crucial small repair on his master's dress uniform, only to find out that all the Jews were still fast asleep. No doubt encouraged by her husband's notorious sympathy for them, they now lacked the elementary decency to make themselves useful on a day that was sacred to the good Christians who were softhearted enough to permit this stiff-necked and alien race to live in their midst.

It was a long-standing tradition in the province that the Count-Governor, his family, and staff all celebrate Christmas and Easter mass in St. Hildegard's chapel in the Castle itself, rather than in the Cathedral in town. No one knew the custom's precise origin, but it was thought to date back to a time when the extent of Vienna's authority over the region was still contested. Like many political crises, this one had been resolved through a purely symbolic gesture: Twice a year, for the two most solemn masses of the liturgical calendar, the representatives of Imperial power would cede their rightful place in the Cathedral to the provincial nobility and withdraw to their private chapel. The special solemnity of this Easter, when so much of the town's attention would be commanded by the Count-Governor and the visiting dignitaries, gave a singular poignancy to his symbolic exclusion at the start of the day.

Although he never said so directly to Marie-Luise, who thought the local custom shockingly disrespectful, Wiladowski was delighted by anything that lessened the time he would have to appear in public. Moreover, services in St. Hildegard's tended to be rather hurried affairs since no one was inclined to linger in such an uninviting place. In spite of attempts by generations of provincial governors and their wives to beautify it, the chapel remained a forbidding structure, ill lit and cold even on the sunniest days and more suited to withstand a siege than to inspire religious devotion. Father Kakuska, who officiated at the Castle services, found himself shortening his sermons so that he could return to his cozy rooms as quickly as his sense of decorum allowed. Wiladowski entirely approved of his priest's inclination, particularly on Easter morning, when the mass took place before breakfast, and everyone was expected to attend on an empty stomach. Most of the visitors housed within the Castle were still asleep when the pealing bells summoned them to mass. Knowing how many other duties awaited his congregants, Father Kakuska outdid himself in his brevity, while still performing all the requisite solemnities. Marie-Luise had ordered a lavish breakfast prepared for the guests, along with Father Kakuska, to enjoy at leisure before they had to get into their dress uniforms for the ceremonial parade.

In spite of the occasion, Wiladowski, as was his custom on regular mornings, took his breakfast alone in his study. He suspected that his absence would provoke hostile comments, but he needed the time by himself before being thrust into the continuous round of festival duties. Besides, he knew how much more the visitors and Marie-Luise would enjoy exchanging Court gossip if he were not there to dampen their pleasure, and he anticipated that by the time the day was over, his guests would have enough other examples of his neglect to make this morning's dereliction fade in their memory. With Tausk laid up in the infirmary, he had no reliable information about the mood in the town, but if a detailed report on the Josef Quarter had been available, he would have found himself in sympathy with the inhabitants' lack of enthusiasm for the Bell Tower ceremony.

As he contemplated the long day ahead, none of the Josef Quarter's different factions could have felt more displeased by the parade Wiladowski was about to head than the Count-Governor himself. He kept getting up from his breakfast to scan the horizon for any sign that it might yet rain, but seeing the cloudless sky stretching all the way to the steppes, he gave up hope and glumly ordered Aloïs to bring in his uniform and help him dress. Like most members of his class, Wiladowski retained an honorary rank in at least one of the elite regiments and was expected to wear its uniform on ceremonial occasions and national holidays. There was always a great deal of competition among the different service branches into which the Imperial army was divided, and the artillery, infantry, engineering corps, and mounted troops all enjoyed periods of relative prestige and decline. Well-placed courtiers like Zichy-Ferraris, Trautmannsdorff, Hohenlohe-Schillingsfurst, and von Kirchstein avoided the risk of being associated with any branch momentarily out of favor by getting themselves appointed honorary regimental colonels to distinguished units in each one, and there was much speculation throughout the Castle about which uniform, among the several to which they were entitled, the visitors would select. They themselves made as great a mystery out of their choices as their wives did about the cut and color of their evening gowns for the first ball of the season, but it was no secret that Zichy-Ferraris had tried to bribe Trautmannsdorff's valet to find out in advance what uniform his master would pick out. Although only Wiladowski had the right to wear the imposing Grand Cross of the Leopold Order, over the years the Emperor had provided all of them with an abundance of decorations and medals, so that when they finally emerged, fully bedecked from their rooms, to begin the great procession into town, an observer might have thought that except for their gray hair and paunches, a column of military heroes, unmatched since the legendary paladins of Charlemagne, was riding by.

In his nightmares, Wiladowski was usually riding in a closed carriage, accompanied by Marie-Luise and at least one aide, when the crash of the windows told him, a second before the actual explosion, that a bomb had been thrown into his coach. But today he would be denied the protection of his specially reinforced carriage since tradition demanded that he lead the procession on horseback. As he thought about what lay ahead, Wiladowski gradually progressed from a mild dislike of riding to an active loathing of horses as a species. He had concluded that his death was as likely to result from a fall from one of these beasts as from an assassin's bullet. As a mordant comment on the absurdity of the whole affair, he had chosen to ride on the gray stallion he had won playing billiards with Lieutenant von Sulzbach. Since the disgraced officer would be on foot duty along the parade route, if he saw the Count-Governor fall to his death from the very horse he himself had squandered away gambling, it might make him feel less regret about that evening, and Wiladowski's existence would end on an act of charitable, if exceedingly reluctant, kindness toward one of his fellow human beings.

The horses chosen for the procession differed in color and size from one another just as much as did the variegated uniforms worn by their riders. No one had the indiscretion to appear on a white stallion that might be mistaken for one of the monarch's renowned Lipizzaners, but with that exception, virtually every equine breed was represented. Trautmannsdorff, after hours of agonized indecision, had been audacious enough to select a cream white uniform with turned-up gold cuffs and a red and white sash that, in Wiladowski's eyes, was unsuitably reminiscent of the famous portrait of Franz Josef himself. At least he had restrained himself from wearing one of the ornate plumed crests on his helmet that the Emperor favored. In any case, compared with the immensely tall, horsehair-topped helmet that Zichy-Ferraris put on to complete his robin's-egg blue artillery uniform with its double row of gold buttons, Trautmannsdorff looked almost chaste. The oddest appearance of all was struck by Konrad von Hohenlohe-Schillingsfurst. Perhaps he was already beginning to fall victim to the streak of madness that surfaced in his line at least once a generation, or perhaps he simply, if somewhat eccentrically, had concluded that since they were there to celebrate the three hundredth anniversary of the rededication of the great Bell Tower, it was only fitting that he dress the way his forebears did on that first splendid occasion. In either case, he had brought out from his family vaults an ornately worked silver and black suit of full body armor, with high white leather boots, a thick scarlet and gold ribbon fixed on the left shoulder to make it flutter loosely behind him as he rode, and hanging at his side, sheathed in an intricate gold and black scabbard, a massive, thick-handled battle sword. His only concession to the calendar was to modify his headpiece by fifty years, so that instead of fitting himself into a helmet that would leave his face invisible to the throng, Hohenlohe-Schillingsfurst chose a dashing black felt cap with a red feather modeled after the one worn by the Cardinal-Infante Ferdinand at the Battle of Nördlingen in 1634, where one of his own ancestors had fought so valiantly. Unfortunately, the practice of learning how to stay seated on horseback in full armor had fallen into disuse in the intervening centuries, and although ceremonial armor was considerably thinner and lighter than anything actually worn into battle, it was, nonetheless, crush-

461

ingly heavy compared with anything in which Hohenlohe-Schillingsfurst had ever tried to move before. As a result, instead of his scarlet ribbon dancing boldly in the breeze, it was the rider who swayed precariously side to side as his black charger advanced. Wiladowski had been trained since infancy to control his features, but when he first caught sight of Hohenlohe-Schillingsfurst in the courtyard, struggling to get on his horse with the assistance of three servants, his eyes widened in stupefaction. Now, riding alongside the man over the Nepomuk Bridge and down the Mariahilferstrasse toward the Radetzkyplatz and the Mendelssohn Club, the Count-Governor was positively alarmed, certain that at any moment Hohenlohe-Schillingsfurst was going to topple sideways off his horse and, in his fall, drag down everyone near him as well.

But if Wiladowski's judgment of Hohenlohe-Schillingsfurst's mental as well as physical balance was ungenerous, his estimation of the man's effect on the crowd lining the streets could not have been more mistaken. The Count-Governor was convinced that as soon as people caught sight of the squat figure, made up like an extra from the Imperial Opera House, a torrent of laughter was sure to break out, and the ceremony would be overwhelmed by the kind of public humiliation that was nearly as dangerous to the government as revolutionary violence. To his amazement, though, it was Hohenlohe-Schillingsfurst who seemed to inspire the unstinting admiration of the spectators. At every stage along the parade route he was greeted with loud applause and shouts of "Hurrah!" in appreciation of his willingness to dress for his part without holding anything back. The moment people caught a glimpse of him, the cheers began, and they swelled in volume until they matched anything heard by his ancestors on their way back into the capital victorious from the battlefield. Hohenlohe-Schillingsfurst himself modestly acknowledged the acclaim, raising, as briefly as possible, an armor-gloved hand from the reins, which he otherwise clutched with the devotion of a holy relic, and swaying his body in apparent appreciation of the accolades before collapsing back onto the red and gold threaded caparison spread decoratively over his saddle.

As Wiladowski's eyes continued scanning the crowd, kept at a respectful distance by a line of regular soldiers in the brown capes and red plumes of their dress uniform, the Count-Governor thought he recognized some of the faces moving among the spectators as belonging to Tausk's men, and he felt more comforted by their presence than by the armed soldiers. Only Karl Gustav von Alpsbach, whom he intended to keep as close to his side as possible, even if it meant riding two abreast rather than letting himself be seen at the parade's head, inspired any confidence in Wiladowski. Occasionally he glanced back enviously toward Marie-Luise and the civilian notables who were following far behind in a row of high-wheeled, ebony carriages and presented a much less inviting target than the men leading the parade on horseback. The "surprise" inspection of the army barracks with which the morning had started had gone remarkably smoothly. After the soldiers had marched past the Count-Governor on the parade ground, there had been an exchange of carefully rehearsed toasts saluting both the senior officers stationed in town and the distinguished visitors. The whole affair had been agreeably short and culminated in a brotherly vow of lifelong fidelity to Church and Throne in which the whole corps and the ceremonial party enthusiastically joined. The Count-Governor, who regarded every public function that he survived without serious harm as a personal triumph, rode away from the barracks with a sense of relief that the day's events had begun on such an encouraging note. It was only as they neared the Schwarzenberg statue that he started worrying about how awkward the whole business with the Mendelssohn Club might prove. He had conceived of the visit to the Jewish club largely as a quid pro quo for Moritz Rotenburg's financial contributions and, secondarily, to annoy Zichy-Ferraris. But with the financier away somewhere in Switzerland, the main reason to make an official stop here was gone. It was impossible to cancel the visit, but he would do his best to abbreviate it as much as possible, while still irritating all those in his party who were offended by the involvement of Jews in an Easter ceremony at all. Wiladowski had no thought of revising his prepared speech, which was devoted largely to extolling Rotenburg's many patriotic contributions to the province and the Empire. "By his public spirit and generosity, this man of humble origins has become more than just a credit to his race; he has demonstrated beyond question how that race, so often misunderstood and persecuted, can be relied upon to produce citizens whose loyalty is in no way inferior to that of any of the Emperor's other subjects." Wiladowski had memorized his lines weeks ago and knew he could deliver them with the required pathos. The immediate problem, though, was that the Count-Governor had no idea to whom he would be addressing his speech, and when the procession came to a halt in front of the club, he unsuccessfully scanned the welcoming committee assembled on the doorstep for any face he might recognize. In the course of his duties he had received numerous delegations of rich Jews at the Castle, but Rotenburg was the only one he had come to know personally, so it was hardly surprising that among the dozen or more men crowding the steps, all dressed in black top hats and dark, formal suits, not a single face was familiar to him. What Wiladowski did register with amusement was the contrast between the rainbow-hued uniforms of his party and the sober restraint of the clothes worn by the Mendelssohn Club's Governing Board. In Zichy-Ferraris's crowd, the innate tendency of Jews to tasteless, Levantine excess in their dress and mannerisms was a frequent source of malicious jokes, and Wiladowski could not resist beckoning Zichy-Ferraris over and asking whether a visitor from a distant country, seeing the two groups and being informed of their putative traits, might not mistake who were the Jews and who the Christian gentlemen.

Of course Wiladowski's readiness to champion his Jews against someone like Zichy-Ferraris was quite different from having any direct acquaintanceship with them. Fortunately, just as one of the oldest members of the delegation approached the procession and bowed elaborately to Wiladowski, an aide-de-camp rode up between Wiladowski and Karl Gustav and whispered in the Count-Governor's ear, "Gerhard Himmelfarb, retired businessman, Your Excellency." That was all the prompting Wiladowski required. He dismounted from his horse and listened with a benevolent smile to the interminable welcoming address—it was impossible to deny that these people really were extraordinarily long-winded!—and when it was finally time to reply, he beamed at the man as though they were familiar acquaintances and shouted out so that everyone nearby could hear, "My dear Himmelfarb, on behalf of all of us here today, I thank you for your most hospitable greeting." As Wiladowski had foreseen, being publicly acknowledged in front of his fellow club members by the Emperor's own representative was the most joyous moment of the fellow's life. In spite of his disagreeably sallow complexion, it was obvious that Himmelfarb was blushing with the embarrassed pride of an adolescent girl. Wiladowski took advantage of Himmelfarb's excitement to rush through his own declamation as quickly as decency allowed. He began by apologizing for not being able to come inside to visit the club after all. He had hoped to do so, but the demands of his numerous responsibilities—and he nodded to Himmelfarb as though he were similarly burdened and so could be relied on to understand the situation fully—compelled him to delay what surely would have been a rare pleasure. But he was determined not to leave until he had told them all of his high regard for their illustrious founding member, unfortunately too ill to be present today. Thereupon Wiladowski delivered his encomium on Moritz Rotenburg, certain that as a fellow businessman Himmelfarb would delight in hearing that a man with whom he shared not only his religion but also his profession could gain the esteem of the highest quarters in the land. "I need say no more"—he concluded sententiously—"than that your compatriot's achievements have been noticed favorably by His Apostolic Majesty himself, and I have no doubt of the deep satisfaction this must bring to you and the other worthy members of your community." Then, helped by Karl Gustav, Wiladowski awkwardly remounted his gray horse. He gave what he hoped was a gallant wave of his arm to signal the procession to move on, leaving Himmelfarb, who had counted on the prestige of personally leading the Count-Governor and the most distinguished of his party upstairs to the executive rooms, where elaborate refreshments were laid out for them, standing at the entrance with a disconsolate expression.

Although the most trying events still lay ahead, Wiladowski was beginning to feel almost cheerful. The visit to the Jewish club had gone quite well. The only regrettable thing was that they had picked such a tedious old man to welcome him in Rotenburg's place. Wiladowski had always been fond of Mendelssohn's vocal music, and no doubt the club had an excellent choir trained to perform his compositions. It would have been a pleasure to hear them instead of this Himmelfarb, but at least he had succeeded in making one of Rotenburg's intimates happy. The final stop before the procession reached the Cathedral Square was politically the most significant of the three, but in a rather indirect way, and was not expected to present any special difficulties. The Greek Orthodox Church of St. Athanasius the Great lay on the carefully maintained Freudenau Crescent, between the Mendelssohn Club and the town Cathedral. It was a relatively modest building, erected seventy-five years ago to serve the small but prosperous community of Greek businessmen and their families who had settled in the province, and it was notable chiefly for a splendid Byzantine icon of St. Athanasius, donated by one of the congregation's founders. The Foreign Minister had suggested the visit only after all the experts, including Wiladowski, had concluded that halting in front of the Russian Orthodox church would have been too provocative. In the language of diplomacy, stopping in front of St. Athanasius signaled the Austrian Emperor's determination to assume responsibility for all his Orthodox subjects, whether they looked to Moscow or Constantinople as their religious center. But diverting the visit to the Greek rather than the Russian church mitigated some of the declaration's sting and left open the possibility of a compromise in other areas. Translated from gesture into words, it amounted to the difference between "assuming a responsibility" and "asserting a right." To the members of the ceremonial party—and, equally important, to the Czar's advisers in St. Petersburg—this language was as clear as it was incomprehensible to St. Athanasius's parishioners or to Father Dimitrios Kastanas Spyridon, their young priest.

The speech Wiladowski had prepared for the occasion differed only slightly from the one he had just delivered with such happy results at the Mendelssohn Club. He intended to commend the entire Greek Orthodox community for its industriousness and fidelity to the Emperor. As the highlight of the visit he would bestow the Empress Elisabeth Medal on Theodor Chorafa, the wealthiest of the Greek merchants, whose grandfather had donated the icon of St. Athanasius and who always made a generous contribution to the Count-Governor's winter relief fund. In a suitably diminished version, Wiladowski could apply to Chorafa some of the phrases he had used in praise of Rotenburg, and such an economy of effort pleased him like an elegant formulation in the text of a political treaty. Here, though, Wiladowski counted on including references to the shared Easter customs binding the Greek Orthodox to the many other Christian denominations in the Empire. He was looking forward to being greeted with a joyous "Christos Anesti! Christ Is Risen!" and to astonishing the congregation by offering the correct ritual response, "Alethos Anesti! Truly, He Is Risen!" But his advisers had neglected to tell him that the Greek Orthodox calendar differed from the Roman one and that for them, Easter Sunday was still a full week away. It was only as the procession was coming in sight of the church that the army chaplain, who, although a Catholic, knew something about these matters from the soldiers in his charge, informed Wiladowski that for the Orthodox, today was only Palm Sunday. No one had briefed Wiladowski about what these people did to celebrate Palm Sunday, and the chaplain confessed that he himself had only a vague notion. As a result, and to the shock of the worshipers, who concluded that he must be prejudiced against their faith, the Count-Governor became too worried about committing a theological faux pas to risk any religious reference at all.

By the time the procession turned the corner onto Freudenau Crescent, St. Athanasius's entrance was flung wide open, and the sound of rejoicing flowed through the open doors into the street. Inside, the whole building was glimmering with candlelight that flickered in hundreds of small red jars. The golden icon of the saint seemed to draw the light to the back of the chancel, where it glowed more brilliantly in its frame than did the church's bronze dome in the sun outside. Neither palm nor olive trees could thrive in the local climate, and so, for the Festival of Palms, the Orthodox had substituted willow branches, which were already in bud at Easter. The whole altar was strewn with pussy willows, brought there to be blessed and then carried home. Wiladowski glanced briefly into the church and nodded his approbation to a serious-looking Father Spyridon. Ordinarily the aesthetic seductions of religion left Wiladowski indifferent, but there was something about this display that appealed to him.

Within a few sentences, he had the disagreeable impression that the visit was not going well. If Himmelfarb had been annoyingly long-winded, Father Spyridon said nothing at all, except to raise his hands and pronounce a blessing in Greek over the visitors. Instead of feeling himself and his flock honored by the procession, he appeared displeased at the interruption and kept staring at the Count-Governor with an impenetable expression. Since nothing he said seemed to effect any change of attitude in the priest, Wiladowski raced through his speech as quickly as he did when toasting one of his numerous aunts on her birthday. He was soon finished, but there was still no reply. After a few embarrassingly silent moments Father Spyridon lifted his hand in prayer once more, and to judge by the direction of his gaze, he must have expected Wiladowski to kneel down in the street to receive his blessing. The Count-Governor had no intention of doing such a thing and was irked at the way the whole encounter was going. Wiladowski's irritation gave him enough energy to mount his horse without any assistance. He curtly gave the order to continue to the Cathedral Square and in his mind, began to compose a letter to the Foreign Minister outlining why it was a grievous mistake for the Emperor to rely on his Orthodox subjects in any conflict with Russia. As they rode along together, Karl Gustav noticed Wiladowski's scowl and, thinking it was due to some anxiety about security matters, assured him that there had been nearly as many guards in the small area in front of the church as there were parishioners. Perhaps it was because he was speaking only to a lieutenant, or perhaps because, like everyone else, he had simply taken a liking to Karl Gustav, but for whatever reason, instead of evading the question with a witticism, Wiladowski admitted that he had found the priest's brusque behavior extremely disconcerting and could not help interpreting it as a bad omen for the ceremony ahead. Karl Gustav looked at him thoughtfully for a moment and then, without any hint of criticism or amusement in his voice, explained that he knew from his mother, who kept up with all the town gossip and was one of Theodor Chorafa's best customers, that Father Spyridon had only arrived from Istanbul less than six months ago and still spoke almost no German. Wiladowski's speech must have been quite incomprehensible to him, especially since, if he might be permitted so personal an observation, His Excellency spoke only in the Theresianum Viennese of the upper classes, which sounded completely different from anything Father Spyridon would have heard from the people he had so far encountered in town. The poor man must have felt absolutely confused and probably kept staring at Wiladowski's face in the hope of deciphering by his expression what the Count-Governor might be talking about.

Rather than feel abashed by his misjudgment, Wiladowski immediately brightened. The important thing was that the visit had not been a catastrophe and so could not count as a bad omen. All the rest was trivial. No one had said anything openly antagonistic at the church, and a brief letter, written in Greek by someone hired for the job, praising the work Father Spyridon was doing in his new parish and inviting him to a luncheon at the Castle, would be entirely sufficient to smooth over any ruffled sensibilities. Perhaps the Cathedral Square ceremony was not doomed to end horribly. At the very least, in Karl Gustav, Count Wiladowski had found a young soldier with whom he could feel comfortable, and he intended to do his best to get him permanently transferred to his own staff with an enticing promotion and the promise of greatly increased responsibilities. With a recovered Tausk in charge of his spy network, and Karl Gustav as commander of his troops, Wiladowski thought he might actually get through the rest of his term of office with an easy mind.

A large crowd had been gathering at the Cathedral Square since daybreak. Many of the townspeople had chosen to attend early-morning Easter mass and then stayed to find a place in the square close to the dais. A contingent of Castle guards, assisted by the security personnel who had accompanied the dignitaries from Vienna, circulated among the waiting audience, making certain that no one who looked suspicious was allowed to remain. Several times, to the vocal approval of the well-dressed people nearby, the police discreetly removed some young man whose shabby clothes suggested an unreliable background. Throughout the square the profusion of monumental Easter hats of every color, flower and lace miracles of millinery ingenuity, was as striking as though, in subtle homage to the great Bell Tower, their owners were competing for who could balance a more complex structure on her head, while their younger daughters stood beside them in simple white dresses with sprays of blue flower blossoms pinned in their hair. Most of the women had brought along brightly decorated spring parasols to shade them from the sun, but since it was almost impossible to open them in such a tightly packed throng, they were handed over for safekeeping to the attendant husbands, standing idly behind their wives, each seeming to wonder if he might just catch a glimpse of his mistress with her own family somewhere in the crowd. Ten rows of wooden chairs, with red silk pillows on the numbered seats, had been set up directly below the platform, but each of these was cordoned off by uniformed officers, and admission required an invitation personally signed by Matthias Pfister. These places were reserved for members of the local nobility and leading middle-class families, who were not important enough to merit a seat on the platform but still needed to be singled out from the general population for special recognition. The rest of the spectators would have to stand at the back, but neither the discomfort of the long wait before the ceremony began nor the difficulty of seeing what was happening at the front of the square through the thick cluster of Easter bonnets and top hats discouraged anyone. Even those with invitations, who might have been expected to come later to emphasize that they had comfortable seats waiting for them, started arriving well before noon, more concerned not to miss any gossip than to make a display of their distinction. The most prominent among them quickly found one another and established an impromptu open-air salon in which no one exactly sat down but rather, hovered near enough to his seat to talk to everyone without having to turn around all the time, while still letting it be seen in which row he had been placed.

Since the Cathedral's massive bronze doors and the famous stone sculptures of the twelve apostles over the portico were blocked off from view by the raised platform, the prominence of the Bell Tower was emphasized more than ever. The building itself had undergone so many alterations, especially after the great fire three hundred years ago and again during the vogue for modernization in the eighteenth century, that very little of its original plan survived. In its latest incarnation, the Cathedral had a floor plan in the shape of a Latin cross with rounded transepts, a large central dome, and six rows of independent chapels on each side of the nave. The interior was lavishly decorated with gilt and ornate stucco, brightly colored frescoes of the life of the Virgin, and, wherever possible, a profusion of intricate embellishments in white, pink, and gold. On a bright day the whole structure was flooded with sunlight, and although it was a smaller Cathedral than many of the visiting officials had seen elsewhere and contained no art a connoisseur would regard as truly first rate, it was nonetheless an appealing building, making up in playfulness and a certain easygoing theatricality what it lacked in grandeur. Initially the Count-Governor had thought of holding the Bell Tower rededication ceremony after midday mass, but Archbishop Hartenstein had persuaded him that it would be more suitable for the representatives of the state first to deliver their speeches and only then, when all the worldly business was done, to lead a solemn procession into the church for a service that would be the fitting emotional climax of such a sacred day. As the cavalcade was coming into sight of the square, Wiladowski was pleased he had accepted Hartenstein's suggestion. The sooner his own part of the affair was done, the sooner he could stop worrying and retreat into his own thoughts. Instead of sitting through another church service right away, anxious about what would follow, he would be greatly relieved to know that once he found the shelter of the Cathedral, nothing more would be required of him until the night's farewell banquet.

As planned, the procession circled the entire square twice, so that all, no matter where they were standing, could see the riders. Wiladowski was no longer surprised that Hohenlohe-Schillingsfurst again received the most heartfelt cheers. The more weary Hohenlohe-Schillingsfurst grew, and the less steady on his horse, the more striking the impression he made, and the applause was perhaps intensified because the continuous rivulets of sweat running down from his forehead onto the black and silver breastplate below so closely resembled the way the seepage from a bloody wound would have looked in an earlier century. The square was barely big enough to accommodate such a large group on foot, so the cavalcade finished its route at the back of the Cathedral, where military orderlies were waiting to look after the mounts and help the women and civilian visitors out of their carriages. The party then arranged itself in pairs, according to rank and precedence and, led by a smiling Wiladowski and Marie-Luise, proceeded into the square and up to the platform along the red carpet that Pfister had prevailed upon the Count-Governor to lay down.

The moment the procession emerged into view again from behind the Cathedral, the military band broke into Haydn's great hymn, adopted by the Habsburgs as their dynastic anthem. The motif was picked up and echoed back from bells in the high tower, until at all once, without any official prompting, the whole audience in the square began to sing the familiar lyrics, "God preserve, God protect, our Emperor and our land." Even Wiladowski, who was rarely stirred by outpourings of devotion toward a family he had known since boyhood, and of whose aptitude for their office he was far from convinced, found himself starting to hum Lorenz Haschka's words under his breath. He felt Marie-Luise's hand momentarily grip his arm more tightly as they walked together up to the dais, stride for stride in instinctive consonance with the music.

The first burst of gunfire cut into the procession simultaneously with a triumphant roll on the large kettledrums. For half an instant people thought the piercing, high-pitched salvo from the guns might be a new musical effect, cunningly introduced by the bandmaster to add a dramatic touch to the column's slow passage through the crowd. Even a moment later, when Zichy-Ferraris's body tottered and crashed forward into the row of chairs, the realization of what was happening did not fully take hold of anyone beyond the immediate witnesses. Only after a terrified scream—no one knew from whom—was heard above the other noise did a surge of fear spread through the tightly packed square. But from that moment on the panic was unremitting. It was impossible to tell how many people were firing, since the shots seemed to be coming from different parts of the square at the same time. The uncertainty intensified the general terror, and people began to rush frantically toward the street, knocking one another down in their desperation to escape, only to collide with a troop of armed soldiers who were attempting to clear a path to the dignitaries in order to protect them. Before anyone else had moved, Wiladowski threw himself on the ground underneath one of the chairs. From there he watched Karl Gustav, already bleeding from a wound in his shoulder, try to shield Marie-Luise when a second bullet, fired from somewhere close by, tore apart half of his head, so that he dropped where he stood, leaving a dazed Marie-Luise alone on her feet, splattered with a mixture of blood and brain tissue. She stood there in shock, seemingly unable to move at all until, finally, one of the guards reached her and pulled her away to safety. With everyone running in the opposite direction, it had been easy for Hohenlohe-Schillingsfurst to make his way up to the platform, where he remained the entire time watching the scene at his feet, serenely confident that his armor would continue to protect him from the bullets. He was luckier than Pfister, who was standing near the back of the procession and should have been safe in his inconspicuous place among the less important civilian guests. To judge by his expression, Pfister must not have considered himself in danger either because when he suddenly crumbled down, like a building whose supports have been pulled away, his face showed only surprise, rather than pain or fear. He looked offended, almost as if he had been forced to witness some incomprehensible breach of etiquette, and the last words heard from him were a puzzled complaint at the undeserved bad luck that had dogged his whole career.

For all its fury, the actual shooting lasted less than a minute. Just as people had been slow to realize they were caught in a lethal crossfire, so it took a while after the last shot had been fired before it became clear that the attack was over. Wiladowski agreed to emerge from his hiding place under the chair only when the ranking officer of the guards assured him that everything was under control again and that a large group of His Excellency's party was safely assembled behind the platform, surrounded by a ring of soldiers. Marie-Luise and Hohenlohe-Schillingsfurst were doing their best to comfort the distraught families. All the wounded had been evacuated immediately to the town hospital, and most of the provincial nobility had chosen to hurry back to their own estates at the same time, without waiting for an additional escort. It would still take a while, though, until the square was completely cleared of spectators. Military reinforcements were expected at any moment, and as soon as they arrived, the rest of the Count-Governor's party would be escorted back to the Castle in closed carriages. They would take a roundabout route, in case there were any terrorists still on the loose, but it was the officer's judgment that the danger had passed. One of the assassins had been caught already on the Mariahilferstrasse. In the excitement he had accidentally discharged his weapon into his own leg and was bleeding heavily from the wound. No doubt it would not take too long before the others were rounded up as well. Wiladowski was dumbfounded to hear that the terrorist, who had been taken off in chains directly to the Castle prison, was young Leo von Arnstein, and he suspected that there might be a mistake in the identification. But all that would be clarified soon enough. What mattered now was bracing himself to hear just how badly things had gone. All in all, Major Tatrallyay permitted himself to tell the Count-Governor at the outset, considering that the procession had allowed itself to be trapped in an escapeproof ambush, it was fortunate that more people had not been killed. "Tell that to the Ministry in Vienna," Wiladowski ungraciously snapped. Now that he was safe, he thought it advisable to take a stern tone with everyone, and he decided to stay with the Major, under the pretense of taking charge himself, rather than join his party under the dais and risk some disagreeable comments. In spite of the Major's attempted words of encouragement, the preliminary report was devastating. There had been three fatalities: Count Zichy-Ferraris, Lieutenant Karl Gustav von Alpsbach, and First Secretary Matthias Pfister had died instantly from their wounds. Four other members of the ceremonial party had been injured, Baron von Kirchstein severely, although the army doctor who examined him said that he had a good chance of recovering. At least a dozen spectators had been hurt in the crush trying to escape, mostly with minor bruises, but unfortunately, one small child had been killed when it had fallen and been trampled by the people behind.

The last detail depressed Wiladowski more than any of the other deaths except for Karl Gustav's. He and Marie-Luise had never had any children, and he was not inclined to be sentimental about them, but Tatrallyay's report filled him with melancholy at so much pointless loss. Later he realized he had not thought of asking whether the infant had been a boy or a girl, but by then it seemed fruitless to pursue the question. Wiladowski glanced at his pocket watch and glumly realized that less than an hour ago he had been exchanging incomprehensible words with Father Spyridon and all these people were still alive. He decided to make his way over to the platform after all and set about trying to help his wife and Hohenlohe-Schillingsfurst, whose absurd armor now seemed somehow reassuring, keep everyone calm until it was safe to return to the Castle. No one said anything to Wiladowski about his abject panic under fire, and even Marie-Luise, who had the most right to reproach him for disappearing, only inquired solicitously if he had been hurt. But Wiladowski was under no illusion. The rebukes would come soon enough, both officially and in private. When the inevitable commission of inquiry had finished its hearings, he would be forced into retirement in disgrace. But since he intended to resign his post before then, they would have to hold their probe without him and forward any questions to Trieste, where he would be living by then, too ill, alas, to come back and testify in person.

Just as Major Tatrallyay had predicted, the ride back to the Castle in the closed carriages was crowded but uneventful. Wiladowski waited until all were settled into their rooms, and the doctor had given Marie-Luise a sleeping draft to calm her nerves, before rushing up to the infirmary to see Tausk. When the Count-Governor got there, the same nurse greeted him and said that the instant her patient had been brought news of what had happened in the square, he jumped out of bed and, without waiting for the doctor's approval or saying another word to her, got dressed and hurried back downstairs. For a moment Wiladowski was tempted to follow Tausk and watch him piece together who was responsible for the attack. But an underground warren of interrogation cells was not a place Wiladowski was in the mood to visit just then, so he went back to his own library and told a guard to bring Tausk to him at once, no matter what the spymaster might be doing.

Outside, the last slivers of sunset were still illuminating the Castle park. A gentle grayness, quite different from the leaden pall of only a few weeks earlier, was starting to hide the outline of the Nepomuk Bridge. No one had bothered to take down the Chinese lanterns decorating the trees along the embankment. Pfister had ordered them for the banquet celebrating the end of the festivities, and Wiladowski winced to see them hanging there now. The evenings were not really cold anymore, but the Count-Governor felt more chilled than in mid-February and noticed with pleasure that Aloïs had built a large fire in the library. When Tausk appeared in the doorway, he stopped and stared for a moment at Wiladowski's exhausted form, hunched in his chair, and although neither of them would have been able to endure any obtrusive display of emotion, Tausk's relief at seeing the Count-Governor back in his usual place was palpable. Wiladowski heard Tausk's footsteps and looked up at him with pleasure. Tausk turned slightly sideways to light a cigarette, and then, instinctively, they both fell into a dry, practical tone. Each suspected that they would not be having many more such conversations, and without directly saying so, they were glad it should be in this room, and alone, that they were talking now.

Wiladowski set out to describe the day from the time the riders had assembled in the front courtyard. He was sure Tausk would already have questioned everyone on the Castle staff but wanted him to understand how events had unfolded from his perspective. He also knew that none of the important visitors, or the security personnel they had brought with them, would agree to report to the Jewish spymaster, whose authority had been irretrievably compromised by the murders. The fact that the assassinations were not Tausk's fault made no difference. On the contrary, the cavalier dismissal of his suggestions about security arrangements in the square made it all the more important to shift as much responsibility as possible on to him. When the Count-Governor had finished, Tausk nodded thoughtfully and thanked him for his continuing confidence. In his own mind, though, Tausk had already come to terms with the ruin of his career. Lying in his hospital bed, he had recognized too late his misjudgment in leaving any of the conspirators at liberty. He should have found a means to keep them all away from town and promised himself that relying on half measures was not a mistake he would make in the future. Tausk was also certain that if he had only been in the Cathedral Square at Wiladowski's side, he would have been able to stop the killers before they could have acted. His own breakdown, the one possibility he had never foreseen, had changed everything. For a terrible moment he recalled Brugger's final look back there in the clearing and wondered how the rebbe would react, wherever he was, when the news of the Cathedral Square murders reached him.

Wiladowski got up to warm himself by the fire. Tausk watched him standing there, holding his hands out in front of him, seemingly lost in his weariness. The flames threw constantly changing shadow patterns over the furniture, and Tausk moved silently around the room to light a few of the lamps. He needed to change the mood in whatever way he could. The thought that this capricious nobleman, whose suspiciousness was legendary, trusted completely in his loyalty, while the spymaster himself was haunted by how much he had kept from Wiladowski, was becoming unendurable. But admitting his culpability would help neither of them now, and Tausk had no temptation to add the burden of a useless confession to their other problems. Instead he decided to continue his report as though there had been no lull in the conversation and was relieved to see the Count-Governor shake off his gloom and return to his chair by the desk, looking as alert as he always did when they were discussing important security matters. Von Arnstein had confessed immediately, Tausk told his master with a contemptuous smile, and betrayed his fellow conspirators almost as quickly. The spymaster could take no credit for breaking him, since so little skill had been required. Tausk discovered him sobbing like a child at finding himself manacled in a filthy jail cell. He seemed completely unprepared for being treated like a common murderer rather than a political prisoner and kept complaining about the shameful humiliations to which he was being subjected. He was also suffering a great deal from the pain of his leg wound, and just the threat of physical coercion helped unnerve him further. In Tausk's opinion, von Arnstein still could not fully comprehend what he had done. His own misery was real enough to him, but all the rest was like an end-of-the-term theatrical performance at the military academy in which he had unaccountably injured himself and gotten into trouble with the school authorities as well. "Listening to him," Tausk said acidly, "I had to keep reminding myself that people had been killed because he and his friends wanted to play at being historical figures."

Instead of being offended by the comparison, Wiladowski simply shook his head. "I am sure you are right about von Arnstein. Only his case is getting less unusual every week. The person who said history is written by the winners was a fool. These days whoever has the loudest grievance wants to write the next chapter, and if there is one thing people like that are certain of, it is their own virtue. The stagehands and understudies are taking over politics, and in the end that always means more bloodshed."

For Tausk, what counted was hearing Wiladowski talk to him in his familiar, ironically didactic tone, a sure sign that for all the pessimism of the Count-Governor's conclusions, emotionally he was himself again. He put von Arnstein's signed confession in Wiladowski's hands and said that as soon as he had obtained the names of the other three terrorists, he had sent his men to arrest them. Joachim Gerling and Manfred Langer had been apprehended two hours ago, trying unsuccessfully to find someone to hide them in the Josef Quarter, and he was just starting to question them when the duty officer summoned him to attend on the Count-Governor. Von Arnstein had told him that Christoph von Hradl was almost certainly at his parents' estate, hiding in a secret room underneath his mother's summerhouse, and within a short while a squadron of soldiers would be arriving at Weidenau with a warrant for the young von Hradl. With any luck, he would be in the Castle prison alongside his comrades later that night.

Wiladowski glanced over the protocol with something of the same morose discouragement he had felt hearing about the young child's death in the square. He had often been a visitor out at Hirschwang and Weidenau and knew the elder von Hradls and von Arnsteins quite well. The other two names were not as familiar, but Wiladowski was sure he had heard Paul Gerling spoken of favorably in government circles as an intellectual one could trust and assumed that this Joachim must be the man's son. He tried to read von Arnstein's explanation of what had prompted them to resort to "direct, illegal, revolutionary means of warfare" but found himself unable to get to the end of the statement. In between expressions of fear for his own future and halfhearted contrition for the harm he had caused, von Arnstein still seemed stirred by the lethal clichés that he took for a political program. For Wiladowski, to be born ignorant and stupid was one thing; deliberately to make oneself so was inexcusable. He pushed the papers back to Tausk with a promise to study them all carefully tomorrow. For the moment, he said, it was expecting too much of him first to be shot at by these gentlemen and then to spend his evening reading their explanation why it had been a fine idea to do so.

"But what about Rotenburg and von Alpsbach?" Tausk asked, not picking up the dossier that the Count-Governor had thrust toward him. "When you get to the end of his statement, Your Excellency will see that the prisoner mentions both Ernst von Alpsbach and Hans Rotenburg as having been aware of the conspiracy. Rotenburg is even named as a ringleader, although I find it difficult to believe that these aristocrats would let themselves be commanded by a Jew, no matter how rich his father. Of course he is an excellent choice for a scapegoat, especially if he is not alive to contradict his accusers. In any case, since we know definitively that neither the young von Alpsbach nor Rotenburg was present at the square, I have not taken any actions concerning them before receiving your instructions."

"What shameless effrontery." Wiladowski had been stirred out of his low spirits into outright anger. "Karl Gustav died in front of my eyes protecting my wife. Alfred and Magdi saw the whole thing too, and I don't believe either of them will ever recover. Magdi refused to let Karl Gustav's fellow officers take away the body and insisted on transporting it back to Brunnenberg in her own carriage to be buried there. The thought of her in that coach, with her dead son beside her, has not left me since I watched them ride off, and I can promise you that without a great deal more proof than an accusation by these cowards, I have no intention of bringing more misery to that poor family. As for Rotenburg, his death makes the whole question moot. But if von Arnstein really believes fables like that will save his neck, he is even stupider than I thought."

"I am not sure that his neck will have much to do with how the boy dies," Tausk answered. "By the time I was done questioning him and had a physician brought in to look at the wound, infection had set in. The doctor performed an immediate amputation, but even with the leg removed, the likelihood of fatal blood poisoning is apparently very high. So it seems we will soon have to add Leo von Arnstein to the list of people killed by the terrorists' bullets. But as far as Hans Rotenburg is concerned, Your Excellency should know that there are rumors circulating in town that it was not his remains that were found in the wreckage."

"What do you believe really happened, Tausk?" Wiladowski asked, perhaps a bit too casually for the spymaster's peace of mind.

Tausk paused for a few moments to consider the question before replying. "I am not sure I am in a position to give Your Excellency a useful answer," he finally said. "The evidence is inconclusive. No doubt the father's refusal to permit a funeral helped start the rumors, and once such stories are put into circulation, they become impossible to contain. But just because something is a rumor does not necessarily mean it is untrue either," he said, emphasizing his readiness to look at the question from every side. "Certainly Hans Rotenburg could have left the area before the explosion without any of us finding out, and someone else been immolated in the shack, but up to now we have no credible grounds for thinking so."

"But if it did happen like that," Wiladowski interjected, "then his father must have known all about it or he would have agreed to the interment. And if Moritz Rotenburg is involved, then Hans's disappearance must be linked to some secret business scheme of the old man's. I certainly wish I knew what the two of them were up to, but whatever its nature, it is hardly likely to involve assassinating Imperial officials. But whether Hans Rotenburg is really dead or conducting some negotiations abroad, he certainly did not shoot at anyone today, and I see no point dragging his name into the case."

Tausk knew better than to agree too quickly to a suggestion that suited him so well. At the risk of irritating Wiladowski, he insisted on returning to the question. "Yes, I agree that involving the Rotenburgs is likely only to complicate matters," he replied. "But if the murderers' defense involves naming either von Alpsbach or Rotenburg as an accomplice, we will end up having to investigate their accusations anyway, so perhaps the most prudent thing would be for me—or for my successor, if Your Excellency believes my immediate resignation would make things easier for you—to look into the matter first, as a preemptive gesture."

While they were talking, it had turned completely dark outside. The curtains were still open, and when Wiladowski looked out the window and saw how late it had become, he abruptly rang for Aloïs to come in and put some more logs on the fire. He leaned against the curved library ladder, contentedly watching his servant busy himself with his regular evening routine. Tausk was standing out of their way, toward the back of the room, and smiled appreciatively at hearing the Count-Governor tell Aloïs to have a box of the spymaster's cigarettes brought up from his quarters, along with mineral water for Tausk and some brandy for himself. When Aloïs had finished and they were alone again, with the bottles of brandy and water placed on a table near the fire, Wiladowski invited Tausk to sit down beside him. The Count-Governor waited until he had finished his cigar before resuming their conversation, but when he did, it was with an acerbity Tausk had not anticipated.

"What makes you think I intend to give these gentlemen a platform from which to accuse anyone?" he asked. "I am sure they would like nothing better than a great public trial in which they would have a chance to make world-historical speeches justifying themselves. For them, it would be better than having a play accepted by the Burgtheater, since in a courtroom they would be both the lead actors and the dramatists. But they miscalculated. By shooting at an official government procession and murdering officers in His Majesty's army, they have subjected themselves to a closed military tribunal, and I intend to convene one as soon as we have them all in custody. If the doctor can give me his word about the outcome, von Arnstein will be allowed to die in bed from his wound, but the others will go directly from the sentencing to their execution."

"What about their families? They will undoubtedly make difficulties and perhaps appeal for clemency directly to the Emperor?" Tausk was certain the Count-Governor had thought of the question already but asked anyway, for the pleasure of hearing Wiladowski's explanation.

"As long as you give me a signed confession from each of the traitors, no one can challenge the legality of our action," Wiladowski told Tausk decisively. "As for their families, I am afraid that our terrorists have murdered above their station. In addition to their other victims, they have killed Zichy-Ferraris and gravely wounded von Kirchstein, both of whom outrank the assassins by far too many grades for their own titles to shield them. And in the provincial council, von Alpsbach will support everything I do to punish the people who murdered his son. As a matter of courtesy, I will talk to him about it, of course, but I think we can assume that we have a free hand."

Tausk knew his master well enough to register that underneath his habitual irony, Wiladowski was consumed with rage and determined to exact whatever revenge he could on the assassins. But it was less the brutality of the murders in the Cathedral Square that moved him to such fury than the thought that the terrorists had dared shoot at him. The Count-Governor had dreamed about an assassination attempt for so long that he had come to regard it as his personal recurrent nightmare, dreadful to endure night after night but, for that very reason, unconnected to events in the daylight world. Wiladowski spoke of being killed the way a brilliant but anxious student tells all his classmates that he has surely failed his examinations or a lover insists on predicting his mistress's infidelity—that is, as a form of sympathetic magic, designed to ensure that the much-talked-about catastrophe will never really happen. Now that the calamity actually had occurred, it was precisely Wiladowski's constant imaginative anticipation that had left him so unprepared for the reality. But although Tausk could sympathize with the Count-Governor's anger, he was taken aback by how cold-bloodedly Wiladowski had already mapped out the quickest way to dispatch the prisoners. "I have a reputation for ruthlessness," Tausk thought, "but when the chance to kill Brugger was handed to me, I could not do it. In my place, Wiladowski or Moritz Rotenburg would have given the order to shoot him down without an instant's hesitation. At a mere glimpse from his rebbe, a nonentity like Sonnenschön sows death wherever he goes, and I haven't even decided what to do about him yet. It is high time I started to learn from my betters." Tausk grimaced at his belated determination to mend his ways. To the Count-Governor, though, he adopted an entirely different tone. Thinking of Sonnenschön had given him a plan that might redress some of his earlier vacillation.

"If Your Excellency has decided on a speedy resolution," he said, "then I can suggest a way to deprive the assassins of the public spectacle for which they are hoping. On Friday night we raided the wonder rabbi's house in the Josef Quarter and arrested his closest followers. There is ample evidence to convict them of multiple murder and arson, and I wonder whether we could not simply try two or three of Brugger's disciples, right along with the Cathedral Square conspirators, in a single session of the court. Then, after sentence has been pronounced, it would be routine procedure to execute them all together as well. Von Arnstein could scarcely believe he was in an ordinary jail cell, and I am sure that to be treated like common hoodlums and thugs and go to their death alongside a pack of Jewish religious zealots is hardly the end that von Hradl and the others fantasized."

Wiladowski nodded grimly. "An excellent notion, Tausk. Yes, that is exactly how we will arrange it. And the sooner the better. Just bring me the confessions, and I will have the tribunal convened immediately. As a matter of prudence, I do not intend to sit on it myself. Karl Gustav's old commanding officer will be glad to serve as presiding magistrate, and I will leave it up to him to appoint two associate judges who can be relied upon to do their duty. But what about this rabbi of yours? I had forgotten all about him until now."

"I took care of everything in light of what Your Excellency and I discussed," Tausk answered. "He will never come back here to trouble us, but since he undoubtedly has followers in other towns on both sides of the border, who knows what stories about him will continue to circulate? Just as they have started doing about Hans Rotenburg, I suppose."

"It is Easter, after all, Tausk." Wiladowski dismissed the topic with a shrug. "Of course new legends will arise. My Church does not have an exclusive patent on such fables. I assume that is how revelation always works, no matter what the religion: the executioners asleep or absent, the mourners secret and guarded, and the tomb vacant. A large hole for competing stories to fill. The Empress Elisabeth has been glimpsed all over Europe in the decade and a half since her murder, and what is just as miraculous, she always seems to look as though she were still in her early forties, instead of the worn-out sixty-one-year-old woman who was stabbed through the heart in Geneva."

"But if Your Excellency intends to proceed with a single trial of the conspirators and the rabbi's followers, I take it you do not want me to resign immediately?" Tausk inquired. He had intended his offer sincerely. He and Wiladowski both knew that his time at the Castle was measurable in weeks, at the most, and whether he left tomorrow or at the end of April made little difference.

"I wish I could get indignant and say that it is up to me, not Trautmannsdorff and his crowd in Vienna, how long you should serve here, but after today's events I probably have lost the authority to protect you. In any case, it is me they are after, not you. I did hear your offer of resignation earlier and will accept it soon in the spirit in which you intended it. But in the meantime I would regard it as a great personal favor if you could stay on until the trial and its aftermath are over."

Tausk noticed that once the conspirators' fate had been decided, the Count-Governor went back to using terms like *aftermath* rather than *execution*. Another principle of statecraft he felt obscurely pleased to have been shown. But Tausk also felt unaccountably moved by Wiladowski's request. He had never heard Wiladowski use words like *a great personal favor* with anyone, let alone a member of his own staff, and rather than take it as a sign of weakness, Tausk recognized it as a kind of leave-taking, a nobleman's last affirmation of their strange companionability.

After Tausk had gone back downstairs to secure his prisoners' confessions, Wiladowski allowed himself a final large brandy. The fire was starting to die down, but for the moment he did not want even Aloïs's barely registerable presence in the room with him. He got up and looked at the letter of resignation that he had been drafting when Tausk came in. He would date it three weeks after the executions, so that Tausk could leave first, with Wiladowski still in office to guarantee his safe departure. He looked around the only room in the entire Castle that did not fill him with repugnance every time he entered it and thought how little he would miss. If his Triestine friends were to ask him how it felt to have left such a position, he would answer them honestly that it was like checking out of an undistinguished hotel from which one had expected little and received even less. He wondered, though, what Tausk would do next. In spite of today's crisis, Wiladowski remained a man of the larger social world and was still convinced that observing a person at an elegant dinner or in a box at the opera revealed as much about his essential character as would his behavior in a prison cell or a religious seminary. Or in a Count-Governor's library, if it came to that. One could gamble with one's future anywhere. Wiladowski was certain that a month ago Tausk would have been more agitated at the impending loss of power. So what had changed? Perhaps, Wiladowski reflected, it was nothing more than a deep-seated inability to accept a subordinate role indefinitely. But even before the murders Wiladowski had caught a suggestion, so faint as to be virtually imperceptible, of Tausk as a man with one eye on the door, seemingly fully engaged in whatever he was doing but somewhere inside already scanning the horizon for the path that would lead him elsewhere. Wiladowski knew the sensation well; it had marked his own career from the beginning, and even in places like Rome, where he had been happiest, he remembered feeling himself a transient, sure that before long he would be looking out onto another landscape and sleeping in a new bed.

In early June, a week after the summary trial and executions, when Tausk left the Castle for the last time, he did so at an hour he thought the Count-Governor would be asleep. A hired coach was waiting in the courtyard, and when Tausk and Roublev got in, they took with them little more than a single suitcase and a military-issue duffel bag each. No one from the Castle staff came out to wave good-bye. Wiladowski watched their departure from his study window. It was better this way, without any prolonged farewells. Tausk was taking with him a substantial letter of credit drawn on Wiladowski's private bank and a scribbled note of appreciation with the Count-Governor's address in both Vienna and Trieste, although Wiladowski doubted Tausk would ever make use of them. It had been difficult to prevent a formal accusation of negligence in the execution of his duties from being leveled at Tausk, but Wiladowski had succeeded in persuading the Ministry that doing so, and thereby giving the spymaster the opportunity to refute the charges in court, would only be embarrassing to everyone involved, including the government's own secret police. To Wiladowski's relief, von Kirchmayr, the Chief of Police, agreed with him, and so, in the best Austrian tradition, the matter was temporarily shelved. Marie-Luise had left for the capital several days before to prepare their house there for Wiladowski's imminent retirement and to try to repair relationships with some of the other families who would never forgive what had happened in the Cathedral Square. Wiladowski himself thought her effort futile as a practical matter and pointless as an emotional one, but he knew it mattered to Marie-Luise and saw no reason to discourage her. Curiously, though, one family that might have been expected to sever all social ties with Wiladowski appeared, on the contrary, to have come to regard him almost as a relative. It seemed as though his final official duty, before departing for Vienna and presenting his resignation in person to the Emperor, would be to attend the hurried marriage of Elisabeth Demetz and Ernst von Alpsbach. By all accounts, it turned out that Dr. Demetz was not so reliable after all. According to the von Alpsbachs, it was not medical scruples but the chance to see his daughter wed to one of the country's great families that had prevented Viktor Demetz from doing what was expected to make a marriage unnecessary. At least it would be a very small affair, with Wiladowski the only person not directly related to the families being asked to attend. In view of the bride's origins and the family's grief at Karl Gustav's death, the von Alpsbachs had decided to hold the ceremony at Brunnenberg with the local parish priest officiating. Wiladowski had been invited at Magdi's insistence, not in his capacity as Count-Governor, but because of his great sympathy for Karl Gustav in the poor boy's final hours and his understanding of her loss. Wiladowski himself felt no desire to attend but saw no decent way to refuse, and so he arranged to be taken directly from Weidenau to catch the express train to the capital as soon as the ceremony was concluded. Since Marie-Luise had ordered their possessions to be packed up and forwarded to them, it was unlikely Wiladowski would ever need to return to the province again.

CODA

1925

It was impossible for him to love this country. Admire it, yes, but nothing here reached him as deeply as the memory of sitting downstairs by the large bay window, watching the snow shift like lace in the December wind as it gently blanketed the branches in his father's garden. Even on the most striking autumn days in England, when the sun would set in a sky of intense salmon pink over blue, he found himself longing to see the pearl gray mist rising from the fields at the end of the von Alpsbach forests. The new moon like a scythe over those same fields, palely illuminating the peasant houses daubed for the holidays with red paint to resemble bull's blood: While he had lived there, he had scarcely been aware of taking any of it in, let alone of loving it so profoundly. But now, when he took long, restless walks through country lanes or along the ridges of the softly rolling hills that everyone assured him were among the loveliest in the world, the thoughts that stirred in him had little connection with what he was actually seeing but arose in response to inner images of an entirely different landscape, half a continent away. London was no different. He still kept the house in Portman Square open and stayed there whenever he was in town on business, but except when he was being driven along the embankment, looking out toward Greenwich, where the houses almost dissolved in the evening fog, the grandeur of this immense city struck him as alien, constructed with an indifference to ordinary human comfort or equanimity. There was ample luxury for those who could pay for it, but if not, the wretchedness here was harsher and more unrelieved than anything he had seen back home. Perhaps it was just that the scale was all wrong for an Austrian. He too had grown up in an Empire, although largely a landlocked one, but a certain careless inefficiency had made it seem less oppressive. His father used to tell him that it was almost impossible to sound pompous in Yiddish. Analogously, perhaps, the much-maligned Habsburg passivity, an ambition not to triumph but merely to survive, took off some of the edge of Imperial power. Here, though, there was no such self-doubt. He knew that by comparison with America, the war had seriously compromised Britain's long-term economic prospects, and for some time now he had been moving significant amounts of his capital to the United States. But the vulnerability of their own role in the world had done nothing to diminish English arrogance. Even for someone with his access to government officials, their assumption of effortless superiority was grating. In the Ministries that Hans had occasion to visit from time to time, the doors of the senior officials never carried anything as vulgar as nameplates. If the caller did not know in advance which room he was seeking, he obviously did not belong in the building. Hans was not certain if it was the fact that he was a Jew, a former citizen of a defeated enemy, or a onetime Red that accounted for some of the odd reactions he elicited, but often he was able to play on the anxieties provoked by each of these categories when it came to negotiating an important contract with the government. He knew that Lord Northcliffe, the newspaper magnate, had once referred to him as "that filthy rich Bolshie Jew," and Hans enjoyed turning that knowledge to his advantage when he needed the man's newspapers to take an editorial stance favorable to the Rotenburg interests. But there was less need of those maneuvers with each year. His subordinates were able to handle many of the day-to-day decisions of his company, and he was finally making use of the country house that he had bought five years ago, more as an investment than a residence. Or at least that was what he had told himself at the time. Now that he and Batya were writing each other again, irregularly at first, but increasingly more often, and always with the confidence of finding a receptive ear, Hans was able to acknowledge that perhaps he had been thinking all along that this was the kind of place she would enjoy visiting.

Batya, who used to love going out into the country so much, came into his mind frequently when he set out, irrespective of the weather, on his long, prescribed walks. For her, the "return to nature" had been directly identified with the Zionist program of "returning to the Nation." Years ago, when they were still going out together and he declined, as he almost invariably did, to join her on her hikes, she would respond by teasing him about his typical shtetl Jew's indifference to anything but abstract thought. Even back then he had been tempted to tell her that money and power were the least abstract things in the world, but he knew it would be futile to argue. Well, indifferent or not, these days he had been forced by his doctors to take up what he skeptically called "the walking cure" to help his circulation. He had never recovered fully from the injuries of the explosion and sometimes at night would wake up in terror from a dream in which he lay in Auer's shack, seeing his own flesh burn off his bones without being able to lose consciousness. Parts of his body were still badly scarred, and the slight limp from where a beam had shattered his hip made hiking anywhere but on flat ground or the gentlest slopes painful. In one of her first letters after they had reestablished contact, Batya asked him whether shame at his disfigurement was why he had never married. He thought for a long time before answering, and when he did, he uncharacteristically said much more than her question required. Hans assured her that his scars hardly amounted to being disfigured and that, as far as he could tell, considerations of that kind had played no part in his choices. There had been a number of women for whom he had cared, and once or twice he had nearly become engaged, but each time differences of background and temperament between him and the woman had made him shy away before proposing. Although Batya did not directly ask, he posed, in her name, the question of whether he had been changed by his different love affairs and wrote back, "As for learning from past mistakes, I don't know. I think my experiences during the past decade are very different from anything that happened when we were young together, but probably not because I understand things better now or have learned anything specific from my failures. I have made horrible mistakes that I deeply regret, some of which you know; others, I have to confess, I am glad you don't. But I think if I have learned at all, it is more the way a stone learns from being worn down by water and wind. I feel myself changed by age and elements, but I also know that fundamentally one remains the same. I certainly have not acquired wisdom with time, or perhaps, at best, a stone's wisdom."

So far the only person to have benefited concretely from Hans's determination to be more tolerant of others was Asher Blumenthal, and that solely because he was far enough away that it was possible to humor him without risking any greater intrusiveness. Asher's regular letters from Haifa were one of Hans's few reliable sources of entertainment, and he was glad to honor the arrangement his father had made to send Blumenthal a regular stipend in exchange for his never coming back to Europe.

Hans had even increased the amount of his support from time to time, less in response to Asher's litany of complaints than as a kind of tribute to his unwavering consistency. Hans was a generous contributor to Zionist causes, and in 1920, when the first postwar Zionist convention was held in London, he had attended several sessions as an interested observer. Asher, though, was living proof that one could remain entirely unaffected either by starting a new life in Palestine or by the destruction of one's old existence in the war. To Hans, Asher did nothing but complain about how unbearable a country he was being forced to live in. His greatest pleasure, he said, was that there were so many Germans in his neighborhood that he could go on conducting his life in his own language. He readily admitted that his Hebrew had never become proficient enough for him to say anything in it beyond the rudimentary phrases found in a schoolboy's primer. "My lack of fluency," he wrote Hans mournfully, "makes me sound like a man who goes walking along the beach when a violent storm breaks out. He sees the waves swelling to enormous heights before crashing thunderously against the rocks and sand, the fierce winds spraying salt water and drenching everything around, and he expresses all this by shouting out, 'Wet!' The result of this ineptitude is that in spite of my evident material advantages—provided by your father's and your own generosity—over the other single men of my age in this insect-infested Levantine backwater, none of the attractive young women are in the least interested in me except as a source of a free dinner. For which, I might point out, they are not even honorable enough to reward me with favors they seem to bestow without a second thought on any Polish immigrant who has decided to transform himself from a tailor into an orange picker."

Poor Asher. He must have been so disappointed when Moritz did not immediately designate him his heir after the explosion. Probably that gave Asher his first clue Hans was still alive. In one of their many long conversations in the sanatorium in Switzerland, where Moritz was dying more quickly from his cancer than his son was regaining his strength and use of his limbs, his father had amused Hans by recounting how Asher had rushed into his study the very evening after Auer's shack blew up to offer condolences and, in the same breath, discreetly remind Moritz that Hans had died owing him a substantial amount of money of which he was in desperate need. Partway through telling Hans the story, Moritz's breathing had become so constricted that his son begged him to stop and rest, but Moritz waved him off, eager to continue, not, as Hans realized only long afterward, because he found the story so entertaining but because until they had managed, tentatively and with much mutual trepidation, to come to understand each other better, Asher offered them a good topic about which they could joke, safe in the knowledge that they already shared a similar view. In that sense, Hans thought, Asher unwittingly fulfilled the role of a generous elder brother helping to reconcile the father and his youngest son.

People frequently talk about how greed blinds one, Hans mused, but in Blumenthal's case, it had given him a clarity denied to everyone else. Something in the evasive way Moritz responded to his perfectly formulaic expressions of condolences convinced Asher that the financier was not as grief-stricken as he tried to pretend. Moritz was unable to let the words *My son is dead* cross his lips, and that was enough for Blumenthal to intuit the truth. About everything else, though, he was wildly off the mark. He became more certain than ever that the Rotenburgs had plotted together to ruin the families of the other conspirators in order to acquire their estates at a fraction of their real worth. Since Hans's supposed death, the rest of the cell had cut off all contact with Asher, so that he had no idea of their plans and had lost any chance of getting paid for informing on them to Tausk. More forfeited income, as he complained piteously to Moritz, evidently hoping the financier would feel obliged to make up for his loss. All in all, Moritz told his son, it was clear that Asher's jumble of shrewd guesswork and absurd speculation was dangerous to them both. The only solution Moritz could see, short of having Tausk dispose of Asher altogether, was to hire Blumenthal on the spot to accompany them to Switzerland in the sealed train carriage and, once there, to give him the choice of emigrating to Palestine, with the promise of a modest but guaranteed lifetime income, or to make his own way back home and see how well he would do opposing himself to the Rotenburgs. Even an indirect threat from such a source reduced Asher to tearful avowals of gratitude for Moritz's generous offer and a promise to accept his terms without question. According to Asher, he felt no regret at leaving their province, which in any case he had always detested. His only sorrow came because Moritz would not permit him to stay in Zurich long enough to see Hans well again. If he went away now, with Hans still needing constant medical attention, he would not be able to bid a proper good-bye to a person whom he had come to know so well and for whom he had developed such strong sentiments of comradeship. The next day, though, Asher returned with a different request altogether. He pleaded all morning to be allowed to change the place of his exile, but Moritz stayed inflexible, promising only the grimmest consequences if Asher should ever set foot outside Palestine. By the time Hans recovered enough to sit with his father on the balcony of their clinic, Asher was on his way to Eretz Yisrael, the only Jew from the Mendelssohn Club to have done so since the first Zionist recruiters had started giving presentations in their town.

Over the years, by turning Asher's continuing misbehavior into the subject of an imaginary conversation with his father Hans was able to overlook it. Occasionally, when Asher had drunk too much, he would go around Haifa insisting that his name was really Asher Rotenburg and that he was the illegitimate son of the great financier, who was paying him off not to embarrass the family by disclosing his real identity. Inevitably some of these stories reached Hans in London, but he decided to take no action beyond making certain all the banks in Palestine knew not to honor any requests for funds beyond the quarterly stipend for which Hans had left standing orders. Asher's futile longing to be anything other than who he was helped Hans understand better what his father had meant in the course of a long conversation a few days before Moritz returned to Austria. Moritz said that while he was sitting watching over Hans, he had come to accept that some of the differences between them did not stem from any deep-seated antagonism between their two natures. For all his wealth, Moritz recognized that he still had an inner image of Jewish life as it had been when he himself was growing up, a continuous struggle to survive amid a crushing labyrinth of restrictions and legal disabilities, whereas Hans had encountered scarcely any barriers. For him, a brilliant life, aristocratic friends, and a seemingly unfettered future all appeared entirely natural, a birthright to be disposed of as he himself saw fit and hence not in need of being preserved and fought for. People like Nathan Kaplansky were always saying that revolutions were made by those who, possessing nothing, had nothing to lose, but as far as Moritz could judge, more often than not they were led by people like Hans, who had grown up with everything and so felt confident enough to risk it all for what they regarded as a higher aim. Far from deriving any comfort from his father's efforts to make sense of what had prompted his actions, Hans only felt more deeply ashamed. The news of what had happened in the Cathedral Square, and the ensuing arrest and execution of his childhood companions, filled Hans with such revulsion at himself that only his father's repeated plea not to throw away still another life stopped Hans from boarding a separate train home and surrendering himself to the police as the conspiracy's instigator.

In the first weeks of his convalescence, during which he and his father spent most of their day together, Hans was frequently startled by how remote he felt himself from the person he had been only a short while before. It required a conscious act of will for him to recall the Hans who had walked into Auer's shack to construct a bomb, and he knew that surviving the explosion had transformed him in ways that he was not yet able to put into words. When they had lived together at home, Moritz's conversation used to enervate Hans almost immediately, but now, as they were saying good night, he already found himself looking forward to seeing his father again at breakfast. Occasionally Hans grew puzzled about how entirely he had turned his back on his former convictions without having found anything compelling to replace them beyond an instinctive, unthinking gratitude for being alive, but feeling his body slowly heal was so powerful a source of joy that he dismissed any other concern as the remnant of an illness that had scarred his mind in the same way that the blast had damaged his limbs. He was so absorbed in the workings of his body that at first he found it hard to concentrate on his father's explanation of the structure of the Rotenburg holdings, but gradually the circle of his interests began to widen outward again from his immediate physical condition, and the idea of taking an interest in his future stopped seeming like a waste of precious energy. By then it was already mid-June. Hans's injuries were healing as well as could be hoped, and his father felt able to leave him to complete his recovery on his own. It was clear to everyone that Moritz had little time left. The doctors were not able to do any more for him, and he wanted to die in his own house, with his affairs in order. The thought that he would have to do so without Hans beside him was so wrenching that neither man ever mentioned it directly, but the ache of that knowledge accompanied everything they talked about in Zurich and remained with Hans for the rest of his life. Hans was still not well enough to see his father off at the station, so their awkward good-bye at the circular tree-lined entrance to the sanatorium, with the hospital staff hovering zealously around both men, was their last glimpse of each other.

The outbreak of the war shortly after Moritz's return did not interrupt the regular exchange of letters between Switzerland and Austria. As Moritz had anticipated, his timely return home enabled him to deflect the growing questions about what had happened to Hans. Rumors implicating

Hans in the Cathedral Square murders were circulating in town; but there was no real evidence connecting him to the killings, and the government, which needed Rotenburg's financial backing more than ever, was reluctant to initiate an investigation whose results were bound to be inconclusive. Moritz simply announced that just before Easter, he had sent Hans abroad on confidential family business, but that his son had been taken gravely ill and for a long time lay near death. The concern everyone had seen Moritz express was for the seriousness of his son's condition, which, although improving, was still far from satisfactory. With the evidence of a letter from the Swiss doctors about the extent of Hans's debility, and Moritz's personal assurance, backed by a substantial contribution toward the costs of the full-scale national mobilization, the Minister of War himself authorized Hans Rotenburg's exemption from the military call-up until such time as his physicians declared the young man fit for active service. First from the hospital and then, when he no longer needed constant medical supervision, from the small house he rented in town, Hans was able to follow his father's pessimistic analysis of the political situation. The Rotenburgs' private couriers continued operating unchecked across Europe throughout the four years of bloodletting during which Franz Josef's Empire disintegrated. But soon it was only business reports that Hans received, since Moritz died less than a year after his return. Except for a few gifts to old employees and some large donations to various Jewish causes, Hans was left sole heir to the Rotenburg fortune. Moritz had invested much of the money in England and the United States, and by the time the war was over and the European borders were again open for travel, the increase in the value of his pound sterling and dollar holdings alone had made Hans wealthier than his father had been in 1914.

The urge to see his home again, if only to visit his father's grave, was often nearly overpowering, but never so much as during the first months after the armistice, before he moved his company's headquarters to London. He booked a ticket on at least three separate occasions but each time ended up canceling at the last moment. Except for Batya, almost everyone he had known well from his own generation had been killed in the war. Even if she were willing to see him—and for a long time he was too afraid of a rebuff to inquire directly—he found himself dreading the thought of their meeting. She was a widow now, with two young children, and belonged to a family to whose suffering he had contributed unforgivably. He had come through the war years and the collapse of their country's economy undamaged, and Hans could not bear seeing in her eyes the question of why he had survived when so many better men, including her husband, had perished. Perhaps such a thought would never occur to Batya; but it was one that came to him often, and he knew he would search for it in whatever she actually said to him. There were too many other ghosts as well, standing between him and even the briefest homecoming. Legally no charges against Hans had ever been filed in connection with the Cathedral Square murders, and after so many millions of dead, the event itself was forgotten everywhere but in his own town. The Gerlings and Langers had moved permanently to Vienna early in the war and quickly lost touch with everyone in the province. But old von Arnstein was still alive out at Hirschwang, and although Philip von Hradl had died during the influenza epidemic, Christoph's mother and his numerous female cousins had survived. Hans knew that both families regarded him as the malignant devil who had corrupted their sons and led them to their deaths. It was a judgment he found himself repeating in his own mind often enough, but he did not feel able to hear it directly from those he had injured.

He only confessed his fear to Batya a few years later, after they already had been corresponding for some time, and was surprised by how openly she was able to talk about everything with him. From her letters he gathered that there was no one in her daily life with whom she could discuss her past without constraint and that Hans's being far away in London, and many years removed from the experiences they had shared, gave her a freedom to put her thoughts on paper that she welcomed.

"I certainly do not feel that way about you now," she wrote to him in Portman Square, "but immediately after the war it might have been different. To have seen you then, prosperous and flourishing, when my children will never know their father and our life here was in ruins, would have been very hard. You know, Ernst was killed in the fighting along the Isonzo River just a year before the war ended. When we found out I was pregnant that April, we talked about having a belated honeymoon in that very area after the baby was born. We were going to visit Trieste and Gorizia, along with Venice, but of course he was called up several months before I was due. I suppose it doesn't really matter where one dies, but I know he must have thought about it when his unit was ordered to the Italian front. At least he got to see Nora when he came home on leave, but by the time Madeleine was born he had been dead for several months. I am not even sure he ever got my letter telling him that I had become pregnant again during his leave. I know a lot of women in my position end up making a kind of shrine to their husbands in their memory—after all, what else do we have left except those memories?—and attribute qualities to their men that they never really noticed while they were alive. But there is no need to imagine Ernst's virtues; they were evident to everyone who knew him. He was a good man who loathed injustice wherever he saw it. He thought the war was a catastrophe from the beginning, and I never once saw him express any of the revolting enthusiasm for going off to fight that so many of the others around here showed. But he felt it was his duty to join up and refused to use his family connections to get transferred to a safe posting away from the slaughter. When he came home on leave and saw Nora for the first time, I have never witnessed a more joyful smile. He suddenly looked like a boy of fifteen. They took to each other from the moment he picked her up, and I am quite sure that if he had survived the war, Nora would have grown to prefer him over me. I said to myself, 'That man was meant to be a father,' which, I suppose, is why I was so glad when I found out I was pregnant again. Somehow, I thought it might help keep him alive. Not that the knowledge of it would make him be more careful, you understand, but superstitiously, I half convinced myself that whatever God there is, whether ours or his Christian one, would not let a man like that be killed before his child is born. But knowing everything I do about Ernst, and even having watched him with Nora, can't make me forget that I had decided to leave him, at least temporarily, that spring before she was conceived. I remember so many complicated, contradictory feelings, but I was not certain enough they included the kind of love I thought a girl my age should feel for the man with whom she chose to spend the rest of her life. I hadn't met anyone else in whom I was interested; that wasn't the problem. I simply did not feel ready for a permanent decision. Or maybe for all his noble qualities, Ernst was not the right man for me. I was never able to make up my mind which and tortured both of us with my indecisiveness. Also—and I can see you smiling as you read this, Hans—although no one took me seriously, I had never completely given up the thought of someday emigrating to Palestine, and of course staying with Ernst would have made that impossible. I suppose that I wanted all my possibilities to stay open and found the idea of having to give up any of them intolerable.

"At first, when I found out I was pregnant, I was not sure I wanted to keep the baby. Unlike me, Ernst never had a moment's hesitation, although I couldn't say for sure whether it was out of love for me, the wish to be a father, or more of the von Alpsbach sense of duty. Of course, Magdi and Alfred were perfectly horrible and accused me and my family of every vileness imaginable, but both Ernst and my father absolutely refused any discussion of an abortion. For a while we played out this bizarre little drama at Brunnenberg, with Magdi, Alfred, and me, who detested one another but for the moment were temporary allies, rehearsing all the reasons why, in the long run, the pregnancy could only bring unhappiness to everyone, and, on the other side, Ernst, looking increasingly more somber and nursing the cold fury I sometimes saw erupt in him, warning that no one would hurt his baby as long as he had strength to defend it. The whole time my own poor father stood by helplessly, no doubt certain we all were quite mad. The most sordid threats and counterthreats were being bandied about. One day the von Alpsbachs would swear they were going to disinherit Ernst in favor of his younger brother, and the next, Ernst would announce his settled decision to give up his claim to the name and estate and leave—with me expected to go along, of course—for some unspecified destination to start a new life. Then Karl Gustav's death changed everything for them. After Magdi came home with his body, there was no more talk of an abortion or opposition to our getting married. No one in either family seemed to notice that I was just as unsure as before of what I wanted. But I went along with everything, so I suppose I must have been if not exactly overjoyed, then at least resigned to what was happening. For me, it was not until Nora's actual birth that everything changed forever. I still don't know from where the woman emerged who wanted only to spend all day beside her child, for whom the sleeplessness that other mothers complain about seemed an easy burden, scarcely worth mentioning, and for whom her own wishes counted for nothing next to her baby's needs. A happily domestic Batya. Who could have guessed? Certainly neither of us, which is perhaps why I can write to you about it so easily. Now, though, late at night, when they both are asleep, I sometimes worry about who I will be—or if I will *be* at all in any way that I can still recognize—when that unfamiliar woman who was born full grown along with Nora and Madeleine in order to take care of them is no longer required.

"I am so glad you immediately noticed the resemblance, even from the stilted photo I was able to send. It was almost impossible to get them both to sit still for the photographer, but I wanted you to see for yourself what they look like. Little Madeleine and Nora often amaze me by being such a blend of Ernst and me on our best days, and they seem a kind of proof that nature, in spite of what everyone says, is much more loyal than history. But I also treasure your loyalty to our personal history, Hans, not least because it is only ours now. I don't think I ever told you that no one except you calls me Batya anymore, and so I delight in seeing that name in your letters more than ever. It is strange to be connected to one's past mostly by a name, but I suppose that is what names are really for, isn't it? To summon us back when we are no longer there."

Hans was dubious about some of what Batya wrote him, but it was all absolutely characteristic of her, and few things gave him as much pleasure these days as one of her letters. Would she have written that about nature's being more loyal than history if she had moved to Palestine? Hans wondered. Probably not. For a moment he imagined her actually having made the journey, and her dismay at meeting Asher Blumenthal in a Haifa coffeehouse, but although he laughed aloud at the thought, his amusement was sympathetic. Her whole description was vintage Batya in its romanticization of whatever she happened to be doing and reminded him of the many hours they had spent passionately debating how best to live one's life. The people he met here thought such questions absurd. Among his English acquaintances, it was almost regarded as bad taste to bring up such matters. "Boring stuff, all that foggy Continental hand wringing," was how even the cleverest of their university-bound children dismissed the question when he sought out their opinion. Yet for Hans, the search for the right life and the right way to live that life remained a powerful impulse connecting him, in spite of all their clashes, far more to Batya, Ernst, and the others of his generation back home than to anyone he knew over here. With Moritz in mind, Hans was willing to concede that perhaps they all had started out driven by little more than a fear of their own superfluousness in a world of such powerful fathers, but if so, their search had outgrown its origin sufficiently to deserve being judged on its own terms. Not that it excused any of their appalling errors, his own least of all. If anything, the importance of what they were seeking only magnified the burden of his culpability. The hurt he had caused others would weigh on him forever, and his responsibility for what had happened in the Cathedral Square was not mitigated by the far greater horrors inflicted on the whole continent so soon afterward. But in Batya's uncertainties about her own future, Hans heard a question that had animated them all when they were young, and he was glad both that she continued to ask it and that her life had given her the right to do so. It struck him now that what he used to regard as little more than irritating self-dramatization came from the same elusively provisional sense of herself that had saved Batya from the doctrinaire answers to which he had succumbed with such catastrophic results.

He took out the picture Batya had sent him from his drawer and looked at it more closely. It had been carefully hand-colored over the photographic image and showed two young girls, the elder posed in a light brown pinafore of fine corduroy, which she wore with an embroidered white cotton shirt and a matching cream-colored ribbon in her hair, while her sister was in a simple blue and white sailor's costume of the kind only boys wore when Hans was young, with her curly hair allowed to fall freely around her cheeks. They looked to Hans like healthy, contented children, but if he had been asked to say whom they resembled, he would have been at a loss. It had been eleven years since he had seen Batya or Ernst, and although he thought of them often, he could not have conjured up their faces. Besides, he always had difficulty making out the supposed resemblance between children and their parents, even when both were standing in front of him and everyone else was remarking enthusiastically on the similarities. But he knew mothers enjoyed hearing such observations and was happy that his comment had pleased Batya. He was certainly young enough that he could still try to have a family of his own, and from time to time the thought of living out his life without a wife or children did seem unbearably lonely. But the prospect of marrying and raising offspring had receded in his imagination until it felt as though it belonged to someone else's future, not his own. Perhaps if Moritz were still alive, Hans would have felt an obligation to give him grandchildren. It was one of the things they had touched on in passing when Moritz finally told Hans of the provisions he had made to secure the family holdings by transferring the bulk of his assets abroad. But they both were temperamentally ill suited for displays of emotion, and quickly—much too quickly, Hans now thought—they had retreated back to a discussion about how the company could be managed from Switzerland until it became clear where Hans intended to establish himself after his recovery. Paradoxically, rather than make them more ready for personal disclosures, the knowledge that they would never see each other again inhibited them all the more. They needed to say too many things for the time they had left and so settled for saying very little at all. Once, though, after a particularly difficult day on which Moritz had found taking in any nourishment almost impossible, he did allow himself to say that with Hans doing so much better, he himself did not especially mind dying, but he was sorry that his illness meant he would never see his grandchildren. Almost at once, though, he waved off the comment with a slightly embarrassed expression, as though he had transgressed one of the unspoken rules that governed their conversations during those final weeks. To his regret, Hans could think of nothing to say in reply and so only reached out briefly to hold his father's hand in his own before releasing it and resuming their previous discussion. Neither of them ever referred to the subject again. But these days Hans sometimes wondered if his childlessness was not a fitting judgment on someone who had been as careless of others' lives as he had been. Perhaps a man who had committed the wrongs he had did not deserve to see his children continue his life into the future, and he was meant to die alone in a strange country, less as an act of atonement than simply as the logical consequence of his own earlier choices. But Hans was also too much his father's son to indulge in such thoughts for long, and he put Batya's photos back into their envelope and shut them in his desk drawer. He would buy a suitable frame for them soon and keep them on the large piano in the music room, but for now he had no wish to look at them anymore.

Fortunately, Batya's letters could always be relied on to dispel Hans's tendency to melancholy. She had kept much of the malicious wit that used to shock everyone at the Mendelssohn Club, and although she frequently brought up troubling questions about her experiences, she also delighted Hans with descriptions of her social life. At first it was difficult for Hans to keep in mind that she was now, after all, the Countess von Alpsbach and mistress of the single largest estate in the area. As happened to many other noble families, a large portion of the von Alpsbach money had vanished in the war when the government bonds became worthless, but at least their property had never been heavily mortgaged. Even before Ernst's death, Moritz had offered Batya the services of one of his shrewdest financial experts, hoping thereby to do something for a family from whom his son had taken so much. Gradually, with the help of Rotenburg's expert, who stayed on to manage the estate for Batya, much of the family's prosperity was restored, and two years after the war's end Brunnenberg again ranked among the great houses in the province. In one of her letters Batya wrote that she was now so firmly established as the region's grande dame that when some of Ernst's relatives came back for one of their rare visits, none of the younger people in town understood their attempts to mock her origins. During a party she gave in their honor, Ernst's surviving sister and his Salzburg cousin Gretel von Wallderdorf commented sarcastically that Batya owed her ascent in society entirely to how shrewdly she had exploited her skill in the bedroom, but the other guests just listened in appalled silence and assumed that the speakers were prematurely senile. Batya of course heard every word but found ample revenge in the general pity with which the two women were regarded. But there was one bit of society malice whose intemperance amused her, even though she was its target, and she was curious what Hans would make of it. When she had paid off the last of the war debts and repaired all the damage to the large house and grounds, Batya held a splendid open-air fête, the first in the district since the armistice. As she strolled alone in and out among the lime tree bowers, lost in her reminiscences of having walked there with Ernst during their first ecstatic days together in a landscape he had loved, she suddenly overheard the Dowager Baroness von Kirchstein, in her loudest stage whisper, telling someone in her entourage whom Batya could not see, "Yes, my dear, this former Jewess, now our much-respected Countess von Alpsbach, has succeeded in coming up in the world so thoroughly that the only person at her parties who does not come from the finest families is the hostess herself."

Hans was less amused by the story than Batya assumed. Living in England had sharpened his antennae for a certain kind of reflex, salon anti-Semitism that seemed one of the few bonds linking this country's aristocracy and its intellectuals. But the scene also reminded him disagreeably of the tone in one of Alexander Garber's plays, *The Jew's Misfortune*, whose West End opening Hans had attended recently. In London there was currently a vogue for everything Austro-Hungarian, and the last days of the Habsburgs had become a fashionable topic. No one satisfied the market for a confectioner's version of that vanished world more thoroughly than Garber, even in the execrable translations in which his works were regularly served up. But to Hans, Garber's dramas seemed cloyingly sentimental, as insubstantial as the multihued spun sugar consumed by tourists on a seaside holiday. Hans had walked out of the theater at the first intermission, disconcerted at hearing the questions that used to torment the best of his generation turned into the stuff of reassuring fairy tales and legends. The play seemed so determined to charm its audience that everything difficult and painful about its subject was dissolved away. According to reports Hans had received from Palestine, in addition to boasting that he was Moritz Rotenburg's illegitimate son, Asher also liked to announce that he was a childhood friend of the famous author Alexander Garber. Hans knew that for once Asher was telling the truth, but he suspected that anyone in Haifa who was familiar with Garber's writing and had also spent an hour in Blumenthal's company would assume that both of Asher's claims were equally far-fetched.

No doubt it was also Batya's mentioning the name von Kirchstein that made Hans so uneasy. Adrian von Kirchstein had recovered from his wounds in the Cathedral Square attack, as the doctor had predicted at the time, only to be killed two years later in the fighting at the Trotus River valley in Romania. The Dowager Baroness, whose mocking comment Batya had overheard, must be his widow, and Hans was surprised that she had returned to the province at all, even for such a party. It could only have been out of loyalty to her late husband's affection for Karl Gustav that she accepted Batya's invitation, and her ill humor was surely prompted as much by bitter memories of what had happened there on her last visit as by resentment at Batya's now being regarded as her equal. But as Hans thought more about Batya's letters, he started to realize that her comic stories about life at Brunnenberg were considerably more anxiety-ridden than he had first assumed and that her amusing anecdotes might represent an attempt not simply to entertain him but also to make light of her own worries. Hans went back into his study and opened the thick sheaf of her letters to read them all consecutively. This time he took away a different impression. It was not exactly the opposite of his initial one, but alongside Batya's high-spirited stories, he now registered more forcefully a kind of secondary, almost subterranean mood, the way a piece of music can let one hear the suggestion of darker, more discordant tones amid a cheerful, festive melody. He had responded more to Batya's carefree voice because that is what he was looking for in a letter from her, not because that was all they contained. But as he let himself imaginatively enter her actual situation, Hans understood how many difficulties she had been forced to endure after Ernst's death and how much effort was required to maintain her easygoing manner.

Although she herself had never converted, Batya had agreed reluctantly to allow her children to be baptized so that they could inherit the von Alpsbach lands without challenge. There was no suggestion that Batya felt directly threatened by the growing electoral success of the anti-Semitic parties in her country, but the memory of the sectarian violence that had swept through the district at the end of the war had never entirely left her. For the past three or four years the situation had appeared relatively stable, but the pitched battles between gangs of right-wing and Communist hoodlums that had terrorized many of the larger towns for months had left her increasingly uneasy about the stability of the new political institutions. The few times she referred to the Cathedral Square killings in her letters to Hans, it was to say how insignificant in scale the pre–Great War terror was in comparison to the bloodletting that followed. Yet at the time it had shaken everyone to the core. "So it must be how deeply an event touches our imagination, not the number of men involved, that matters," she ventured. Then she immediately corrected herself: "But that can't be entirely true either, can it, Hans?" she asked. "How can the millions of dead, including my husband and most of his friends, not make an absolute difference? Of course it does. Only I don't have any way to think about the war without its diminishing everything we experienced before, and that seems terribly wrong to me as well."

Unlike her comic scenes, which she seemed to enjoy writing for their mutual amusement and which she allowed herself to unfold at leisure, Batya rarely elaborated on her fears beyond a few, fragmentary descriptions. But a single sentence stayed in Hans's mind from her account of barricading the gates at Brunnenberg and hiding with her two children and a few old family servants during a violent clash between rival political squads in 1919. "Murder does not scare one so much, but its legitimization does," she told him, and on his rereading, although Hans was certain that she had not intended it as a rebuke, her phrase struck home more sharply than any explicit critique of his own former beliefs would have done. No wonder he had overlooked that strand in her letters. When they had started corresponding, he was not prepared yet to hear such words from her directly—or at least she must have feared that about him—and so she put them in almost as throwaways for him to find and take up or not, depending on his own inner readiness. It was always much easier for Hans to accept blame on paper than in person, and if Batya were sitting across from him, he was far from certain that he would make no effort to defend himself.

Like his father, Hans had taken to using one of the large downstairs rooms directly off the front entrance of his house as a private library and office. But to the displeasure of his visitors, he refused to allow the fireplace either at Portman Square or in the country house near Headington to be stocked with an adequate quantity of logs. Irrespective of the weather, there were never more than a few, unimpressive pieces of wood burning at one time, and guests often went home muttering about such undignified Hebraic parsimony. But Hans himself had spent so many hours in Moritz's study that he could not breathe comfortably in an overheated atmosphere. One night in late November, Hans found himself unable to sleep and went downstairs to his study, where he put a single log, on which pieces of old moss were still clinging, onto the almost extinct embers of its predecessor. The wood smoked unpleasantly for a few seconds before bursting into flame, but Hans appeared not to notice as he wrapped himself more tightly in his silk bathrobe. He went over to his large desk and set out to draft a preliminary memorandum to his lawyer. After years of being urged to do so, Hans finally had made up his mind to write his will. The results would shock everyone he knew, but he himself had no doubt that he was doing the right thing. He intended to name the Countess von Alpsbach and her two children as his principal beneficiaries, leaving them all his shares in the family company, as well as sole possession of his various private holdings in England and the United States. The house in Headington was to be turned over to her as her own property immediately, with Hans undertaking to pay for its upkeep during his own lifetime. Upon Hans's death, Asher Blumenthal would be given an immediate cash payment representing five years of his normal annual allowance. This amount was to be his, free and clear, no matter where he decided to move. Should he choose to remain in Palestine, his yearly grant was to be continued on the prior terms, to be doubled once an additional five years had passed. The remaining details, including the exact amounts to be given to various Zionist charities, he would work out with the lawyer to whom he intended to send the memorandum in the morning, along with instructions to meet him in Portman Square by the end of the week with a formal document ready for his signature.

Hans was far from certain how Batya would respond. He had mentioned nothing about his plan to her so far, and as he looked over his letter, he could easily imagine her refusing altogether. Worst of all would be if she misunderstood his motives, yet he himself was not at all sure that he could describe them clearly. It was much easier for him to say what they were not. He certainly did not entertain any hope that he and Batya would ever become intimate again, nor even that they would see much of each other in the future. He was giving her the country house simply as a refuge, in case she ever needed a change from her situation at home. He would have to discuss the whole decision with her in person, but he intended to leave it entirely up to Batya whether he should travel to Brunnenberg or whether she would prefer to visit London. Hans himself was not sure which solution he hoped she would pick and was inwardly prepared for either one. But at least it had become clear to them both that it was high time they met. In one of her recent letters, Batya mentioned that no less a figure than Alexander Garber had just written her from Salzburg with the oddest questions. She remembered going with Hans years ago to see a one-act curtain raiser by Garber and disliking it, but she had not kept up with his writing since then and knew him only by reputation as an important author whose works were often set in their district. Apparently, Garber had become interested recently in the Cathedral Square murders—no doubt for some new piece of his own—and Batya assumed he had gotten in touch with her as the sister-in-law of one of the victims. It was evident from his letter that Garber knew very little else about her, and she was uncertain whether or not to reply to his request for information. In any case, she intended to do nothing about it without first consulting Hans. Batya admitted that she found Garber's inquisitiveness unsettling since she herself had been toying with the idea of writing a memoir about what had happened to all of them in the months before the war. She wanted to be completely candid about her feelings toward Hans and Ernst, about what it had been like when she became pregnant, and then, later, when she was widowed, about her struggles to maintain Brunnenberg for Nora and Madeleine. Her aim was mostly to leave her children a written record about the world of their parents, and she had not thought a great deal about whether to publish her recollections. But it was a possibility she did not want to exclude altogether, and the idea that if it did appear in print, her story would be regarded as competing with Garber's was intimidating. She wanted Hans's advice whether to go ahead at all or not, and although she did not say so directly, it was also evident that she was afraid he might end up being hurt by some of what she would write about him.

Rather than be worried, though, Hans found himself unreservedly excited at the idea of Batya's composing her memoirs, and no matter how he came out in them, he was glad to encourage her in any way he could. He intended to bring her his will to look over, but whether they met in London or Brunnenberg, now there would be something else of equal importance to them both to talk about. As he finished a short note to Batya proposing a meeting, he could not resist adding that as far as he was concerned, there was no reason for her to cooperate with Garber. On the contrary, she should think of Garber's new project as an additional inducement to finish her own memoir before he fixed everyone's impression of what their lives had been like when they were young. "I can't predict whose version will seem more credible to people who were never there," he wrote Batya. "But I think it is important that more than one choice exist. For myself, I have no doubt whose judgment I trust, and I admit that I am very curious to hear what you think is worth remembering."